Praise for
SUN OF SUNS

A Kirkus Best of 2006
A Romantic Times Top Pick
A 2007 Campbell Award Finalist

"Outrageously brilliant and absolutely not to be missed."
—*Kirkus Reviews* (starred review)

"Over the years, science fiction has provided us with awesome environments, the best ones based on careful logic. There were Hal Clement's *Mission of Gravity* and Robert Forward's *Dragon's Egg*. Karl Schroeder's new novel is in a class with these masterpieces. The longer one ponders *Sun of Suns*, the less paradoxical—and the more intricately sensible—it comes to be."
—Vernor Vinge, author of *A Fire Upon the Deep*

"Schroeder has accomplished the enviable task of creating a fascinating new universe for readers to explore: a spaceborne steampunk environment that conjures up images of neo-Victorian-era flying vehicles traveling among piecemeal floating communities. A rousing, old-fashioned, pulplike adventure yarn."   —*Starlog*

"Schroeder brilliantly adds another level to an absorbing adventure as the complexities of Virga are slowly revealed."
—*Rocky Mountain News*

"We already knew that Karl Schroeder could do Kubrick. Now it turns out he can do Dumas as well. And more: not since Middle Earth have I encountered such an intense and palpable evocation of an alien world. *Sun of Suns* puts the world-building exercises of classic Niven to shame."   —Peter Watts, author of *Blindsight*

"Full of marvelous images and cutting-edge ideas. Schroeder has the rare and invaluable ability to develop wholly new concepts and turn them into compelling narratives. The scientists are already studying Schroeder's ideas. Take him very seriously."
—Stephen Baxter, author of *Ark*

"Schroeder's deft alchemy fuses scrupulously detailed, mind-expanding world-building with unabashed, rip-roaring pulp adventure to produce a twenty-four-carat story sparkling with science fiction's finest virtues."

—Paul McAuley, author of *The Quiet War*

Praise for
QUEEN OF CANDESCE

"Set against one of the lushly realized worlds that are rapidly becoming [Schroeder's] trademark. *Queen of Candesce* has a backdrop that's simultaneously steampunk and space opera, a complex and believably flawed lead character, and plenty of action and intrigue."

—Interzone

"Damned good . . . The strong prose supports a skillfully developed plot and a number of complex, yet easy-to-follow, political intrigues. The hard SF rigorously governs Virga, but it never becomes so dominant that it bores those readers more interested in high adventure than in engineering puzzles. The characterizations are sharp, and the protagonist, Machiavellian genius Venera Fanning, is excellent company as she plots her escape, plans her revenge on her husband's enemies, and grows and changes despite her worst intentions. . . . Confirms that Karl Schroeder belongs in the front ranks of SF world-builders."

—SciFi

"Comparable to classic SF epics like John Varley's Gaean trilogy and Jack L. Chalker's Well of Souls series, Schroeder's saga is an awe-inspiring example of masterful world-building. A myriad of themes, from rogue artificial intelligences to the evolution of human bodies and culture, make this futuristic epic one to reckon with."

—*Publishers Weekly* (starred review)

VIRGA
Cities of the Air

KARL SCHROEDER

VIRGA

Cities of the Air

A TOM DOHERTY ASSOCIATES BOOK NEW YORK

VIRGA: CITIES OF THE AIR

Sun of Suns copyright © 2006 by Karl Schroeder
Queen of Candesce copyright © 2007 by Karl Schroeder

A Tor Book
Published by Tom Doherty Associates, LLC
175 Fifth Avenue
New York, NY 10010

www.tor-forge.com

Tor® is a registered trademark of Tom Doherty Associates, LLC.

ISBN 978-0-7653-2670-6

First Trade Paperback Edition: July 2010

Printed in the United States of America

0 9 8 7 6 5 4 3 2 1

SUN OF SUNS

TO THE INDISPENSABLE:

Cory Doctorow, Phyllis Gotlieb, Sally McBride,
David Nickle, Helen Rykens, Sara Simmons,
Michael Skeet, Hugh A. D. Spencer, Dale Sproule,
Allan Weiss, and Theresa Wojtasiewicz

Acknowledgments

As always, I'd like to acknowledge the hard work and good advice of my editor, David Hartwell, as well as Denis Wong at Tor Books; my agent, Donald Maass, for having the good grace to run with this project when I unexpectedly dropped it in his lap; and of course, Janice and Paige for their patience during my extended periods of impractical musing and daydreaming.

HAYDEN GRIFFIN WAS plucking a fish when the gravity bell rang. The dull clang penetrated even the thick wooden walls of the corporation inn; it was designed to be heard all over town. Hayden paused, frowned, and experimentally let go of the fish. Four tumbling feathers flashed like candle flames in an errant beam of sunlight shooting between the floorboards. The fish landed three feet to his left. Hayden watched the feathers dip in a slow arc to settle next to it.

"A bit early for a spin-up, ain't it?" said Hayden. Miles grunted distractedly. The former soldier, now corporation cook, was busily pouring sauce over a steaming turkey that he'd just rescued from the oven's minor inferno. His bald skull shone in the firelight. "They might need me all the same," continued Hayden. "I better go see."

Miles glanced up. "Your ma left you here," he said. "You been bad again. Pick up the fish."

Hayden leaned back against the table, crossing his arms. He was trying to come up with a reply that didn't sound like whining when the bell rang again, more urgently. "See?" he said. "They need somebody. Nobody in town's as good with the bikes as I am. Anyway, how you gonna boil this fish if the gravity goes?"

"Gravity ain't gonna go, boy," snapped Miles. "It's solid right now."

"Then I better go see what else is up."

"You just want to watch your old lady light the sun," said Miles.

"Don't you?"

"Today's just a test. I'll wait for tomorrow, when they light it for real."

"Come on, Miles. I'll be right back."

The cook sighed. "Go, then. Set the bikes going. Then come right back." Hayden bolted for the door and Miles shouted, "Don't leave that fish on the floor!"

As Hayden walked down the hall to the front of the inn another stray beam of sunlight spiked up around the plank floorboards. That was a bad sign; Mom would have to wait for deep cloud cover before lighting the town's new sun, lest the Slipstreamers should see it. Slipstream would never tolerate another sun so close to their own. The project was secret—or it had been. By tomorrow the whole world would know about it.

Hayden walked backward past the well-polished oak bar, waving his lanky arms casually at his side as he said, "Bell rang. Gotta check the bikes." One of the customers smirked doubtfully at him; Mama Fifty glared at him from her post behind the bar. Before she could reply he was out the front door.

A blustery wind was blowing out here as always, even whistling up between the street boards. Sunlight angled around the edges of the street's peaked roof, bars and rectangles of light sliding along the planking and up the walls of the buildings that crammed every available space. The street boards gave like springs under Hayden's feet as he ran up the steep curve of the avenue, which was nearly empty at this time of day.

Gavin Town came to life at dusk, when the workers who slept here flooded back from all six directions, laughing and gossiping. Merchants would unshutter their windows for the night market as the gaslights were lit all along the way. The dance hall would throw open its doors for those with the stamina to take a few turns on the floor. Sometimes Hayden picked up some extra bills by lighting the streetlights himself. He was good with fire, after all.

If he went to work on the bikes Hayden wouldn't be able to see the sun, so he took a detour. Slipping down a narrow alleyway between two tall houses, he came to one of the two outer streets of the town—really little more than a narrow covered walkway. Extensions of houses and shops formed a ceiling, their entrances to the left as he stepped into the way. To the right was an uneven board fence, just a crack open at the top. An occasional shuttered window interrupted the surface of the fence, but Hayden didn't pause at any of them. He was making for an open gallery a quarter of the way up the street.

At moments like this—alone and busy—he either completely forgot himself or drowned in grief. His father's death still weighed on him, though it had been a year now; was it that long since he and his mother had moved here? Mother kept insisting that it was best this way, that if they'd stayed home in Twenty-two Town they would have been surrounded by reminders of Dad all the time. But was that so bad?

His father wouldn't be here to see the lighting of the sun, his wife's completion of his project—their crowning achievement as a family. When Hayden remembered them talking about that, it was his father's voice he remembered, soaring in tones of enthusiasm and hope. Mother would be quieter, but her pride and love came through in the murmurs that came through the bedroom wall and lulled Hayden to sleep at night. To make your own sun! That was how nations were founded. To light a sun was to be remembered forever.

WHEN HAYDEN WAS twelve his parents had taken him on his first visit to Rush. He had complained, because lately he'd come to know that though Slipstream was a great nation, it was not *his* nation. His friends had jeered at him for visiting the camp of the enemy, though he didn't exactly know why Slipstreamers were bad, or what it meant to be a citizen of Aerie instead.

"That's why we're going," his father had said. "So that you can understand."

"That, and to see what they're wearing in the principalities," said Mother with a grin. Father had glowered at her—an expression his slablike face seemed designed for—but she ignored him.

"You'll love it," she said to Hayden. "We'll bring back stuff to make those pals of yours completely envious."

He'd liked that thought; still, Father's words had stuck with him. He was going to Rush to understand.

And he thought he did understand, the moment that their ship had broached the final wall of cloud and he glimpsed the city for the first time. As light welled up, Hayden flew to a stoutly-barred window with some other kids—there was no centrifuge in this little ship, so everybody was weightless—and shielded his eyes to look at their destination.

The nearby air was full of travelers, some riding bikes, some on prop-driven contraptions powered by pedals, and some kicking their feet to flap huge white wings strapped to their backs. They carried parcels, towed cargos, and in the case of the fan-jets, left behind slowly fading arcs and lines of white contrail to thatch the sky.

Their cylindrical frigate had emerged from the clouds near Slipstream's sun, which it made an inferno of half the sky. Seconds out of the mist and the temperature was already rising in the normally chilly ship's lounge. The other boys were pointing at something and shouting excitedly; Hayden peered in that direction, trying to make out what was casting a seemingly impossible shadow across an entire half of the view. The vast shape was irregular like any of the rocks they had passed on their way here. Where those rocks were usually house-sized and sprouted spidery trees in all directions, this shape was blued with distance and covered with an even carpet of green. It took Hayden a few seconds to realize that it really was a rock, but one that was several miles in diameter.

He gaped at it. Father laughed from the dining basket, woven of wicker, where he perched with Mother. "That's the biggest thing you've ever seen, Hayden. But listen, there's much bigger places. Slipstream is not a major state. Remember that."

"Is that Rush?" Hayden pointed.

Father pulled himself out of the basket and came over. With his broad laborer's shoulders and calloused hands, he bulked much bigger than the kids, who made a place for him next to Hayden. "The asteroid? That's not Rush. It's the source of Slipstream's wealth, though—it and their sun." He leaned on the rail and pointed. "No . . . *That* is Rush."

Maybe it was because he'd never seen anything like it before, but the city simply hadn't registered in Hayden's mind until this moment. After all, the towns of Aerie were seldom more than two hundred yards across, and were simply wheels made of wooden planks lashed together and spoked with rope. You spun up the whole assembly and built houses on the inside surface of the wheel. Simple. And never had he seen more than five or six such wheels in one place.

The dozens of towns that made up Rush gleamed of highly polished metal. They were more cylindrical than ring-shaped, and none was less than five hundred yards in diameter. The most amazing thing was that they were tethered to the forested asteroid in quartets like mobiles; radiating from each cylinder's outer rim were bright sails of gold and red that transformed them from mere towns into gorgeous pinwheels.

"The asteroid's too big to be affected by the wind," said Father. Hayden shifted uncomfortably; Father was not trying to hide the burr of his provincial Aerie accent. "The towns are small enough to get pulled around by gusts. They use the sails to help keep the wheels spun up." This made sense to Hayden, because wind was the result of your moving at a different speed than whatever airmass you were in. Most of the time, objects migrated outward and inward in Virga to the rhythm of slowly circulating rivers of air. You normally only experienced wind at the walls of a town or while flying. Many times, he had folded little propellers of paper and let them out on strings. They'd twirled in the rushing air. So did the towns of Rush, only much more slowly.

Hayden frowned. "If that big rock isn't moving with the air, won't it drift away from the rest of Slipstream?"

"You've hit on the very problem," said Father with a smile. "Slipstream's more migratory than most countries. The Slipstreamers have to follow their asteroid's orbit within Virga. You can't see from here, but their sun is also tethered to the asteroid. Ten years ago, Slipstream drifted right into Aerie. Before that, we were a smaller and less wealthy nation, being far from the major suns. But we were proud. We controlled our own destiny. Now what are we? Nothing but vassals of Rush."

Hayden barely heard him. He was eagerly staring at the city.

Their ship arrived at midday to find a traffic jam at the axis of one of the biggest cylinders. It took an hour to disembark, but Hayden didn't care. He spent the time watching the heavily built-up inner surface of the town revolve past. He was looking for places to visit. From the axis of the cylinder, where the docks sat like a jumble of big wooden dice, cable-ways radiated away to the other towns that made up the city. One wheel in particular caught his eye—a huge cylinder whose inside seemed to be one single building with balconies, coigns and glittering glass-paneled windows festooning it. This cylinder was surrounded by warships, which Hayden had seen in photos but never been close to before. The massive wooden vessels bristled with gun ports, and they trailed smoke and ropes and masts like the spines of fish. They were majestic and fascinating.

"You'll never get there," said Father drily. "That's the pilot's palace."

After ages they were finally able to descend the long, curving, covered stairway to the street. Here Hayden had to endure another interminable wait while a man in a uniform examined Father's papers. Hayden was too distracted at the time to really notice his father's falsely jovial manner, or the way his shoulders had slumped with relief when they were finally accepted into the city. But after some walking he turned to Mother and kissed her, saying quietly, "I'll be back soon. Check us into the hotel, but don't wait for me. Go and do some shopping, it'll take your mind off it."

"Where's he going?" Hayden watched as Father disappeared into the crowd.

"It's just business," she said, but she sounded unhappy.

Hayden quickly forgot any misgivings this exchange might have raised. The town was huge and fascinating. Even the gravity felt different—a slower turnover of the inner ear—and there were points where you couldn't see the edges of the place at all. He followed his mother around to various outlets and while she haggled over wholesale paper prices for the newspaper she helped run, Hayden was happy to stare out the shop's windows at the passing crowds.

Gradually, though, he did begin to notice something. Mother was dressed in the layered and colorful garments of the Aerie outer districts and, like Father, made no attempt to hide her accent. Even her black hair and dark eyes marked her as different here in this city of fair-haired, pale-eyed people. Though the shopkeepers weren't actually hostile to Mother, they weren't being very friendly either. Neither were the other kids he saw in the street. Hayden smiled at one or two, but they just turned away.

He could have forgotten these details if not for what happened next. As they approached the hotel late that afternoon—Hayden laden with packages, his mother humming happily—he spotted Father at the hotel entrance, standing with his hands behind his back. Hayden felt his mother clutch his shoulder even as he waved and shouted a hello. It was only then that he noticed the men standing with his father, men in uniform who turned as one at the sound of Hayden's voice.

"Shit," whispered Mother as the policemen converged on her and a very confused Hayden.

The rest of the trip mostly consisted of waiting in various pale-green, bare rooms with his mother, who sat white-faced and silent, not answering any of Hayden's increasingly petulant questions. They didn't go back to the hotel to sleep, but were given a couple of rough cots in a small room in the back of the police station. "Not a cell," said the sergeant who showed them to it. "A courtesy apartment for relatives."

Father had reappeared the next day. He was disheveled, subdued, and had a bruise on his cheek. Mother wept in his arms while Hayden stood nearby, hugging his own chest in confused anger. Later that day they boarded a passenger ship considerably less posh than the one they had arrived on, and Hayden watched the bright pinwheels of Rush recede in the distance, unexplored.

Later Father had explained about the Resistance and the importance of assembling the talent and resources Aerie needed to strike out on its own. Hayden thought he understood, but what mattered was not the politics of it; it was the memory of walking through Rush's crowded streets next to his father, whose hands were bound behind his back.

THE GALLERY WAS just a stretch of street empty of fence, but with a railing you could look over. Mother called it a "braveway"; Miles used the more interesting term "pukesight." Hayden stepped up to the rail and clutched it with both hands, staring.

A gigantic mountain of cloud wheeled in front of him, nearly close enough to touch. The new sun must be behind it; the ropes of the road from Gavin Town to the construction site stabbed the heart of the cloud and vanished inside it. Hayden was disappointed; if the sun came on right now he wouldn't see it.

He laughed. Oh, yes he would. Father had impressed it upon him again and again: when the sun came on, there would be no missing it. "The clouds for miles around will evaporate—poof," he'd said with a wave of his fingers. "The temperature will instantly shoot up, in fact everything within a kilometer is going to catch fire. That's why the sun is situated so far from any towns.

That, and security reasons, of course. And the light . . . Hayden, you have to promise not to look at it. It's going to be brighter than anything you can imagine. Up close, it could burn your skin and dazzle you through your closed eyelids. Never look directly at it, not until we've moved the town."

The cloud appeared to rotate as Hayden gazed at it; Gavin Town was a wheel like all towns, after all, and spun to provide its inhabitants with centrifugal gravity. It was the only form of gravity they would ever know, and it was a precious resource, costly and heavily taxed. Grant's Chance, the next nearest town, lay a dozen miles beyond the sun site, invisible for now behind cloud.

Cloud was why the Griffins had come here. At the edges of the zone lit by Slipstream, the air cooled and condensation began. White mist in all its shapes made a wall here separating the sunlit realm from the vast empty spaces of winter. This was the frontier. Here you could hide all manner of things—secret projects, for instance.

The town continued to turn and now sky opened out beyond the barrier of mist—sky with no limits, either up, down, or to either side. Two distant suns carved out a sphere of pale air from this endless firmament, a volume defined by thousands upon thousands of clouds in all shapes and sizes, most of them tinged with dusk colors of rose and amber. There were ragged streamers indicating currents and rivers of air; puffballs and many-armed star shapes; and many miles away, its outlines blurred by intervening dust and mist, a mushroom head was forming as some current of cold impacted a mass of moist air. Below and above, walls of white blocked any further view, while whatever lay on the other side of the suns was obscured by dazzle and golden detail.

As it radiated through hundreds of miles of air, that light would fade and redden, or be shadowed by the countless clouds and objects comprising the nation of Aerie. If you traveled inward or up to civilized spaces, the light from other distant suns would begin to brighten before you ran out of light from yours; but if you went down or back, you would eventually reach a point where their light was completely obscured. There, a creeping chill took over. In the dark and cold, nothing grew. There began the volumes of winter that made up much of the interior of the planet-sized balloon of air, called Virga, where Hayden lived.

Gavin Town hovered at the very edge of civilization, where the filtered light of distant fires could barely keep crops alive. It wasn't lonely out here, though; above, below, and all about hung the habitations of Man. Three miles up to the left, a farm caught the suns' light: within a net a hundred feet across, the farmer had gathered pulverized rock and soil, and was growing a crop of yellow canola. Each plant clutched its own little ball of mud and they all tumbled about slowly, catching and losing the light in one another's shadow. The highway that passed near the farm was busy, a dozen or more small airships sailing along guided by the rope that was the highway itself. The rope extended off into measureless distance, heading for Rush. Below and to the right, a sphere of water the size of a house shimmered, its surface momentarily ridged by a passing breeze. Hayden could see a school of wetfish swirling inside the sphere like busy diamonds.

There was way too much to take in with a single glance, so Hayden almost didn't spot the commotion. Motion out of the corner of his eye alerted him; leaning over the railing and sighting left along the curving wall of the town, he saw an unusually dense tangle of contrails. The trails led back in the direction of the sun and as he watched, three gleaming shapes shot out of the cloud and arrowed in the same direction.

Strange.

Just as he was wondering what might be happening, the gravity bell rang again. Hayden pushed himself back from the rail and ran for the main street. It wouldn't do for somebody else to get the bikes running after he'd promised Miles he'd be there.

The stairwell to the gravity engines led off the center of the street. Gravity was a public service and the town fathers had insisted on making its utilities both visible and accessible to everyone. Consequently, Hayden was very surprised when he clattered down the steps into the cold and drafty engine room and found nobody there.

Bike number two still hung from its arm above the open hatchway in the floor. It wasn't a bike in the old gravity-bound sense; the fan-jet was a simple metal barrel, open at both ends, with a fan in one end and an alcohol burner at its center. You spun up the fan with a pair of pedals and then lit the burner, and you were away. Hayden's own bike lay partly disassembled in the corner. He'd been meaning to get it running tonight.

When started and lowered through the hatch, bikes one and two would produce enough thrust to spin Gavin Town back up to a respectable five revolutions per minute. This had to be done once or twice a day so normally the engine room would have somebody in it either working, topping up the bike's tanks, or doing maintenance. Certainly if the gravity bell rang, somebody would always be here in seconds and the bike operational in under a minute.

The wind whistled through the angled walls of the room. Hayden heard no voices, no running feet.

After a few seconds, though, something else came echoing up through the floor. Somewhere within a mile or two, an irregular popping had started.

It was the unmistakable sound of rifle fire.

A CRACKING ROAR shook the engine room. Hayden dropped to his stomach to look out the floor hatch, just in time to see a bike shoot by just meters below. It flashed Slipstreamer gold. A second later another that gleamed Aerie green followed it. Then the town had curved up and away and there was nothing out there but empty sky. The firing continued, dulled now by the bulk of the town.

Now he heard pounding footsteps and shouting from overhead. Shots rang out from nearby, making Hayden jump. The volleys were erratic, undisciplined, while in the distance he heard a more even, measured response.

As he ran back up the steps something whistled past his ear and hit the wall with a *spang*. Splinters flew and Hayden ducked down to his hands and knees, knowing full well that it wouldn't do any good when this section of the town rotated into full view of whoever was firing. The bullets would come straight up through the decking.

He emerged onto the still-empty street and ran to the right, where he'd heard people firing. A narrow alley led to the town's other outer street. He skidded around the corner to face the braveway—and saw bodies.

Six men had taken up firing positions at the rail. All were now slumped there or sprawled on the planks, their rifles carelessly flung away. The wood of the rail and flooring was splintered in dozens of places. There was blood everywhere.

Something glided into view beyond the railing, and he blinked at it in astonishment. The red and gold sails of a Slipstream warship spun majestically there, not two hundred yards below. Hayden could make out the figures of men moving inside the open hatches of the thing. Beyond it, partly eclipsed, lay another ship, and another. Contrails laced the air between and around them.

Hayden took a step toward the braveway and stopped. He looked at the bodies and at the warships, and took another step.

Something shot past the town and he heard a shout from the empty air outside. Gunshots sounded from below his feet and now a wavering contrail dissipated in the air not ten feet past the railing.

He ran to the braveway and took one of the rifles from the nerveless fingers of its former owner. He vaguely recognized the man as someone who'd visited the inn on occasion.

"What do you think you're doing?" Hayden whirled, to find Miles bearing down on him. The cook's mouth was set in a grim line. "If you poke your head out they're gonna shoot it off."

"But we have to do something!"

Miles shook his head. "It's too late for that. Take it from some-body who's been there. Nothing we can do now except get killed, or wait this out."

"But my mother's at the sun!"

Miles jammed his hands in his pockets and looked away. The sun was the Slipstreamers' target, of course. The secret project had been discovered. If Aerie could field its own sun, it would no longer be dependent on Slipstream for light and heat. Right now, Slipstream could choke out Aerie's agriculture by shading their side of the sun; all the gains that Hayden's nation had made in recent years—admittedly the result of Slipstream patronage—would be lost. But the instant that his parents' sun came on the situation would change. Aerie's neighbors to the up and down, left and right would suddenly find a reason to switch allegiances. Aerie could never defend its sun by itself, but by building it out here, on the edge of darkness, they stood to open up huge volumes of barren air to settlement. That real estate would be a tremendous incentive to their neighbors to intercede. That, at least, had been the plan.

But if the sun were destroyed before it could even be proven to work . . . It didn't matter to Hayden, not right now. All he could think was that his mother was out there, probably at the focus of the attack.

"I'm the best flyer in town," Hayden pointed out. "These guys made good targets 'cause they weren't moving. Right now we need all the riflemen we can get in the air."

Miles shook his head. "Listen, kid," he said, "there's too many Slipstreamers out there to fight. You have to pick your battles. It ain't cowardice to do that. If you throw your life away now, you won't be there to help when the chance comes later on."

"Yeah," said Hayden as he backed away from the braveway.

"Drop the rifle," said Miles.

Hayden spun and raced down the alley, back to the main street. Miles shouted and came after him.

Hayden clattered down the stairs to the engine room, but only realized as he got there that his bike was still in pieces all over the floor. He'd planned to roll it out the open hatch and fire it up when he was in the air. The spin of the town meant he would leave it at over a hundred miles an hour anyway; plenty of airflow to get the thing running, if it had been operable.

He was sitting astride the hoist that held bike number two when Miles arrived. "What do you think you're doing? Get down!"

Glaring at him, Hayden made another attempt to pull the pins that held the engine to the hoist. "She needs me!"

"She needs you alive! And anyway, how are you gonna steer—"

The pin came loose, and the bike fell. Hayden barely kept his hold on it, and in doing so he dropped the rifle.

Wind burst around him, blinding him and taking his breath away. Fighting it, he managed to wrap his legs around the barrel shape of the bike and used his own body as a fin to turn it so that the engine faced into the airstream. Then he grabbed the handle-bars and hit the firing solenoid.

The engine caught under him and suddenly Hayden had a new sense of up and down: down was behind the bike, up ahead of it—and it was all he could do to dangle from its side as it acceler-ated straight into the nearby cloud.

His nose banged painfully against the bike's saddle. Icy mist roared down his body, threatening to strip his clothes away. A sec-ond later he was in clear air again. He squinted up over the nose of the jet, trying to get a sense of where he was.

Glittering arcs of crystal flickered in the light of rocket-trails: Aerie's new sun loomed dead ahead. Jet contrails had spun a thick web around the translucent sphere and its flanks were already holed in several places. Its delicate central machinery could not be replaced; those systems came from the principalities of Can-desce, thousands of miles away, and used technologies that no one alive could replicate. Yet two Slipstream cruisers had stopped directly over the sun and were veiling themselves in smoke as they launched broadside after broadside into it.

Mother would have been topping up the fuel preparatory to evacuating her team. Nobody could enter the sun while it was running; you had to give it just enough fuel for its prescribed burn. The engineers had planned a two-minute test for today, providing there was enough cloud to block the light in the direction of Slipstream.

A body tumbled past Hayden, red spheres of blood following it. He noticed abstractly that the man wore the now-banned, green uniform of Aerie. That was all he had time for, because any second now he was going to hit the sun himself.

Bike number two had never been designed to operate in open air. It was a heavy-duty fan-jet, powerful enough to pull the whole town into a faster spin. It had handlebars because they were required by law, not because anybody had ever expected to use them. And it was quickly accelerating to a point where Hayden was going to be ripped off it by the airstream.

He kicked out his legs, using them to turn his whole body in the pounding wind. That in turn ratcheted the handlebars a notch to the left; then another. Inside the bike, vanes turned in the exhaust stream. The bike began—slowly—to bank.

The flashing geodesics of the sun shot past close enough to touch. He had a momentary glimpse of faces, green uniforms, and rifles, and then he looked up past the bike again and saw the formation of Slipstream jets even as he shot straight through them. A few belated shots followed him but he barely heard them over the roar of the engine.

And now dead ahead was another obstacle, a spindle-shaped battleship this time. It flew the bright pennants of a flagship. Behind it was another bank of clouds, then the indigo depths of winter that lurked beyond all civilization.

Hayden couldn't hold on any longer. That was all right, though, he realized. He made sure the jet was aimed directly at the battleship, then pulled up his legs and kicked away from it.

He spun in clear air, weightless again but traveling too fast to breathe the air that tore past his lips. As his vision darkened he turned and saw bike number two impact the side of the battleship, crumpling its hull and spreading a mushroom of flame that lit a name painted on the metal hull: *Arrogance*.

With the last of his strength Hayden went spread-eagle to maximize his wind resistance. The world disappeared in silvery gray as he punched his way into the cloud behind the flagship. A flock of surprised fish flapped away from his plummeting fall. He waited to freeze, lose consciousness from lack of air, or hit something.

None of that happened, though his fingers and toes were going numb as he gradually slowed. The problem now was that he was soon going to be stranded inside a cloud, where nobody could see him. With the din of the battle going on, nobody would hear him either. People had been known to die of thirst after being stranded in empty air. If he'd been thinking, he'd have brought a pair of flapper fins at least.

He was just realizing that anything like that would have been torn off his body by the airstream, when the cloud lit up like the inside of a flame.

He put a hand up and spun away from the light but it was everywhere, diffused through the whole cloud. In seconds a pulse of intense heat welled up and to Hayden's astonishment, the cloud simply vanished, rolling away like a finished dream.

The heat continued to mount. Hayden peered past his fingers, glimpsing a silhouetted shape between him and a blaze of impossible light. The Slipstream battleship was dissolving, the flames enfolding it too dim to be seen next to the light of Aerie's new sun.

Though he was slowing, Hayden was still falling away from the battle. This fact saved his life, as everything else in the vicinity of the sun was immolated in the next few seconds. That wouldn't matter to his mother: she and all the other defenders were already dead, killed in the first seconds of the sun's new light. They must have lit the sun rather than let Slipstream have it as a prize.

The light reached a peak of agony and abruptly faded. Hayden had time to realize that the spherical blur flicking out of the orange afterglow was a shockwave, before it hit him like a wall.

As he blacked out he spun away into the blue-gray infinity of winter, beyond all civilization or hope.

2

THE HEADACHE WASN'T so bad today but Venera Fanning's fingers still sought out the small scar on her jaw as she entered the tiled gallery separating her chambers from the offices of Slipstream's admiralty. A lofty, pillared space, the hall ran almost the entire width of the royal townwheel in Rush; she couldn't avoid traversing it several times a day. Every time she did she relived the endless time after the bullet hit, when she'd lain here on the floor expecting to die. How miserable, how abandoned.

She would never enter the hall alone again. She knew it signaled weakness to everyone around her, but she needed to hear the servant's footsteps behind her here, even if she wouldn't look him in the eye and admit her feelings. The moaning of the wind from outside was the only sound except for her clicking footsteps, and that of the man behind her.

While that damnable hall brought back the memories whenever she entered it, Venera hadn't had the place demolished and replaced as her sisters would have. At least, she would not do that until the pain that radiated up her temples morning, noon, and night was ended. And the doctors merely exchanged their heavy-lidded glances whenever she demanded to know when that would be.

Venera flung back the double doors to the admiralty and was assailed by noise and the smells of tobacco, sweat, and leather. Right in the doorway four pages of mixed gender were rifling a file cabinet, their ceremonial swords thrust out and clashing in unconscious battle. Venera stepped adroitly around them and sidled past two red-faced officers who were bellowing at one another over a limp sheet of paper. She dodged a book trolley, its driver invisible behind the stacks of volumes teetering atop it, and in three more steps she entered the admiralty's antechamber, there to behold the bedlam of an office gearing up for war.

The antechamber was separated into two domains by a low wooden barrier. On the left was a waiting area, bare except for several armchairs reserved for elderly patrons. On the right, rows of polished wooden tables were manned by clerks who processed incoming reports. The clerks passed updates to a small army of pages engaged in rolling steep ladders up and down between the desks. They would periodically stop, crane their necks upward, then one would clamber up a ladder to adjust the height or relative position of one of the models that hung like a frozen flock of fish over the clerks' heads. Two ship's captains and an admiral stood among the clerks, as immobile as if stranded by the hazard of the whizzing ladders.

Venera strolled up to the rail and rapped on it smartly. It took a while before she was noticed, but when she was, a page abandoned his ladder and raced over to bow.

"May I have the key to the ladies' lounge, please?" she asked. The page ducked his head and ran to a nearby cabinet, returning with a large and ornate key.

Venera smiled sweetly at him; the smile slipped as a pulse of agony shot up from her jaw to wrap around her eyes. Turning quickly, she stalked past the crowding couriers and down a rosewood-paneled corridor that led off the far side of the antechamber. At its end stood an oak door carved with bluejays and finches, heavily polished but its silver door-handle tarnished with disuse.

The servant made to follow her as she unlocked the door. "Do you mind?" she asked with a glower. He flushed a deep pink, and only now did Venera really notice him; he was quite young and handsome. But, a servant.

She shut the door in his face and turned. The lounge's floors were smothered in deep crimson carpet, its walls of paneled oak so deeply varnished as to be almost black. There were no windows, only gaslights in peach-colored sconces here and there. While there were enough chairs and benches for a dozen ladies to wait in while others used the two privies, Venera had never encountered another woman here. It seemed she was the only wife in the admiralty who ever visited her husband at work.

"Well?" she said to the three men who awaited her, "what have you learned?"

"It seems you were right," said one. "Capper, show the mistress the photos."

A high-backed chair had been dragged into the center of the room and in it a young man in flying leathers was now weakly rifling through an inner pocket of his jacket. His right leg was thickly bandaged, but blood was seeping through and dripping on the carpet, where it disappeared in the red pile.

"That looks like a main line you've cut there," said Venera with a professional narrowing of the eyes. The youth grinned weakly at her. The second man scowled as he tightened a tourniquet high on the flyer's thigh. The third man watched this all indifferently. He was a mild-looking fellow with a balding head and the slightly pursed lips of someone more used to facing down sheets of paper than other people. When he smiled at all, Venera knew, Lyle Carrier lifted his lips and eyebrows in a manner that suggested bewilderment more than humor. She had decided that this was because other people's emotions were meaningless abstractions to him.

Carrier was a deeply dangerous man. He was as close to a kindred spirit as she'd been able to find in this forsaken country. He was, in fact, the one man Venera could never completely trust. She liked that about him.

The young man hauled a sheaf of prints out of his jacket with a grimace. He held it up for Venera to take, his hand trembling as though it were lead weights he was handing her and not paper. Venera snatched up the pictures eagerly and held them to the light one by one.

"Ah . . ." The fifth photo was the one she'd been waiting to see.

It showed a cloudy volume of air filled with spidery wooden dock armatures. Tied up to the docks was a row of stubby metal cylinders bristling with jets. Venera recognized the design: they were heavy cruisers, each bearing dozens of rocket ports and crewed by no less than three hundred men.

"They built the docks in a sargasso, just like you said," said the young spy. "The bottled air let me breathe on the way through. They're pumping oxygen to the work site using these big hoses . . ."

Venera nodded absently. "It was one of your colleagues who discovered that. He saw the pumps being installed outside the sargasso, and put two and two together." She riffled through the rest of the pictures to see if there was a better shot of the cruisers.

"Clearly another secret project," murmured Carrier with prim disapproval. "It seems nobody learned from the lesson we gave Aerie."

"That was eight years ago," said Venera as she held up a picture. "People forget. . . . What's this?"

Capper jerked awake in his chair and with a visible effort, sat up to look. "Ah, that . . . I don't know."

The image showed a misty, dim silhouette partly obscured behind the wheel of a town. The gray spindle shape suggested a ship, but that was impossible: the thing dwarfed the town. Venera held the print up to her nose under one of the gaslights. Now she could see little dots scattered around the gray shape. "What are these specks?"

"Bikes," whispered the spy. "See the contrails?"

Now she did, and with that the picture seemed to open out for a second, like a window. Venera glimpsed a vast chamber of air, walled by cloud and full of dock complexes, towns, and ships. Lurking at its edge was a monstrous whale, a ship so big that it could swallow the pinwheels of Rush.

But it must be a trick of the light. "How big is this thing? Did you get a good look at it? How long were you there?"

"Not long . . ." The spy waved his hand indifferently. "Took another shot . . ."

"He's not going to last if I don't get him to the doctor," said the man who was tending the spy's leg. "He needs blood."

Venera found the other photo and held it up beside the first. They were almost identical, evidently taken seconds apart. The only difference was in the length of some of the contrails.

"It's not enough." Frustration made hot waves of pain radiate up from her jaw and she unconsciously snarled. Venera turned to find only Carrier looking at her; his face expressed nothing, as always. The leather-suited spy was unconscious and his attendant was looking worried.

"Get him out of here," she said, gesturing to the servants' door at the back of the lounge. "We'll need to get a full deposition from him later." Capper was roused enough to lean on the shoulder of his attendant and they staggered out of the room. Venera perched on one of the benches and scowled at Carrier.

"This dispute with the pilot of Mavery is a distraction," she said. "It's intended to draw the bulk of our navy away from Rush. Then, these cruisers and that . . . thing, whatever it is, will invade from Falcon Formation. The Formation must have made a pact of some kind with Mavery."

Carrier nodded. "It seems likely. That is—it seems likely to me, my lady. The difficulty is going to be convincing your husband and the pilot that the threat is real."

"I'll worry about my husband," she said. "But the pilot . . . could be a problem."

"I will of course do whatever is in the best interest of the nation," said Carrier. Venera almost laughed.

"It won't come to that," she said. "All right. Go. I need to take these to my husband."

Carrier raised an eyebrow. "You're going to tell him about the organization?"

"It's time he knew we have extra resources," she said with a shrug. "But I have no intention of revealing our extent just yet . . . or that it's my organization. Nor will I be telling him about you."

Carrier bowed, and retreated to the servants' door. Venera remained standing in the center of the room for a long time after he left.

A thousand miles away, it would be night right now around her father's sun. Doubtless the pilot of Hale would be sleeping uneasily, as he always did under the wrought-iron canopy of his heavily guarded bed. His royal intuition told him that the governing principle of the world was conspiracy—his subjects were conspiring against him, their farm animals conspired against them, and even the very atoms of the air must have some plan or other. It was inconceivable to him that anyone should act from motives of true loyalty or love and he ran the country accordingly. He had raised his three daughters by this theory. Venera had fully expected that she would be disposed of by being married off to some inbred lout; at sixteen she had taken matters into her own hands and extorted a better match from her father. Her first attempt at blackmail had been wildly successful, and had netted her the man of her choice, a young commodore of powerful Slipstream. Of course, Slipstream was moving away from Hale, rapidly enough that by the time she consolidated her position here she would be no threat to the old man.

She hated it here in Rush, Slipstream's capital. The people were friendly, cordial, and blandly superior. Scheming was not in fashion. The young nobles insulted one another directly by pulling hat-feathers or making outrageous accusations in public. They fought their duels immediately, letting no insult fester for more than a day. Everything political was done in bright halls or council chambers and if there were darker entanglements in the shadows, she couldn't find them. Even now, with war approaching, the Pilot of Slipstream refused to beef up the secret service in any way.

It was intolerable. So Venera had taken it upon herself to correct the situation. These photos were the first concrete validation of her own deliberately cultivated paranoia.

She resolutely jammed the pictures into her belt purse—they

stuck out conspicuously but who would look?—and left by the front door.

Her servant waited innocently a good yard from the door. Venera was instantly suspicious that he'd been peering through the keyhole. She shot him a nasty look. "I don't believe I've used you before."

"No, ma'am. I'm new."

"You've had a background check, I trust?"

"Yes, ma'am."

"Well, you're going to have another." She stalked back to the admiralty with him following silently.

Bedlam continued in the admiralty antechamber, but it all seemed a bit silly to her now—they were in a fever of anticipation over a tiny border dispute with Mavery, while farther out a much bigger threat loomed. Nobody liked migratory nations, least of all Slipstream. They should be ready for this sort of thing. They should be more professional.

A page jostled Venera and the photos fell out of her purse. She laid a backhanded slap across the boy's head and stooped to grab them—to find that her servant had already picked them up.

He glanced at two that he held, apparently by accident, then did a double-take. Venera wondered whether he'd tripped the page behind her back just so he could do this.

"Give me those!" She snatched them back, noting as she did that it was the mysterious photos of the great, dim gray object that he'd looked at. She decided on the spot to have him arrested on some sort of trumped-up charge as soon as she reached the Fanning estate.

Blazing with anger, Venera elbowed her way through the crowd of couriers and minor functionaries, and took a side exit. Cold air wafted up from the stairs that led up to the cable cars connecting the other towns in this quartet. Fury and cold made her jaw flare with pain so that she wanted to turn and strike the insolent young man. With a great effort she restrained herself, and gradually calmed down. She was pleased at her own forbearance. *I can be a good person*, she reminded herself.

"Fifteen hundred feet," murmured the servant, almost inaudibly.

Venera whirled. He was trailing a few yards behind her, his expression distracted and wondering. "What did you say?" she hissed.

"That ship in the picture . . . was fifteen hundred feet long," he said, looking apologetic.

"How do you know that? Tell me!"

"By the contrails, ma'am."

She stared at him for a few seconds. He was young, certainly, and his high-cheeked face would have seemed innocent but for the weatherbeaten skin that reddened his brow and nose. He had a mop of black hair that fell like a raven's wing across his forehead and his eyes were framed with fine lines in an airman's perpetual squint.

He was either far more cunning than she'd given him credit for, or he was an idiot.

Or, she reluctantly admitted to herself, maybe he really had no idea that she'd met with someone in the ladies' room, and didn't expect a lady like herself to be carrying sensitive information. In which case the photos, to him, were just photos.

"Show me." She fished out the two shots of the behemoth and handed them to him.

Now he looked doubtful. "I can't be sure."

"Just show me how you reached that conclusion!"

He pointed to the first picture. "You see in the near space here, there's a bike passing. That's a standard Gray forty-five, and it's running at optimum speed, which is a hundred twenty-five knots. See the shape of its contrail? It only gets that feathered look under optimum burn. It's passing close by the docks so you can tell . . ." he flipped to the second picture, "that here it's gone about six hundred feet, if that dock is the size it looks to be. It means the second picture was taken about two seconds after the first.

"Now look at the contrails around the big ship. Lady, I can't see any bikes that *aren't* Gray forty-fives in the picture. So if we assume that the ones in the distance are Grays too, and that they're going at optimum speed, then these ones skimming the surface of the big ship have traveled a little less than half its length since the first picture. That makes it a bit over twelve hundred feet long."

"Mother of Virga." Venera stared at the picture, then at him. She noticed now that he was missing the tips of several fingers: frostbite?

She took back the pictures. "You're a flyer."

"Yes, ma'am."

"Then what are you doing working as a body servant in my household?"

"Flying bikes is a dead-end career," he said with a shrug.

They resumed walking. Venera was mulling things over. As they reached the broad clattering galleries of the cable car station, she nodded sharply and said, "Don't tell anybody about these, if you value your job. They're sensitive."

"Yes, ma'am." He looked past her. "Uh-oh."

Venera followed his gaze, and frowned. The long cable car gallery was full of people, all of whom were crowding in a grumbling mass under the rusty cable stays and iron-work beams that formed the chamber's ceiling. Six green cable cars hung swaying and empty in the midst of the throng. "What's the holdup?" she demanded of a nearby naval officer.

"Cable snapped," he said with a sigh. "Wind shear pulled the towns apart and the springs couldn't compensate."

"Don't drown me in details, when will it be fixed?"

"You'd have to ask the cable monkeys, and they're all out there now."

"I have to get to the palace!"

"I'm sure the monkeys sympathize, ma'am."

She was about to erupt in a tirade against the man, when the servant touched her arm. "This way," he murmured.

With a furious *hmmph*, Venera followed him out of the crowd.

He was heading for an innocuous side entrance. "What's down there?" she asked.

"Bike berths," he said as he opened the door to another windy gallery. This one was nearly empty. It curved up and out of sight, its right wall full of small offices with frosted-glass doors, its left wall opening out in a series of floor-to-ceiling arched windows. Beyond the windows was a braveway and then open turning air.

The gallery floor was full of hatches. About half had bikes suspended over them. The place smelled of engine oil, a masculine smell Venera found simultaneously rank and intriguing. Men in coveralls were rebuilding a bike nearby. Its parts were laid out in a neat line across a tarpaulin, their clean order betraying the apparent chaos of the opened chassis.

She was in a place of men; she liked that. "You have your own bike?" she asked the servant.

"Yes. It's right over there." He took a chit to the dock master and traded it in for a key and a worn leather jacket. They went over to the bike and he knelt to unlock the hatch beneath the gently swaying machine.

"Let me guess," she said. "A Gray forty-five?"

He laughed. "Those are work-haulers. This is a racer. It's a Canfield Arrow, Model fourteen. I bought it with my first paycheck from your household."

"There's a passenger seat," she said, suddenly thrilled at the prospect of riding the thing.

He squinted at her. "Have you never flown a bike, lady?"

"No. Does that surprise you?"

"I guess it's always been nice covered taxis for you," he said with a shrug. "Makes sense." He winched open the hatch and she took an apprehensive step back. Venera had no fear of the open air; it was speed that frightened her. Right now the air below the hatch was whipping by at gale force.

"We'll get blown off!"

He shook his head. "The dock master's lowering a shield ahead of the hatch. It'll give us several seconds of slipstream to cruise in.

Just hunker down behind me—the windscreen's big—and you'll be fine. Besides, I won't take us flat out, too dangerous inside city limits."

He straddled the bike and held out his hand. Venera suppressed her grin until she was seated behind him. There were foot straps but she had nothing to hold on to with her hands except him. She wrapped her arms tightly around his waist.

He pushed the starter and she felt the engine rumble into life beneath her. Then he said, "All set?" and reached up to unclip the winch.

They fell into the air and for a few seconds the curve of the town's undersurface formed a ceiling. There was the shield, a long tongue of metal hanging down but pulling up quickly. "Head down!" he shouted and she buried her face in his back. Then the engine was roaring to drown all thought, the vibration rattling up through her spine, and they were free in the air between the city cylinders. The wind wasn't tearing her from this man's grasp, so Venera cautiously leaned back and looked around. She gave an involuntary gasp of delight.

Contrails like spikes and ropes stood still in the air around them. Tethers with gay flags on them slung here and there, and everywhere taxies, winged humans, and other bikes shot through the air. The quartet of towns that included the admiralty was already receding behind them; she turned to look back and saw that the cable car system, whose independent loop touched the axle of the vast spinning cylinder, was indeed slack. Men floated in open air around the break, their tools arrayed in constellations about them as they argued over what to do. Venera turned forward again, laughing giddily at the sensation of power that pulled her up and up toward the next quartet.

They passed heavy steel cables and then the broad cross-shaped spokes of a town's pinwheel. Up close the brightly colored sails were torn and patched. In far too little time the bike was rising under another town, the long slot of a jet entrance visible overhead. Venera's flyer expertly inched them into a perfect tangent course, and it seemed as if the town's curving underside simply reached out and settled around them. Her flyer shut down the engine and held up a hook, clipping it to an overhead cable just as they began to fall again. And there they were, hanging in a gallery almost identical to the one they just left. A palace footman ran up and began winching them away from the slot. They had arrived.

Venera dismounted and staggered back a few steps. Her legs had turned to jelly. Her servant swung off the back of the bike as though nothing had just happened. He grinned happily at her. "It's a good beast," he said.

"Well." She cast about for something to say. "I'm glad we're paying you enough that you can afford it."

"Oh, I never said I could afford it."

She frowned, and led the way out of the gallery. From here she knew the stairs and corridors to take to reach Slipstream's strategic command office. Her husband, Admiral Fanning, was tied up in meetings there, but he would see her, she knew. She thought about how much she would tell him regarding her spy network. As little as possible, she decided.

At the entrance to the office she turned and looked frankly at the servant. "This is as far as you can go. Wait down at the docks, you can run me back home the same way you brought me."

He looked disappointed. "Yes, ma'am."

"Hmm. What's your name, anyway?"

"Griffin, ma'am. Hayden Griffin."

"All right. Remember what I said, Griffin. Don't talk about the photos to anyone." She waggled a finger at him, but even though her head was pounding she couldn't summon any anger at the moment. She turned and gestured for the armed palace guard to open the giant teak doors.

As she walked away she thought of the beautiful freedom Griffin must have in those moments when he flew alone. She'd caught a glimpse of it when she rode with him. But entangled as she was in a life of obligation and conspiracy, it could never be hers.

HAYDEN WATCHED HER go in frustration. So close! He'd gotten to within a few yards of his target today. And then to be thwarted at the very entrance to the command center. He eyed the palace guard, but he knew he couldn't take the man and the guard was eyeing him back. Reluctantly, Hayden turned and headed back toward the docks.

He'd nearly blown it picking up those pictures. Obviously he'd underestimated Lady Fanning. He wouldn't do it again. But since he had been assigned to her, he hadn't been able to get anywhere near Fanning himself. If she liked him, though . . .

It was only a matter of time, he decided. Admiral Fanning would come within arm's reach one day soon.

And then Hayden would kill him.

3

A FLOCK OF fish had wandered into the airspace inside Quartet One, Cylinder Two. Disoriented by the city lights spinning around them and caught in the cyclone of air that Rush's rooftops swept up, they foundered lower and lower in a quickening spiral, until with fatal suddenness they shot between the eaves of two close-leaning, gargoyle-coigned apartments. They banged off window and ledge, flagpole and fire escape, to end flapping and dying in a narrow street along which they'd scattered like a blast of buckshot.

Hayden ignored the cheering locals who ran out to scoop up the unexpected windfall. He paced on through the darkened alleys of Rush's night market, noticing nothing, but instinctively avoiding the grifters and thieves who also drifted through the crowds of out-country rubes. He felt slightly nauseated, and twitched at every loud laugh or thud of crate on cement.

The market was stuffed into a warren of small streets. Hayden loved walking through the mobs; even after living here for two years, the very fact that the city comprised more than one cylinder amazed him. The rusting wheels of the city provided gravity for over thirty thousand souls. Throw in the many outlying towns and countless estates that hung in the nearby air like sprays of tossed seed, and the population must push a hundred thousand. The anonymity this afforded was a heady experience for an unhappy young man. Hayden could be with people yet aloof and he liked it this way.

He was dead tired after another long day at the Fanning estate; but if he went back to the boarding house now, he would just pace until his downstairs neighbors complained. He would pull at his hair, and mutter to himself as if he were mad. He didn't want to do that.

He paused to buy a sticky bun at a vendor he favored, and continued on down a twisting run sided with fading clapboard. Slipstream's sun was on its maintenance cycle, and darkness and chill had settled over the city. Here and there in the alleys, homeless people kept barrel fires going and charged a penny or two to anyone who stopped to warm their hands. Hayden sometimes stopped to talk to these men, whose faces he knew only as red sketches lit from below. They could be valuable sources of information, but he never revealed anything about himself to them, least of all his name.

To be so close to his goal and yet be unable to act was intolerable. He walked through the Fanning household like a dutiful servant for hours while his mind raced through scenarios: Fanning walking by distracted in a hallway; Hayden slipping into the Admiralty unnoticed by the omnipresent security police . . . It was all useless. The chances never came, and he was getting desperate.

He'd driven Venera Fanning again today—unnecessarily, for she could easily have taken a cable car. He wondered at her motives in riding with him. When he'd returned to his room he'd discovered that a faint scent of her perfume still hovered on his jacket. It was alluring, as she was with her porcelain complexion—marred only by the scar on her chin—and her hair the color of winter skies. Attractive she might be, but she was also without doubt the most callous human being he'd ever met. And she traded on her beauty.

How strange that she should be the first woman he'd given a ride to since arriving in Rush.

Halfway down the alley was a cul-de-sac. A knife seller had set up his table across its entrance, and had mounted targets on the blank wall at the dead end. Hayden stopped to balance a sleek dart knife on his finger. He held it out facing away from him, then at right angles to that.

"It's good in all the directions of gravity," said the vendor, who in this light was visible only as a black cutout shape with a swath of distant lamplight revealing his beige shirt collar. The black silhouette of an arm rose in an indistinct gesture. "Try it out."

Hayden balanced the knife for a second more, then flipped it and caught it behind the guard fins. He threw it with a single twitch of his wrist and it buried itself in the center of a target with a satisfying thump. The vendor murmured appreciatively.

"That's not our best, you know," he said as he waddled back to retrieve the knife. His mottled hand momentarily became visible as he pulled the knife from the wall. "Try this." Back at the table, he fished in a case and drew out a long arrow shape. Hayden took it from him and turned it over with a professional eye. Triangular cross-section to the blade, guards that doubled as fins for throwing, and a long tang behind that with another fin on its end. Its heft was definitely better than the last one.

He thought of Admiral Fanning and his purpose in coming to this city. With a muttered curse he spun and let fly the knife. It sank dead center in the smallest target.

"Son, you should be in the circus," said the vendor. Hayden heard the admiration in his voice, but it didn't matter. "Say, do you want to hang around a while and throw for the crowd? Could bring in some business."

Hayden shook his head. He wasn't supposed to have skills like knife throwing. "Just dumb luck," he said. "I guess your knives are just so good that even an idiot can hit the bull's-eye with one." Ducking his head and aware of the lameness of his excuse, he backed away and then paced hurriedly down the alley.

"That wasn't smart," said a shadow at his elbow.

Hayden shrugged and kept going. "What's it to you?"

The other fell into step beside him. Hayden glimpsed a tall, rangy figure in the dim light. "Somebody you owe a favor, Hayden."

He stepped away involuntarily. "Who the—"

The man in the shadows laughed and moved into a pale lozenge of candlelight that squeezed out between the cracks of a low

window. The profile revealed was of a lean, bald man with bushy
eyebrows. "Don'tcha recognize me, Hayden? Last time I saw you,
you were dropping out of Gavin Town on a runaway bike!"

"Miles?" Hayden just stood there, painfully aware of how meetings like this were supposed to go: the prodigal and the old soldier, laughing and slapping each other's backs in surprise and
delight. They would head for a bar or something, and regale each
other with stories of their exploits, only to stagger out again singing at three the next morning. Or so it went. But he'd never much
liked Miles, and what did it matter, really, to find out now that one
other person had survived the attack on the sun? It didn't change
anything.

"What are you doing here?" he asked after the silence between
them had stretched too long.

"Looking after you, boy," said the ex-soldier. "You're not happy
to see me?"

"It's not that," he said with a shrug. "It's . . . been a long time."

"Well, long or not, I'm here now. What do you say?"

"It's . . . good to see you."

Miles laughed humorlessly. "Right. But you'll be thanking me
before long, believe me." He started walking. "Come on. We need
to find a place to talk."

Here it came, thought Hayden: the bar, the war stories, the
laughing. He hesitated, and Miles sighed heavily. "Kid, I saved your
ass today. If it weren't for me, you'd be on your way out of Rush by
now with a permanent deport order issued against you."

"I don't believe you."

"Suit yourself." Miles started walking. After a moment Hayden
ran after him.

"What do you mean?" he asked.

" 'It's so good to see you, Miles. How are you doing, Miles?
How did you survive Gavin Town?' " The ex-soldier glared at
Hayden as they crossed a busy and well-lit thoroughfare. "Jeez, you
were always a surly little runt, but let me tell you, I'm wondering

whether I should have bothered faking the docs for your background check."

"What background check?" He'd had two of them already, he knew, a cursory one when he first applied for Rush residency, and a more thorough check after he answered the call for work at the Fanning residence. It seemed all too plausible that somebody somewhere should want to do more digging—and now he realized who. "Venera Fanning. She had me investigated."

"But not by the legal authorities," said Miles as he ducked into another alley. This one was empty, and meandered in the general direction of one of the town spokes. The spoke jabbed into the heavens above all rooftops, a tessellation of wrought-iron girders barnacled here and there by shanty huts built by desperate homeless people. Some spokes had municipal elevators in them and were quite well-kept; this one was a rusty derelict unlit from any source.

"It's just lucky we have a man in Fanning's network." Miles had disappeared in the darkness ahead. Hayden followed his voice, idly wondering if he'd been lured in here to be mugged. "This time they weren't going to just hold your papers up to a light and check the birth registries. Friends, family, coworkers—I had to come up with them all at the last minute."

"But how did you know about it?"

"Ah, finally, a sensible question. Here, watch your step." They had reached the gnarled fist of beam and cable that was the spoke's base. Someone had built a crude set of stairs by simply jamming boards into the diamond-shaped gaps in the ironwork. Miles plodded up this, wood bending and twanging under his feet.

His voice drifted down from overhead. "I review intercepted dispatches about security checks. It's my job in the Resistance."

Hayden stopped climbing. "Resistance? You still believe in that?"

Miles spun around, glaring. "Hayden, how can you of all people say that? You were born into the Resistance—you were the first baby born of two members, didn't you know that?"

He shrugged uncomfortably. "That's not the point, is it? When they blew up the sun they beat us. It was our last hope."

"Is that what you thought?" Miles sounded outraged. "Son, we were just getting started! And after the attack we needed you more than ever. We searched for you for days after the attack . . ."

"I didn't know. I fell into winter." He looked down, noticing distractedly how the rooftops looked from just overhead, with their shingled peaks and streamlined eaves. From here the whole circular geometry of the town spread out below him, with its mazes of close-packed buildings, streetlights glowing overhead and on two sides, and the permanent winds of Slipstream whistling from the dark open circles of night to left and right. A gust shook him and he realized that he'd fall hard enough to be killed if he got blown off this precarious vantage point. Keep following Miles or go back? Hayden reluctantly groped for the next ladder-like step. "Where are we going, Miles?"

"There." The lean ex-soldier—who, when it came right down to it, Hayden didn't know that well—pointed straight up. The inside of the open-work spoke was blocked by a wood ceiling ten feet farther up. The surface was white with strange, broad black bands painted across it. With a start Hayden realized they were intended to look like shadows; this box was supposed to be invisible if looked at from some particular perspective—probably from the direction of the Office of Public Infrastructure.

Miles ascended the last distance by ladder and raising his fist, knocked it against wood. A square of light appeared above his head, and he clambered up. "Come on in, Hayden."

He cautiously raised his head above the lip of the trapdoor, and then, for the first time in many years, he entered a cell of the Resistance.

"No, it's not our headquarters," said Miles as Hayden looked around the little room. "Just a watching post. We're at a rare spot that lets us look down the window of the semaphore room in the Admiralty. But we also store sensitive materials here—like guns." He gestured to a stack of long boxes on the floor.

The place was little more than ten feet on a side, though a ladder led up to what was presumably a second level. Blackout curtains covered three walls. A little chair in the out-of-fashion Lace style perched in front of a desk where a man with thick glasses and a halo of white hair sat muttering over a pile of paper. In the opposite corner crouched a lanky man dressed entirely in black. He was walking his fingers over a map of Rush, evidently trying to gauge distances in one of the cylinders.

"Meet Hayden Griffin. He's the son of the original sunlighters."

The man in black just grunted; but the balding fellow at the table sat up straight and cranked his glasses down to get a look at Hayden. "Grace! So it is! You probably wouldn't remember me, Hayden, but I babysat for you when you were four."

"Martin Shambles," said Miles. "And this one, he's V.I.P. Billy. Our assassin."

Hayden nodded to them both, trying not to sneak another look at Billy. Shambles stood up and held out his hand. "Well met, Hayden! Looks like we saved your ass today."

"I wasn't aware it needed saving," said Hayden. But he shook the offered hand.

"'Course, it would have been easier if we'd known you were still alive." Shambles sat back down, chuckling. "And working in the Fanning house, no less! That caused a stir. Some of our boys went so far as to claim you'd turned, gone over to their side—"

"But we know you wouldn't do that, would you?" asked V.I.P. Billy, who was now standing. Hayden suddenly realized that he was unfavorably placed with his back to a corner, with Miles and Billy on either side of him.

"Of course, there's the question of where you've actually been the past several years," continued Shambles, who was unconcernedly peering at his papers again. "We had a back story ready for somebody else, papers, friends—it's the sort of in-depth investigation Venera Fanning goes in for. She's much more thorough than the Admiralty that way. I mean, we traced you as far as we could, but that wasn't far. Not far at all, in fact."

Despite the cold air, Hayden was starting to sweat. "But—but I could ask you the same thing," he said. "Where were you? When the sun blew up and I fell into winter, where were you? It wasn't the Resistance who found me and nursed me back from frostbite. Hell, I fell *four hundred miles* before I finally hit a mushroom farm run by this weird old couple. . . . Nobody came after me. Did you even look?"

Miles nodded gravely. "We looked. Your falling into winter was one possibility. Being captured by one of Fanning's ships was another. It was fifty-fifty which had happened."

"These people . . ." Hayden had trouble thinking of what to say. He knew his life was on the line here. "They were exiles. A man and woman named Katcheran. Said Aerie had kicked them out twenty years ago. They had no gravity, they were as fragile as birds. They grew mushrooms on this little rock they'd found in the emptiness, and occasionally they'd jet over to the outskirts of Aerie to drop some off for supplies. But it took them ages to ferment enough alcohol for fuel . . . he tended to drink it away."

Miles looked skeptical, but Shambles perked up. "Did you say Katcheran?" Hayden nodded. Shambles pursed his lips. "Haven't heard that name in years." He tilted his head to one side and looked at Hayden shrewdly. "Go on."

Hayden did his best to describe his stay in the dark regions outside civilization. The volumes of air there were vast, and not all of it was cold, or dark. The little mushroom farm was just a cave to live in hollowed out of a clay ball no more than fifty feet in diameter. Katcheran and his wife bickered in a constant, monotonous murmur. Hayden had spent most of his time outside, watching the skies for any sign of a passing ship.

The distant beacons of Aerie teased him whenever he looked in its direction. But every now and then dawn would come as clouds parted around some distant sun. Then he could see just how far away from home he'd come. Hazy depths of emptiness opened out to all sides, not even a stray boulder or water ball visible for miles upon miles. He was stranded in a desert of air, and a few times he'd curled into a ball, hovering above the stinking fungus, and wept.

On two or three occasions, though, he saw more. The shells of cloud that enveloped the center of Virga sometimes parted, revealing the sun of suns, Candesce. Daylight would suddenly flash out to fill the entire volume of winter. Each time, Hayden had stood on the air, amazed at the brilliance of it—at the sheer size of an ancient, untended fusion engine that put all other suns in Virga to shame. Dozens of civilizations depended on that single central light, he'd heard. It was the greatest source of heat in the world; it drove the circulation cells in which Aerie and the other nations migrated slowly inward and outward.

The core components of his parents' sun had come from Candesce; the sun of suns was the wellspring for all of Virga's lesser lights.

"It was a year before Katcheran had enough fuel for us to fly back, and then he followed the beacons he knew, which brought us in a hundred miles away from Gavin Town. Of course, the town was a legend by then, but nobody knew much about it. Any pieces that were left after Slipstream attacked had been dismantled or drifted away. I didn't have anybody to go to . . . any way to get in touch with the Resistance, unless I came to Rush, and I didn't have any money to travel. I got a job in a kitchen in Port Freeley and saved until I could get passage here.

"But you know what I found out when I finally got back to Aerie? Nobody knew about our sun! Nobody knew. We'd built it in secret, and Slipstream attacked in secret, and nobody told the people what had happened. If they'd known . . . something might have been done." He shook his head. "Maybe the Resistance couldn't have kept Slipstream from finding the sun and destroying it. I don't know. But you could have told—you had the responsibility to tell the people of Aerie what had happened.

"How could I get involved with you again after that?"

Miles looked troubled, but Billy just raised an eyebrow. "So why are you working for the Fannings? It took you a lot of effort to do it—you even forged your Slipstream citizenship yourself, by the looks of it."

Hayden stared at him. "Well, why do you think I came here? I came to kill Admiral Fanning."

There was a brief silence while the other three looked at one another. Then Billy cracked a slight smile. "Why in Virga would you want to do that?"

"Because he's the one." Hayden didn't care that the man in black was a killer. The indignity of having his motives suspected was just too much. "I saw the name on the side of the flagship that attacked us. The *Arrogance*. It was Fanning's ship when he was still commodore. He blew up our sun! He killed my mother! I care about that. Don't you care? What have you been doing here, all these years? What kind of a resistance is this? You're supposed to be an assassin, why haven't you killed him?" He stepped over to Shambles's table and tossed some of the papers in the air. "What, are you gonna *plan* them all to death? Is that the idea? Well, while you've been squatting on your asses in your little box, I've been doing something with my time. I was ten feet away from him today; tomorrow I'll be right there, and then he'll be dead."

He glared at them. "That's why I came here. That's what I'm doing. So what are you doing?"

Shambles adjusted his glasses and patted down the papers. "Well, Hayden my lad, we're trying to save our country. That would seem like a very different goal from yours, now wouldn't it?"

"Oh, please," said Hayden, crossing his arms. "What's to save? Slipstream annexed Aerie ages ago. I don't even *remember* how it was before that happened. It's ancient history."

"What you say is very true," said Shambles with a thoughtful nod. "However, it is also true that, since Slipstream is a migratory nation, it will someday migrate its way out of Aerie. Our concern is with what happens when that occurs."

Hayden looked at him blankly.

"Hmm." Shambles turned in his chair, crossing his legs. "It is a fact of youth that it has no concept of the future. Yet that is what we are here to discuss. The future of Aerie—and your future."

Hayden snorted.

"Tell me," said Shambles, "what is it, fundamentally, that keeps a nation together?"

Hayden decided to take the bait. "A sun."

Shambles shook his head. "No. It's *formation flying*. That is what keeps a nation together. If all your towns and farms and water balls are sailing off in different directions, it hardly matters if you've got a sun of your own, does it? What's essential is that you keep everybody flying on the same heading, maintaining the same altitude and position above the Sun of Suns. Aerie is still doing that—for now. The danger is that the presence of the Slipstream sun in our skies will cause parts of the nation to drift away, leave the formation, and join other countries. Hayden, that is a threat far greater than any police actions or propaganda by Slipstream could be."

"For ten years now we've been keeping Aerie in formation," said Miles. "That's what the Resistance does. What possible good would revenge do us? If you kill Fanning, he'll just be replaced."

"Yes," said Hayden, "but he'll also be dead."

Miles sighed. "I brought you here tonight because I hoped we could bring you back into the net. With your position in the Fanning household, you could be invaluable to us—especially now that Slipstream's finally moved close enough to our neighbors that it's been perceived as a threat. Mavery is moving against Slipstream. Slipstream will move into Mavery territory in a year or two and at that point they'll find themselves fighting a two-front war, against Mavery and us. Our job is to prepare for that, and to make sure that when the time comes, we either win or convince them to commit all their forces to Mavery, and leave us behind. If we had a spy in the very heart of the Admiralty . . ." His expression was greedy.

"Aerie is gone," Hayden said. "When Slipstream leaves they'll take their sun with them. Without a sun, Aerie will freeze in the dark. The people will leave. I've lived in winter. I know what it's like."

"We're working on that," said Shambles. "With the right components we could—"

Hayden shook his head. "I'm only here to do one thing. And after that . . . I don't care."

"But, Hayden my boy," purred Billy as he put an arm around Hayden's shoulder, "the problem is, we care. It's a worry, you know—the vision of you shooting Fanning and then being caught and tortured. You might talk about us, you see."

"Oh! No, I—"

"Now it would be supremely gauche of me to threaten your life at this point," Billy went on. "After all, as you say, you have your own path to take. That's fine. But if you're not going to join us, then we have one simple request."

"What's that?"

"If you're going to kill Fanning up close and personal like, say in the middle of the Admiralty itself . . . Just make sure you kill yourself too, hmm? As a favor to us, you see. So we don't have to."

Hayden bolted to the trapdoor and flung it up. "You know where to find us if you change your mind," Shambles called cheerfully.

"You won't hear from me," snapped Hayden as he lowered himself down to the invisible ladder. Slamming the trapdoor he began clumsily backing his way down to the city, fuming and muttering as he went.

He was just above the rooftops when a lurid orange flash lit up the sky. A distant grumble like thunder reached his ears. Hayden paused, clinging to the swaying planks, and listened.

The tearing sound of a jet could be heard fading in the distance. Then another one, growing closer. Funny; he knew all about bikes, but he couldn't identify the type from this one's sound.

Then something flashed by outside the iron stanchions. He poked his head out between the girders in time to see something bright shoot straight into the lit window of a mansion near the far end of the cylinder. To his amazement, the outer wall of the house seemed to dissolve in flame and the whole roof lifted off.

Another missile tore past, this one miraculously threading its way through spokes, guy wires, and ladder-ways to exit the other end of the cylinder. Seconds later he heard gunfire, and a distant bloom of light signaled the missile's destruction.

A head poked out next to his. The windburned homeless man spared Hayden a single glance before gaping at the next missile to appear out of the darkness. Belatedly, sirens were starting up throughout the city, animal voices Dopplered weirdly by distance and rotation.

The new missile hit one of the other spokes. The unfolding red flower lit the stubbled face next to Hayden's, tiny arcs of reflection glinting in the man's eyes.

Then he heard shouts from above. Miles and the others were coming down. Hayden pulled his head in and clambered the rest of the way down to the street, where people were now running back and forth shouting.

He felt a momentary surge of exultation. Slipstream was paying at last! He hid his grin; laughing out loud would probably be a bad idea right now.

Hayden walked through the chaos for a few minutes. No more missiles appeared but firefighting crews were battling their way through the mob and fights were breaking out. All lights were on and somewhere engines were throbbing. He felt a pull to the right and creaking, groaning sounds echoed through the street as his weight diminished. The hit on that spoke must have spooked the gravity department.

His feet had unconsciously led him toward the docks. When he realized where he was, he frowned. He should just go home—ride this out. But where would Fanning be just now? This attack meant that the fleet would be mobilized. For all he knew, the admiral might be aboard his flagship already, and then Hayden would never get a chance at him.

With a curse he ran for the docks, where he had parked his bike.

4

AT THE DOCKS the master was screaming, "No civilian craft, no civilian craft!" at a hundred panicked men crowding the doors. Hayden showed the security guard his pass to the Fanning estate and the grim-faced man reluctantly let him by. Once through the press of people he leaped on the back of his jet and kicked it into life. He dropped into turbulent air and the wail of attack sirens.

The sky was a storm of vehicles. Hayden had to twist and turn to avoid colliding with flocks of police bikes and ambulances. He kept his speed way down and held up his pass as he shot through narrow checkpoint gaps in ship-catcher nets that hadn't been there an hour before. In the distance other nets were slowly unfurling, distance making them appear like gray stains spreading in water.

Hayden never tired of flying between the cylinders of Rush at night. Even in this emergency, he found himself turning his head to watch the running lights of Quartet One, Cylinder Two as it showed him its black underside and, after he passed it, a crescent-shaped vision of glowing city windows and rooftops inside. The air was normally full of lanterns showing where invisible cables and stations waited in the dark; the lights were doubling, tripling now as he flew. To complicate matters, it looked as though a lightning storm was moving in: the sky below him was lit with intermittent flickers of white.

He was coming up underneath the Admiralty cylinder when bright radiance slapped his shadow against the town's spinning metal hull. He nearly missed the entrance slot in surprise: they'd turned the sun on, seven hours early!

After he'd hooked his bike to its crane and climbed off, he saw that this wasn't a normal dawn cycle. The skies visible through the arched windows of the dock were still a deep indigo. There must be some sort of spotlight feature to the sun that he'd never heard of before; Rush was pinioned in a beam of daylight but the rest of the world was a cave of night.

Another pilot was standing by the windows. "Now I believe it happened," he muttered under his breath. Hayden frowned and hurried out of the dock and up the stairs.

He could hear the tumult in the Fanning household before he even opened the servants' door. Inside, the kitchen staff were running back and forth piling cutlery in boxes, searching for anything with the Fanning monogram on it.

"What's going on?" Hayden asked mildly, sitting down at the large table beside the stove.

"They're going to war," said a maid on her way past. At that moment the chief butler swept into the kitchen and immediately spotted Hayden. "Griffin! Get into uniform. We're going to need you."

"Yes, sir."

He felt a pulse of resentment, but as he turned to go to the cloakroom Lynelle, another of the maids, passed close by and whispered, "This throws all my well-laid plans to waste."

"Uh, what?" He turned to look at her as she leaned in the kitchen doorway. She was pretty, he hadn't failed to notice that. But maybe he'd failed to notice her noticing him.

"I was going to throw a little party at my place on our shift's off-day. And I was going to invite you when I saw you tonight." She shrugged sourly. "Can't do it now."

"I—, I guess not." He backed away.

She followed. "Was it really an attack by Mavery?" she asked.

"I don't know. Listen, I . . . I have to get ready for work."

"Oh. All right, see you." He knew she was watching him walk away; his ears burned.

Hayden had been careful to cultivate a respectful attitude since being hired. In truth, he hated it when the other servants were nice to him. How could good people, in all conscience, work for a monster? It seemed perverse and incomprehensible to him. He went to his locker in the men's cloak room and donned the livery of the Fanning household. Once he was dressed, he sat down on the dressing bench for a moment to gather his courage.

Obviously, he would never get a better chance than this—if Fanning was home. Chances were he was in the Admiralty office or the palace right now. But Hayden would have to assume otherwise, and do what so far he had not had a chance to do: venture unescorted into the Fanning's living quarters. He checked that the knife in the back of his belt was accessible, then stood up.

One little detail kept nagging at him. Hayden's search for his mother's killers had led him here. He had verified that the *Arrogance* was under Fanning's command at the time of the attack on Aerie's new sun. But there was a troubling photograph in one of the hallways of this mansion. It showed Chaison Fanning standing with an academy graduating class, his easy smile contrasting their own serious pride. He had given a speech and attended a dinner there, six hundred miles away from the edge of Aerie.

The picture was dated the very day of the attack.

His hands were trembling. With a curse he strode out of the cloakroom and made for the stairs. Somebody shouted after him, but he ignored them. Let them think he had business upstairs—well, it was true anyway.

He was feeling lightheaded. The lamps in their amber sconces throwing rings of light on the ceiling; the looming portraits of ancestral Fannings glaring at him from all sides; the distant shouting and clanging, all lent an unreal atmosphere to the night. Hayden passed several people on the stairs, one of whom was an admiralty attache; they all ignored him. As he reached the landing to the second floor he heard muttering sounds coming from the admiral's office. So Fanning was here after all.

But not alone. Hayden paused outside the door, which was ajar. Fanning was talking to someone in low, clipped tones. It came to

Hayden that this was exactly where Miles and the other Resistance members would have wanted him to be, had he agreed to join their cause. For a moment the wild thought came to him that he might be able to kill Fanning and escape, and that if so, he could pull a double coup if he returned to Miles with strategic information. So he listened.

". . . Won't accept any of it. He's getting way too trusting in his old age." Hayden recognized Fanning's voice, which he had only ever heard from behind closed doors. Was the admiral talking to only one person, or was there a full-blown staff meeting going on in there? Hayden couldn't find an angle where he could look around the door without being seen.

"But our orders are clear," said another man. "We're to take the Second Fleet into Mavery and deal with them now."

"We don't need the Second Fleet to eradicate Mavery," said Fanning contemptuously. "And the old man knows that. He's afraid that the First Families are going to side with me and order the fleet to investigate this buildup of ships in the sargasso. If he moves us all into Mavery we can't do that."

"He doesn't believe the sargasso fleet's a threat?"

"He doesn't believe it's *real*." Hayden heard papers shuffling. "So. Here are your orders."

There was a pause, then Hayden heard a sharp intake of breath from the other man. "You can't mean this!"

"I can. We'll deal with Mavery, like the old man wants. But I'll be damned if I'm going to sit in the air occupying a second-rate province while somebody else moves in full force against Rush."

"But—but by the time we do this—"

"The sargasso fleet's not ready. That's clear from the photos. And we won't be able to put Mavery down right away; it'll take a minimum of two months before we're inextricably engaged with them, and whoever's behind this knows to wait for that to happen. We have the time."

The other muttered under his breath, then seemed to catch himself. "Sir. It's audacious, Admiral, but . . . I can see the logic of it."

"Good. Well, go to it, Captain. I'll join you when I've completed preparations here."

Hayden just had time to close the door of the linen closet as a captain of the navy in full dress attire strode out of Fanning's office and down the stairs.

As soon as he was gone, Hayden was out and sidling up to the door to the office. There was no one but Fanning in there now, he was sure of it. His mouth was dry, and his pulse pounding in his ears as he steeled himself for what he had to do. In all likelihood he wouldn't survive the night, but he had a debt to pay.

Taking a deep breath, he reached for the doorknob.

"There you are!"

He snatched his hand back as if it had been burned, and turned to find Venera Fanning standing at the head of the stairs. She had a hand on one cocked hip, and was glaring at him in her usual withering way. She was dressed in traveling attire, complete with trousers and a backpack thrown over her shoulder.

"I'm going to need a good driver," she said as she stalked up to him. "You're the only one I know who can handle himself outside of an air carriage."

"Uh—thank you, ma'am?"

"Wait here." She swept past him and into the office, leaving the door wide open. This gave Hayden his first glimpse of Fanning's office; it was not what he'd expected. The place was a mess. All four walls were crammed with bookshelves of differing pedigree. Books swelled out of the shelves and sheets of paper stuck out between the volumes like the white leaves of some literary ivy. More papers stood in precarious stacks on the floor, all leaning left to accommodate the Coriolis tilt of the town's artificial gravity. The admiral himself was leaning back in his chair, one foot propped up next to the table's only lamp. He scowled up at Venera as she walked in.

"This is low even for you," he said as he tossed a sheaf of papers onto the desk. He looked older in person than in the photos Hayden had seen, with crow's-feet around his eyes, and his hair was starting to recede. Whipcord thin, he nonetheless moved gracefully under gravity, unlike people who spent most of their time in freefall.

"Oh, come now," Venera was saying. "I'm just asserting my prerogative as a wife, to be with her husband."

"Wives don't travel on ships of the line, especially when they're going into battle!" As if to emphasize his words, a flash of lightning lit the sky outside the office's one narrow window.

"I admit I underestimated you, Venera," continued Fanning. "No—actually, I misunderstood you. This intelligence network you created, it's . . ." He shook his head. "Beyond the pale. Why? What's it for? And why are you so insistent on joining the expeditionary force that you're willing to blackmail your own husband to guarantee that I'll say yes?"

"I did it all for us," she said sweetly as she came around the desk to lean over him. Venera smoothed the hair away from Fanning's forehead. "For our advantage. It's the way we do things back home, that's all."

"But why come along? This will be dangerous, and you'll be leaving the capital just when it would be most advantageous for you to remain here as my eyes and ears. It's a contradiction, Venera."

"I know you hate mysteries," she said. "That's what makes you good at your job. But I'm afraid this particular mystery will have to remain unsolved for a while. You'll see—if all works out as I hope. For now, you'll just have to trust me."

He laughed. "That's the funniest thing you've said in a long time. Well, all right then, pack your things and get down to the docks. We'll be sailing tonight."

"Under cover of darkness?" She smiled. "You do some of your best work then, you know."

Fanning just sighed and shook his head.

Venera returned to the hallway, and taking Hayden's arm, drew him away from the office and toward the stairs. He let her do it. "I'm going to send a man around to your flat," she said to Hayden. "Tell him what to collect for you. You're not to leave the house today; wait for me by the main doors at six o'clock tonight, or your contract is terminated. Is that understood?"

"But what's—"

She waved a hand imperiously, indicating that he should retreat down the stairs.

She stood between him and the man he'd come to murder.

"Well?" she said. Venera seemed to see him for the first time; a muscle in her jaw flexed, causing the star-shaped scar there to squirm. "What are you waiting for?"

Hayden took a step down. He'd been planning this moment for years. In his mind it had always been clear: the traitor revealing his cowardice at the end, Hayden making some pronouncement—different every time—of just vengeance for his people's loss. An execution, clean and final.

But in order to get at the admiral now, he would have to leave Venera Fanning bleeding out her own life in the hallway.

He took another step down.

Something came over Venera's face. Softness? Some subtle giving-in to an interpretation of his actions that he didn't understand? "It will all be made clear tonight," she said in as soothing a tone as she was likely capable of.

He could have retreated around a corner, waited for her to leave. He might have staked out Fanning's office for the rest of the night. Instead he found his feet take another step and another, and then he was turning and clattering down the steps as though he actually had some other place to go. Somehow he ended up passing the photograph of Fanning posing with a graduating class. He stopped and stared at the date written on it until a hand descended on his shoulder and someone spoke his name.

He pushed past the other manservant as the world spun around him—and when he came to himself again he was kneeling in one of the servant's washrooms vomiting wretchedly into the privy.

ADMIRAL CHAISON FANNING pulled himself hand over hand up the docking rope and did a perfect free-fall flip to land on the quarterdeck of the *Rook*. He'd practiced that maneuver many times when he was younger, just as he'd practiced wearing the uniform of the Admiralty, keeping the cut of the jacket just so, the toeless boots polished to perfection and his toenails manicured and clean. The men watched for weakness using every possible standard—some couldn't follow a man with a thin voice, others couldn't respect an officer who didn't occasionally smile. Sometimes it seemed he'd spent the past two decades learning sixty varieties of playacting, with a special role for every rung on the ladder to his success.

There was a particular style to be cultivated when you were leaving port; he needed to project confidence and purpose to the airmen so that they didn't look back and obeyed his orders without question.

Rook was not the flagship of the fleet. A midsized cruiser, she was beginning to show her age, and several years ago had been refitted to buttress Slipstream's dwindling winter fleet. Still, she was a good ship: a hundred feet long, thirty in diameter, basically cylindrical but with curving ends that terminated in vicious spiked rams. Her thick wooden hull was festooned with hatches and ports through which could be thrust rifles, rocket racks, jet engines, braking sails, or mutineers as the situation warranted. Many of the hatches were open as she hung in the air next to the docking scaffolds, a mile from the Admiralty. The sun was glowering from behind the docks, whose caged catwalks cast long curving shadows across the amber hull of the ship, while tongues of light had found and lit random intricacies of its interior. Inside, the ship was a series of interlocking cells, most of them made of wooden lattices through which you could see men working or the tanned sides of tarpaulined and lashed crates. Some of the cells were big blocks of metal, such as the armory and the rocket magazine. And to the fore of the ship, just behind the bridge, an exercise centrifuge spun lazily. Its side walls made a turning mandala of Admiralty notices, wooden walls, and plumbing. The men were required to spend a few hours a day in the centrifuge, and he would too; nobody was going to lose their fighting trim on this voyage.

Captain John Sembry saluted the admiral. His staff were lined up in midair behind him, their toes pointed precisely in the same direction. "The ship is ready, sir," announced Sembry.

A quick glance told Chaison that everything was where it should be, and the men were all working hard—or at least giving the impression of working hard. That was all that mattered, if things were truly ready. "Very good, Captain. I'll be on the bridge. Carry on." He turned and did a hand-over-hand walk through a narrow passage under the centrifuge, heading for the prow.

On the way to the bridge he checked his cabin. Venera was not there. Neither was her luggage. Fuming, he continued on up to the cylindrical chamber just behind the fore rocket battery. The navigator and helm were waiting, looking expectant. They hadn't yet received their orders and were expecting to be told to set a course for Mavery. He was going to surprise them.

But not, apparently, yet. "Where is she?" he demanded of a petty officer. The man snapped to attention, slowly drifting upward and away from his post.

"Semaphore said, on her way, sir!"

"And when was that?"

"Half—half an hour ago, sir."

He turned away, composing himself before the man could see his mask of professionalism slip. He was looking for something to do—a tie-down to criticize, a chart crib to fold—when the navigator said, "She's here, sir," with some relief in his voice. He was floating next to a porthole; Chaison stepped over fifteen feet of empty air to join him there, and look where he pointed.

Hanging limbs akimbo in the cage of a docking arm twenty meters away was a long-haired woman with an imperious nose and heavily made-up eyes. She wore an outlandishly bright jumpsuit that was also too tight in all the right (or, on a ship like this, wrong) places. Her hands were twisting nervously, but her expression was intent and focused as she directed some navvies to push a small mountain of crates and trunks through the narrow exit of the docking arm.

Aubri Mahallan was not the "she" Chaison had been hoping to see. He'd assumed this particular passenger was already on board. Forgetting himself he frowned virulently at her, as if she could see him behind the sun-drenched hull.

"That . . . costume . . . will not do," he muttered under his breath.

"Two women on board, sir," said the navigator neutrally. "It's—"

"Far from unprecedented," Chaison finished smoothly. "There's a great tradition of female ship officers in Virga, Bargott—just not of late in the enlightened principality of our beloved pilot."

"No, sir, ah, yes, sir."

"Summon the armorer to the chart room when she boards. I'll meet her there." Chaison left without another glance at the bridge staff.

Located behind the bridge, the chart room was the traditional inner sanctum of the ship's commanding officer. Nobody was allowed in here except the bridge staff and Chaison himself—nobody except for the one person he did find when he entered the drum-shaped room. Gridde, Chaison's chart-master, was fabulously old and bent over—so much so that he retained the stoop even in freefall. As Chaison entered he was teasing a tiny ruby clip out of its nestle in the crook of two fine hairs inside the chamber's main chart box. "Ah, Admiral," he said without turning around, "it's an interesting challenge you've given me this time."

Chaison's irritability evaporated, as it always did around Gridde. "It would have been a shame for you to retire without helping us navigate winter."

"I've done it before," wheezed Gridde, smiling at Chaison's surprise. "Thirty-five years ago," continued the chart-master. He returned his attention to the large glass chart box. Inside the box was a three-dimensional lattice of fine, almost invisible blond strands—actual hairs, harvested from the rare young lady whose locks met Gridde's standard. Clipped to these strands were dozens of tiny jewel-clusters: a single sapphire stood for a small town, double-sapphires for larger towns, and so on. The box was a scintillating galaxy of light: sapphires, rubies, emeralds, topaz and jet, pale quartz and peridot. At the very center of the chart was a large diamond, which stood for the Slipstream sun. Gridde was adjusting the position of a ruby according to the latest semaphore information.

"Well, don't leave me drifting," said Chaison, crossing his arms and smiling. "What happened thirty-five years ago?"

Gridde snorted. "Why, the whole damn nation nearly drifted into winter! Don't they teach you any history at that academy? I remember a day when half the chart box was empty!" Despite the vehemence of his tone, his fingers were absolutely steady as they gripped the tiny ruby between a pair of wires and moved it infinitesimally to the left. "There. That ought to hold you for a day or two."

Chaison gripped the side of the chart table and pulled himself close to examine the three-dimensional representation of the one hundred miles of air surrounding Rush. "And our course?"

"Don't push me." Gridde slowly withdrew his wires and shut the case. "See, if this was one of those new gel charts, just drawing the wires out would move everything! You can't let them standardize on gel charts, sir. Would be a disaster."

"I know, Gridde, you've only told me a thousand times."

The chart-master sailed over to the wall and shut the metal bullet shield over the porthole. Now the room was lit only by the gleam of a gas lantern. Chaison wound up the lantern's little fan, without which it would starve itself of oxygen in seconds, and handed it to Gridde. The chart-master closed the metal door of the lantern, and now light only shone out of a tiny pipette. He carefully arranged this miniature spotlight in a set of flexible arms attached to the chart table, and aimed it.

Only a narrow column of jewels was lit now; the big diamond gleamed at its end. "The way-point," said Gridde, "is Argenta Town, the double-ruby." The two little red gleams were the only town within the beam of light. The beam represented the course the expeditionary force would take; Chaison could see that they would pass unseen by the majority of the local population.

"Good—" Chaison turned his head at a rap on the door. "Enter!"

Sunlight washed away the illusion of hovering above a miniature world. Silhouetted in the doorway was the curving shape of Aubri Mahallan. "That will be all, thank you, Gridde," said Chaison. "Come in, Armorer."

AS VENERA FANNING'S small party wound their way through the labyrinth of docking arms, Hayden stared at their destination with claustrophobic dread. Above him, below, and to all sides hung the bannered cruisers of Slipstream. These were the very ships that had invaded and conquered Aerie. He found himself searching the nearest ship for some sign of a scar—of burned hull, long since painted over—though the ship he had flown Can Two into six years ago had been incinerated before his eyes. He would not have been surprised had it turned up here, intact, a malignant ghost. Indeed, the cluster of bloated cylinders that shadowed the walkway seemed more nightmarish than real. This was the very last place in Virga he would have chosen to go.

"I'm definitely going to miss those Friday evening soirees," Venera was saying to some acquaintance of hers who had come to see her off. "Strange. The crowd has stopped cheering."

Only a low muttering came from the wall of people who pressed against the naval base's security netting. Hayden knew exactly why, but he was obligated to hold his tongue in the presence of his mistress. The crowd had come out to watch the fleet depart. They were eager for spectacle—for the proof that the Pilot was acting decisively after last night's outrageous attack on the city. People had been arriving all day, forming a curving half-shell made of human beings like tiles in a mosaic, that gradually came to obscure the backdrop of Rush's whirling towns. Charged up and indignant, they periodically broke into chants and songs, while continuously flinging sandwiches, drinks, and children up and down the surface of the wall. Bikes and folded wings, picnic baskets and man-sized wicker spheres containing food and souvenir vendors made a kind of base coat behind the human surface.

The fleet had been due to depart an hour ago. The sun was shutting down for the day, its light sputtering and reddening. The light made the docks seem like an alternation of photographs with different exposures and tints—now sepia, now plum-red, now black-and-white. As soon as the sun shut down, heat would flee the air. Few in the crowd had dressed for that. So now they were complaining.

Also muttering were the noncoms and military police who were hurrying Venera's party down the arm to the shadow-striped Rook. As they approached, the ship's jets growled into life for a moment, and it began to rotate until it was vertical compared to the approaching party. The rest of the ships began executing the same turn as word of their initial course and heading was relayed from the Rook.

"Ooh, Venera," said the socialite clinging to Fanning's arm, "they're excited to see you!" She waved at the crowd, which had burst into song again at the sight.

The grumbling engines and motion of ships made Hayden's head spin—but he kept going. There was only one way for him to redeem himself for his earlier cowardice. Fanning was leaving Rush, and Hayden had to follow.

And if—an idea so heretical he refused to take it seriously—if he should be unable to kill Fanning (he would never *choose* not to!), then Hayden could still do some good by acting as a spy aboard the *Rook*. If what he'd heard outside Fanning's office was any indication, there was more to this expedition than met the eye.

They reached the end of the docking arm. Hayden hauled on the rope to halt the forward drift of Venera's trunks while she showed her papers to the waiting deck officer. He barely glanced at them, waving her on.

"Now don't forget my camera!" shouted the socialite from behind the shoulders and arms of the MPs. Venera's other friends waved and shouted similar platitudes, as though Lady Fanning were going on a Sunday cruise and not leaving the country under mysterious circumstances. Hayden gathered the two trunks, each by its leather handle, and stepped across the two-meter gap between the arm and the ship.

As the big doors swung shut behind him Hayden was met by a chaos of detail: beams and ropes in gaslight, the smell of jet fuel and soap, racks of rifles and swords, the flickering motion of a giant centrifuge wheel—and everywhere people, a mob of silent men all of whom seemed to be looking at him.

He spun around, because it was Venera Fanning they were staring at. She stared back for a second, a half-smile crinkling the scar on her chin. Then she turned and shot in the direction of a narrow corridor that passed under the centrifuge. Hayden was left holding her bags.

As he moved to follow her he realized that only one other person had accompanied them on board: a nondescript, passive-faced man of middle age. He looked like some minor bureaucrat. Now he smiled at Hayden.

"But the other servants—" They had come here in a large group. Surely Hayden wasn't the only one who was going?

"You're the driver?" asked the bland man; his voice was as colorless as his appearance.

"Uh . . . yes."

"Stow the bags in the captain's cabin and then go to the centrifuge. You bunk with the carpenters."

"Ah." He stuck out his hand tentatively. "I'm Hayden Griffin."

The man shook it distractedly. "Lyle Carrier. Get going, then."

Hayden grabbed the trunks in an awkward embrace and went to find Venera Fanning.

DARKNESS SHUTTERED THE sky well before the last ship had left the docks. Chaison Fanning sat in the command chair, chin on his fist. He had no duties at this moment: the ship was in the hands of Captain Sembry. Sembry's voice rang out confidently, sending commands down the speaking tubes to the engines and rudder gangs. All eyes were on him just now, and that was a relief.

Chaison rotated a little cup-shaped object in his fingers. It had been given to him by that problematic armorer, Mahallan, a few minutes ago. This device was intended to make real for him an idea he'd thought ridiculous when Venera had first brought it to him. He supposed he should try it.

It was hard to focus past his anger, however. He glanced around; nobody was looking at him. No, they wouldn't. But it would be all through the fleet in hours. This was a humiliation he wouldn't be able to escape.

Why had she done it? He wondered. More importantly: why had he let her? He could have set sail and forced her to catch up. Except that she had information that she could—and would—use against him, her own husband, if he didn't do exactly what she said. He had no doubt she would move against him, he had known Venera long enough not to doubt her ruthlessness.

He gripped the cup tightly and almost threw it at the wall. But that would just add to the talk later, he knew. With a sigh he held it up to his ear.

The sound was surprisingly loud—he pulled the cup away, then gingerly replaced it. What he heard was a roaring din—a steady hissing, weird warbling noises that came and went, and a sound like giant teeth grating. Overlaid on all this was a deep tearing sound, like some impossibly heavy fabric being ripped. It went on and on, hypnotic, an argument between demons.

He took the speaker away from his ear. This was supposed to explain everything, this incessant grumbling. He did admit it was a compelling demonstration, but in no way did it lend credence to any of the wild claims Venera had made.

Anyway, he didn't care. All Admiral Fanning could think of right now was the fact that his wife had, no doubt deliberately, made the national fleet of Slipstream . . . late.

A COLUMN OF ragged clouds twisted like smoke in the night. The shapes wheeled grandly like wary duelists, occasionally testing one another's defenses with half-hearted lightning bolts. Every now and then, a transient corridor of clear air would open to some distant sun through the shuffle of gray shapes that receded for thousands of miles in every direction. Then the flanks of one or another silent combatant would momentarily throw the rest into invisibility as it shone in shades of dusty rose and burgundy.

These were young clouds, the progeny of a mushroom-shaped column of warmer air that had penetrated into Slipstream territory earlier in the day. Being young, these banks and starbursts of mist had just begun to condense. The realm through which they drifted was filled with the remnants of an earlier mass of clouds: its droplets had come together and fused over the hours and days, each collision making fewer and larger drops. Now great spheres of water, some head-sized, some as large as houses, punched through the clouds like slow cannonballs, adding to the chaos of the mixing air.

Wakeful citizens on bikes hovered outside the two towns and a farm that were the only habitation for miles. The sentries kept a watch out for any large mass of water that might loom out of the dark on a collision course with the spinning wheels, or the dark nets of the farm. For one sentry, the only sound was the whirring of the little fan that kept his lantern alive as he waited in silence, cloak drawn around his shoulders to ward off the damp, feet ready on the pedals to kick his bike into motion.

Thus huddled, he at first didn't notice something nose out of a cloud shaped like a bird's head. When he finally spotted it he muttered a curse, because initially it looked like a town-wrecker of a water ball. He reached for his horn with numb fingers, but as he raised the brass horn to his lips he hesitated. The shape no longer appeared rounded, but rather like an extra beak to the diaphanous bird, this one hard and sharp. It was the prow of a ship.

Now that he could see what it was he realized he'd been hearing it for a minute or two already—a distant whine in several keys from its engines. He could also see two spotter bikes weaving in spirals ahead of it. You never knew what might lurk inside a cloud, so the spotters went ahead of the ship to ensure that there were no rocks, water balls, or habitations in the way. On dark nights like this, spotters sometimes found obstacles by running into them. So ships tended to move slowly at night.

They also used headlights to probe the blackness—that was simple prudence. This ship, however, was running dark. As it left the cloud in a whirl of eddied mist, another nose appeared behind it, and another.

The sentry raised the horn again, suddenly fearing an invasion; then he saw the lantern-lit sigil of Slipstream on the hull of the lead vessel. He slowly lowered the horn and clipped it to his saddle. He was a citizen of Aerie; he would not pick a fight with Slipstream tonight. In fact, he would be happy not to be noticed by them at all.

Seven big vessels passed by, all dark except for their running lights. As they disappeared into the black the sentry shivered and turned his attention back to his watch. This would be a story for the morning, perhaps, but he wasn't about to fly over to the other watchers to compare notes. Somehow he felt it better not to speak of these ships while darkness reigned.

HAYDEN HID IN his coffin-sized bunk for as long as possible. He'd spent an uneasy and unpleasant night, but staying here was preferable to climbing out and facing the reality of the situation.

He had been shanghaied—pressed into service to the same enemy he was sworn to destroy. It was all some sort of absurd nightmare.

His bunk was at the bottom of a stack in the exercise centrifuge. He felt like a disused book shelved away in a particularly cramped library. He couldn't sit up because the bunk above his was only inches away from his nose. Each time he rolled over the world seemed to turn in the opposite direction—a familiar enough sensation from town living, but magnified by the small size of this wheel. The thing rotated five times a minute but only provided a tenth of a gravity for all that effort. Its axles had creaked monotonously, men on either side of him had snored in different rhythms, and someone had created prodigious amounts of bad smell that hovered in the air for what seemed hours.

Now his bedding was vibrating with footfalls as an endless parade of airmen ran laps around the wheel. The sleeping level had only one narrow aisle between the stacks of bunks, so the runners' feet slammed down inches from Hayden's head. Finally, when someone stumbled and kicked his shelf, he cursed and rolled out into the narrow space between the bunk stacks.

"Out of the way!" The shark-faced boatswain pushed Hayden as he made to step into the aisle. For the next few minutes he ducked from bunk stack to bunk stack as other airmen made a game of trying to hit him on the way by. Their crude laughter followed him as he scrambled up the ladder to the upper level of the wheel.

Last night the boatswain had made it very clear that on board this ship, Hayden was little more than dead weight. He had gone to bunk with the carpenters as ordered, but they didn't want him around either. He'd found an empty berth in the centrifuge, but clearly he would have to locate some less trafficked part of the ship or he was going to be covered in bruises before the end of the day.

The upper level of the wheel was simply a barrel fifteen feet in diameter. Half of it was taken up with crates, the other half was bare flooring where men with swords were circling one another under the watchful eye of a drill sergeant. Hayden eyed the crates, and finally climbed up on a stack, losing weight with every step. He settled in to watch the fencing technique of the men below.

"You!" He looked down. It was the boatswain again. He was a florid man with a crisp uniform and a shock of carrot-red hair. His eyes protruded when he glared, which was most of the time. Now his lips flapped as he said, "That's delicate equipment, get off it!"

Hayden sighed and hopped from the crates up to the centrifuge's entranceway, at its hub. Surely there must be a quiet spot somewhere.

All the ship's ports were open, it seemed, and a cold wind blew through the interlocking chambers of its interior. Everywhere he looked men were hauling ropes, shifting boxes, or hammering something. He decided that an open cargo door was his best bet and flew over to perch on its inside. A stiff wind flapped past just a foot away but he'd found a pocket of relatively still air. He curled up to look out.

The sun glowed far to aft. It was dim and red with distance; they must be near the border. The clouds they passed threw hazy shadows like fingers pointing the way ahead.

Dotting the sky around him were other ships. He counted six; there might be more on the other side of the vessel, but this was a far cry from the dozens that had left port. As the *Rook* slowly rotated around its axis he was able to verify that there were only seven ships in this group, counting his own. Where was the rest of the fleet?

They skirted the sides of a cloud-mountain and suddenly the air ahead opened up, clear of obstructions. Hayden blinked in surprise. He faced a deep blue abyss—a span of darkness that ran from infinity below to infinity above, and stretched endlessly to both sides. The *Rook* was driving straight into winter.

He couldn't understand how he'd come to be here. He'd had the chance to kill Fanning, and he hadn't done it. That made him a coward—but, undeniably, there was also something big going on, something beyond an imminent attack on Mavery. He might be the only spy Aerie had aboard these ships. As he'd tossed and turned last night, he'd kept coming back to the conclusion that it was his duty to find out what he could, and report it back.

"Hey you!" He turned to find himself facing a boy with a rat-like face who wore an airman's uniform several sizes too big for him. "You Griffin?" he asked belligerently. When Hayden nodded, he jabbed a thumb in the direction of the centrifuge. "Yer wanted in the lady's chamber." He smirked.

"Thanks. You can call me Hayden. What's your name?"

"Martor," said the boy suspiciously. "I'm the gopher."

"Good to meet you, Martor. By the way, where can a guy get a meal around here?"

Martor laughed. "You missed it. That was six o'clock. Not that you could have et with us men, anyway. Yer gonna hafta find yer own meals."

"How much to get that arranged for me?"

Martor's eyebrows lifted. He thought about it. "Six. No less."

"Done." Hayden went forward, a little less deferential to the other men now that he had a destination.

It wasn't Venera waiting for him outside the captain's quarters, but the bland Carrier. He stood on the air with his arms crossed, toes pointed daintily. He frowned at Hayden. "You have duties," he said without preamble.

"I, uh—yes?"

"Lady Fanning has secured a bike for our use. This is not a military machine but a fast racer with sidecars. You are to familiarize yourself with it. Three hours a day, no more no less."

"Yes, sir!" So they wanted him to fly? Well, it would be their funeral. "What model is it?"

Carrier waved a hand negligently. "Don't know. Anyway, the rest of your time will be spent assisting the new armorer. We were told," he said with a faintly unpleasant moue, "that you were mechanically minded."

"Well, I tinker with bikes—"

"Good. You are to report to the armorer immediately. That's aft," Carrier added helpfully.

"Okay, but what will I—" Carrier didn't even frown; he just turned his head away almost imperceptibly. Hayden got the message.

A little of the stifling gloom that had settled on him last night lifted as he headed aft, but he was still bewildered at how quickly and thoroughly he'd gotten himself into this situation. If he'd had any sort of courage he'd have killed Fanning yesterday. The fact that he hadn't, and was now effectively working for the enemy, made him feel deeply sick.

"Know where you're going, do you?" said somebody. Hayden looked down to find Martor squinting at him. "It's this way," he continued, pointing past the drooping bellies of a row of fuel tanks.

"Thanks. Hey—when I looked outside earlier, I saw we were headed into winter. What's all that about?"

Martor looked uncomfortable. "Don't know. Nobody's telling us anything, not yet anyway. You saw we split off from the main fleet? Rumor is we're going to come around behind the enemy. But that don't make no sense. Enemy's farther into the suns, not out here."

"You mean Mavery?"

"Who else would I mean?"

Martor was trailing Hayden now, shifting his weight and fiddling with his hands, much more like the boy he was than the tough man he tried to be. "Winter's nothing to worry about," said Hayden. "I've been there."

"You have? Is it true that there's capital bugs with suns in their bellies? And whole countries frozen solid, guys about to stick each other with swords when their suns went out and their whole armies covered in ice now?"

"Never saw anything like that . . ."

"But how would you know, since it goes on forever?"

"*Forever?*" Somebody laughed. "I don't think so."

An irregularly shaped box was stapled to the outer hull under a mad web of netting. The box had a perfectly ordinary door in one of its facets. The laughter had come from that direction. It sounded suspiciously like a woman's.

"You're gonna tell me that's the armorer," Hayden whispered to Martor. Martor nodded vigorously. "Thought so."

He stuck his head through the door. There was indeed a woman fitted into the intricate mess like a main cog in a watch. She was opening one of several dozen boxes crammed in around her, and was currently upside down compared to him so that all that registered at first was the halo of writhing brown hair that surrounded her face and the fact that she was dressed entirely in black save for a glimpse of scarlet silk that peeked out below her collar. He rotated politely to match her orientation and stuck out his hand. "I'm Hayden Griffin. I was told to assist you."

Her hand was warm, her grip strong. "Aubri Mahallan. Who told you to assist me?"

"Um, man named Carrier."

"Oh, him." She dismissed the man's entire existence with those two words. Mahallan had a heavy accent, bearing hard on sounds like er and oh. Right side up, she looked as intriguing as she sounded, her skin pale and perfectly unblemished like the most pampered courtier, her eyes wide in a perpetually startled look and overemphasized with black makeup. Her mouth was broad and was always twisting into one or another expression so that a constant parade of impressions flickered across her face. Just now she was pursing her lips and squinting at Hayden. "I suppose I can use you for something. And you!" She aimed her expressive gaze past Hayden at the open door. "This is the fifth time you've blocked my light this morning. Guess I'm going to have to find something for you to do as well."

"Yes, ma'am," came Martor's voice faintly from somewhere outside.

"But I can't have ignorant savages working for me," continued Mahallan as she spun and opened a porthole to let a blast of fresh air into the junk-filled cell. "Winter does not go on forever—or rather, it does, but only in the sense that you could go around the outside of a dinner plate forever. Do you understand?"

"No, sir!" said Martor, still invisible.

"Come in here!" Martor peeked around the doorjamb. Somewhere outside, a gang of airmen was engaged in a swearing contest. "And close the door, will you?" added the armorer. Hayden shifted to let Martor do that, and found himself close enough to Mahallan that he could smell her perspiration.

Her attention was fixed on Martor. "Do you believe this world goes on forever in all directions?"

"Yes, ma'am," said Martor with no trace of irony. "Rush came out of Forever, two generations ago, and we attacked the countries here. After we've cut through them all, we're going back to Forever, out the other side of the countries."

"I see we have our work cut out for us," said the armorer with an amused glance at Hayden. "Young man, do you know what a balloon is?"

"A bag for storing gas," said Martor instantly.

"Good. Well, Virga, your world, is a balloon. It is an immensely big balloon, in fact, fully five thousand miles across and orbiting in the outer reaches of the Vega star system. Virga is artificial. Man-made."

"Ma'am, that's very funny," said Martor with a stilted grin.

"It's utterly true, young man. Is it not a fact that your suns are artificial? So, then, why not the rest of the world, too?" Martor looked a little less sure of himself now. "Now, the problem is that even a fusion sun capable of heating and lighting everything out to a distance of several hundred miles is just a tiny spark in a volume this size. Especially when clouds and other obstacles absorb the light so readily. Sixty, eighty, even a hundred suns aren't enough to illuminate the whole interior of Virga. So, we have large volumes of air that are unlit, unheated—volumes of winter."

"I'm with ya," said Martor.

"But these volumes don't go on forever. They end, one way or another, at the lighted precincts of some other nation, or at Candesce if you head straight toward the center of Virga. Or they end at the skin of the world, where icebergs crowd and grind like the gnashing teeth of a god. And your asteroid, Rush, orbits very slowly around the middle of this world, tugged by the almost imperceptible gravity the air creates."

"Now you're having me on," said Martor.

Mahallan sighed extravagantly, but couldn't hide a smile. "Go on. You're taking up my air. You," she said to Hayden, "stick around and help me unpack some of these boxes."

THE SEVEN SHIPS killed their engines a dozen miles into winter. They drifted for a few minutes, then with slow grumbles of their turning engines they slid into a star formation, each one pointing out from a central point. Lines were cast from nose to nose, and the captains of six ships hand-walked across to an open port in the side of the Rook. In all directions, darkness swallowed distance and detail.

When Admiral Fanning entered the Rook's chart room he was pulled up short by the vision of the captains clinging to floor, walls, and ceiling like wasps in a paper nest. They were all identical in their black uniforms, rustling and moving slightly. He could practically hear a subliminal buzz coming from them.

He shook off the impression and glided to his chair by the chart table. "You've all been very patient with our secrecy," he said as the last visiting captain ducked past him to loop a hand through a velvet wall-strap. Now that he thought about it, the idea of these men as wasps seemed more and more apt. They were dangerous, focused—and for the most part, dumb as planks. Perfect for the job he had in mind.

"I'm sure you've had your suspicions about where we're going. I'm equally sure," he said with a smile, "that your crews have been devising all kinds of extravagant ideas of their own." There was a polite smile from the swarm in return.

"Now that we're out of semaphore-range of any potential spies, we can make a general announcement."

"It's about time!" Captain Hieronymous Flosk, the oldest and least patient of the company, leaned into the light from the chart table. The glow made his face a mask of crevasses and pitted plains. "This secrecy is ridiculous," he grated. "We don't have to skulk around hiding from Mavery. Hit them direct, and hard. You'd think that would be obvious," he sniffed.

"Well, you'd be right," said Fanning, "if Mavery were our target."

Several of the captains had been muttering together, but these words shocked them silent. "What do you mean?" asked Flosk, his voice momentarily reduced to a whine. "After the damned sneak attack the other day—"

"Almost certainly not them," said Fanning drily. "Oh, their munitions, right enough. But Mavery's border dispute with us has been trumped up by a third party—one with deep pockets and spies throughout Slipstream." He took one of the slides his wife had prepared for him and slipped it into the hooded lantern under the chart box. Opening a little door on the side of the lantern, he projected the image onto the wall behind him.

"This," he said, "is a secret shipyard of Falcon Formation. One of, uh, our spies took this photo less than a week ago." Several of the captains rotated in place to try to find a better view of the picture. Fanning glanced back to verify that he'd chosen the correct slide: it was Venera's picture of the giant warship.

"The dreadnought you see in the deep background is fifteen hundred feet long," he announced. Again, the captains went still. "Nothing like it has ever flown in Virga. It's big enough to be a carrier for midsized hunter sloops, as well as a substantial assault force. We believe she will be the flagship of a fleet aimed at Slipstream. We have learned that they are using the dispute with Mavery as a ruse to draw our forces away from Rush. Once our

fleet is entangled in Mavery, they will move in and take the city."
He didn't have to add that Rush *was* Slipstream. Take one and you
had the other.

There was a long silence. Then Flosk said, "Who's this 'we'
who believes all of this crap? You and the Pilot?"

"The Pilot, yes," Fanning lied. "He is well aware of our nation's failings in the espionage area. He's taken steps—hence the
pictures." He changed the slide for another that showed the shipyard itself. "That's the strategic situation. I'm sure you can appreciate how important it's been to keep our knowledge of the situation
secret."

"Wait," said someone. "You mean we're going to attack *Falcon?*"

"Suicide," someone else mumbled.

"Clearly we need any advantage we can get," said Fanning
with a reluctant nod. "Your ships were either designed as winter
ships or have been refitted as part of a winter fleet. These up-
grades have been going on for some years, since my predecessor
discerned a need for such a fleet."

"But these are hardly the best winter ships," objected Flosk.
"The new ones are off with the force that's heading to Mavery."

"Naturally. Mavery and Falcon will notice if our finest winter
ships don't show up for the border dispute. Your ships—and I
hate to put this indelicately, gentlemen—are the inconspicuous
ones. Not very powerful, not very important. Nonetheless, they
are all rigged for operations in cold, darkness, and low-oxygen
conditions. They will be sufficient."

He closed the cover on the projector and restored the light to
the chart box. "This is the local constellation of nations," he said.
"We are here. Falcon is there." The chart box contained dense
clouds of colored sparks, each hue representing a different nation.
The nations coiled around and pressed against one another in in-
tricate contact, like the internal organs of some creature of light.
"The chief nations of Meridian all follow the rise and fall of the
Meridian Five Hadley cell that's powered by heat from the Sun of
Suns, which is below the table in this view. Rush Asteroid is

largely unaffected by the air currents and continues to follow its orbit around Candesce, at something less than walking speed. As you can see, Rush will soon leave Aerie and migrate into Mavery's territory. But after that . . ." He turned the box to show a mass of glittering green stars that took up much of one side of the box. "After that we will, by force of celestial mechanics, have to pass through Falcon."

Three suns—diamonds among emeralds—gleamed within the broad dazzle of green.

"Now, here is the location of the secret shipyard we discovered." He flipped a lever in the base of the map box. All the little pinpricks of light dimmed save for one amethyst that lit up deep inside Falcon territory.

The captains broke into a babble of complaint. Flosk burst out laughing. "How are we expected to get to that spot without fighting our way through the whole of Falcon?"

"Simple," said Fanning. "The location of the shipyard is secret because it's in an underpopulated area—a volume filled with sargassos. It's really at the terminus of a long tongue of winter that extends hundreds of miles into Falcon. The sargassos shade this volume and much of it is oxygen-poor. A wilderness. We're going to circle all the way around the Meridian constellation and sneak in through this alley of dead air."

". . . And raid the shipyard," said somebody. There were nods all around.

"Well, it's bold," said Flosk grudgingly. "Still suicidal. But then we're not too many ships. Slipstream can afford to lose us."

"I have no intention of sacrificing us," said Fanning.

"But how are we going to survive and get home again?"

"That's a part of the plan that has to remain secret for now," said the admiral. "But what it means in the short term is that, before we circle around through winter, we have to make a . . . a detour."

7

IT MIGHT HAVE been two thousand miles away; it could have been twice that. They were never able to tell her for sure. But somewhere, and not too long ago, there had been a war.

Nobody knew whether the shot was fired by a lone sniper, or whether it was one of a salvo loosed in the midst of a confused melee involving thousands of men. But it was a military-grade weapon of some sort, that much was sure. The bullet had come out of its muzzle at a velocity of more than a mile per second. It outran its own sound.

She knew what had happened next. The bullet had gathered its experiences with it as it flew, remembering what it saw and where it went; and these memories came to Venera Fanning now and then, as dreams and nightmares. They must be from the bullet, there was no other possible source for them. She herself could never have imagined the vision of fantastically prowed vessels ramming one another and tumbling in burning embraces into bloodred clouds. Nor could she have thought up the rope-connected freefall city the bullet had sailed through shortly after being fired. The city owned no wheeling towns. Its towers and houses were nodes in a seemingly infinite lattice of rope, and its scuttling citizens were long as spiders, their bones fragile as glass. The bullet passed through the city going hundreds of miles per hour, so the faces and rippling banners of the place were blurred and unidentifiable.

The bullet shot past farms and forests that hung in the air like green galaxies. In places the entire sky was alive with spring colors as distant suns lit the delicate leaves of billions of independently floating plants, each one clinging by its roots to a grain of dirt or drop of water. The air here was heady with oxygen and, for the humans who tended the farms, redolent with the perfume of growing things.

In contrast, the vast expanses of winter that opened up ahead of the bullet were clear as crystal. Falling into them was like penetrating a sphere of purest rainwater, a deep fathomless blueness wherein the bullet cooled and shrank in on itself just a little. It threaded through schools of heavily feathered, blind fish and past the nearly identical birds that fed off them. It entered a realm of sky-spanning ice arches, a froth of frozen water whose curving bubbles were tens of miles on a side. Black gaps pierced their sides. Snow nestled in the elbows of icicles longer than Rush's shadow. Here the air was dense, exhausted of oxygen as well as heat. The bullet slowed and nearly came to a halt as it reached the farther edge of this shattered cathedral of ice.

But as it began a slow tumble and return to the blue intricacies behind it, an errant beam of light from Candesce welled up from below. The glow heated the air behind the bullet just enough to make a sigh that welled out and pushed it away. Again it tumbled into dark emptiness.

Winter did not rule all the empty spaces of Virga. There were columns of warm air hundreds of miles long that rose up from the Sun of Suns. Before they cooled enough for their water to condense as clouds, they were transparent, and Candesce's light followed them up, sometimes penetrating all the way to Virga's skin. The bullet strayed into one such column and changed course, rising now and slowly circumnavigating the world.

It was the passage of an iceberg that galvanized the bullet into motion again. An eddy of the passing monster put a sustained wind at its back and soon the bullet was cruising along at a respectable thirty miles an hour. On the crest of this wavefront it entered a dense forest that had supersaturated itself with oxygen. It narrowly missed a hundred or so of the long spiderweb filaments of trunk and branch whose weave made up the forest. But then it happened: the bullet rapped a solitary, tumbling stone a few miles in and some sparks swirled after it. One spark touched a dry leaf that had been circulating in the shadowed interior of the forest for ten years. The leaf turned into a small sphere of flame, then the other leaves floating nearby lit, and then a few nearby trees.

An expanding sphere of fire pushed the bullet faster and faster. Mile after mile the storm of flame pushed through the super-charged air, in seconds consuming threadlike trees bigger than towns. The forest transformed itself into a fireball bright as any sun in Virga. When it burned out its dense core of ashes and smoke would contain a sargasso—a volume of space sheltered from the wind by leagues of charred branch and root, where no light nor oxygen could be found.

The bullet was indifferent to this fate. It rode the explosion all the way out of the forest. When it left the roaring universe of flame it was once again speeding at nearly a mile a second. Several minutes later it entered the precincts of Aerie. It flashed past the towns and outrider stations of Slipstream. It narrowed its focus to a quartet of towns in the formation known as Rush. It lined up on a single window in the glittering wheel of the Admiralty.

It stopped dead in Venera Fanning's jaw. Some blood tried to continue on, but that only made it a few meters farther. And while the doctors did dig it out of Venera's throat, it had remained in the Admiralty ever since.

Until now. As Venera slept uneasily and dreamed her way back down the long trajectory of the projectile, it bumped slowly back and forth inside the lacquer box in her luggage where she kept it. Its journey was not over yet.

8

THE *ROOK*'S HANGAR was a deep pie-shaped chamber taking up one-third of the length of the ship. Most of the space was bikes, all lashed to the walls like somnolent bees in a hive; but two big cutters made the stern area into a well of shadows, each boat a forty-footer armed to the teeth. Hayden eyed these as he slammed an access panel on the bike Venera Fanning had brought for him. The cutters were weapons, of course, and so distasteful to him; but they were also ships, and he couldn't help wondering how fast they were and how maneuverable they'd be to steer.

The bike was ready. He gave it one last appraising look. This wasn't his bike, but it was a racer, complete with two detachable sidecars and a long spool of grounding thread for those situations where you outran your own rate of static charge drain.

Hayden had been staying up late so as to be awake during nightwatch—there were fewer people around—so he was startled when Martor's thin face popped over the bike's small horizon like some parody of the sun. "Watcha doin?" said the gopher in his usual challenging way.

"Shouldn't you be asleep?" Hayden unclipped the bike from its drydock clamps and hefted it, judging its mass. There were traces here and there of red paint, but sometime very recently it had been redone a glossy black. He didn't mind that.

"Could say the same about you." Martor hand-walked around the clamps to look at what Hayden was doing. As he did the wind keened particularly loudly past the ship's outer hatches. Martor jerked his head in that direction.

"Still worried about winter? It's a bit late for that," Hayden pointed out. "We've been in it for days."

"You're not taking that out in it?" Martor watched in distress as Hayden dragged the racer in the direction of the forward bike hatch. "Ain't it'll freeze you like a block of ice?"

"It's not that cold." The bike started to drift as they passed the center of the chamber so Martor steadied it with his own mass. "Clouds insulate the air," said Hayden. "So it only gets so cold. Usually doesn't even get down to freezing, most places. Hey, why don't you come along for the ride? I'm just taking her out for a practice run."

Martor snatched his hands back from the bike. "You crazy? I'm not going out there."

"Why not? I am."

A couple of members of the hatch gang had heard this and laughed. They were lounging next to the big wooden doors, awaiting any order to open them. Hayden nodded and they reluctantly abandoned their cards to man the winch wheel.

"Hang on there!" Both Hayden and Martor turned. The eccentric armorer, Mahallan, was poised at an inside doorway. Her silhouette was very interesting, but she only perched there a moment before flying over to the hatch. "You boys going for a night flight?"

Hayden shrugged. "All flights are night flights right now."

"Hmm. Glad to see you've overcome your fear of winter," she said to Martor. The boy blushed and stammered something.

"Listen," continued Mahallan, "I'd like you to do something for me. While you're out there—I know it'll be dark so you probably won't see them—if you spot anything like this, could you bring it back?" She opened her fist to reveal a bent little glittering thing, like a chrome wasp.

Martor leaned close. "What's that?" Hayden plucked it from the air and turned it so its wings rainbowed in the gaslight. "I've seen these before," he mused. "But I don't know what they are. They're not alive."

"Not by ordinary standards, no," said Mahallan. She was perched on his bike, an angel in silhouette; rearing back she said with some obscure sense of satisfaction, "They're *tankers.*"

Martor smiled weakly. "Ha?"

"Tankers. That little abdomen is an empty container. Usually when you catch one and open it, you'll find the tank full of ugly chemicals like lithium pentafluorophenyl borate etherate, methoxyphenylboronic acid or naphthylboronic acid. Very interesting. And where do you suppose they're taking it?"

"Couldn't tell ya," said Martor, whose eyes had gone very wide as the multisyllabic chemical names tripped off Mahallan's lips.

"They're going in," said the armorer. "Toward Candesce." She snatched the metal wasp out of the air. "Find me some more. If you can."

"Yes, ma'am." Martor saluted and turned to Hayden. "Let's get goin', then."

The hatch gang spun their wheel and the bike door opened into total darkness. As Mahallan kicked away to presumably return to her little workshop, Hayden leaned in to Martor and whispered, "You forgot the passenger saddle. It's over there." He pointed.

"Ah. Uh, thanks."

Mahallan left, and Hayden waited for Martor to back out of his impulse to come along. But he returned with the saddle and dutifully waited while Hayden strapped it to the side of the bike. And he climbed aboard meekly and waited while Hayden guided the fan-jet to the open hatch and shoved it out into the light breeze, following himself a second later.

"IT'S NOT COLD at all!" Martor squinted over his shoulder as Hayden opened the throttle a bit. They shot away from the *Rook.* The bike was admirably quiet, so Hayden was able to lean back and say, "Like I said, the clouds trap the heat."

Now that they were in winter, the ships of the expeditionary force had all their lights on. Distant clouds made a tunnel that curled away ahead of them, but the air was clear for miles around. It was an opportunity to open up the ships' throttles that their pilots were stolidly ignoring. True, they were making twenty or thirty miles per hour, but each could do five times that without straining.

"Shall we see what she'll do?" Hayden asked. He didn't wait for Martor's answer, but gripped the throttle and twisted it. The fan-jet's grumble became a roar and they shot ahead and into the full blaze of the Rook's headlamp.

Martor pounded him on the back. "Quit showin' off!"

Hayden laughed. "No! Look back!"

Martor turned awkwardly and gasped. Hayden knew that their corkscrew contrail would be gleaming in the cone of the Rook's headlight like a thread of fire.

"Come on, Martor. Let's do some stitching!"

The bike was capable of nearly two hundred miles an hour, and he tested it to this limit over the next few minutes, running lines back and forth parallel to the Rook's course. Laying down parallel lines like this was called stitching. Following his own contrail was the safest way to test the bike's speed; if he entered cloud or deviated too far from air he knew was clear, he could kill himself and Martor if he ran into something unseen.

Hunkered down behind the windscreen, he could nonetheless feel the rip of the air inches away, and cautioned Martor not to stick his head—or hands or feet—out lest he get them ripped off. The bike performed well and he quickly got a feel for it.

"Right!" he said eventually. "Let's do a bit of exploring." He eased back on the throttle and nosed them in the direction of the encircling clouds. As they were about to enter a huge puffball he turned the bike and hit the throttle again; the ground wire trailing behind them whipped ahead into the cloud, and sparks flew.

"Is this a good idea?" Martor had been whooping with delight a minute before. He seemed afraid of anything new, Hayden mused.

"It's a great idea." Now that they'd shed their static potential, it was safe to push the bike into the cloud, a transition noticeable only in the drop in temperature and sudden appearance of the cone of radiance from the bike's headlight. Hayden glanced back; the Rook was invisible already.

Martor shook Hayden's shoulder. "H-how are we going to find the ship again?"

"Like this." He reached down and shut off the engine. As the whine faded, he heard a distant grumble—the other ships—but it seemed to be coming from all around them at once. "Wait for it."

The foghorn's note sounded low and sonorous through the darkness. "Where did that come from?" he asked Martor.

"That way?" The boy pointed.

"Right. Now, we're not going far. I just want to see if there's another side to these clouds." He spun up the bike again.

The mist seemed to go on forever, an empty silver void. After a few minutes, though, Hayden began to see pearl-like beads gleaming in the headlight. They shot by on either side, and at their lower speed Martor was able to reach out and grab one. It splashed into a million drops in his hand.

The water spheres grew more numerous and larger. "Could they stall the engine?" asked Martor nervously.

"A big one could," he replied. "Like that one." He dodged the bike around a quivering ball the size of his head.

Visibility was improving. They were now idling their way through a galaxy of turning, shivering drops, some of them tiny, some big as men. Reflections and refractions from the bike's headlamp lit the water cloud in millions of iridescent arcs and glints.

Martor was silent. Hayden looked back at him; the boy's jaw was slack as he gaped at the sight.

"Look." Hayden cut the engine and with the last of their momentum steered them over to a water-beaded stone that hung in solitary majesty amid the water. The rock was less than two feet in diameter.

"Well?" he said to Martor. "Aren't you going to claim this piece of land for Slipstream?"

The boy laughed and reached up to grab the stone. "Not like that!" Keeping one hand on the bike, Hayden flipped himself out of the saddle and wrapped his legs around the rock. "You've got to sit on a piece of land to claim it, you know.

"I decree this land the property," he said, "of . . ." *Aerie.*

"Of Hayden Griffin!" shouted Martor.

"Okay. Of the sovereign state of Hayden. Uck, it's wet." He kicked it away and settled into a perch on the windscreen of the bike.

"I didn't know it was like this out here," said Martor. "I grew up in Rush."

"What are you doing here, anyway? You're—" He was about to say "just a boy" but figured Martor would resent that. "—not a volunteer."

"Press-ganged," said Martor with a shrug. "I don't mind. It was that or the orphanage. I been in the fleet a year now, but this is the first time I've been out of dock."

"So you don't know much about the fleet—say, the admiral?"

"I do." Martor glared at him. "Admiral Fanning's the youngest one to take that job. Got it by doing some sort of secret mission for the Pilot, years back. 'Cept he really doesn't like to talk about that, I saw him get all red in the face one time when somebody just mentioned his promotion."

"Maybe it was his wife who got it for him," speculated Hayden. "She's at least as dangerous as he is."

"Ah," said the boy, "she's pretty, that's sure."

"Actually," said Hayden drily, "I meant put-a-bullet-in-you dangerous. But yes, she's pretty."

Hayden sighed and looked off into the dark. "Well, I hope you get a chance to see more of the world. It's not all like this out here." He smiled slyly. "There's . . . things in the dark, you know."

Martor looked alarmed. "I thought you said there wasn't!"

"Well, I've never seen anything. But you hear stories. Like the ones about the black suns. Ever heard of them?"

Martor's eyes had gone round.

"Pirate suns. They're small and weak, they only heat a few miles around them but it's enough for several towns to thrive. And they only shine through a few portholes, to spotlight the towns and nothing else. Black suns, they call them, each one surrounded by the ships the pirates have captured, in a cloud of wreckage that hides the glow of the towns. . . . They're migratory, like Rush, and they could be anywhere. . . ."

"You're making that up."

"Strangely enough, I'm not." The chill was starting to eat at him, so Hayden swung back into the saddle and pedaled the engine to life again. "We should get back."

They flew in the direction of the most recent foghorn, not talking for a while. As the water cloud tapered out, replaced by mist again, Martor said, "Do you think we'll be coming home? After whatever it is we're out here to do, I mean."

Hayden frowned. "I don't know. I . . . wasn't counting on it, personally." *What's there to come back to?* But he didn't say that.

"Do you suppose there's something in winter that's threatening Slipstream?"

"Seems unlikely."

"And what about the armorer?"

"Huh? What about her?"

"I overheard some of the officers talking. They said she's . . . not from here. Not from the world."

"What do you mean, not from the world?"

"Not from Virga. That doesn't make any sense, does it?"

Hayden thought about it. She did have a funny accent, but that didn't mean anything. He dimly remembered his parents talking about a wider universe beyond Virga; he tried to recall what his father had told him. "There's other places, Martor. Places that are all rock or all water, just like Virga's all air. It could be that she's from somewhere like that. After all, they say we all were, originally."

"Oh, now you're—" Martor swallowed whatever he was going to say, as a giant shape loomed up ahead of them. It was one of the ships, though not the *Rook*.

"Home again," said Hayden. "Let's find our own scow."

"Hey! Don't call the Rook a scow!" They accelerated past the ship and into its light. Hayden intended to make a spiral and locate the other ships by their lights, so he took them ahead of this ship's outrider bikes, into the night.

So it was that he had several seconds in which to be surprised as he saw a gleam of light shooting straight for him, a gleam that quickly resolved into the light of a bike—a light that quavered and shook—and time to shout a curse and turn the racer, nearly toppling Martor off his saddle. Time to hit the collision warning on his horn and narrowly miss plunging them into the solid wall of black water that blocked the sky in all directions.

Time enough to turn and watch as the ship they'd passed sounded its own alarm and began to deploy its emergency braking sails. Too late: it flew in stately majesty into the wall of water and disappeared in a cloud of foam and spray.

SPOTLIGHTS PINIONED THE crashed ship—although it wasn't so much crashed in the small sea as embedded. The surface of the sea curved into the mist in four directions, and clouds formed another wall directly behind the six free vessels whose headlamps were aimed at it. The cones reflected off its intact sides and into the water, making a diffuse blue aura there that was attracting fish.

The Tormentor was stuck three-quarters into the water, its forlorn tail orbited by a halo of water balls. As Hayden and Martor watched from the hangar hatchway of the Rook, gangs of engineers and carpenters were slinging lines to the other ships to pull her out. A breeze, chilly and damp through and through, teased and prodded at the warmer air inside the ship, and intermittently ruffled the surface of the sea.

"Who sounded the alarm?" somebody asked behind Hayden. Without thinking, he said, "I did."

"You're not one of their outriders." He turned and found

himself facing Admiral Fanning, who floated in the hangar in a cloud of lesser officers.

"W-what?" Hayden felt like he'd been kicked in the stomach. He'd hated this man at a distance for so many years that the very idea of talking to him seemed impossible.

"He was doing a practice flight on my instructions." Venera's bloodless servant, Carrier, hung in the shadows to one side.

"Ah." Fanning rubbed his chin. "I can't decide whether the warning helped or did more damage. If they hadn't tried to extend the braking masts they wouldn't have snapped off when they hit the water. However, doubtless your heart was in the right place." He peered at Hayden, seeming to notice him for the first time. "You're one of the civilians."

"Yes, Admiral, sir." Hayden's face felt hot. He wanted to squirm away and hide somewhere.

The admiral looked disappointed. "Oh. Well, good work."

"Lights!" someone shouted from the absurd jut off the Tormentor's tail. "Lights!"

"What's he going on about?" Fanning leaned out, right next to Hayden, his face a picture of epicurean curiosity.

"Shut down! All! Lights!" It was one of the foremen, who while yelling this was pointing dramatically at the water.

They looked at one another. Then Fanning said, "Well, do as the man says." It took several minutes, but soon the spotlights and headlights were going out, one after another, leaning shadows back and forth through the indigo water.

"There!" The faint silhouette of the foreman was pointing again. Hayden craned his neck with the others. The man was indicating a patch of water near the Tormentor—a patch where suddenly, impossibly, a gleam of light wavered.

When Hayden had seen the size of this sea, he'd wondered. Now he was sure.

"It's just a glowfish!" somebody yelled derisively. But it wasn't. Somewhere in the depths of the miles-wide ball of water that the Tormentor had hit, lanterns gleamed.

"Do a circuit!" shouted Fanning to a waiting formation of bikes. Their commander saluted and they took off, contrails spreading to encircle the spherical sea like thin grasping fingers. Almost immediately one of the bikes doubled back. It shut down and did a high-speed drift past the *Rook*. "There's an entrance!" shouted its rider. "Half a mile around that way."

Hayden nodded to himself. You could dig a shaft into a water ball as easily as a dirt or stone pile. Farmers regularly used such shafts as cold-storage rooms. From the faintness of the shimmer here, though, the ones who'd dug this tunnel had taken it deep into the sea. And the extent of the lights suggested more than just a few rooms carved out of the cold water.

"*Warea*," he muttered. He turned to Martor. "This might be Warea."

"Huh?" Martor goggled at him. "What you talking about?"

"Warea. It's one of the towns I . . . heard about back when . . . when I lived with some folks who traded into winter. I heard that Warea was dug into a small sea, as a defense against pirates."

"You know this place?" Fanning had noticed him again. Hayden silently cursed himself for speaking up.

"It's a small independent station," he told the admiral. "Paranoid about pirates and military raids—they won't take kindly to seeing your ships out here, sir."

"Hmm. But they could have some of the supplies we need to fix the *Tormentor's* masts, eh?" Fanning squinted at the distant glow. "They've probably got divers in the water now, watching us dig her out. Can't hide that we're military . . ." He thought for a second, then nodded. "You, the boy, Carrier, and two carpenters. Go in, negotiate a purchase. Foreman'll give you a manifest. Tell them we've no interest in them beyond buying what we need."

"But why us?"

"You because you know the place. The boy because he looks harmless. Carrier because he also looks harmless, and because you and he are obviously civilians." He looked down his nose at Hayden's shabby shirt and trousers.

"Sir!" It was the armorer, Mahallan, coming up from below. "This settlement—they might have some of the things I need."

"Go on with you, then." Venera Fanning had also appeared. As she sailed in from the left the admiral glared at her and said, "Not a chance."

"He's my pilot." She indicated Hayden. "He takes orders from me."

"I'm the only one who gives orders on this ship." Fanning turned away from her. Venera's eyes narrowed, but then she smirked good-naturedly, and Fanning grinned back for a second. Hayden was surprised; he'd never seen Venera acquiesce like that, hadn't even known it was possible for her.

One of the carpenters thumped a hand onto his shoulder. "Stop gawking and get your coat, boy. We're going to town!"

9

"THERE'S NO SIGN," muttered Slew, the head carpenter. Hayden shot him an incredulous look. There certainly was no garish, brightly colored sign over the entrance to Warea. "You mean one that says 'Loot Me'?" he asked.

"How does it work?" Mahallan climbed down from one sidecar of the bike as Hayden reached out to clip a line to the nearest strut of the entrance framework. They floated just outside the dark shaft that led into Warea; nobody had come out to greet them. Mahallan's question was unnecessary, though. The scaffolding of the entrance shaft stuck ten feet out of the water, far enough to make it plain how it was constructed.

"Look, it's simple," he said, slapping the translucent wall of the shaft; it made a faint drumming sound. The builders of Warea had taken a simple wooden skeleton, the sort the Rush docking tubes were made of, and wrapped it in wax paper. Then they'd stuck the assembly into the side of the sea, like a needle into the skin of a giant. Up this close, he could see faint striations of tangleweed matted under the surface of the water. Warea probably cultivated the stuff—which was an animal, not a plant—to provide structural integrity to the vast ball of water in which they lived. Without it, a stiff breeze could tear the sea apart.

The shaft made an impenetrably dark hole in the water, unlit, possibly leading nowhere—except that a tickle of air teased Hayden's brow, and his bike was slowly being sucked inward.

"We're wasting time." Carrier kicked forward, his foot-fins driving him quickly into the dark. Hayden flipped off the bike and gestured for Martor to follow. Mahallan was already inside the tunnel, flanked by the carpenters.

Inside there was little to tell they were entering a world of water. The tunnel was a lattice of beams, like those of any freefall scaffold. The surface stretched between them could have been stone in the dimness of lamplight. Only the clammy chill suggested the nearby presence of the sea.

"I would have thought the walls would bulge inward or something," said Mahallan. "But of course they don't. No gravity, no pressure."

"I've heard that word before," said Martor in an overly casual way. "Gravity. Spin makes it, right?"

Mahallan had been doing a hand-over-hand walk along the struts. Now she stopped to look at Martor, and in the dim light he saw her eyes had gone wide. "Sometimes I forget," she murmured, "that the strangest of things here are the ones I talk to."

"Now what's that supposed to mean?" But she had turned away already. Ahead, Carrier shouted for them to be quiet.

He was silhouetted by flickering lamplight from a number of fan-driven lanterns. Beyond him the tunnel opened up into a broad space—a cubic chamber walled in wax paper and about forty feet on a side. This was a hangar, Hayden realized, for it was filled with bikes and other flying devices. The air here was cold and damp but the six men who were pointing their rifles at the newcomers didn't seem to feel it. They were uniformly dressed in dark leathers, and their narrow pale faces had the sameness of kin. It seemed like a small welcoming committee, but Hayden was sure that the faint motion of the paper walls next to him indicated more men hiding in the water outside.

"State your business," said their leader, who was clearly the oldest. The father of the others, perhaps?

"Trade," said Carrier. "Carpentry supplies. We can pay you whatever you think is appropriate."

"We're not trading," said the older man. "Be on your way."

There was a momentary silence; Carrier hung perfectly still. "What now?" Mahallan whispered to Hayden. "Does he threaten them?"

Hayden shook his head. "It's hardly worth our while to fight a pitched battle for some nails and wood, and they know it. I don't know what he'll—" He stopped, because Carrier was speaking again.

"As you can plainly see," he said, "our charting expedition is well-enough supplied that we don't *need* your help. But it'll shorten our stay if you do help us."

"Charting?" The older man looked alarmed. "Charting what?"

"Oh, just the various objects in this part of winter," said Carrier with a negligent wave of his hand. "Forests, rocks, lakes— anything that might drift into our space someday. Or that might be useful or militarily significant."

"We're of no use to nobody," said the leader. He was visibly tense now. "We want to be left alone."

"Well, then," purred Carrier, "I'm sure our captain could be persuaded to leave one or two objects off of the charts. If, that is, we received something in return."

"Wait here." The man turned and left through a prosaic-looking door that opened out of the hangar's far wall. A few minutes later he returned, looking unhappy. "Come ahead," he said. "You can trade."

So it was that they entered Warea and learned how the cast-out and the fugitive lived in the empty spaces between the nations. The walls of the short corridor between the hangar and the town complex glowed from distant lamplight; long shadows cast on the paper walls suggested some sort of layered barrier between the cold of the sea and the town. In fact as they passed through the next door the temperature rose and the dampness receded. The silhouetted bodies of the people in front of Hayden split off one by one, opening more and more of the space to his view until he was there himself, gaping about at the cave that was Warea.

Mostly it was just a cube like the hangar, but several hundred feet across. Floating in this space in a disorganized jumble were various multisided houses, each one tethered to its neighbors or the space's outer struts. Numerous openings led off from the main cube, some terminating almost immediately in walls of gelid water, others twisting away, their lamplit outlines faintly visible through the paper walls of the cave. The place reeked of burning kerosene and rot but it was reasonably warm, and the big industrial lanterns with their grumbling fans at least prevented an aura of total gloom from overtaking the citizens.

Some of these were staring in open hostility as Carrier led his group into their crowded airspace. The town elders who had decreed that they could enter had discretely retreated, or chose to remain anonymous within the mass of people. Carrier stopped to ask directions and while he did, Hayden examined the people. They had a familiar look: sallow, overstretched, and glum. For the most part they were exiles who remembered growing up within the light of a sun. Unhappy they might be, but few of them showed the signs of weight-deprivation.

In a few minutes he saw why. The far wall of the cube was moving—swinging up and to the left with a constant rumble that quivered the walls. The cube was only part of Warea. An entire town was embedded in the sea, and on part of its rotation the wheel passed through the cube like a giant saw cutting into a block of wood. Hayden watched houses, shops, and markets pop out of the cube's wall and swing up to vanish through the ceiling in steady and relentless motion.

"It's not a small place," muttered Carrier. "There's two markets. Dry goods on the wheel, Armorer. Building materials here."

"We'll split up, then," said Mahallan helpfully.

"I'll join you in a few minutes," said Carrier with a disapproving frown. "Watch yourselves."

Hayden, Martor, and the armorer watched the others vanish into a cloud of people in the building market. The place was crowded with huge baskets filled with white bricks and beams.

"Looks like they'll find what they need right off," said Mahallan worriedly. "Let's hurry, we wouldn't want to keep them waiting."

Hayden shrugged and turned to coast in the direction of the wheel's axis. "I didn't see any wood back there," he commented.

"But what was all that white stuff?"

"Same as these houses are built with." He did a course correction by slapping one on the way by. Its white brick surface undulated slightly. "Paper. They fold origami bricks and beams in triangular sections and then fill them with water. You get beams and bricks that are stiff and incompressible."

"Really?" She seemed inclined to stop and admire the buildings. Hayden pressed on; now that he'd escaped Carrier's roving eye, he could run an errand of his own.

Mahallan and Martor caught up to him as he was entering the big barrel-shaped axis of the wheel. A sullen local flapped by on ragged foot-wings, and the armorer watched him go. "Who are these people?" she asked. "They don't seem happy to see us."

"Refugees, most of them," he said. "A lot of them will be from Aerie, which was conquered by Slipstream about ten years ago. And some are pirates."

"This is a *pirate* town?" Mahallan laughed in apparent delight as they hand-walked down the top few yards of the yin-yang staircase that led to the rim of the wheel.

Where the curve of the staircase began to flatten out the rungs of the staircase were replaced with steps, at first improbably tall ones. As Hayden flipped over and began using his feet he said, "You asked who these people are. Can I ask who you are? You don't seem to know the first thing about how the world operates, and yet you're our armorer. That's more than a little . . ."

"Odd?" Mahallan shrugged. "It's a fair question. But I'm surprised nobody told you. I'm not from Virga."

"Told you," mouthed Martor behind her back.

"Then where . . . ?"

The nearly vertical staircase rapidly leveled out as they descended past the town's rooftops. Weight and the familiar, homey sensation of vertigo increased with each step. As she entered gravity, Mahallan seemed to shrink. Her normally cheerful face was clouded by unhappiness.

"Where is a difficult thing to answer," she said. "My world isn't like yours. Oh, I expect you'd think I mean that I come from a planet, with land and mountains and so on." Hayden had never heard either of these words before, but he kept his expression neutral as Mahallan went on. "But the rules . . . of reality . . . you might say . . . are different in my world. Identity and location are very fluid things. Too fluid. Too arbitrary; I prefer it here."

He shook his head. "I don't understand."

"Good," she said with a sad smile. "That means we can still be friends."

They had reached the street. Down had made itself forcefully known, and if it wasn't quite perpendicular to the decking but heavily skewed in the direction of the town's rotation, it was still comfortable to Hayden. "That looks like the market up there," he said, pointing.

"Excellent." Her smile was back. "Let's look for some chemicals I need. They'll likely be lurking in ordinary household materials—"

"Listen, I'll catch up to you," said Hayden. "I need to, uh, use the privy."

"Oh, well, whatever. We'll just be up here." She and Martor walked away, heads leaning together in intense dialogue. Hayden watched them go for a minute, then paced in the opposite direction.

He'd had time to scribble a few lines while fetching his coat. The folded scrap of paper in his pocket seemed to weigh a hundred pounds. Even now, as he hurried to find the local post office, he doubted the wisdom of his decision.

The paper read:

The Occupants
Strut Fourteen, Tromp L'oeil Elevated Platform
Quartet 1, Cylinder 2
Rush, Slipstream

6th Recession, Year 1580 A.V.

Seven Ships of the Slipstream Expeditionary Force split off from the main party near the diametric border of Aerie on 1st of Recession. The ships are the Severance, the Tormentor, the Unseen Hand, Rush's Arrow, the Clarity, the Arrest, and the Rook. *ADMIRAL FANNING IS COMMANDING THE ROOK.*

These ships continued on a diametric course outward from Aerie for four days before stopping at the winter town of Warea. Their destination after this is UNKNOWN, but they are all equipped for winter navigation and well supplied. The expedition appears urgent. Also aboard are Lady Fanning and an armorer from outside Virga named Aubri Mahallan.

Regardless of the ultimate purpose of this force, its absence from the main body of the fleet may make for a strategic advantage.

Yours,
A reluctant recruit

Mail was an adventurer's game in winter. There were no regular lines, just bags exchanged by ships and the occasional courier who flew dedicated runs, dodging pirates, weather, and the beasts of the void. These men were used to hand-deliveries—and to not asking questions. Provided Hayden paid well enough, he was reasonably sure his little envelope would get through.

The town didn't have a post office as such, but after asking a couple of locals he was directed to the mendicant's lodge. The bartender there handled what little mail came out of the town.

He had just found the place and was tensely walking up to the doors when a hand fell on his arm.

"You're a bit late," someone snarled.

Hayden whirled to face the man. "Do I know . . ." But he did know him.

Bright gray eyes in a pasty-white face stared up at him. "You were due to meet us at the docks, what . . . a year ago, was it? Just come to trust you, and the first day we let you loose on your own, you fly."

"I got detained, Milson," said Hayden as he backed away.

"Detained, sure." Milson sneered. "Desertion's a crime, little rat." He loosened his sword in its scabbard. "You better come with me."

"Excuse me," said Carrier, who had appeared out of nowhere. He smiled vapidly at Milson then turned to Hayden. "Where are the others?"

"Er, just up the street. Listen, I—"

"Come, then." Carrier took Hayden's elbow and turned him about, smiling at Milson in a dismissive manner.

"Oh no you don't—" Hayden heard the scrape of a sword being drawn behind them; then suddenly Carrier wasn't at his side anymore. He heard a swishing sound and a faint "urk" but in the second it took for him to turn he missed all the action. Carrier and Milson were walking together toward an alley; Carrier had one arm around Milson's greasy shoulder and only an observant man would have noticed that Milson's feet weren't quite touching the ground.

The two men entered the alley. One, two, three, four . . . Carrier emerged, dusting his hands, every bit the mild bureaucrat again. He smiled at an old woman as he passed her and fell into an easy stride next to Hayden.

"What was that all about?" he asked. His voice was flat, completely belying his jovial expression.

"Uh . . . apparently they resent the presence of battleships outside their doors," Hayden improvised. "I think I was about to get mugged. Thanks."

"I'm not here to clean up your messes," hissed Carrier. "Understand this: if there's a next time, I'll laugh along with the crowd when they stick you." He smiled. "Now, let's make sure the other two aren't being similarly harrassed."

Hayden put a hand in his pocket. Before they'd gone twenty feet he'd balled the message into a tight wad; when Carrier turned his head away for a moment, he angrily flicked it onto a pile of trash.

So much for joining the Resistance.

10

BY HAYDEN'S RECKONING, the ships were making barely fifteen miles per hour—nosing cautiously through the dark clouds, occasionally stalling while the commanders tried to figure out their current position by peering with narrowed eyes at the tracks their gyroscopes had made through tanks of glycerine. Twice great oceans of clear air opened up in front of them. The admiral took the opportunity and ordered full speed ahead. Hayden tracked down Martor on these occasions and took him for rides aboard his bike, opening it up to top speed and once tearing the poor boy loose entirely. Hayden circled back to find him arrowing on through the dark, sleeves rippling in the wind and utterly calm in his certainty that Hayden would return for him.

In the quietest hours of the nightwatch, he and Martor would meet Mahallan in her little box-shaped workshop. She had them building things—though what those things were, she wouldn't explain. "It's to do with electricity," was all she'd said. The devices (significantly, there were seven of them) were boxes full of metal wires that poked into and through various other, smaller boxes and tubes. Mahallan spent most of her time working on these little containers, filling them with carefully mixed pastes and powders that stank of oils and metal. Every now and then she would get Martor or Hayden to pedal a stationary bike that was attached to a big metal can connected by more wires to one of the boxes, and then she would poke about inside the new device using some metal prods. It was by turns fascinating and boring to watch. So, they whiled away the time by talking.

Hayden wanted to know about the strange outside world where

Mahallan was from, but he could barely get a word in edgewise, what with Martor's constant babbling. The boy was thoroughly infatuated with the armorer.

When Hayden did get a chance to ask her about her past, Mahallan was evasive. But on the third night, as they hovered around one of her strange boxes watching an expanding sphere of smoke extrude out of its side, she sighed and said, "This is the most wonderful thing, for me."

"What's that, lady?" Martor had turned to fetch a leather curtain. She waited as he deftly scooped the smoke into it and glided over to the porthole to squirt it outside. When he returned, she pried open the lid of the box and said, "It's wonderful to me that we can sit here and build things whose behaviors we design ourselves. Like this ship." She patted the wall. "Things like this are made using *knowledge*." She savored the word.

"Don't you have knowledge where you come from?" Hayden asked the question facetiously, but to his surprise, she shook her head.

"No, we don't. Not about the physical world, anyway. The systems of Artificial Nature make it unnecessary for us to know anything." She saw his look of puzzlement and grimaced. "I know, it's hard to explain. That's why I haven't talked about where I come from. Listen, in the worlds beyond Virga, humans no longer have to make things for themselves. Artificial Nature makes them for us. And no two devices or machines are alike; each one evolves in its own pre-physical virtual world. Even two tools intended to do the same job, while they may look identical, might work in totally different ways. And because each device is evolved, not . . . *designed*, is the word you use here . . . no one can say how a given one works. You could spend years studying how one engine operates, but that wouldn't tell you how other engines necessarily function. So there's no incentive to try. It's been this way on most worlds for thousands of years.

"So Hayden, Martor, you can't begin to imagine the excitement I felt when I came here and first saw two of your ships sailing out of the clouds. They were *identical!* They worked the same way, used exact copies of the same machines. Here were people who could take their own mental models of objects, and make them physically real. Virga is a wonder to me, because here you have knowledge and you use it to make more than one of things. Every time I see a new one of something I've seen before—like these ships—I'm thrilled all over again." She beamed at them. "You live in a very special world."

As she had been speaking the box she'd been working on had been slowly, strangely, drifting toward one wall. She noticed it and seized it. "*That's* not a good sign," she muttered.

Martor rubbed at his chin, considering. "Is that why you seemed surprised that I'd heard of gravity, the other day?"

The armorer nodded. "Gravity, exactly. Uh . . . yes, most of the worlds I know are replacing concepts like gravity with new mythologies their artists are crafting." Hayden and Martor must have really looked lost at this point, because Mahallan laughed richly when she glanced over at them.

"I'd heard," ventured Hayden, "that the people from beyond Virga live forever, can travel anywhere in the universe, and can do anything."

Mahallan shrugged. "Oh sure. And that means we have no more need to know anything. That's a tragedy. I spent years learning what you call the *sciences* but it was difficult to find entities who knew how to teach them. Most such knowledge is implicit in the construction of things . . . not written down, as it were. In fact, that's why I came to Virga. It was the one place I knew where there was no Artificial Nature."

"Why is that?"

She leaned forward like a conspirator. "Candesce disrupts the systems of Artificial Nature. It was refitted to do that centuries ago, in order to keep my people's civilization out of Virga. There's side effects that aren't good for your civilization, though—and that's why we're building these." She waggled the burnt-out box.

"What do they do?" Hayden had asked this very question a

dozen times now, and she'd sidestepped the issue every time. Maybe now that she wanted to talk, she'd give it away.

But Mahallan just smiled enigmatically and said, "They'll help us win."

At that moment there was a knock on the door. Before any of them could move, Venera Fanning poked her head into the tiny chamber. "Aha," she said. "The night owls are up, as promised."

"Venera," said Aubri neutrally. The admiral's wife swept into the room, frowning as she spotted Martor.

"So, the little spy-for-hire has wormed his way into your good graces. Get out, or I'll have the boatswain chop off your fingers."

Martor scrambled past her and out the door. With a faint smile of satisfaction, Venera closed it behind him. Turning to the other two, she clasped her hands before her and said, brightly, "How is it coming along?"

"It was coming along just fine, until you ejected my assistant," said Aubri.

"Bah!" Venera waved away the problem. "You still have this one. Though not for long, I need him to pilot me tomorrow. We're going on a little trip. You're coming too."

Aubri carefully placed the device she'd been working on in a dark wooden case and shut it. "Where is it that we're going?"

"Our first stop. First official stop, I mean. I want you to come with us because you've been here before."

"Really?" Aubri shifted uncomfortably. Hayden thought she looked very unhappy all of a sudden. "Have we circled back to Slipstream, then?"

Venera barked a laugh. "You know that's not where I mean. We're coming up on the tourist station! That was your first home when you came to Virga, wasn't it? You should know your way around it pretty well."

"As a matter of fact, I don't. And I don't appreciate being taken back to it without consultation. Unless—" She paled suddenly. "You're not sending me back . . ."

"Of course not, silly woman. I need you to find someone for

me—talk to them, make a deal. That's what this is all about, isn't it? Our deal?"

"Yes," murmured Aubri. To Hayden's astonishment he saw that she wouldn't look Venera in the eye. Venera either didn't notice this, or accepted it as normal. She turned to Hayden, smiling her predatory smile.

"Be ready to fly at eight o'clock sharp. We'll be taking the bike and sidecars, so they'd better be put together."

"Yes, ma'am."

"Good." Without another word, Venera left. As soon as the door closed Aubri spun and went to the porthole. She yanked it open and stuck her head outside. Hayden heard muffled cursing coming from beyond the hull. "What's going on?"

She pulled her head back in and grimaced at him, gesturing at the open porthole. He slipped by her and put his own head out into the cold whispering wind.

For a moment he saw nothing but the usual darkness and clouds. Then with a start he realized that what he had taken to be a giant puffball of vapor was made of facets and sweeping curves of glittering ice. They were sailing past a frozen lake: an iceberg as big as any of the cylinders of Rush.

He brought his head back in. "There's an iceberg outside."

Aubri shook her head dejectedly. "Look again." Puzzled, Hayden looked out again. Well, there was the iceberg, and actually there was another one on the other side of it. And another—they were attached tip-to-top, making a kind of chain.

A wreath of cloud slipped over and past the ship, and in the opening that followed he saw what Aubri wanted him to see— and gasped.

The Rook's running lights reflected faintly from shimmering planes of ice, a thousand angles of it receding into blackness. The ship's cyclopean headlight cast a cone of radiance into the dark and where it lit, Hayden beheld a forest of icebergs. They clung to one another by merest filaments and blades; a dense fog insinuated itself into every hollow and space between them. The Rook wove slowly around the giant spires of ice, each giant receding into the haze as others emerged ahead.

Hayden's eye followed a line of bergs as they passed it, and he realized that they thickened and converged miles away until they were jammed together cheek by jowl. Dark crevasses gaped between them. He was reminded of the forest that carpeted Slipstream's asteroid, only instead of the crowns and cones of trees rising up from darkness, here was endless ice.

"It's like a wall," he said. Just then his chin bumped the edge of the porthole. For some reason he'd started to drift into the ship—probably the air pressure.

"It's not a wall," said Aubri sourly. "It's a ceiling. The ceiling, to be precise."

"The . . ." He got it then. "This is the world's skin?"

"The skin of the balloon, yes. Everything else in Virga is below us here. That's why we're feeling gravity. I should have realized it from the way the engines were straining."

In the distance a thunderous crack! echoed through the berg forest. Hayden looked out again, and beheld a mountain of ice majestically disengage itself from its neighbors. He watched it as it faded into the ice fog behind them; he was almost sure he could see it moving away from its brothers.

"Candesce drives convection currents in Virga," said Aubri, startling Hayden because she was right next to him, just below the porthole. "Rising water vapor condenses into lakes, and if it makes it all the way up here, it freezes. The skin of Virga is very, very cold. But the skin is also the top of Virga's gravity well, slight though that may be. As these bergs grow they become heavy. Eventually they dislodge and fall, melting as they go. The biggest of them make it almost to Candesce before they evaporate."

Hayden contemplated the gargantuan icicles—for that was what they were—for a long time. Then he drew his head into the ship and said, "Why are we here?"

Aubri's face was only inches from his own. He had never been this close to her, and it gave him an uncomfortable pleasure—but she was looking miserable. "What's wrong?"

She pulled herself back to her workstation and fiddled with the lamp for a moment. "If I'd known we were coming here, I wouldn't have joined this expedition."

Hayden crossed his arms and waited. After a few seconds Aubri sighed heavily and said, "Look, I came to Virga to get away from that world." She jabbed a thumb hullward, aiming, he supposed, past the skin at the universe beyond. "I'm a refugee here, and I don't like to be reminded of what I left. Even less do I want to revisit that insipid tourist station."

He descended to sit on the air next to her. After musing for a few moments, he said, "I think I understand. I was born and raised in Aerie. Slipstream conquered it when I was still a boy. But I remember it—and there's reminders of it everywhere you look, from the crafts they sell in the market to the accents of people in the streets. They're . . . painful. You start avoiding them. And then you feel guilty about it."

She shook her head. "It's not like that. Not quite like that, but yeah, I don't like to be reminded." She smiled suddenly. "I didn't know you were from Aerie."

"Well, neither did anybody else before tonight," he said, clasping his hands in front of him. "Are they going to know by morning?"

Aubri raised an eyebrow. "No—no reason why they should."

They sat in companionable silence for a while. Then a faint shudder went through the ship, and simultaneously the whine of the engines changed tone.

Aubri groaned. "Are we there already?"

The howl of the alarm Klaxons drowned out any reply Hayden might have had, or any thought. He bounded to the window and looked out in time to see bright streaks converge on one of the other ships from inside a vast cloudbank. Bright flashes lit the side of the ship. He was able to close and dog the porthole before the staccato noise of explosions reached the *Rook*.

"We're under attack," he said unnecessarily, but there was no reply as Aubri Mahallan had already left the room.

CHAISON FANNING THREW on a jacket while an aide with a hand on his back steered him through the connecting passage to the bridge. Behind him the whole ship was awake and churning with activity. "How many are there?" he shouted ahead at the suddenly alert nightwatch. "What weapons?"

"Admiral, it looks like winter pirates," said the frightened-looking Helm. He was a junior officer on one of his first watches. Probably more afraid of messing up than of the enemy.

Chaison glided to the main periscope and took hold of its handles, slipping his feet into the stirrups below without having to look for them. For a few seconds he blinked, trying to figure out what he was looking at. Then practiced reflexes took over and he began counting and evaluating.

"I see ten enemy craft. It's a whole fucking fleet. I bet there's more maneuvering inside that cloud bank."

"Somebody at Warea must have told them about us," said Captain Sembry from behind him. "We're probably the biggest prize that's ever wandered into their territory."

"It's pure foolishness—they're not a navy, just a ragged flock of crows. What makes them think they can outmaneuver us? . . . Ah." He laughed humorlessly as he made out more details of the distant ships. "Some of them look like Aerie frigates. I take it back, they're not after booty. At least some of these people are carrying a grudge."

He spun and offered the periscope to Sembry. "Captain, it's a classic night engagement. They've got us trapped in the center of a cylinder of cloud. Their ships have plumbed those clouds, and I don't doubt at all that there's some big icebergs lurking in there if we were foolish enough to follow them. They're going to hit and run out of the fogbanks because they know what's inside them. We have to take away that advantage."

He turned to the disheveled but alert semaphore team. "All ships: launch bikes. Bikes to reconnoiter clouds, not to engage enemy unless attacked. All ships: rolling torus formation. All ships: ready rocket barrages.

"Fire at will."

"CIVILIANS TO QUARTERS!" The boatswain waved his sword at Hayden for emphasis. "That means you, errand boy. And strap yourself in—we're going to be pulling heavy maneuvers."

After a few moments of hesitation, Hayden retreated back to Mahallan's workshop. This was probably the only place in the ship where he'd be left alone. He nearly missed his grab for the door as the entire vessel shuddered. The sound of the engines was momentarily deafening, and a squeal of seldom-used brakes echoed from the fore. They were stopping the centrifuge so the Rook could maneuver without having to take gyroscopic effects into account. Somewhere in the distance he heard crashing sounds as the personal effects of dozens of airmen slid and tumbled inside the wheel.

He stuck his head out the porthole, wary of getting it shot off. What he saw was a jumble of ships, lit intermittently by rocket fire, moving at all angles to one another with no way at first to tell friend from foe. Some of those silhouettes were familiar, however. Hayden knew the sleek forms of the winter pirate vessels all too well, having spent some time on one of them during the years of his exile. He'd lied when he told Miles and the other Resistance fighters that he'd spent all his time sitting on a mushroom farm in the middle of nowhere. The truth was more dangerous to admit.

More details resolved as his eyes adjusted to the darkness. Clouds of bikes were tumbling out of the ships now, their tearing buzz filling the air as they swarmed around one another. The whole tableau was framed by black cloudbanks that pressed in on all sides. And now a huge frigate emerged as if by magic from one of those clouds, tongues of red fire erupting from its side as it fired a salvo of rockets point-blank into the stern of a Slipstream vessel. A good half of the rockets bounced off the cone-shaped end of the ship, drawing scarves of light on the darkness, but the remainder exploded. Beams and planking flew everywhere. The pirate rolled, jets screaming, and lined up its dorsal rocket battery. This time the bulk of the volley shot straight down the length of the Slipstream ship's exposed interior. A chain-reaction of explosions convulsed the victim and then the clouds flashed into flame-lit visibility as the ship burst like an overripe fruit. Men and materiel tumbled into the cold air while thunder banged and rolled around them.

Hayden smiled in grim satisfaction. That was one less Slipstream ship. On the other hand . . . he suddenly realized that the expeditionary force might lose this battle. If they were overwhelmed, there would be no prisoners taken. Everyone would be killed, from Admiral and Lady Fanning to Martor and Aubri Mahallan.

He would cheer the deaths of the Fannings—or at least of the admiral. Venera . . . he didn't know what to think of her. But her fate was out of his hands, he realized with a pang. She would never agree to escape with him. But maybe he could convince Martor and Aubri Mahallan to climb into the sidecars of his bike. They could arrow out of here, make for the tourist station, which he could now see through a gap in the clouds. It was miles away yet, an inverted, glittering landscape of towers; a city not rolled into cylinders but flattened out across the black ceiling of Virga.

They could make for that swirl of light. They could survive.

He turned and bolted for the workshop's door.

"WHO KNEW THERE were this many pirate ships in all of Virga?" muttered a crewman. Chaison Fanning didn't acknowledge the comment, but he'd been wondering the same thing. Had they gathered this fleet from all over the world, just to attack his little expeditionary force? Right now it seemed that winter really was the vast dark empire of freebooters and privateers that some popular stories and songs made it out to be.

Unbelievably, they'd already lost Rush's Arrow. The effect of the ship's explosion on the men had been immediate and dire. Chaison was now on his way through the ship, hurling orders and optimistic quips to the men as he went. He needed them to know that he trusted Sembry to command the Rook, and that his primary concern was them. But he was followed by a stream of staffers and he paused at every porthole to stare out at the battle, and occasionally issue a terse order for the semaphore team.

He stuck his head into the bike hangar. The place had been emptied out, all bikes in the air except for Venera's absurd racer with its sidecar, which her driver was laboring over. The hangar doors were wide open and men with rifles perched on them at various angles, haphazard gargoyles ready to fend off any comers. On his orders the ships had tossed out flares and so the clouds outside were lit a lurid green.

Actually, the view from here was excellent, better than the bridge, even. Chaison leaped over to one of the doors and anchored himself next to a surprised airman. "Do you have any more of those?" he said, pointing to the man's rifle. "I'm aiming to take some personal vengeance for the Arrow."

The airman grinned and shouted back, "A rifle for the admiral, boys!" One was passed up, the last several hands being those of his staffers, who looked uneasy and disapproving.

He motioned for them to join him. "Run a speaking tube from here to the bridge," he said. Just then the Rook's rotation brought the black-sided hull of a pirate corsair into view. The ship was less than three hundred feet away; he could see lights through its open rocket ports.

"Hit that ship!" he yelled, and opened fire with his rifle. The men cheered and a satisfying volley erupted around him. Moments later the bright darts of rockets followed from the Rook and from somewhere behind it. That would be the Severance, he guessed, which should be in triad formation with the *Rook* and the *Unseen Hand*.

"Concentrate your fire on the engines!" He squeezed off several shots to demonstrate. In a battle like this you kept moving, but you were also rolling the ship constantly to bring the rocket batteries to bear on the enemy. In order to do this the ship had to stick its engine nacelles out and turn them ninety degrees; this made them vulnerable to rocket and small-arms fire.

The *Rook* was rolling now and it made for a bit of gravity; Chaison had to turn himself around and cling to the hatch because *out* was now *down* and he was firing past his own feet. This was why you lashed yourself to any handy ring during a battle. You could easily fall out of the ship.

As the hangar rotated out of sight of the corsair Chaison caught a glimpse of one of his bikers plunging in from behind it. The man held a grenade over his head and as he passed the corsair at over a hundred miles an hour, he threw it. The green-lit ball disappeared into one of the corsair's engines and it blew up, just as the out-thrust hangar doors cut off Chaison's view.

But now the rest of the battle swung into sight again. *Tormentor*, *Clarity*, and *Arrest* had good crews and had maintained their triad even though they were surrounded now by six ships. One of those ships was on fire and as Chaison watched it veered away into the safety of the clouds. A coordinated volley of rockets from the triad enveloped another pirate and its sides buckled under the explosions. Silent and dark, it began to drift.

The ships and cloudbanks were lit flare-green but now yellow and red lights also glowed inside the clouds. Those were locator flares his bikes had dropped where they'd found ice or other hazards inside the mist. The bikes should be returning now. He turned to his staffers. "All bikes: attack enemy at will."

Seconds later he heard the buzzing snarl of jets as bike formations began to appear, swirling into the disorganized knots of the pirates' own riders.

The roar of a bike sounded, very close. It might be one of the *Rook*'s boys coming back, maybe wounded, or . . . He swung down and looked around the edge of the hangar door. Not thirty feet away, a black can trailed flame as it tried to match the rotation of the *Rook*. Its rider wore a lime-green jacket and burgundy trousers. He was straining to snag a passing porthole with a hook lashed to a grenade.

Chaison leaned way out, standing now on the very bottom of the open door with only a rope around his waist tying him to the *Rook*. He aimed and fired in one motion, and saw the rider convulse and the bike veer away. Before he swung back up he verified that the grenade had followed them into the dark.

Dangling there, vaguely aware of cheering coming from up above, he watched the battle progress. His forces had a clear advantage in weaponry, armor, and discipline, but they were outnumbered. The pirates—or expatriate Aerie airmen—kept swinging in and out of the cover of the cloudbanks. They had men on bikes tracking down the flares Slipstream's own bikes had laid down; as Chaison watched, the glows that marked the location of obstacles in those clouds were snuffed one by one. Having previously set the positions of those ice and rock chunks in their inertial navigation systems, the pirates themselves had no need of lamps to know where they were.

Another swing around and *Severance* and the *Unseen Hand* appeared, locked into a fierce rocket battle with three black cylinders. Their formation was broken and the two ships were drifting away at a quickening pace. As Chaison was about to ask why Sembry wasn't pursuing them, the *Rook*'s rotation took them out of sight, and something huge cut off any further view of the sky.

It was the black hull of a pirate, and it was barely yards away. The bastard had somehow snuck up on Sembry. Looking to the side, Chaison realized that the pirate had already looped rope around the spinning *Rook*. If friction or snags didn't break them, the pirates could drag the *Rook*'s hull into contact with the jagged rams that were even now being thrust out of its rocket ports.

"Sembry!" roared Chaison. He'd have the man towed for a day behind his own ship for this. The riflemen around him were gaping, so he yelled, "Fire on those ports!" and did so himself as an example.

Then he turned to his staffers. "Ready the ship for boarders. And find out why Sembry's not moving us!"

"It's mines," somebody said. "They've mined the air between us and the others."

Sure enough, as the ship spun around again he caught glimpses of green-lit star shapes tumbling in the space between the *Rook* and the receding *Severance*. "I need those cleared!" Even as he said this he realized that none of Slipstream's bikes were nearby. The bulk of them were caught up in a gigantic dogfight at the opposite end of the battle. Some drifted, dead or burning. The rest were missing.

He whirled and pointed at Venera's driver. "You! Get out there and clear those mines."

"W-what?" The young man blinked at him dumbly. Of course, he was just a civilian.

Chaison appealed to the riflemen. "Can anyone else here fly a bike?"

"No, wait, I'll do it." The driver was glaring at Chaison as though he'd received a mortal insult. "But . . ." The black-haired young man glanced to one side slyly. "I'll need help." He indicated the bike's two sidecars.

"Whatever," said Chaison with a negligent wave of the hand. "Take whoever you need.

"Bring me a saber and a pistol," he said. As he waited he watched the driver manhandle his bike toward the open hangar doors. *Venera's not going to be happy if I wreck her nice little taxi*, he thought. The idea made him smile.

11

"MARTOR!" HAYDEN WAVED frantically as he saw the boy pass the inside door to the hangar. "Get in here!"

"But I gotta go to—she's got nobody to—"

Hayden grabbed him by the arm and aimed him at the bike. "Are you talking about Aubri Mahallan?" he asked. Martor nodded quickly. "Well then go get her and bring her here. Fast!"

He did his best to be slow about winching the bike over the open doors. Every few seconds the scarred hull of the pirate would flash into view and the ships would exchange rifle fire. Bullets hummed past on all sides when that happened and Hayden hid behind the substantial metal of the bike.

When he poked his head out the third time he saw Martor literally dragging Aubri Mahallan into the hangar. "What's this all about?" she asked impatiently as the two came to land on the sidecars.

Hayden turned to Martor. "Martor, can you fetch us an extra set of stirrups?"

The boy looked suspicious. "But why—" Hayden turned away from him, to face Mahallan. In a low voice he said, "We're going to lose this battle. Come with me if you want to live."

Her eyes widened. She glanced at the opened doors below them just as black hull appeared there. "Down!" Hayden grabbed her shoulders and pushed her into the open mouth of the bike's jet as gunfire sounded all around them. Abstractly he noticed how fine-boned her shoulders were. Behind them, two of the Rook's riflemen convulsed and tumbled forward to hang at the end of their lines.

Aubri cried out and covered her eyes.

"We have to go," Hayden said to her, "and we have to go now! The *Rook*'s about to be boarded. You have no idea what they're going to do with a woman if they catch you."

The gunfire subsided as the pirate swung out of sight again. Aubri Mahallan looked out at the bullet-scarred space, its air blue with gunsmoke, and bit her lip in obvious indecision. Then she pushed Hayden aside angrily. "Get out of my way," she hissed. "I'm needed here."

"What are you talking about? You'll be killed if you stay!"

"I can't go," she said, looking frantic. "Too much has happened—is at stake now. It would be—"

"You have to choose your battles, Aubri."

She shook her head angrily. "Fine. I choose this one. You run away, if that's what you want."

Hayden was too astonished to stop her as she jumped back up to the inner door. Martor was coming back with the spare stirrups and gaped at her as she went by. "What did you say to her?" he yelled at Hayden. At the same time, another heavy body landed on the bike next to him, making it rock.

"Hey!" shouted the red-haired boatswain, who held a bundle of rope and rockets under his arm. "Cut us loose, errand boy!"

Hayden cursed and mounted the bike. "Come on, Martor! We need you!" He and the boatswain dragged the protesting boy onto the bike. Hayden glanced down to make sure the pirate wasn't below them, and then pulled the pin on the winch. The bike did its curving fall into the dark air, and he spun up the fan and lit the burner without thinking.

His two passengers were having a shouted conversation past his back. ". . . Tied to the nets," said the boatswain as the jet lit and they surged forward just in time to avoid the approaching hull of the pirate. "Snag a mine with the net and light the rocket. Make sure you aim the rocket away from the *Rook* first. If you can aim it at a pirate, great!"

The boatswain spun in his seat and hit Hayden in the midriff. "Get us out there! The *Rook*'s about to be boarded!"

Hayden complied silently. This bike was dangerously fast, even with sidecars on it, so he was compelled to approach the mined air in a series of short bursts. This drew more insults from the boatswain. Meanwhile the battle continued to rage around them, at near points such as the *Rook*, and far away in flashes like lightning on distant clouds. Grumbling and roaring noises echoed strangely off the ice field that made a half-visible wall beyond the mists.

In the light of flares that Martor held over his head, the first mine hove into sight just yards ahead. Hayden puffed the engine a couple of times and the boatswain leaned out with his net to encircle the studded metal sphere. The net was tied to a rocket the length of his forearm; the boatswain lit it and the bike was showered with sparks. Hayden shielded his eyes for a second then watched as the rocket surged away, towing the mine into winter.

"Next!" roared the boatswain. Hayden turned the bike, glancing back at the *Rook* as he did. It and the smaller pirate seemed locked together now and men were spilling into the air between them.

He looked in the opposite direction. Far out there, the glittering lights of the tourist station beckoned. There was life for Martor and Aubri, if only he could figure out a way to get her off the *Rook*.

It was too late for her, he realized with a pang. But not for Martor.

The boatswain fired off another rocket. "Next! We've got to clear a tunnel for the *Rook* to fly through!"

"All right, all right!"

Hayden's heart was pounding. It was happening again: start to know someone, and all you got was the chance to lose them. True, he barely knew Aubri Mahallan. And true, a month ago he'd been willing to sacrifice his own life just to strike a blow against Slipstream. His most hated enemy was fighting for his life in the *Rook*, and Hayden should fervently wish nothing but disaster for that ship and all aboard it.

But he'd flown out from Gavin Town with a rifle in his hand and attacked Slipstream's cruisers while his mother decided her own fate in Aerie's unlit sun. And as Hayden had tumbled helplessly away into winter she had died. Was he really going to let Aubri go in the same way?

He swore, twisting his grip on the bike's handlebars. "Next!" yelled the boatswain and he turned the bike to find another glint of green in the light of Martor's flares.

Momentarily, he had an audience's grand view of the battle. Slipstream's ships were giving better than they took and several pirates were now drifting hulks surrounded by clouds of debris and dead men. The superiority of Fanning's disciplined crews was beginning to tell. The problem was that the pirates were able to use the cover of the clouds; they emerged just far enough to fire off a salvo, then retreated into invisibility.

Now that he could see the whole vista, though, Hayden realized that the pirates were only hiding in the clouds on one side— the side where the icebergs lay hidden in mist. They could use those bergs safely because the things didn't move, they were really giant icicles hanging from the outer skin of Virga. He had seen one of them begin a slow majestic fall just before the battle.

That gave him an idea.

"Next!" He looked around. There were dozens of mines, and there was no way they were going to clear a path for them before the boarding action on the Rook was decided one way or another. He turned toward a nearby mine, but made sure that he brought it up to the bike on Martor's side. "You take it, rat," said the boatswain as he handed Martor a rope and rocket. The boy grinned fiercely and leaned out to lasso the mine.

Hayden pulled out his knife and cut the strap tying the boatswain to his seat. The man was watching Martor and didn't notice. Then Hayden took a net and threw it over the boatswain's head.

"Hey! You bastard, watch what you're—"

Hayden lit the rocket tied to the net just as Martor was lighting his own. Sparks showered everywhere and they both ducked down covering their eyes. When Hayden looked up again, both the mine and the boatswain were gone.

Martor stared at the empty seat. "Where'd he go?"

"I don't know." Hayden spread his hands, looking surprised. "One second he was here, then he was gone. Must have caught a stray bullet."

Far out there, if you knew where to look, the fading ember of a rocket poked into a cloudbank and disappeared. Hayden watched it go then turned to Martor. "Listen," he said, "this isn't going to save the Rook. I've got a better idea."

He took them over to the next mine and Martor netted it. "Don't light the rocket," Hayden told him. "Just string it out behind us." They did the same with the next mine, and the next. Soon they had five of them dangling in their way.

"Now we get out of here," said Hayden.

"But the admiral told us to—" Martor hastily grabbed the sides of his car as Hayden put on the power. They shot up and away from the mined air—and the battle—heading straight for the mists that hid the bergs.

"Light more flares. We'll need to see where we're going." He slid them into the clouds at an incautious speed, trusting to his own skill to avoid hitting anything. The flares made a sphere of leaf-green light around them, and only the occasional wisp of moisture fluttering past showed that they were moving at all.

It was freezing in here, and Hayden took inspiration from that: follow the chill. He slowed the bike and let it drift in the air currents until he felt it enter a river of cold. Then he cautiously nudged them forward.

Out of the darkness, a vast turquoise shape emerged—a long sleek fish-shaped mountain of ice covered with knobby protuberances. Hayden could make out its tip off to the right, a dangerous white spike intermittently lit by distant explosions. To the left, the shape wove off into blackness.

He wrestled the bike in that direction. Martor was silent now, puzzled but obviously intrigued. As Hayden circled the berg he saw what he was looking for: there was a spot where the giant icicle narrowed to a thickness of only a few yards. In the minuscule gravity created by Virga's collective air and water, this neck was enough to hold up the rest of the bulk.

"Martor, I want you to fire a mine at that crimp there." He pointed. Now the boy's eyes widened with understanding and he hurried to obey.

Hayden ducked away from a cascade of sparks, then looked up to see that Martor's aim was good. The mine sailed silently at the ice, contacted it and—

A flash of orange lit the night and moments later the thunderous bang of the explosion made Hayden flinch. As the smoke cleared he saw that the neck of ice had been severed. A white splinter shot past his head, barely a foot away, but he hardly noticed. He was watching the gap that now existed between the ice attached to Virga's skin, and the long berg that had hung down from it.

"It's widening," he said after a few seconds. "Martor, do you see it? It's starting to fall."

The boy grinned. "Let's do another one."

THE SHIP WAS a madhouse full of screaming, gunshots, and the clash of swords. Chaison Fanning had his sword out, but his staffers were in the way. One of them interposed himself between Chaison and the silhouetted form of a pirate whom he was about to attack.

Chaison had a savage moment in which he considered stabbing the man to get at the pirate. What he needed above all else was to take the heads off a few of those swine who were threatening his ship, his men, and his mission.

Chaison slipped past the well-meaning fool and his sword fight, and dove for the hangar. A knot of men was struggling unsuccessfully to prevent the pirates from gaining access to the ship proper. Chaison flew over to join them, being careful to look past the heads and struggling arms in his way and assess the enemy. The hangar was mostly full of low-lifes and bullies who were unused to an even fight, but they seemed to be led by a tight vanguard of ex-Aerie naval officers who had thrown themselves across the space between the ships with no regard for bullets or blades.

"Shoot the leaders!" He grabbed a rifle and aimed past a pair of men who were fighting a freefall sword fight, blade in one hand, long curving belaying hook in the other.

"But sir!" The damned fly who'd buzzed around him earlier was back, panting but unscathed. "What about the fleet? Your orders?"

He whirled, murderous rage causing him to level the rifle at the man. To his credit, the officer paled but stood his ground. "They need an order," he said.

Chaison cursed and grabbed him by the throat. "Don't ever," he hissed, "make the mistake of thinking I can't fight and plan at the same time." Then Chaison dove past him, making for the bridge.

The way was blocked. He blinked in surprise at the staved-in beams and boards that filled the narrow passage beneath the centrifuge. That didn't look like rocket damage. A prow? Had they been rammed while he was looking the other way?

It hardly mattered. He pried some planks out of the way and stared out at the dark. The battle was going much as he'd expected; the pirates had the advantage of available cover and were using it shamelessly. But the five ships on the other side of the mined zone were making mincemeat out of them anyway. *They don't need my help,* he decided. Taking a moment to run down his list of priorities, he turned to the staffers and said, "Where's my wife?"

"Uh, the bridge, sir."

"All right. We're going to have to get there, that's where the scuttling triggers are located. Time to do a little outside climbing, boys."

He kicked at the broken planking and soon had made an opening big enough to worm through. The staffer who'd confronted him earlier put a hand on his arm as he made to go through it. "Let me go first, sir. We don't know what's out there."

Chaison looked at him in surprise. "What's your name?"

"Travis, sir." He looked more like an actor playing some idealized naval officer than a real man. Why, they were in the middle of a battle and his uniform wasn't even scuffed! But he looked calm and composed, unlike the rest of his team.

Chaison grinned at him. "You've got a fine sense of propriety, Travis, but you're a bit impertinent." Travis looked crestfallen and Chaison laughed. "Get going! We'll talk later."

Travis made it outside and apparently didn't die; his hand reached back through the gap to help Chaison and the other staffers clamber out. They found themselves at the bottom of a huge dent in the Rook's hull. Nothing that the carpenters couldn't take care of. Chaison looked out and saw that both the Rook and the pirate had stopped spinning. They were lashed together now by dozens of ropes. The nearest hatches on the pirate were twenty feet away, and while men were popping out of those every few seconds, none looked forward and spotted Chaison's small group. It was tempting to start picking them off, but that would be a fool's game; they wouldn't last a minute before somebody sniped them from behind a porthole.

"There's a fine irony," commented Chaison as he groped for purchase on the streamlined hull. All around was nothing but air, the endless abyss of Virga; a misgrab here would send you on a slow trip around the world, with the birds, bugs, and fish making a moving feast of you along the way.

"What's that, sir?" Travis appeared next to him. Both of them clung by their fingernails to the gaps between hull planks, moving themselves forward with slow swings so as not to lose that purchase.

Chaison shrugged and said, "We came out here to find a pirate's treasure, but it looks like we're going to become such a treasure instead."

Travis nearly lost his grip. "Pirate's . . . *treasure?* Admiral, sir, what are you talking about?"

Chaison gazed past him. Another of his ships was disappearing behind a pall of smoke. He doubted that it was a deliberate ploy, it wasn't evenly enough distributed. That did not look good.

They were approaching the portholes to the bridge. There was an impenetrable hatch there; they would have to talk their way in. *Shouldn't be hard,* Chaison thought absently. *Venera's not mad at me for anything at the moment.*

He risked another glance at the battle. Yes, that was definitely the *Clarity* on fire out there. Three pirates had it under sustained attack. They were using a wheel formation, he saw—that was far too sophisticated a maneuver to be undertaken by untrained privateers. The three ships had let out ropes and tied them together at a central point. With their engines on full they'd begun to spin around that central pivot point. Spinning up like that was easy; it was a standard way for groups of ships that lacked centrifuges to create gravity while on long voyages. What was hard was spinning and twisting while you spun to present a difficult target to attackers. These ships were doing that.

Two-thirds of the wheeling formation were inside the cloudbank. The net effect was that a pirate would swing out of the white wall at a fierce clip, fire a volley of rockets, and then dive back into the mist in a much steeper turn than would normally be possible. The *Clarity* was firing rockets at the center of the formation, hoping to cut the ropes that held the three ships together. That was a long shot, however.

Travis had given up asking about the treasure and was pounding on the armored hatch. Chaison hardly noticed, mesmerized as he was by the drama unfolding in that distant patch of sky. *Get out of there,* he willed the *Clarity,* but its engines must be damaged. It was a hanging target, like a driver fallen off his bike and vulnerable in clear air. In seconds it could all be over.

The cloudbank pulsed orange once, twice, then dozens of times in rapid succession. Chaison had seen fireworks reflecting off clouds; that was what this looked like. He'd been mentally timing the appearance of each ship from within the clouds, and the next one was late. No, not late—it wasn't coming out. Seconds passed, and the second of the three should have appeared, but it didn't.

Finally one appeared. The pirate left the cloudbank in an uncontrolled tumble. Flashes of rocket fire showed long streamers of rope trailing behind it.

"They hit something," he said. Travis looked up, puzzled. Chaison pointed, and as he did so another flash lit the clouds, this one miles away.

"Somebody moved the icebergs," he whispered. Then he started to laugh. Two spokes of the wheel had been lost within seconds— two pirate ships flown at full speed into an unexpected obstacle. The fools were too confident in their charts, and now they were blindly running into the mountains of ice they had been using to hide their maneuvering. It served them right.

"*I don't see what it is you find so amusing about the situation,*" said a cold voice behind Chaison.

"Travis, cease your work," he said quietly. Turning, he raised his hands. "We have visitors."

VENERA FANNING CROUCHED on the inside of the bridge's hatch. She could hear voices outside; one had sounded like her husband's. Captain Sembry refused to undog the hatch, however, and she didn't have the strength. The damn thing was designed to resist an invading force. Opening was about the last thing it was capable of doing.

Rhythmic pounding came from the inner doors as well. A minute ago an explosive charge had gone off behind one of those doors, but it hadn't been enough to break the hinges. It was only a matter of time, though.

Well, she thought, *this will be an interesting new chapter in my life. Captured by pirates!* The prospects of various fates worse than death outraged and angered her, but Venera wasn't afraid. She was already wondering what leverage she could use to make the best of the situation.

"The gas?"

Venera came alert at those words. She looked over at the bridge crew, who were clustered around a set of valves and pipes at the back of the can-shaped chamber. Captain Sembry was shaking his head at whoever had spoken.

"Too late for that," he said. "We'd kill the boarders, but the rest of the pirates would just blow the stuff out and come in again."

"The charges, then."

Sembry nodded, reaching into his jacket for something.

"Captain?" Venera put on her best maiden-in-distress act. "What's happening?"

Sembry turned, looking patriarchal and sad. "I'm sorry, dear," he said, "but we can't allow a Slipstream ship to fall into enemy hands. I'm going to have to scuttle the *Rook*."

She widened her eyes. "But we'll all be killed, won't we?"

He sighed. "That is the nature of military service, I'm afraid."

"How do you scuttle a big ship like this?" she asked.

Sembry showed her the key in his hand. He nodded to a set of metal boxes on the wall behind him. "These charges can only be set off by electrical current," he explained. "This key—"

He blinked in surprise at the pistol Venera had produced from inside her silk pantaloons. Sembry opened his mouth to speak but Venera never learned what he might have said because at that moment she shot him in the forehead.

The rest of the bridge crew was nicely packed together, and consequently picking them off was just as easy.

Twitching bodies and drops of blood caromed around the bridge. Venera ducked through it all and grabbed Sembry, who still had a surprised look on his face.

First order of business, she thought: dispose of this key.
Second: open the doors and let in the pirates.

HAYDEN'S PLAN HAD worked. He and Martor hovered high above the action, at the only spot he'd found where they could see past cloud, contrail, smoke, and darkness. Four icebergs were nosing out of the mist now, trailing fog as they slowly gathered momentum in their long fall toward the Sun of Suns. The pirates had lost their advantage and were in disarray. The battle might have turned.

Something he hadn't anticipated was happening, though: as the icebergs fell, they brought their weather with them. The battle scene was fast disappearing in a vast billow of cloud. Already foghorns were sounding through the dimness as the ships struggled to avoid one another.

Martor was squirming with impatience. "Now back to the Rook!"

Hayden nodded and spun up the engine; but he was uneasy. With the ships separated by mist and mines it could be a long time before the Rook was relieved. He nudged them cautiously through the layers of mist, listening for the sound of gunfire or rockets. Ominously, he heard nothing.

A black hull loomed up suddenly and he had to spin the bike and hit the gas to stop in time. "It's the pirate!" said Martor as he groped for the sword he'd stowed in the sidecar. "Sounds like we've won!"

Hayden eased them around the hull, as quietly as he could. The pirate and the Rook were still bound together with rope, and lights burned in the portholes of both. He could see the gray shapes of men working on the Rook's engines, so the fight must indeed be over.

Martor was nearly bursting. "Come on, what are you waiting for?"

"Shh!" Cutting the engine entirely, Hayden let them drift toward the aft of the ships. The working figures resolved slowly, like images he'd once seen on a photographic emulsion.

"Hey, those aren't—" Quickly Hayden grabbed Martor's arm, putting a finger to his own lips. The boy pulled away.

"But that can't be! We have to do something."

"Martor, they've taken the *Rook*," Hayden whispered. "We can't go back now."

"But somebody has to protect Aubri! Listen," pleaded Martor, "we can catch a ride on the hull, like tired crows, and when they least expect it—" Hayden shook his head.

Martor tried again. "Then let's hang back in the clouds and follow them . . . What?"

"We have another ten minutes' worth of gas, tops. If they aren't out there already, the pirates are going to send out bikes any minute now to look for any followers. And you know perfectly well they'll check every inch of the hull, inside and out, for stowaways."

"You want to run back to one of the other ships? No! I'm staying to fight."

"Martor, that's ridiculous. You wouldn't last ten seconds." Let the boy think they were returning to the other ship. By the time he realized that their true destination was the tourist city, it would be too late.

Hayden felt sick at the thought of leaving. Consigning Aubri Mahallan to these monsters was another defeat in a lifetime of defeats. And for some reason, the thought that Admiral Fanning was dead or soon would be, was no consolation. *Who cares about him?* some unexpected part of him said. *Only you, and what do you matter?*

"I hate to do it," he said sincerely. "But we've got to—"

He glanced up just in time to see the black cylinder of a rocket, held in Martor's hands, swing toward his face. Then everything burst and went dark.

12

WHEN VENERA FANNING was a girl she lived in a room with canary-yellow walls. Little trees and airships were painted on them, and her bed had a canopy of dusty velvet and sat against one wall.

At night, if she pressed her ear to the uneven plaster, she could hear the screams of men and women being tortured in her father's dungeon.

She'd been reminded of home many times over the past day. Now, though, the sounds of screaming echoing through the Rook had died out. In the relative silence that followed she could hear someone big approaching through the lamplit dimness—whoever it was was banging back and forth off the walls in a freefall tantrum. As the figure passed the doors to the hangar where Venera was tied up, she saw that it was the pirate captain, Dentius was his name. It was apparent that he wasn't pleased with the results of the torture session.

Venera took the opportunity. "By now," she said loudly, "you'll have noticed that the crew have absolutely no idea where we were going."

Dentius whirled. His already small eyes narrowed further and his lips pulled back from his teeth. Swinging into the hangar he stopped himself by wrapping his legs around Venera's hips. He grabbed her by the throat.

"What do you know?" he shouted. "Tell me or you're next."

"Now, Captain," she croaked, rearing back, "there are easier ways. I'm quite willing to tell you . . . for a little consideration."

He sneered. Dentius wore the faded and patched uniform of

an Aerie ship captain. His face, however, bore no traces of ever having been exposed to sunlight. Like most of his crewmen, his skin was as white as the inside of a potato, except where it was crisscrossed with pink scars. To Venera he looked like some giant, writhing grub stuffed into an officer's jacket.

She knew he was already inclined to treat her differently than the crew, who were mostly crammed into empty rocket racks or water lockers, out of sight and momentarily out of mind. Whether Chaison was with them, or whether he even lived, she had no idea.

Venera and Aubri Mahallan were tied up and on display in the hangar, "as an inspiration to the lads," Dentius had said— though both were still clothed because, he'd said, "there's a fine line between inspired and obsessed." Still, Mahallan was lashed spread-eagled in the center of the space and seemed dazed and despairing. Venera merely had her wrists fastened to a stanchion near the door.

It was clear what the captain had in mind for Mahallan. If he had no clear idea of what to do with Venera, she wanted to provide him with some alternatives before he thought about it too much.

He peered at her for a moment, then sucker-punched her in the kidneys. The pain was astonishing—but through Venera's mind flashed a memory of herself lying on marble tiles, moaning through a ruined mouth and staring at the blood-shrouded shape of a rifle bullet that lay next to her. While nobody came and her fury grew and grew . . .

Dentius grabbed her hair and pulled her head back. "Tell me!" he roared at her. "Or I'll kill you right now!"

"Th-that's the problem, isn't it?" She managed to smile, though her neck and jaw pulsed with pain and she could feel the hairs in her scalp starting to pull out. "You're going to kill me anyway. So why should I cooperate?"

Dentius grunted and drew back. He had the mentality of a shark, she'd decided: all straight-ahead brute force, but stupid and immobile when stopped. Her bravado seemed to have stymied him—or at least, it had reminded him of what she'd already done.

"Why'd you shoot the captain?" he asked suddenly.

Venera smiled. "Why? Because he was the one other person on board who knew our destination."

Dentius let go of her hair. At that moment one of his obsequious mates appeared in the doorway. "Inventory's done, Captain," he said in a familiar accent she couldn't quite place. "Strictly military, except for some paintings. Probably going to trade those at the voyeur's palace."

Dentius nodded, eyeing Venera speculatively. Then he drew a knife out of his boot. She drew back, but he merely reached up to cut the length of rope holding her to the beam. "We'd best talk further," he said, as he towed her out of the hangar and into the remains of battle: drifting droplets of blood and hanging balls of smoke, wood splinters, and tumbling scarves of bandage.

As he dragged her with bumps and jerks through the wooden ribs of the ship, Venera tried to keep her wits. She needed a sense of who was still alive, and where they were. The rocket racks were essentially iron cages, so it was easy to see their inhabitants. None of the senior officers was visible, only able airmen who stared at her listlessly or with fear. Was Chaison dead, then?

Dentius hauled her into the axle of the centrifuge, which had been spun up. Exhausted or wounded pirates lolled in hammocks at the rim of the wheel; she heard both moaning and laughter. "My cabin," she said to Dentius, pointing with her tied hands.

"Captain's cabin," he said. "You his woman?"

She shook her head. Chaison Fanning had appropriated Sembry's cabin, causing the *Rook*'s captain to have to bunk elsewhere. "I was the admiral's wife," she admitted. "But he's dead and lost in the clouds now."

Venera had no doubt that Dentius would have asked the tortured men about her. There was no point in trying to deny her status.

Without comment Dentius shoved her into the cabin, which

was a shambles of overturned chests and jumbled clothing. Most of the contents had been Sembry's of course; Chaison traveled light.

Her jewel box lay on the floor, its lid up, the fated bullet that had struck her jaw still on its velvet bed inside. The centrifuge's spin was making her nauseated so Venera went to sit on the edge of the bed, making a show of straightening her clothes.

"So . . ." Dentius gnawed at one calloused knuckle. "Why'd you kill the rest of the bridgers?"

She shrugged. "They . . . objected to my tactics."

Dentius laughed. "Venera Fanning, that's your name, isn't it?"

"Aye," she said, lifting her chin. Her heart was hammering in her chest; raised though she was in the arts of deceit, Venera doubted she could keep her calm demeanor for long.

Dragging over a chair, Dentius sat down and clasped his hands in his lap. "So," he said in a horrible parody of politeness, "what brings you to our winter, Venera Fanning?"

"Treasure," she said promptly. "Somewhat ironically . . . pirate treasure, to be exact."

Dentius shook his head. "If there were anything worth having out here, I'd have taken it and built a fleet to reconquer Aerie years ago. Nobody brings treasure into winter. Anybody here who's got it, takes it somewhere sunny."

"I know," she said. "But that wasn't always the case. There've been times when convoys ran through winter regularly, shipping goods between the principalities of Candesce and the outer nations. And during those periods, there was treasure to be had."

Dentius thought for a while. His face, which had appeared that of a brutal simpleton just minutes ago, relaxed by degrees into that of a weary, disappointed man. After a while he said, "I've heard the fairy tales. We all have. There was even a time when I believed in such things." With a faint smile he added, "It's Anetene, isn't it? You're talking about the—how would you put it, 'the fabled treasure of Anetene.'"

Venera frowned past his tired skepticism. "I was," she said.

"We were on our way to the tourist station, because that's where the map is."

Dentius laughed. "You've got to be out of your mind," he said. "Anetene's a legend. Sure, he lived and he was a great pirate. The less intellectually endowed members of my crew swear by him. But the treasure's pure myth."

"Maybe," she said with a shrug. "But the map to it is real."

His lips curled in sly indulgence. "And what would an admiral of Slipstream be doing hunting pirate treasure in winter?"

"As to that . . ." She looked away, making a faint moue. "Slipstream's finances are not in the greatest of shapes at the moment, if you get my meaning. The Pilot is not the cleverest of men when it comes to state funds."

"You've a deficit to pay off?" Dentius grinned.

"It's more like, the Pilot has a deficit he's told the people about . . . and then there's the real deficit."

"You're wanting to forestall a political scandal, I get that." Dentius shook his head. "The whole story is preposterous on the face of it, and you know it. So why are you trying to put this one over on me?"

"Because the treasure is real," she said. "But I realize that I can't convince you of that." Now she hesitated: how far could she push this man? If she played the next hand, he might kill her. But if she gave in to fear he would have won; the bullet would have won. "There's another consideration," she said slowly. "I saw how you and your men fared during the battle. You have your own deficit now, Captain Dentius: you've just paid far more in men and ships than you've gotten back. Am I wrong in thinking that this is going to cause you some . . . political problems . . . of your own?"

Dentius's face flushed with anger. He stood up, knocking over the chair. "We're going to kill all of you for starters," he said. "Very bloody, very visible. My men will have their revenge."

"Yes but will that be enough?" Venera allowed herself a small, ironic smile. "You know that the other captains won't be impressed. You lost ships, Dentius."

He didn't answer. "Killing us will be a good diversion," Venera continued. "But you need a better diversion. One that will last longer, until the memories of this debacle have faded. You've got to give your men *hope*, Captain Dentius, or else you may be out of a job."

"In other words," he said, "it hardly matters at this point whether the treasure of Anetene really exists . . ."

"As long as there's a map. Something to give the other captains." She nodded. "And there *is* a map."

Dentius leaned against the wall for a while; he was obviously not comfortable in gravity. Finally he nodded once, sharply. "Done. You show us to the map, you get to keep your life."

"And my virtue."

"Can't guarantee that. But let's say it's on the table." He grinned and turned to leave. "Cabin's yours. Anything else your grace requires?"

Life, not death, lay ahead—at least for now—so Venera decided to ask about the one thing that Dentius might be willing to indulge. "There is something . . ."

Dentius turned, surprised. Venera knelt down and retrieved her jewel box. She plucked out the bullet and held it up, next to her jaw.

"We have a history, this bullet and I," she said. "If I live, and if someday I gain my freedom again, I want to know where it came from."

He was obviously impressed. "Why?"

There was no pretense behind her smile now. "So that I can go there," she said, "and kill everyone connected to it."

A BLACK WING lifted. Hayden blinked at a blurred jumble of shadows and silhouettes. Mumbles and tearing sounds came to his ears; someone was tugging at his shirt. He couldn't feel any surface under him so he must be weightless. He was also very cold. And in the distance, the faintly annoying two-tone sound of the Rook's engines rumbled.

That meant something bad. "Hey!" he tried to shout. The word came out slurred and weak.

"He's awake." He recognized the voice behind the tense whisper. "Pardon us, Griffin, we're sacrificing the hem of your shirt to a better cause."

"Wha—" Admiral Fanning's voice had been dry, almost raspy. But why was he of all people here? Hayden shook his head, which filled him with an awful vertigo and a pounding pain that radiated forward from behind his left ear. *Don't throw up*, he beseeched himself. *Don't throw up. There's no gravity today.*

The gray blurs became a bit clearer. He was curled in the fetal position in some cramped space defined by metal bars. There was no light source nearby, everything was shades of speckled gray with no color. Crammed into this unlikely place with him were three men and a boy. One of the men was Fanning. Another—he wasn't sure—might be Venera's manservant, Carrier.

Hayden's stomach did another flip, but not because of his own pain. The third man held Martor by a hand and a foot, stretching him out like a sheet about to be folded while Fanning tried to staunch a dark liquid welling from his flank. Martor's foot stuck out one side of the cage, his hand out the other.

"He's . . . stabbed?"

"Shot," muttered Fanning. "The bullet's still inside."

The sight had brought Hayden alert like a dash of cold water. "We need to dig it out," he said, focusing on making his uncooperative lips form the syllables.

"Really?" Yes, that was Carrier all right, his tone dripping sarcasm. "Keep your voice down," he added in a hiss.

Hayden wanted to ask why they were in this cage, but didn't want to hear any of the possible answers. The strange electric silence of the ship, the way these men flinched any time there was a noise in the distance . . . But overriding that curiosity was the need to know that Martor would be all right.

"Cut the man some slack," Fanning said quietly to Carrier. "He's concussed." He turned to Hayden. "The problem is that I can't reach the bullet with my fingers. And the only other thing we have is a couple of splinters of wood I pried off the hull." He held up two sharp spikes of wood. "If I go noodling around in your friend's abdomen with these, I'm going to puncture something for sure, and probably leave some splinters behind. That's bound to fester."

"Maybe you can help," said the man who was holding Martor like a sheet. Hayden recognized him as one of Fanning's staff. "We could heat the wood to sterilize it—without setting it on fire, of course. If we could reach that." He pointed.

Now Hayden realized where they were: crammed into the framework of a rocket rack, somewhere near the stern of the ship. The rack was mounted to the hull and surrounded by boxes that blocked the light. But where the staffer pointed, the corner of one crate was brightly silhouetted. Just around that corner was a lantern. Hayden held out his hand and felt the faint movement of air coming from its wind-up fan.

A cough sounded nearby and gruff voices spoke. The men in the cage froze, only their eyes darting in the direction of the sound. Seconds ticked by, and eventually they all sighed as one and relaxed from their positions.

"None of us can reach that lantern," said Fanning, as if nothing had happened. "But you're young and lanky. Care to try? We need these splinters heated but not burned."

"Ah." He took them in one shaking hand. "Okay." Drops of Martor's blood were drifting past his nose, scented of iron. Hayden carefully ducked around them and pressed his shoulder to the bars of the cage. Once again in middistance he heard grating, accented voices: that was not the crew of the Rook. The pirates might see his hand groping around the corner of the crate—it was going to be brightly lit, after all—but he'd be damned if he was going to seize up like a busted engine every time one of them sneezed. He had to try his part to save Martor.

By straining until spots appeared in his eyes, he was able to get his hand around the corner of the crate. He knew the shape of the little lanterns intimately: they were like tiny bikes, open-ended cylinders with a wind-up fan at one end to move air past the lamp's wick. He pictured the device in his mind, and moved one of the splinters until he figured it was near the flame. He waited a moment, then brought it back.

The splinter was still cool. He tried again, shifting position slightly. Five tries and he put it right into the flame, making it catch light so that he had to quickly blow on it while Carrier cursed him for a fool. But he was getting the hang of it now.

A few minutes later he gingerly handed two hot lengths of wood to Fanning, who grunted in approval. Hayden felt proud of himself, happy for the implied praise, and then angry at himself for valuing Fanning's opinion.

Now that Fanning was at work, Hayden felt he could finally ask the questions that were burning in him. "Who shot him?" he asked Fanning's staff member. The man looked over Martor's arm at him with a bemused look on his face.

"We were going to ask you the same question," he said. "They threw you both in with us an hour after we lost the fight. I'd heard a shot. . . . Were you outside the ship?"

Hayden nodded. "Clearing mines. . . . Now I remember. He hit me on the head because I refused to return to fight. You'd . . . already lost."

"Wisdom is often rewarded with a blow to the head," said the other. "My name is Travis. This is Carrier. You probably know the—uh, Ensign Fanning, here." Travis smiled ruefully. "You have the privilege of being stuck in the cage reserved for troublemakers. Fanning and I were caught sneaking outside the ship. Carrier made it all the way into the bridge of the enemy ship and killed six people before they subdued him. And apparently, you two attacked a fully armed pirate ship with one bike and two pistols. We're a pretty worrisome lot, I guess."

"But we're alive," said Carrier in a flat voice. "Stupid of them."

"They don't know—" Fanning's voice was distracted "—which of us might be valuable."

"They don't know who he is," Travis whispered, jabbing a thumb at the admiral. "But they know there was an admiral on board. His ransom might be the only profit they see off this escapade."

"Thought I was him," said Carrier with the first trace of amusement he'd shown. "Why they didn't shoot me on the spot."

"Ah!" Fanning hunched over, gritting his teeth as he slowly inched his hands back. At last he drew a gleaming metal slug into the dim light. "That's it. Let's patch him up."

They'd each torn strips off their shirts. Hayden reached to hand some to Fanning, and his hand faltered. "Just a sec—" he said.

Then the black wing descended again over everything.

"I'M NOT SURE that's such a good idea," said somebody. Hayden felt his body twitch once, then he was blinking around at a half-familiar vision of dimly lit bars and crowded bodies.

"Travis, I let you talk me out of surrendering myself when these criminals started torturing our men and now I feel ashamed of myself." Admiral Fanning sat on the air, knees up and his hands tightly gripping them. His breath misted in the cold air as he spoke.

Martor drifted, face pale and limbs akimbo, in the center of the cage.

"But it was to protect the details of the mission—"

"Hang the mission! These men are my responsibility. If I can spare just one of them the agonies we heard earlier, then I have to."

"Not if that ultimately kills them," murmured Carrier. "Quiet, someone's coming."

Hayden had been about to ask how Martor was. The sound of someone hand-skipping off the beams of the ship silenced him.

After a moment a lean, pale face appeared outside the cage. The pirate was young, almost grotesquely spindly, and dressed in layers of patched jackets, vests, and pantaloons. Keeping a safe distance, he shoved a couple of flasks in the general direction of the cage. "One's fer pissing, one's fer drinking," he said as they sailed over. "Don't get 'em mixed up."

Admiral Fanning cleared his throat. "Where are we going?" he asked in a calm tone.

"Voyeur's palace," said the pirate. "After we catch up to the rest of our fleet." He pushed off from the cage and began climbing away like a four-limbed spider.

"What's the voyeur's palace?" whispered Travis.

"I think he meant the tourist station," said Fanning. "That's bad news. It means they found out what we're up to."

Travis sighed. "Great. So you're telling me the pirates know the purpose of our mission in winter, while your senior staff still do not?"

Martor was breathing regularly, Hayden saw. He turned his attention to Fanning, who was looking chagrined.

"The revelation that we were looking for a famous treasure was to be kept from the men until we were actually there," said Fanning. "We felt it might . . . affect discipline . . . among the press-ganged members of the crew."

Carrier guffawed. "They might mutiny so they could set themselves up like kings, you mean."

"Yes, Mr. Carrier. That is what I mean."

Hayden stared from one man to the other. What was this about a treasure?

"But why undertake such an expedition now?" Travis shook his head. "We're at war with Mavery. There's indications that Falcon Formation is going to take advantage of the fact and stage an invasion. Why go running halfway around the world for gold? Unless . . ."

"Belay that thought, Travis," said Fanning. "We're doing this for the survival of Slipstream, and our present client nation."

Hayden started at this mention of Aerie. "The fact is," Fanning continued, "our navy is no match for Falcon's. We need an edge, and since our Pilot has successfully alienated all our current neighbors, that edge can't be diplomatic. It has to be military."

"But a pirate's *treasure?*"

"Oh, forget the treasure, man. We'll divide that up between the men, I don't care about that. It's what's said to be kept with the treasure that interests me. Something that would be valueless to any of these men—or to pirates, for that matter."

"And that is . . . ?"

Fanning smiled enigmatically. "We sometimes forget, Travis, that we live in an artificial world—a world sustained by mechanisms so vast that we seldom realize that's what they are. And mechanisms built by man have doors, and locks. . . . I've said too much. Suffice it to say, if we find what we're looking for, Falcon Formation should be easy to handle."

Travis—and Hayden—waited. When nothing more was forthcoming, Travis said in annoyance, "Didn't you say 'hang the mission' a few minutes ago? Now you're being protective of it again."

"That's because our benefactor there," Fanning nodded in the direction the pirate had gone, "gave me an idea."

Hayden decided to reveal the fact that he was awake. "How's the kid?" he asked—though he also wanted to hear more about this treasure. His voice came out as a croak; he realized as he spoke how terribly thirsty and hungry he felt.

"The boy will recover," said Carrier. "What are you thinking, Admiral?"

Fanning reached up to pull on the bars of the rocket rack where they were riveted to the hull. "This ship wasn't originally designed for winter," he said. "It's a retrofit. Now, I once saw a rack like this pull free of the wall during a maneuver in winter. It was due to frost-heaving in the planks."

"Oh?"

"If we inject water in between the boards, here and here . . ." The admiral pointed. "It may push the wood apart when it freezes."

Carrier looked disdainful of the idea, but Travis appeared to be giving it some thought. "Since the ship's been winterized, the chinks have been sealed with tar against bad air coming in," he pointed out. "The water will have nowhere to go."

"Exactly," said the admiral. "Now, I don't propose that we use our drinking water, here." He held up the other flask. "Everybody piss. We'll use that."

Hayden shook his head as Fanning unlaced his own codpiece and proceeded to demonstrate. Maybe he was hallucinating. That would explain why he seemed to have heard Admiral Fanning talking about a treasure hunt, and why that same admiral was now proposing that they piss in the walls.

"What are you suggesting?" he asked sarcastically. "Are we four going to take the ship back with the strength of our own arms?"

Fanning shook his head. "Of course not. We will scuttle the *Rook*. Can't allow Slipstream military hardware in the hands of the enemy."

"Ah . . . And how do we do that?"

"Got to get to the bridge. I suggest we find a porthole and crawl outside to the—" Fanning noticed Hayden vigorously shaking his head. "Why not?"

"Because when winter pirates have a lot of prisoners they hang the excess off the hull. So they'll have a man or two out there to keep watch."

All three men turned to look at him. "And how do you know that?" asked Carrier.

Hayden hesitated, but his last reserve of cunning was exhausted. "Because," he admitted, "I was press-ganged by pirates five years ago."

Now they just frankly stared. Finally Carrier shrugged and looked away. "Things begin to become clear. Knew you weren't what you seemed. Pirates planted you in Fanning household?"

"No! Nothing like that." He'd done it now. Even if the pirates didn't kill him, Fanning would have him towed until he froze, or shot in front of the crew. There was just the faintest chance, if he told most of the truth—but not all of it—that he could avoid such a fate. "I . . . I eventually escaped and made my way back to Rush. And yes, I made up a cover story, that's true, I'd learned how to do that from a station infiltrator I worked for. But I wasn't spying for anybody. I really did need a job."

Carrier raised one eyebrow. "Interesting," he said. "You actually expect us to believe that?"

"We'll deal with that question later," said Fanning. "Right now I want to know why you're familiar with how winter pirates deal with their prisoners."

"Uh . . ." Hayden blinked. Fanning didn't care that he'd wormed his way into the service of his wife under false pretenses? Or was he really as focused on the here and now as he appeared? "Well, sir," he said, "I was brought on board the pirate ship *Wilson's Revenge*, somewhere in between being a slave and an apprentice. I couldn't leave; but I had the run of the ship."

Fanning waved a hand indifferently. "Press-ganged," he said. "Get to the bit about the prisoners."

Hayden took his turn at the flask and tried to organize his thoughts. "Ah. Um, being a pirate turned out to be the most unglamourous job you could imagine. It consisted of bullying fishing boats and birdcatchers and selling their tackle and nets at places like Warea. You could barely buy food, you had to hoard your ammunition, and beer was out of the question unless you brewed it yourself. Mostly it was just dark, dismal, and hopeless."

Fanning dug at the caulking between the planks, at the spot where the frame of the rocket rack was mounted to the hull with bolts. Once he had a finger-sized hole, he jammed the neck of the now-full flask into it and squeezed. "Go on," he said.

"Once in all that time I spent with these men, we heard about a yacht that was trying to sneak through the cloudbanks of the nations near Candesce. It was some young noble kid trying to reach his lover, who lived in a nearby nation the kid's nation was at war with. . . . You get the picture. My infiltrator boss had the word from one of his spies. So we went on the hunt and we found the yacht right where it was supposed to be. We . . . took it."

He didn't like being reminded of that incident, but now that he'd started talking about it, it seemed he couldn't stop. "Our ship was a modified birdcatcher, the same dimensions as the *Rook* but mostly hold—empty space. Thirty crew, tops. The yacht had that many plus a ridiculous number of manservants and cooks and such for the noble kid. The hold was full of bikes, so my captain made most of the survivors ride outside."

Without realizing it, Hayden had hunched around himself and drifted into one corner of the cage. "Most of them froze to death in the first day," he murmured. "I know; I had to stand one watch."

To his suprise, Fanning asked no more questions about his past. Instead, the admiral called a huddle to discuss tactics. Hayden supplied his best guesses about where the guards would be stationed, and Travis provided a detailed description of the inside of the ship, including sight lines. Reaching the bridge undetected from the inside would be difficult, but it could be done.

While they talked, Hayden periodically checked on Martor. The boy was breathing more easily now, and though he remained pale and cold, he was at least alive. Hayden wrapped his own jacket around Martor's feet to help keep him warm; out of the corner of his eye he saw Fanning nod approvingly as he did so.

That fanned the smouldering spark of his anger. Who was this murderer to deign to approve of his decency?

Something had been festering in the back of Hayden's mind ever since the attack. Now he turned to Admiral Fanning. "Sir, how did the pirates know we were here? They must have amassed that fleet with some foreknowledge of its target."

Fanning mused. "Don't think I haven't been wracking my brains over that. As best as I can figure, somebody in Warea sent the word that we were there. They might have dispatched a bike in secret before we'd even reconnoitered the lake."

Just then a sharp crack sounded from the hull. The rocket rack quivered and all four men turned to stare at the planking. A long splinter had popped up and the crack ran right under the bolted frame. "I don't believe it," whispered Fanning. "The damned thing worked."

"I'll never doubt you again," said Carrier. He almost smiled—but Fanning turned and looked down his nose at the man.

"Your confidence is not required, Mister Carrier," he said. "Now help me lever this thing aside. We need the youngest and nimblest of our party to slide under here."

They braced their feet against the hull and hauled on the bars of the rack. The bolt pulled free with a groan and a space opened between the bars and the hull. Hayden didn't feel particularly nimble at the moment, with his head pounding like a malfunctioning sun, but he eagerly wriggled his way into the opening.

He was through up to his hips and already thinking about how to deal with the guards he knew were lurking around these crates, when the sound of the ship changed. The engines changed pitch, and the sound of a ringing bell echoed through the space. Moments later the engines cut out entirely.

"Back, get back in!" Three sets of hands dragged him back under the pressing rust of the rack. Scratched and breathless, Hayden pressed himself against the hull as three pirates with pistols in their hands rounded the crates.

"Here's the catch of the day," said one with a laugh. "You gentlemen have the privilege of witnessing a grand display of fireworks to celebrate our reunion with the rest of our fleet.

"Well, okay," he admitted with an ironic wink at his companions. "You won't really be witnessing the fireworks. You're gonna be the fireworks."

They all laughed, and he came to unwind the chains holding the rack closed. "Get out!" he commanded.

"It's execution time."

13

"IT'S A TRADITION of mass executions to sail into port leaving a trail of blood in the sky," said Captain Dentius to his audience. "But that only works when you're near a sun. It's the visibility that's important, you see—justice must be seen to be done, eh?" He looked down at Venera and grinned. The grin had the intense focus of a man who's on stage and acting a part.

"So," he declaimed, "we pirates of winter have invented an alternative method. Rather than tying you all to the outside of your ship and riddling you with bullets, or slicing your arteries with knives and then flying into port trailing a grand banner of blood . . . rather than that, we choose to announce our executions with fire.

"This will be a truly grand spectacle!" he shouted. Dentius had his feet hooked into two leather straps on a T-bar that surmounted a long pole. The pole had been thrust out the side of the *Rook* so that he stood outside it, in commanding view of both his own ship and the *Rook*. Two of his lieutenants were similarly perched, and tied to the crosspiece by their wrists were Venera Fanning and Aubri Mahallan.

"Dentius, please," murmured Aubri. "You won't lose face if you spare these men. It—"

"Silence," he hissed at her. "I've already lost face." He turned back to the vista of the rope-twined ships. The portholes and hangar doors of the pirate were wide open, and everywhere lanterns were aimed at the *Rook*. The bright light obscured whatever waited in the darkness; it was as if only these two ships existed in the entire universe. *As far as we're concerned*, Venera thought, *that might as well be true.*

The crew of the *Rook* were tied in nets that trailed behind the ship on long ropes. Three pirates carrying a bag of kerosene and a mop were moving systematically around the nets, slopping fuel over the men of Slipstream.

Venera had also asked Dentius to spare the men. Not that she'd begged; he might have felt he had leverage on her if he thought she cared overmuch for them. And she didn't, of course; but one pair of eyes glaring up at her from the bullet-scarred hull of the *Rook* belonged to Chaison. He had survived and his men had not given him away. Both facts impressed Venera.

"Have you considered that some of these airmen might make good converts?" she asked now.

"They're Slipstreamers," Dentius said. "The original pirates. You execute pirates when you catch them, you know."

It was humiliating to be tied at the feet of these odorous maggot-colored men. She'd see them dead as soon as humanly possible. The thought cheered her somewhat, until she glanced back at the tangles of bodies hanging from the *Rook*.

Would her plan work with the degree of uncontrolled fire that was likely to be trailing the *Rook* in the next hour or so? She somehow doubted it; after all, if she played her hand now Dentius could always belay the fire and have the Slipstreamers shot instead.

She almost opened her mouth anyway to give Dentius her ultimatum—but he was addressing the crowd. "We will be rendezvousing with the rest of our ships within the hour," he shouted. "We've seen their semaphores blinking in the night air. The little Slipstream fleet has been utterly destroyed. To celebrate, as we sail into formation with our brothers, you will light our way. And your smoke will trail behind us for a hundred miles—two hundred miles!" His men cheered and Dentius raised a fist.

Dentius had come to her last night, and she'd submitted to his dark attentions. Venera's revulsion for the man had reached an almost religious pitch; she hadn't felt such intensity of emotion since the bandages were removed and she first saw her scar in the mirror. Yet she'd known he was waiting for her to try something. He would have happily taken the pretext to kill her, she knew. So instead of reaching for a hatpin or the comfortable heaviness of her jewel box, she had lain there and listened to him talk. He was a man crushed beneath the weight of his own history.

Dentius had once been a captain in the Aerie navy. Upon the fall of his nation he had escaped into winter along with some of his compatriots. But he still dreamt of a triumphant return, someday. Despite his own better judgement, the notion that the treasure of Anetene might be real had seized his imagination. He couldn't help talking about what he might do with a king's ransom in money: build a fleet and free his homeland. In his own mind, Dentius was still an embattled airman, biding his time. He was not *really* a pirate, though he acknowledged that he must play the role.

Venera had lain there with an arm across her eyes, willing him to shut up and die while he tried to justify and magnify his own existence.

Now he was clinging to the attention his men were giving him. "Are you ready?" he bellowed. The torch men raised their fists over their heads. "All right then. Light 'em up!"

Venera had to speak now or it would be too late. But it would do no good. As the first screams rose from the nets, Venera could only look away. Beside her, Aubri Mahallan was sobbing.

"All engines ahead slow," directed Dentius. "We want just a whiff of a breeze to stroke that fire back over the rest of them." The crew of the pirate were whistling and hooting now, a din to match that of the screaming coming from the *Rook*. Dentius looked down over it all like some pale bird on his perch, and laughed.

Venera became aware of the cracking sound only after something flickered in her peripheral vision. She turned to look but it was gone. Then, turning back, she blinked at the sight of twenty bikes swooping out of the darkness. Flashes from rifle fire lit them and suddenly Dentius's pirates were tumbling from the nets. Red dots of blood gleamed in the firelight.

"Get them!" Dentius began hastily clambering down the long pole, his lieutenants behind him. That left Venera and Aubri Mahallan pinned like targets between the ships.

The deep thrum of engines signaled the appearance of five cylindrical shadows. The *Severance*, the *Tormentor*, the *Unseen Hand*, the *Clarity*, and the *Arrest* fell into a star formation around the Rook and its captor. Droning bikes and gunfire filled the air.

The fires on the nets were going out. At the same time, the ropes connecting them tautened and the helpless men were drawn in until they were pressed against the hull of the Rook.

Now the pole holding Venera and Mahallan wobbled and began to move. They were being drawn into the Rook, she thought in relief. It was better armored than Dentius's own ship. Moments later she found herself on the bridge with Mahallan, Dentius, and his lieutenants. One of them slammed the metal hatch and the horrible sounds coming from outside dampened somewhat.

"Wait for it," said Dentius with a nervous chuckle. He pretended to count off seconds on his fingers. Before he reached ten, the sound of gunfire ceased.

He blew out a sigh of relief. "We've lashed their men to our hull," he said with satisfaction. "The bastards know they can't fire on this ship or they'll hit their own crew. We've got 'em by the balls." He turned to the pilot. "Let's get the hell out of here."

"If you try to leave they're likely to fire anyway," Venera pointed out. "They'll target the engines."

Dentius shrugged angrily. "Who cares?" He turned to the boy who'd taken over the semaphore chair. "Send 'em a message. Tell 'em if they fire we'll start shooting the prisoners. The ones we lit up have gone out, right? Maybe they'll take that as a good sign." He rubbed his chin. "All we have to do is make the rendezvous and we're home free."

Venera felt a languorous wave of spiteful pleasure wash over her. "No, Dentius, you're trapped," she said with a smile. "Just one rocket in the wrong place and this ship is going to explode."

He had looked away from her and was about to say something to his men. Now Dentius turned, a quizzical look on his face. "What did you say?"

"You really think I shot the bridge staff because they knew our destination?" She laughed. "They were going to scuttle the ship, Dentius. I stopped them. But after I did that, I armed all the charges myself—and broke off the key in the control box's lock." She pointed.

Everybody turned to look at the inconspicuous metal panel on the bridge's inside wall. "Once the charges are armed, any kind of disturbance could set them off," she said. "They're *supposed* to be on a hair trigger."

A new salvo of gunfire sounded outside. "That would be your men, shooting at the bikes," said Venera. "You know there's going to be return fire."

One of the pirates was crouched over the control box. "It does appear to be a scuttling panel, Captain," he said. "And there's a key broken off in the lock."

Dentius swore softly.

"Close your mouth, you look like a fool," said Venera.

"Belay that message!" Dentius dove for the semaphore chair. "Tell them we request a ceasefire!"

"But . . . but . . ." Dentius's lieutenants looked at one another; at him; at Venera.

"Those five ships have no idea how fragile the *Rook* is right now," Venera pointed out. "And they've just watched their own men be set on fire. Do you really think they're going to be polite?" She shook her head. "It's time to come to terms, gentlemen. You can always threaten to blow us all to smithereens, so your situation's not hopeless. In fact, I'm betting you can escape with your skins and maybe even your own ship. But you'd better start talking fast."

Dentius's eyes were bulging and his face was bright red. He drew his sword and launched himself toward her.

She ducked behind the navigator. "You'd better negotiate with my husband, the admiral," she said quickly. "He's, ah, waiting outside. And Dentius, he'll be more inclined to accept your proposal if he knows I'm alive."

Dentius snarled. Then he turned to the semaphore man. "Send this: 'Request immediate ceasefire. Admiral to negotiate disengagement.' And somebody tell our men to stop firing!"

He glared down the length of his sword at Venera. "Be as smug as you want right now, lady. But I'm putting a price on your head that'll have every thug and cutthroat in Slipstream after you. I'll see you dead in a year, one way or another."

She shrugged out of the navigator's grip. "It'll be just like life back home, then," she said insouciantly. "But I wouldn't count on you living to put out that contract. Not once your own men are done with you."

There was silence after that, and then the outside hatch was opened and one of the lieutenants went out to fetch Admiral Chaison Fanning.

SLEW, THE HEAD carpenter, nodded in greeting as Hayden eased the bike into the hangar. The man was standing with the hatch gang, who all waved. One of them even grinned at Hayden.

Come to think of it, there hadn't been the usual delay in getting the hatch opened when he returned from his search run.

What was all that about?

Hayden was bone weary, having logged ten hours in the air at his own insistence. All the Rook's bikes were out looking for the pirates; so far there had been no sign of them. Dentius and his mates had made a clean getaway, having negotiated a small head start as part of their terms of disengagement. None of the other ships had been seen either; Travis's theory was that they had a hideout somewhere among the icebergs.

Venera's racing bike was riddled with bullet holes and made an odd whistling noise now when it ran. It hadn't lost any performance, though. The thing was developing enough character that Hayden was beginning to think he should give it a name.

"Here, let me." One of the hatch gang whose name he didn't know reached out to help him hook the bike to its winch-arm. Hayden blinked at him in surprise.

"Thanks." He didn't know what else to say, so he ducked his head at the gang and left the hangar. Sick bay was at the back of the ship; he went that way.

A small mob of airmen, silhouettes in the lantern light, crowded around the angular box that was the sick bay. Somebody must have died, Hayden thought—and in a sudden rush of anxiety he elbowed his way through the crowd.

But no, he heard Martor's voice well before he got to the door. The boy was awake and talking. Not just talking: his voice wove up and down in pitch and volume, like a master storyteller's.

". . . So we's got this bag of mines, now, see. And Hayden sez, 'Let's take 'em and blow those icebergs!' So there we are weaving our way in and out of the rest of the mines, voom voom, and we're in the clouds. And sure as itches, there's this great awful wall of ice comes at us out of the mist. Got this little tiny neck holding it to the wall of the world and Hayden sez, 'Let her rip!' so I do. Boom!—Ow! Oh, that smarts."

"In my report," came the surgeon's dry voice, "I shall state that Master Martor died of an excess of hand gestures."

"Yeah," somebody shouted over the laughter, "tone down the jumping about, boy. I want to hear how this ends."

Hayden paused at the doorway, uncertain of whether to go in. He didn't like that Martor had been talking about him, although that might explain why the hatch gang had been so polite just now.

Suddenly worried about what the boy had been saying, he tapped the man in the doorway on the shoulder. "Well, here he is, the man hisself," said the airman as he shifted to let Hayden past. He glided into the sick bay and grabbed the back of a cot to stop himself.

Wounded men tiled the floor, walls, and ceiling of the place. Nearly all of them were awake and apparently listening to Martor, who had pride of place, propped like some parody of a doorman by the entrance to the surgery.

"Hayden, I was just telling the guys how we blew the icebergs and saved the fleet!" Martor's ferretlike face was twisted into a quite uncharacteristic smile. "The pirates flew right into 'em, blam blam blam!" He laughed and immediately winced. "And then," he said to the general crowd, "he sez, 'Now let's go back and save the Rook!' Just the two of us, can you imagine? But he—"

"I did no such thing," Hayden said sternly. "I wanted to get the hell out of there."

"But Hayden," stage-whispered Martor. His eyes darted at the listening men. "Tell 'em how we attacked the pirates, huh?"

Hayden crossed his arms and gave his best adult's frown at Martor. "I don't remember us attacking the pirates, because after we saw that the Rook had been taken, this little snake rapped me over the head with a rocket when I tried to fly him away to safety."

He couldn't have said what he expected, but Hayden was vastly surprised as the assembled men broke into peals of laughter.

Someone clapped him on the shoulder. "Ah, Martor, I wondered just how far your lying instinct would take you this time," said one of the officers. "Too bad you had a witness this time."

"But it's true about the icebergs," Hayden said quietly. "At least—we did blow them. I can't vouch for whatever else he might have worked into the tale."

"Like the emergency stop at the whorehouse?" someone asked.

"Or the sword fight with the hundred pirates on bikes?"

"Or the—"

"I never said that stuff!" Martor tried to get out of his bed, grimaced, and let the elastic sheet flatten him back against the wall.

"This has gone too far!" shouted the surgeon. "The lad really is going to bust a kidney if you all keep this up. Out! Out! That goes for you too," he said, waggling a finger at Hayden.

Hayden couldn't suppress his grin. "Since I know you're not dead, I'll be on my way," he said to Martor. "But no more lies about me, you hear?"

"Yes, sir," said the boy sullenly.

Hayden headed for Aubri Mahallan's little workshop. All around him the ship was abuzz with talk. He knew this, he'd seen it before after the few one-sided fights he'd been in when he was a pirate himself. The trauma of the battle and captivity had to be exorcized somehow; there were some fights, the settling of scores, but mostly, the airmen were exchanging their stories. In the process they were building a whole mythology around the battle.

It seemed that Hayden had unwittingly placed himself at the heart of the myth.

He nodded at another airman who had casually saluted him on the way past, and knocked on the door to Mahallan's wooden cube. There was no answer.

Was she hiding? Hayden hadn't talked to her since the battle. He had only seen her, looking starkly grim and pale, her hair a rat's-nest and her fingernails chewed to the quick. She had avoided his eyes. He was worried about what might have been done to her by the pirates, but so far that part of the incident had not been worked into any shipboard stories.

"She ain't there," said the airman who had saluted him. Hayden turned, eyebrow raised.

"Up at the bow, talking to the lady," said the airman. Venera Fanning was another hero of the day; her quick thinking in palming Captain Sembry's key when the pirates burst into the bridge and killed everyone had ultimately saved the Rook. A craftsman was apparently on the bridge right now, delicately teasing the broken key out of the lock to the scuttling panel.

"Lucky thing the admiral gave a good account of himself in the fight," someone had said earlier, "else we'd all be saluting his wife instead of him."

"Well go on," said the airman now. "They'll be wanting you

anyway. We're arriving at that weird tourist city, and Mrs. Fanning wants to visit it."

ADMIRAL CHAISON FANNING felt very small in this place. He didn't like the sensation at all.

The tourist "station" was really a city that dwarfed any place he'd seen—or even heard of—in Virga. It spread for miles across the ceiling of Virga, a glittering chandelier of towers like fiery icicles, globular dwellings hanging from long tethers, and vast spinning cylinders, each one three or four times the size of the towns of Rush. It was to the axis of one of these cylinders that the *Rook* had gone, under Aubri Mahallan's instruction. Now Chaison walked the streets of a city that seemed more delirium dream than reality.

Some cunning of artifice had hidden the shape of the town; it didn't appear to be rolled up and spun, as it really was. Above Chaison was an endless sky of blue, and the city's confectionary towers were laid out on a seemingly flat surface. The streets converged in perspective until they blurred into the hectic detail of buildings, people, and floating unrecognizable glowing things. Signs, some of those—but more were mobile, and some, he'd noticed, could speak.

The people were just as bizarre. They were dressed—when dressed at all—in sloppy imitations of Virga's fashions. They came in all sizes and skin tones, including unlikely shades like blue and vermillion. They crowded the streets in their millions, gabbling and waving their hands at faint squares of flickering light that buzzed around their heads like bees. Images flashed across these squares like heat lightning and everywhere there was a chaos of noise.

He and Venera had to hurry to keep up with Aubri Mahallan, who stalked through the crowd with her head down and her shoulders hunched. The strange gatekeeper who had met the *Rook* at the docks had insisted that no more than two natives accompany her. "Take no pictures," he had said in a sibilant accent while smaller versions of himself—identical right down to the clothes—perched on his shoulder or ran laughing down the hall behind him. "Take no items, leave anything you want."

"We've come to recover a work of art loaned to one of your museums two hundred years ago," Venera had said. "It's ours, not yours."

He'd raised an eyebrow while one of his smaller selves stuck out its tongue. "Take it up with the museum," he'd said. "Not my area of concern."

Chaison quickened his pace until he was walking abreast of Mahallan. She still looked drawn and grim. He cast about for something to say, finally deciding to directly confront her most likely complaint. "I had to let the pirates go," he said. "We might have reneged on our bargain and blown them up as they left, but then they might have gotten a rocket or two into the *Rook* at the same time."

After a few moments she looked over at him, an expression of distaste on her face.

"Is that why?" she asked. "Because you were afraid they'd blow up the *Rook*?"

"It's a sufficient reason," he said. "But no, that's not all. We did make an agreement. And while my entire crew and all of my officers howled for revenge, I am bound as a gentleman to keep my word. Even more importantly than that, I just had no desire to cause any more deaths this week."

Mahallan mulled this over, but the dark expression on her face had not lifted. "Are you happy to be back among your own people?" he asked her.

"No."

The silence drew out. Clearly companionable solicitations were not going to work. "Well, you've seen the ships of the fleet in a real engagement," he said after a while. "If your opinion about the usefulness of your devices has changed at all, I hope you'll tell me."

Mahallan glared at him. "Is that all it was to you? An 'engagement'? Something to be picked apart afterward, analyzed and stuffed for future consideration?"

Her anger didn't impress Chaison. "As a matter of fact, it's a requirement of my position that I view it that way. Why? Because understanding everything that happened is the only way that I can hope to save more lives next time we're forced to fight. And saving lives is my job, Lady Mahallan. I bend every effort to achieve military objectives with the least possible loss of life. That is why we are in this city, walking these streets, isn't it?"

She stopped and pointed down a shadowed and empty side street. "There. The entrance to the Museum of Virgan Culture's storage depot." Then she took off down the narrow way at a renewed pace.

"I—I'm sorry you had to be part of that, Ms. Mahallan," he said before she could get out of earshot. "The incident has been hard on us all."

"Don't bother," said Venera cheerfully as she took him by the arm and sauntered after Mahallan. "She's bitter. People enjoy being bitter. It gives them license to act childishly."

"Aren't you the philosopher," he said with a laugh. "Are you unscathed by, ah, recent events?"

"I wouldn't say that," she said, glancing down.

"Dentius didn't touch you, did he? I know you told me not when we were negotiating with him, but you knew I'd have run him through if I thought he had."

She looked him in the eye. "He didn't lay a finger on me."

"I didn't want you to come," he said. "Things like this happen. This is no society outing, Venera."

"I coped."

At the end of the street was a reassuringly real-looking door. Mahallan was waiting impatiently for them in the shadows.

"Admiral and Lady Fanning, this is Maximilian Thrace, the curator of the museum," she said in a voice that had suddenly gone sweet.

Beside her hovered a ghost. That, at least, was Chaison's impression of the apparition; he could see right through it. Thrace bore many resemblances to a human being, but there was no color to him, only stark white and shades of gray. His head was disproportionately large and he had huge eyes. "Max is a Chinese Room persona from a very old and respected game-church," Mahallan whispered. Chaison nodded politely.

He bowed to the vision. As he was straightening, Venera said, "We've come to recover an artifact you've had on display here for a long time. It's called the . . ." She turned to Chaison, one eyebrow eloquently raised.

"*The Winding Tree of Fate*," he said with a smile. "It's important to a small but influential group of artists in Slipstream, our home. Our documents show that it was placed on loan here, two centuries ago."

Thrace's frown was magnificently overdone, a great downturning of the mouth that distorted his whole jaw. "You wish us to return all representations, versions, models, simulations, and copies of the piece? That could be difficult, it will require viral legislation that could take months—" Mahallan was shaking her head.

"We just want the original."

Thrace's eyes narrowed ever so slightly. "The what?"

"The artwork itself," said Venera. "The item that your, ah, copies are based on."

"That's why we asked to meet you here," added Mahallan, "at the storage depot."

"You just want the original? Nothing more?" Thrace looked tremendously amused. "You could have just sent us a . . . what do you call them? A letter. We'd have mailed it back to you!" He turned and gestured, and the door in the wall opened by itself. Chaison jumped at this, but nobody seemed to notice.

As Maximilian Thrace drifted into the dark hallway revealed by the open door, he said, "Space is expensive here. It would have cost us less to send it back to you than to continue to store it. We could even have hired escorts if you wanted."

Chaison stopped walking. Thrace's ghost continued on; Venera had given him her arm, so apparently he had some solidity although his tiny feet waved impotently some inches above the floor. Chaison shook his head and looked away. There was nothing else in this long narrow corridor to look at, except Aubri Mahallan, who had paused to look back at him.

"Did you know this?" he asked her. She looked apologetic.

"I doubt he's telling the truth about the escort," she said, falling back to walk beside him. "I knew they would ship it to us if we asked. But we'd have had to send a courier ship here to do that, and then wait . . . time was tight. It didn't seem practical."

"In the future," he said tightly, "please allow me to make such judgements."

"Sorry."

Civilians! He hated them as a species. Chaison trudged along, thinking about the lives lost in getting here. They were all ultimately his responsibility. But it was an awful thing to make choices in ignorance of potential alternatives.

Mahallan seemed to just be realizing her mistake. "Listen, if I had known—"

"What is he?" Chaison gestured at the wraith who was walking and laughing with his wife. "Is he a real person?"

"Ah." Mahallan shrugged awkwardly. "Define 'real.' Max is a Chinese Room persona, which makes him as real as you or I." She saw his uncomprehending stare, and said, "There are many game-churches where the members of the congregation each take on the role of one component of a theoretical person's nervous system—I might be the vagus nerve, or some tiny neuron buried in the amygdala. My responsibility during my shift is to tap out my assigned rhythm on a networked finger-drum, depending on what rhythms and sounds are transmitted to me by my neural neighbors, who could be on the other side of the planet for all I—" She saw that his expression hadn't changed. "Anyway, all of the actions of all the congregation make a one-to-one model of a complete nervous system . . . a human brain, usually, though there are dog and cat churches, and even attempts at constructing trans-human godly beings. The signals all converge and are integrated in an artificial body. Max's body looks odd to you because his church is a manga church, not a human one, but there's people walking around on the street you'd never know were church-made."

Chaison shook his head. "So this Thrace is . . . a fake person?"

Aubri looked horrified. "Listen, Admiral, you must never say such a thing! He's real. Of course he's real. And you have to understand, the game-churches are an incredibly important part of our culture. They're an attempt to answer the ultimate questions: what is a person? Where does the soul lie? What is our responsibility to other people? You're not just tapping on a drum, you're helping to give rise to the moment-by-moment consciousness of a real person. . . . To let down that responsibility could literally be murder."

He looked at her sidelong. "You seem awfully passionate about this for a voluntary exile. Did you belong to one of these churches before you came here?"

"Oh!" She looked like someone who had just realized that she'd said too much. "No, it's just that—"

"They told me you were here!" said a voice behind them.

Chaison turned quickly, hand going to his waist where his sword should be—but wasn't. An ordinary-looking man of medium height and age had come up behind them as they talked. His accent had not been like Aubri's, Chaison realized. He had sounded like he was from Virga.

"Aubri Mahallan," he said now, arching one eyebrow. "What could you possibly be doing back at the station?" She shrank back.

Stepping between them, Chaison said, "And you are . . . ?"

"Aston Shen," he said, holding out his hand for Chaison to shake. "Virgan home guard."

"Home guard?"

"You've never heard of us? Good! Then we're doing our job." Shen smiled at Chaison's expression. "There are always some people of every generation who become curious about the outside world, you know. A few hundred find their way here every year. Some emigrate and never return. But some of us . . . find a higher calling. The home guard exists to protect Virga from outside influences. We try to ensure that no bad elements enter our world." Deliberately, he looked past Chaison at Mahallan. "And when they do . . ." He eased past Chaison. "So, Aubri, what have you been up to?" he asked. She shrugged.

"Just living my life, Aston. As best I can, now that I'm here."

"So? And the purpose of your business in the station?"

Chaison interposed himself again. "She is here on my business. We needed a native guide. I'd kindly ask you not to interfere."

Shen held his hands up solicitously. "Wouldn't think of it, old man. As long as you know to be careful with this one. She's not to be trusted."

"Oh really? I—" They were interrupted again as Venera returned carrying something. She held it up triumphantly and beamed at Chaison.

"We got it!" The thing appeared to be an intricate branch with extremely tiny leaves, if those finest bifurcations were leaves at all. Jewels glinted here and there inside its tangles.

"I'll expect delivery of the paintings tonight, then?" Thrace was saying to her. Venera nodded vigorously. "Come dear, we should get back." She noticed Shen. "Well, hello."

"Ma'am." Shen turned back to Mahallan. "We'll do a full-pass sweep of you and your companions before you're allowed to leave. I thought it polite to let you know." Seeing Chaison's expression, he smiled and bowed. "You won't even know it's happening. Just remember," he said to Mahallan, "we're watching you." He walked away.

Venera watched him go. "What an unpleasant person," she said. She had that appraising look that Chaison had learned meant that her instincts for paranoid intrigue had been triggered. "Let's get out of this place," she said to him as she smiled again at Thrace.

As they walked back to the ship Chaison tried to sort out everything he'd just seen and experienced. But he was tired, and Venera's excitement just too infectious. By the time they reached the *Rook*, he had forgotten Mahallan's explanation of her people's churches, and couldn't bring himself to speculate about the Virga home guard or Shen's cryptic warnings.

None of it mattered anyway. They had the map they had come to find.

14

THE SCENE WAS an eery repeat of Dentius's call to execution, only now it was Chaison Fanning who perched atop the T-bar and addressed all six of the ships. The vessels were temporarily lashed together into a loose star formation. Their crews sat or stood on their hulls, dark silhouettes casting long shadows from the spotlights that lit Fanning.

The admiral gestured with his bullhorn. "We are a long way from home. We have gone through the trials and tribulations of a minor war, and yet I have not told you why.

"Now, I will tell you why."

A murmur went through the assembly. Hayden Griffin, who sat astride his bike comfortably invisible in the dark air, strained to hear what the crewmen were saying. Resentment battled respect among them, he knew. Fanning was known to have fought gallantly against the pirates, but then he had also let Dentius and his men escape. There were airmen listening now who would always bear the scars of Dentius's torturer.

This had better be good, Hayden thought, knowing that the same thought must be going through everybody else's minds as well.

"Before I explain our mission in full," said the admiral, "I'm going to tell you a story." He held up a hand, face slightly turned away. "This is no cocktail-party anecdote, designed to soften up an audience. I know you're exhausted. This story is vital to your understanding our purpose. It's a story that concerns pirates, in fact.

"Two hundred years ago, winter was not the quiet place that it is today." If he expected a laugh at this point, Fanning didn't get it.

"We've tangled with a modern pirate armada. But Dentius's force is nothing compared to the old ones. Once, pirate navies fought their way into the heart of civilized nations. They plundered suns. Their blades reached all the way to the precincts of Candesce itself. And the greatest of the pirates of that age was Emile Anetene.

"Anetene was a fop. He was an educated man, with refined tastes. Such men become the most savage of killers, and Anetene was the finest at it. He plundered the principalities of Candesce; he terrorized Slipstream's borders; and eventually, he inspired the wrath of the whole world, so that a vast navy was assembled, comprising ships from most of the worlds of Virga. And they hunted him down.

"Now, you might think that it was Anetene's depredations that caused the nations to finally react so. Most people think so; we in the government have always encouraged the impression that it was out of compassion for our set-upon citizens that we hunted Anetene down. But that's not true.

"Anetene stole one particular thing—a small, seemingly insignificant object. When the heads of Virga's states found out—particularly the principalities of Candesce—they acted instantly. No amount of rapine and slaughter could have galvanized them to do so. One theft did."

Fanning paused. The men were silent now, confused but also curious. The admiral looked away into the darkness, appearing to gather his thoughts. His expression was serious.

"This expedition was undertaken after certain facts came to the admiralty's attention," he said. "We knew all about the threat from Mavery, and you and I know that this threat was never great. We were always able to defend ourselves against the likes of them. But let me ask you something. Their rocket attack on Rush—the one that so surprised us all, and that precipitated the Pilot's order to send out the fleet . . . many of you were there. You are military men. Did that attack *make any sense to you?*"

Fanning nodded, as though to himself, and said, "That attack was a deliberate provocation. It was designed to draw us out. But why would Mavery do that? —When we were sure to make mincemeat of their navy in the ensuing battle?"

Now the murmurs started again. "Somebody's with 'em!" someone shouted.

"Exactly. They've got allies. To be precise, they have one ally that intends to join them to crush Sliptream. That ally is Falcon Formation."

Shouts of anger and dismay met this news. Hayden nodded to himself. He remembered now the photographs he had seen in Venera Fanning's hand. A fleet being commissioned.

"Slipstream's very existence is threatened!" shouted Fanning. Hayden leaned forward, his mouth dry. For years he had dreamed of hearing such news—but that it should be the Formation . . .

"Falcon Formation is our most powerful neighbor," said the admiral. "We've had little to do with them because our long journey of exile has taken us on a tangent course. It's a good thing we never attracted their attention before, even when we were conquering their neighbor Aerie. The Formation is a dark bureaucracy, a super-Confucianist state ruled by a hereditary caste of bloodless clerks. They are fanatics who are determined to one day rule over all of Virga. And they have decided that Slipstream is a prize worthy of their ambitions.

"We might be able to hold off an invasion by the existing Formation fleet. I beseeched the Pilot not to fall for Mavery's diversion. We would need all our ships to thwart an attack by the Formation. But a month ago we learned that Falcon Formation is building a new weapon that they are going to use to crush us."

As Fanning told the men about the Formation's secret shipyard and the dreadnought being built there, Hayden found himself wracked with conflicting emotions. The prospect of Slipstream being conquered was exhilarating. On the other hand, if Falcon Formation moved in on the conquered territories of Aerie, they would never give them up. Aerie's people would be assimilated into the cold dictatorship of that notorious bureaucracy, and Aerie itself would be erased from the history of Virga.

". . . No allies will come to our aid," Fanning was saying. "Therefore, we need a miracle. You, men, are here in winter to provide that miracle.

"The stories they'll tell about you! Each and every one of you will be entered into the roster of Slipstream heroes when our journey is done. For we are on our way to destroy the navy of Falcon Formation!"

A stunned silence greeted these words. Fanning looked around slyly. "Is he mad? That's what you're wondering. How are six ships—and the ghost of a seventh whom we will never forget—how will such a tiny force prevail against the hundred cruisers and carriers of Falcon?

"I will tell you how.

"There exists a weapon that will give us an unassailable tactical advantage over Falcon's ships. It will allow us to maneuver in darkness and fog as though we were in clear and empty air. It will let us fly and bank and turn in utter darkness at two hundred miles an hour, all the while keeping Falcon Formation's ships centered in our crosshairs. We have come to winter to acquire that weapon!"

A babble of protests, shouts of delight, and heated arguments wafted through the dark. Fanning gestured for silence. "Please! I've heard all the objections before. If such a weapon existed, why isn't it being used? Why doesn't Falcon Formation have it?

"The reason," he said more quietly, "has to do with Candesce. The Sun of Suns emits radiation that interferes with certain types of machine. *Radar* is one of the devices that won't work within Virga—though it works everywhere else in the universe. Anybody can build a radar set, it's just an electrical device. You've all seen electricity, we use it for lighting and electrolysis. But getting anything but noise out of a radar set, that's another matter, here in Virga.

"But there is a way to make electrical devices work cleanly. The secret was lost two hundred years ago—stolen from the flagship of one of the principalities of Candesce by one of the most legendary figures in history."

Fanning laughed. "Yes. We come back to Emile Anetene. His

story is almost mythological—indeed, it wasn't until we visited the tourist city and I saw the map with my own eyes, that I allowed myself to really believe that the legend of the treasure of Anetene is true."

Hayden had to smile at the muted reaction to this. The men had heard too much that was unbelievable already. One more preposterous notion piled on top of the rest made little difference.

That is, it didn't at first. Fanning explained how Emile Anetene had stolen something—a key, though to what he didn't say—and hidden it with the rest of his hoard. He then died in a hail of rockets, cornered by the allied navies of Candesce. Almost from the first there were rumors about the hoard. No one had plundered it, the legend went, because Anetene had left the only map with one of his women—and she had hidden it somewhere no one would ever find it.

"We found the map," said Fanning. "We have it. Within the week, you will be plundering Anetene's hoard." He laughed again briefly. "At this point, you needn't believe my story. Just lend me seven days of service, and we'll all know for sure if the legend is true. And if it is . . . then the treasure is yours."

"Now that's more like it!" yelled an airman with a broken arm. The others laughed.

"We will return with the treasure and working radar. We will demolish Falcon Formation's secret shipyard and anybody else who gets in our way. We will save Slipstream and you will return to your homes rich as Pilots.

"Anybody object to that?"

HAYDEN SPUN UP the bike and drifted it to the *Rook's* open hangar doors. Fanning continued to field questions, though he wouldn't answer any more about how this radar thing was going to work. Many of the men considered his story a ridiculous fabrication, but they agreed that giving him a week to prove it was fair.

Having worked with Aubri Mahallan to build the radar units, Hayden already believed.

After securing his bike he sought her out. The two of them still hadn't spoken properly, and he intended to find out why. Her workshop's door was tightly closed, so he rapped on it smartly. He waited, and when she didn't answer, he rapped again.

"I can keep doing this," he said loudly.

There was a long pause, then the door flew back. Aubri was braced just inside. Her eyes were red. "What?" she snapped.

"Can I come in?"

Silently, and with obvious reluctance, she drew back to allow him to enter. Her workshop was a shambles. The pirates had evidently ransacked it, but surprisingly little was actually broken—or not so surprisingly, he remembered now. Pirates had so little of their own that they prized, rather than destroyed, whatever they could steal of others'.

"I just wanted to see whether you were all right," he said after a long and awkward silence. Aubri shrugged, and finally nodded.

"Why did you come back after the battle?" she said in a subdued voice. "To make sure you were right? —About the Rook being taken?"

"I was hoping it wasn't."

"Or maybe you didn't come back at all," she continued. She wasn't watching him, but was nervously organizing the debris in the room. "Maybe you were on your way to the station when Martor figured out you'd abandoned us all. And that's why he knocked you out."

Anxious, but unwilling to back out now, Hayden shrugged. "Think what you will. I wasn't wrong, was I? The Rook lost the battle. The ship was boarded. If it hadn't been for Venera's quick thinking . . ."

"She's as savage as the pirates," said Aubri with a rueful smile. "I've never seen such ugliness as I saw here. Brutality . . . You people are animals."

"I couldn't agree more." She looked at him in surprise. "If the world needed saving it wouldn't be worth doing it," said Hayden. "Everything worthwhile ends up getting stolen by someone evil. You hate the pirates who tried to take the Rook and its people? Well, some pirates are so powerful they get to call themselves by other names. Names like 'Pilot of Slipstream.' What's Slipstream if not the biggest pirate armada in the world? So big that they don't capture and plunder ships, but whole nations."

"What are you talking about?"

He sighed. "Do you know anything about the people you're working for?"

Aubri narrowed her eyes, searching his face. "This is some sort of justification for why you wanted to abandon your friends, isn't it? They're bad people, so you're justified in only being in it for yourself, is that it?"

Angry now, he said, "I tried to save you. There's nothing for me out there. I haven't got a future. I just thought it might be worth saving the life of somebody who did have one."

"Then you picked the wrong person to save."

It took a few seconds for her words to register with Hayden. "W-what did you say?"

Aubri sighed heavily. "Listen, I don't need this right now. And I don't need your help at the moment, *assistant*. You know our machines are ready." She put her hand in the center of his chest and pushed. Confused and angry, Hayden let himself sail out the door.

Slew the carpenter had watched his exit and now smiled. "They're all trouble, kid. Take my word for it, that's as good as you're gonna get from her."

"Shut up." But Slew just laughed at him, and Hayden, ears burning, retreated to the hangar again.

FINDING ITSELF IN a stray beam of sunlight from distant Candesce, the capital bug shrugged awake. It unfolded its six legs and stretched them ineffectually into the cold air. There was nothing to grab on to for a hundred miles in any direction, but it didn't care much; it lived on stray flotsam and jetsam and could hibernate for months at a time. The heat of a sun could waken it, though, and as it felt the distant rays of Candesce it spread its diaphanous wings, and began to hum.

"Batten the hatches!" The *Rook*'s new boatswain leaped from one side of the vessel to the other, following his own order. The lads in the hangar were hastily dogging the doors as well; but it did little good. The world-shattering drone of the capital bug wormed its way into every nook and cranny of the ship. The crewmen cursed and clapped their hands over their ears, but the buzz seemed to resonate all the more inside their skulls. One by one, across the ship, the windup lantern flames flickered in the choppy air and went out.

Hayden had been asleep on his bedroll in the ship's centrifuge. He was used to all its noises now, and even the thunder from test firings and target practice couldn't wake him. But the sound of the capital bug had him instantly alert.

As he exited the now-shaking wheel he saw Travis's face floating in the solitary illumination of the last opened porthole. "Will you look at that!" said the officer—or at least, those were the words his mouth shaped. Hayden couldn't have heard him from six inches away.

Over the past few days Hayden had discovered that Travis liked or at least respected him. The feeling was mutual; the man didn't treat the presence of civilians on his ship as a threat to his authority. So Hayden didn't worry that he was tempting fate by putting his head next to Travis's and looking out the porthole.

Dots of cloud patterned the air around the capital bug, throwing small lozenges of shadow on the vast, distance-blue curve of its abdomen. That flank was all Hayden could really see at the moment; any details about the rest of the beast faded into darkness or blue to either side. Cruising up and down the vast wall of flesh were flocks of birds or fish, apparently immune to the drone that could kill any man who came too close. Closer to the *Rook*—only a few miles away—a number of large black spheres turned lazily in the sudden sunlight. These were surrounded by wreaths of yellowish mist and swarming dots.

The buzzing stopped, leaving a ringing silence that was, in its own way, just as painful as the noise.

Travis grinned. "That's a real capital bug, isn't it?" It sounded like he was on the other end of one of the ship's speaking tubes.

Hayden nodded, digging in his ears and then checking his fingertips for blood. "Good thing we weren't any closer," he shouted.

"What're those things?" Travis pointed at the town-sized spheres of black in the middle distance.

"Bug shit," said Hayden. "You don't want to go near it. Great for growing mushrooms, though."

"I can't believe anything that huge could be alive."

"They're mostly empty space. A big balloon, like the world itself I guess. The bugs even have their own forests and lakes and stuff inside them, or so they say."

Travis gave one last wistful look out the porthole, then turned away to attend to his duties. Hayden stayed where he was as up and down the *Rook* men threw open the rest of the portholes. The heat of Candesce was very faint, but it was sunlight on his face, and its very presence was vastly soothing.

"Don't get too comfortable," said a voice next to him. Hayden turned, blinking, to find Lyle Carrier hovering in the shadows.

"What?"

"I know you think you've made friends in high places," said Carrier, nodding at Travis's retreating feet. "But it's not really that they trust you, you know. They're happy to smile and chat with you because they know I'm watching you."

Hayden scowled at him. "What's that supposed to mean?"

"There's a lot of unanswered questions about you, boy," Carrier said, his mouth pursed in a by now familiar moue of distaste. "And what answers you have given just don't add up. You see," he leaned in close, "I know you're up to something, and Venera knows

I know. She has every confidence that I'll find out what it is. So she and your other betters are happy to indulge you for the moment. They know you're well taken care of."

Hayden stared back at him. It had taken him a long time to get Carrier's proper measure. He regretted not sizing the man up properly right at the beginning. Carrier was a killer; but Hayden wasn't afraid of him.

He cocked his head to one side. "You mean you've spent all this time skulking around watching me and formulating hypotheses on your own? And you never once thought to just *ask*?"

The slightest tremor passed over Carrier's left eyelid. It was enough discomposure to make Hayden smile.

"What are you up to, then?" said Carrier.

"None of your business," snapped Hayden. He turned back to the view.

"So that's the way you want to do it," murmured Carrier. "All right. Later, Griffin."

Hayden didn't hear him leave, but he refused to turn his head to check. For one thing, the sight outside was beautiful: the light from Candesce wasn't fading, if anything it was brightening, and no wonder for that was where the *Rook* and its sister ships were going.

But also, he didn't want Carrier to see his face right now. Carrier would have seen that Hayden knew he was now marked for death. You didn't insult a man like Lyle Carrier and get away with it.

So be it. Right now he needed an enemy he could hate unreservedly. His feelings about Admiral Fanning were too mixed to be satisfying. Carrier . . . that was another matter.

Hayden watched the *Rook*'s sister ships skirting the precincts of the gargantuan capital bug. They set their prows in the direction of the Sun of Suns, and as the air continued to be clear and fortunately lighted, they all opened up their throttles and arrowed toward Candesce.

TWO DAYS LATER, and the way ahead was bathed in perpetual light. First one, then two, then four suns peeked out from behind the somber cloudbanks of winter. At first each was little more than an orange smear on the sky, its light diffused and filtered by hundreds of miles of air, water, and dust. Over the hours they sharpened, becoming in time tiny pinpricks of actinic light embedded in discs and arcs of silver and green which were the collective reflection of thousands upon thousands of individual houses, towns, forests, lakes, and farms.

Gridde, the ancient chart-master, emerged from his velvet-lined chamber to hold up prisms to the light of these suns. He examined the miniature rainbows so created and consulted tables in a huge book that he had carried strapped to his back for so long that it had permanently dented the shoulder of his jacket. Then he pointed at each of the suns in turn and said, "The Nation of Tracoune, the Principality of Kester, the March Collective of the Hero Reeve and, er, what was the other damn one . . . that one's the Upstart Breakaway Republic of Canso."

The crewmen who had gathered to watch this procedure nodded and muttered sagely to one another. Few had heard of any of these nations, and none had heard of all of them. They were halfway around the world from Slipstream and its neighbors. More importantly, these were countries that steered their way through the intermediate airs of Virga, hundreds of miles above the principalities of Candesce but hundreds more below the layers flown by Aerie and other familiar places. Between were layers of winter—dark, cold, and choppy air that had proven over the centuries to be unlucky for the founding of nations.

"Gridde told me it's because there's cyclones, jet streams," Martor said later. "Things drift apart too easy. I guess if they didn't there'd be no winter, just suns and countries packed from one end of the world to the other." He smiled wistfully. "Imagine that."

"Hmmpf." For lack of anything better to do, Hayden was polishing the racing bike for the tenth time. Now he looked at Martor with a sour expression. "There's too much junk floating around in civilized spaces. You can't take a bike above sixty miles an hour without getting somebody's discarded chamber pot in the forehead—or worse, the loose contents of one. Plus there's police every five miles waiting to ticket anybody who opens up their throttle. Far be it that you should rattle the windows of some rich man's house."

"I hadn't thought about it that way," said Martor.

"That's 'cause you haven't got enough bike time in yet. When you own your own someday you'll curse the density of civilized spaces."

Over the next few days Hayden's dim assessment of civilization was confirmed: the expeditionary force made little headway through increasingly populated air. Habitation began on the lowest level with basement spiders who wove long scarves of web that attracted flecks of soil and trash, gradually growing into rafts the size of dinner tables on which myriad other creatures thrived. The webs tangled in the Rook's vanes and had to be swept off with brooms. Birds, fish, and insects, most thumbnail-sized but some big as boats wove and ducked around the mats. As the light of the suns brightened the mats were seen to be festooned with grass and wildflowers. In the distance the watchmen began to spot trees and farms. And everywhere, now, there was ship traffic.

Most of the local suns followed the diurnal rhythm of Candesce, otherwise there would be no darkness here at all. Some renegades did use their own time scales, for historical or political reasons. The result was that the nights here were more glorious than any Hayden had known. The air and clouds deepened to azure tinged with shades of turquoise, mauve, and peach, and in this twilight a thousand town and house beacons glimmered. Hayden overheard Aubri say something about "the stars" as she gazed at the view from the Rook's hangar. He didn't approach her to find out what she meant.

Nor were there any fights or loud arguments among the men. A spell of grace had settled over the ships, all the more precious because they knew it wouldn't last. For a few days they were just airmen, entering strange and wonderful skies.

They didn't approach any of these suns; their destination lay farther in. The six cruisers threaded their way between border beacons, staying in international air as they approached the shell of civilization enshrouding the Sun of Suns. The principalities of Candesce became visible as a vast haze that curved away to all sides—the misty outline of a bubble hundreds of miles in radius with Candesce at its center.

The man-tended suns of the outlying nations fell behind as Candesce's radiance grew. Here were dense forests like gargantuan heads of broccoli, each dozens of miles in extent. There were equally big lakes, some shaped by scaffolding into lens shapes that focused the light of Candesce into town-sized zones of incandescence for industry or waste control. The air began to smell hot and rich with life.

This was the most ancient part of inhabited Virga. Candesce had been here since the founding of the world, and some of the nations now visible had existed almost as long. The crew traded stories of fabled places and legends, of town wheels made of solid gold and forests as big as nations. The air was speckled with ships in all directions, and now they even spotted flying humans, intrepid individuals using leg-powered wings mounted on their backs, like angels, to travel between towns and houses. Ship traffic became constrained by beacon lanes and the six Slipstream ships dutifully kept within their boundaries.

Finally Gridde emerged from his cell again and went to perch like some ragged black bird on a hangar door. He measured the angles between Candesce and the suns they had passed, and eventually nodded. "Gehellen," he announced, "lies two days' journey that way." He pointed toward a part of the crescent of haze surrounding Candesce that looked to Hayden like any other part. As he folded himself back into the ship Hayden overheard him mutter to Admiral Fanning, "It's there that you'll find Leaf's Choir."

Two days later, the Rook and its sister ships stopped at a border beacon. The beacon itself was a wrought-iron and glass ball forty feet in diameter. Since it was day, its fires were banked, but the air smelled of kerosene for miles around. The lane markers had funneled all ship traffic into a choke-point here; all travelers had to pass near the rocket racks of an ancient, moss-encrusted fortress built of stone in a crude cube shape. Tethered to this were four baroque, heavily carven cruisers flying banners Hayden had never seen before.

As the Slipstream vessels arrived, a squadron of bikes exited the fortress and moved to surround them. The cruisers's engines coughed into life and they began to edge forward, blocking the way. And deep within the shadowed stones of the fortress itself, the noses of rockets slid into view.

"So," said Slew the carpenter, who was sitting with Hayden in the hangar, "welcome to Gehellen."

15

". . . LADY AND BARON Castermond." Heads turned to acknowledge the new arrivals. Chaison Fanning bowed, but by now Venera couldn't be bothered. She looked beautiful today, so she could get away with bad behavior. She intended to.

This ballroom was a chamber to equal anything in Rush, constructed of stone and glass, with all the extra spin-up cost that implied; of course, grand reception halls were intended to intimidate. Anybody who thought their purpose more innocent was an idiot.

"You see? I told you all the best people would be here," said Ambassador Richard Reiss. Slipstream's representative in Gehellen was a portly man with a wine-stain birthmark on his cheek. He wore local apparel, with flounces at the wrists and ruffles at the throat. For once Venera Fanning was grateful for the austerity of Slipstream military uniform; her husband looked positively rakish next to the ambassador.

"It's just a shame that your exotic passenger wasn't able to attend," continued Reiss. "What was her name again?"

"Mahallan," said Chaison absently. He tilted his glass to greet someone he didn't know.

"She had . . . research to attend to," said Venera. "This isn't a holiday for us, Ambassador."

"Of course, of course. Nonetheless I'm glad we were able to throw this little soiree at such short notice." Reiss gently cupped Venera's elbow and led her toward a drinks table. "This evening's festivities could be essential to greasing the wheels of progress. You know, your ships . . ."

He hardly had to remind her. The *Rook* and its sisters were sitting idle at the military shipyard on the other side of Gehellen's capital city of Vogelsburg. They had been there for three days now, ever since the Gehellen navy had escorted them in under watchful guns. Venera couldn't really blame them for being cautious; you didn't just let foreign warships traipse through your territory. Not without giving them every inspection and putting the question to their crews. Chaison should have thought of that before they got here.

Still . . . the delay did have its advantages. Venera's first sight of Vogelsburg had electrified her. She had dreamed of this place.

This was the weightless city she had visited in her sleep so many times—she was sure of it. Vogelsburg's buildings came in all shapes and sizes, but very few spun to provide local gravity. They had confectionary shapes, with many honeycombed sides, frescoes, statues, and minarets that stuck out all over. They looked like the diatoms her oldest brother had once shown her in a microscope. Joined together by ropes and kept apart by their minarets, they jostled in slow motion in the perpetually golden light of distant Candesce, just like in the dream. Vogelsburg's people flitted like birds in their thousands between the shifting structures.

The people themselves made Venera uncomfortable. Only the rich and powerful had regular access to gravity in Gehellen. Even they were much taller than she was used to—spindly and bandy, for the most part, though some of the women achieved a state of ethereal grace whose effect on her husband she didn't fail to notice. The lower classes were instantly recognizable: the servants in this ballroom could barely lift their heads, much less the drinks and canapes they served. They loomed like giant spiders over their betters, appearing uncomfortable and worried.

Venera could understand this dichotomy as the result of a deliberate policy to keep the poor weak. History was rife with examples of aristocracy reserving physical health and power for themselves, after all. What disturbed her was the possibility that this state of inequality might have come about through simple neglect. That would imply a shameful decadence on the part of the principalities of Candesce.

As Reiss grazed over the drinks table, Venera took her husband's arm and leaned in close. "This is a very strange assemblage," she said.

"You've never been here before," muttered Chaison. "So how do you know?"

"It's the mix of people, dear. My father threw a little banquet like this once, for some of the outlying provinces' tax collectors. He brought them all together in one place, sealed the doors, and had them shot from the gallery."

Chaison gazed off into space. "Sounds like your father."

"Anyway, I don't like it. Look around yourself. We're cut off from the ships. All the officers are here. There's guards on the entrances."

He looked askance at her. "But they left us our sabers."

"As if that will help. Oh, mark my words, Chaison, I'm sure there's not going to be some sort of massacre. These people value their architecture far too much to risk chipping it with bullets. But something's not right, I'm sure of it."

"Well," said Chaison. "You keep an eye on things, then. Worry all you like. Meanwhile, I'm going to enjoy the afternoon. These people have done nothing to threaten us."

"That's only because we have six fully armed warships sitting in their port," she whispered. At that point Reiss returned, a tall glass in his hand.

"Look who I just spotted." He nodded in the direction of a stiff-looking older gentleman who stood alone under one of the vast rose windows that dominated the ballroom's end walls. Colored lozenges of light from the stained glass dappled this man's dress uniform, and just now half his face was lit green. "General Harmond is here. I'll have to tell your husband—"

"Oh, I'll tell him myself," said Venera as she headed straight for the military man. Reiss made a surprised "Oh" sound as Venera outpaced him. Stopping in front of the general, she bowed. He instantly snapped to attention.

"General Harmond, isn't it?" she said, eyes wide. "I've heard so much about you."

"Oh?" He looked surprised and wiped his palms on his hips before extending a hand for her to shake. "You're with the Slipstream party. Sorry about locking down your ships like that, it's uh, protocol."

"Oh I'm sure it's necessary," she said, waving a hand to dismiss the whole affair. "Protocol isn't one of my strong points. But I do have my hobbies, General, and I was hoping to meet someone authoritative enough to be able to indulge one of them."

"Oh, indeed? And what hobby might you be talking about?" The poor man looked like he wanted to flirt, but had no idea how.

"Small arms," said Venera brightly. "I have a fascination with rifles, pistols—small bore weapons."

"Really?" He goggled at her.

"I'm also a bit of a history buff," she said. "Wars interest me, and I'm afraid I've not kept up with recent events in this part of the world. I was hoping that you might be able to enlighten me—and fill in some sad gaps in my knowledge of Candesce armaments."

The general preened. "I'd be delighted. Just as long as you don't ask me about any military secrets, you know."

"Oh, I wouldn't know it if I was," she said demurely. "I'll have to trust you to correct me if that happens."

"Hmmf. Well, then. Rifles, you say? Our armorers are unmatched in all of Candesce, if I do say so myself. Take the Matchley forty-five, for instance . . ."

Venera listened intently, while Chaison Fanning wove his way through a maze of courtiers and ingenues, now faintly worried.

THE ROUND WINDOW of the palace's reception hall flashed crescent rainbows for a moment as it rotated up and away. Hayden turned resolutely away from the government town; the Fannings were behind that intricate glass and for once, were not his problem. Now that the bike had been ejected from the wheel's small hangar it drifted under him as he took his bearings.

· "The library's over there," said Aubri Mahallan, pointing.

"Yeah yeah."

She held up her hands, palms out. "Just trying to help," she said.

Aubri wore flame-red today, an outfit of silk with harem pants whose long slit sides showed off her legs. Fanning wouldn't allow her to wear anything like this on the Rook. Hayden was determined not to let her know he'd noticed.

She was his passenger reluctantly; the Gehellens refused to let any of the Rook's military bikes fly through Vogelsburg. In fact, they wouldn't let any of the crew off their ships. Once again, Hayden was benefitting from his ambiguous relationship to the expedition.

He had seen and learned a lot since he joined the Rook. It was time to send a report about his experiences back to the Resistance. Once he dropped off Mahallan he planned to find a local post office and draft some sort of letter. The problem lay in deciding what to write.

The bike's fan was whirring, so he leaned back and pumped on the ignition to send a spark into the bike's alcohol burner. It lit with a whoosh and the bike reared forward.

"Slow down!" Mahallan snatched at her handlebars.

"It always kicks like that when it starts. Don't worry, I'm not going to drop you."

"I'm more worried that you'll run into something. This place is dense."

"No denser than where I grew up."

There was a momentary silence as they wove their way into the slower traffic of foot-powered wings and propellers that streamed into the disordered jumble of the city. Then Aubri said, "You grew up in Aerie, didn't you?"

"Yes. And Aerie has its cities too. Or, it did—before Admiral

Chaison Fanning and his fleet dispersed them and killed or drove out everyone I ever knew."

"He wasn't admiral when Slipstream invaded Aerie," said Mahallan. "I do know my history. He was promoted after the conflict ended."

"You've been reading," he sneered.

She held his gaze defiantly, then said, "Talking to the crew. Because you were right to criticize me for not knowing enough about the people I'm working for."

This simple statement knocked most of the wind out of Hayden's sails, but by now he wouldn't back down. "They only told you their side, though," he said, "and haven't told you some things at all. Things like the reason Fanning was promoted. It seems he found a secret Aerie sun we were building and destroyed it, killing all the workers in the process. Some hero!"

"You know about that?" She shook her head. "But you've got the facts wrong. After a few drinks one night the admiral told his officers—I was there—how his promotion came about. He's quite bitter about it. Fanning was against the attack on the Aerie sun—it was the Pilot's idea. In fact the Pilot insisted on leading the expedition himself and even took potshots with a rifle from the flagship! He treated the whole thing like a sporting event but afterward he realized his misstep; everyone involved was horrified at the outcome. So since Fanning had gotten in his face about it, he proclaimed to the upper house that the whole thing had been Fanning's idea. They promoted Fanning but the promotion came with a reputation as a butcher. It's hung like a weight around his neck ever since. He despises the Pilot."

Hayden nearly ran them into a forty-foot-wide food net that was being towed across his path by a flock of tame, feathered barracuda. As he fumbled with the controls he stammered incoherent curses. "My mother," he heard himself saying. "He killed my mother. The Pilot ordered my father executed, never saw him again. Killed them."

"*What?*" Mahallan leaned around the curve of the bike, un-balancing it so that Hayden nearly crashed them again. "Who killed your mother?"

He shut down the bike, turned, and glared at her. "Fanning. Fanning killed her. I was there, at the new sun, when he came out of the sky and killed everyone I knew."

She drew back. Angrily he spun up the engine again and opened up the throttle all the way, dodging them around startled people and cargo nets. "Don't tell me what happened because I know what happened," he said even though she wouldn't hear him over the rip of the wind. "I was there!"

The library, her destination, came up all too quickly. It would be petty of him to overshoot it, or circle it; reluctantly, Hayden cut the engine and deployed the bike's parachute.

"Hayden . . . of course I didn't know," she said. "This is the burden you carry everywhere, isn't it? If you'd only told me sooner—"

"It was years ago," he said, trying to pull back from the emotions she had stirred up. "There's nothing to be done—or said, really. Here's your stop."

For a few seconds he was absorbed with judging the final yards of their approach to the library. This was not so much a building as a concretion: perhaps it had originally been a box, or pyramid or sphere of wood with ordered rooms inside it. If that were true, there was no way to tell. Over the centuries, individual rooms had been screwed or nailed onto the original structure, jutting out like barnacles. Whole floors were canted onto it and make-shift galleries built to connect them to the whole. Shafts had been dug through existing levels while other municipal buildings that possessed their own logic of construction had been towed over and added to the assembly. The whole bizarre pile rotated by slow increments causing the light from Gehellen's sun to tangle in con-fusing ways in its interior. People drifted like flies in and out of this migraine-inducing architectural disaster, and smaller flecks drifted too in their thousands: loose books not yet snagged by the haggard and overwhelmed library staff who chased them down in ones and twos using nets on poles.

"So," he said awkwardly, "what do you hope to find here?"

She gazed at him sadly as he grabbed a strand of the big rope cone that framed the library's entrance. "The admiral wants me to research the destination our map points to," she said quietly as she unwound herself from the embrace of the bike. "But all I was really after was distraction."

"Well." He made to turn the bike around. "When would you like me to pick you up?"

"Wait!" Aubri stretched out to put a hand on his arm. "Stay, please. I'd appreciate the company—and the help."

On the way here Hayden had been telling himself that he would leave her here for a few hours while he tried again to contact the Aerie Resistance. He would report the important information that Slipstream was threatened by Falcon Formation. What, though, was the Resistance going to do with that information? Hayden had run through various scenarios in his head as he lay on his bunk listening to the snores of Slew the carpenter. His thoughts had not been reassuring. The Resistance was likely to take the information and try to cut a deal with Falcon; they wouldn't have any faith in this mad venture of the Fannings. Maybe, if Hayden were some sort of hero, he could steal whatever it was that Fanning was after, and bring a radar set or two home with him. Then what? Give them to Falcon? He couldn't see any deal with the Formation that wouldn't seal the fate of Aerie once and for all.

Aubri had seen Hayden's hesitation, and frowning she turned away. "Wait!" He hand-walked up the netting of the entrance funnel to join her.

They drifted into a long cylindrical space with branching entrances leading off to all sides. The entrances were marked by subject matter. Ropes with handhold loops crisscrossed the space and bright lanterns lit the walls, their windup fans gently whirring.

Whatever the chaos of its facade, inside at least the library seemed remarkably well organized.

Aubri was watching him sidelong. "Slipstreamers are your mortal enemies, aren't they?" He nodded.

"And all this time you believed it was Admiral Fanning who led the attack on your sun? I can't imagine what it must have been like to be trapped on the *Rook* with him."

"It was intolerable," he admitted. At that moment Hayden was near having some internal dam burst and he knew it; one more sympathetic word from her and he would blurt out his whole life story like some maudlin teenager. He cast about for a way to change the subject. "Things haven't exactly been easy for you either."

She half-smiled. "Are you referring to the pirates? It was . . . bad, I admit. But that whole incident's over with, isn't it?" Her smile held sadness. "You should be grateful for traumas that have a definite ending to them. Some don't, you know."

"Believe me," he said, "I know." Then he narrowed his eyes. "You did this to me before."

"What?"

"Danced around the subject of why you're unhappy."

"Ah."

He grabbed a rope, and her hand, and stopped them above a square shaft that had the words MUNICIPAL ENGINEERING carved around it. For a long moment he felt her warm fingers wrapped around his; their eyes met. Then she drew her hand away.

He had to say something; what came out was, "I came aboard the *Rook* planning to kill Admiral Fanning, but you see I never expected to survive doing it. That's what I meant before, when I said I had no future. But when I said that, you suggested you didn't have one either. What did you mean?"

Aubri's expressive face twisted in eloquent distress. "I can't explain. Not in a way that you'd understand."

He crossed his arms and let himself hang in the air before her. "Is it because I'm an 'ignorant savage'? I believe you used that phrase to describe Martor a few days back."

She bit her lip. "It's not that. . . . I don't know how to explain it to you." She looked around, spotted something, and said, "I think we need to go that way."

Hayden thought she was changing the subject again, but as they flew down the hexagonal wood-paneled corridor to the library's history department, Aubri said, "I didn't come to Virga willingly. Not entirely willingly; I wasn't lying when I told you I had studied science and admired your people for their knowledge."

They entered a vast circular room that would not have seemed out of place under gravity—if one ignored the usual crisscross of ropes that various readers were using as perches. Light was provided by bright lanterns which lit the endless ranks of books lining the walls.

"It was my love of ancient arts like manufacturing that got me into trouble," continued Aubri. In this light she looked very beautiful to Hayden, a troubled doll drifting in lamplight. "Along with some others, I tried to overthrow Artificial Nature—locally, at least. We wanted to go back to noble pursuits like industry and construction! Work with our minds and hands again. I confess that . . . entities died. Not humans, you wouldn't understand them, they were surfers, standing waves in the stuff of A.N. Taking down A.N. killed them. As punishment, I was exiled here."

"I understand something about being an exile," said Hayden. Aubri smiled.

"Before I can return I have to fulfil a mission for Artificial Nature," she added with a sudden frown. "It hangs over my head like a sword. If I don't do it . . . I'll die."

"What? They'll send an assassin or something?"

She shook her head. "The assassin is already here, inside my body. It waits and watches. If I don't play my role to its end, it will strike me down."

This revelation was the last thing Hayden had expected from Aubri. He tried to imagine some alien machine coiled in her throat, watching him through the veil of her skin. The thought made his scalp prickle. "So what's this mission?" he asked after a long silence.

"I can't tell you," she said simply. "It might activate."

Confused and upset, he followed her to a cage mounted on one wall. There perched a bored-looking woman with arms like birds' legs, her prehensile foot crooked around a strap while she filed books in various slots in the cage. "Can I help you?" she asked, looking down her nose at Aubri.

"Hello, I'm not from around here. I'm looking for information about Leaf's Choir."

The woman's face brightened. "My, what an interesting accent! Well, welcome to Gehellen. And welcome to the library. Did you know we've been continuously open now for two hundred forty-seven years?"

"That doesn't surprise me at all," said Hayden.

"What about Leaf's Choir?" Aubri asked.

The librarian yawned. "The novels start over there, and wrap halfway around. Children's stories over there. Opera and plays, there."

"What about aereography?"

"Maps? That would be that section there." She pointed to the opposite side of the room. "But you won't find much, comparatively speaking. Leaf's Choir is much more interesting as a story than as a place."

"Why's that?"

"It's just a burnt-out shell now. Nobody can go in very far because of lack of oxygen, and occasional flare-ups. And whatever was in the outer layers was stripped decades ago. Leaf's Choir is a sargasso."

Suddenly Hayden understood. The extra fittings on the Rook weren't just for winter travel; they included air tanks and sealant for the portholes. The ship had a furnace but it also had a rock-salt battery for storing heat.

We're going in there, he thought, in sudden wonder.

"It must have quite a history to be the subject of all those novels," said Aubri as she gazed at the stacks. The librarian nodded.

"The original story's as fabulous as the novels," she said. "Once upon a time, two suns burned in the heart of Leaf's Choir. The suns were invisible from outside the nation because they were surrounded by a single, vast forest: millions of weightless trees connecting and reconnecting like the threads of a spiderweb through an intricate network of lakes and rock bits. The forest made a sphere over fifty miles across and within it were dozens of towns and hundreds of villages built out of the living branches of the trees." The librarian shaped the forms with her hands, long shadows cast by the lamps interpreting her gestures on the bookshelves behind her. "The impenetrable barrier of foliage provided protection as well as wealth to the citizens of Leaf's Choir, and they prospered.

"After centuries of peace, rumor began to circulate of the beauty of an heiress from Leaf's Choir, and that rumor attracted the attention of a warlord who determined to have her for himself. He laid siege to Leaf's Choir and was finally able to seize the giant air-pumping stations that kept the forest from supersaturating itself with oxygen. He threatened to blow up the stations unless the young lady was turned over to him. The government refused but the heiress secretly fled the capital and made her way to the warlord's encampment, and there gave herself up.

"To punish the nation, the warlord ordered the pumping stations blown up. Then he left—and behind him, the millions of trees of the forest continued to bask and produce oxygen. Leaf's Choir had cultivated them for centuries, to the point where it needed the artificial circulatory system of the pumps to ensure that oxygen did not build up to dangerous levels within the nation. Without the pumps, the least spark might set off an impossible conflagration—and so it happened, weeks after the warlord left. The fire raged out from the heart of Leaf's Choir and consumed everything, town, tree, and sun. All that was left when it was over was a sphere of charred wood and ash thirty miles across. That sphere is now tethered at the edge of Gehellen's territory; we've been mining it for its charcoal for centuries. It's very slow work because the heat of combustion is still trapped in airless pockets deep inside the sargasso. If oxygen reaches them, they break into flame again; so Leaf's Choir remains choked with stagnant, dead air. We have special ships that can go in, but navigation is a nightmare; it's all just black twisted wreckage that goes on forever. Leaf's Choir is ugly now—like a scar on the sky. Nobody goes there, unless it's for mining."

"That's very sad," said Aubri.

Yet somewhere deep inside it, Hayden mused, was the hidden treasure of the pirate king.

They spent several hours poring over maps of the place. The librarian was very helpful—Hayden and Aubri were a blessed break in her routine, it seemed. They both began to relax in each other's presence again. Hayden couldn't help but be distracted by occasional flashes of thigh or calf when Aubri reached for something; she pretended not to notice him noticing. The time went quickly.

Still, Hayden couldn't stop thinking about the assassin thing she had described. He wondered whether there were some way to pull the monster out of her, or poison or blind it. Aubri spoke no more of it, and he said nothing further about his own troubles. Perhaps out of a mutual need to turn their thoughts away, they focused with great intensity on comparing photos of Venera's map to the various charts. The charts were all centuries out of date. As the librarian had pointed out, the outer shells of the sargasso had been stripped away long ago, and the inner ways were char. It would take a miracle of navigation to find the treasure.

"I wish Gridde were here," Hayden said eventually. "He'd be able to sort all this out." As he said this he realized he'd felt a pang of affection for the crabby old man. Well, why not? Gridde was no soldier, he was just in love with his work. He was an innocent.

Finally they had compiled enough information to satisfy Aubri.

"I think we've earned a break," she said. "There should be a restaurant near here, don't you think?"

They followed the librarian's instructions and soon found themselves back in the crowded sky of Vogelsburg. Distant Candesce was cycling into its evening phase, its light reddening slowly. Where the librarian had directed them, the air was so crowded with structures as to be nearly impassable. Blocks and spheres, triangles and loose basket-farms were jammed in together, all jostling for sunlight and air. People sailed every which way, and as they nearly collided they would reach out to push off from one another without rancor or pause. The air was full of the scent of cooking and of waste, as well as shouts and laughs overlaid with the distant, ever-present rumble of buildings grinding together.

Hayden had just spotted the wicker restaurant the librarian had recommended when suddenly Aubri clutched his arm. "Someone's following us," she murmured.

He restrained the urge to turn and look. "Are you sure? How can you tell in this crowd?"

"Because he followed us into the library. I spotted him dawdling in the history room when we were working. He was trying to see the maps, I'm sure of it. Now he's behind us again."

"Well . . ."

"He looks like one of them." He looked at her blankly. "One of the pirates!" she whispered.

Now he did contrive to glance casually behind him. Hayden spotted a shock of yellow hair moving through a swatch of sunlight and felt his scalp prickle with recognition.

"Come on." Hayden led them in a complicated path between buildings, just to see if their tail would keep up. He did, a constant in the churning flow of faces and clothing.

"Okay, forget about lunch. We'd better get back to the bike and tell the others about this." He grabbed a municipal rope to change his course; less gracefully, Aubri followed.

She touched his ankle. "Look, there's a police station. Should we . . . ?" Hayden wasn't inclined to trust the constabulary, but today might be a good time to make an exception. He grunted and they jumped in that direction.

"He's gaining on us."

"Wants to keep us from getting to the station, maybe?" Hayden didn't look around, but redoubled his efforts to get to the building, which was a cube built of stone and rust-streaked iron.

"He's right behind us!"

Hayden looked back, and hissed with shock: he recognized this man. He had been one of the two who had doused the Rook's crewmen with kerosene. Now he was only yards back, moving with great easy bounds between the buildings and carefully not looking at Hayden or Aubri.

The police station was just on the other side of a great crumbling apartment held together by rope and stretched burlap—but they weren't going to make it. "Fuck it," said Hayden; he grabbed the corner of the building and stopped himself. Then he reached for his sword.

The pirate dove toward him, but passed a good ten feet away, still looking the other way. "What the—" Hayden and Aubri watched in disbelief as their follower sailed on through empty air; with no ropes to catch and change course, he had only one possible destination.

"I don't believe it," said Aubri as the pirate disappeared into the funnel-shaped entrance of the police station. "What do you suppose that means?"

"I think I know exactly what it means," said Hayden as the entrance suddenly boiled with uniformed officers wearing powerful foot-fins. Somewhere behind the building he heard jets whining into life.

"We've got to get back to the bike!"

Aubri sat perched on the side of the apartment, staring at the cloud of oncoming policemen. "But what's—"

"He's working with them! Aubri, come on!"

"Oh, I think you'll find it's too late for that," said a familiar voice behind them.

Hayden spun around.

Captain Dentius stood on the building, not fifteen feet away. He was flanked by two policemen, and he looked very pleased with himself. "Hello again," he said in his grating voice. "It's always a pleasure to run into former clients . . . especially when you've got unfinished business with them."

"Bastard!" Hayden's anger finally had a focus. It was with something like joy that he drew his sword and leaped at the man, ignoring the policemen.

He spun until he was going feetfirst and nearly managed to put his blade through the captain's throat, but Dentius ducked out of the way at the last moment. The policemen couldn't react before Hayden planted both boots on Dentius's chest and kicked hard. He sailed back to Aubri with extra momentum on his side. "Come on!"

She took his hand and they careened around the corner. Angry shouts followed.

"I can't believe you just did that!" she shouted. A gunshot sounded very close by, and here came the police bikes, a black swarm emerging from behind the police station.

"Take the initiative and you turn bad odds around," laughed Hayden. "First thing they teach you in pirate school!"

"Apparently Dentius skipped that class. Now what do we do?" They were trapped on the plain of the apartment block, with men closing in on all sides. There was just one obvious direction to go; Hayden smashed the wooden filigree of a window with his sword, and Aubri climbed in ahead of him as the police yelled at them to stop.

They found themselves in a strange apartment shaped like the cells of a wasp's nest. Shouts erupted from the half-dressed couple in the nearby bed-nest. Their limbs grotesquely long and curving, they looked like spiders as they reached out for any handy objects to throw at the intruders.

"Sorry!" Hayden and Aubri ducked past as policemen and pirates crammed into the window behind them.

Out in the tubelike hall, Hayden saw doors opening in both directions. The shouting and shots had alerted the whole building. He and Aubri went as quickly as they could from rope-hold to rope-hold but in seconds all the doors were open, and the citizens of Gehellen poured into the air around them.

16

"THAT'S A PRINT from the second dynastic era of Keppery," said the courtier helpfully, indicating the garish splash of lime-green and beige plastered like an insult on the banquet hall's wall. Venera was about to give some vapid reply (something on the order of "it's very nice") when she noticed what was happening near the doors.

"Excuse me." She sought out her husband, who was placidly sipping his fourth glass of wine next to Reiss. Gravity was taking its toll on them both. Venera leaned close and snapped, "They're locking us in."

"Wonderful news, dear," said Reiss obliviously. "The government of Gehellen has agreed to grant shore leave to your shipmates. Why, I believe if we visit the postern window over there we might even be able to see them disembarking."

Chaison was staring over Venera's shoulder with a puzzled expression on his face. "I do believe you're right, dear. And who are those people who just came in?"

Without glancing around, Venera said, "Compact, nondescript faces, no expressions, efficient movements, simple clothing?"

"Why yes, how did you—"

"Father bought a few of those from Falcon Formation, if I recall. They're secret policemen, love, you wouldn't recognize them because of your appalling lack of education in certain areas." She kept the smile on her face—in truth, it was no more false now than it had been ten minutes ago. "We're about to be arrested, I believe, and our men are being herded off the ships."

Ambassador Reiss sputtered. "They can't do—"

"Think of something, fast," hissed Venera as she heard some-one with slow confident steps approaching from behind. "Excuse me," said a voice that might have been stamped out of the same press as Carrier's.

Venera looked into Chaison's eyes, and saw something she'd never seen before—he was furious in some silent and calculated way that he'd never shown her. They had been separated during the battle with the pirates but she had heard he'd shot some men from the Rook's hangar. The leader who had done that was not the man she bickered with over dinner, who gave in so easily on do-mestic matters that it drove her to distraction. She'd hoped to meet that man someday, but under better circumstances.

Chaison Fanning was about to kill someone. Venera realized that it was time for her to get out of his way. She began to step to the side, saw his eyes widen, and felt a hand descend on her shoulder—

—And then a concussion sent her to her knees as stone and glass cascaded over her like water.

She looked up, blinking away dust, to see Chaison leaping over her as though she were a discarded chair in some bar brawl. A fa-miliar roar filled the banquet hall, its presence here such a shock-ing violation of the order of things that it froze Venera in place for a moment. She whirled, one hand still on the grit-spalled floor, and saw indistinct figures struggling in a tunnel of spiraling dust. The stink of burning kerosene filled the air.

"Come on!" Hayden Griffin reached out of the cloud. His grim face and jacket's torn shoulder blazed into perfect clarity in a shaft of Candesce's light. Just as she moved to take his hand, however, he spun around and the sword in his other hand flashed a blur over her head. Someone screamed in the white opacity of dust that surrounded him.

"Officers to me!" That was Chaison's voice.

A pistol shot startled Venera into standing up. Aubri Mahallan appeared, smoking weapon in her hand. "Sir, it's a trap," Griffin was telling Chaison. "Dentius got here ahead of us. He must have cut a deal with Gehellen for part of the treasure."

"Details later," said Chaison. "Officers, to me! We have to get back to the ships!"

Venera looked up. There was a jagged hole in the wall where the intricate stone and stained-glass rose window had been. "Ah," she said to no one in particular. "But what—?"

Something in the corner was rolling around belching fire and heat and the cloying odor of kerosene. Suddenly Venera realized that it was the black racing bike she had Griffin flying, and everything came together for her.

"You came through the *window?*"

Mahallan grinned tightly. "It was his idea."

A chaos of screaming men and clashing swords surrounded her. Venera was standing at the pivot-point of an actual sword fight, not one of those staged duels from her father's house that ended in a scratched cheek. Men were dying. For some reason she was shaking, which hadn't happened even when she shot the captain of the *Rook.*

"How are we getting out of here?" she asked Mahallan. "Climb out the window and jump off the town? Then we're in the city, I guess we could fly back to the ships . . ." But Mahallan was shaking her head.

"We'd be easy targets in the open air," she said. "We have to get a vehicle."

"There." Venera pointed at the rattling, smoking bike.

"Not sure we can get it up to the window," said Mahallan, "and anyway, it'll only carry three."

Venera pressed her hand. "I'm sure you can hold them off long enough for Chaison and me to escape."

The armorer stared at her. "I'm going to assume that you're joking."

"Sometimes I don't know myself." Just then a wall of *Rook* officers reared into view out of the dust. They were being forced back by a mass of men pouring in from the opened doors at the far end of the ballroom. The Slipstreamers were already outnumbered three to one and it was just going to get worse.

"This is hopeless!" shouted the handsome one, Travis. His sword was bloody and his hair matted to his forehead. "There's a whole army coming the way we need to go."

"We need to clear that hallway," said Chaison. "Oh, for a rocket."

"How about a jet?" It was Hayden Griffin, appearing again out of the dust. This time his face was in shadow and he looked savage with his sword and ripped leathers.

He ran to the corner and dodged the angry lunges of the downed bike until he could grab its handlebars. Then he was in its saddle, feet skidding across the floor as he tried to manhandle it into submission. "Out of the way!" he screamed. Travis turned, yelled, and grabbed the shoulder of the man next to him. They hit the floor exposing several startled Gehellen swordsmen.

"Aerie!" That wasn't the battle cry Venera had expected but she didn't care—the vision of Griffin opening the throttle all the way and shooting across the ballroom in a shower of sparks would stay with her for the rest of her life. Men flew through the air but the bike continued to accelerate as it crossed the hall. Venera screamed something that was half cheer, half obscenity, and reached for an enemy sword that had fallen at her feet. Travis and the other Rook officers were also screaming as they poured into the breach Griffin had made in the enemy's line.

The building shook to a deep *whoomp!* and a flash of light pierced the corridor down which the bike had shot. Mahallan gave a shriek and Venera thought, *So much for my driver.* But no, when they entered the corridor in a knot of Rook officers it was to find Hayden Griffin lying among the soldiers he had knocked aside. He levered himself to his feet as Venera placed the tip of her sword against the throat of an enemy who had the temerity to try to do the same. "Stay there," she said to the man cheerfully.

"Jumped off the bike when it cleared the doors," Griffin was saying to Mahallan. "Come on." He limped ahead. Mahallan just stood there for a moment, hands to her face.

Venera clapped her on the shoulder. "Well, what are you waiting for? Let's kill some men."

To her surprise Mahallan laughed and readied her pistol. "Yes!" They ran after the officers.

The end of the corridor was a mass of flame; the bike's kerosene tank had burst. Behind the flames cursing soldiers waited. Several fired random shots and one of the Slipstreamers went down with a bullet to the neck. Meanwhile Travis was vigorously kicking down the paneled sidewall a few feet from the fire. "This way!"

They piled into what looked like a servants' corridor. Chaison indicated left with his sword. "But that's where the soldiers are coming from!" Venera objected.

"It's the way to the entrance," he said. "I'm not about to end the day with my back to a wall." He ran in that direction without waiting for an answer.

Startled servants jumped out of the way; they were almost comical with their stiltlike legs and frightened looks. Venera felt powerful and alive, galvanized by the knowledge that she was probably going to die here. For the moment, following her husband through shouting and screams, she didn't care.

HE ONLY HAD time for quick glances as they ran, but what Hayden saw of the Gehellen's servants' rooms was strange and disturbing. There were pulley systems that people raised gravity-free could use to glide from room to room. They passed one nine-foot man—who couldn't have weighed more than one hundred fifty pounds—dangling helplessly from one of these, weak feet scuffing the floor frantically as he tried to get out of the way. Nobody hurt him. There were lots of rolling carts, crutches and soft seats, and most of the side rooms had big tanks of water in which men and women floated, exhausted, during their infrequent duty breaks.

"It's like a fucking hospital," muttered Travis as they passed a group of servants who cowered on their cots.

Gunfire ripped at them from up ahead. "They've blocked us," said Fanning with no trace of surprise.

Somebody cursed colorfully. Hayden turned to see an elaborately dressed man with a wine-stain birthmark gesturing from a side door. "This way, you fools!"

Fanning raised an eyebrow. "Well, follow the man," he directed.

This man, a dignitary of some sort, had circled around through unknown means and now held open a door to the palace's formal spaces. Hayden found himself in a huge atrium with curving staircases sweeping up to either side. The portraits on the wall were double or triple life-sized. Fanciful beasts were carved into the banister posts. There was distant shouting, but so far no enemy feet had disturbed the deep red pile carpet. "Don't stand there gawking, up, up!" raged the dignitary. As he followed the mob of officers he added, "You might have thought to ask directions from the *one* man among you who's familiar with the layout of this place."

"Thought you were dead, Reiss," said Fanning with a shrug.

"In there!" Hayden allowed himself to be herded through a stout-framed door in the cavernous upstairs hallway. This brought him into a tall galleried library whose far wall was entirely composed of beveled-glass windows. There was only one other door and immediately some men ran to secure it. "Now where?" Fanning asked Reiss.

While the two talked and gestured, Hayden sought out Aubri. She was standing with Venera Fanning, who looked calm and composed as always. "Are you all right?"

Aubri nodded. "I honestly didn't think that window-crashing thing was going to work."

"I only did it because you didn't tell me not to. You're the technical one! I assumed you'd have said something."

"Oh."

Venera laughed. "You *have* to tell me how all of this came about."

Hayden was distracted by nearby shouting. Fanning was yelling at Reiss. "But we've got to keep moving!"

The ambassador stood his ground. "Admiral, sooner or later, we're going to have to jump off this town. There is no way to get to the docks. This library juts out from the edge of the wheel; it's the best jumping-off point."

"Trapped!" One of the men at the far door waved. "They're coming this way in force."

"This way too!"

"Well, that's just splendid," muttered Fanning.

"Richard, what is going on here?"

All conversation stopped for a moment. Two richly dressed women, unnoticed until now, stood with fans in their hands in the center of the room. When Reiss saw them he blanched (wine stain momentarily fading) and stammered, "L-Lady Dristow, what a surprise! I, I mean—"

The older of the pair strode forward, fan flicking above her robin's-egg-blue bodice. "We came here hoping to have a quiet conversation, Richard. Not to be burst in upon by a covey of hysterical barbarians with swords." She looked down her nose at Admiral Fanning. "You are disturbing the peace, sir."

"Secure the doors," said Fanning. "And tear down those curtains! They might come in handy." Then he turned to the women. "Our apologies, madam. Circumstances have forced us to commandeer your library for a few minutes. I suggest you leave before the shooting starts."

"We will do no such thing!" The matron pointed her fan at the admiral, stabbing it rhythmically at him as she spoke. "Richard, tell this man how out of his depth he is. He does not speak to one such as myself. You must leave this place, sir, not I!"

The crack of a gunshot made Hayden jump. Lady Dristow shrieked as the fan she was holding exploded in a thousand flinders.

Hayden turned. Venera Fanning stood with one hand behind her back, the pistol straight-armed and aimed at Lady Dristow's head. "Shut," she said slowly, "up."

Chaison Fanning seemed to be suppressing a smile. "Reiss, do these women have hostage value?"

"Do these . . . ?" Reiss seemed to have lost the use of his voice. He shook his head, fluttered his hands at the ends of his arms, and then hurried over to take the shredded remains of the fan from the matron's fingers.

"We'll look into that later," said Fanning with a sigh. "For now, put them up top. Build a fort around them using books, it might stop a few bullets."

"What have you done?" squeaked Reiss.

"If we do have to jump, those curtains will have to serve as parachutes," continued the admiral. "I have no desire to tour the city at two hundred miles per hour."

". . . Just like the dream," Venera was muttering, her eyes wide and fixed on nothing.

"What have you *done!*" Reiss's anger had caught like a reluctant engine. He reared back, seeming to grow an inch, and his birth-mark flushed deep red. "Twenty years I've been here, serving my country loyally. Letters I've penned to the Pilot, all this time— 'Gehellen is a natural ally to Slipstream, we should increase trade connections'—slowly gaining these people's confidence and trust. Why, when I arrived they thought everyone outside of Candesce's light was a hopeless barbarian! It took two years just to set up my first cocktail party. And now you come sailing in here with a fleet of ships armed to the teeth, blow a hole in the palace wall and you ask me whether the dowager baroness of Cordia might make a good *hostage?*" He grabbed his hair and yanked it.

Venera shifted her aim and raised an eyebrow at her husband. Fanning pursed his lips and waggled a finger at her.

"Ambassador, if I even suspect that you led us in here in order to prevent us from escaping, I will shoot you myself," said Fanning quietly. Behind him, Travis was leading the matron and her cowering friend up the wrought-iron steps to the gallery.

"Admiral, I am loyal to Slipstream," raged Reiss. "Are you?"

"Unless I complete my mission, there will be no Slipstream,"

Fanning snapped. These words seemed to penetrate Reiss's fury. He crossed his arms and turned away.

"So, we may have to jump," said the admiral. He strolled over to the glittering windows. "We'd best line up our trajectory, then."

Venera jammed her pistol into the silk sash of her outfit. "You were going to tell me what led up to this," she said to Aubri. Behind her the air was assaulted by the sound of shattering glass as someone knocked out some windowpanes.

Aubri described how they had been followed by what turned out to be one of Dentius's pirates, and then had encountered the man himself. Venera's eyes widened at the mention of the name; Hayden could see muscles tightening under the scar on her jaw.

She didn't hide her disappointment when Hayden told of just missing Dentius's neck with his sword. "You'll have to do better than that next time, Griffin!"

"Aubri saw an open window and dived for it," he continued. "They chased us through the building—we were just a few feet ahead of them at one point." In the pandemonium the building's residents had swarmed out of their rooms, "And we thought we were done for. But they started throwing furniture and cutlery back at the police! They made enough chaos that we were able to get away."

Aubri shrugged. "I guess the people don't like their authorities very much."

"Well," said Venera with a shrug, "if they're deliberately kept without gravity then why would they? Ugh, I don't like the image you're conjuring—like a nest of bugs."

The image was indeed apt, Hayden thought. The residents had stuck out long and warped limbs, had thrown chamber pots and boxes, and cheered when Hayden and Aubri made it out a window on the far side of the place. "This put us in a cavity made by six or seven jammed-together buildings; the police bikes couldn't get in so we were able to jump to another building and escape into a crowded marketplace. From the market we made it back to the library and my bike."

"We knew the reception here was supposed to run into the evening," added Aubri, "and we couldn't get back to the docks because the police were blocking that direction."

"Did you at least do the charting I asked for while you were out?" asked Venera. Both Hayden and Aubri glared at her. "What?"

"The sky's packed with bikes," said an officer who'd stuck his head out the broken window. His hair was all tangled and his eyes were watering from the force of the wind. "They'll pick us off with no problem at all if we jump."

"Please, we have to negotiate!" Reiss was clasping his hands together in distress. "Give them the information they need, Admiral, and we stand a chance of getting home again."

"Unacceptable." Fanning was staring out the window. He grabbed the man next to him and pointed at something. "Besides," he said, "there may be another way."

He ran over to the downed curtains and crouched atop them, gathering a handful and staring around at the other furnishings of the room. "Colors! I need the right color combination! And I need a man who knows semaphore like his own speech."

Travis leaned over the railing and waved. "I'm your man. What have you got in mind?"

"I can see several of our ships from here—the docks aren't that far away. There's people filing off them now, but I can't tell how many have disembarked. We need to get their attention and signal them. Are you up for it?"

"I'll need a bigger opening than that." Travis strode to the stairs, drawing his pistol. The gallery crossed the windows; methodically, Travis shot the panes out, showering leather armchairs and ancient side tables with glass. The wind from the palace's rotation tore at the leftover edges, growling and hissing like some monster trying to get in.

"Slipstreamers!" The voice came from the main hallway, beyond the barricade of stout tables and bookshelves that Fanning's officers were completing. "This doesn't have to end in bloodshed! You know the information we're after. It's ours by right, just as

Leaf's Choir is ours. Give it up and I promise you'll be unharmed. You'll be escorted to the border and freed, along with your ships."

"You see," exclaimed Reiss. "Admiral, these are civilized people. They'll keep their word."

"Civilized people don't lay traps for visitors," said the admiral. "But tell him we're seriously considering his offer. It'll slow them down, and give you something to do." He turned to the others. "I want a salvo out that window. The sound has to carry to the ships, so every available man put his pistol outside."

They began firing, while Travis stood on the gallery overhead, waving makeshift flags as the wind tried to pull him out of the building. Meanwhile Reiss stood by the barricaded door and stammered out a wonderful string of vague promises and apologies; even Fanning had to smile at his tortuous negotiating style. "The man could buy us an hour at this rate," he said.

"Sir, something's happening at the docks." Fanning ran back to the window. "Everybody quiet! Listen." Travis stood stock-still, his hair fluttering in the wind. Faintly, through the constant roar of the air, Hayden could hear a distant, irregular pop-popping sound.

"Gunfire! And some sort of commotion by the ships. I think they're trying to cast off."

At that moment the dowager baroness of Cordia stood up and shrieked, "It's a trick! They're just trying to buy time, you dolts. You're letting them get away."

Venera spun and fired. The baroness fell back with a cry. Then the main door's barricade shuddered under an explosion that knocked paintings off the walls and books out of the shelves. The heavy tables that made up the barricade stepped forward several feet, knocking some of the defenders aside in a spray of smoke and splinters.

Fanning leveled his pistol and fired into the cloud. "Shore that up!" The Gehellens had misjudged the amount of powder it would take to blow the barricade, but next time they were likely to overcompensate. The door was going to open soon no matter what the Slipstreamers did.

"They're moving! The ships are moving!" A cheer went up at this announcement. The door defenders were back on their feet and using up the last of their ammunition to prevent anyone coming through as they shoved the smoking furniture back into the gap. It was too late, though—blades and bullets shot out of the smoke, taking down two of the officers.

Fanning stood on a central table and pointed with his saber. "Cut up those curtains. I want parachutes."

Men were smashing out the remaining panes of glass on the library's lower level. The wind now had free reign and it began sucking up everything—shards of glass, glowering portraits of Gehellen royalty, the buzzing pages of books. Gunfire ripped through both barricades, scattering the men there. Somebody screamed, "They're coming through!"

Suddenly the younger of the two Gehellen women leaped onto the gallery banister, wailing incoherently as she leveled a gun at the people below. The hand of the man left to guard her hung limply through the banister posts. She aimed at something over Hayden's head and fired, the recoil causing her to lose her footing. She fell off the gallery into the chaos of broken furniture and Hayden turned in time to see Travis, clutching his shoulder, stagger into the embrace of the wind and be snatched away by it.

Through the howl of the wind Hayden heard someone yell, "The *Tormentor* is coming," just as the barricades fell and armed men leapt into the room. Fanning leaped off his table and ran for the windows. "Junior officers first, get ready and line up your jump!" He handed large swatches of torn curtain to the young men then pushed them at the window. That was all Hayden had time to notice before he was faced with a grinning enemy with a sword and had to parry a cut to his throat.

The Gehellens were weak. It took long seconds for the fact to register with Hayden. As he cut and parried he realized that he outmatched his opponent in both strength and speed and that the same was true in the other duels being fought around him. Gravity was a precious commodity here, metered out unwillingly by the upper classes. These soldiers hadn't trained nearly enough in it.

He sent his opponent down with a slice to the ribs and turned to the next one. For a few seconds there was only the narrow world of slash-and-dodge; then someone screamed his name.

Glancing around, he saw Aubri holding one hand out to him. She stood next to the window with several others; in one hand she clutched a crimson swath of curtain. Hayden cut madly at the man he fought, then dove back to take Aubri's hand. She pulled them both out the window, and the library, the palace, and the royal town of Gehellen swept up and away at awful speed.

17

SNARLING BIKES TRAILED banners of vapor through the city. Chaison Fanning expected bullets to strike him any second; he focused on holding on to the corners of the scarlet curtain that fought to leap out of his hands. This close to a town wheel, there was usually a zone of empty air for safety reasons; if only he didn't lose the sheet he might be able to slow down to a reasonable velocity before he plastered himself against some window in the weightless part of the city.

The riveted iron belly of the royal town wheel receded with alarming speed, but he could see no puffs of smoke to signify that his people were being fired upon. In fact, he heard no shots at all now, just the bikes and the juddering of the wind.

One bike slid across the air toward him. *Here comes the end*, he thought. But as the can-shaped jet closed the last few feet to run parallel with his fall, he saw the Slipstream crest on its side. Its rider leaned over and held out an open palm for him to catch.

Chaison let go of the recalcitrant cloth and grabbed at the offered hand. It took a while to make the catch but before he expected it he was astride the hot metal cylinder, hanging on with white knuckles while he tried to jam his feet into the passenger stirrups.

Everywhere he looked, bikes were picking up falling officers. He even spotted Venera by the color of her clothes as she wrapped her arms around the waist of her rescuer. In the middle distance— between the bikes and the tumbled shapes of the city—six battered cruisers were circling.

He clapped his driver on the shoulder. "The *Rook*, if you can."

"Yes, sir." The man hunched forward and they took off. "That's a mighty fine dress uniform if I do say so myself."

"One of the things they give you when you get to be admiral," yelled Chaison over the wind.

"Yeah? What else they give you?"

"Headaches!"

With a few seconds to spare, Chaison examined the tactical situation. A navy's worth of bikes, cutters, and strike boats was stitching just beyond the Slipstream ships. And at the naval shipyard, a dozen battleships at least were casting off their moorings. But so far, nobody had fired a shot.

"They're afraid we'll blow up their city," he said. Indeed, the Slipstreamers' rocket racks were all open and aimed, some at the palace.

Chaison began to smile.

The bike dropped him off at the familiar hangar; the hatch gang gawked at him as though he'd returned from the dead as they helped him inside. "Senior officers to the bridge as soon as they arrive," he said to them. "Prepare to get under way."

There was no way everyone had made it back on board. If the fight at the docks had gone the way it had looked, a sizeable knot of Slipstreamers might have been left behind when the ships lifted off. This presented Chaison with a bitter decision, and he considered it unhappily as he hand-walked up to the bridge.

"Admiral on the bridge!" He ignored the jubilant cries of the staffers and strapped himself into the command chair. He was sitting thus, glowering, when the wounded and adrenaline-fired officers began straggling in, laughing and shouting and embracing one another. To his astonishment, Travis was with them, pale and clutching his wounded arm, but otherwise intact.

Trailing them all came Ambassador Reiss, who appeared to be in a state of shock.

"Listen!" Chaison hammered the arm of the chair to get

everyone's attention. "We have about one minute to make a major decision. We have a choice now. I understand that some of our men are still at the docks and may be scattered through the city if the bikes didn't get to them in time. We can recover all of them if we take a stand here and threaten to blow up the royal palace of Gehellen."

He had their full attention now. "Now, with luck and a little negotiation, we might then secure an escort to the border and escape this nest of traitors. But during all the talking and threatening, the Gehellens will have plenty of time to deploy their ships to best effect. We will have to give up any hope of reaching Leaf's Choir."

"Then they'll have won!" wailed a junior staffer.

"But we'll have our men."

They looked at one another unhappily. "On the other hand," continued Chaison, "if we abandon the stragglers, we can set a course directly for the Choir. The Gehellens will give chase and there may be a running battle, but at top speed the sargasso is only an hour or two away. Once in it we can hide—and hunt for our objective."

The door opened and Aubri Mahallan entered. Her harem pants had ballooned and ripped in the fall, her hair was a mad tangle, and her eyes were red—but she looked calm as she presented Chaison with a leather folder. "Best guess for the location of the treasure, based on the maps we found in the library," she said.

All eyes were on the folder as Chaison opened it. He noticed that, and half-smiled. "It seems," he said, "that we all know what we have to do. Perhaps later we can repatriate our men by offering the Gehellens some of their treasure back. Anyone here want to pledge a tithe to that purpose?"

Everyone shouted "Aye!" —Everyone, that is, except Richard Reiss, who merely hung his head.

"Good," Chaison said with satisfaction. "Make the same offer to the general crew, and get these ships under way! Maximum speed, use rockets to blow any obstacles out of the way—and prepare to lock down for sargasso running!"

In that small space, the cheer was almost deafening.

HAYDEN HELD THE handles next to a porthole and stared out at the dark. Candesce was fading as the Rook and its sisters lofted past the last pendant towers of the city. The mauve-and-rose-colored sky went on forever, its perfect symmetry broken by the glitter of countless home and town lights. The air was dense with rope highways and navigation beacons, vast and diffuse farm nets and weaving flocks of fish and birds. The ships did not slow down for any of these hazards; in fact, they accelerated into the dimming air, recklessly daring fatal collision with stone, water, or tree. The entire Gehellen navy came screaming after them with only a little more caution.

Far in the distance, veiled by evening color, a vast black smudge polluted a full thirty degrees of sky. The sargasso of Leaf's Choir ate all the light shone at it, and cast an indigo shadow across hundreds of miles of air. Minor wars had been fought over the significant zone of winter caused by that shadow; among the principalities of Candesce a significant minority favored the idea of towing Leaf's Choir into a final incineration at the central sun. The majority was horrified at the prospect of smothering the Sun of Suns in that much ash, and predicted dire consequences from prolonged darkness, and as the purified residue fountained back up. Arguments about what to do with the Choir had seesawed for centuries.

No one had ever seriously suggested that the Choir be sent the other way, into the outer volumes of winter. To dispose of the sargasso among barbarians would sully the memory of one of the greatest nations of Candesce.

For all Chaison Fanning's intentions, there was no way that the expeditionary force could reach the Choir in only two hours. Darkness and the crowded air slowed them, forced detours and unpredictable maneuvers. Rockets began to appear from behind, red streaks zipping past in ominous silence as any second now an explosion might convulse the *Rook*; and yet you could only take so much fear. Hayden watched as long as he could, but eventually drowsed, and dreamed confused half-dreams of Aerie, his parents, and the destruction of their half-built sun.

The impressions stayed with him even as he woke to find someone shaking his shoulder. "Armorer wants you," said a crewman. Hayden grunted his thanks and levered himself away from the window. The thrum of the engines continued; apparently they weren't dead yet. But it was impossible to tell where they were or how long this chase would last.

As he made his way through the ship he saw men sealing portholes and cracks with thick gummy tar. Others were hooking hydrogen peroxide tanks to the engines and checking the air distribution hoses, preparing for sargasso running. There was little conversation, just a muted hum of urgency.

It all seemed reassuring, somehow. Without noticing, he had come to think of the *Rook* as his home—and it was hardly surprising. Hayden hadn't had a home in many years; certainly the various bug-ridden flats and one-room bachelor's nests he'd slept in hadn't counted. He had been alone for so long that he'd forgotten what it was like to be among friends. But the atmosphere of the *Rook* reminded him of Gavin Town. Ironic that it was a ship of the enemy.

He passed Martor, who slept strapped to a beam just behind the hangar. The boy looked younger than his fifteen years. A few hours before he had told Hayden about the fight at the Gehellen naval shipyard. The Gehellens had begun offloading the crews along a narrow metal scaffold, a barred cage with troops hanging in the air outside of it. It was a shooting gallery, really, had they all been in it when the shots from the palace had been heard. Luckily there were still men in the ships able to man the rocket racks, and they had blasted the troops who had tried to disengage the cage and sail it away to a nearby blockhouse. Men had spilled into the air and a fierce swordfight erupted. Martor had described this in his usual way, waving his arms and making stabbing motions. But his heart didn't seem in it; he'd known men who had died in this battle and he seemed to be beginning to realize what real death meant.

Hayden turned away from the boy, shaking his head. No—these people weren't the enemy, no matter what their homeland had done to his. Aerie deserved its freedom, and Slipstream as a nation deserved to be knocked down. But the people of Slipstream and the people of Aerie deserved equal respect and consideration. They were only human, even the loyal crewmen of the Slipstream navy whom he now counted as friends.

Somehow, he mused, there must be a way to separate the political from the personal. His bitterness over the past years seemed increasingly to have come from not believing that such a thing was possible.

He passed one other person on his way: the forlorn figure of Richard Reiss curled up next to a porthole, where he watched the skies in mourning for the life of luxury and prestige he had so suddenly lost.

Hayden rapped on the door to Aubri Mahallan's box-shaped workshop. The wooden panel squeaked open an inch, then widened, letting loose a fan of lamplight. He squeezed inside and the silhouetted shape of Aubri shut the door behind him.

And latched it.

"What can I do for you?" He reached out and somehow she had swirled closer and his outstretched fingers slid up her arm and onto her shoulder—which was bare.

He started to snatch his hand back but she held it, and now his fingers strayed onto the smooth soft skin of her pectoral. "You stuck with us through everything," Aubri murmured. "I thought you needed some sort of reward."

With the permission of her fingertips on his wrist, his own fingers slipped further onto the satin slope of her breast. With a simple scissoring motion Aubri reached around his waist with her legs and drew herself to him. His other hand reached down to cup her hip and encountered warm skin.

"Now we must be very, very quiet," she whispered. "Or we'll be the crew's main topic of conversation for days."

"Um," he said; but then she was kissing him, and he was spared having to think of any clever replies.

SPOTLIT BY SMOKING electric torches, men braced themselves in the hangar doors of the ships and waved flags at the dark silhouettes of their sister vessels. The flags fluttered and buzzed in the fearsome headwind, but the messages that flickered across the rushing air were clear and measured. Encoded status reports, inventories, updates to the chart numbers, all flowed steadily between the members of the force, routine and controlled.

—Until one message to the *Rook* caused the duty officer to curse under his breath. Reluctantly, he sent Martor to knock on the admiral's door.

Hayden Griffin was drifting in a timeless haze of pleasure in Aubri Mahallan's arms when the *Rook* shook from some sort of collision. They were both instantly awake. There was another bump and then the grating sound of hull-against-hull contact. Hayden heard shouting.

Aubri's eyes were wide. "We're being boarded!"

He shook his head. "No gunshots. Something's up, though." They both hastily dressed. "Stay here," he said. "It might be the Gehellens after all."

She shuddered. "If we really are being boarded, I'm going out the window this time."

He flipped out the doorway and closed the portal, immediately encountering Martor. "Come on!" shouted the boy. "We're taking on passengers." He bounded back toward the hangar.

The *Rook* and the *Unseen Hand* were lashed together, door to door. The ships bucked and strained against the ropes and wind whined through the gap. Men were leaping between the ships carrying boxes and rockets. The *Rook*'s new boatswain yelled and pointed, face red and sweating, as crates and bedrolls bounced and tumbled through the air.

"What's going on?" Hayden asked one of the *Unseen Hand*'s crewmen. The man grimaced and waved at his ship.

"Oxygen system's busted. We'll suffocate if we take the *Hand* into that place right now. Admiral ordered us to transfer over to the *Rook*, leave a skeleton crew on board. With fewer people breathing over there, they might stand a chance." He looked around at the crowded interior of the *Rook*. "Where can I strap my bedroll?"

"Martor, take care of him," said Hayden. He headed for the hangar doors, intending to help with the transfer. Glancing forward between the ships, he was startled to see nothing but blackness ahead of them. "Where are we?"

"Hard to say," said one of the hatch gang. "Word is that it's too dark for sighting and we don't know the local navigation beacons. The sargasso could be ten miles away, or we might be about to run into it at full speed."

Hayden spent a few minutes jumping back and forth between the ships carrying supplies—crates of food, coils of rope, and rolls of canvas for the braking sails. He was untying a barrel of hydrogen peroxide near the back of the *Hand* when the shouting in the hold took on a hysterical edge.

"Cast off! Cast off! Just cut it!" Hayden let go of the barrel and bounded up to the *Hand*'s hangar. Men were frantically slashing at the ropes that bound the two ships together. He opened his mouth to ask what he could do to help and was drowned out by the sound of both ships' collision horns going off. "Brace for impact!" someone screamed.

Something like a giant black claw swept through the narrow space between the ships. One crewman who had been jumping the gap was suddenly gone. At the same time, both ships lurched and a series of loud rattling bangs shook the *Hand*.

"We're in the trees!" They had reached Leaf's Choir; apparently the navigators had misjudged the distance after all. More bangs, rattles, and cracks signaled impacts with the charred branches of the former forest. The *Hand* shuddered and began to slow.

The gap between the ships suddenly expanded. Hayden realized he was holding tight to a beam aboard a vessel that had no oxygen supply. Everyone he knew was on board the *Rook*, including Aubri. In seconds they would be separated and he might never see her again.

He spun and put his feet against the beam. Looking up he saw the square of light that was *Rook's* open hangar door. Men crowded there, but only one was looking in his direction. It was Carrier.

For a moment he and Venera's servant locked gazes. Hayden saw Carrier hesitate—just for a second—and then he extended his hand.

Hayden jumped. For a second he was in turbulent air, surrounded by lashing black branches and the scent of charcoal. Then Carrier had him by the wrist and was pulling him into the *Rook*. The hatch gang cheered.

Carrier let go and turned away. The boatswain pushed Hayden toward the inner door while shouting, "Shut the hatch! Tar it! Stand by for sargasso running."

Hayden looked back as the hatch closed. Carrier had disappeared. Through the closing hatch he could see the lights of the *Unseen Hand* flickering through a chaos of whipping branches. The *Hand* veered away, its light guttered and was lost; then the hatch slammed shut and the gang moved to seal it.

They had reached Leaf's Choir.

MOST OF THE Gehellen vessels fell back to circle the black forest in frustration, but some sargasso-equipped ships continued to follow the Slipstreamers. This made it risky for the *Rook* to slow down—but it was equally risky to continue at speed. The outermost layers of Leaf's Choir had been picked over by charcoal harvesters for centuries, and now consisted mostly of long spearlike trunks, denuded of branches, that wove and curved through the air for hundreds of feet at a time. These spears could puncture the hull of even an armored warship, if struck at high speed.

Each tree had originally been rooted to a small clump of asteroidal dirt. As they grew they wound branches around one another, like swimmers grasping for companions. With no sense of up or down, the trees had used Candesce and the local suns as their targets, sending threadlike stalks and branches through the empty air, spreading nets of leaves to catch light and passing moisture. Gradually, they had formed a vast and diffuse substance that made its own weather, caught drifting dust and stones and assimilated them, and greedily sucked up the carbon dioxide and smoke of the industries that thrived among them. Humans had woven the pliable branches into elaborate structures, entire cities of living green that went on, chamber by beautiful breathing chamber, for miles. Generations of gardeners cultivated their home trees, adding flowers and liana. Giant spheres and rods of water filled the central spaces, cupped by a thousand delicate fronds, in which fish and people swam. The people of Leaf's Choir had cleverly fashioned gigantic mirrors out of water—simply by stretching nets and wetting them until the water clinging to neighboring strands met and merged into a single surface—and used these to reflect the light of Candesce and their own two suns many miles into the forest.

All of it had burned. All was now black and sunless, the air replaced by stagnant smoke that never settled, merely eddied and spiraled around itself in an eternal dance of mourning.

The ships' navigators soon started cracking under the strain of finding their way through this gargantuan, mazelike tomb. They spent hours staring out at the advancing lines of black lit by the ships' headlights. Odd objects would appear in the light and slide by like hallucinations: window lintels, blackened shoes, spoons, and bedposts. The men began to swear they saw figures beckoning to them from the darkness beyond the branches.

And all the while, the Gehellens followed.

Chaison Fanning locked himself in the chart room with

Gridde and Aubri Mahallan. They compared photographs of the measureless spaces and distant, branching buttresses of forest growth to the charts Aubri had found in the library. The precious treasure map from the tourist station waited in a glass case beneath the chart table. "It all hinges on finding the city of Carlinth," Gridde said over and over. "Find the city, we can find the rest of the way. If we don't . . ."

There were reports of men collapsing suddenly. Unless the air was kept moving, carbon dioxide, monoxides, and smoke from outside seeped in and pooled. You could put your head into an invisible cloud of death without knowing and just pass out. It was as though some unseen monster stalked the ship. Everybody watched everybody; nobody slept unless their face was near a fan.

Dangerous as it was, some men found themselves obsessively watching out the portholes. Hayden was one. He had no duties since the bikes were useless without oxygen. Though he hungered to be with her, Aubri was busy with the charts. The only way he could feel he was contributing was by maintaining some sense of where they were.

Of course he'd heard of sargassos. They happened whenever a forest became too large and caught fire. Normally, though, a sargasso didn't last long. Air moved through it chasing the smoke away. The charred raft of branches broke up or was taken apart and everything went back to normal. It was terrifying to think that a forest could become so large that its sargasso could never be healed. As he watched he thought about the fact that an entire civilization was entombed here in the dark: the Rook hummed past chalk-white stone house cubes and blackened town wheels where only ghosts now dwelt.

There were hints in the lines and buttresses of the forest that Leaf's Choir had once been a realm of grand sculptured bubbles made up of smaller bubbles, a fractal palace with living walls. At times the perspectives became dizzying. Miles-wide chambers and arches had walls made up of buildings—houses as bricks, towers as pillars, the city as building material. It was almost reassuring that their full extent was no longer visible; the grandeur and the feeling of loss that must go with seeing it would be unbearable.

At times it seemed as though the *Rook* had entered some other plane of existence. Home, friends, ordinary cares no longer existed. There was only the breathing of the pumps and the distant roar of the engines. Faces were side-lit or merely imagined on silhouetted figures passing between the active workstations of the ship. And maybe this otherworldliness was what caused the crew of the *Tormentor* to let down their guard.

Hayden didn't see the missile itself. The *Tormentor* was somewhere out of view on the other side of the *Rook*. He did see a row of distant house windows, previously black, light up in lurid reds one after another—a quick whipcrack motion from right to left—and then the ghostly network of dead branches was thrown into stark relief by a burst of white light.

The roll of thunder followed moments later.

The illusion of peace was shattered by shouts, warning horns, and furious activity. The porthole suddenly moved away from Hayden as the *Rook* began to roll over. "Running lights off!" the boatswain was shouting. "Headlight off!"

"What are we doing?" demanded the airman from the *Unseen Hand* who Hayden had spoken to earlier. "Aren't we going to stand and fight?"

The boatswain shook his head. "Admiral's orders. The others are going to draw them away while we make a run for the treasure. Don't worry. He planned for this."

"He plays fast and loose with our lives," muttered the crewman.

"Right here, right now," replied the boatswain, "caution'll get you killed."

Roars and rumbles could be heard through the hull for many minutes, but the light of battle faded behind quickly, and eventually the relentless silence of Leaf's Choir settled back over the ship—worse than before, if that were possible, because the *Rook* was barely moving now. The navigator and pilot sat with their noses to the bridge portholes, staring into the darkness until their eyes watered. Occasional thumps on the hull and the sharp snap of breaking branches signaled their mistakes. The ship would shudder at such times and slow, and the fire crew would rush around looking for broken seams, cracks, or punctures—anything that might let in the toxic mix that passed for air in this place. It was fully two hours before the admiral allowed the *Rook*'s headlight to be lit again.

By that time, Hayden was certain they were lost.

CHAISON FANNING HAD begun to feel unpleasantly familiar with the back of Gridde's head. The old man had his eye glued to the periscope in the chart room and hadn't moved in ten minutes; Chaison suspected he was asleep. Would that Chaison could be.

He was hiding here, he had to admit. It was just too nerve-wracking to be on the bridge right now. After all, the entire mission—and possibly the future of Slipstream itself—was riding on the events of the next day. Or rather, no, it wasn't the direness of the situation that was keeping his nerves on edge. He'd already fought several battles to get here, and none had affected him like this interminable waiting. No, it was the prospect of being proven a fool that bothered him. In all likelihood there was no pirate treasure; the very phrase was an oxymoron, for pirates were outcasts, the poorest of the poor.

If it turned out that he had betrayed his men's trust by luring them halfway across the world on a bootless quest, Chaison would willingly step out of the *Rook*'s aft hatch without a gas helmet and make Leaf's Choir his tomb. Or give himself up to his men's wrath. It wouldn't matter which at that point.

"There it is!" Gridde had been awake after all. He said nothing else, until Chaison put a hand on his shoulder and said, "What, man? What do you see?"

"It's the city," the old man whispered. "Dead as a forgotten legend. Your wife's map starts here. From here, I can find our way."

Chaison went to one of the portholes to look out. There had been nothing but relentless black out there for hours now as the *Rook* searched for landmarks in the open central cavity of the Choir. Once, two suns had lit this space, but it had shrunk until it was only fifteen miles across. Cities, farms, and palaces had soared through the luminous air. Now, any light you made was quickly eaten by the permanently drifting smoke.

Impatiently, he bounced over to a speaking tube and said, "I want flares, in all six directions. Air-free white." He waited impatiently by the porthole until the lights stuttered on.

And a ghostly image began to emerge from the frozen billows of smoke and killed air: the bone-white shape of a city, its arcs and curves embedded in shadows of perfect black.

This was Carlinth, once the second-largest city of Leaf's Choir. As Chaison examined it he realized he was looking at one of the legendary architectural forms of the principalities of Candesce. Carlinth was a geared town.

Six town wheels surrounded a seventh like the petals of a flower. Their rims touched and an elaborate scaffolding, shadowed behind them, indicated some fixed connection between them. When they turned, they would have turned in synchrony. You could step off one wheel and onto the rim of another—no cable cars for these people.

Each town wheel was twice the size of any of Rush's. They were crowded with mansions and minarets, and many more free-floating buildings hung in the surrounding dark. But it all looked unreal, like an ivory child's toy, because there was no color at all to the scene. Every object and structure was the same shade of purest white.

Gridde hissed as he squinted through his periscope. "It's ash, sir. Finer than smoke, it's like paint when it settles. The whole place is layered in it."

A shroud, thought Chaison with a shudder.

"But I can see the way," continued the chart master. He held up the long branchlike map Venera had taken from the tourist station. "I can navigate us from here."

The knot in Chaison's stomach began to unwind, just a bit.

The Rook slid silently past the dead town wheels. Just as the flares began to gutter Chaison began to catch glimpses of discolored areas on the motionless structures, places where objects had been removed, doors forced, and windows broken. Someone had come here to strip the dead city, but whoever it was had not come in force and hadn't stayed long.

Was it ghosts that had scared them away? Skittering sounds in the darkness, half-glimpsed movement down streets that had once thronged with people? Or was it just the silence, relentless and oppressive, that had made men begin by talking in whispers and end up not speaking at all? —Leaving, abandoning their ambitions of getting rich off the death here; shamed and uneasy, fleeing Leaf's Choir never to return?

Carlinth perched on the tip of a four-mile-long outthrust of foliage. As the beam of the Rook's headlamp grazed this bleached tangle it became clear that the fires had not reached the city. Perhaps through some heroic effort, the citizens of Carlinth had fended off the flames; if so, they had only postponed their fate as the air turned foul and smoke invaded from all directions, sliding under doors and through cracks until eventually everyone succumbed. He could only imagine the tragic tableaux that must still be on display in bedrooms and plazas throughout the city.

The unburnt forest was a porcelain filigree full of infinite detail; but Chaison was tired, and happy to leave the navigation to Gridde. He retired to his tiny cabin on the Rook's wheel to find Venera sprawled diagonally across the bed, snoring. When he tried to move her she awoke, grinned raffishly at him, and drew him down. Their lovemaking was passionate and fierce; all the words that stood between them during the day were erased by moments like this. They reaffirmed their loyalty to one another through caress and kiss, and said nothing.

When he awoke it seemed as though no time had passed. Venera was asleep. At least, he assumed it was sleep, and checked her pulse just in case. You never knew, with the pernicious gases that were lurking about.

The chart room stank of unwashed old man, and Gridde looked deathly ill, but he was still at his post. "Nearly there," he said hoarsely. His right hand clutched the end of a speaking tube and he alternated between sighting along the branchlike map and peering through the periscope. His eyes, when Chaison saw them, were hollow but burning with fierce intensity.

"The map works?" Chaison couldn't keep the surprise out of his voice.

Gridde laughed, a rattle like water through old pipes. "Get up to the bridge, boy. We can't be more than a half-hour away now."

Chaison grinned. He did feel like a boy, responsible to no one but himself. He was hungry—better get a meal sent up. He resisted the urge to laugh out loud. It's working!

On the way out of the chart room he paused to glance out the porthole, and gasped.

Color had returned to the world outside the Rook.

Here, the forest had not burned. Stifled and enmeshed in darkness, the trees had died slowly. It could be that one of the little suns had continued to burn for a time after the fire, because the myriad leaves now swirling past the Rook were all autumnal, like those of a forest that had strayed too far from its sun. They blazed red, shone gold, or were touched with delicate browns and tans. Little clouds of them danced in the vortex caused by the Rook's passage. The tunnel of foliage down which they were travelling was dappled in rich hues that burst into view as the headlight caught them, then faded to black as they slid past.

It was a mesmerizing sight; but he couldn't dally.

Chaison made sure he was well groomed and had a confident air as he entered the bridge. The bridge crew looked up blearily, then snapped to attention. "Sound general quarters," he said as he strapped himself into the captain's chair. "I want the excursion teams suited up and ready to go." He thought of sending someone to wake his wife, but an unfamiliar but pleasurable spitefulness stopped him. Let her sleep through the discovery. It would serve her right.

For a while he presided over the rousing of the ship. Ultimately he couldn't resist, though, and returned to a porthole to watch. And so he was one of the first to see it as they rounded a knee of forest that almost blocked the vast autumnal tunnel, and the fabled treasure of Anetene hove into view.

18

THE ANCIENT SHIP hung in the center of a cave of leaves six hundred feet in diameter. In the dancing light of lanterns waved by the gang of red-suited sargasso specialists, Venera could see occasional flashes of the ropes that suspended the old corsair like a fly in a spider's web.

"They're taking too long," she grated. "What's the holdup?"

Her husband rested his hand lightly on her shoulder and peered out the porthole. "They're testing for booby traps, dear. On my orders."

"And then we go over?"

"I go over. To find the box."

"*We* go. This expedition was my idea. The box was my discovery. You can't let me miss out on the final moment."

He sighed. "Have you ever worn a sargasso suit?"

"Have you?"

One of the little figures out there was waving its lantern in a strange pattern. The others were clustered around a dark opening in the side of the ship. The craft was smaller than the *Rook*, and unornamented; but the lines seemed archaic, even to Venera's untrained eye. "What's he doing?" She pointed.

"Signaling the all-clear. Apparently Anetene decided the sargasso was a big enough booby trap all by itself." The little figures began disappearing one by one into the dark hatch. Little glints of light on the hull revealed portholes hidden in shadow around the curve of the ship.

"It'll be there," she said confidently. Either that, or she'd have to find a new home. Rush would no longer be a suitable dwelling once Falcon Formation took over.

Venera tried to pretend that this would be a mere matter of convenience. But she kept imagining herself returning to her father's court with her exiled husband. They would eat him alive, those back-biting courtiers, the kohl-painted ladies with their poisoned hairpins, the gimlet-eyed men with their ready poniards. Chaison would be used as sport by the jaded or the marginalized, and he would have no one to defend him.

It would surely be a personal humiliation for her, if he were killed.

"Well, if it's safe, let's go then," she said, but a commotion from the chart room distracted Chaison. Venera scowled at him as he turned away.

"It's Gridde!" Travis was waving frantically at the admiral. "He's collapsed."

Chaison dove for the doorway. "Was it bad air?"

"I don't think so. Exhaustion, more like."

Venera followed the whole bridge staff back to the map room. This was a tiresome interruption, but she had to be supportive of her husband. She affected a look of concern as she entered the room. The air in here was close, stinking, but then so was the rest of the ship by now. Grídde hung limply in midair, tendrils of white hair haloing his head.

"I got you there," he whispered as Chaison moved to hold him by the shoulders. The old man's face quirked into a half-smile, though his eyes were half-closed. "Rest now."

"Slipstream will survive, because of you," said Chaison.

Gridde's head rose and his eyes focused on the admiral. He managed a weak laugh. "Don't give me platitudes, boy. Just make sure those damn fools in the academy hear about this. I proved it." He began to gasp. "Old ways—better than—gel charts . . ."

"Get the surgeon!" cried Chaison, but it was too late. Gridde shook and sighed, and then went still.

Some of the bridge staff began to weep. Venera crossed her

arms impatiently, but there was nothing she could do but wait. The brief agony of military grief would burn itself out in a few minutes and then everyone would get back to work.

They had come too far to let one more death stop them now.

HER BREATH AND the suit pumps roared in Venera's ears. Every few minutes a loud bell sounded and she had to reach down to wind the clockwork mechanism that ran the pumps. She could barely see out the brass helmet's little window. The unfamiliar oilcloth sack of the suit felt like prison walls against her skin, its chafing creating a subliminal anxiety that fed back with weightlessness and the dark to make her jaw throb.

She didn't care. Venera was in a state of rapture, gazing into the most wondrous place she had ever seen.

The others' bull's-eye lanterns sent visible shafts of blue light up and down, flicking from side to side—each darting motion lifting a cascade of sparkling reflections and refractions from the contents of Anetene's treasure trove.

Venera had seen clouds rub past one another and throw up a cyclone; at either end these looked like tubes full of turbulent snatches of vapor. The interior of the treasure ship was like that— except that here, it wasn't clouds that formed the spiral down which she gazed. It was jewelry, gold coin, faience, and ivory figurines by the thousand.

The nets that had once held the treasure to the walls had decayed over the centuries, and so every week or two a gem or coin would disengage from its neighbors and drift into the ship's central space. Once there, it would be caught up in the almost imperceptible rotation in which everything inside Virga participated. Something to do with orbits and tides, that was all she knew of that. But the vortex had grown and remained stable for centuries, the drift of its objects slower than a minute hand but inexorable. The spiral pattern, so delicate, was now being erased by the blundering passage of treasure seekers.

For the moment, though, garnets, emeralds, and rubies made in the fires of Candesce trailed in lines and arcs through the air. Here and there gleamed dry-amber from sargassos on the other side of the world; chains of diamond like runnels of light flashed in her lantern's beam. The currency of two dozen nations sat fixed in air as though in solid glass (the stamped profiles of pilots and kings layered into shadow like a history lesson) among clouds of platinum and buttons of silver. Beneath the ragged netting the hull was still plated with paintings, skyscapes half-covering formal portraits whose eyes awoke like a sleeping ghost's when her light touched them. One painting, only one, had broken free, and so it was that at the center of the cyclone stood a tall stern man in dark dress, his black eyes those of a contemptuous father gazing accusingly at the looters. Only the gilt frame surrounding him spoiled the illusion of reality. There was a fresh bullet hole in his chest, put there by the first man of Slipstream to enter the ship.

They'd be joking about that startled shot for weeks, she was sure.

Chaison had swam indifferently through the shining constellations and disappeared into the ship's bridge. Venera followed, not without plucking a few choice items from the air on the way.

Chaison's hand-light floated free in the air, slowly turning to illuminate the fixtures of the old-style, cramped bridge. Venera kept expecting to see skeletons, but there was no evidence of violence here; apparently Anetene had been compulsively neat. In the center of the room was a chart pedestal, and clipped to the top of this was an ivory box, its sides inlaid with fantastical scenes out of mythology: men and women under gravity, riding beasts she remembered were called horses. Chaison's hand hovered over the lid of the box.

"Oh, just open it!" Of course he couldn't hear her; even to herself, Venera's voice sounded muffled in the suit. She bounced over to grab the box just as Chaison reached down and flipped back the lid. Both of their lanterns lit the contents through the blue air.

The object was simple, a white cylinder a little longer than her hand with a single black band around its center, and a loop for grasping at one end. It was made of some translucent crystal that made it gather the light mistily. Chaison hesitated again, then grasped the handle and pulled it out.

He leaned his helmet against hers. "The key to Candesce," she heard, the distorted words barely audible through the metal. "Just as the old books described."

"Let's hope it works," she said.

"Candesce still works. Why shouldn't this?" He put it back in the case and closed it. Then he hung there in the air for a while, head down, as if praying.

Puzzled, Venera touched her helmet to his again. "What's wrong?"

Did she imagine the sigh or was it real? "I'm just trying to figure out what to do next," he said. "The Gehellens will be circling Leaf's Choir waiting for us to come out. How are we going to get to Candesce?"

"You're not one to live in the moment, are you?" she said. It was true she hadn't thought that far ahead, herself. Maybe she should have—for he was right, this was a problem.

A wide moat of empty air lay between the principalities of Candesce and the Sun of Suns itself. Venera knew they would have to cross two or three hundred miles of open space to reach the ancient sun. Candesce was so hot that no clouds could persist in this zone, and no living thing nor habitation within a hundred miles. As the battered ships of the expeditionary force crossed this span they would be easy targets for the Gehellen navy.

"If we send the others out as decoys again, and just take the Rook . . ."

His helmet grated against hers as he shook his head. "We'll be seen. Not even a bike could get to Candesce right now."

"We'll have to hide, then. Wait them out."

"But there's another problem," he said. "We're almost out of time."

"What?"

"That dreadnought . . . Based on the progress your photos showed, it'll be ready to fly by now. And in a few days the Slipstream fleet is going to be thoroughly entangled in the fight with Mavery. If Falcon Formation intends to invade Slipstream, they will be amassing their forces as we speak."

Venera scowled at the little box. Their original plan had been to visit Candesce during its night cycle and let Aubri Mahallan work the magic she swore she could perform with the Sun of Suns. Then they would take the most direct possible course at full speed to Falcon Formation, and the secret shipyard there. Mahallan claimed that she could set a timer on the mechanisms of Candesce that would trigger the correct action after a predetermined number of days and hours.

"Someone's going to have to stay behind," she said. "Wait until after our ships have left and the Gehellens have given chase. Then go into the sun."

"That's what I'm thinking," he said. "Mahallan, of course. And someone to keep her in line. Your man Carrier is the natural choice there."

"Me," she said quickly.

"No, dear, I absolutely—"

"Why? You think I'm going to be safer on board the Rook when you go into battle against Falcon? Besides, love, this is our plan, yours and mine. Who are we to trust to see it through, if not one another? When you go up against that dreadnought, you need to focus on the task at hand and not worry about whether Mahallan's done her job, or whether Lyle Carrier really is loyal. You need someone you can trust."

"And I can trust you."

"Why Chaison, that almost sounded like a question." She laughed and punched him in the arm. "It's the best plan, admit it."

He admitted it and they turned to go. As Chaison pulled the ivory box away from its moorings, something small tumbled out. He didn't notice. Venera waved her lamp around until the thing flashed; there it was, twirling away toward a forward porthole.

She reached out and snatched it out of the air, then held it up between two fingers.

It was a ring, a signet made for a man's hand. The stone was opaque bloodred and the design was of a horse standing on its back legs. The horse had wings.

She slipped the ring over the bulky glove of her suit and followed her husband out of the bridge.

HOWLS OF DELIGHT echoed through the Rook as a spew of gold and jewelry flew from the wooden airlock door. Moments later a man in a red sargasso suit squeezed out waving his hands over his head. A muffled "unh, unh" sounded from inside his round brass helmet, but nobody was paying any attention to him. Crewmen and officers, the press-ganged and the volunteers, all abandoned civility and leaped on the ricocheting treasure. The man in the suit finally levered off his helmet and yelled, "This is just the dregs, boys! There's tons of it there! Tons!"

A light hand descended on Hayden's shoulder. "Hey," said Aubri in his ear. Hayden felt himself flushing, and his heart beat a bit faster.

"Admiral wants to see you," she continued. Peering past him, she said, "They look happy, don't they?"

He had to laugh at the absurd understatement. The men were weeping, fighting over trinkets, screaming, and bouncing off the walls.

Then her previous words penetrated his consciousness. "Fanning wants to see me?"

"Yes, he's in the chart room." She gave him a little push in the lower back and he began to glide through the center of the rioting crewmen.

He bounced off several people and ducked around the worst of the fighting—just in time, as the airlock opened again and another bag of gold was dumped into the air.

The forward section of the ship was relatively empty by the

time Hayden reached the chart room. He knocked and Fanning's muffled voice said, "Come in."

The presence of numerous lanterns did nothing to brighten the can-shaped chamber. To Hayden's surprise, Fanning was alone, hovering with one foot in a strap near the map table. In the dim light he was a study in muted shades, his eyes and the folds of his uniform blended into shadow. He had his arms crossed and seemed to have acquired new lines of care around his eyes and mouth.

"I hear that you have gotten to know our armorer very well," said Fanning, his face deadpan.

How did he know? Was news of Hayden's tryst with Aubri all over the ship already? "Well enough," said Hayden cautiously. What did this mean?

"Maybe. Maybe well enough, for the task I've got in mind." Fanning waved him inside. "Shut the door, if you will." Hayden could still faintly hear the sounds of revelry through the walls after he did so; he glided over to a strap near the admiral's and stuck his foot through it. The two men faced one another over the glowing map table.

"I'm about to let my wife out of my sight for an extended period of time," said Fanning with a cryptic smile. "Months, probably. Do you know the details of our plan? —Why we're here?"

"No more than anybody else, sir."

"Hmm." Fanning stared off into the darkness for a moment. "What this is all about, Mr. Griffin, is defeating a numerically superior foe. When Venera first came to me and told me how she'd put together a collection of old clues and documents, and now believed that radar might be possible in Virga, I wasn't much interested. It's a technology that would have only marginal utility in a fair fight—in daylight, in clear air, I mean. But the evidence that Falcon Formation was about to invade changed everything. With no guidance from the Pilot, we were about to commit a strategic blunder and lose our nation."

"I can't much care about that, sir. I was born in Aerie." It was a half-hearted challenge, but he felt he had to make it.

To his surprise the admiral merely nodded at the revelation. "That explains some things about you, though by no means all. You're a good airman, Hayden, but I've been wondering if I could trust you. We fought side by side on the way out of Gehellen, but you know that proves little."

It was Hayden's turn to look away. "I considered you my enemy for many years," he said.

Fanning smiled. "Well, I probably still am your enemy, politically. But I don't feel like you're a personal enemy of mine, Griffin. And that makes a world of difference in the current situation. Tell me: what do you suppose will happen to Aerie if Falcon Formation conquers Slipstream?"

"It'll be as if we never existed," he replied. Fanning caught his eye and Hayden shrugged. "I know that you're the only hope for my people right now."

"And what do you think of my wife?"

Surprised, Hayden said, "Well, I like her well enough, if that's what you mean."

Fanning sighed. "In order to carry out our plan, I have to leave her here while we make a run for the Gehellen border," he said. "She needs to sneak by the locals, get into the Sun of Suns and turn a switch that will make it possible for us to use those radar units that Aubri Mahallan has constructed. Actually, Venera's not the one who has to throw the switch; she doesn't have the technical expertise. Aubri Mahallan does."

Into the Sun of Suns? And Aubri too? Hayden's face must have betrayed his surprise, because Fanning smiled.

"You understand. I'm not at all comfortable leaving my wife here, Griffin, but it was always her plan and one of us has to supervise Mahallan. Am I right in assuming that you'd feel just as uncomfortable leaving Aubri behind?"

Hayden chewed his lip. He'd been caught totally off guard by the notion that the expedition would be headed for Candesce. Old emotions and new questions were starting to boil up in him. Focusing on the matter at hand, he said, "I suppose. What are you getting at?"

"I want you to fly them into Candesce, and then find a way back to Slipstream when you're done," said Fanning earnestly. "I don't have anybody else I can trust to do the job. In fact, logic tells me you're the very last person on this expedition that I should trust. But I think I'm right about you, so I'm asking you straight up: can I trust you to do it?"

"You're not going to damage Candesce, are you? That would be—"

"Insane. Suicidal. Genocidal." Fanning shook his head. "I don't think we could damage Candesce, even if we wanted to. No, our change will be small, temporary, and unnoticed by anyone in Virga. If you agree to go, you have a chance to guarantee that yourself."

Hayden couldn't believe what he was hearing. Fanning trusted him! Surely he didn't deserve that trust, not with all that he'd planned and tried to do. There was no way he should accept an offer such as this; he was bound to betray it, by honor and the momentum of his long-held purpose.

Yet, Aubri would be going. She might need his protection. It was with a sinking feeling of guilt that he said, "Yes, I'll do it.

"I'll take them in," he said, unsure of whether he believed himself, "and I won't interfere with your plans. As long as Candesce remains safe."

And then, to shame Hayden even further, Fanning smiled at him. "I know I can count on you to bring them home safely," he said.

Hayden smiled, and nodded, but did not believe it of himself.

THE AIR IN the ship was stagnant and heavy by the time the Rook made its rendezvous with the other vessels. All six met under the empty gaze of Carlinth's windows. Huge nets full of treasure were towed to the partially repaired *Tormentor* and its sisters while in the *Rook's* chart room Admiral Fanning read reports of the skirmish with the Gehellens. The dangerous diversionary tactic had worked well and nobody had been killed, although two more ships had suffered hull breaches and their crews were only now able to take off the oxygen masks they had worn while they repaired them. They didn't care; there was jubilation over the treasure and cheers echoed through the sunless streets of Carlinth for the first time in centuries.

While Admiral Fanning shouted an inspirational speech through a bullhorn mounted into the hull of the *Rook*, Hayden camped out in the hangar. With the help of Martor, he was modifying one of the military bikes. Fanning's words came muffled through the walls; nearly everyone else on all the ships had their ears to their hulls and was listening intently.

"... *Falcon Formation will destroy* ..." Fanning was saying as Hayden held up an afterburner housing for Martor to see. "Designed for speed but built for reliability," said Hayden. "Typical military. These are tough bikes, but that extra armor and framing's gotta go."

"... *Only the most extraordinary measures can save* ..."

Martor was wiring two extra saddles onto the bike. "But the armor's insulation too, ain't it?" He tapped the outer shell of the cylinder. "I damn near burnt my foot off on your racer, and there was insulation on that."

"... *Up to us to do the job* ..."

Hayden shrugged. "Saddle, foot straps, and handlebars will be it. Touch the bike at any other point and it'll burn you. But it's the price we pay for decent speed with this baby."

"... *Not only rich, but heroes* ..."

Hayden reached out to flip a gold chain that looped around Martor's neck. "What are you going to do now that you're rich?" In the absence of gravity, the trinkets hung off the boy every which way, making an absurd tangled cloud in front of his face that he wiped to the side every few moments.

"I dunno," he said. "I always been navy. . . . Buy a ship, I guess. Explore."

Hayden grinned. "Hunt pirates?" But Martor shook his head.

"I didn't like the fighting, come right down to it," he said seriously. "Some things are great to talk about, but awful to see or do." He looked away shyly. "But, you know . . . talking about it was great fun. The lads loved my stories and they were easy to think up. I was thinking, maybe when we get back, I might try to learn to read and write."

"You, a storyteller?" Hayden nearly laughed, but he could see that the boy meant it. "That's a great idea," he said. "You'd be good at it. Uh, hand me that wrench, will you?"

"Hi." Hayden looked up as Aubri entered the hangar. She wore practical leather flying gear including an airman's cap with goggles. She swam over to the bike and stopped herself with one hand on it and one on Martor's shoulder. "How are you?" she asked the boy. Martor stammered something incoherent.

"You need to stay out of trouble while we're gone," she told him. "No fighting and no profiteering, you hear? We're going to check up on you when we get back."

Martor smiled at her shyly. "I'll survive—if only to see you again, Ms. Mahallan."

Aubri looked troubled for a moment, then smiled as well. "It's only ten days," she said. "That's how long it'll take for you to get to Falcon Formation, assuming you escape the Gehellen dragnet. And assuming you don't run into anything, and assuming that the navigation team can find your sun and you don't end up wandering around and around in winter til the end of time." She grinned at Martor's expression. "Don't worry. We've got it timed down to the minute."

"That's what worries me," muttered Hayden. This was the weakest part of the plan: Fanning would have to get back to Falcon Formation in time to attack the secret shipyard at an exactly predetermined moment. With all the vagaries of travel in Virga—navigation errors, collisions, breakdowns, fuel shortages, and piracy—it would be a miracle if they could do that in time. By contrast, Hayden's own part in the plan was simple.

Just fly straight into the Sun of Suns.

"And what are you gonna do after?" Martor asked suddenly. Hayden looked over; he'd been focused on his work and didn't know who the boy had asked. He opened his mouth and saw Aubri doing the same.

Hayden shrugged. "Haven't thought that far ahead." He avoided Aubri's gaze, though she also seemed to be looking elsewhere.

THE NIGHTWATCH WAS well under way when Hayden came back to the hangar. The *Rook* and its sisters were creeping toward the outskirts of Leaf's Choir, much more cautiously than when they'd entered. The hatch gang had left the hangar, but the place resounded to the snores of the various *Unseen Hand* crew members who'd been billeted here. Hayden wove in and out of the men who hung like pupae from the walls, floor, and ceiling, until he came to his bike. Then he eased the folded cargo net and heavy coil of cable off his shoulder and parked it in midair next to him. Unfolding his tool kit, he selected a wrench; he dug in his pocket for a moment and brought out some brackets and bolts. Quietly, so as not to wake the men, he proceeded to bolt the brackets onto the back of the bike, over the afterburner.

Hayden had been taken aback by Admiral Fanning's request that he shepherd Venera and Aubri to Candesce—so taken aback that for almost an hour afterward, he hadn't realized what doing that could mean. When he did, it was in the midst of a conversation with the new boatswain; Hayden had lost his train of thought in midsentence, and just stared slack-jawed at the dark hull until the boatswain said, "What's up? You having a stroke or something?"

He'd stammered some sort of reply and extricated himself from the conversation. Going to a porthole, he stared out at the blank nothingness of the sargasso, as an unfamiliar sense of lightness crept over him.

Words whispered in his mind; was he thinking them, or were they a memory of long ago? It might have been his father's voice saying, *"Candesce is the mother of all suns. If Aerie is to have a new sun, its core will come from there."*

No one had ever told Hayden how Candesce gave up its treasures; but he had heard that collecting them was easy. "Like picking fruit," one of the Resistance engineers had said.

Now as he worked as quietly as he could, he reflected upon the irony that Fanning himself would probably approve of what he was doing. If he got caught, he could in fact appeal to the admiral. Carrier was the one more likely to object, but Hayden wasn't afraid of Carrier. No, he was doing this in secret and on his own time not because he was afraid of being caught but because this particular task was his alone. It was personal.

He plucked out the stuffing of the bike's saddle and replaced it with the coiled cargo net. Little tufts of stuffing started floating away and he jammed them in his pockets. Then he reached around the bike's exhaust vent and began coiling the thin cable inside the bike's housing. He wired it in tightly and leaned back with a satisfied smile to admire his work.

Miles and his cronies in the Resistance had been right about one thing: it wasn't what you fought that mattered; the only thing that mattered was what you built. Hayden's own parents had known that, but he'd forgotten it for years after their deaths. Wasted years? —No, they had brought him here, now, to finish something that should have been done a long time ago.

He put away his tools, patted the bike, and headed for the ship's centrifuge to sleep under gravity for the last time in a long while.

19

CANDESCE BLAZED BENEATH Hayden's feet. Even here, hundreds of miles away, the heat from the Sun of Suns was almost intolerable. If he shielded his eyes and looked near the light, Hayden could just make out the bright tails of infalling lakes that were boiling away as they approached that point of incandescence. "They look like comets," Aubri had said when she first saw them.

Other things moved near Candesce. Ships from all the principalities hovered just outside its zone of heat, moving in after sunoff. Among the principalities it was common custom to consign the coffins of the dead to the Sun of Suns; Hayden imagined that they too must become comets at the last, never reaching their goal but evaporating back into the stuff of Virga to become places and people again. So must his mother have gone when Aerie's new sun exploded. His father would have become compost for some Slipstream farm.

Some of the ships hiding in Candesce's light would be funeral vessels. But some had another purpose.

"What are you doing?" Aubri looped an arm around his waist. "You'll burn your eyes out doing that. Come inside."

Hayden had been thinking about the ships that ventured close to Candesce during darkness. They were the harvesters—boats that scrounged the garbage cast out of the Sun of Suns. That garbage was Virga's chief source of sun components. His parents had used fusion-core pieces bought from the principalities to build Aerie's secret sun.

For now, Hayden would not let his speculations run away with him. He let Aubri draw him inside the charcoal-harvester's hut they had found on the outskirts of Leaf's Choir. It perched like an angular bug on the black branch of a tree whose roots lay miles away in darkness. Venera Fanning and Carrier had taken up residence in another harvester's hut some distance away; the bike was hidden there in a ball of sticks. Carrier would not trust Hayden to be its keeper.

He didn't care. It had been strange and wonderful this morning to wake to the first glow of Candesce coming through the one shuttered window of the hut, and find himself wrapped in Aubri's arms and in silence. He had slept with women before; he had never awoken the next morning to find one still with him. So he dwelt in this moment for a long time, breathing slowly and contentedly with her beside him.

The now-familiar hum of the Rook's engines was gone, and not even birdsong signaled dawn here. When Hayden pulled himself over to the window (sleeping Aubri coming along like she was tied to him) he looked out on an astonishing vista. It was as if he were a mite clinging to a giant's hair; for miles in every direction thin black trunks reached toward Candesce from a place of shadow and blackness. The giant's hairs twisted and intertwined as they strained toward the light; many still had branches though the harvesters were systematically stripping them. None had leaves, but life was not completely absent here. Wildflowers nestled in the crooked elbows of branches, and bright green bushes dotted many trunks. Aubri had discovered wild raspberries on this very tree, which might explain why the hut had been positioned here. It was too hot for fish, but a few birds cruised in the distance.

After an hour or two Hayden had started to wonder if there might be a beehive or wasps' nest hidden somewhere nearby, because he'd realized that it wasn't completely silent here. A deep basso thrum filled the air, faint but unwavering. He hadn't heard it last night.

When he mentioned it to Aubri she just shrugged and said, "It's Candesce. Up close it must be like a god singing."

He was in awe of Aubri's knowledge and said so. "You truly know how to control Candesce? You could make it your toy, like a bike?"

She shook her head. "Ride it like a rocket, more like. But Hayden, Candesce was designed before Virga existed. Those designs are still available to anyone willing to leave Virga to find them. I had them with me when I first came here."

That conversation had happened a few hours ago, and had trailed off into kissing and more personal intimations. But her words had stuck with Hayden, growing stranger and stranger the more he thought about them. Now, as they settled in the cooler shadow of the hut, he said, "Why would you have the plans for Candesce with you? Did you already know you were going to visit it?"

She frowned, just slightly, and looked around at the wicker walls. But when she met his gaze again she wore a carefree smile.

"I came here with every piece of information we'd ever collected on Virga," she said. She held up two fingers and pinched them close together. "All that data could be contained in something much smaller than a grain of sand, so why not carry all of it? Of course, when I got here, the memory store was disabled by Candesce's emissions. So I'll have to go on what little I remember when we get there. But I remember enough."

He nodded, still thinking about it. Suddenly Aubri grabbed his arm. "Look!"

Buzzing in the doorway was one of those odd little chrome insects that one saw sometimes. *Tankers,* Aubri had called them. Hayden reached out a hand. "Should I catch it?"

She shook her head. "I don't have my instruments with me, I couldn't study it now." The little tanker spun around and zipped off. A sudden cloud of similar bugs flicked past the window.

"You were right," Hayden said. "They're headed for Candesce."

"Carrying fuel," she said with a nod. "For the Farnsworth Fusors."

———

THEY FLOATED TOGETHER inside the hut, exhausted after making love, and were silent together. He was acutely aware that much had gone unspoken between him and Aubri.

At last he turned and laid his hand, gently, on her breastbone. "Does it listen?" he asked her. He had no need to say what it was.

She shrugged. "I need to be careful. But . . . it doesn't care. Not really. It's just a dumb mechanism."

He thought about that. Then he nodded to the window. "Was this your mission? To visit Candesce?"

She looked him in the eye and said, "No. In fact . . . it's the opposite. If there's anywhere in Virga where I might find a way to free myself from this . . ." She tapped her throat. "Then it would be there."

Hayden shook his head in confusion. "You don't need to be careful about telling me that?"

"No. The assassin-bug only cares whether I tell people what my real mission is. It's not able to care about anything else."

"Not even its own life?"

"It's not alive. So, no." She quirked a smile. "Look at it this way: some things trigger it, some don't. That's all."

"So . . ." He mused. "You think we might find a way to kill it in Candesce?"

"It's why I pushed the Fannings to do this. A selfish reason, maybe." She shrugged, grinning. "But it worked."

He laughed. "Can I help?"

She kissed him. "Just keep guard. I'll do the rest."

"You can help me too," he said seriously. Aubri cocked one eyebrow. "Both of us, really," he added. "Aubri . . . have you actually thought about what you'd do if you got free of that thing? Would you stay, or would you go?"

She hesitated. "Stay," she said finally. "I would stay."

Hayden sighed. He took a moment to compose his thoughts. "I have a reason for going into Candesce too," he told her. He felt his heart lifting as he described his plan to locate sun components in Candesce and return them to Aerie. "I want to finish my parents' work. Light a new sun on the edge of winter, that the people of Aerie can gather around. Let them leave Slipstream and the rest of Meridian behind. Save my people."

It would have sounded like an arrogant, impossible dream to Hayden—had not his mother and father confidently pursued that same dream.

"I'll need an engineer," he said. "You could be invaluable."

"Oh." She looked away. "Is that all you want me for? My engineering skills?"

"No!" He laughed and pulled her to him. "More. I want much more. We could found a new nation together, Aubri. Is that something you could want?"

She wrapped her arms around him and buried her face in his shoulder.

"More than anything," she murmured, "I would want that."

THEY BOTH AWOKE with a start. It was the middle of the night, and absolutely black inside the hut. Somewhere, far in the distance, something had screamed.

"Did you hear that?" Hayden asked. He felt rather than saw Aubri's nod. They both listened in perfect stillness for a while; then she relaxed against him.

"Maybe Venera's cohabitation with Carrier is not so chaste as we'd been led to think," she said.

"Ugh," he said. "Don't say that. I—" He stopped, as a long, ululating sound crept through the night to enwrap the hut.

They were both at the window a second later, peering out into the gloom. "That wasn't any person," said Aubri needlessly. There was nothing to see outside the hut, however—nothing at all, an extravagant blackness Hayden couldn't remember encountering even in winter. For a moment he wondered if the hut had somehow slid backward into the depths of Leaf's Choir. How would they know, before they suffocated?

The cry came again, and this time it was accompanied by the

sound of branches shattering. The roar built—it seemed that entire trees were being thrown aside by something huge that approached through the darkness. The hut began to shake.

Then as quickly as it began, the roaring ended.

They stayed at the window for a long time, but nothing further happened. After an hour or so, a bobbing flashlight beam meandered up the trunk of the tree, and Carrier and Venera appeared. Both looked grim.

"Any ideas?" Carrier asked without preamble. Hayden shook his head.

"Maybe we should stick together tonight," he said. Then, with sudden urgency: "Where's the bike?"

Carrier waved a length of twine Hayden hadn't seen he was holding. It stretched off into the blackness. "I towed it over," he said. "Thought it best." Hayden nodded.

They all crowded into the little hut and sat there looking at one another for a while. "This is ridiculous," Venera said after the uncomfortable interlude had stretched on for fifteen minutes. "We have to do something. Talk, at least."

"I agree," said Aubri.

There was another long silence.

"Let's tell stories," said Venera brightly.

They all stared at her in the feeble glow of the flashlight. "Ghost stories," amended Venera; then she laughed. "Oh, come on. Can you think of a better time to do it?"

Everyone laughed, and a minute later, Hayden found himself relating the story of the black pirate suns, and of the strange monsters reputed to live in winter.

After his turn Venera spoke, and somehow Hayden wasn't surprised when it turned out that she knew lots of such stories, and relished telling them.

In one of Venera's stories, Candesce itself had gone roving one night; the sun had been hungry after shining for so many centuries, and it ate several of the neighboring principalities before being talked out of a further meal by a brash young farm boy. Venera tailored her description to the night's events: the unseen sun passing in majestic noise, a skyscape of sounds, no sign of what had caused its devastation after it returned to its station and lit again.

Aubri clapped her hands when the story ended. "You have hidden talents, Venera!"

The admiral's wife preened, examining her nails with ostentatious care. "I do, don't I?"

"I hope you don't mind my asking, but I've been wondering all along how you managed to convince Chaison to bring you on the expedition." Aubri looked genuinely puzzled. "During our planning sessions he seemed adamant about leaving you behind."

"Ah," said Venera with a smile, "but that was before I blackmailed him."

"Ah—what?" Aubri and Hayden both laughed nervously. Venera waved a hand dismissively.

"Back when he was a student, my Chaison wrote a few seditious pamphlets denouncing the Pilot. Nobody knows that, of course—no one who would talk about it." She eyed Carrier, whose face was as wooden as always. "I found out about it from an old drinking companion of his, and I held it over his head to get him to take me along. That's all." She said this in a modest sort of way.

Hayden couldn't resist a grin. "Chaison Fanning . . . denounced the Pilot?"

Carrier, however, was glaring at Venera. "You never told me about this," he said.

She shrugged. "Why should I?" Venera looked at him archly. "In any case, it's your turn, Lyle. Don't you have any ghost stories to share?"

Carrier stammered something, then looked down. After a moment, he met Venera's eye and said, "Ghost stories are for kids. Things that really happened are far more harrowing than any story."

Some line had been crossed, Hayden thought, but Venera didn't seem to have noticed. She pouted at Carrier and said, "For instance?"

"For instance," he grated, "take the story of a man who discovers that his son doesn't have the stomach for the things that need to be done to protect his people. The boy joins the Resistance of a conquered foe, and tries to convince his father to do it too."

Venera arched an eyebrow. "What's so horrible about that?"

Carrier took a deep breath. "The father plays along with it. In the end the Resistance comes to trust the boy, and of course he trusts his father—enough that one day he tells him the location of the new sun his friends are building. And the father," he said with a grim smile, "he does what any loyal man would do. He tells the Pilot."

Belatedly, Venera was realizing how angry Carrier was. "Youthful zeal," she said. "They grow out of it."

"Only if they live," said Carrier. "Only if they live."

Aubri shifted, half-reaching out to Carrier. "What happened to your son?" she asked quietly.

"He died when the Aerie bastards blew up their new sun," said Carrier; his voice carried no emotion, no inflection at all. "But you know what? If I had to do it all again, I would. Because a loyal citizen of Slipstream will do nothing against the Pilot; will do anything for his nation." Again, he was watching Venera as he said this.

The silence that followed was long and awkward. Aubri tried to salvage the mood by telling a humorous anecdote about her brief days in Rush, but her delivery was wooden and it fell flat.

The damage had been done; all they could do now was sit in silence and wait for dawn. This was just fine as far as Hayden was concerned; he didn't want to talk anymore. He just sat in the corner, nursing his shock.

The man he had sworn to kill sat next to him. For the moment, nothing else mattered.

But then a curious thing happened. As the hours dragged on, Hayden's anger lessened. When Candesce finally ignited in a stuttering dawn Hayden even allowed himself to exchange a wondering glance with Carrier as they gazed out at a vast gash that had opened up in the miles-long trunks of the dead forest.

"It's like some monster was *grazing* on the trees," said Aubri.

"Capital bug?" asked Carrier, but clearly he didn't believe it. Capital bugs were big, the way clouds were big, but they were not strong. Whatever had done this could eat whole cities.

"Candesce, walking," said Venera smugly. They all laughed, and the tension of the night broke.

Later, he watched Carrier and Venera fly back to their hut. Hayden felt curiously light, as if some huge responsibility had been lifted from his shoulders. Lyle Carrier was just a man, after all, and a sad one at that.

What had drained his anger? He wondered about that for a while, seeing Aubri, and Candesce burning at the center of the sky, there was really no doubt. Somehow in the past weeks Hayden had learned to look past yesterday and today. It was the possibility of a future that had changed him.

Maybe he could fulfil his promise to Chaison Fanning after all.

A SWARM OF bikes spiraled through winter. Each flyer had a large magnesium lamp mounted in front of his saddle and great spears of light pierced the gloom as they searched for safe passage. Behind them, recklessly fast, came the expeditionary force itself. Dew beaded on the sleek hulls of the ships and tumbled away in their wakes. Their contrails could have been followed by anyone who cared to pursue them; but the Gehellen navy had given up at the border. The chase had been half-hearted anyway, since the Slipstream ships had gone many miles under cover of night before they were spotted.

Giant multilimbed clouds reared out of the black, too big to circumnavigate. The bikers' flight leader leaned down to let off a sounding rocket and watched as its yellow eye receded into the mist. If it hit anything it would explode in a shower of phosphorous. He watched the contours of the cloud intently, heedless of the icy air tumbling past his limbs. After a moment he waved an all-clear and underscored the rocket's contrail with his own.

Some miles behind the bikes, Chaison Fanning climbed out a side hatch of the Rook and hooked his feet through a ring on the hull. He stared out across a hundred miles of cloud-dotted air at the hint of silver in the darkness that identified Mavery's sun. Faint flickers and flashes lit the sky far up and to one side of that silver area.

It could just be a lightning storm—but the colors were wrong. Some of those pinpricks were red, some vivid orange. The light came from the border between Mavery and winter. It was too far away for Chaison to hear the explosions, of course—but the battle must be huge, and fierce. He should be there.

After a while Travis clambered through the hatch with a blanket fluttering in his good hand. "Begging your pardon, Admiral, sir, but you'll freeze out here," he shouted as he tried to drape the blanket one-handed over Chaison's shoulders.

"Look at it," said Chaison. The tiny stars that signaled explosions had only been able to keep his attention for so long, despite what imagination and reason had told him must be happening there. His gaze had inevitably drifted forward and eventually he'd realized that framed by the cross-hatch lines of bike contrails was the collected light of nations. Half the sky was awash with luminescence in circles too broad to encompass with out-thrown arms. Their outer edges faded to dusk and black, their centers shone sky-blue and here and there a sun appeared for seconds at a time. There were a dozen such realms of light in the cluster of nations known as Meridian, but the farthest countries were hidden behind the nearer.

The pearlescent zone of sky next to Mavery was Slipstream—had been Aerie, once. Obscured behind the Rook's hull was multisunned Falcon Formation. Chaison had climbed around the hull several times to look at it.

"The men want to go," said Travis, nodding at the sparkling battle. "They know we have another destination, but they're not happy."

Chaison sighed. "I'm not happy either. The fleet will be cursing my name that I'm not there. All of us—we've probably been branded traitors by now. If we don't bring back the figureheads of Falcon's flagship, the Pilot will have me publicly flogged. At the very least."

He made sure his feet were anchored, then stood up into the *Rook*'s headwind. "That's where we go," he yelled, pointing to the vast span of light that was Falcon Formation. "And chances are we'll never see the light of Slipstream again. So enjoy the view while you can, Travis!"

"Come inside, sir!"

He shook his head. "When I'm good and ready. Leave me alone."

Travis retreated, a concerned frown on his face.

Chaison Fanning stood alone on the hull of his ship, feeling alone. Venera wasn't with him for the first time in many months, and he found the ache of missing her far more intense than expected. She was infuriating and inescapable; yet she made him smile as often as she outraged him.

They hadn't said good-bye as they parted; but the last of her he'd seen was a backward glance as she looked for him and spotted him watching from the hangar doorway. Her eyes had gone wide, and then she'd turned away again.

He smiled, as the wind tore salty droplets from his eyes and cast them into the vortex of the *Rook*'s contrail.

CANDESCE WAS FADING like an ember when the four travelers climbed into their saddles and Hayden lit the fan-jet's burners. Back became down, and they shot away from the threadlike trees of Leaf's Choir, seemingly straight up toward the sun. Hayden turned for a last look at the harvester's hut, and smiled. Then he adjusted the goggles on his nose and opened the throttle.

They weren't leaving a contrail, he'd noticed. That was probably due to the heat of the air near the Sun of Suns; whatever the reason, they would be less noticeable to the Gehellen cruisers that still patrolled the air here.

—Or so he was able to tell himself for the first ten minutes of the flight; then he saw Carrier's hand waving from the opposite side of the bike.

Hayden craned his neck around the metal cylinder and at first saw only the normal traffic of funeral ships and scroungers cautiously edging toward the sun. After a moment he saw what Carrier had spotted: eight sparks of light rising over the black furze of the sargasso. They were the color of the sun, their backdrop the mauve air of dusk.

Carrier leaned past Venera to shout, "Bigger than bikes!" But smaller than commercial vessels; Hayden nodded. These looked like catamarans—twin engined, with both pilot and gunner. They'd be fast, and they could reduce the bike and its riders to splinters in seconds if they got close enough.

Hayden tapped the throttle, feeling for the bike's response. Then he leaned in as close to the hot metal as he dared and kicked in the afterburner. The women on either side of him pressed their noses to the hull as well while the air began to thunder past and Candesce seemed to get perceptibly brighter.

For a few minutes, that is; then the Sun of Suns began to go out.

It didn't do so all at once. In fact, as Hayden squinted past the handlebars he began to make out structure to the radiance ahead. Candesce, he realized with a start, wasn't one sun but rather a cloud of them. He tried to count them, but they were guttering faster than he could keep up. Each one left a fading red spot and, in the eye, a lozenge of retinal overload.

But the heat remained. He could feel it first in the places where the wind didn't penetrate: in the hollow of his throat, along his calfs. As the minutes passed heat piled up against the bike as if they were pressing into a resilient surface made of exhaust and fire. They crossed fifty miles of air and were swaddled in it; a hundred miles and it was becoming hard to breathe. The commercial ships had fallen behind but the catamarans still followed, their gemlike highlights wavering in the rippling air.

Little flashes started to appear in the corner of Hayden's eye. He was alarmed—was he about to pass out?—and then saw the contrails that were sketching across the sky like meridian lines.

Venera waved frantically. When he caught her eye she held up her hand in a gun-shape. He nodded and began slaloming the bike from side to side, gently at first so as not to shake off his passengers—then more and more violently as bullets stitched the air to all sides.

After a minute the gunfire stopped. He glanced back to see their pursuers close, but keeping a decent distance.

Hayden smiled. There was nowhere for him to go—or so those men thought. They believed that if they hung on his tail long enough he would have to give up. After all, there was no place to hide here, and no way to get inside Candesce.

They were in for a surprise.

A LONG WING of shadow swept into winter behind Sargasso 44. The gnarled black fist of burnt forest, its outlines softened by mist, wasn't much to look at after Leaf's Choir, but it was still a respectable three miles across. The *Rook* and its sisters crept up to the hidden shipyard from its unlit side, their running lights off. Two bikes jetted out of Chaison Fanning's modest flagship to reconnoiter and he waited, not on the bridge but in the hangar, for their return.

Propriety be damned. He glanced at the ticking wall clock, then at his men. Two hours until Falcon's suns dimmed into their night cycle. In two hours the plan would succeed or fail. And everybody knew it, but nobody would speak of it.

They'd installed the radar casting machines in the nose of each ship and tried them. Of course they didn't work—there was only a bright fuzz on the hand-blown cathode ray tubes bolted next to the Rook's pilot station. But as each sister ship turned its own radar on or off, the fuzz had brightened or dimmed. Some sort of invisible energy was in play here. Chaison had been cheered by that tiny hint of future success.

And the men . . . He looked at them again. They'd been running drills for days now to perfect the art of firing blind according to orders from the bridge. The rocketeers looked confident.

He shook his head and laughed. "Men, I don't mean to be insulting, but you look like pirates." Some were wounded, others had hasty repairs to their uniforms to cover sword and bullet holes. It was the jewelry, though, that set them apart from any other crew Chaison had worked with. As battle approached the men had been sneaking off to their lockers to collect their treasures, as if the talismanic weight of future wealth would keep them alive through the coming battle.

It was so far from regulation that he could validly have any one of them whipped for it. Necklaces might get in the eye, or tangle a hand at a crucial moment.

Nobody was going to be disciplined, and they all knew it. Perversely, knowing they knew it pleased Chaison. He felt an affection for this crew he hadn't known for any other he'd worked with.

The bikes' contrails hit the side of the sargasso and vanished. Sargasso 44 was too small and old to have retained a toxic interior, especially with transport ships coming and going and all the industry happening inside it. Chaison had nonetheless insisted that the men on the bikes wear sargasso suits. It would be a fine irony if they were knocked out by fumes and sailed their bikes right into the shipyard.

"Now we wait," said Travis. Chaison shot him an amused look.

"We've been reduced to cliches, have we?" he said.

Travis stammered something but Chaison waved a hand in dismissal. "Don't mind me," he said. "I'm feeling free for the first time in weeks."

"Yes, sir." Then Travis pointed. "Sir? Look."

The bikes were returning already. Falcon's shipyard must lie closer to the sargasso's surface than he'd thought.

"All right." Chaison clapped his hands briskly. "Let's see where we stand."

HAYDEN HAD SEEN clouds bigger than these rising spires, but nothing else, not even the icebergs at Virga's skin, could compare. On the outskirts of Candesce long arcing stanchions connected many glittering transparent spines, which soared into the surrounding air like the threads of the jellyfish that hid in winter clouds. These spines were miles long but they were not anchored to a single solid mass. Candesce, he was surprised to see, was not a thing, but a *region*. Hundreds of objects of all shapes and sizes gleamed within the sphere of air sketched by the giant spires. Candesce was an engine open to the outside world.

So what was Venera's key intended to unlock? They glided in between the outreaching arms at a sedate pace. The enemy catamarans were hanging back, confident in being able to catch the bike and curious to see what Hayden would do. The moment was strangely peaceful, or would have been if not for the savage heat that radiated from those needles of crystal.

"Are they glass?" he wondered aloud. Beside him, Aubri shook her head.

"Diamond," she said. "Re-radiators."

As they passed the spires dim orange glows from the dormant suns revealed traceries of intricate detail farther in: ribs and arching threads of cable, mirrored orbs the size of towns, and long meandering catwalk cages. With all the suns lit, internal reflection and refraction must double and redouble until it was impossible to separate real from mirage. Drowned in light, Candesce would disappear as a physical object. These spars and wires were like the crude ghost of something else that had no form. That something had left, for now—perhaps stalking the distant air to devour a principality or two. But it would return to its den come morning, and then this diamond and iron would give over to a greater reality, one made of light. Any person foolish enough to be here would disappear as well.

Venera and Carrier had raised their heads to stare too. Hayden breathed in little sips; the heat was making him dizzy. "Where?" he asked Aubri with renewed urgency.

She scanned the unlikely bauble of the Sun of Suns. "There." Where she pointed, a dark rectangle lay silhouetted by one of the suns. It was nestled against the diamond point at the base of one of the spines. "That should . . . should be the visitor's center."

Hayden barked a laugh and instantly regretted it as the air seared his throat. "Another tourist station?" But Aubri shook her head.

"This one"—she gasped spasmodically—"is for education and maintenance. No remote control. No tourists."

"Nobody waiting for us, I hope."

She shook her head. Hayden fired up the bike and they shot through the glittering clouds of machine and cable. Now, though, he heard the sound of other engines. The Gehellen catamarans were closing in.

He guided them down the curve of the spire, alert for anything familiar. The rectangle ahead slowly resolved into a boxy structure about thirty meters on a side, made of some white substance. The crystal spike pierced its side, and next to that spot was a small square on the box. Hayden blinked in the wavering air; was it real? Yes, it was there: a door.

Sleek blue spindles eased into sight on either side of the bike: the catamarans. They were like streamlined rockets with outrider jet engines and a cockpit on either side. Both cockpits had heavy machine guns mounted next to them; two of these now swivelled to aim at Hayden's bike. One of the Gehellens gestured for him to turn around.

He waved *yes*, and kept going.

The square door was only yards away when one of the Gehellens fired a warning shot. The bullet *pinged* off the diamond wall.

Hayden took his hands off the bike's handles and raised them in surrender, while at the same time gripping the bike with his knees to steer it.

Another warning shot and this time Hayden looked down to see a puncture in the bike's cowling, inches from Aubri's face.

He reached to cut out the bike's engine and saw Carrier lean casually around the bike. There was a *bang!* loud in the sudden absence of engine noise, and then Carrier was off the bike and spinning in midair and firing again.

Both machine gunners were dead, with identical holes in the center of their foreheads. Carrier was yanking Venera off her saddle; he aimed her at the black outline of the door and pushed himself the other way into open air. Hayden yelled a warning and saw that Aubri was drifting off her own saddle, unconscious. Quickly he took one foot out of its stirrup and lunged for Carrier. They locked hands and he pulled the larger man back just as both catamarans rolled over—trailing spirals of blood—to expose their pilots, and the pilots' machine guns.

Venera had found an indentation in the wall and jammed in the white cylinder she'd been guarding. Both catamaran pilots opened up and bullets flew—sloppily as the recoil moved the gun platforms. A bullet hit Carrier's pistol and it shattered in his hand. He drew back, cursing.

Hayden grabbed Aubri's shirt with one hand and with the other, the bright edge of a suddenly opening door in the diamond wall. He hauled Aubri and the bike into dazzling light to the ear-shattering accompaniment of machine gunfire.

The sound cut off abruptly as the door shut and four humans and a bike tumbled onward into light.

"NOTHING? NOTHING AT all?" Chaison felt sick. The two bike pilots weren't looking much better; the crew had formed a half-dome around them, and were looking stricken as well.

"It's abandoned, sir. Shut down, except for one or two huts that look like security buildings. All the ships are gone—except the tugs, but . . ."

"They weren't just out of sight, hidden somewhere else in the sargasso?"

The two men looked at one another. They made identical shrugs. "Nowhere to put them, sir. We looked. Sir . . . sir, they're gone."

Gone. A Falcon Formation dreadnought and a fleet of new warships were on their way to Slipstream. Maybe they were there already. And Chaison Fanning had taken seven ships that might have helped defend his home, and frittered them away in a useless quest for an advantage that had now proven chimerical. He had lost.

"Sir? What do we do now?"

Chaison Fanning had no answer.

20

COOL AIR WASHED over Hayden's face. For a second he reveled in that, drawing in deep breaths and running his hands over his sweat-stained scalp. Then he turned to Aubri.

"She's not been shot." Carrier was already there, turning her over in midair like something he was inspecting at market. He was right, there was no blood.

Was it the assassin-bug she carried inside her? Had Aubri crossed some invisible line, or begun to say something that had triggered it? For a moment Hayden was sure that such a thing had happened, and that she was dead.

Then Carrier put his hand on her forehead. "Hot. Her pulse is a bit fast. She's not sweating; looks like she fainted from the heat."

Aubri coughed weakly and opened her eyes. "Oh, my head," she murmured. She looked around herself in confusion. "How did we get back to—oh." She pawed at the air, seeking something to hold on to. Hayden put out his hand and she took it, oriented herself upright with respect to the two men. "We're in Candesce."

"And we have a schedule to keep." Venera was waiting impatiently at a nearby doorway. The military bike hung in the air next to her, popping and pinging as it cooled. Hayden counted bullet holes as he pulled Aubri past it; there were at least twenty. A glance told him that the fuel tanks hadn't been punctured, but he wasn't sure about the burners or fan.

"Come on," said Venera. "Mahallan, are you awake enough to do your job?"

"Yes yes," said Aubri peevishly. But Carrier shook his head.

"She needs water and cold compresses," he said. "We don't want her making mistakes at a crucial moment."

Venera drew an ornate watch out of her silk tunic. "We have an hour," she said. "And I'm grudging you that."

They went to explore. It was easy for Hayden to tow Aubri, who seemed feverish and vague; if they'd been under gravity she might not have been able to walk.

"Familiar enough design," Venera said as they moved down a bright, white-walled corridor. The interior of what Aubri had called the visitor's center was divided into numerous chambers and corridors, but only in a loose sort of way by walls and floors that generally did not quite meet. Instead of the enclosed boxes one found under gravity, here were rectangles of pastel-colored material that were suspended in midair to suggest rooms and floors without limiting mobility. In many places you could slip over or under a "wall" into the next room, or glide through a gap in the floor into a room "below." Electric lights in many colors floated here and there, casting shadows that softened the edges of the space. This sort of plan was common in freefall houses and public institutions—but in those places you could always see the ropes or wires that kept the rectangles in place. Hayden could see no means of support for this place's walls.

The rooms were in turn subdivided by screens into different functional areas: eating and cooking alcoves, entertainment centers, even shadowed nooks for sleeping. It didn't take them long to find fresh cold water for Aubri. She splashed it over herself and began to look more alert.

"This place could house hundreds," said Carrier. "Are you sure no one ever comes here? It all looks a bit too well kept."

Aubri laughed. "After maintaining the suns of Candesce, taking care of this place must be light work."

"But light work for whom?"

"For what, you mean. Nothing we're likely to meet while we're here, Carrier. Nothing human."

He looked uneasy. "It's too empty in here. I don't like it."

Hayden searched the cupboards for something to help Aubri. To his surprise he found them well stocked, but the packages and boxes were lettered in an unfamiliar language.

Aubri was shrugging off any more help anyway. "I'm feeling better, Venera. Let's do what we came to do." She glided out of the kitchen alcove and slid through the loop of a large couch sling in the living area next door.

Venera frowned at Aubri. "Well then, what are you waiting for? Where's the . . . bridge, command center, or what have you?"

Aubri gestured at a blank picture frame that took up much of the ceiling. "It's wherever you want it to be, Venera. Watch." She spoke several words in a language Hayden had never heard before, and the picture frame swirled with sudden inner light. Then it seemed to open like a door or window, and Hayden found himself staring into the gleaming interior of Candesce.

Lit by some magical un-light, Candesce's interior teemed with motion like the little creatures Hayden had seen once when he looked through a teacher's microscope. The suns themselves resembled diatoms, spiky and iridescent; though they were quiescent, all around them things like metal flowers were opening. Their petals fanned like the hands of mannered dancers, hundreds of feet wide, to reveal complex buds of machinery that must have hibernated in tungsten cocoons during the day's heat. Bright things poured out of them like seeds from a pod—or bikes from a hangar.

Other things were moving too—long spindly gantries delicately picked crystalline cylinders out of the air and stuck them together end to end. Hayden glimpsed more machinery inside the cylinders.

"What are they doing?" he asked.

"Repairing," said Aubri in a distracted tone. "Rebuilding. Don't look at anything too closely, you could break it."

Hayden sent her a worried glance; he noticed Carrier squinting at her as well. But she looked more alert and lucid than she had a few minutes ago. Hayden decided to let her strange comment go.

"There!" Aubri pointed. Hayden squinted, and saw two catamarans peeling away from the awakening machinery. The Gehellens had been unable to follow their quarry into the Sun of Suns, and were giving up the chase. Maybe they intended to wait for morning outside Candesce's unnerving heart. Well, they would face that possibility when it came.

He turned his attention back to the unfurling non-life of Candesce. Hayden was looking for something, and after a few minutes he spotted it. One of the salvage ships from the principalities was nosing cautiously into the zone of mechanical activity. It flew a flag he'd never seen before, but he ignored that and its strange lines, and watched where it was going.

"Well?" Venera was asking impatiently. "Where are the controls, Mahallan? Hadn't you better get started?"

"Shush, Venera," said Aubri. "I've already started."

Hayden had heard that all the suns in Virga made use of discarded components of Candesce. He wasn't sure what he was expecting to see, but was still surprised when the principality ship swung in close to one of the big translucent cylinders as it was being hoisted near a sun. Some complex exchange had just taken place between the cylinder and one of the flowers; a door had opened in the crystal and swarms of metal insects swirled between it and the "flower." Now another hatch opened in the tesselated side of the sun, and another exchange began.

As it did, the hangar doors of the principality ship flew open and men in sargasso suits—star shapes at this distance—flung themselves into the stream of packages. They wrestled something away from its insectile courier; he could have sworn he'd seen the arcs and bands of that device before, in the half-constructed heart of his parents' new sun.

But wouldn't the metal bugs object? It seemed suicidal folly to try to steal from them. He waited for the swarm to turn and attack the men. After a long moment it began to happen: the remaining drones let go of their cargoes and turned toward the humans, who seemed oblivious to the threat.

Get away, get away, he willed them, even as the steel insects opened their claws and flung themselves at the men.

"Hayden, whatever you're doing, stop it," said Aubri. She was waving her hand in front of his eyes.

"Huh? I'm not doing—look at the ship, there!" He pointed.

Aubri turned and looked toward the principality ship. "Oh. You didn't, did you?" She sounded disappointed. "Let's stop that."

At the last second, the metal insects veered away from the men. "Hayden, stop it," said Aubri. "Look away, Hayden." She grabbed his shoulder and spun him around.

"What are you—"

"Hayden, we're looking into a command mirror. Don't you know what that is?" Aubri saw the blank looks on three faces and sighed. "No, you don't. Sorry. Listen, the command mirrors are the control system for Candesce. Whatever you look at in the mirror, that thing will do what you imagine it doing—insofar as it's capable of it and only inside Candesce. Hayden, you disrupted the movement of those cargo handlers by worrying whether they would stop what they were doing."

Venera laughed. "You made the bugs attack those men! You're meaner than I thought."

"Hey, I didn't mean to—"

"Command mirrors are sensitive," said Aubri. "Maybe it would be better if none of you looked into it for a while. I have to figure out which component of Candesce to switch off. It could take me a few minutes."

The three natives of Virga left the couch and returned to the food-preparation area. "How are we going to know if she's done the job or not?" whispered Carrier. Venera rolled her eyes.

"It's pretty late for you to worry about that. Chaison and I talked about it months ago. Mahallan's not the only person who knows something of old technologies; we had a professor at the University build this." She reached into her tunic and brought out a simple metal tube. It had a switch on its side and a single glass eye, like a bull's-eye lantern. "When I throw this switch, nothing happens. If Mahallan does her job, I'm told that a light will go on inside the tube when you switch it." She flipped the switch. Nothing happened.

"Does she know about this thing?" asked Carrier. Venera snorted derisively.

"No. Why would I tell her?" Idly, she turned the switch again. This time, the glass eye immediately glowed red. Venera yelped in surprise and let go of the rod, which tumbled slowly in the air between them. "Well," she said. "Well, well, well."

Hayden watched as the two of them hovered over the tube, talking excitedly. Venera's little indicator didn't impress him; he was thinking about his experience with the wish-mirror. The glass panels were scattered throughout this building; he tried to remember the words Aubri had used to light hers.

"Listen," he said, "the bike is full of bullet holes. If something's broken we need to know now, while there's still time to fix it. I'm not sure this place is going to still be safe for us once the suns start coming back on." Mother and Father had talked a lot about radiation; he remembered that. Even if it remained cool in here throughout the day, it might be lethally radioactive while the suns were operating.

Carrier was nodding. "Go check it out, then."

Hayden took one more look at Aubri. She was perched in mid-air, staring at the glowing images on the screen. Her face was masklike, expressionless.

Heart pounding, Hayden slipped under a wall and away from the plots of Slipstream.

"WHEN YOU'RE OUT of ideas, just give another order." Chaison Fanning recalled the cynical advice of one of his academy teachers as the helmsman moved to execute his latest command. The expeditionary force was sweeping the air around Sargasso 44 using sophisticated spiral search patterns. He had all the bikes out hunting for contrails. It was all he knew to do. Meanwhile he retained a mask of professional calm, as though he'd expected this and had a plan. He had no plan. There was nothing left but to run for home.

"Bike brigade sixteen reports no sightings, sir," reported the semaphore team. Chaison nodded. There was nothing but gray mist outside the forward portholes. The clouds on the edge of winter were to have been his greatest advantage if he'd succeeded in luring the Falcon Formation ships out of their den. Ironically, that dense pack of wraithlike mists was now obscuring any chance he had of finding where the enemy had gone.

The light outside the portholes was fading: night was coming to Falcon. The Formation synchronized its day and night cycle with Candesce, so the Sun of Suns must be going out now too. If Aubri Mahallan had done her job, in a few minutes the subtle distortions of space-time ringing out from Candesce would cease. This night, technologies long banned in Virga would become possible here again. Radar might now work.

The radar man Mahallan had trained was looking at him expectantly. Chaison gave a half-smile. Why not? "Begin radar sweep," he said, chin on his fist. It was nice to know that his voice was still calm, despite his desperate disappointment.

Even now the newly minted Falcon dreadnought might be bearing down on Rush. There was nothing in Slipstream that could stop it. The Pilot richly deserved to be deposed—Chaison knew he would get no argument from his men on that score— but Falcon Formation would eat everything if it conquered Slipstream. They had done it before: art would be repainted according to the arbitrary standards of the bureaucracy, literature rewritten to match the ideology of the Collective. Architecture would be chipped away and eventually, even the language itself distorted to match Falcon's vision of a perfect world.

A horrible sick feeling filled Chaison. He wondered if the citizens of Aerie had felt that way when the Pilot had uttered his ultimatum to them.

A younger Chaison Fanning would never have considered such a thing.

"It's working!" He shot the radar man an annoyed look. "Sorry, sir. I mean, we have a signal. The screen is clear! Look."

Despite himself Chaison was intrigued. Aubri Mahallan had made toy versions of the system that showed how things were supposed to look. Now as he unstrapped himself and glided over he saw little glowing smudges on the two green circles of the display, very similar to the ones Mahallan had displayed. She had drilled the bridge staff in the meanings of the various shapes, and so Chaison had no difficulty in recognizing the other ships of the expeditionary force as spindle-shaped lozenges of lighter green. The two screens showed the results from rotating beams that were at right angles to one another. Comparing them, you could roughly guess at the position of objects in three-dimensional space.

The bridge staff were all staring over his shoulder. Chaison ignored them. "What's that?" he asked, pointing at a broad smudge well behind the centerpoint that represented the *Rook*.

"I believe that's the sargasso, sir."

"Hmm." He stared at the display for a few seconds. "All right then," he said, "if these shapes are us," he pointed, "and that shape is the sargasso," he pointed again, "then what, exactly, is *that?*"

Right at the edge of the displays, a collection of tiny dots scintillated. One by one they were leaving the screen, which suggested they were moving very quickly.

Chaison and the radar man looked at one another. Then the admiral jumped back to his seat. "All hands! Prepare for maximum acceleration! Recall all bikes! Semaphore team, order all ships to activate their radar! Tell them, if you want to have a place to spend that treasure you're wearing, then follow us now!"

AFTER CHECKING OUT the bike and spending an hour or so repairing it, Hayden drifted back into the corridors of the station. He dithered over whether to look in on Aubri—but she had insisted that only she could find a way to excise the dark thing coiled in her throat. He didn't want to interrupt her in that crucial task. No, he had his own responsibility, and he had best fulfil it.

He found a small room far from the place where Aubri was working. It was dark here, but there was a command mirror on the wall. He strapped himself opposite it and tried to remember the words Aubri had spoken to activate hers.

It took several tries, but soon the rectangle began to glow. "Huh." Hayden couldn't believe he was actually here, in Candesce, doing something no one had ever told him was even possible. Controlling the Sun of Suns itself.

The twisting ballet of Candesce's night machines revealed itself to him and he scanned the air for the things he sought. It seemed like many years since he had played in the half-built sun while his mother ordered construction crews about. Not that long a time, in adult terms. He remembered the day the precious inner components had arrived, shipped at horrendous expense and in secret from the principalities of Candesce. The crates with their exotic stamps and lettering were more interesting to Hayden than their contents, but he remembered those as well. Now, he examined the interior of Candesce looking for similar mechanisms.

From what he'd seen earlier, Hayden had surmised that the crystalline cylinders were factories of a sort, manufacturing new pieces for the suns. Now as he examined them—the display zooming into fine focus if he wished it to, zooming out again just as easily—he began to understand the logic of the Sun of Suns. Those tiny glittering clouds spiraling into the cylinders, they were the bugs Aubri had called tankers, only here they swarmed by the million. They were bringing in supplies. Inside the cylinders and unfolded metal flowers, the metal foremen and laborers of Candesce forged new wicks for the sun, and when they were done they handed them off to other machines that installed them.

All that Hayden had to do was locate the pieces he wanted and then imagine them being brought here. *Park them outside the door,* he commanded. With mounting excitement he watched as his orders were obeyed.

No wonder no one was allowed in here! You could destroy Candesce on a whim from this place; and if Candesce went, so would go all of Virga.

The thought was disturbing. Hayden's excitement soured as he watched the slow parade of machines sidle through the air toward the visitor's center. This was too easy—there was too much power to be had here. It made him wonder what Venera Fanning would do once this episode was over. Or what the Pilot of Slipstream would do if he demanded and received the Candesce key from the Fannings.

After assuring himself that the machines were doing as he'd asked, Hayden left the little room. He flipped over and under walls, around floors, hurrying back to the entrance and his bike.

Double-check the bike to make sure it was flight-worthy. Tie the sun components he'd found into the cargo net and tie it to the back of the bike. And then . . . rehearse what he was going to say to the others when they saw what he'd acquired.

They would need convincing—particularly Carrier. His plan was to get to the man through his mistress, Venera. If he could convince her that these components were his just payment for his part in this adventure, then maybe she could restrain Carrier.

He flipped around a corner and spotted the entrance.

It was open.

Hayden slowed down and cautiously drew his sword. Had the Gehellens somehow managed to force the door? That didn't seem likely; why now, after so many centuries? Or maybe—the thought gave him a chill—maybe now that it was unlocked, anyone could get in here. He hadn't thought of that. Were the Gehellen airmen inside?

Hayden could see the first of the packages he'd ordered bobbing in the darkness outside. Despite his worry, the sight made him smile. He looked around the room. There was the bike, seemingly untouched. There was no one else in sight. He moved carefully toward the door.

Carrier swung in from outside to brace himself on the two

sides of the entrance. Night was at his back. "So there you are," he said. "I wondered what exactly you were going to try. Of course, I had no doubt that you'd try something."

"This doesn't concern you," said Hayden.

"A new sun for Aerie does concern me."

Carrier drew his sword.

THE *ROOK* ROARED through blackness with exhilarating recklessness. Chaison imagined statutes and naval regulations fluttering in the ship's wake, centuries of rules about how fast to travel in cloud all broken in an instant. He pushed the Rook to one hundred miles an hour, then two hundred, and watched the dots of the Falcon Formation navy grow into circles, then distinct ship shapes.

The bridge crew were white-faced. Travis perched next to Chaison, his lips drawn thin while his fingers gripped the edge of the chair. Logic said they would run into something at this speed—but of everyone in the bridge, it was the radar man who was now the calmest. "Bear two degrees to port, five south," he would say, or "six degrees starboard right now." The pilot, flying blind, obeyed with frantic sweeps of the wheels.

"Getting secondary signals," said the radar man abruptly. "Just like she said."

"All right." Chaison smiled grimly. "You know what to do."

Falcon's fleet was creeping slowly through an ocean of cloud; nobody could tell how far the mist extended. He didn't need the cloud, of course, it was night anyway. But if they could strand the target vessels of the Falcon fleet in opaque fog they would still be vulnerable when daylight returned. —If the battle still raged at that point.

Meanwhile, he had to deny the enemy all their other assets. "Line up on those bikes," he said. " 'Ware our other ships, they'll be doing the same. We're going to scrape the sentries off Falcon's fleet like old scabs."

The engines whined as they accelerated one more notch. There was a sudden dark flicker outside the portholes and then *bang!* The ship twitched to the impact, but ran on.

Chaison winced. They were running over the Falcon Formation's sentry bikes. As when the *Tormentor's* bikes had flown ahead to watch for obstacles—unsuccessfully, in that case—the Falcon fleet was feeling its way by sending them ahead and to the sides. Lacking radar, the bikes were its only means of safe travel through darkness and cloud.

Another crash against the hull, and another. On the radar Chaison could see the shapes of *Rook's* sister ships overtaking the dots of Falcon bikes, which simply vanished as they passed.

Ahead was the huge but indistinct blob that must be the new dreadnought—a weapon of terror no one from Slipstream had ever seen except in blurry photos. Ironically, they were unlikely to see it now. If all went well the men of Slipstream would never make visual contact with the enemy they were destroying.

The *Rook* swept out and around in a great circle. Chaison was reassured to see no clear air ahead as they came around for another pass. "Prepare to deploy mines," he said. Then, "Brake, brake!" He heard the flutter-chop of the braking sails being thrust out of the hull and then he was nose-down, Travis clinging to the back of the chair as the *Rook* groaned and began to decelerate. "Engines off!"

In sudden silence save for the rush of wind and the whuffing breath of the braking sails, the *Rook* slid past the invisible dreadnought and directly into its path.

"Deploy mines! Out out out now now now!"

There was the sound of wind in open hangar doors, and a distant rattle like some monster clearing its throat.

Then thunder.

21

A RIBBON OF Hayden's blood twisted in the center of the room, as if blindly trying to find him. Carrier had connected with a slash to his cheek.

"Wait!" Hayden backed away. The man's first lunge had taken him by surprise, but he had his own sword out now. Yes, it would be satisfying to counterattack Carrier, who had killed his family; so much more satisfying to change his mind.

"You still have a chance to save yourself," said Hayden as Carrier braced himself for another leap.

"Save myself?" Carrier laughed. "I'm the better swordsman by far!"

"That's not what I mean. I'm talking about your son."

Carrier's face went ashen white. "Wh—"

"You betrayed him! Betrayed him and had him killed. And it eats away at you. Your life has been barren since that moment, hasn't it? Anyone can see it in the way you walk, hear it in the tone of your voice. I just didn't know *why*, until the other night."

"My life's not your concern," grated Carrier. "Look to your own."

"You don't believe there's any way you could make up for what you did to him. I'm saying there is. Can you even imagine such a thing anymore? There *is*."

Carrier visibly fought to control himself. "No."

"How would your son feel if he knew that, in the end, you took back your choice? —That you let his project succeed?"

Now Carrier was silent, his eyes wide.

"Slipstream will leave Aerie in a few years. Why not leave a viable nation behind? That was all he wanted. Let me bring back the pieces of a new sun for my people; it won't be ready in time to be a threat to you. Why not? Your son's spirit will be reborn in that light. You'll have him back in that way. It's not too late."

Carrier lowered his sword, his face eloquently puzzled at a possibility he'd never even considered. Then, gradually, Hayden saw his features harden again, as if in the end his guilt were all he was really comfortable with.

"Nice try!" he shouted, and then he leaped again.

FOUR SLIPSTREAM CRUISERS glided silently through the dark. Horns and gunshots sounded in discontinuous bedlam, but in the impenetrable night it was impossible to put direction or distance to any of the sounds.

The courses of the cruisers began to diverge; observers on one ship watched the other silhouettes flicker and fade into the clouds. Now odd objects began twirling past, momentarily flame-lit: men, their limbs akimbo; smouldering flinders; the crumpled rings of military bikes. They shot by the ships with frightening speed, yet it was not they that moved, but the ships.

An order went out: *brake!* The cruiser strained and shook as the shuttlecock vanes of the braking sails tumbled into the airstream.

Next came the hardest thing. It was drilled into the minds and reflexes of naval gunnery teams never to fire a rocket blindly. Once loosed, ordnance just kept on going and in any military engagement in populated air, shots that missed the enemy would eventually hit another friendly ship—or civilians.

For weeks Admiral Fanning had tried to undo this training. Now the rocket teams waited tensely for the order, uneasily watching each other, the walls, the rocket racks—anything but the depthless black outside the square firing ports. When the order came it was a shock, however expected it had been. "Ten degrees by forty-three!" barked the officer at the speaking tube. The team cranked the racks around and up. "Fire!"

Sere lines of orange light leapt into the mist—five, ten, fifteen in less than a second. Backwashing fumes billowed over the team. Used to this, nobody coughed or moved. Mist swallowed the contrails.

The cruiser's engines whined into life; it was already turning by the time chattering bangs indicated a hit. By the time the enemy triangulated on the incoming rockets' contrails and fired back, the *Rook* would be gone.

Chaison Fanning looked up from the radar screens. Travis was staring at the glowing green circles, shaking his head minutely and muttering. Chaison caught his eye and smiled.

"Look at them all," said the officer. Travis had circles under his eyes; evidently his injured arm was giving him trouble but he hadn't complained, probably hadn't even noticed.

Look at them all. The navy of Falcon Formation spread away into indeterminacy in all directions; knots, clusters, and clouds of ships of all sizes and designations. The *Rook* was weaving recklessly through them at two hundred miles an hour, a falcon among pigeons. The enemy would see the glow of the cruiser's engines for seconds at a time as it lunged out of nothing and before they could train their weapons on it, it would be gone again.

"Admiral, sir!" He glanced back to see the boy Martor saluting him from the doorway. "Sir, we've had to restrain Slew."

"What? The head carpenter? What's he done?"

"Running around telling us to stop. Said it weren't natural to fight a battle this way." The old Martor would have smirked while he reported something like this; this new version, his side still taped up where Chaison had removed a bullet, looked very serious as he held his salute.

"Very good. Keep him out of our way until after the battle." He turned back to the radar.

"These vessels," said Chaison, indicating some boxy shapes on the edge of the screen. "They're troop carriers, aren't they?"

Travis nodded. "They've got the profile. No reason to send those on maneuvers. And they move like they're full."

The fleet had been driving in the direction of Slipstream. Venera's spies had been right, it was an invasion force. Of course, Chaison had known the spies' reports were accurate—or he would never have undertaken this mad escapade. Somehow, though, seeing the ships and their heading made him furious with Falcon Formation for the first time. As though he hadn't really known at all.

"More mines, sir. We can avoid the cloud this time, but they're going to disperse soon. It'll be harder to find a way around them next time."

"Hmmph." The dreadnought had not stopped when it realized Rook had mined the air ahead of it. To Chaison's astonishment and dismay, the huge vessel had simply plowed through the cloud, enduring a staccato barrage of explosions without apparent effect. It was not to be stopped that way; and if it kept going, sooner or later it would reach clear air, and Slipstream's advantage would diminish.

So Chaison was targeting its engines. He'd emptied barrage after barrage of rockets into them but so far the dreadnought hadn't slowed significantly. Having realized what was happening—if not how it was being done—Falcon was now mining the air around their ships. The mines were tuned to ignore impacts at less than fifty miles an hour, so the fleet continued to grind forward and maneuvering became harder and harder for Slipstream.

"I want to stop the dreadnought," said Chaison, "but I want those troop carriers taken out as well. Without them there's no occupying force." He gave the order to the semaphore team, who had reluctantly given up their flags and were cheerlessly using an electromagnetic signaling technique called "radio telegraph" that was based on Mahallan's radar. It let the Slipstream ships communicate instantly, with no interference from clouds.

Travis glanced up at Chaison. "Bit of a surprise about Slew, isn't it?"

Both men smiled—and Chaison was about to say something

witty when the green light of a thousand tumbling flares burst through the portholes. The Rook had entered clear air.

HAYDEN LEAPT TO the side careless of where he might end up. Free of doubt now, Venera's spymaster was relentless, economical in his movements, and expressionless as he pursued Hayden around the room.

It didn't help that this place was so bare of ornament. The antechamber where the bike had been left had only a few hand-straps on the walls, ceiling, and floor, as well as some cabinets and shelves that didn't make good purchase. The key to a gravity-free sword fight was never to let yourself become stranded in midair—and in this place, that was not so easy. As they circled one another Hayden tried to ensure that he had one hand or foot on a strap or piece of furniture at all times. With blank wall at your back, all you could do was jump straight out, and the enemy would know in advance where you were going. And when you dove at your enemy, you made your whole body a missile but you also could not stop until you'd made contact with something; your opponent would attempt to ensure that the something was his sword blade.

Carrier seemed unhurried. There was no indication that adrenaline powered him; it was more like he was going through a set of mechanical motions, cut, parry, dodge, cut. He would keep doing it until Hayden was dead.

Hayden dove for the door but Carrier anticipated him. They came together in the center of the room, thrusting with their sword-arms while reaching to try to catch sleeve or foot with the other hand. For frantic seconds they tumbled and then a thrust by Carrier took Hayden through the left bicep. He shouted at the jolt of pain.

Carrier gave a grunt of satisfaction. Hayden tried to pull back but Carrier fluidly moved with him, keeping the blade embedded in flesh as Hayden cursed.

Not so gracefully, Carrier flailed at a wall-strap with his other hand. He caught it—barely—and swung his sword, with Hayden attached, outward. Hayden knew he was seconds away from being placed motionless in midair, out of reach of the walls, at which point Carrier could bounce around and cut him to pieces at his leisure.

Desperately Hayden let go of his own sword, grabbed the blade of Carrier's, and pushed. The metal slid out of his skin, dotting the air with blood, and then Carrier yanked it out of his grasp, slicing Hayden's fingers open to the bone. Hayden writhed out of the way of the backhanded cut that followed. He tried to snatch his own sword out of the air but it had drifted too far away. He saw then that he really was stranded, two meters from the nearest handhold.

Carrier sneered and stood up from the wall-strap which he'd hooked with his foot. Hayden twisted around again and managed to kick the older man in the face. As Carrier cursed and spat blood, Hayden very slowly drifted across the room.

Carrier dove past him again with a vicious slash. Hayden did as Katcheran had drilled him to do: he rolled into a ball in the air and presented his feet to the blade. The sword chopped right through the tough leather but a cut foot wasn't going to kill him. And the pressure of the blow put him closer to the bike.

His sword twinkled as it turned on the far side of the room. Carrier perched at the inner door now, and was carefully lining up his next jump. This time he would thrust rather than cut, Hayden knew; there would be no evading the blow.

He stretched out, reaching for the bike. Carrier laughed. "Even if you can reach that what are you going to do?" he asked. "Throw it at me? Bounce somewhere? I'll never let you get your sword, you know."

Hayden's taut fingers brushed the curving metal of the bike. And Carrier jumped.

———

"FULL ABOUT!" CHAISON dove for the portholes, missed his grip, and banged his chin on the wall. He pressed his face up against the glass, staring out at vast sensual curves of green-lit cloud. He still had the advantage here, because the dozens of flares drifting out of the cloudbanks lit only a small volume; the plan had counted on the fact that there were many smaller clouds dotting the edge of winter. His ships could dive through them with impunity. But while the six battered, obsolete Slipstream vessels still had an advantage of speed and maneuverability here, it wouldn't be enough. Falcon simply had too many ships.

The *Rook* pivoted in midcourse, air tearing at its hull, and Chaison strained to catch a glimpse of what was behind her. Lurid tumbles of cloud; arms and arches of vapor. And emerging from it only one other ship, so far.

"All batteries, target that ship! Don't give it a chance to sound!"

Too late. Even as the first rockets lurched toward the distant cruiser, a faint echo of its clear-air signal came to Chaison's ears. He cursed. "Take it out!" The noise of battle would prevent most of the other vessels from hearing that lone horn—but if only one picked it up, it would repeat it, and so would every other one that heard. Soon the clouds would be ringing with the signal that open air had been found.

He went back to the radar display. The shadow of Falcon Formation's giant ship still lay some miles inside the cloud, and it was slowing. "All ships: put everything into stopping the dreadnought. Release parachute nets ahead of it, mine the air—*anything!*"

—Hammering sound of bullets hitting the hull. Sudden flame of a missile veering past. He heard the *Rook*'s own machine-gunners opening up at something. "Put us back in the cloud deck," Chaison commanded as he regained his chair.

The ship took a hit before they managed to escape into the mist. There was chaos over the speaking tube for about a minute, then an all-clear. Chaison frowned at the indiscipline, but most of his attention was on the radar.

They had arrived at this battle late. Daybreak was little more than an hour away. By the time Falcon's suns were glowing full, Venera would have had Mahallan switch Candesce's defensive systems back on.

During this long night of dark maneuvering, Slipstream had thrown the Falcon Formation fleet into disarray, had wiped out its bikes and smaller vessels, and scored crippling blows on a number of midsize ships. The troop carriers appeared damaged as well. But that was all—and it was nothing.

If they didn't score a decisive blow to Falcon's invasion plans in the next minutes, the whole mission would have been for nothing.

"Sir!" It was the radar man. "We—I think we've lost a ship."

Chaison looked where he was pointing. One of the fast-moving dots on the screens had broken in two pieces. As he watched, the pieces subdivided and disintegrated. The dots dissolved into smudges on the screens.

"Any idea who that was?" Chaison asked into the sudden silence. He scowled at the display. *The damn fools flirted with a mine cloud.*

There was silence in the bridge; the men glanced at one another. "Back to the dreadnought," Chaison commanded. "I want the cutters packed with explosives—warheads, bullets, everything we've got. Rockets haven't had much effect on it, so we're going to ram something bigger down its throat."

And if those don't work, we'll make the Rook itself into a missile.

CARRIER JUMPED.

Hayden grabbed the seam of the bike's saddle and pulled as hard as he could.

The cargo net he'd stuffed under the saddle flowered into the air and he spun as best he could, throwing it at Carrier. The spymaster shouted and tried to evade it but he was in midleap now and there was nothing he could do. Tangled, swearing furiously, he bounced off the bike and back into the air.

Hayden planted both feet on the metal and pushed. The dive took him across the length of the room and he plucked his sword out of the air before spinning and kicking off from the far wall. Carrier was struggling to free his sword from the net; his awkward parry went bad and suddenly he was staring down at Hayden's sword which stuck out of his chest.

"Wh—" He tried to reach up; failed, and looked in Hayden's eyes. Carrier was trying to speak.

"Don't talk to me," said Hayden. "The one you need to explain yourself to isn't here. You'll see him soon enough." He let go of the sword, turned, and jumped back to the bike. Reaching around the exhaust vent, he caught a loop of the thin cable he'd stashed there before they had left the Rook. He pulled out the loop and began to unreel it.

When he was sure Lyle Carrier was dead he unwove the net from around him, and attached the cord to it. Then he moved to the door and looked for the first of the packages he'd ordered Candesce to provide.

AUBRI MAHALLAN WAS acting very nervous, and it was driving Venera crazy. After the tenth time that the woman bounced a circuit around the room, Venera said, "Is there something you need to do?"

Mahallan shook her head, becoming very still. "No. Nothing."

"Then settle down. It's not your husband who's in the middle of a battle right now. Your man's just down the hall."

"He's not my man," said Aubri quickly.

Venera raised an eyebrow. "Oh? He thinks he is."

Now Mahallan looked uncomfortable; as far as Venera was concerned, that was a definite improvement.

"You don't think the waiting gets to me?" continued Venera. She crossed her arms, glancing once at the indicator device she had stashed in her bag by one wall. It still glowed steadily. As long as it was on, Chaison retained his advantage; so in a sense, its light was her lifeline to him. But she would have to shut it down soon, when dawn came.

"I'm not you," said Aubri, scowling. "I've done a great deal for your little project, Venera. Have you ever asked yourself what I'm going to get out of all this?"

Venera shrugged. "You never asked for anything, did you? Which is odd, except that you're an exile for whom everywhere is the same. . . . But why not take Hayden Griffin? He's a fine catch for someone from the servant classes. Is that your problem with him? That he's not one of your own kind?"

"You wouldn't understand," said Mahallan.

Venera laughed. "On more than one occasion I've been told that my problem is that I do understand people, I just don't feel for them. Which is probably true. But you're right, I don't get it. We've completed our project, you're free and as rich as you want to be. In just a few minutes you can switch the sun's defenses back on, and then all you have to do is take your money and your man and go enjoy yourself. What could be simpler?"

Mahallan looked startled. "Is it time already?"

Venera checked her pocket watch. "Getting there."

"Okay." Aubri smiled; it seemed a bit forced to Venera. Mahallan glided over to the command mirror. "I'll get ready to shut it down, then," she said brightly.

"All right." Venera watched her, keeping her face neutral. As the strange outsider woman gazed into the mirror, Venera let herself drift over to her bag. She made sure that she could see the glow of her indicator, and Mahallan, without turning her head.

Just in case, she loosened the scabbard of her sword.

THE DREADNOUGHT WAS tangled in parachutes and trailed debris in a long smoking beard of rope and timber. Its engines were tangled knots of metal belching black smoke into the air. Its rudders were useless flags.

There were no significant holes in its hull.

The mist ahead of it was brightening as it approached open,

flare-lit air. Just a few hundred yards and it would be free of the nightmarish disadvantage of the clouds. Its enemy would no longer be invisible. One shot from the rifled ten-inch guns mounted along its sides and the smaller ships would be matchwood. All it needed was the sight lines.

As the *Tormentor* slid into position to unloose a salvo, the dreadnought got its chance. The Slipstream ship had been relying on the veils of mist to let it do what it had done ten times already: stand off, hidden, and pummel the larger vessel before moving to another firing position. This time, though, the intervening clouds proved to be just a thin curtain and when it parted suddenly, the *Tormentor* was unluckily right in the way of a searchlight. The dreadnought's gunners had been waiting for this.

The first shell convulsed the cruiser with an internal explosion. The next broke it in half. Six more followed, pulverizing the twisting remains before the shockwave from the first blast had died out. The *Tormentor* and all its men were simply erased from the sky.

Rockets continued to rain on the dreadnought from other directions—but the gun crews were emboldened now and began firing wildly. If some of their own ships were close by, well, too bad; any sane Falcon Formation craft would be headed for that brightening in the clouds by now. Only the enemy would lurk in the darkness, and so into that darkness they fired.

A lucky shell clipped the *Unseen Hand*'s stern and blew its engines off. Its crew bailed out, flapping away with foot-wings, but the *Hand*'s captain was old, mean-tempered Hieronymous Flosk. He drew a pistol and aimed it at the bridge door. "Any man who tries to leave, dies!" he bellowed. "We're going in! Man your posts, you cowards! Make your lives count for something!"

The *Hand* still had steering and was doing over a hundred miles an hour. When it lunged out of the cloudbank the dreadnought's gunners had only a few seconds to fire and the one shell that hit bounced off the cruiser's streamlined hull. Then the *Unseen Hand* slammed into the side of the great ship and exploded.

In a zone of half-mist, where towering banks of cloud interspersed with pockets of clarity, the dreadnought shuddered and sighed to a stop.

"SIR." THE RADAR man sounded puzzled. Chaison looked up from trying to catch the flailing straps of his seat belt. The whole ship was rattling now as their airspeed peeled away planks behind the open wound of the hangar doors. They had to reduce their velocity, but a few bikes and cutters were still pursuing.

The radar man held up his chronometer. "Sir, it's daybreak in Falcon. The radar shouldn't be working anymore, but it's holding steady."

Chaison stared at him. What did this mean? Was Venera giving him a gift of extra time? Or had something gone wrong in Candesce?

He might have radar for as long as he needed it . . . or it might cut out at any second. It no longer mattered: daylight was here.

The clouds were an abyss of pearl dotted with instants of black—men, burnt-out flares, and wreckage only half-glimpsed as the Rook shot by them. And coalescing out of the writhing whiteness were the iron contours of the dreadnought. The great ship seemed determined to keep a pall of night around itself; it had drawn a cloak of smoke and debris around its hull. With each broadside it let loose, the smoke thickened.

"I bet they never thought of this," Travis said, shaking his head. "Rockets take their exhaust with them when they go. But guns . . . They're blinding themselves with smoke."

"It's a gift," said Chaison. "Let's take it while it's offered." He moved to the speaking tube. "Are the cutters loaded and ready? Good. Wait until I give the order and then let them fly."

The Rook spiraled around the motionless dreadnought just ahead of cannonades of deadly fire. Chaison stared through the portholes, looking for any vulnerable spot through the wavering lines of tracer rounds that subdivided the air. Enemy bikes shot past, snarling like hornets, and the *Rook* bucked to some sort of impact.

"Enemy closing from all directions, sir," said the radar man. "It looks like they've got another of ours boxed in too . . . I think it's the *Arrest*. I can't see the *Severance*, but they're still broadcasting."

"Bring us closer," Chaison told the pilot. He'd seen what he was looking for—a triangular dent, yards wide, in the hull of the dreadnought. The surrounding metal was scored and burnt; something bigger than a rocket had impacted there. He reached for the speaking tube—

—And everything spun and hit at him, walls furniture the men rebounding with the shock of a tremendous explosion. Half-deafened, Chaison shook himself and grabbed for a handhold, abstractly noticing that the bridge doors were twisted, half-ajar. *Slew's not going to fix this one,* he thought.

He struggled back to the commander's chair. The pilot was unconscious and Travis was shoving him aside to reach the controls. Chaison grabbed the speaking tube and shouted, "Report, report!"

A thin voice on the other end said, "They're dead."

"Who's dead?"

"The . . . everybody that was in the hangar, sir."

"Is this Martor? What about the cutters?"

"One's intact, sir." There was a pause. "I'll take it out, sir."

Chaison turned away for a moment, unable to speak. "Son," he said, "just aim it and jump clear. Make sure you've got a pair of wings and just get out of there. That's an order."

"Yes, sir."

Travis had the ship under control and was banking tightly to avoid a fusillade of shells from the dreadnought. "Sir, here comes the rest of Falcon," he said tightly. Chaison glanced at the portholes and saw a white sky crowded with ships. Just then a large shape obscured the view: the explosives-laden cutter had soared ahead of the *Rook* and was curving down toward the iron monstrosity.

Chaison couldn't look away. Tracer rounds and the shocked air of shell fire outlined the cutter; he saw pieces of its armor shattering and flying away. Then it was suddenly not there, and Chaison blinked away afterimages of a flash that must have been visible for miles.

The roar overtook the *Rook*, shaking the hull and starring another porthole. Chaison simply stared at the absence and coiling serpents of smoke. He felt a crush of grief and for a few moments was paralyzed, unable to think.

But everything rested on his decision. He shook off his feelings and turned to Travis.

"Prepare to scuttle the ship," he said.

22

HAYDEN TIED THE last of the sun components into the cargo net. His hands were shaking. As he fumbled with the cords, he noticed his shadow, hunched and vague, wavering against the gray wall of the visitor's station. He looked over in time to see the metal flowers of Candesce's strange garden closing. Silhouetting one of them was an orange glow that hadn't been there a minute ago.

"Oh no." He finished the knot hastily and climbed back along the cargo net's cables to the open entrance of the station. The bike was tethered there; it too had a shadow—no, two shadows. He looked down and saw that a second sun was opening its glowing eye.

He'd thrown Carrier's body into the open air. His story was going to be that the Gehellens had come back and there'd been a fight at the entrance. The attackers had been driven off but Carrier was killed. He had rehearsed his story over and over during the past hour, while he struggled against the pain of his wounds to fill the nets with sun parts. As he'd done so he'd found himself crying.

He no longer wondered at such tears. As he rehearsed the lie about the Gehellens, Hayden found himself wondering whether he was reluctant to tell the truth to Venera, or Aubri or himself. Either way, he felt no satisfaction at Carrier's death. The only thing he was proud of was his attempt to talk the man out of attacking him.

So in his head he began to rehearse a second story. This one would not be told until he was an old man, if he got things right.

It began and ended with, "Carrier was the last man I killed, or ever wanted to kill."

Once inside the station he climbed quickly from strap to strap, heading for the inner chambers. "We have to go!" he called as he went. "Come on, the suns are waking up!"

Nobody answered. What were Venera and Aubri up to? From his own experience with the wish-mirror, he'd seen that once you set something in motion here, you could pretty much ignore it and go on about your business. Aubri shouldn't have had to nurse Candesce after shutting down its defenses against Artificial Nature.

"Aubri! Venera! Where are you? We have to leave, now!"

He heard a thump from somewhere ahead. Hayden ducked under and over walls, passing through several rooms that seemed familiar. Then, as he was gliding across a half-lit room filled with hammocks and rest nooks, he heard a woman's voice growl a single word:

"Bitch!"

More thumps and a gasp from the other side of this wall. Hayden perched there for a moment, blinking, then swung down to climb into the next room. He stopped, straddling the wall.

Aubri Mahallan and Venera Fanning clung to straps on opposite walls. Both women had swords in their hands, and those swords were pointed at one another. Venera's face was twisted into a rictus of fury, muscles jumping in her famous jaw.

"Turn it on!" Venera screamed. "Turn it back on!"

Aubri silently shook her head.

Hayden somersaulted into the room. "What's going on?" He made to join Aubri, but she dove out of his way.

"Stay back," she murmured.

"Stay . . . ? What's going on?" By now, he was too tired and in too much pain to catch her.

Venera pointed to where her special indicator lamp tumbled in midair, its light glowing steadily. "She won't turn it back on. Candesce's defenses! She was willing to turn them off all right, but she won't bring them back. She's opened the gates to her friends from beyond Virga."

"Aubri?" He stared at her, but she wouldn't return his gaze.

He should have figured this out. He realized now that she had given him enough clues over the past week—but he'd been so consumed with the idea of finding components for a new Aerie sun that he hadn't thought through the things Aubri had told him. She had told him that she had not been sent to Virga to enter Candesce; but in the same breath she had told him that the assassin-thing coiled inside her was listening for any hint that she might reveal her true mission. Her denial should have tipped him off; but he hadn't been smart enough to see it.

"I'm sorry," she said in a low, shaking voice. "If I turn it back on, I'll die."

"You were sent to bring Artificial Nature to Virga," he said. "That's what you couldn't tell me." She nodded.

Hayden's thoughts were racing. Should he try to stop this? Or should he side with Aubri? "What happens now?" he asked her. "When you let them in . . . What are you letting in?"

Now she looked at him, her expressive features crumpled into sadness. "A trillion ghosts will come first," she said. "The disembodied AIs and post-humans will flood into Virga, make it their playground. They're hungry for resources. They'll transform everything they touch—and everybody. When that transformation happens, your reality will fade away. The walls of Virga will disappear. The suns, the darkness, the towns, and ships . . . They'll be erased by virtual realms. Glorious beauty, places like Heaven brought into being around every man, woman, and child. Whatever you imagine will come to pass. Everything and anything, except Virga itself. Everything you knew will be gone, replaced by fantasies made real."

Venera shuddered. "We won't survive it," she said.

Aubri shook her head. "Not as you are now," she said. "Whatever your hopes and dreams were, they're obsolete now. You'll need new ones. New reasons to live." Her mouth twisted in grief. "And that's the one thing the system can't make for you."

"No!" Venera launched herself across the room. Before Hayden could reach them the two women were twisting in the air, Venera slashing madly at Aubri who tried to parry. Hayden cried out as he saw Venera's sword slide into the muscle under Aubri's left shoulder.

Hayden's lover, the Rook's armorer, tumbled backward streaming blood.

He screamed and jumped, too late, as Venera cursed and kicked off from Aubri's limp body. Venera reached a corner and ducked around the offset panels with one wide-eyed look back at Hayden.

He wrapped his arms around Aubri and turned so his own back took their impact on the far wall. She was jerking in his grasp, twists of blood reaching out of her with each breath.

"I'm—sorry," she gasped. "I was too afraid."

"Hush," he said, smoothing back her hair. "It's not your fault. It's theirs for making you and then condemning you for being who you are."

She closed her eyes and whimpered. "Hush," he said again, holding her close.

"No." She pushed against him. "No! Let me go. Get me to the, the command mirror." She pointed at a glassy rectangle on the ceiling.

"Stay still."

"No. Let—" She writhed in his arms, turning to glare at him. "Let me beat them."

THE BRIDGE WAS full of drifting grit and the stench of smoke. Deafening explosions rattled the beams; all the portholes had shattered. Chaison clung to the arms of his chair and glared out into gleaming sunlight as the Rook came apart around him.

"Ready, sir!" Travis was holding onto a pipe with his toes, one-armed as he was with his hand in a sling; his free hand was poised over the scuttling console.

Chaison felt infinitely weary. It wasn't as though it mattered whether Falcon Formation got its hands on the radar sets. There wasn't anything they could do with them. Assuming, of course, that Aubri Mahallan did her job. The idea that she might not seemed distantly worrying, but he couldn't bring himself to focus on abstractions. Instead, he frowned past the jagged glass rimming the porthole, at the obstinately solid silhouette of the dreadnought that was even now turning to aim its biggest guns at the *Rook*.

All I wanted, he thought with an ironic smile, *was to get rid of that thing*.

As the dreadnought turned it exposed the dented portion of hull where something had collided with it. Sunlight angled around the dark hull and Chaison saw that the ship's armor had split at the bottom of that dent; there was a three-sided hole there.

"Wait a second, Travis," he said. Chaison frowned, then reached for the speaking tube.

"Rocket batteries one and two, are you there?" he shouted.

"Y-yes, sir. What do you want us to do, sir?"

"Don't bail out," he said. "You'll be shot to pieces in open air. I have a plan. Load the racks and get ready."

"Sir!"

He turned to Travis, who was watching him with a raised eyebrow. The radar man and the semaphore team were also staring. "Get to the helm," he told Travis. "We've still got power. We're going to ram her."

"Ah. I see." Travis looked faintly disappointed. Chaison had to laugh.

"No, you don't see," he said. "We're going to ram her *there*." He pointed. Travis began to smile.

The *Rook* ducked out of the path of the big guns, angling up and shooting straight at the line of Falcon Formation battleships that was bearing down on her. They were momentarily safe since the ships would not want to miss *Rook* and hit the dreadnought.

The *Rook* groaned as Travis spun them around and lined up on the dreadnought. "They're going to get at least one good shot at us, sir," he said.

Chaison shrugged. "Have you got a better idea?"

Travis didn't answer, but merely pushed the control levers forward. Chaison heard the distant engines whine toward full power.

"If you do want to bail out," he said to the semaphore team and the radar man, "now would be the time to do it."

Nobody moved.

"All right then."

Holed, dripping splinters and chunks of armor, the *Rook* accelerated for the last time. The air it crossed was layered with smoke and debris, the bodies of men and unexploded ordnance. Chaison watched it all pass in disgust. *How pointless.* He wasn't sure whether it was Falcon's invasion that he meant, or his own attempt to stop it.

"Brace for impact!" He strapped himself in and spun the chair around. It was designed to handle collisions like this; the *Rook*, like her sister ships, had a substantial ram on her prow. She was never intended to ram something as big as a town, though. This whole gambit might just provide a good laugh to the Falconers, if *Rook* simply splatted against the dreadnought's skin like a bug on a porthole.

He closed his eyes, and thought of the home he would never see again.

The impact, when it came, was surprisingly gentle. A vast grinding sound filled Chaison's ears and the ship shuddered and bucked. Then it eased to a stop. In the swaying light of the gas lamp, he met Travis's eyes and grinned.

"Let's see where we are." The portholes were blocked by wreckage. Both men jumped over to the bridge doors and Travis flung them open. Chaison gasped at what he saw.

The *Rook* was holed in dozens of places. Its interior was in shambles, with dead men and parts of men, tangled coils of rope, broken bulkheads, and spars thrusting every which way. Way down past where the hangar had been, streams of sunlight made bluish shafts across the space. Nearer, the holes in the hull revealed only darkness.

"We're jammed inside it," Travis said wonderingly. "More than halfway."

Chaison nodded. "That's what I had in mind." He clambered through the wreckage, heading for the rocketeers who huddled next to their bent racks. "Ready to fire, men?" They stared at him.

Chaison laughed recklessly. "Come on!" he shouted. "This is the stuff of legends! We're going to rake this bastard of a ship with a barrage that'll tear it to pieces—and we're going to do it from the inside!"

Still they hesitated—and then a loud voice burst out, "What are you waiting for?"

It was Slew, smoke-stained and trailing a broken chain from his wrist as he flew up from the aft. Beside him, helping him maneuver past the wreckage, was Ambassador Reiss. Both men had swords in their hands; both looked grimly determined.

"You heard the admiral!" yelled Slew. The men looked at each other, then leaped to their posts. Already Chaison could hear gunshots, and just behind Slew soldiers in Falcon Formation uniforms began pushing their way through gaps in the hull. The irate crew. Well, they were too late.

"Reiss, Slew, behind you. You men—fire!"

The port and starboard racks unleashed their rockets and the Rook's hull tried to collapse as everything outside blew up. Some of the rockets must have found their way down long passageways, exploding hundreds of yards away. Some didn't get ten feet. But the dreadnought had never been designed to withstand this kind of attack. As the rocketeers cleared their tubes and made to load another round, the Rook was hammered by new explosions, much bigger than those they had caused. Now the hull really was collapsing, Travis grabbing at a stanchion, Reiss and Slew's faces lit with surprise and all of them disappearing into bright sunlight as the ship sheared in two and the sky filled with gouts of smoke and flying darkness.

Somehow, Chaison had caught a rope and found himself dangling over the infinite airs of Virga, watching while the aft half of the dreadnought fell away and wrenched itself to pieces with explosion after explosion. Mesmerized, he didn't look away from the sight until he felt the rope being tugged from the other end. He glanced up.

The shattered half-hull of the *Rook* still stuck out of the fore half of the dreadnought, right at the spot where the great ship had been torn in two. Smoke billowed out of the forward section but it hadn't exploded. Three Falcon airmen were hauling in the rope Chaison held, murder in their eyes. Of the rest of his crew, there was no sign.

"Gentlemen," Chaison said as he held out his hand, "meet the man who beat you."

VENERA WATCHED HAYDEN Griffin weep. A fluttering sense of disquiet plucked at her; she fought against it fiercely.

Aubri Mahallan moved feebly in the young man's arms, gesturing at the command mirror in front of which they floated. Venera clutched her sword in sweating hands and wondered why Lyle had not shown up yet.

The indicator light for Candesce's defenses still spun lazily in the air. Without fanfare, it suddenly went out. Venera frowned at it. Had its little battery died, or . . . She looked at Aubri Mahallan.

The woman's limbs drifted free now, and her head slowly tilted forward. Griffin gave one last wracking sob and then spun to look at the command mirror. It was a rectangle of white light now, all details washed away by the awakening suns.

Griffin turned again, and now he looked straight at Venera. Despite herself, she flinched from his glare. But all he said was, "We have to go."

The words made no sense at all; Venera could barely believe she'd heard them. "I killed your woman," she said. "If I come near you, you'll kill me."

"No," he said.

She sneered. "Oh? Where's Lyle?" Griffin looked away, and Venera's heart sank. "He's not coming, is he? You boys finally settled your little dispute, whatever it was?"

He gathered Mahallan's body in his arms again, and kicked off toward an open corner. "What choice did I have?" she called out after him. "You know what she tried to do!"

"Shut up," he said without looking back. "Just shut up."

Venera was furious and, yes, scared; but she wasn't going to back down. Not to this servant. "So strand me, or shoot me," she cried. "I did what I had to do."

Now, just before disappearing around the corner, he did look back. He looked sad, and puzzled. "Venera, I'm not going to kill you," he said. "There's room on the bike. Come with me."

"That would mean trusting you," she said.

"Yes."

Venera laughed, and hunkered down a little more in the shadows. "I've never done that in my life," she said. "I'm not about to start now."

"Suit yourself," he said with broken weariness. Then he was gone.

Venera remained where she was for long seconds. Outside, Candesce was rousing itself to full power. She couldn't feel the rain of invisible particles that Mahallan had said would flood this place during the day, but she imagined them like virulent poison seeping through the walls. Even if the heat didn't kill her . . .

But trust a man whose lover she had just killed? The idea was insane. Trust Griffin? Trust *anyone*? There were fools who did it and survived somehow. She could not be so lucky, she knew.

Venera fingered her jaw angrily. She would die here, miserable, abandoned.

When the bullet hit her and she lay moaning on the stone she had waited—waited for someone to come to her, to discover her in pain. She had waited for the cries of distress, the solicitations of her rescuers. Nobody came. There was no rescue for Venera Fanning. So in the end she had crawled, herself, unassisted, through the corridors and into the Admiralty. At the last second she had fainted, before knowing whether the ones who found her had cared enough to hold her as Griffin had held Mahallan, whether they wiped her drying tears and murmured that she would be all right. When Chaison tried, much later, it was too late.

Venera spat a curse, and uncoiled from her defensive knot. As quietly as she could, she crept after Hayden Griffin through the dimming rooms of the station.

HEAT AND INTOLERABLE light met Hayden at the entrance. The bike's handlebars were almost too hot to touch and he had to squint and grope for a loop of cable to wrap around Aubri.

He didn't have enough to tie her to the saddle, so he looked around for another solution. Put her in the cargo nets? Maybe—if he could get to them. The heat scored his face whenever he turned toward the suns; the very air was attacking his mouth and lungs. He wasn't sure he could jump over to the nets and get back before the heat took him.

You've lost her already. Like he'd lost everyone else in his life. He should be used to this by now.

Heartsick, he gave her body the slightest of shoves, and she slipped through his fingers—waist, shoulders, finally one trailing hand smoothing his before the moment of separation. She seemed to be turning to look at him, face calm and lips parted as if to tell him it would be all right, while past her shoulder the mechanical flowers of Candesce curled behind their mirrored petals. As the eyes of the suns opened all around, Aubri Mahallan vanished into light.

Hayden turned and climbed onto the bike.

He spun up the fan and the burner started immediately. As the jet's whine escalated he clung to familiar routines, listening to it, judging the health of the machine. He jiggled it with his knees, estimating how much fuel was left. Hayden knew his machines, and this one still had some life in it. A few refuelings and it would get him back to Rush, he was sure of it.

And then . . . He fingered the pockets of his jacket, which were full of jewels and coins from the treasure of Anetene. He probably had enough to hire the artisans he'd need. The core components of Aerie's new sun were already in his possession. He might not even need the help of the Resistance to get it built.

Unsmiling, he opened the throttle and began to move away from the visitor's station. There was a lurch as the cable tautened and the nets fell in line behind the bike. That cargo would slow him down, of course.

He might meet the Gehellens on the way out. —What if they got into the visitor's center? Better close the door. He glanced back, and saw that the entrance to the visitor's station was already shut. Crouched beside it in a hurricane of radiance was Venera Fanning.

The cargo net was passing her, just a few yards away. Her eyes met his; there was no appeal in her gaze, just defiance. Hayden nodded once, then deliberately turned back to his piloting. After a moment he felt a slight jerk translate up the cable and through the bike as Venera caught and clung to the passing net.

He opened the throttle and the bike accelerated, but slowly, too slowly as the inferno of dawn welled out from the heart of Candesce. He imagined he could hear the familiar low hiss of the Sun of Suns, even over the scream of the bike. In minutes it became impossible to see; then he could no longer breathe except in shallow gasps; and then he started to tear at his clothing as it burned him wherever it touched. All the while, the air rushed past faster and faster. Before he completely lost his senses he stopped himself from throwing away his jacket and shirt. The light burned his bare skin as much as their touch had.

Gradually the agony abated. Candesce was reaching out to ignite hundreds of miles of air, but he was escaping it, barely.

Squinting ahead, he could see many long fingers of shadow reaching past him. Catamarans or bikes? He turned his head, trying to make out what they were.

Everywhere, the sky was full of shrouded human bodies, all gliding silently in toward Candesce. Joining Aubri. The faint specks of a hundred funeral ships receded into the distance, returning to their ports after unloading their cargoes.

When he was finally able to regain his flapping shirt and jacket, and look around himself, Hayden found that he had no idea where he was. Originally they had planned to navigate by keeping Leaf's Choir in view. They would head for one of Gehellen's neighbors, and from there return to Slipstream. Hayden could be going in the opposite direction now, for all he knew.

It didn't matter. He would find his way, eventually. He couldn't imagine spending the days and nights without Aubri beside him; it seemed impossible that he had done so before. But he had to try. He had responsibilities now.

A few minutes later he felt another vibration through the cable. He looked back, shielding his eyes with one hand.

Venera Fanning made a black cross against the Sun of Suns as she launched herself into the air. They were doing a good sixty or seventy miles an hour at that moment; she swept her arms ahead of her in a diving posture and arrowed away, clothes fluttering.

With luck she would make it to the principalities of Candesce. Though he wished achingly that it could be Aubri silhouetted in exuberance against that light, he hoped Venera would survive and find her way home.

Hayden turned back to his own task. He was done with fighting, done with brooding over the past. His nation and his life had been in shambles for too many years; it was time to rebuild.

He had too much to do to waste his time on resentment.

He settled into the bike's saddle, and opened the throttle wide.

QUEEN OF CANDESCE

Prologue

GARTH DIAMANDIS LOOKED up and saw a woman in the sky.

The balcony swayed under him; distant trees wavered in the hot afternoon air though there was no breeze. A twist of little clouds pirouetted far overhead, just beneath the glitter and darkness of the city that had exiled Garth, so many years ago, to this place. Well below the city, only a thousand feet up at this point, a single human form had appeared out of the light.

She rotated up out of Garth's view and he had to wait several minutes for her to come back around. Then, there she was: gliding with supernatural grace over the tall, ragged wall that rimmed the world at its nearer end. Behind her, infinite air beckoned, forever out of reach of Garth and the others like him. Ahead of the silent woman, a likely tumble into quickly moving trees, broken limbs, and death. If she wasn't dead already.

Someone tried to escape, he thought—an act that always ended in gunshots or bloody thrashing beneath a swarm of piranhawks. This one must have been shot cleanly by the day watch for she was spiraling across the sky alone, not attended by a retinue of blood droplets. And now the spin-gale was teasing the fringes of her outlandish garment, slowing her; bringing her down.

Garth frowned, for a moment forgetting the aches and pains that bedeviled him all day and all night. The hovering woman's clothes had been too bright and fluttered too easily to be made of the traditional leather and metal of Spyre.

As the world turned the woman receded into the distance, frustrating Garth's attempt to see more. The ground under his perch was rotating up and away along with the whole cylindrical world; the black-haired woman was not moving with it but rather sailing in majestically from one of the world's open ends. But Spyre made its own winds as it turned, and those winds would pull her to its surface before she had a chance to drift out the other side.

She would have sped up by that time, but not enough to match Spyre's rotation. Garth well knew what happened when someone began clipping the treetops and towers at several hundred miles per hour. He'd be finding pieces of her for weeks.

The ground undulated again. Frantic horns began echoing in the distance—an urgent conversation between the inner surface of Spyre and the city above.

Watching the woman had been an idle pastime, since it looked as though she was going to come down along the rail line. People with more firepower and muscle than Garth owned that; they would see her in a few moments and bring her down. Her valuable possessions and clothes would not be his.

But the horns were insistent. Something was wrong with the very fabric of Spyre, an oscillation building. He could see it in the far distance now: the land heaved minutely up and down. The slow ripple was making its way in his direction; he'd better get off this parapet.

The archway opening onto the balcony had empty air behind it and a twenty-foot drop to tumbled stones. Garth hopped over the rail without hesitation, counting as he fell. "One pilot, two pilot, three—" He landed among upthrusts of stabbing weed and the cloudlike brambles that had taken over this ancient mansion. Three seconds? Well, gravity hadn't changed, at least not noticeably.

His muscles creaked as he stood up, but climbing and jumping were part of his daily constitutional, a grim routine aimed at convincing himself he was still a man.

He stalked over the crackling grit that painted a tiled dance floor. Railway ties were laid callously across the fine pallasite stones; the line cleaved the former nation of Arbath like a whip-mark.

Garth stepped onto the track daringly and stared down it. The great family of Arbath had not reached an accommodation with the preservationists and had been displaced or killed, he couldn't remember which. Rubble, ruins, and new walls sided the tracks; at one spot an abandoned sniper tower loomed above the strip. It now swayed uneasily.

The tracks converged in perspective but also rose with the land itself, a long graceful curve that became vertical if he followed it far enough. He didn't look that far but focused on a scramble of activity taking place about a mile distant.

The Preservation Society had planted one of their oil-soaked sidings there like an obscene graffito. Some of the preservationists were pouring alcohol into the tanks of a big turbine engine that squatted on the tracks like an idol to industrialism. Others had started a tug and were shunting in cars loaded with iron plating and rubble. They were responding to the codes brayed out by the distant horns.

They were so busy doing all this that none had noticed what was happening overhead.

"You're crazy, Garth." He hopped from foot to foot, twisting his hands together. When he was younger he wouldn't have hesitated. There was a time when he'd lived for escapades like this. Cursing his own cowardice, Garth lurched into a half-run down the tracks—in the direction of the preservationist camp.

He had to prove himself more and more often these days. Garth still sported the black cap and long sideburns that rakes had worn in his day—but he was acutely aware that the day had come and gone. His long leather coat was brindled with cracks and dappled with stains. Though he still wore the twin holsters that had once held the most expensive and stylish dueling pistols available in Spyre, nowadays he just carried odd objects in them. His breath ratcheted in his chest and if his head didn't hurt, his legs did, or his hands. Pain followed him everywhere; it had made crow's-feet where once he'd outlined his eyes in black to show the ladies his long lashes.

The preservationist's engine started up. It was coming his way so Garth prudently left the track and hunkered down beneath some bushes to let it pass. He was in disputed land, so no one would accost him here, but he might be casually shot from a window of the train and no one would care. While he waited he watched the dot of the slowly falling woman, trying to verify his initial guess at her trajectory.

Garth made it the rest of the way to the preservationist camp without attracting attention. Pandemonium still reigned inside the camp, with shaven-headed men in stiff leather coats crawling like ants over a second, rust-softened engine under the curses of a supervisor. The first train was miles up the curve of the world now and if Garth bothered to look down the length of Spyre, he was sure he would see many other trains on the move as well. But that wasn't his interest.

Pieces of the world fell off all the time. It wasn't his problem.

He crept between two teetering stacks of railway ties until he was next to a pile of catch-nets the preservationists had dumped here. Using a stick he'd picked up along the way, he snagged one of the nets and dragged it into the shadows. Under full gravity it would have weighed several hundred pounds; as it was he staggered under the weight as he carried it to a nearby line of trees.

She was going by again, lower now and fast in her long spiral. The woman's clothes were tearing in the headwind and her dark hair bannered behind her. When Garth saw that her exposed skin was bright red he stopped in surprise, then doubled his efforts to reach the nearest vertical cable.

The interior of Spyre was spoked by thousands of these cables; some rose at low angles to reattach themselves to the skin of the world just a few miles away. Some shot straight up to touch down on the opposite side of the cylinder. All were under tremendous tension and every now and then one snapped; then the world rang like a bell for an hour or two, and shifted, and more pieces fell off of it.

Aside from keeping the world together, the cables served numerous purposes. Some carried elevators. The one Garth approached had smaller lines draped and coiled around its frayed black surface—some old, rusted, and disused pulley system. The main cable was anchored to a corroded metal cone that jutted out of the earth. He clipped two corners of the roll of netting to the old pulley. Then he jogged away from the tracks, unreeling the net behind him.

It took far too long to connect a third corner of the huge net to a corroded flagpole. Sweating and suffering palpitations, he ran back to the flagpole one more time. As he did she came by again.

She was a bullet. In fact, it was the land that was speeding by below her and pulling the air with it. If she'd been alive earlier she might be dead now; he doubted whether anyone could breathe in such a gale.

As soon as she shot past Garth began hauling on the pulleys. The net lurched into the air a foot at a time. Too slow! He cursed and redoubled his effort, expecting to hear shouts from the preservationist camp at any moment.

With agonizing slowness, a triangle of netting rose. One end was anchored to the flagpole; two more were on their way up the cable. Had he judged her trajectory right? It didn't matter; this was the only attachment point for hundreds of yards, and by now she was too low. Air resistance was yanking her down and in moments she would be tumbled to pieces on the ground.

Here she came. Garth wiped sweat out of his eyes and pulled with bloody hands. At that moment the shriek of a steam whistle sounded from the preservationist camp. The rusted engine was on the move.

The mysterious woman arrowed in just above the highest trees. Garth thought for sure she was going to miss his net. Then, just as the rusted engine sailed by on the tracks—he caught snapshot glimpses of surprised preservationist faces and open mouths— she hit the net and yanked it off the cable.

A twirling screw hit Garth in the nose and he sat down. Sparks shot from screaming brakes on the tracks and the black tangling form of the falling woman passed between the Y-uprights of a jagged tree, the trailing net catching branches and snapping them as she bounced with astonishing gentleness into a bed of weeds.

Garth was there in seconds, cutting through the netting with his knife. Her clothes marked her as a foreigner, so her ransom potential might be low. He probably couldn't even get much for her clothes; cloth like that had no business being worn in Spyre. Oh well; maybe she had some adornments that might fetch enough to buy him food for a few weeks.

Just in case, he put a hand on her neck—and felt a pulse. Garth cursed in astonishment. Jubilantly he slashed away the rest of the strands and pulled her out as a warning shot cracked through the air.

Unable to resist, he teased back the wave of black hair that fell across her face. The woman was fairly young—in her twenties—and had fine, sharp features with well-defined black eyebrows and full lips. The symmetry of her face was broken only by a star-shaped scar on her jaw. Her skin would have been quite fair were it not deeply sunburnt.

She only weighed twenty pounds or so. It was easy to sling her over his shoulder and run for the deep bush that marked the boundary of the disputed lands.

He pushed his way through the branches and onto private land. The preservationists pulled up short, cursing, just shy of the bushes. Garth Diamandis laughed as he ran, and for a precious few minutes he felt like he was twenty years old again.

A LOW BEAMED ceiling swam into focus. Venera Fanning frowned at it, then winced as pain shot through her jaw. She was definitely alive, she decided ruefully.

She was—but was Chaison Fanning also among the living, or was Venera now a widow? That was it, she had been trying to get back to her husband, Chaison Fanning. Trying to get home—

Sitting up proved impossible. The slightest motion sent waves of pain through her; she felt like she'd been skinned. She moaned involuntarily.

"You're awake?" The thickly accented words had the crackle of age to them. She turned her head gingerly and made out a dim form moving to sit next to her. She was lying on a bed—probably—and he was on a stool or something. She blinked, trying to take in more of the long low room.

"Don't try to move," said the old man. "You've got severe sunburn and sunstroke too. Plus a few cuts and bruises. I've been wetting down the sheets to give you some relief. Gave you water too. Don't know what else to do."

"Th-thanks." She looked down at herself. "Where are my clothes?"

His face cracked in a smile and for a second he looked much younger. He had slablike features with prominent cheekbones and piercing gray eyes. Eyes like that could send chills through you, and from his confident grin he seemed to know it. But as he shifted in the firelight she saw that lines of care and disappointment had cut away much of his handsomeness.

"Your clothes are here," he said, patting a chair or table nearby.

"Don't worry, I've done nothing to you. Not out of virtue, mind; I'm not a big fan of virtue, mine or anyone else's. No, you can thank arthritis, old wounds, and age for your safety." He grinned again. "I'm Garth Diamandis. And you are a foreigner."

Venera sighed listlessly. "Probably. What does that mean around here?"

Diamandis leaned back, crossing his arms. "Much, or nothing, depending."

"And here is . . . ?"

"Spyre," he said.

"Spyre . . ." She thought she should remember that name. But Venera was already falling asleep. She let herself do it; after all, it was so cool here. . . .

When she awoke again it was to find herself propped half-upright in a chair. Her forehead, upper body, and arms were draped with moist sheets. Blankets swaddled her below that.

Venera was facing a leaded-glass window. Outside, green foliage made a sunlit screen. She heard birds. That suggested the kind of garden you only got in the bigger towns—a gravity-bound garden where trees grew short and squat and soil stayed in one place. Such things were rare—and that, in turn, implied wealth.

But this room . . . As she turned her head her hopes faded. This was a hovel, for all that it too seemed built for gravity. The floor was the relentless iron of a town foundation, though surprisingly she could feel no vibration from engines or slipstream vanes through her feet. The silence was uncanny, in fact. The chamber itself was oddly cantilevered, as though hollowed out of the foundations of some much larger structure. Boxes, chests, and empty bird cages were jammed or piled everywhere, a few narrow paths worn between them. The only clear area was the spot where her overstuffed armchair sat. She located the bed to her left, some tables, and a fireplace that looked like it had been clumsily dug into the wall by the window. There were several tables here and the clutter had infected them as well; they were covered with framed pictures.

Venera leaned forward, catching up the sheet at her throat. A sizzle of pain went through her arms and shoulders and she extended her left arm, snarling. She was sunburned a deep brick red that was already starting to peel. How long had she been here?

The pictures. Gingerly, she reached out to turn one in the light. It was of a young lady holding a pair of collapsible wrist-fins. She wore a strange stiff-looking black bodice, and her backdrop was indistinct but might have been clouds.

All the portraits were of women, some two dozen by her estimation. Some were young, some older; all the ladies seemed well-off, judging from their various elaborate hairdos. Their clothes were outlandish, though, made of sweeping chrome and leather, clearly heavy and doubtless uncomfortable. There was, she realized, a complete absence of cloth in these photos.

"Ah, you're awake!" Diamandis shuffled his way through the towering stacks of junk. He was holding a limp bird by the neck; now he waved it cheerfully. "Lunch!"

"I demand to know where I am." She started to stand and found herself propelled nearly to the ceiling. Gravity was very low here. Recovering with a wince, she coiled the damp sheet around her for modesty. It didn't help; Diamandis frankly admired her form anyway, and probably would have stared even if she'd been sheathed in plate armor. It seemed to be his way, and there was, strangely, nothing offensive about it.

"You are a guest of the principality of Spyre," said Diamandis. He sat down at a low table and began plucking the bird. "But I regret to have to inform you that you've landed on the wrong part of our illustrious nation. This is Greater Spyre, where I've lived now for, oh . . . twenty-odd years."

She held up the picture she had been looking at. "You were a busy man, I see."

He looked over and laughed in delight. "Very! And why not? The world is full of wonders, and I wanted to meet them all."

Venera touched the stone wall and now felt a faint thrum. "You say this is a town? An old one . . . and you've turned gravity way down." Then she turned to look at Diamandis. "What did you mean, 'regret to inform me'? What's wrong with this Greater Spyre?"

He looked over at her and now he seemed very old. "Come. If you can walk, I'll show you your new home."

Venera bit back a sharp retort. Instead, she sullenly followed him through the stacks. "My temporary residence, you mean," she said to the cracked leather back of his coat. "I am making my way back to the court at Slipstream. If ransom is required, you will be paid handsomely for my safe return . . ."

He laughed, somewhat sadly. "Ah, but that it were possible to do that," he murmured. He exited up a low flight of steps into bright light. She followed, feeling the old scar on her jaw starting to throb.

The roofless square building had been built of stone and steel I-beams, perhaps centuries ago. Now devoid of top and floors, it had become a kind of open box, thirty feet on a side. Wild plants grew in profusion throughout the rubble-strewn interior. The hole leading to Diamandis's home was in one corner of the place; there was no other way in or out as far as she could see.

Venera stared at the grass. She'd never seen wild plants under gravity before. Every square foot was accounted for in the rotating ring-shaped structures she called towns. They were seldom more than a mile in diameter, after all, often built of mere rope and planking. There was no other way to feel gravity than to visit a town.

She scanned the sky past the stone walls. In some ways it looked right: the endless vistas of Virga were blocked by some sort of structure. But the perspective seemed all wrong.

"Come." Diamandis was gesturing to her from a nearly invisible set of steps that ran up one wall. She scowled, but followed him up to a level area just below the top of the wall. If she stood on tiptoe, she could look over. So she did.

Venera had never known one could feel so small. Spyre was a rotating habitat like those she had grown up in. But that was all she could have said to connect it to the worlds she had known. Diamandis's little tower sat among forlorn trees and scrub grass in an empty plain that stretched to trees a mile or more in each direction. In any sane world this much land under gravity would have been crammed with buildings; those empty plazas and tumbled-down villas should have been awash with humanity.

Past the trees, the landscape became a maze of walls, towers, open fields, and sharp-edged forests. And it went on and on to a dizzying, impossible distance. Diamandis's tower was one tiny mote on the inside surface of a cylinder that must have been ten or twelve miles in diameter and half again as long.

Sunlight angled in from somewhere behind her; Venera turned quickly, needing the reassurance of something familiar. Beyond the open ends of the great cylinder, the reassuring cloudscapes of the normal world turned slowly; she had not left all sense and reason behind. But the scale of this town wheel was impossible for any engineering she knew. The energy needed to keep it turning in the unstable airs of Virga would beggar any normal nation. Yet the place looked ancient, as evidenced by the many overgrown ruins and furzes of wild forest. In fact, she could see gaps in the surface here and there through which she could glimpse distant flickers of cloud and sky.

"Are those holes?" she asked, pointing at a nearby crater. Leaves, twigs, and grit fogged the air above it, and all the topsoil for yards around had been stripped away, revealing a stained metal skin that must underlie everything here.

Garth scowled as if she'd committed some indiscretion by pointing out the hole. "Yes," he said grudgingly. "Spyre is ancient and decaying, and it's under an awful strain. Tears like that open up all the time. It's everyone's nightmare that one day, such a rip might not stop. If the world should ever come to an end, it will start with a tear like that one."

Faintly alarmed, Venera looked around at the many other holes that dotted the landscape. Garth laughed. "Don't worry, if it's serious the patch gangs will be here in a day or two to fix it—dodging bullets from the local gentry all the while. They were out doing just that when I picked you up."

Venera looked straight up. "I suppose if this is Greater Spyre," she said, pointing, "then that is Lesser Spyre?"

The empty space that the cylinder rotated around was filled with conventional town wheels. Uncoupled from the larger structure, these rings spun grandly in midair, miles above her. Some were "geared" towns whose rims touched, while others turned in solitary majesty. A puff of smaller buildings surrounded the towns.

The wheels weren't entirely disconnected from Greater Spyre. Venera saw cables standing up at various angles every mile or so throughout the giant cylinder. Some angled across the world to anchor in the ground again far up Spyre's curve. Some went straight past the axis and down to an opposite point; if you climbed one of these lines you could get to the city that hung like an iron cloud half a dozen miles above.

She didn't see any elevator traffic on the nearest cables. Most were tethered inside the mazelike grounds of the estates that dotted the land. Would anyone have a right to use those cables but the owners?

When Diamandis didn't reply, Venera glanced over at him. He was gazing up at the distant towns, his expression shifting between empty adoration and anger. He seemed lost in memory.

Then he blinked and looked down at her. "Lesser Spyre, yes. My home, from which I am exiled for life. Always visible, never to be achieved again." He shook his head. "Unlucky you to have landed here, Lady."

"My name," she said, "is Venera Fanning." She looked out again. The nearer end of the great cylinder began to curve upward less than a mile away. It rose for a mile or two then ended in open air. "I don't understand," she said. "What's to prevent me—or you—from leaving? Just step off that rim yonder and you'll be in free flight in the skies of Virga. You could go anywhere."

Diamandis looked where she was pointing. Now his smile was condescending. "Ejected at four hundred miles per hour, Lady

Fanning, you'll be unconscious in seconds for lack of breath. Before you slow enough to awake you'll either suffocate or be eaten alive by the piranhawks. Or be shot by the sentries. Or be eviscerated by the razor-wire clouds, or hit a mine. . . .

"No, it was a miracle that you drifted unconscious through all of that, to land here. A once-in-a-million feat.

"Now that you're among us, you will never leave again."

DIAMANDIS'S WORDS MIGHT have alarmed Venera had she not recently survived a number of impossible situations. Not only that, he was manifestly wrong about the threat the piranhawks represented; after all, hadn't she sailed blithely through them all? These things in mind, she followed him down to his hovel where he began to prepare a meal.

The bird was pathetically small; they would each get a couple of mouthfuls out of it if they were lucky. "I'm grateful for your help," Venera said as she lowered herself painfully back into the armchair. "But you obviously don't have very much. What do you get out of helping me?"

"The warmth of your gratitude," said Diamandis. In the shadow of the stone fireplace it was impossible to make out his expression.

Venera chose to laugh. "Is that all? What if I'd been a man?"

"I'd have left you without a second thought."

"I see." She reached over to her piled clothes and rummaged through them. "As I suspected. I've not come through unscathed, have I?" The jewelry that had filled her flight jacket's inner pockets was gone. She looked under the table and immediately spotted something: it looked like a metal door in the floor, with a rope loop as its handle. Her feet had been resting on it earlier.

"No, it's not down there," said Diamandis with a smile.

Venera shrugged. The two most important objects in her possession were still inside her jacket. She could feel the spent bullet through the lining. As to the other—Venera slipped her hand in to touch the scuffed white cylinder that she and her husband had fought their way across half the world to collect. It didn't look like it was worth anything, so Diamandis had apparently ignored it. Venera left it where it was and straightened to find Diamandis watching her.

"Consider those trinkets to be payment for my rescuing you," he said. "I can live for years on what you had in your pockets."

"So could I," she said levelly. "In fact, I was counting on using those valuables to barter my way home, if I had to."

"I've left you a pair of earrings and a bracelet," he said, pointing. There they were, sitting on the table next to her toeless deck shoes. "The rest is hidden, so don't bother looking."

Seething but too tired to fight, Venera leaned back, carefully draping the moist sheet over herself. "If I felt better, old man, I'd whip you for your impudence."

He laughed out loud. "Spoken like a true aristocrat! I knew you were a woman of quality by the softness of your hands. So what were you doing floating alone in the skies of Virga? Was your ship beset by pirates? Or did you fall overboard?"

She grimaced. "Either one makes a good story. Take your pick. Oh, don't look at me like that, I'll tell you, but first you have to tell me where we are. What is Spyre? How could such a place exist? From the heat outside I'd say we're still near the sun of suns. Is this place one of the principalities of Candesce?"

Diamandis shrugged. He bent over his dinner pot for a minute, then straightened and said, "Spyre's the whole world to those of us who live here. I'm told there's no other place like it in all of Virga. We were here at the founding of the world, and most people think we'll be here at its end. But I've also heard that once, there were dozens of Spyres, and that all the rest crumbled and spun apart over the ages. . . . So I believe we live in a mortal world. Like me, Spyre is showing its age."

He brought two plates. Venera was impressed: he'd added some cooked roots and a handful of boiled grains and made a passable meal of the bird. She was ravenous and dug in; he watched in amusement.

"As to what Spyre is . . ." He thought for a moment. "In the cold-blooded language of the engineers, you could say that we live on an open-ended rotating cylinder made of metal and miraculously strong cables. About six miles from here there's a giant engine that powers the electric jets. It is the same kind of engine that runs the suns. Once, we had hundreds of jets to keep us spinning, and Spyre's outer skin was smooth and didn't catch the wind. Gravity was stronger then. The jets are failing, one by one, and wind resistance pulls at the skin like the fingers of a demon. The old aristocrats refuse to see the decay that surrounds them, even when pieces of Spyre fall away and the whole world becomes unbalanced in its turning. When that happens, the Preservationist Society's rail engines start up and they haul as many tons as needed around the circle of the world to reestablish the balance.

"The nobles fought a civil war against the creation of the Preservation Society. That was a hundred years ago, but some of them are still fighting. The rest have been hunkered down on their estates for five centuries now, slowly breeding heritable insanities in the quiet of their shuttered parlors. They're so isolated that they hardly speak the same language anymore. They'll shoot anyone who crosses their land, yet they continue to live, because they can export objects and creatures that can only be made here."

Venera frowned at him. "You must not be one of them. You're making sense as far as I can tell."

"Me? I'm from the city." He pointed upward. "Up there, we still trade with the rest of the principalities. We have to; we've got no agriculture of our own. But the hereditary nobles own us because they control the industries down here." The bitterness in his voice was plain.

"So, Garth Diamandis, if you're a city person, what are you doing living in a hole in the ground in Greater Spyre?" She said it lightly, though she was aware the question must cause him more pain.

He did look away before smiling ruefully at her. "I made the cardinal mistake of all gigolos: I cultivated popularity among women only. I bedded one too many princesses, you see. I was kindly not killed nor castrated for it, but I was sent here."

"But I don't understand," she said. "Why is it impossible to leave? You said something about defenses . . . but why are they there?"

Diamandis guffawed. "Spyre is a treasure! At its height, this place was the equal of any nation in Virga, with gravity for all and wonders you couldn't get anywhere else. Why, we had horses! Have you heard of horses? And dogs and cats. You understand? We had here all the plants and animals that were brought from Earth at the very beginning of the world. Animals that were never altered to live in weightlessness. Even now, a breeding pair of house cats costs a king's ransom. An orange is worth its weight in platinum. We had to defend ourselves and prevent our treasures being stolen. So, for centuries now, Spyre has been ringed with razors and bombs to prevent attack—and to prevent anyone smuggling anything out. And believe me, when all else has descended to madness and decadence, that is the one policy that will remain in place." He hung his head.

"But surely one person, traveling alone—"

"Could carry a cargo of swallowed seeds. Or a dormant infant animal in a capsule sewn under the skin. Both have been tried. Oh, travel is still possible for nobles of Lesser Spyre and their attendants, but there are body scans and examinations, interrogations and quarantines. And anyone who's recently been on Greater Spyre comes under even more suspicion."

"I . . . see." Venera decided not to believe him. She would be more cheerful that way. She did her best to shrug off the black mood his words had inspired, and focused on her meal.

They ate in silence for a while, then he said, "And you? Pirates or a fall overboard?"

"Both and neither," said Venera. How much should she tell? There was no question that lying would be necessary, but one must always strike the right balance. The best lies were built of pieces of truth woven together in the right way. Also, it would do her no good to deny her status or origins; after all, if the paranoid rulers of Spyre needed money then Venera Fanning herself could fetch a good price. Her husband would buy her back or reduce this strange wheel to metal flinders. She had only to get word back to him.

"I was a princess of the kingdom of Hale," she told Diamandis. "I married at a young age—he is Chaison Fanning, the admiral of the migratory nation of Slipstream. Our countries lie far from here—hundreds or thousands of miles, I don't know—far from the light of Candesce. We have our own suns, which light a few hundred miles of open air that we farm. Our civilizations are bounded by darkness, unlike you who bask in the permanent glory of the Sun of Suns . . ."

Some audiences would need more—not all people knew that the whole vast world of Virga was artificial, a balloon thousands of miles in diameter that hung alone in the cosmos. Lacking any gravity save that made by its own inner air, Virga was a weightless environment whose extent could easily seem infinite to those who lived within it. Heat and light were provided not by any outside star but by artificial suns, of which Candesce was the oldest and brightest.

Even the ignorant knew it was a man-made sun that warmed their faces and lit the crops they grew on millions of slowly tumbling clods of earth. But the world itself? One glance up from your own drudge-work might encompass vast, cloud-wreathed spheres of water, miles in extent, their surfaces scaled with mirror-bright ripples; thunderheads the size of nations, which made no rain because rain required gravity but rather condensed balls of water the size of houses, of cities, then threw them at you; and a glance down would reveal depths of air painted every delicate shade by the absorption and attenuation of the light of a dozen distant suns. How could such a place have an end? How could it have been made by people?

Venera had seen the outer skin of the world, watched icebergs calve off its cold black surface. She had visited the region of machine-life and incandescent heat that was Candesce. The world was an artifact, and fragile. In her coat pocket was something that could destroy it all, if you but knew what it was and how to use it.

There were things she could tell no one.

A thing she could tell was that her adopted home of Slipstream had been attacked by a neighboring power, Mavery. Missiles had flashed out of the night, blossoming like red flowers on the inner surface of the town-wheels of Rush. The city had been shocked into action, a punitive expedition mounted with her husband leading it.

She explained to Diamandis that Mavery's assault had been a feint. He listened in mesmerized silence as she described the brittle dystopia known as Falcon Formation, another neighbor of Slipstream. Falcon had conspired with Mavery to draw Slipstream's navy away from Rush. Once the capital was undefended, Falcon Formation was to move in and crush it.

The true story was that Venera's own spy network had alerted them to this plot. Chaison and Venera Fanning had taken seven ships from the fleet and left on a secret mission to find a weapon powerful enough to stop Falcon. The story she told Diamandis now was that her flagship and its escort were pursued by Falcon raiders, chased right out of the lit air of civilization into the darkness of permanent winter that permeated most of Virga.

That had been a month ago.

After that, more things she could tell: a battle with pirates, being captured by same; escape, and more adventures near the skin of the world. She told Diamandis that they had sailed toward Candesce in search of help for their beleaguered country. She did not tell him that their goal was not any of the ancient principalities that ringed the sun. They were after a pirate's treasure, in particular the one seemingly insignificant piece of it that now rested in Venera's jacket. They had come seeking the key to Candesce itself.

In Venera's version, the Slipstream expedition had been met with hostility and chased into the furnace-like regions around Candesce. Her ships had been set upon and half of them destroyed by treacherous marauders of the nation of Gehellen.

In fact, she and her husband had orchestrated the theft of the pirate's treasure from under the noses of the Gehellens and then fled with it—he back to Slipstream and she into the Sun of Suns. There she had temporarily disabled one of Candesce's systems. While it was down, Chaison Fanning was to lead a surprise attack on the fleet of Falcon Formation.

Slipstream's little expeditionary force was no match for the might of Falcon—normally. For one night, the tables should have been turned.

Venera had no idea whether the whole gambit had been successful or not. She would not tell Diamandis—would not have told anyone—that she feared her husband was dead, the force destroyed, and that Falcon cruisers ringed the Pilot's palace at Rush.

"I was lost overboard when the Gehellens attacked," she said. "Like much of the crew. We were close to the Sun of Suns and as dawn came, we burned. . . . I had foot-fins, and at first I was able to fly away but I lost one fin, then the other. I don't remember anything after that."

Diamandis nodded. "You drifted here. Luckily the winds were in your favor. Had you circulated back into Candesce you'd have been incinerated."

That much, at least, was true. Venera suppressed a shudder and sank back in her chair. She was infinitely weary all of a sudden. "I need to sleep."

"By all means. Here, we'll get you to the bed." He touched her arm and she hissed in pain. Diamandis stepped back, concern eloquent on his face.

"There are treatments—creams, salves . . . I'm going to go out and see what I can get for you. For now you have to rest. You've been through a lot."

Venera was not about to argue. She eased herself down on the bed and, despite being awash in burning soreness, fell asleep before hearing him leave.

2

NEAR DAWN, THE lands of Greater Spyre were lit only by the glitter of city lights high overhead. In the faint glow, the ancient towers and forests seemed as insubstantial as clouds. Garth paused in the black absence beneath a willow tree. He had run the last hundred yards and it was all he could do to keep his feet.

Silhouettes bobbed against the gray outline of a tower. Whoever they were, they were still following him. It was unprecedented: he had snuck through the hedgerows and fields of six hereditary barons, each holding no more than a square mile or so of territory but as fanatical about their boundaries as any empire. Garth knew how to get past their guards and dogs, he did it all the time. Apparently, these men did also.

It must have been somebody at the Goodwill Free Clinic. They'd waited until he was gone and then signaled someone. If that was so, Garth would no longer be able to count on the neutrality of the kingdom of Hallimel—all six acres of it.

He moved on cautiously, padding quietly onto a closely cropped lawn dotted with ridiculously heroic statues. It was quiet as a tomb here, and certainly nobody had any business being out. He allowed himself a little righteous indignation at whoever it was that was following him. They were trespassers; they should be shot.

It would be most satisfying to raise the alarm and see what happened—a cascade of genetically crazed hounds from the doorway of yon manor house, perhaps, or spotlights and a sniper on the roof. The trouble was, Garth himself was a known and tolerated ghost in only a few of these places, and certainly not the one he was passing through now. So he remained discreet.

A high stone wall loomed over the garden of statues. Its bricks were crumbling and made an easy ladder for Garth in the low gravity. As he rolled over the top he heard voices behind him—someone exclaiming something. He must have been visible against the sky.

He landed in brambles. From here on the country was wild. This was disputed territory, owned by now-extinct families, its provenance tied up in generations-old court cases that would probably drag on until the end of the world. Most of the disputed lands were due to the railway allotments created by the preservationists; they had needed clearances that ran completely around the world, and they had gotten them, for a price of blood. This section of land had been abandoned for other reasons, though what they were Garth didn't know. He didn't care, either, as long as the square tower he called home was left in peace.

His intention was to reach it so that he could warn the lady Fanning that they had company—but halfway across the open grassland he heard thuds behind him as half a dozen bodies hit the ground on his side of the wall. They were catching up, and quickly.

He flattened and rolled to one side. Grass swished as dark figures passed by, only feet away. Garth cursed under his breath, wishing there were some way to warn Venera Fanning that six heavily armed men were about to pay her a visit.

VENERA HEARD THEM coming. The darkness wasn't total—Diamandis had left a candle burning—so she wasn't completely disoriented when she awoke to voices saying "Circle around the other side" and "This must be his bolt-hole." A flush of adrenaline brought her completely awake as she heard scratching and scuffling just outside the hovel's door.

She rolled out of bed, heedless of the pain, and ran to the table where she snatched up a knife. "Down here!" someone shouted.

Where were her clothes? Her jacket lay draped across a chair, and on the table were the bracelet and earrings Diamandis had left her. She cast about for her other things, but Diamandis had apparently moved them. There they were, on another table—next to the opening door.

Venera's first inclination would normally be to draw herself up to her full five foot seven and stare these men down when they entered. They were servants, after all, even if they were armed. If she could speak and make eye contact, Venera was completely confident in her ability to control members of the lower classes.

At least, she used to be. Recent events—particularly her unwelcome dalliance with Captain Dentius of the winter pirates—had made her more cautious. Plus which, she was sore all over and had a pounding headache.

So Venera snatched up the candle, her jacket, and the jewelry and knelt under the table. The rope ring scraped her raw skin as she yanked on it; after a few tugs the mysterious hatch lifted. She felt down with her foot, making contact with a metal step. As men blundered into Diamandis's home she billowed the damp sheet behind her, with luck to drape over the hatch and hide it.

The candle guttered and nearly went out. Venera cupped a hand around it and cautiously felt for the next step. She counted seven before finding herself standing in an icy draft on metal flooring. A constant low roar made it hard to hear what was going on above.

This small chamber was oval, wider at the ceiling than at the floor, and ringed with windows. All the panes were flush with the wall, but a couple vibrated at a high speed, making a low braying sound. They seemed to be sucking air out of the room; it was the walls that soaked cold into the place.

Diamandis evidently used the room for storage because there were boxes piled everywhere. Venera was able to make her way among them to the far end, where a metal chair was bolted to the floor. The windows here were impressive: floor-to-ceiling, made of some resilient material she had never seen before.

The candlelight seemed to show a dense weave of leaves on the other side of the glass.

She was going to freeze unless she found something to wear. Venera ransacked the boxes, alternately cursing and puffing out her cheeks in wonder at the strange horde of broken clocks, worn-out shoes, rusted hinges, frayed quills, moldy sewing kits, left socks, and buckles. One crate contained nothing but the dust jackets of books, all their pages having been systematically ripped out. It was a small library's worth of intriguing but useless titles. Another was full of decaying military apparel, including holsters and scabbards, all of it bearing the same coat of arms.

At least the activity was keeping her warm, she reasoned. The faint clomp of boots above continued, so she moved on to a new stack of boxes. This time she was rewarded when she found it packed with clothing. After dumping most of that onto the floor she discovered a pair of stiff leather pants, too small for Diamandis but sufficient for her. Getting into them wasn't easy, though—the material scoured her already-raw skin so that it hurt to move. The leather cut out the wind, however.

Once she had donned the flight jacket Venera sat down in the metal chair to wait for whatever happened next. This was much harder; it wasn't in Venera's nature to remain still. Staying still made you think and thinking led to feeling, which was seldom good.

She drew her knees up and wrapped her arms around her shins. It came to her that if they took away Diamandis and she couldn't get out of here, she would die and no one would ever know what had happened to her. Few would care, either, and some would rejoice. Venera knew she wasn't well liked.

More stomping up above. She shivered. How far away was her home in Slipstream? Three thousand miles? Four? An ocean of air separated her from her husband and in that ocean gyred the nations of enemies, rising, lowering, drifting with the unpredictable airs of Virga. Awaiting her out there were the freezing abysses of winter, full of feathered sharks and pirates. Before the Sun of Suns had roasted her into unconsciousness, she had been determined and sure of her own ability to cross those daunting distances alone. She had leaped from the cargo nets of Hayden Griffin's jet and soared for a time like a solitary eagle in the skies of Virga. But the sun had caught up to her and now she was here, trapped and in pain hardly any distance from where she'd started.

She climbed off the chair, fighting a wave of nausea. Better to surrender herself to whoever waited above than die here alone, she thought—and she almost ran up the steps and surrendered. It was a pulse of pain through her jaw that stopped her. Venera drew her fingertips across the scar that adorned her chin, and then she backed away from the steps.

Her heel caught the edge of a box she'd dropped, and she stumbled back against the icy windows. Cursing, she straightened up, but as she did she noticed a gleam of light welling up through the glass. She put her cheek to it—which dampened the pain a bit—and squinted.

The windows were covered with a long-leafed form of ivy. The stuff was vibrating with uncanny speed—so quickly that the leaves' edges were blurred. Diamandis had said that Spyre rotated very fast; was she looking into the air outside?

Of course. This oval chamber stuck out of the bottom of the world. It was an aerodynamic blister on the outside of the rotating cylinder, and that chair might have once fronted the controls of a heavy machine gun or artillery piece mounted outside. It still might. Frowning, Venera clambered over the mounds of junk back to the metal seat and examined it.

There was indeed a set of handles and levers below the chair, and more between the windows. She didn't touch them but peered out through the glass there, as light continued to well through the close-set leaves.

Candesce was waking up. The Sun of Suns lit a zone hundreds of miles in diameter here at the center of Virga. Past the trembling leaves Venera could see a carousel of mauve and peach-painted cloud tumbling past with disorienting speed; but she could also see more.

The oval blister was mounted into a ceiling of riveted metal, as she'd expected. That ceiling was the hull of Spyre, and a few feet above it was soil, trees, and the foundations of the buildings she had seen yesterday. Covering this surface in long runnels and triangles was the strange ivy. Its leaves were like knives, sharp and long, and they all aligned in the flow of the wind. Venera had heard of something called speed ivy; maybe that was what this was.

The ivy seemed to prefer growing on things that projected into the airstream. Sheets of metal skin were missing here and there—in fact, there were outright holes everywhere—and the ivy clustered on the leading and trailing edges of these, smoothing the airflow in those places. Maybe that was what it was for.

This view of Spyre was not reassuring. The place was showing its age—dangling sheets of titanium whirred in the wind and huge I-beams thrust down into the dawn-tinted air, whole sagging acres just waiting to peel off the bottom of the world. It was amazing that the place kept itself together.

Next to the blister, a rusted machine gun was mounted on the surface. It faced stoically into the wind and didn't move when Venera tried the controls in front of the chair.

Well. All this was interesting, but not too interesting. She headed back to the stairs, but the light coming through the ranked leaves was considerable now and she could see more of the blister's interior. So the little passage that opened out behind the stairs was now obvious.

Venera gnawed her lip and rolled her eyes to look at the closed hatch overhead. One hand was on her hip; even here, with no audience, she posed as she thought.

She needed shoes—but she'd recovered the important items, the key to Candesce and her bullet. Venera was quite aware that she was obsessed with that bullet, and who wouldn't be, she usually reasoned, if one like it had flown a thousand miles or more across Virga to randomly spike through a window and into their jaw? This particular projectile had been fired in some distant war or hunting party and missed its target; since there was no gravity nor solid ground to stop it the thing had kept going and going until it met her. From that encounter Venera had gained a scar, regular crippling headaches, and something to blame for her own meanness. She'd kept the bullet and over time had become consumed with the need to know where it had come from. It was not, she would admit, a healthy need.

She patted the jacket, feeling the heavy shape inside it; then she slipped past the steps and into the narrow passage, and left Diamandis and his invaders to their own little drama.

IT WAS MORE of a crawlway than a corridor. Venera walked bent over, gasping as the old leather chaffed her hips and knees. Why didn't these people dress sensibly? Lit only by intermittent portholes, the passage wormed its way a hundred yards or so before ending in a round metal door. It was all so obviously abandoned—stinking of rust and inorganic decay—that Venera didn't bother knocking on the door, but turned the little wheel in the middle of it and pushed.

She stepped down into a mirror image of the blister she had just left. She half-expected to find another maze of boxes on the other side of the steps, with another junk-framed hovel and another Garth Diamandis waiting for her above. But no, the blister was empty save for a half-foot of stagnant water and a truly revolting gallery of fungus and cobwebs. The windows were hazed over but provided enough light for a tiny forest that was trying to conquer the metal chair at the far end. The stairs were jammed with soil and roots.

The prospect of dipping her bare feet into that horrid water nearly made her turn back. What stopped her was a tiny chink of light visible in the midst of the soil plug. After wading cautiously and with revulsion through the stinking stuff, she reached up and pulled at the roots. Gradually, in little showers of dirt, worms, and fibrous tubers, she widened a hole big enough for her to shimmy through. A minute later she dragged herself up, out, and into the middle of a grassy field.

Too bad about Diamandis, but with luck he was still off on his errand and the interlopers wouldn't be there when he got back. Anyway, he'd been more than compensated for taking care of her; that had been a Pilot's ransom of gems and faience he'd taken from her jacket. She half-hoped those loud burglars found the stuff—it would serve him right.

Venera's own destination was clear. Spyre being a cylinder, it had ends and one of those was only half a mile away. There, the artificial land curved up hundreds of feet in a gesture that would close off the end if continued. The curve ended in a broad gallery above and beyond which the winds of Virga shuddered. Venera had only to make it up that slope and hop off the edge and she would be in free flight again. She would take her chances with the piranhawks and snipers. She doubted any of them could hit one small woman leaving Spyre at four hundred miles per hour.

In this case, wearing leather would serve her well.

Between Venera and the edge of the world lay a chessboard of estates. Each had its tottering stone walls, high hedges, towers, and moats to defend its two or three acres from the ravages of greedy neighbors. Constrained by space and what Venera sensed was deep paranoia, the estates had evolved into similar designs— the larger ones walled, with groves surrounding open fields and a jumble of towers, annexes, and greenhouses at the center; small ones often just a single square building that took up the entire demesne. These edifices were utterly windowless on the outside, but higher up the curve of the world she could see that most contained courtyards crammed with trees, fountains, and statuary.

The walls of some estates were separated by no more than twenty feet of no-man's-land. She ran through these weed-choked alleys, dodging young trees, past iron-faced pillbox gates that faced one another across the minor space like boxy suits of armor. The footing was treacherous, and she suspected traps.

Venera was used to higher gravity than Spyre's. Tired and sore though she was, it was easy for her to leap ten feet to the top of a stone wall and run its length before dropping to the grass beyond. Her feet barely felt brick, root, and stone as she wove in and out of the trees, sprinted around open ponds under windows that were just beginning to gleam yellow in the light of Candesce. As she ran she marveled that such distances could exist; she had never run so far in a straight line and could hardly believe it possible.

The birds were the only ones making sound, but as she ran Venera began to notice a deep rushing roar that came from ahead of her. It was the sound of the edge of the world, and with it there came the beginnings of a breeze.

She heard surprised shouts as she crossed one fanatically perfect lawn, bare feet kissing wet grass. Glancing to the side, Venera caught a glimpse of a small party of men and women sitting on curlicued iron chairs in the morning light. They were sipping tea or something similar.

They stood up—stiff ornamented garments ratcheting into their standing configurations like portcullises slamming down—and the three men howled "Intruders!" as if Venera were an entire army of pirates. After a moment sirens sounded inside the looming stone pile behind them.

"Oh, come on!" She was panting with exhaustion now, her head swimming. But there were only two more estates to pass and then she would be on the slope to the world's edge. With a burst of speed she raced by more lighting windows and opening doors, noting abstractly that the considerable mob of soldiers who had spilled out of the first place's doors had stopped at the edge of their property as if they'd slammed into an invisible fence.

So she had only to outrace the alarm in each particular property. It could be a game and Venera actually would have enjoyed the chase if she hadn't been on the verge of fainting from exhaustion and residual heatstroke. If only she had the breath to taunt the idiots on the way by!

Gunshots cut the air as she passed the last estate. This was one of the big single-building affairs, all gray asteroidal stone drizzled with veins of bright metal. Its only external windows were murder slits that started fifteen feet up, and she saw no doors. Empty upward-curving fields beckoned on the other side of the edifice; she staggered onto what Diamandis had called "disputed territory" and paused to catch her breath. "Ha! Safe!"

The wind was now a harsh constant moan, flickering past her in gusts. It spun in little permanent tornadoes over gaps and holes in Spyre's skin. There were more and more such holes as the slope rose to the edge. The edge itself was ragged, a crenelation of collapsed galleries, upthrusting spars, and flapping plates that added to the din.

She heard something else too. A regular creaking sound seemed to be coming from overhead. Venera looked up.

Six wooden platforms had been lowered over the top of the stone cube and were being winched down. Each was crowded with men in tall steel helmets and outlandish spiked armor. They clutched pikes and rifles with barrels longer than they were tall. Several were pointing at her excitedly.

Venera swore and took off up the rubble-strewn slope. The wind was at her back and it became stronger the closer she got to the edge. Several gusts lifted her off her feet. Venera noticed that the metal skin of Spyre was completely exposed in the final yards leading up to the edge. Only fair-sized rocks inhabited the area behind it. As she watched, a stone the size of her foot rolled up the metal and spun off into the air. A few more yards and the wind would take her too.

Her foot sank into the slope and Venera fell in ridiculous slow-motion. As she pried herself upright again she saw that the metal plate bent by her foot was vibrating madly in the square hole it had made. Then with a loud pop it disappeared and suddenly a hurricane was howling into the bright aperture it had left.

Venera was sucked down and slid forward until she was right over the hole. She reached out and braced her hands on either side of it while the air screamed past her. It was trying to escape Spyre with even more passion than hers. For a few seconds she could only stare down and see what faced her if she made it to the edge and jumped.

Many long flagpole-like beams thrust out below the edge of the world. They trailed wire nets into the furious wind; anyone caught on those nets would suffocate before they could be pulled up. Far beneath the nets, where scudding clouds spun past, Venera glimpsed thousands of black specks and grayish veins in the air. Mines? More razor wire? Diamandis had not been lying, after all.

"Damn! Shit!" She tried to scream more curses—every one she could think of—but the air was being pulled out of her lungs. She was about to faint into the hole and die.

Strong hands took her by the arms and legs and hauled her back. Venera was hoisted onto someone's back and unceremoniously toted back down the slope. With every jolting step escape, home, and Chaison receded past the frame of her grasping fingers.

3

ALTHOUGH HE WAS her favorite uncle, Venera never saw much of Prince Albard. He was a mysterious figure on the periphery of the court, sweeping into Hale in his yacht to regale her with tales of strange cities and the outlandish women he'd met there (always sighing when he spoke of them). His face was split down the center by a saber scar, putting his lips into a permanent twist that made it look like he was smirking. Unlike most of the people who encountered him, Venera knew that he *was* smirking—laughing inside at all the pointless desperation and petty recrimination of life. In that regard he was the polar opposite of her father, a man with a mind focused by a single lens of suspicion; maybe that was why she clung to Albard's knees when he did appear, and treasured the odd-shaped dolls and toys he brought.

They recognized each other, this vagabond prince in his motley and the pouting princess in clothes she systematically tattered as soon as she was in them. So maybe it was natural that when the time came, it was in her bedroom that Albard barricaded himself.

He only noticed her after he had dragged her wardrobe in front of the door and piled some chairs and tables around it. "Damn, girl, what are you doing here?"

Venera had cocked her head and squinted at him. "This is my room."

"I know it's your room, damnit. Shouldn't you be at lessons?"

"I bit the tutor." Banished and bored, she had (not out of anger but a more scientific impulse) been beheading some of her dolls when Albard swept in. Venera had assumed that he was there to talk to her and had politely waited, limp headless body in one hand, while he proceeded to move all the furniture. So he wasn't there to see her? What, then, was this all about?

"Oh, never mind," he said irritably, "just stay out of sight. Things could get ugly."

Now she could hear shouting outside, sounds of people running. "What did *you* do?" she asked.

He was leaning back against the pile of furniture as though trying to propel it out of the room. "I bit someone too," he said. "Or, rather, I was about to, and they found out."

Venera came and sat down on the fuschia carpet near him. "My father, right?"

His eyebrows rose comically. "How did you guess?"

Venera thought about this for a while. Then she said, "Does that mean that everybody who makes Father mad has to come to this room?"

Albard laughed. "Niece, if that were true, the whole damn kingdom would be in here with us."

"Oh." She was slightly reassured.

"Give it up, Albard!" someone shouted from outside. It sounded like her father. There was some sort of mumbling discussion, then: "Is, uh . . . is Venera in there with you?"

"No!" The prince put a finger to his lips and knelt next to her. "The one thing I absolutely will not do," he said gently, "is use you as a bargaining chip. If you want to leave I will tear down this barricade and let you go."

"What will they do to you?"

"Put me in chains, take me away . . . then it all depends on your father's mood. There's a black cloud behind his eyes lately. Have you seen it?" She nodded vigorously. "It's getting bigger and bigger, that cloud, and I think it's starting to crowd out everything else. That worries me."

"I know what you mean."

"I daresay you do." There followed a long interval during which Albard negotiated with the people on the other side of the furniture. Venera retreated to the window, but she was far from bored now. At last Albard blew out his cheeks and turned to her.

"Things are not going well," he said. "Do you have a pen and some writing material?" She pointed to the desk that perched on top of the barricade. "Ah. Much obliged."

He clambered up and retrieved a pen and some paper. Then, frowning, he dropped the paper. He went to his knees and began hunting around for something, while Venera watched closely. He came up with one of her dolls, a favorite that had a porcelain head and cloth body.

"Do you mind if I borrow this for a minute?" he asked her. She shrugged.

Albard rubbed the doll's face against the stone floor for a while, while crashing sounds started from the hallway. The barricade shook. Holding the doll up critically, the prince grunted in satisfaction. Then he hunched over and began delicately pressing the pen against its face.

He was standing in the center of the room with his hands behind his back when the barricade finally fell. A dozen soldiers came in and they marched him out; he only had time to look back and wink at Venera before he was gone.

After they'd taken him away some members of the secret police ransacked her room. (That it looked substantially the same when they left as before Albard had arrived was a testament to her own habits.) They seized everything that could write or be written on, even prying the plaster off the wall where she'd scribbled on it. Venera herself was frisked several times and then they swirled out, all clinking metal and bandoliers, leaving her sitting in the exact spot where he had been standing.

Neither she nor anyone she would later meet would ever see Albard again.

Eventually she moved over to the window and picked up a particular doll. Its tunic was ripped where the secret policemen had cut it open looking for hidden notes. Venera held it up to the window and frowned.

So that was what he'd been doing. Albard had rubbed its eyebrows off against the stone. Then, in meticulous tiny lines and curls, he had repainted them. From a distance of more than a few inches they seemed normal. Up close, though, she could see what they were made of:

Letters.

THE NATION OF Liris curled around its interior courtyard as though doubled up in pain. Every window stared down at that courtyard. Every balcony overhung it and the six towers that surmounted the building were built to overlook it as well. The bottom of this well would be in permanent shadow if not for the giant mirrors mounted on the roof, which were aimed at Candesce.

Venera could plainly see that the courtyard was the focus of everything—but she couldn't see what was down there. For the first two days of her stay she was shuttled from small room to small room, all of them lined up in a short hallway painted institution green. After a brief interview in each chamber she was taken back to a drab waiting room, where she sat and ate and slept fitfully on the benches. She was startled awake every morning by a single gunshot sounding somewhere nearby. Morning executions?

It seemed unlikely; she was the sole inhabitant of this little prison. Prison it clearly was. She had to fill out forms just to use the one washroom, a cold cube with wooden stalls defaced by centuries of carven graffiti. Its high grated windows gave her a view of the upper stories of the inner courtyard. They hinted at freedom.

"B-b-back to waking?" Venera sat up warily on the third morning and tried to smile at her jailor.

He was tall, athletically muscled, and possessed the sort of chiseled good looks one saw in actors, career diplomats, or con artists. As dapper as could be expected for a man dressed in iron and creaking leather, he might have melted any lady's heart—provided she never looked in his eyes or heard him speak. Either of those maneuvers would have revealed the awful truth about Moss: his mind was damaged somehow. He seemed more marionette than man and, sadly, appeared to be painfully aware of his deficit.

Just as he had yesterday, Moss carried a stack of forms in one hand, bearing it as though it were a silver platter. Venera sighed when she saw this. "How long is it going to take to process me into your prison?" she asked as he clattered to a stop in front of her.

"P-p-prison?" Moss gaped at her. Carefully, as though they were gold, he placed the papers on the peeling bench. His metal clothing gnashed quietly as he straightened up. "You're n-not in p-p-prison, my lady."

"Then what is this place?" She gestured around at the sound-deadening plaster walls, the smoke-stained light sconces, and the battered benches. "Why am I here? When do I get my things back?" They'd gone through her jacket and taken its contents—jewelry, key, and bullet. She wasn't sure which loss worried her most.

Moss's face never changed expression as he spoke, but his eyes radiated some sort of desperate plea. They always did, even if he was staring at the wall. Those eyes seemed eloquent, but Venera was beginning to think that nothing about Moss's looks or demeanor meant anything about his inner state. Now he said, in his intensely flat way, "This is the im-immigration department of the g-g-government of Liris. You were brought here to t-t-take your citizenship-ip exams."

"Citizenship?" But now it all made sense—the forms, the sense of being processed, and the succession of minor officials who'd taken up hours of her time over the past days. They had grilled her mercilessly, but not about how or why she had come here, or about what her plans or allegiances might be. They didn't even want to know about her peeling sunburns. No, they'd wanted to know the medical histories of her extended family, whether there was madness in her line (a question that had made her laugh), and what was the incidence of criminality among her relatives.

"Well, my father stole a country once," she had answered. She had of course asked them to let her go, in perhaps a dozen different ways. Her assumption was that she would be ransomed or otherwise used as a bargaining chip. With this in mind she had sat anxiously for hours, wondering about her value to this or that state or person. It had never occurred to Venera that she might be adopted by Liris as one of its own.

Now as she realized what was going on, Venera had one of the strangest moments of her life. She felt, for just a second, relief at the prospect of spending the rest of her life hidden away here, like a jewel in a safe. She shook herself, and the moment passed. Disturbed, she stood and turned away from Moss.

"B-b-but the news is good," said Moss, who looked like he was begging for death as he said it. "D-don't fret. You have p-p-passed all the t-t-tests so far. J-just one set of forms to g-go."

Venera gnawed at her knuckle, each bite sending little pulses of pain up her jaw. "What if I don't want to be a citizen of Liris?"

Moss proceeded to laugh, and Venera swore to herself she would do anything to avoid seeing that again. "F-Fill these out," he said. "A-and you're done."

It wasn't eagerness to become a citizen of a nation the size of a garden that made her sign the papers. Venera just wanted to get her things back—and get out of the waiting room. What she'd felt a moment ago was just a craving for anonymity, she told herself. Citizenship of any nation meant nothing to her, except as a sign of lowly status. Her father was hardly a citizen of Hale, after all; he *was* Hale and other people were citizens of him. Venera had grown up believing she too was above such categories.

"Come" was all Moss said when she was finished. He led her out into the hallway and at its end he unlocked the great metal door with its wire-mesh window. Before pushing the portal open, he picked up an open-topped box and held it out to her.

Inside were the necklace and earrings he'd confiscated from her jacket when she arrived. Rolling next to them was her bullet.

The key to Candesce was not there.

Venera frowned but decided not to press the matter just now. Moss gestured with one hand and she edged past him into her new country.

Shafts of dusty sunlight silhouetted tall stone pillars. Their arched capitals were muted in shadow, but the polished floors gleamed like mirrors. Save for a wall where the edge of the court-yard should be, the whole bottom floor of the great cubic build-ing seemed open. Filling the space were dozens and dozens of cubicles, desks, worktables, and stalls.

Indeed, it seemed as if all the roles of a midsized town were duplicated here—tailor over here, doctor there, carpenters on this side, bricklayers on that—but all gathered in one room. Bolts of cloth were stacked with bags of cement. Drying racks and looms had been folded up under the ceiling to make way for chopping blocks and flour-covered counters. And working in de-termined silence throughout this shadow-cut space was a small army of silent, focused people.

Each was isolated at some chair or desk, and Venera had the startled impression that these workstations had grown up and around some of the people, like shells secreted around water creatures. It must have taken years for that man there to build the small ziggurat of green bottles that reared above his desk; nearby a woman had buried herself in a miniature jungle of ferns. Mirrors on stands and hanging from strings cunningly directed every stray beam of light within ten feet at her green fronds. Each position had its eruption of individuality or downright eccentricity, but their limits were strictly kept; nobody's keepsakes and oddities spilled beyond an invisible line about five feet in radius.

Moss led her to an outer wall, where he opened a dim cham-ber that reminded her of Diamandis's warren. Here were crates and boxes full of what looked like armor—except she knew it for what it was. "You are required to wear four hundred fifty p-p-pounds of mass during the day," said Moss. "That will offset our r-reduced g-gravity and maintain the health of your bones." He stood back, arms crossed, while Venera rooted through the mess looking for something suitable.

It seemed that Spyre's tailors were an unimaginative lot. The room contained an abundance of blouses, dresses and skirts, pants, and jackets, but all were done in intricately tooled and hinged metal. Only undergarments—those directly in contact with the skin—were made of suppler materials, mostly leather, though to her relief she did find some cloth. Venera tried on a vest made of verdigrised copper scales, added a skirt made of overlapping iron plates and weighed herself. Barely a hundred pounds. She went back and found greaves and wrist bracers, a platinum torque, and a steel jacket with tails. Better, but still too light. Moss waited patiently while she layered herself like a battleship. Finally when she topped the scales at one hundred pounds weight—five hundred pounds mass—he grunted in satisfaction. "B-but you need a h-h-hat," he said.

"What?" She glared at him. He had something like a belaying pin tied to his head; it wobbled when he moved. "Isn't all this humiliating enough?"

"We m-must put p-p-pressure on the s-spine. For l-long-term health."

"Oh, all right." She hunted through a cache of ridiculous alternatives, ranging from flowerpots with chin straps to a glass fishbowl, currently empty but encrusted with rime. Finally she settled on the least offensive piece, a chrome helmet with earflaps and crow's wings mounted behind the temples.

With all of this on her, Venera's feet made a satisfactory smack when they hit the ground. She could feel the weight and it was indeed nearly normal, but spread all over her surface instead of internally. And she quickly discovered that it took a good hard push to start walking and that turning or stopping were not operations to be taken lightly. She had a quarter-ton of inertia now. After walking into several walls and doorjambs she started to get the hang of it.

"N-now," said Moss in evident satisfaction, "you are f-fit to see the b-b-botanist."

"The what?" He threaded his way among the pillars without further comment. Venera nodded and smiled at the men and women who were putting down their work to openly stare as she passed. She tried to unobtrusively discern what they were working on, but the light here was too uneven. Shadow and glare thwarted her.

Sunlight reflecting off the polished floor washed out whatever was ahead. Venera glanced back one more time before entering the lit area. Blackness and curving arches framed a dozen white ovals—faces—all turned toward her. On those faces she read every emotion: amazement, curiosity, anger, fear. None avoided her gaze. They goggled at her as though they'd never seen a stranger before.

Maybe they hadn't. Venera's scalp prickled, but Moss was waving her ahead. Blinking, she stepped from the dark gallery into the courtyard of Liris.

For a moment it seemed as if she'd entered one of the paintings on the ceiling of her father's chapel. This one came complete with scented pink clouds. She reached out a hand to touch one of these and heard the sharp click of a weapon being cocked. Venera froze.

"It would be very unwise of you to complete that gesture," drawled a voice from somewhere ahead. Slowly, Venera retracted her hand. As her eyes adjusted to the brightness she saw the barrels of three antique-looking rifles aimed her way. Grim men in iron held them.

The soldiers made a shocking contrast to their setting. The entire courtyard was full of trees, all of one type, all in full flower. The scent and color of the millions of blossoms was overwhelming. It took Venera a moment to notice that the branches of many of the trees were hung with jewels, and gold rings encircled some of the trunks. It took her another moment to realize that a throne sat in the sole bare patch at the center of the courtyard. The woman lounging there was watching her with obvious amusement.

Her gown was of gold, silver, and platinum; on her head was a crown touched with gems of all shades that flashed in the concentrated light of Candesce. She appeared to be in early middle age, but was still beautiful; a cascade of hair dyed the same color as the blossoms wound down her shoulders.

"You seem reluctant to step into sunlight," she said with evident amusement. "I can see why." She tapped her own cheeks, eyes twinkling.

Venera eyed the soldiers, thought about it, and walked over. Since this was evidently a throne room of sorts, she bowed deeply. "Your . . . majesty?"

"Oh. Oh no." The woman chuckled. "I am no queen." She waved a hand dismissively. "We are a meritocracy in Liris. You'll learn. My name is Margit, and I am Liris's resident botanist."

"Botanist . . ." Venera straightened and looked around at the trees. "This is your crop."

"Please." The lady Margit frowned. "We don't refer to the treasure of Liris in such prosaic terms. These beings *are* Liris. They sustain us, they give us meaning. They are our soul."

"Pardon, m'lady," said Venera with another bow. "But . . . what exactly *are* they?"

"Of course." Margit's eyes grew wide. "You would never have seen one before. You are so lucky to gaze upon them for the first time when they are in flower. These, Citizen Fanning, are *cherry* trees."

Why was that word so familiar? There'd been a ball once, and her beloved uncle had approached her with something in his hand. . . . A treat.

"What are cherries?" she asked as guilelessly as she could.

"An indulgence of the powerful," said Margit with a smile. "A delicacy so rare that it evidently never made it to your father's court."

"About that," said Venera. "The court, I mean. My family are fantastically rich. Why make me a . . . citizen of this place, when you could just ransom me back? You could get a boatload of treasure for me."

Margit scoffed. "If you were the princess of a true nation then perhaps we would consider it. But you're not even from the principalities! By your own admission during the interviews, you come from the windswept wastes of Outer Virga. There's nothing there, and I find it hard to believe your people could own anything that would be of interest to us."

Venera narrowed her eyes. "Not even a fleet of battle cruisers capable of reducing this place to kindling from twenty miles away?"

Not only Margit laughed at this; the soldiers did as well. "Nobody threatens Spyre, young lady. We're impregnable." Margit said this so smugly that Venera swore she would find a way to throw her words back at her.

Margit snapped her fingers and Moss stepped forward. "Acquaint her with her new duties," said the botanist.

Moss stared at her, slack-jawed. "W-what are those?"

"She knows the languages and cultures of other places. She'll be an interpreter for the trade delegation. Go introduce her." Margit turned away, lifting her chin with her eyes closed so that a beam of sunlight flooded her face.

ON HER SEVENTEENTH birthday, Venera snuck out of the palace for the first time, acquired the means to blackmail her father, killed her first person, and met the man she was destined to marry. She would later tell people that "it all just sort of happened."

The capital of Hale was a collection of six town-wheels—spinning rings, each two thousand feet in diameter—surrounded by an ever-shifting cloud of weightless buildings and smaller rings. The main sound in the city was the rumbling of jet engines, as various rings and large municipal structures struggled to keep their spin and to avoid colliding. The scent of kerosene hung in the air; underlying it were other industrial and biological odors, just as under the rumbling of the engines you could hear shouts, horns, and the laughter of dolphins.

Venera had grown up watching the city life from afar. When she traveled between the town-wheels it was usually in a closed taxi. Sometimes one or another of the nobility hosted weightless balls; then, she and the other ingenues donned fabulous wings that were powered by stirrups, and flew intricate dances in the warm evening air. But that flight always took place within careful limits. Nobody strayed.

She was of marriageable age now—and had recently come to realize that in Hale, marriageable also meant murderable. Venera had three sisters and had once had three brothers. Now she had two of those, and the once-close girls of the family were starting to actively plot against one another. With the boys, it was all about succession; with the girls, marriage.

Someone had used a marvelous word at a dinner party just a few days before: *leverage*. Leverage was what she needed, Venera had decided. And so her thoughts had turned to old family tragedies and the mysteries that had consumed her as a girl.

Today she was dressed in the brown blouse and pantaloons of a servant girl and the wings on her back were not butterfly orange or feathered pink, but beige canvas. Her hair was tied down with a drab cloth and she soared the air of the city barefoot. In her waist bag she carried some money, a pistol, and a porcelain-headed doll. She knew where she was going.

The bad neighborhoods started remarkably close to the palace. This fact might have had something to do with the royal habit of simply dumping waste off the palace wheel without regard to trajectory or velocity. The upper classes couldn't be entirely blamed for the stench that wafted at Venera as she flapped toward her destination, however. She wasn't disgusted; on the contrary the smell and the sound of arguing, shouting people made her heart pound with excitement. Since she was little she'd sat for hours with her eye glued to a telescope, watching these citizens and this neighborhood roll by as the palace turned past it. She knew the place—she had simply never been here.

What Venera approached looked like nothing so much as an explosion frozen in time. Even the smoke (of which there was plenty) was motionless, or rather it moved only as quickly as the air that oozed slowly between the hundreds of cubes, balls, and disheveled shapes that counted as buildings here. Anything not tied down hung in the air and drifted gradually, and that meant trash, animal hair, balls of dirty water, splinters, and scraps of cloth all contributed to the cloud. When the doldrums of summer broke and a stiff wind finally did snake through the place, half the mass of the neighborhood was going to simply blow away, like chaff. For now it roiled around Venera as she ducked and dove toward the gray blockhouse that was her destination.

Her business in the building was brief, but every detail of the transaction seemed etched in extraordinary detail—for here were people who didn't know who she was. It was marvelous to be treated like servants and ordinary folk treated one another, for a change—marvelous and eye-opening. Nobody opened the door to the place for her; she had to do it herself. Nobody announced her presence; she had to clear her throat and ask the man behind the counter to help her. And she had to pay, with her own money!

"The contents of locker six-sixty-four," she said, holding out the sheet of paper she'd written the information on. The paper was for his benefit, not hers, for she'd memorized the brief string of letters and numbers years ago. Deciphering the letters Uncle Albard had penned on her doll's forehead had been one of her primary motivations to learn to read.

The keeper of the storage lockers merely grunted and said, "Get 'em yourself. If you've got the combination, you get in, that's the rule." He pointed to a doorway at the end of the counter.

She made to go that way and he said, "Back pay's owing on that one. Six hundred." He grinned like a shark. "We were about to clear it out."

Venera opened her bag, letting him see the pistol as she rummaged for the cash. He took it without comment and waved her through the door.

The only thing in the dingy locker was a water-stained file folder. As she stood in the half-light flipping through it, Venera decided it was all she needed. The documents were from the College of Succession at the University of Candesce, two thousand miles away. They included DNA analyses that proved her father was not of the royal line.

She barely saw the tumbled buildings as she left the blockhouse; maybe that was why she got turned around. But suddenly Venera snapped to attention and realized she was in a narrow chute formed by five clapboard structures, on her way down, not up toward the palace. Frowning, she grabbed a handy rope to steady herself and turned to go back the way she'd come.

"Don't." The voice was quiet, and came from above and to the left. Venera flipped over to orient herself to the speaker. In the gray reflected light from shingle and tar paper she saw a youth—perhaps no older than herself—with tangled red hair and the long bones of someone raised in too little gravity. He smiled toothily at her and said, "Bad men coming behind you. Keep going and take your first hard right, and you'll be safe."

She hesitated, and he scowled. "Not shittin' ya. Get going if you know what's good for you."

Venera flipped again, planted her feet on the rope, and kicked off down the chute. As she reached the corner the boy had indicated she heard voices coming from the far end of the chute—opposite the way he'd said the bad men were coming from.

This side way led quickly to well-traveled airspace and had no niches or doors out of which someone could spring. Feeling momentarily safe, Venera peeked around the corner of the chute. Three men were flying slowly up from the left.

"I really think you've gotten us lost this time," said the one in the lead. He was in his late twenties and obviously noble or rich from his dress and demeanor. One of his companions was similarly dressed, but the third man looked like a commoner. She couldn't see much more in the dim light. "The palace is definitely not this way," continued the leader. "My appointment is at two o'clock. I can't afford to be late."

Two o'clock? She remembered one of the courtiers telling her that a commodore from some neighboring country would be calling on her father in the early afternoon. Was this the man?

Suddenly one of the other men shouted, "Hey!" He had barely writhed out of the way of a sword that had suddenly appeared in the third one's hand. "Chaison, it's a trap!"

Four men shot down the chute from the right. They were rough-looking, the sort of thugs Venera had watched roaming the neighborhood through her spyglass and sometimes fantasized about. All had drawn swords and none spoke as they set upon their two victims.

The one named Chaison whirled his cloak into the air between himself and the attackers and drew his sword as his friend parried a thrust from their erstwhile guide. After the initial warning from Chaison's friend, nobody spoke.

In a free-fall swordfight, the blade was as much propulsion as weapon. Each of the men found purchase in wall or rope or opponent with hand, foot, shoulder, or blade as they could. Each impact sent them in a new direction and they tumbled and spun as they slashed at one another. Venera had watched men practice with swords and had even witnessed duels, but this was totally different. There was nothing mannered about it; the fight was swift and brutal. The men's movements were beautiful, viscerally thrilling, and almost too fast to take in.

One of the attackers was hanging back. As his face intersected a shaft of light she realized it was the boy who had warned her. He held his sword up, wavering, in front of his face and ducked away from the embattled older men.

It took Venera a few seconds to realize that two of the men bouncing from wall to wall were now dead. There were black beads dotting the air—blood—and more was trailing the bodies, which continued to move but only languidly, from momentum. One was the guide who had brought the two noblemen here; another was one of the attackers.

"Stand down!" Chaison's voice startled Venera so much that she nearly lost her grip on the wall. The remaining three attackers paused, holding onto ropes and bent shingles, and stared at their dead compatriots. The boy looked sick. Then one of his companions grabbed his arm and, with a roar of anger, jumped.

He spun away, slashed in the face by Chaison's companion. The other man had his sword knocked out of his hand by Chaison, who finished the uppercut motion with a blow to his jaw.

The boy was hanging in midair with his sword held out in front of him. Chaison glimpsed him out of the corner of his eye, spun and—stopped.

The blade trembled an inch from the boy's nose. He went white as a sheet.

"I'm not going to hurt you," said Chaison. His voice was soft, soothing—in total contrast to the bellow he had given moments ago. "Who sent you here?"

The boy gulped and, seeing that he still held his sword, he let go it spasmodically. As it drifted away he said, "B-big man from palace. Red feather in his hat. Didn't give a name."

Chaison made a sour face. "All right. Now off with you. Find another line of work—oh, and some better friends." He reached for his companion's wrist and they locked arms to coordinate their flight. Together they turned to leave.

The man who'd been struck in the chin suddenly snapped his head up and raised his arm. A snub-nosed pistol gleamed in his grimy fist. The boy gasped as he aimed it point-blank at the back of Chaison's head.

Bang! A spray of blood filled the air and the boy shrieked.

Venera peered through the blue cloud of gunsmoke. Chaison's

would-be assassin was twitching in the air, and both noblemen were staring past him, at her.

She returned the pistol to her carrying bag. "I-I saw you were in trouble," she said, surprised at how calm she sounded. "There was no time to warn you."

Chaison glided over. He looked impressed. "Thank you, madam," he said, graciously ducking his head. "I owe you my life."

In her fantasies Venera always had a perfect comeback line at moments like this. What she actually said was, "Oh, I don't know about that."

He laughed.

Then he extended his hand. "Come. We'll need to explain ourselves to the local police."

Venera flushed and backed away. She couldn't be caught out here—quite apart from the scandal, her father would ask too many questions. The papers she had just recovered might come to his attention and then she was as good as dead.

"I can't," she said and, turning, kicked off from the corner as hard as she could.

She heard him shouting for her to stop, but Venera kept on and didn't look back until she had passed through three crowded markets and slipped down five narrow alleys between soon-to-collide buildings. Cautiously, she worked her way back to the palace and changed in the guardroom while the man she'd bribed to let her out and in again waited nervously outside.

The next time she saw Chaison Fanning it would be two nights later, over the rim of a wineglass. He told her much later that his astonishment when he recognized her completely drove out all thoughts of the new treaty with Hale that he was celebrating. Certainly the expression on his face was priceless.

Venera had her own reason to smile, as she had learned who had tried to have this handsome young commodore killed. And as she danced with Chaison Fanning, she mused about what exact words she would use when she confronted her father. She already knew what it was she would be asking him for in exchange for her silence regarding his non-royal origins.

For the first time in her young life, Venera Fanning began to conceive of an existence for herself away from the intrigue and cruelty of the Court of Hale.

4

A THICK CABLE rose from the roof of the nation of Liris. Venera squinted at it, then at the blunderbusses the soldiers cradled. Another, larger blunderbuss was mounted on a pivot under a little roof nearby. That must be the damnable gun whose firing kept waking her up in the morning.

None of those ancient arms looked very accurate. She could probably just jump off the roof and run for it . . . but run where? Chances were she'd be snapped up by some neighbor worse than these people.

She decided—for the tenth time today—to remain patient and see what happened. No one in Liris seemed to have any immediate desire to harm her. Her best strategy was to play along with them until the moment came when she could escape.

"Now pay attention," whined Samson Odess. The fish-faced little man had been introduced yesterday as her new "boss." The very idea of a commoner giving her orders without an immediate threat to back them up struck Venera as both bizarre and funny. She had so far done the things he had asked but Odess seemed to sense that she wasn't taking him seriously. He was becoming ever more defensive as the morning wore on.

"This is our lifeline to Lesser Spyre," Odess said, slapping the cable. Venera saw that he stood on a low platform, at the center of which was a boxy machine that clamped the cable with big ratchet wheels. "By means of this engine, we can rise to the city above, where the Great Fair is held once a week. Visitors from everywhere in the world come to the Fair. It is the trade delegation's sacred task to ensure that we conduct the most advantageous transactions in the name of Liris." As he spoke the rest of the delegation popped up through the roof's one hatch. Four heavily armed men bracketed an iron box that must have held pithed cherries. Flanking them were two men and two women, the women veiled like Venera and dressed in ceremonial robes of highly polished silver inlayed with crimson enamel.

"Is the gravity the same up there as it is here?" Venera asked. If it was a standard g, they wouldn't be able to move. Odess shook his head vigorously.

"You can see the spin rate from down here. We'll shed our heavy vestments for city clothes once we're up there."

"Why not change down here?" she asked, puzzled.

Odess goggled at her in astonishment. He'd stared exactly that way yesterday, when he was first introduced. Moss had taken Venera to Odess's office, a glorified closet that made her wonder if Diamandis's pack-rat ways might not be the rule here, rather than the exception. Odess had filled the small space over the years, perhaps his whole lifetime, with oddments and souvenirs that likely made sense to no one but him. What was the significance of that single shoe, mounted as though it were a trophy and given its own little niche in the wall? Could anyone read the faded text on those certificates hung behind his chair? And was that some sort of exotic mobile that drooled from the dimness overhead, or the hanging mummified remains of some sort of animal? Books were stacked everywhere, and a pile of dishes three feet tall teetered next to a rolled-up mattress.

Odess's first words were addressed to Moss, not Venera. "You expect us to accept this . . . this *outsider* in our midst?"

"Is th-that not what you d-do?" Moss had asked. "G-go *outside?*" Startled, Venera had sent him a sidelong look. Was there somebody home behind those glazed eyes, after all?

"B-besides, the b-botanist commanded it."

"Oh, God." Odess had put his head in his hands. "She thinks she can do anything now."

Any slight deviation from routine or custom threw Odess into a panic. Venera's very presence was upsetting him, though the rest of the delegation had been pathetically happy to meet her. They would have partied until dawn if she hadn't begged off early, pointing out that she had not yet seen the room where she was expected to sleep for the rest of her life.

Eilen, Mistress of Scales and Measures, had shown Venera to a closet just outside the delegation's long, cabinet-lined office. The closet was seven feet on a side—its walls of whitewashed stone—and nearly twelve feet high. There was room for a bed and a small table, and there was no window. "You can put your chest under the bed," Eilen said, "when you get one. Your clothes you can hang on those pegs for now."

And that was all. If Venera were inclined to sympathy with other people, she would have been saddened at the thought that Eilen, Odess, and the others accepted conditions like these as the norm. After all, they had likely been born and raised in such tiny chambers. Their playgrounds were dusty servants' ways, their schoolrooms window niches. Yet of all the citizens of Liris, they were the privileged ones, for as members of the delegation they were allowed to see something of the world outside their walls.

While Odess sputtered and tried to explain why tradition demanded that they rise to Lesser Spyre in full ceremonial gear, Venera watched the soldiers deposit their precious cargo on the platform. After the rest of the delegation was on board, they flipped up railings on all sides (to her relief) and one bent to examine the archaic engine. This was what really interested her.

"If we're all ready, we will sing the 'Hymn of Ascension,'" said Odess portentously.

Venera looked around. "The what?"

He looked as though he'd been slapped—but Eilen put a hand on his arm. "We didn't tell her about it, so how would she know?"

"Anyone in Spyre could see us arise, hear the . . ." He realized his mistake. "Ah yes. A true foreigner." Shaking himself, he put both hands on the rail and puffed out his cheeks. "Listen, then, and learn the ways of a civilized society."

While they sang their little ditty Venera watched the soldier spark the hulking rotary engine into life. Its chattering roar immediately drowned out the miniature choir, who didn't seem to notice. The wheel turned, gripping the cable, and the platform inched slowly into the air.

The purpose of the railings soon became clear. Only a few yards above the rooftop they caught the edge of the howling gale that swept toward the open end of Spyre. This steady hurricane was produced by the rotation of the great wheel, Venera knew; she'd seen its like in smaller wheels like those of Rush. A wind came in at the cylinder's axis of rotation and shot out again along the rim. If she simply jumped off the platform at this point, she would be propelled out of Spyre entirely, and at goodly force.

The four soldiers were here to shoot anyone who tried that. And now that they were higher up she could see other guarantors of obedience: gun emplacements were suspended in the middle air by more cables, and some of them were visibly manned. Hanging in the sunny clouds beyond the wheel were more bunkers and turrets. It seemed a miracle now that she had, unconscious, threaded her way between them all to land here.

"Father would love this place," she muttered.

Chaison Fanning, her missing husband, would probably consider Spyre a moral obscenity and would want to blow it up.

They rose some miles, through filigrees of cloud, puffballs that hovered like anxious angels between the incoming and outblowing gales; past houses and pillboxes, bolted to other cables, whose glittering windows revealed nothing of what might be taking place inside them. The lands of Greater Spyre widened and widened below Venera, its patchwork estates becoming a mesmerizing labyrinth: the blockhouses of a dozen, a hundred and more nations of Liris, it seemed, painted the inside of the cylinder. Slicing through these, leaving ruin and wildflowers on their sidings, were the railways of the preservationists.

All the while, Lesser Spyre came closer.

Venera had seen a geared town once before—in the dead

hollow heart of Leaf's Choir Chaison Fanning's ships had moored next to the asphyxiated city of Carlinth. But Carlinth's pale grandeur couldn't match the wonder of Lesser Spyre because that other city had been motionless in death, and Lesser Spyre lived. Its great wheel-shaped habitats, each a half-mile or more in diameter, turned edge to angled edge like the meshwork of a vast clock. The citizen of one wheel could stroll to its edge and simply step onto the surface of another as their rims came within touching distance. The wheels were kept in configuration by a lattice of giant spars and thick cables, from which black banners fluttered.

The cable car eluded gravity entirely after a while, and its passengers clipped their metal costumes to the railing and waited until their destination hove into sight. The cable terminated in a knot of dozens of others, at a complicated cagework that threaded the axle of a town-wheel. Venera could see other people embarking and disembarking there. They moved in small groups that gave one another a wide berth.

She saw something else, though, that gave her hope for the first time in days: ships were berthed here. Sleek yachts, for the most part, of many different designs and flying diverse colors—but all foreign. They signaled the possibility of escape, real escape, for the first time since her arrival.

She tapped Odess's tin shoulder and pointed. "Our customers?"

He nodded. "Pilgrims from all the principalities of Candesce come to us, hoping to leave again with some trinket or token of ours. Do you recognize any of those ships?"

Venera nodded. "That one is from Gehellen." It was the only one she knew, but Odess was obviously impressed. "I know that we'll trade them cherries," she went on. "But what do the rest of Spyre's countries sell?"

He laughed, and just then the platform came to rest at its terminus. As they clambered over to the axle like so many iron spiders, Odess said, "What do they trade? You ask that with refreshing innocence. If we knew what half our neighbors traded, we might arrange some extra advantage for Liris. The fame of many of Spyre's commodities is spread far and wide—but not all. There are sections of the Fair no stranger can enter without providing a guarantee of circumspection."

"A what?"

"A hostage, sometimes," said Eilen. They had entered a long cylindrical chamber with many small doors spiraling up its interior. Odess found one of these and, producing a massive key, unlocked it. Inside was a slot-shaped locker, its walls encrusted with rust and cobwebs, with one incongruously bright mirror at the far end. Odess and the others proceeded to strip off their metal shells, trading them for ornately tooled leather equivalents—except that in place of veils, each costume came with an elaborate mask. Odess passed a kit to Venera and she turned her back modestly to change. Her mask had a falcon's beak.

"There are nations," Odess said, "that average one customer every ten years. Whatever it is they trade, it is so fabulously valuable that the whole country lives off the sale for a generation. That's an extreme example, but there are many others who guard the nature of their produce with their lives. Liris used to be one such. Now everyone knows what we produce, but that's actually worked to our advantage."

"But what can those others be selling?" Venera shook her head in incomprehension. She was stretching a black jacket over a silver-traced vest, admiring herself in the mirror. With the mask in place she looked intimidating. She liked the effect.

"*She* is from one of them." It was one of the soldiers who said it. He didn't have to say who *she* was; Venera knew he meant the botanist.

Venera raised an eyebrow. "She wasn't born in Liris?"

The soldier shook his head, glancing uneasily at Odess. "Our previous botanist . . . the trees were languishing, m'lady. They were dying, until she came." Odess was scowling in obvious warning but the soldier shrugged. "Five years now, she's brought them back to health."

"And you don't know anything about where she came from?"

"Of course we do!" Odess laughed loudly. "She's a lady of the nation of Sacrus. We know the families and lineage of Sacrus, we know who she is . . . even if we don't know what it is that Sacrus *does*."

"You need better spies," said Venera. Nobody laughed, but the thought intrigued her. Spyre, it seemed, was an investigator's playground. She would love to develop a network here, the way she had in secret in her adopted home of Slipstream.

They moved from the locker cylinder to the axle of the townwheel. Here, dozens of yin-yang stairs and elevator shafts ran down to the copper-shingled roofs of the vast building lining the wheel. Odess showed their letters of transit to a succession of inspectors and gradually they worked their way over to one of the elevators.

"Stay alert, everyone," Odess said as the wrought-iron doors grumbled shut behind them and they began to move down. "Watch for any signs of change. In particular, our new interpreter"—he nodded at Venera—"is going to cause a stir. We need to stick to our agreed story. You," he said to Venera, "must only speak to the customers and then only when we ask you to. We don't want to give our rivals any clues about our capabilities or what's been going on inside Liris."

This paranoia reminded Venera of Hale and the darkened corridors of her father's palace. "But why?" she asked in irritation. "Why this skulking?"

"Questions might be asked," said Odess darkly. "About where you came from. About why our people might have ventured outside our walls. Where we might have gone, what we might have seen. What *you* might have seen." He shook his head. "Your story is that you were born and raised in Liris."

"But my accent—"

"Is why you will only speak to the customers."

There was silence for the rest of the ride. Venera adjusted her mask, glanced around, and noted the tightening of shoulders, straightening of stances as gravity rose until it neared the level she was used to. And then the elevator clunked to a halt, and the doors opened.

The trade delegation of Liris edged cautiously into the Great Fair of Spyre.

FABULOUS BEASTS SWEPT across the dance floor, their skirts wheeling in time to the deep drumbeat of Spyre's music. The beasts had the faces of monsters, of animals, of gods. They danced in pairs, sometimes pausing in midpose as the music paused. It was during those pauses that business was transacted.

One slender figure with a hawk's face stood at the foot of a gold-chased pillar, her backdrop a blue trompe l'oeil vista of wheeling towns. She watched the dancers alertly, aware of the deep strains of paranoia and deceit that must run through Spyre for it to have developed this custom. For this filigreed and gleaming ballroom and its whirling dancers was the Great Fair itself.

True, there were display rooms. Out of the corner of her eye she saw Odess emerging from the doorway that led to Liris's. He was alone, and doubtless his errand had been to check on the disposition of the glass cases and lights there. No customers had passed that door since she had been here.

Venera had spent some hours in the display room, helping the others set up. A solitary cherry tree dominated the marbled parlor; it sat in a broad stone bowl, the glow of its pink blossoms the first sight that greeted a visitor. It was a fake, made of silk and common woods.

While Liris's soldiers played cards behind a screen in the display rooms, the rest of the delegation danced. The music was loud, the dances fast and close; so conversation consisted of quick whispers in your partner's ear, quips at arm's length, or brief nose-to-nose exchanges. Eavesdropping was impossible in these circumstances—and the soldiers of Spyre watched carefully for any sign of it. Venera had been told that visitors were carefully screened, and the penalty for revealing secrets here was death. Ironically, the whole setup seemed designed for cheating, for who could tell what any two dancers were telling one another?

She had heard that the dances were occasionally interrupted by spontaneous duels.

The denizens of Spyre took their masque very seriously. Not all the visitors did; most eschewed disguises, and so Venera was able to tell how many principalities were represented here. She even recognized one or two of the national costumes they wore.

A gavotte ended and the dancers broke up. Gorgon-headed Eilen headed Venera's way. A waiting footman handed her a drink as she paused, panting. "Is it always like this?" Venera asked her. "Interested customers seem a bit thin on the ground."

"We have our regulars," said Eilen. "It's not the season for any of them. Oh, this gravity! It pulls at my stomach."

Venera sighed. These people were so immersed in their traditions that they couldn't see the insanity of it all. In the brief pause between dances, some of the customers had drifted off with outlandishly masked delegates—salesmen, really. Venera had been keeping track of who went through which doorways. Many of the portals around the vast chamber had never opened. They might be locked or even bricked up on the other side, for all she knew.

She couldn't figure out the architecture of the fair. It seemed that the sprawling, multiwinged building had been renovated, rebuilt, and reimagined so many times over the centuries that it had lost any sense of its original logic. Corridors ran into blank walls; stairwells led nowhere; elevator shafts opened onto roaring air where lower floors had once been. Behind the public walls countless narrow passages twisted their ways to the offices, storage lockers, and panic rooms of the trade delegations. Liris's domain extended several floors above and below their public showroom; Venera had glimpsed in passing a huge chamber, like a collapsing ballroom, its dripping casements lost in gloomy shadows. Eilen had told her that this was where they met customers back when their cherries were a state secret. The ballroom was on one of the high-security levels of the Fair; Liris still owned title to it but had no use for it now.

Venera had scoffed at this. "Has no one had the courage to drill spy holes in the walls to find out what your neighbors are up to?" Odess had sent her one of his disapproving, frightened looks, but nobody had said anything.

—Oh, something was happening—Capri, Eilen's apprentice, was leading four people in rich clothes toward the Liris door. The little surge of excitement was absurd, and Venera nearly laughed at herself. Now Odess was bowing to them. He was opening the door. Venera imagined cheering.

"Who are they?" she asked Eilen.

"Oh! Success! That's . . . let's see . . . the delegates from Tracoune."

Venera ransacked her memory; why was that word familiar? Ah, that was it. It was only a couple of weeks ago that Venera and her husband had attended a soiree in the capital of Gehellen. The event had been unremarkable up until the shooting started, but she did remember a long conversation with a red-faced admiral of the local navy. He had mentioned Tracoune.

"Excuse me, I'd like to watch this," she said to Eilen. The woman shrugged and turned back to the dance. Venera threaded her way around the outskirts of the ball and pushed open the door to the Liris showroom. It was at the end of a long hallway, seventy feet at least in length. Random words echoed back at her as Venera walked down it.

Odess was showing them the tree. Now he was opening a lacquered box to reveal the cherries. Capri hovered nervously in the background.

The visitors didn't seem too impressed. One of the four—a woman—wandered away from the others to stare idly at the paintings on the walls. They seemed to be marking time here, perhaps taking a break from dancing. Even Venera, with no experience in sales, could tell that.

She approached the woman. "Excuse me . . . ," said Venera. She deliberately did not stand or move the way Odess and Capri were—clasping their hands in front of them, darting hesitantly like servants. Instead, Venera bowed like an equal.

"Yes?" The customer looked surprised, but not displeased, at being approached in this way.

"Do I have the pleasure of addressing a citizen of Tracoune?"

The woman nodded.

"I had the most illuminating conversation recently," Venera continued, "at a party in Gehellen. We talked about Tracoune."

An edge of calculation came into the woman's gaze. "Oh, really? Who were you talking to?"

"An admiral in the Gehellen navy, as it happens." Venera saw Odess notice that she had accosted a customer (his expression said, "The new one's loose!") and then he started trying to make eye contact with her while pretending to give his full attention to his own people.

Venera smiled. "I'm so sorry that you've had to cancel the Feast of St. Jackson this year," she said to her prospect. "The Gehellenese are speculating that you won't be able to afford to feed your own people this time next year. Gauche of them, really."

"They said that?" The woman's face darkened in anger. "The Incident at Tibo was hardly that serious!"

"Ah, we thought not," said Venera in a conspiratorial way. "It's just that appearance is so important to international relations, isn't it?"

Ten minutes later the visitors were signing on the dotted line. Venera stood behind the astounded trade delegation of Liris, her arms crossed, inscrutable behind her beaked mask.

Odess stepped back to whisper furiously to her. "How did you do it? These people have never been customers before!"

She shrugged. "You just have to know people's weaknesses. In a few weeks Tracoune will throw some minor party for visiting officials, and among other things they'll give away a few cherries . . . as if they could afford boatloads of them. A very discreet message, on a channel so private that almost no one on either side will know why when the Gehellens decide not to call in their outstanding loans to Tracoune. . . . Which they've been thinking of doing."

He glared at her. "But how could—"

She nodded. "The levers of diplomacy are very small. The art lies in knowing where to pry."

Venera chatted with the clients while a soldier loaded a carrying case with dry ice and Odess measured out the pithed cherries. ". . . Speaking of Gehellen," Venera said after a while, "we heard about some sort of commotion there a couple of weeks ago."

The head of the Tracoune expedition laughed. "Oh, that! They're the laughing stock of the principalities!"

"But what happened?"

He grinned. "Visitors from one of the savage nations . . . Oh, what was the name?"

"Slipstream," said the woman Venera had first dealt with.

"Slipstream, that was it. Seems an admiral of Slipstream went mad and took to piracy with some of his captains. They fought a pitched battle with the Gehellen navy in the very capital itself! Smashed their way out of the palace and escaped into Leaf's Choir, where it's rumored they found and made off with the hoard of Anetene itself!"

"But that part's too preposterous, of course," said the woman. "If they'd found the hoard, they would have a key to Candesce as well—the last one is supposed to be the centerpiece of the hoard. With that they could have ruled all of Virga from the Sun of Suns itself!"

"Well." The man shrugged.

"What happened to them?" asked Venera. "Did they escape?"

"Oh, they evaded the Gehellen navy right enough," he said with another laugh. "Only to be cut to ribbons in some barbarous nation near the edge of the world. None escaped, I hear."

"None . . ." Venera's pulse was racing, but she chose not to believe this man. His story had too many of the facets of rumor.

"Oh, no, I've been following this one," said the woman with

evident enjoyment. "It seems the Slipstreamers ran afoul of a place called Falcon Formation. The admiral suicidally rammed his flagship into some sort of dreadnaught of Falcon's. Both ships were obliterated in the explosion. Of his six other ships, only one got away."

"Its name?" Venera put her hand out to steady herself. Her fingers met the false bark of the fake cherry tree.

"What name?"

"The . . . the ship that escaped. Did you hear which one escaped?"

The woman looked affronted. "I didn't follow the story that closely." Now it was her turn to laugh. "But they foolishly ran for home, and the Pilot of Slipstream had them arrested the instant they came into port. For treason! What foolishness of them to even try to go home."

Venera was glad of the mask she wore. It felt like her heart was slowing and would stop at any second. It was all she could do to keep up appearances until the Tracoune delegation left with their first consignment of cherries. Then she rushed back to the screened alcove, ignoring the jubilant congratulations the others were lavishing on her.

Even though the mask would have hid them, she shed no tears. Venera had learned many years ago never to do that in the presence of another human being.

5

THAT EVENING THERE was a celebration in a gallery over-looking the cherry trees. Amber light poured into the blued central shaft, glinting off windows and outlining shutters and balconies above and below, while small gusts of air still warm from Candesce's light teased the diaphanous drapes. Like every-where else in Liris, the party room was small, crammed with memorabilia and eccentric furnishings, and reachable only through a labyrinth of stairs and corridors. It reminded Venera of her childhood bedroom.

She had not wanted to come. All she wanted to do was sit alone in her closet. But Eilen insisted. "Why so gloomy?" she asked as she leaned hipshot in Venera's doorway. "You did great service to your country today!" Venera didn't speak as they walked; and she did her best to be the ghost at the wedding for the remainder of the night.

Her sorrow wasn't catching. Most of Liris turned out for the event, and a dizzying parade of strange and neurotic characters passed in front of Venera as she systematically drank herself into a stupor. There were the hereditary soldiers with their peaked helmets and blunderbusses; the gray sanitation men who spoke in monotones and huddled together near the drinks table; the seam-stresses and chandlers, carpenters, and cleaners who all spoke a secret language they had developed together in their childhood. And there were children too—grave, wide-eyed gamins who skirted around Venera as though she had stepped out of one of their fantasy books.

She watched them all go by, numb. *I knew that this might happen,* she told herself. *That he might die.* Yet she had gone ahead with her plan, dragging Chaison reluctantly into it. It had been necessary if they were to save Slipstream; she knew that. But the decision still felt like a betrayal.

"It's so *electric*," said Eilen now, "having a new face in our world!" Quite drunk, she balanced on one foot near Venera, waving excitedly at people she had seen every day of her life. Of those people, a few had approached and introduced themselves, halting and stammering; most stayed back, muttering together and eyeing Venera. Foreigner. Strange beast. New darling of the botanist.

And yes, the botanist was here too. She glided through the celebrants as though on rails, nodding here and there, speaking strategic words on the outskirts of discussions, the same mysterious smile as always hovering just behind her lips. Eventually she made her way over to Venera. She hove to just this side of Eilen. Eilen herself moved away, suddenly quiet.

"I've always said that it pays to know your customers," the botanist said. "I judged your potential rightly."

Venera eyed her. "Is that what you feel you do? Judge people's potential? Like the buds of flowers that might bloom or whither?"

"How apt. Yes, that's exactly right," said the botanist. "Some are to be encouraged, others cut from the branch. You nod as though you understand."

"I've done a certain amount of . . . pruning . . . in my day," said Venera. "So I've achieved a great victory for your tiny nation. Now what?"

"Now," said the botanist in a breathless sort of sisterly way, "we talk about what to do next. You see, you've vindicated my methods. I believe Liris needs to be more open to the outside world. We need to send our delegates farther, even outside Spyre itself."

The fog of Venera's sorrow lifted just a bit. "Leave Spyre? What do you mean?"

"I would like to send a trade mission to one of the principalities," said the botanist. "You, of course, would lead it."

"I'd be honored," said Venera with a straight face. "But isn't it Odess's job to arrange such things?"

"Odess?" The botanist waved her hand dismissively. "Prattling whiner. Take him if you'd like, but I can't see what good he'll do you. No, I picture you, perhaps Eilen, and one or two loyal soldiers. And a consignment of our treasure to tempt potential customers."

"That sounds reasonable." Venera couldn't believe what she was hearing. Did the woman seriously believe she would come back if she got out of this place? But then, everyone in Spyre seemed dangerously naive.

"Good. Say nothing of this to the others," instructed the botanist severely. "It won't do to let old wounds fester."

What did that mean? Venera thought about it as the botanist strolled away; but then Eilen returned and spilled her drink on Venera's shoes. The evening went downhill from there, and so she didn't really ponder the botanist's unlikely offer until she got back to her closet, near dawn.

She had just closed the ill-fitting door and was about to climb under the covers when there was a polite knock on the jamb. Venera cracked the door an inch.

Moss leaned like a decapitated tree outside her door. "Citizen F-F-Fanning," he said. "I j-just wanted to give you th-th-these."

In the faint lamplight of the hallway, she could just make out a tiny bouquet of posies in his hand.

The juxtaposition of his chiseled features with the emptiness of his eyes made her skin crawl. Venera slipped her hand out to snatch the little bundle of flowers from his nerveless fingers. "Thanks. You're not in love with me, are you?"

"I'm s-s-sorry you're so s-sad," he murmured. "T-t-try not to be so s-s-sad."

Venera gaped at him. His words had been so quiet, but they seemed to echo on and on in the silent corridor. "Sad? Why do you think I'm sad?"

Nobody else had noticed—not even Eilen, who had been watching Venera like a mother hawk all evening. Venera narrowed her eyes. "I didn't see you at the party. Where were you?"

"I w-w-was there. In the c-corner."

Present yet absent. That seemed to sum Moss up. "Well." Venera looked down at Moss's present. Somehow she had clenched her fist and had crushed the little white blossoms.

"Thank you," she said. Moss turned away with a muted clattering noise. "Moss," she said quickly. He looked back.

"I don't want you to be sad either," said Venera.

He shambled away and Venera closed the door softly. Once alone, she let loose one long shuddering sigh, and tumbled face-first onto the bed.

THE NEXT MORNING, Venera wore the half-crushed posies on the breast of her jacket. If anybody noticed they said nothing. She ate her breakfast with the members of the delegation in their designated dining room—a roofed-over air shaft lined floor to invisible ceiling with stuffed animals—and followed them silently to their offices. She had discerned the routine by now: they would sit around for the rest of the day, occasionally engaging in desultory, short-lived dialogs, have lunch and then supper, and turn in.

If she had to live like this for more than a couple of days, Venera knew she would snap. So, at ten o'clock, she said, "Can't we at least play cards?"

One of the soldiers glanced over, then shook his head mournfully. "Odess always wins."

"But I'm here now," said Venera. "What if I were to win?"

Slowly, they roused into a state resembling the attentive. With much cajoling and brow-beating, Venera got them to reveal the location of the cards, and once she had these she energetically pulled a table and some chairs into the center of the room. "Sit," she commanded, "and learn."

This was her opportunity to grill her compatriots properly—
the party last night had been too hectic and strange, with everyone playing pal in transparent ways—and Venera made the best
of it. After ten minutes Odess emerged from his office, looking
bleary and cross, but his eyes lit up when he saw her shuffling the
cards. Venera grinned sloppily at him and he drew up a chair.

"So," she said as the others examined their cards. "Tell me
about the botanist."

THE PANTRY WAR had been dragging on for five years. Liris
and the Duchy of Vatoris both claimed a five- by seven-foot room
off one of the twisting corridors of the Fair. The titles went back
a hundred years, and the wording was ambiguous. Neither side
would back down.

"War?" said Venera as she peered over her cards. "Don't you
mean feud?"

The other players all shook their heads. No, explained Odess, a
feud was a family thing. This was a conflict between professional
soldiers, and it took the form of pitched battles. —Even if those
battles were between a dozen or so soldiers on either side, which
was all the manpower the tiny nations could muster. After years
of ambushes, raids, firefights, and all manner of other mayhem, it
had settled into a war of attrition. Barricades had been thrown up
in the disputed corridor; a no-man's-land of broken furniture and
cracked tile stretched for thirty feet between them. The entrance
to the closet beckoned only yards away, and either side could capture it in seconds. The trick was to hold it.

The two sides dug in. The barricades were ramified and reinforced, then backed up with cannon and rifles. Days might pass
without a shot fired, but the other tenants of the Fair got used to
sudden flurries of gunfire. Rarely was anyone actually hurt. The
loss of a single man would constitute a disaster.

These things happened. Even now, the Fair was riddled with
strange tensions—empty passages paved in dust where no one

had walked in generations because of just such disputes as this; neighbors who would think nothing of murdering one another in quiet corners if they had the chance; victims walled up in alcoves; and everywhere, conspiracies.

It was a random bullet that had changed everything. The walls around the disputed hallway had never been strong, but the combatants had hired a neutral third party to shore them up at regular intervals. Perhaps it was inevitable, though, that chinks and cracks should develop. One day, a bullet fired from the Vatoris barricade slipped through such a crack, ricocheted sixty feet down an abandoned air shaft, and killed the heir of a major nation as he stood at a punch bowl.

Venera rubbed her jaw. "I can imagine the reaction."

"I'm not sure you can," said Odess portentously. The nation in question was the mysterious Land of Sacrus, a country of "vast size," according to Eilen.

"How vast?"

"Fully three square miles!"

Sacrus traded in power—but exactly how, no one was quite sure. They were one of the most secretive of countries, their fields being dotted with windowless factories, the perimeter patrolled by guards with dogs and guns. Small airships bristling with guns bobbed above the main complex. The Sacrans emerged from their smoke-wreathed towers only once or twice a year, and then they spoke almost exclusively to their customers. They were one of the few nations that had withstood the full force of the preservationists—in fact, nobody in the preservationist camp would talk about just how badly that particular battle had gone.

Sacrus was enraged at the death of their heir. Three days after the incident, the Vatoris barricade fell silent. The soldiers of Liris fired a few shots and got no response. When they cautiously advanced on the Vatoris position, they found it abandoned.

Discreet inquiries were made. No one had seen any of the

Vatorins since the day of the fateful gunshot. In a moment of supreme daring, Liris sent its troops directly to the Vatoris apartments. They were empty.

At this point, rumors of a great stench rising from Vatoris itself reached Odess's ears. "I was sitting in our showroom," he said. "I remember it like it was yesterday. One of the scions of a minor nation entered and told me that his people were walking up and down along the border with Vatoris, sniffing the air and exchanging rumors. The smell was the smell of death."

Odess returned home that night to warn his people. "But it was too late. As I lay down to sleep that evening, I heard it—we all did." A hissing sound filled the chambers of Liris. It was faint, but for someone like Odess who had lived behind these walls his whole life, it had the effect of a siren.

"I stood, tried to run to the door. I fell down." The others related similar experiences, of sudden paralysis, landings behind desks or next to wavering doors. "We lay there helpless, all of us, unable to even focus our eyes. And we listened."

What they heard, after an hour or so, was a single set of footsteps. They moved smoothly from room to room, up stairs and down, not as if seeking anything, but as though whoever walked were taking inventory—committing every passage and chamber of Liris to memory. Eventually, they came to a stop. Silence returned.

The paralysis faded near dawn. Odess rose, retched miserably for a few minutes, and then—trembling—crept in the direction those footsteps had taken. As he went he saw others emerging from their rooms, or rising from where they had fallen in midwalk. They converged on the place where the footsteps had halted: in the cherry tree courtyard.

"And there she sat," said Odess, "exactly as she sits these days, with the same damned smile and the same damned air of superiority. The botanist. Our conqueror."

———

"AND NO ONE has challenged her?" Venera barked a laugh of disbelief. "You fear reprisals, is that it?"

Odess shrugged. "She ended the war, and under her leadership the cherries bloom. Who else are we going to have lead us?"

Venera scowled at her cards. A pulse of pain shot up her jaw. "I thought you were a meritocracy."

"And so we are. And she is the best botanist we have ever had."

"What happened to the one she replaced?"

They exchanged glances. "We don't know," confessed Eilen. "He disappeared the day Margit came."

Venera discarded one card and took another from the deck. The others did the same, then she fanned out her hand. "I win."

Odess grimaced and began to shuffle.

"She came to me last night," said Venera. She had decided that she needed information more than discretion at this point. "Margit was pleased with the work I did." Odess snorted; Venera ignored him and continued. "She had a proposal."

She told them about Margit's idea of an extended trade expedition into the principalities. As she did, Venera watched all movement around the table stop. Even Odess's practiced hand ceased its fanning of the cards. They were all staring at her.

"What?" She glanced around defensively. "Does this violate some ancient taboo? —I'm sure; everything else does. Or is it something you've been trying to get done for years, and now you're mad that the newcomer has achieved it?"

Eilen looked down. "It's been tried before," she said in a quiet voice.

"You must understand," said Odess; then he fell silent. Knitting his brows, he started furiously shuffling.

"What?" Now Venera was seriously alarmed. "What's wrong?"

"To travel outside Spyre . . . is not done," said Odess reluctantly. "Not without safeguards to guarantee one's return. Hostages, if one is married . . . but you're not."

Venera was disgusted. "The pillboxes, the guns, and razor

wire—they really aren't to keep people *out*, are they? They're to keep them in."

"Yes, but you see if Margit is willing to send you out despite you having no ties here, no hostages, or anything she could hold over you . . . then she's obviously willing to try it again," said Odess. He slammed the deck down on the table, kicked his chair back, and walked away. Venera watched him go in startled amazement.

The soldiers were standing too, not making eye contact with anyone.

Venera pinned Eilen with her gaze. "Try *what*?"

The woman sighed deeply. "Margit is a master of chemistry and biology," she said. "That's why she is the botanist. Three years ago she conceived the idea of sending an expedition like the one you're describing. She chose a man who was competent, intelligent, and brave, but one whom she didn't completely trust. To guarantee that he would return, she . . . injected him. With a slow poison that was not supposed to begin to act for ten days. If he returned within those ten days, she would give him the antidote and he would be fine."

Venera eyed the splayed cards. "What happened?"

"The return flight was delayed by a storm. He made it back on the eleventh day."

Venera hesitated—but she already knew the answer when she asked, "Who was it that Margit sent?"

"Moss," said Eilen with a shudder. "She sent Moss."

6

"I HAVE TO admit I was expecting this," said Margit. Venera stood in the doorway to her apartment, dressed down in close-fitting black leathers. Two soldiers hulked behind her, their meaty hands resting heavy on her shoulders.

"In retrospect," Venera said ruefully, "I should have anticipated the trip wires." The inside walls of the courtyard were just too enticing a surface; freed of her metal clothing, Venera weighed only twenty pounds or so and she could easily clamber hand over hand up the drainpipe that ran next to Odess's little window. "There's no other way in or out of the building but up that wall. Naturally you'd have alarms."

". . . I just wasn't anticipating it so soon," said Margit. She twitched a housecoat over her lavender nightgown and lit another candle off the one she was holding. Even in the dimness of midnight Venera could see that her apartment was sumptuous, with several rooms, high ceilings, and tiled mosaics on the floor beneath numerous tapestries.

Of course Margit wouldn't live like the people she ruled. Venera wouldn't have either. She understood Margit enough by now that staying here in Liris had not been an option. So, after bidding her coworkers good night, she had retired to her closet and waited. When the building was silent and dark, Venera had crept out and jimmied open a window that led onto the courtyard.

She hadn't been thinking clearly. The revelation about Moss had shaken her and she had acted rashly. If she didn't regain control of this situation she would be in real trouble.

"Come in, sit down. We need to talk," said Margit. "You may

leave us," she said to the soldiers. They lifted their hands off Venera's shoulders and retreated past the heavy oak door. They would have a long walk down the winding steps that led down to Liris's ground floor. *Good*, thought Venera.

She sat down on a decadent-looking divan; but she kept her feet braced against the floor, ready to leap up instantly if that was required.

The first step to taking control of the situation was taking control of the conversation. Margit opened her mouth but Venera spoke first: "What is an heir of Sacrus doing running a minor nation like Liris?"

Margit narrowed her eyes. "Shouldn't I be asking the questions? Besides, what's your interest?" she asked as she gracefully sat opposite Venera. "Professional curiosity, perhaps? —You are a noble daughter yourself, are you not? A nation like Liris would be an interesting playground for someone learning how to use power. Are you interested in rulership?"

"In the abstract," said Venera. "It's not an ambition of mine."

"Neither is assisting your new countrymen, I gather. You were trying to escape us."

"Of course I was. I was press-ganged into your service. And you admit yourself you expected me to try it." She shrugged. "So what could we possibly have to talk about?"

"A great deal, actually," said Margit. "Such as how you came to be here at all."

Venera nodded slowly. She had been thinking about that, and the conclusions she had come to had motivated her to run as much as the facts about Moss. "I arrived here through an odd chain of events," she said. "At the time I wasn't prepared to wonder why there were armed troops sneaking over the lawns of Spyre during the nighttime. I was mostly concerned with evading them. I didn't know enough to ask the right question."

Margit raised an eyebrow and sat back.

"It's my father, you see," said Venera in a confessional tone. "He's flagrantly paranoid and he wanted his daughters to be as well. He raised me to disbelieve coincidence. So if I was herded here, what could the reason be? The troops who were following me weren't from Liris. In fact, I assumed they weren't after me at all but were chasing down another trespasser whom I had met. It wasn't until today that I realized that those other soldiers had been from Sacrus."

Margit laughed. "That truly is paranoid. You would implicate my nation in every one of your misfortunes?"

"No, just this one." She sat forward. "Since we're talking, though, I'd like to ask you a couple of questions." Smiling her maddening smile, Margit nodded. "The first question is whether you maintain constant contact with your nation. I've been told you don't, but I don't believe that."

Margit shrugged. "It would be easy. So what if I did? Can't a daughter talk to her parents?"

"The second question," said Venera, "is whether Sacrus itself travels regularly into the principalities." Seeing Margit's suddenly guarded expression, Venera nodded. "You do, don't you?"

"So what?"

"Someone guessed where I had come from," marveled Venera. "More than likely the Gehellens have circulated descriptions of myself and my husband throughout the principalities. They seek us, and it's an open secret why."

Margit grinned in obvious delight. "Oh, you are smart! I was right to bring you into Liris in the way I did."

Venera cocked her head. "What other way was there?"

"Oh, I think you can guess."

"Under duress. Tortured," said Venera. "Why do you think I tried to flee just now? It suddenly made no sense to me that I was walking around freely. And your offer to let me travel outside Spyre . . . made even less sense."

"You became alarmed. That's understandable. I was told to learn everything you know about the key to Candesce," said Margit. "You figured that out, of course."

Venera looked innocent. "Sorry, the what?"

Margit stood up and paced over to a side table. "Drink?" Venera shook her head.

"Something happened a short time ago," said the botanist. She stood with her back to Venera and in those seconds Venera looked around quickly for anything that might give her an advantage. There were no handy hat pins, letter openers, or pistols lying on the pillowed furniture. She did spot a battered wooden cabinet that looked markedly out of place compared to the rest of the pieces, but had no time to get to it before Margit turned again, drink in hand.

"Something happened," Margit repeated. "A fight in the capital of Gehellen, rumors of a stolen treasure, and then an event that our scientists are starting to refer to as the *outage*."

Venera tensed. She hadn't expected Margit to know this part of the story.

"Candesce does many things besides light our skies," said the botanist. "We watch the Sun of Suns closely; we have to, our very lives depend on it. So when one of Candesce's many systems shuts down, even for a moment, we know about it. Even though such an event has not occurred in living memory."

She sat down again. "Only someone with a key could enter Candesce and manipulate it. And the last key was lost centuries ago. You can imagine the uproar that the outage has caused, here and abroad. The principalities are mobilizing, and agents of the Virga home guard have been seen nosing around, even here."

Home guard? She wanted to kick herself for failing to realize that the gambit she and her husband had played would alert all the powers in the world. *Hit another trip wire,* she mused.

"It was only a matter of days before we had your name and description, and that of your husband and others in your party," said Margit. "We pay our spies well. So when a woman fitting that description miraculously appeared in the skies of Greater Spyre, we mobilized."

"Clearly I've been a fool," said Venera bitterly. "Then it was Sacrus troops who drove me here?"

"I actually don't know for sure," Margit admitted. "Our men were out that night, I know that much. But there may have been others as well. In any case, once I communicated that I had you, I was told to hand you and the key over. I couldn't very well refuse my masters the key—but you, I declined to part with."

Venera felt a pulse of anxious anger as she realized what Margit was saying. "Then the key is—"

"Locked away in the Grey Infirmary, where Sacrus keeps all their new acquisitions," said Margit with some smugness. She drained her wineglass and tilted it at Venera. "But you're here. I took Liris in order to have a base from which to grow my own power. You provide potential leverage. Why should I give you up?"

"And the offer to let me travel . . . ?"

"I increase my leverage and buy some insurance by getting you out of Spyre and to a safe place that only I know about," said Margit. "But you should really be happy that I haven't tortured you for what you know. I'd prefer to have you on my side. You must admit, I've treated you well."

Cautiously, Venera nodded. "It was too risky to keep the key to Candesce for yourself. But a lesser piece of leverage . . ."

". . . Who knows something vital about it that I can trade . . . that's useful to me at the moment." Margit smiled, catlike.

It still didn't quite add up. "Why did you let me go up to Lesser Spyre?" Venera asked. "Why risk exposing me at the Fair?"

"That was to prove that I had you," said Margit with a shrug. "While I was negotiating what to give up. Sacrus was at the Fair. I told them to watch for you, but with the guards and defenses that surround the Fair they couldn't snatch you from me. It was the safest place in Spyre to display you."

Someone unused to being used as a political pawn might have been surprised at these revelations. For Venera, discovering that she had been played was almost reassuring. It placed her in a familiar role.

She knew exactly what Sacrus was going to do now. Venera had fantasized about it herself: you took the key and entered Candesce, and then shut down the Sun of Suns. As the darkness and cold began to seep into the principalities, you made your demands of the millions whose lives depended on Candesce. You could ask for anything—power, money, hostages, or slaves. Your leverage would be total.

It would help to have enough experienced men to crew a navy, though, because one of your first demands would be that the principalities deliver up their own ships. "Sacrus doesn't have any ships, do they?" she asked. "Surely not enough to run the blockade that the principalities would put in place."

Margit shrugged. "Oh, we have several. Sacrus is a big nation. But in terms of weapons . . ." She laughed, and it wasn't a pleasant laugh. "I doubt we would have to worry much about any fleet of the principalities."

Her confidence was suddenly unnerving. Margit sauntered over to the battered wooden cabinet and opened the top. "Since you're here," she said, "let's talk about the key to Candesce."

"Let's not." Venera stood up. "My knowledge is my only bargaining chip, after all. I'm not going to squander that."

This time Margit didn't answer. She pulled a bell rope that hung next to the cabinet.

The gravity was low enough and Venera still strong enough that she could probably make it to the window in one leap. Then, she could scale the stonework by the tips of her fingers if she had to and make it to the roof in under a minute. Not, however, faster than the soldiers could climb a flight of stairs to retrieve her.

Margit was watching her calculate her options. The botanist laughed as the door opened behind Venera and a large, heavily armored soldier entered.

"I'm not going to hurt you," said Margit. Something glittered in her hand as she approached Venera. "I just want to guarantee your compliance from now on."

"The way you tried with Moss?" Venera nodded at the syringe Margit held. "Is that the same stuff you used on him?"

"It is. His outcome was an accident," said the botanist as the

soldier stepped forward and grabbed Venera's wrists from behind. "I'll be more careful with you."

His outcome was an accident. Venera was familiar with that sort of
logic; she often blamed others for the things she did to them. For
some reason, the argument didn't work this time.

Margit had to round a large couch as she approached Venera.
She took a step to do so, and Venera made fists, bent her forearms
forward, and then raised her arms in an egg-shaped curve that
Chaison had once showed her. The startled soldier clung tightly
to her wrists but suddenly found himself pulled forward and off-
balance as Venera lifted his hands over her head. And then she
turned and her hands were over his as he lost his grip and
she pushed down and he thumped onto his knees.

She kicked him in the face. His helmet ricocheted across the
room as Margit shouted and Venera hopped the couch, snatch-
ing up the open wine bottle and swinging it at the botanist's
head.

Margit slashed out with the syringe, nicking Venera's sleeve.
They circled for a second, then Venera grabbed for her wrist and
they tumbled onto the floor.

The wine bottle skittered away, gouting red. Venera pulled
Margit's arm up and bit her wrist. As the botanist let go Venera
made a grab for the syringe. Margit in turn lunged for the bottle.

"I was just going to kill you," hissed Venera. She landed on
Margit's back as the botanist closed her fingers on the bottle. "I've
changed my mind!" She jammed the needle into Margit's shoulder and pushed the plunger.

Margit shrieked and rolled away. Venera let her. The botanist
had let go of the wine bottle and Venera took it and upended it
over the wooden cabinet.

Cursing and holding her shoulder, Margit ran over to the soldier, who was sitting up. When she saw Venera reach for one of
the lit candles she screamed "No!" and backpedaled.

It was too late, as Venera touched the candle flame to the wine-
soaked cabinet and the whole thing caught. In the orange light of

the fire Venera ran through a nearby arch. She wanted to know whether that cabinet was all there was to Margit's power.

"Ah . . ." She stood in a large private pharmacy—dozens of shelves covered in glass bottles of all sizes and colors hung above long worktables crowded with beakers, petri dishes, and test tubes. Venera joyfully swept her arm across a table and tossed the candle into the cascading glasswork as Margit clawed at her from behind.

There was fire behind them, now fire ahead, and smoke wafting up to the ceiling as Margit pushed and kicked at Venera and tried to get past her. When the soldier finally appeared out of the smoke, Venera stood over the botanist, her nose bleeding but a grin of utter savagery on her face. She brandished a long knife she'd found on the table.

"Back away or I'll cut her throat!" Venera's backdrop was flames. The soldier backed away.

Shouts of alarm and clanging bells were waking the house. Venera dragged Margit out of the inferno and threw her to the floor in front of the smouldering cabinet.

"Ten days." She pointed to the door. "You have ten days to convince your people to save you. I have no doubt that Sacrus has the antidote to your poison, but you'll have to go to them on bended knee to get it. For your sake I hope they're in a forgiving mood."

People were crowding in the doorway—men and women carrying buckets of sand and water, all shouting at once and all clattering to a halt at the sight of Venera standing over the all-powerful botanist.

"You are no longer the botanist of Liris!" Venera raised her arm, summoning everything she had learned from her father about how to intimidate a crowd. "Let no one here ever grant entry to this woman again! Run! Run home to Sacrus and beg for your life. This place is closed to you."

Margit staggered to her feet, clutching her shoulder. "I'll kill you!" she hissed.

"Only if you've a mind to do it," said Venera. "Now go!"

The botanist ran for the door, pushing aside the stunned fire-fighters.

"Get with it!" Venera yelled at them. "Before the whole house goes up!"

She walked through them and as more came up the stairs she politely eased to the side to let them pass. She reached the main floor of Liris to find all the lights lit and a confused mob swirling around the strangely decorated desks and counters.

"What's happened?" Odess emerged from the rush of faces. The rest of the trade delegation were behind him.

"I've deposed the botanist," said Venera. They gaped at her. She sighed. "It wasn't *that* hard," she said.

"But—but how?" They crowded around her.

"But why?" Eilen had grabbed her arm.

Venera looked up at her. Suddenly she felt tears in her eyes. "My . . . my husband," she whispered through a suddenly tight throat. "My husband is dead."

For a while there was silence, it seemed, though Venera knew abstractly that everyone was shouting, that the news of Margit's sudden departure was spreading like fire through Liris. Eilen and the others were speaking to her but she couldn't understand anything they said.

Strangely calm, she looked through the rushing people at the one other person who seemed still. He was giving orders at the foot of the stairs to Margit's chambers, putting out his arm to prevent people without firefighting tools from going up, pointing out where to get sand or buckets to those just arriving. His face was impassive but his gestures were quick and focused.

"What are we going to do?" Odess was literally wringing his hands, something Venera had never actually seen anyone do. "Without the botanist, what will happen to the trees? Will Sacrus forgive us for what you did? Could we all be killed? Who is going to lead us now?"

Eilen turned to Odess, shaking his shoulder crossly. "Why shouldn't it be Venera?"

"V-Venera?" He looked terrified.

Venera laughed. "I'm leaving. Right now. Besides, you already have your new botanist." She pointed. "He's been here all along."

Moss looked up from where he was directing the firefighting. He saw Venera, and the perpetually desperate expression around his eyes softened a bit. She walked over to him.

As shouts came down the stairs saying that the fire was under control, she laid a hand on the former envoy's arm and smiled at him. "Moss," she said, "I don't want you to be sad anymore."

"I-I'll t-try," he said.

Satisfied, she turned away from the people of Liris. Venera traced the steps Margit had taken only minutes before, pausing only to arm herself in Liris's barracks. She walked up the broad stone steps over which towered row after row of portraits—centuries of botanists, masons, doctors, and scholars, all of whom had been born here, lived here, and died here leaving legacies that might have been known only to a handful of people but were meaningful nonetheless. She trod carefully patched steps whose outlines were known intimately by those who tended them, past arches and doors that figured as clearly as heroes out of myth in the dreams and ambitions of the people who lived under them—people to whom they were the very world itself.

And on the dark empty roof, cold fresh air blew in from the abandoned lofts of winter.

She threw back the trapdoor and stalked to the roof's edge. These were the final steps of her old life, she felt. Venera was about to mourn, something she had never done and did not know how to do. She stepped onto a swaying platform and began winching it down, feeling the uncoiling certainty of her husband's death in her gut. It was like a monster shaking itself awake; any moment now it would devour her and who knew what would happen then? Her only defense was to keep turning the wheel to winch herself down. She focused her eyes on the tall grass that swayed at the foot of Liris, willing it closer.

In the dim light cast by Lesser Spyre, Venera Fanning walked into the wild acres of the disputed territories. She moved aimlessly at first, admiring the glittering lights overhead and the vast arcs of land and forest that swept up and past them.

When she lowered her eyes it was to see the black silhouette of a man separate itself from a grove of trees ahead of her. Venera didn't pause but turned slightly toward the figure. He came out to meet her and she nodded to him when he offered his arm for her to lean on.

"I've been waiting for you," said Garth Diamandis.

They strolled into the darkness under the trees.

7

VENERA DIDN'T REALLY notice the passage of the next few days. She stayed with Diamandis in a clapboard hut near the edge of the world and did little but eat and sleep. He came and went, discreet as always; his forays were usually nocturnal and he slept when she was awake.

Periodically she stepped to the doorway of the flimsy hideout and listened to the wind. It tore and gabbled, moaned and hissed incessantly, and in it she learned to hear voices. They were of people she'd known—her father, her sisters, sometimes random members of the crew of the *Rook* whom she had not really gotten to know but had heard all about during her adventures with that ship.

She strained to hear her husband's voice in the rush, but his was the only voice she could not summon.

One dawn she was fixing breakfast (with little success, having never learned to cook) when Garth poked his head around the doorjamb and said, "You've disturbed a whole nest of hornets, did you know that?" He strolled in, looking pleased with himself. "More like a nest of whales—or capital bugs, even. There's covert patrols crawling all over the place."

She glared at him. "What makes you think they're after me?"

"You're the only piece out of place on this particular board," said Diamandis. He let gravity settle him into one of the hut's two chairs. "A queen in motion, judging by the furor. I'm just a pawn, so they don't see me—and as long as they don't, they can't catch you either."

"Try this." She slammed a plate down in front of him. He eyed it dubiously.

"Mind telling me what you did?"

"Did?" She gnawed her lip, ignoring the stabbing pain in her jaw. "Not very much. I may have assassinated someone."

"May have?" He chortled. "You're not sure?" She simply shrugged. Diamandis's expression softened. "Why am I not surprised?" he said under his breath.

They ate in silence. If this day were to follow the pattern of the last few, Diamandis would now have fallen onto the cot Venera had just vacated, and he would immediately commence to snore in competition with the wind. Instead, he looked at her seriously and said, "It's time for you to make a decision."

"Oh?" She folded her hands in her lap listlessly. "About what?"

He scowled. "Venera, I utterly adore you. Were I twenty years younger you wouldn't be safe around me. As it is, you're eating me out of house and home and having an extra mouth to feed is, well, tiring."

"Ah." Venera brightened just a little. "The conversation my father and I never had."

Hiding his grin, Diamandis ticked points off on his fingers. "One: you can give yourself up to the men in armor who are looking for you. Two: you can make yourself useful by going with me on my nightly sorties. Three: you can leave Spyre. Or, four—"

"I thought you said I could never leave," she said, frowning.

"I lied." Seeing her expression, he rubbed at his chin and looked away. "Well, I had a beautiful young woman in my bed, even if I wasn't in there with her, so why would I let her go so easily? Yes, there is a way out of Spyre—potentially. But it would be dangerous."

"I don't care. Show me." She stood up.

"Sit down, sit down. It's daytime, and I'm tired. I need to sleep first. It's a long trek to the bomb bays. And anyway . . . don't you want to hear about the fourth option?"

"There is no other option."

He sighed in obvious disappointment. "All right. Let me sleep, then. We'll visit the site tonight and you can decide whether it's truly what you want to do."

THEY PICKED THEIR way through a field of weeds. Lesser Spyre twirled far above. The dark houses of the great families surrounded them, curving upward in two directions to form a blotted sky. Venera had examined those estates as they walked; she'd hardly had the leisure time to do so on her disastrous run to the edge of the world. Now, as the rust-eaten iron gates and crumbling battlements eased by, she had time to realize just how strange a place Spyre was.

On the steep roof of a building half-hidden by century oaks, she had seen a golden boy singing. At first she had taken him for some automaton, but then he slipped and caught himself. The boy was centered in bright spotlights and he held a golden olive branch over his head. Whether there was an audience for his performance in the gardens or balconies below, whether he did this every night or if it were some rare ceremony she had chanced to see—these things she would never know. She had touched Garth's shoulder and pointed. He merely shrugged.

Other estates were resolutely dark, their buildings choked in vines and their grounds overgrown with brambles. She had walked up to the gate of one such to peer between the leaves. Garth had pulled her back. "They'll shoot you," he'd said.

In some places the very architecture had turned inward, becoming incomprehensible, even impossible for humans to inhabit. Strange cancerous additions were flocked onto the sides of stately manors, mazes drawn in stone over entire grounds. Strange piping echoed from one dark entranceway, the rushing sound of wings from another. At one point Venera and Garth crossed a line of strange footprints, all the toes pointed inward and the indentations heavy on the outside as if the dozens of people who had made them were all terribly bowlegged.

It did no good to look away from these sights. Venera occasionally glanced at the sky, but the sky was paved with yet more estates. After each glance she would hunch unconsciously away, and each time, a pulse of anger would shoot through her and she would straighten her shoulders and scowl.

Venera couldn't hide her nervousness. "Is it much farther?"

"You whine like a child. This way. Mind the nails."

"Garth, you remind me of someone but I can't figure out who."

"Ah! A treasured lover, no doubt. The one that got away, perhaps? —Wait, don't tell me, I prefer to wallow in my fantasies."

". . . A particularly annoying footman my mother had?"

"Madam, you wound me. Besides, I don't believe you."

"If there really is a way off of Spyre, why haven't you ever taken it?"

He stopped and looked back at her. Little more than a silhouette in the dim light, Diamandis still conveyed disappointment in the tilt of his shoulders and head. "Are you deliberately provoking me?"

Venera caught up to him. "No," she said, putting her fists on her hips. "If this exit is so dangerous that you chose not to use it, I want to know."

"Oh. Yes, it's dangerous—but not that dangerous. I could have used it. But we've been over this. Where would I go? One of the other principalities? What use would an old gigolo be there?"

"Let the ladies judge that."

"Ha! Good point. But no. Besides, if I circled around and came back to Lesser Spyre, I'd eventually be caught. Have you been up there? It's even more paranoid and tightly controlled than this place. The city is . . . impossible. No, it would never work."

As was typical of her, Venera had been ignoring what Garth was saying and focusing instead on how he said it. "I've got it!" she said. "I know why you stayed."

He turned toward her, a black cutout against distant lights— and for once Venera didn't simply blurt out what was on her mind. She could be perfectly tactful when her life depended on it but in other circumstances had never known why one should bother. Normally she would have just said it: *You're still in love with someone.* But she hesitated.

"In there," said Diamandis, pointing to a long low building whose roof was being overtaken by lopsided trees. He waited, but when she didn't say anything he turned slowly and walked in the direction of the building.

"A wise woman wouldn't be entering such a place unescorted," said Venera lightly as she took his arm. Diamandis laughed.

"I am your escort."

"You, Mr. Diamandis, are why escorts were invented."

Pleased, he developed a bit of a bounce to his step. Venera, though, wanted to slow down—not because she was afraid of him or what waited inside the dark. At this moment, she could not have said what made her hesitate.

The concrete lot was patched with grass and young trees and they scuttled across it quickly, both wary of any watchers on high. They soon reached a peeled-out loading door in the side of the metal building. There was no breeze outside, but wind was whistling around the edges of the door.

"It puzzles me why there isn't a small army of squatters living in places like this," said Venera as the blackness swallowed Diamandis. She reluctantly stepped after him into it. "The pressures of life in these pocket states must be intolerable. Why don't more people simply leave?"

"Oh, they do." Diamandis took her hand and led her along a flat floor. "Just a bit farther, I have to find the door . . . through here." Wind buffeted her from behind now. "Reach forward . . . here's the railing. Now, follow that to the left."

They were on some sort of catwalk, its metal grating ringing faintly under her feet.

"Many people leave," said Diamandis. "Most don't know how to survive outside of the chambers where they were born and bred. They return, cowed, or they die. Many are shot by the sentries, by border guards, or by the preservationists. I've buried a number of friends since I came to live here."

Her eyes were starting to adjust to the dark. Venera could tell that they were in a very large room of some sort, its ceiling ribbed with girders. Holes let in faint light in places, just enough to sketch the dimensions of the place. The floor . . .

There was no floor, only subdivided metal boxes with winches hanging over them. Some of those boxes were capped by fierce vortices of wind that collectively must have scoured every grain of grit out of the place. Looking down at the nearest box, Venera saw that it was really a square metal pit with clamshell doors at its bottom. Those doors vibrated faintly.

"Behold the bomb bays," said Diamandis, sweeping his arm in a dramatic arc. "Designed to rain unholy fire on any fleet stupid enough to line itself up with Spyre's rotation. This one chamber held enough firepower to carpet a square mile of air with bombs. And there were once two dozen such bays."

The small hurricane chattered like a crowd of madmen; the bomb bay doors rattled and buzzed in sympathy. "Was it ever used?" asked Venera.

"Supposedly," said Diamandis. "The story goes that we wiped out an entire armada in seconds. Though that could all be propaganda. If true, I can see why people outside Spyre would despise us. After all, there would have been hundreds of bombs that passed through the armada and simply kept going. Who knows what unsuspecting nations we strafed?"

Venera touched the scar on her chin.

"Anyway, it was generations ago," said Diamandis. "No one seems to care that much about us since the other great wheels disintegrated. We're the last, and ignored the way you pass by the aged. Come this way."

They went up a short flight of metal steps to a catwalk that extended out over the bays. Diamandis led Venera halfway down the long room; his footfalls were steady, hers slowing, as they approached a solitary finned shape hanging from chains above one of the bays.

"That's a bomb!" It was a good eight feet long, almost three in diameter, a great metal torpedo with a button nose. Diamandis leaned out over the railing and slapped it.

"A bomb, indeed," he said over the whistling gale. "At least, it's a bomb casing. See? The hatch there is unscrewed. I scooped out the explosives years ago; there's room for one person if you wriggle your way in. All I have to do is throw a lever and it will drop and bang through those doors. Nothing's going to stop you once you're outside; you can go a few hundred miles and then light out on your own."

She too leaned out to touch the cylinder's flank.

"So you'll go home, will you?" he asked with seeming innocence.

Venera snatched her fingers back. She crossed her arms and looked away.

"The people who ran this place," she said after a while. "It was one of the great nations, wasn't it? One of the ones that specialize in building weapons. Like Sacrus?"

He laughed. "Not Sacrus. Their export is *leverage*. Means of political control, ranging from blackmail to torture and extortion. They have advisors in the throne rooms of half the principalities."

"They sell torturers?"

"That's one of the skills they export, yes. Almost nobody in Spyre deals with them anymore—they're too dangerous. Keep pulling coups, trying to dominate the council. The preservationists are still hurting from their own run-in with them. You met one of theirs in Liris?" She nodded.

Diamandis sighed. "Yet one more reason for you to leave, then. Once you're marked in their ledgers, you're never safe again. Come on, I'll give you a boost up."

"Wait." She stared at the black opening in the metal thing. The thought came to her: *this won't work.* She could not return to Slipstream and pretend that things that had been done had not been done. She could not in silence retire as the shunned wife of a disgraced admiral. Not when the man responsible for Chaison's death—the Pilot of Slipstream—still sat like a spider at the center of Slipstream affairs.

Thinking this made her fury catch like dry tinder. A spasm of pain shot up her jaw, and she shook her head. Venera turned and walked back along the catwalk.

Diamandis hurried after her. "What are you doing?"

Venera struggled to catch her breath. She would need resources. If she was to avenge Chaison, she would need power. "Yesterday you said something about a fourth choice, Garth." She rattled down the steps and headed for the door.

"Tell me about that choice."

YOU MUST BE ready for this, Garth had said. It is like no place you have ever been or ever imagined. Near dawn, as they approached the region of Spyre known as the airfall, she began to understand what he meant.

The great estates dwindled as they threaded their way through Diamandis's secret ways; even the preservationists avoided this sector of the great wheel. Ruins dotted the landscape and strange trees lay nearly prone like supplicants.

The ground shook, a constant wavering shudder. The motion reminded her with every step that she stood on thin metal sheeting above an abyss of air. She began to see patches of speed ivy atop broken cornices and walls. And the loose soil thinned until they walked atop the metal of the wheel itself.

Wind pushed at her from behind; Venera had to consciously set her feet down, grinding them into the grit to prevent herself starting to run. Giving into that run would be fatal, Diamandis assured her. The reason why emerged slowly, horribly, from around the collapsed walls and tangled groves of once-great estates.

She clapped Diamandis on the shoulder and pointed. "How long ago?"

He nodded and leaned in so that she could hear him over the roar. "A question important to our enterprise. It happened generations ago, in a time of great unrest in the principalities. Back when the great nations of Spyre still traveled—before they began to hide in their fortresses."

A hundred yards or so of slick decking extended past the last broken stones, then the first tears and gaps appeared. Long sheets of humming metal extended out, following the lines of the girders that underlay Spyre's upper skin. Soon even they disappeared, leaving only bright shreds and the girders themselves. A latticework of metal beams was all the ground there was for the next mile.

Below the plain of girders dark clouds shot past with dizzying speed. Propelled by Spyre's centrifugal force, a ceaseless hurricane roared in and down and through the empty windows of the broken ruins and leaped out of a vast hole in the world.

"Behold the airfall!" Diamandis gestured dramatically; but there was no need. Venera stood awestruck at the sheer savagery of the permanent storm that warred about her. If she lifted one foot or straightened her back she might be caught and yanked out and then down, and shot out of Spyre through this screaming, gouting wound.

"This—this is insane!" She hunkered down, clutching a boulder. Her leathers flapped up around her ears. "Am I expected to run into that?"

"No, not run! Crawl. Because up there—do you see it? There is your fourth alternative!" She squinted where he pointed and at first didn't see anything. Then she blinked and looked again.

The skin of Spyre had been stripped away for at least a mile in every direction. The hole must have unbalanced the whole wheel—towers, farms, factories, and even perhaps whole towns being sucked out and flung into the depths of Virga in a catastrophe that threatened to destroy the entire structure. For some reason the peeling and collapse had propagated only so far and then stopped—but the standing cyclone of exiting air must have unbalanced Spyre so much as to threaten its immediate destruction.

This, if anything, explained the preservationists and the fierce war they had fought to lay their tracks around Spyre. The unstable wobble of the wheel could only be fixed by moving massive weights around the rim to balance it. There was no patching this hole.

Everything above had been sucked out as the skin peeled away—except in one place. One solitary tower still stood a quarter mile into the plain of girders. It had the great fortune to have been built overtop a main intersection point for Spyre's skeletal system. Also, the place might once have been a factory with its own reinforced foundation, for Venera could see huge pipes and tanks splayed like the roots of a tree below the girders. The tower itself was dark as the clouds that framed it, and it slowly swayed under the force of the winds. The girders bounced it like an acrobat in a net.

Just looking at it made her nauseated. "What is that?"

"Buridan Tower," said Diamandis. "It's our destination."

"Why? And how are we going to get there through . . . through that?"

"Using our courage, Lady Fanning—and my knowledge. I know a way, if you'll trust me. As to why—that is a secret that you will reveal, to both of us."

She shook her head, but Venera had no intention of backing out now. To do anything else but go forward in this mad adventure would be to invite relaxation—and thought. Grief drove her on, an active refusal to think. She waited, eyes tearing from the wind, and eventually Diamandis nodded sharply and gestured come on.

They crept across the last acre of intact skin, grabbing onto every rock and jammed tree branch that might offer purchase. As they approached a great split in the metal sheeting, Venera saw where Diamandis was going, and she began to think that this passage might be possible after all.

Here, a huge pipe ran under Spyre's topsoil and skin. It was anchored to the girders by rusting metal straps and had broken in places but extended out below the skinless plain. It seemed to head straight for swaying Buridan Tower.

Diamandis had found a hole in the pipe that was sheltered by a tortured dune. He let himself down into the black mouth and she followed; instantly the wind subsided to a tolerable scream.

"I'm not even going to ask how you found this," she said after dusting herself off. He grinned.

The pipe was about eight feet across. Sighting down it she beheld, in perspective, a frozen vortex of discolored metal and sedimented rime. Behind her it was ominously dark; ahead, hundreds of gaps and holes let in the welling light of Candesce. In this new illumination, Venera eyed their route critically. "There's whole sections missing," she pointed out. "How do we cross those?"

"Trust me." He set off at a confident pace.

What was there to do but follow?

The pipe writhed in sympathy with the twisting of the beams. The motion was uncomfortable, but not terrifying to one who had ridden warships through battle, walked in gravities great and small throughout Virga, and even penetrated the mysteries of Candesce. —Or so Venera told herself, up until the tenth time her hand darted out of its own accord to grip white-knuckled some peel of rust or broken valve rim. Rhythmic blasts of pain shot up her clenched jaw. An old anger, born of helplessness, began to take hold of her.

The first gaps in the pipe were small and thankfully overhead. The ceiling opened out in these places, allowing Venera to see where she was—which made her duck her head down and continue on with a shudder.

But then they came to a place where most of the pipe was simply gone, for a distance of nearly sixty feet. Runnels of it ran like reminders above and to the sides, but there was no bottom anymore. "Now what?"

Diamandis reached up and tugged a cable she hadn't noticed before. It was bright and strong, anchored here and somewhere inside the black cave where the pipe picked up again. Near its anchor point the line was gathered up and pinched by a huge spring, allowing it to stretch and slacken with the twisting of the girders.

"You did this?"

He nodded; she was impressed and said so. Diamandis sighed. "Since I've had no audience to brag to, I've done many feats of daring," he said. "I did none in all the years when I was trying to impress the ladies—and none of them will ever know I was this brave."

"So how do we . . . Oh." Despite her pounding headache, she had to laugh. This was a zip line; Diamandis proposed to clip rollers to it and glide across. Well, at least the great girder provided a wall to one side and partial shelter above. The wind was not quite so punishing here.

"You have to be fast!" Diamandis was fitting a pulley-hold onto the cable. "You can't breathe in that wind. If you get stranded in the middle you'll pass out."

"Wonderful." But he'd strapped her in securely, and falling was not something that frightened people who lived in a weightless ocean of air. When the time came she simply closed her eyes and kicked off into the white flood of air.

They had to repeat this process six times. Now that he had someone to give up his secret to, Diamandis was eager to tell her how he had used a powerful foot-bow to shoot a line across each gap, trusting to its grip in the deep rust on the far side to allow him to scale across once. After stronger lines were affixed it was easy to get back and forth.

So, walking and gliding, they approached the black tower.

In some places its walls fell smoothly into the abyss. In others, traces of ground still clung tenaciously where sidewalks and outbuildings had once been. They clambered out of the pipe onto one such spot; here, thirty feet of gravel and plating stretched like a splayed hand up to the tower's flank. Diamandis had strung more cables along that wall, leading toward a great dark shadow that opened halfway around the wall's curve. "The entrance!" Battered by wind, he loped over to the nearest line.

The zip lines in the pipe had given Venera the false impression that she was up for anything. Now she found herself hanging onto a cable with both hands—small comfort to also be clipped to it—while blindly groping with her feet on the side of a sheer wall, above an infinite drop now illuminated by full daylight.

Only a man with nothing to lose could have built such a pathway. She understood, for she felt she was in the same position. Gritting her teeth and breathing in shallow sips in vortices of momentary calm caused by the jutting brickwork, she followed Diamandis around Buridan Tower's long curve.

At last she stood, shaking, on a narrow ledge of stone. The door before her was strapped iron, fifteen feet tall and framed with trembling speed ivy. Rusting machine guns poked their snouts out of slits in the stone walls surrounding it. A coat of arms in the ancient style capped the archway. Venera stared at it, a brief drift of puzzlement surfacing above her apprehension. She had seen that design somewhere before.

"I can't go back that way. There has to be another way!"

Diamandis sat down with his back to the door and gestured for her to do the same. The turbulence was lessened just enough there that she could breathe. She leaned on his shoulder. "Garth, what have you done to us?"

He took some time to get his own breath back. Then he jabbed a thumb at the door. "People have been pointing their telescopes at this place for generations, all dreaming of getting inside it. Secret expeditions have been mounted to reach it, but none of them ever came via the route we just took. It's been assumed that this way was impossible. No . . ." He gestured at the sky. "They always climb down the elevator cable that connects the tower to Lesser Spyre. And every time they're spotted and shot by Spyre sentries."

"Why?"

"Because the nation of Buridan is not officially defunct. There are supposed to be heirs, somewhere. And the product of Buridan still exists, on farms scattered around Spyre. No one is legally allowed to sell it until the fate of the nation is determined once and for all. But the titles, the deeds, the proofs of ownership and provenance . . ." He thumped the iron with his fist. "They're all in here."

Her fear was beginning to give way to curiosity. She looked up at the door. "Do we knock?"

"The legend says that the last members of the nation live on, trapped inside. That's nonsense, of course, but it's a useful fiction."

It began to dawn on her what he had in mind. "You intend to play on the legends."

"Better than that. I intend to prove that they are true."

She stood up and pushed on the door. It didn't budge. Venera looked around for a lock, and after a moment she found one, a curious square block of metal embedded in the stone of the archway. "You've been here before. Why didn't you go in?"

"I couldn't. I didn't have the key and the windows are too small."

She glared at him. "Then why . . . ?"

He stood up, smiling mysteriously. "Because now I do have the key. You brought it to me."

"I . . . ?"

Diamandis dug inside his jacket. He slid something onto his finger and held it up to gleam in the light of Candesce.

One of the pieces of jewelry Venera had taken from the hoard of Anetene had been a signet ring. She had found it in the very same box that had contained the key to Candesce. It was one of the pieces that Diamandis had stolen from her when she first arrived here.

"That's mine!"

He blinked at her tone, then shrugged. "As you say, Lady. I thought long and hard about playing this game myself, but I'm too old now. And anyway, you're right. The ring is yours." He pulled it off his finger and handed it to her.

The signet showed a fabulous ancient creature known as a horse. It was a gravity-bound creature and so none now lived in Virga—or were they the product that Buridan had traded in? Venera took the heavy ring and held it up, frowning. Then she strode to the lockbox and placed the ring into a like-shaped indentation there.

With a mournful grating sound, the great gate of Buridan swung open.

8

GUNNER TWELVE-FIFTEEN WRAPPED his fingers around the dusty emergency switch and pulled as hard as he could. With a loud snap, the red stirrup-shaped handle came off in his hand.

The gunner cursed and half-stood to try and retrieve the end of the emergency cord that was now poking out of a hole in his canopy. He banged his head on the glass and the whole gun emplacement wobbled, causing the cord to flip out into the bright air. Meanwhile, the impossible continued to happen outside; the thing was now a quarter mile above him and almost out of range.

Gunner Twelve-fifteen had sat here for sixteen years now. In that time he had turned the oval gun emplacement from a cold and drafty purgatory into a kind of nest. He'd stopped up the gaps in the metal armor with cloth and, later, pitch. He'd snuck down blankets and pillows and eventually even took out the original metal seat, dropping it with supreme satisfaction onto Greater Spyre two miles below. He'd replaced the seat with a kind of reclining divan, built sunshades to block the harsher rays of Candesce, and removed layers of side armor to make way for a bookshelf and drinks cabinet. The only thing he hadn't touched was the butt of the machine gun itself.

Nobody would know. The emplacement, a metal pod suspended above the clouds by cables strung across Greater Spyre, was his alone. Once upon a time there had been three shifts of sentries here, a dozen eyes at a time watching the elevator cable that ran between the town-wheels of Lesser Spyre and the abandoned and forlorn Buridan Tower. With cutbacks and rescheduling, the number had eventually gone down to one: one twelve-hour shift for each of the six pods that surrounded the cable. Gunner Twelve-fifteen had no doubt that the other gunners had similarly renovated their stations; the fact that none were now responding to the emergency meant that they were not paying any attention to the object they were here to watch.

Nor had he been; if not for a random flash of sunlight against the beveled glass of a wrought-iron elevator car he might never have known that Buridan had come back to life—not until he and the other active sentries were hauled up for court-marshal.

He pushed back the bulletproof canopy and made another grab at the frayed emergency cord. It dangled three inches beyond his outstretched fingers. Cursing, he lunged at it and nearly fell to his death. Heart hammering, he sat down again.

Now what? He could fire a few rounds at the other pods to get their attention—but then he might kill somebody. Anyway, he wasn't supposed to fire on rising elevators, only objects coming down the cable.

The gunner watched in indecision until the elevator car pierced another layer of cloud and disappeared. He was doomed if he didn't do something right now—and there was only one thing to do.

He reached for the other red handle and pulled it.

In the original design of the gun emplacements, the ejection rocket had been built into the base of the gunner's seat. If he was injured or the pod was about to explode, he could pull the handle and the rocket would send him, chair and all, straight up the long cable to the infirmary at Lesser Spyre. Of course, the original chair no longer existed.

The other gunners were startled out of their dozing and reading by the sudden vision of a pillowed divan rising into the sky on a pillar of flame. Blankets, books, and bottles of gin twirled in its wake as it vanished into the gray.

———

THE DAY-WATCH LIAISON officer shrieked in surprise when Gunner Twelve-fifteen burst in on her. The canvas she had been carefully daubing paint onto now had a broad blue slash across it.

She glared at the apparition in the doorway. "What are you doing here?"

"Begging your pardon, ma'am," said the trembling soldier. "But Buridan has reactivated."

For a moment she dithered—the painting was ruined unless she got that paint off it right now—then was struck by the image of the man standing before her. Yes, it really *was* one of the sentries. His face was pale and his hair looked like he'd stuck it in a fan. She would have sworn that the seat of his leather flight suit was smoking. He was trembling.

"What's this about, man?" she demanded. "Can't you see I'm busy?"

"B-Buridan," he stammered. "The elevator. It's rising. It may already be here!"

She blinked, then opened the door fully and glanced at the rank of bellpulls in the hallway. The bells were ancient and black with tarnish and clearly none had moved recently. "There was no alarm," she said accusingly.

"The emergency cord broke," said the gunner. "I had to eject, ma'am," he continued. "There was, uh, cloud; I don't think the other sentries saw the elevator."

"Do you mean to say that it was cloudy? That you're not sure you *saw* an elevator?"

He turned even more pale; but his jaw was set. As the liaison officer wound up to really let loose on him, however, one of the bellpulls moved. She stared at it, forgetting entirely what she had been about to say.

"... Did you just see ..." The cord moved again and the bell jiggled slightly. Then the cord whipped taut and the bell shattered in a puff of verdigris and dust. In doing so it managed to make only the faintest tinking sound.

She goggled at it. "That—that's the Buridan elevator!"

"That's what I was trying to—" But the liaison officer had burst past him and was running for the stairs that led up to the elevator stations.

Elevators couldn't be fixed to the moving outer rim of a town-wheel; so the gathered strands of cable that rose up from the various estates met in a knotlike collection of buildings in freefall. Ropes led from this to the axes of the towns themselves. The officer had to run up a yin-yang staircase to get to the top of the town (the same stairway that the gunner had just run down); as her weight dropped the steps steepened and the rise became more and more vertical. Puffing and nearly weightless, she achieved the top in under a minute. She glanced out one of the blockhouse's gunslits in time to see an ornate cage pull into the elevator station a hundred yards away.

The gunner was gasping his way back up the steps. "Wait," he called feebly. The liaison officer didn't wait for him, but stepped to the round open doorway and launched herself across the empty air.

Two people were waiting by the opened door to the Buridan elevator. The liaison officer felt an uncanny prickling in her scalp as she saw them, for they looked every bit as exotic as she'd imagined someone from Buridan would be. Her first inclination (drummed into her by her predecessor) that any visitation from the lost nation must be a hoax, faded as one of the pair spoke. Her accent wasn't like that of anyone from Upper Spyre.

"They sent only you?" The woman's voice dripped scorn. She was of medium height, with well-defined brows that emphasized her piercing eyes. A shock of pale hair stood up from her head.

The liaison officer made a midair bow and caught a nearby girder to halt herself. She struggled to slow her breathing and appear calm as she said, "I am the designated liaison officer for Buridan-Spyre relations. To whom do I have the honor of addressing myself?"

The woman's nostrils flared. "I am Amandera Thrace-Guiles, heir of Buridan. And you? You're nobody in particular, are you . . .

but I suppose you'll have to do," she said. "Kindly direct us to our apartments."

"Your . . ." The Buridan apartments existed, the officer knew that much. No one was allowed to enter, alter, or destroy Buridan property until the nation's status was determined. "This way, please."

She thought quickly. It was years ago, but one day she had met one of the oldest of the watch officers in an open gallery on Wheel Seven. They had been passing a broad stretch of crumbling wall and came to a bricked-up archway. "Know what that is?" he'd asked playfully. When she shook her head he smiled and said, "Almost nobody does, nowadays. It's the entrance to the Buridan estate. It's all still there—towers, granaries, bedrooms, and armories—but the other nations have been building and renovating around and over it for so long that there's no way in anymore. It's like a scar, or a callus maybe, in the middle of the city.

"Anyway, this was the main entrance. Used to have a sweeping flight of steps up to it, until they took that out and made the courtyard yonder. This entrance is the official one, the one that only opens to the state key. If you ever get any visitors from Buridan, they can prove that they are who they say they are if they can open the door behind that wall."

"Come with me," said the officer now. As she escorted her visitors along the rope that stretched toward Wheel Seven, she wondered where she was going to get a gang of navvies with sledgehammers on such short notice.

THE DEMOLITION OF the brick wall made just enough of a delay to allow Lesser Spyre's first ministers to show up. Venera cursed under her breath as she watched them padding up the gallery walk: five men and three women in bright silks, with serious expressions. Secretaries and hangers-on fluttered around them like moths. In the courtyard below, a crowd of curious citizens was growing.

"This had better work," she muttered to Diamandis.

He adjusted his mask. It was impossible to read his expression behind it. "They're as scared as we are," he said. "Who knows if there's anything left on the other side of that?" He nodded to the rapidly falling stones in the archway.

"Lady Thrace-Guiles!" One of the ministers swept forward, lifting his silk robes delicately over the mortar dust. He was bejowled and balding, with a fan of red skin across his nose and liver spots on his lumpish hands. "You look just like your great-great-great-grandmother, Lady Bertitia," he said generously. "Her portrait hangs in my outer office."

Venera looked down her nose at him. "And you are . . . ?"

"Aldous Aday, acting chairman of the Lesser Spyre Committee for Public Works and Infrastructure," he said. "Elected by the Upper House of the Great Families—a body that retains a seat for you, kept draped in velvet in absentia all these years. I must say, this is an exciting and if I do say so, surprising, day in the history of Upper—"

"I want to make sure our estate is still in one piece," she said. She turned to Diamandis. "Master Flance, the hole is big enough for you to squeeze through. Pray go ahead and tell me that our door is undamaged." He bowed and edged his way past the workmen.

He and Venera wore clothing they had found preserved in wax paper in the lockers of Buridan Tower. The styles were ancient, but for all that they were more practical than the contraptions favored by Spyre's present generation. Venera had on supple leather breeches and a black jacket over a bodice tooled and inscribed in silver. A simple belt held two pistols. On her brow rested a silver circlet they had found in an upstairs bedchamber. Diamandis was similarly dressed, but his leathers were all a deep forest green.

"It's a great honor to see your nation again after so many years," continued Aday. If he was suspicious of her identity, he wasn't letting on. She exchanged pleasantries with him through clenched teeth, striving to stay in profile so that he and the others could not see her jaw. Venera had done her best to hide the scar and had bleached her hair with some unpleasant chemicals they'd found in the tower, but someone who had heard about Venera Fanning might recognize her. Did Aday and his people keep up on news from the outside world? Diamandis didn't think they did, but she had no idea at this point how far her fame had spread.

To her advantage was the fact that the paranoid societies of Spyre rarely communicated. "Sacrus won't want anyone to know they had you," Diamandis had pointed out one evening as they sat huddled in the tower, an ornate chair burning merrily in the fireplace. "If they choose to unmask you, it's at the expense of admitting they have connections with the outside world—and more important, they won't want to hint that they have the key to Candesce. I don't think we'll hear a peep out of them, at least not overtly."

The workmen finished knocking down the last bricks and stepped aside just as Diamandis stuck his head around the corner of the archway. "The door is there, ma'am. And the lock."

"Ah, good." Venera stalked past the workers, trying to keep from nervously twisting the ring on her finger. This was the proverbial moment of truth. If the key didn't work . . .

The brick wall had been built across an entryway that extended fifteen feet and ended in a large iron-bound door similar to the one at Buridan Tower. The ministers crowded in behind Venera, watching like hawks as she dusted off the lockbox with her glove. "Gentlemen," she said acidly, "there is only so much air in here. —Though I suppose you have some natural skepticism about my authenticity. Put that out of your minds." She held up the signet ring. "I am my own proof—but if you need crass symbols, perhaps this one will do." She jammed the key against the inset impression in the lockbox.

Nothing happened.

"Pardon." Diamandis was looking alarmed and Venera quashed the urge to make some sort of joke. She must not lose her air of confidence, not even for a second. Bending to examine the lock, she saw that it had been overgrown with grit over the years. "Brush, please," she said in a bored tone, holding out one hand. After a long minute someone placed a hairbrush in her palm. She scrubbed the lock industriously for a while, then blew on it and tried the ring again.

This time there was a deep click and then a set of ratcheting thumps from behind the wall. The door ground open slowly.

"You are the council for . . . infrastructure, was it not?" she asked, fixing the ministers with a cold eye. Aday nodded. "Hmm," she said. "Well." She turned, preparing to sweep like the spoiled princess she had once been, through the opened door into blackness.

A loud bang! and fall of dust from the ceiling made her stumble. There was sudden pandemonium in the gallery. The ministers were milling in confusion while screams and shouts followed the echoes of the explosion into the air. Past Aday's shoulder Venera saw a curling pillar of smoke or dust that hadn't been there a second ago.

With her foot hovering over the threshold of the estate, Venera found herself momentarily forgotten. Sirens were sounding throughout the wheel and she heard the clatter of soldiers' boots on the flagstones. In the courtyard, someone was crying; somebody else was screaming for help.

Expressionless, she walked back to the gallery and peered over Aday's shoulder. "Somebody bombed the crowd," she said.

"It's terrible, terrible," moaned Aday, wringing his hands.

"This can't have been planned," she said reasonably. "So who would be walking around on a morning like this just carrying a bomb?"

"It's the rebels," said Aday furiously. "Bombers, assassins . . . This is terrible!"

Someone burst into the courtyard below and ran toward the most injured people. With a start Venera realized it was Garth

Diamandis. He shouted a command to some stunned but other-wise intact victims; slowly they moved to obey, fanning out to examine the fallen.

It hadn't occurred to Venera until this moment that she could also be helping. She felt a momentary stab of surprise, then . . . was it anger? She must be angry at Diamandis, that was it. But— she remembered the mayhem of battle aboard the *Rook* when the pirates attacked, and the aftermath. Such fear and anguish, and in those moments the smallest gesture meant so much to men who were in pain. The airmen had given of themselves without a mo-ment's thought—given aid, bandages, and blood.

She turned to look for the stairs, but it was too late: the medics had arrived. Frowning, Venera watched their white uniforms fan out through the blackened rubble. Then she lit her lantern and stalked back to the archway.

"When my manservant is done, send him to me," she said qui-etly. She strode alone into the long-sealed estate of Buridan.

IN AN ABANDONED bedchamber of the windswept tower while the floor swayed and sighs moaned through the huge pipes that underlay the place, Diamandis had told Venera histories of Buridan, and more.

"They were the horse masters," he said. "Theirs was the ulti-mate in impractical products—a being that required buckets of food and endless space to run, that couldn't live a day in freefall. But a creature so beautiful that visitors to Spyre routinely fell in love with them. To have a horse was the ultimate sign of power, because it meant you had gravity to waste."

"But that must have been centuries ago," she'd said. Venera was having trouble hearing Diamandis, even though the room's door was tightly closed and there were no windows in this cham-ber. The tower was awash with sound, from the creaking of the beams and the roaring of the wind to the deep basso-profundo chorus of drones that reverberated through every surface. Even before her eyes had adjusted to the darkness inside the building, before she could take in the clean stripped smell of chambers and corridors scoured by centuries of wind, the full-throated scream of Buridan had nearly driven her outside again.

It had taken them an hour to discover the source of that basso cry: the nest of huge pipes that jutted from the bottom of Buridan Tower acted like a giant wind instrument. It hummed and keened, moaned and ululated unceasingly.

Diamandis slapped the wall. This octagonal chamber was filled with jumbled pots, pans, and other kitchen utensils; but it was quiet compared to the bedchambers and lounges of the former inhabitants. "Buridan's heyday was very long ago," he said. He looked almost apologetic, his features lit from below by the oil lamp they'd brought. "But the people of Spyre have long memories. Our records go all the way back to the creation of the world."

He told her stories about Spyre's ancient glories that night as they bedded down, and the next day as they prowled the jumbled chaos of the tower. Later, Venera would always find those memories entwined within her: the tales he told her accompanied by images of the empty, forlorn chambers of the tower. Grandeur, age, and despair were the setting for his voice; grandeur, age, and despair henceforth defined her impressions of ancient Virga.

He told her tales of vast machines, bigger than cities, that had once built the very walls of Virga itself. Those engines were alive and conscious, according to Diamandis, and their offspring included both machines and humans. They had settled the cold black spaces of a star's outskirts, having sailed for centuries from their home.

"Preposterous!" Venera had exclaimed. "Tell me more."

So he told her of the first generations of men and women who had lived in Virga. The world was their toy, but they shared it with beings far more powerful and wiser than themselves. It was simple for them to build places like Spyre—but in doing so, they used up much of Virga's raw materials. The machines objected.

There was a war of inconceivable ferocity; Virga rang like a bell, its skin glowed with heat, and the precarious life forms the humans had seeded inside it were annihilated.

"Ridiculous!" she said. "You can do better than that."

Spyre was the fortress of the human faction, he told her. From here, the campaign was launched that defeated the machines. Sulking, they left to create their own settlement on the far side of the solar system—but some remained. In faraway, frozen, and sunless corners of the world, forgotten soldiers slept. Having accumulated dust and fungus over the centuries, they could easily be mistaken for asteroids. Some hung like frozen bats from the skin of the world, icebergs with sightless eyes. If you could waken them, you might receive powers and gifts beyond mortal desire; or you could unleash death and ruin on the whole world.

The humans slowly rebuilt Virga's ecology, but they were diminished from their original, godlike power. Nations were spawned by the dozen, hot new suns springing into life in the black abyss. They turned their backs on the past.

Then, rumors began of something strange approaching across the cold interstellar wastes . . . a new force, spreading outward like ripples in a pond. It came from their ancient home. It had many names, but the best description of it was *artificial nature*.

"Ah," said Venera. "I see."

They made their rounds as Diamandis talked. Each foray they made began and ended in the central atrium of the old building. Here, upward-sweeping arches formed an eight-sided atrium that rose fifteen stories to the glittering stained-glass cupola surmounting the edifice. Lozenges of amber and lime, rose and indigo light outlined the dizzying succession of galleries that rose to all sides.

On the second day, as they were exploring the upper chambers, they came across traces of a story Garth Diamandis did not know. As Venera was poking her head in a closet she heard him shout in alarm. Running to his side she found him kneeling next to the armored figure of a man. The corpse was ancient, wizened and dried by the wind. A sword lay next to it. And in the next chamber were more bodies.

Some dire and dramatic end had come to the people here. They found a dozen mummified soldiers, all lying where they had fallen in fierce combat. Guns and blades were strewn about among long-dried pools of black liquid. The disposition of the bodies suggested attackers and defenders; curious now, Venera followed the path the interlopers must have taken.

High in the tower, behind a barricaded door, a blackened human shape lay on the moldering coves of a vast four-poster bed. The white lace dress the mummy wore still moved in the wind, causing Venera to jump in startlement whenever she glanced at it.

She systematically ransacked the room while Diamandis stood contemplating the body. Here, in desk drawers and cabinets, were all the documents and letters of marque Venera needed to establish her identity. She even found a genealogy and photos. The best of the clothes were stored here as well, and that evening, rather than listening to a story, Venera began to make up her own—the story of a generations-long siege, a self-imposed exile broken finally by the last member of the nation of Buridan, Amandera Thrace-Guiles.

THE DARKNESS YIELDED detail slowly. Venera stood in what had once been a cobblestoned courtyard overlooked by the pillared facade of the Buridan estate. Black windows looked down from the edifice; once, sunlight would have streamed through them into whatever grand halls lay beyond. At some point in the past dark buttresses had been leaned onto the smooth white flanks of the building to support neighboring buildings—walls and arches that had swathed and overgrown it in layers, like the accumulating scales of some vast beast. For a while the estate would have still had access to the sky, for windows looked out from many of the encircling walls. All were now bricked up. Stone and wrought-iron arches had ultimately been lofted over the roofs of the estate, and at some point a last chink must have let distant sunlight in to light a forlorn cornice or the eye of a gargoyle. Then that too had been sealed and Buridan encysted, to wait.

It was understandable. There was only a finite amount of space on a town-wheel like this; if the living residents couldn't demolish the Buridan estate, they'd been determined to reach other accommodations with it.

Two glittering pallasite staircases swept up from where Venera stood, one to the left, one to the right. She frowned, then headed for the dark archway that opened like a mouth between them. Her feet made no sound in the deep dust.

Certainly the upstairs chambers would be the luxurious ones; they had probably been stripped. In any case she was certain she would learn more about the habits and history of the nation by examining the servants' quarters.

In the dark of the lower corridor, Venera knelt and examined the floor. She drew one of her pistols and slid the safety off. Cautiously she moved onward, listening intently.

This servants' way ran on into obscurity, arches opening off it to both sides at regular intervals. Black squares that might once have been portraits hung on the walls, and here and there sheet-covered furniture huddled under the pillars like cowering ghosts.

Sounds reached her, distorted and uncertain. Were they coming from behind or ahead? She glanced back; silhouettes were moving across the distant square of the entranceway. But that sliding sound . . . She blew out the lantern and sidled along the wall, moving by touch.

Sure enough, a fan of light draped across the disturbed dust of the corridor revealed a shadow play of figures moving against the opposite wall. Venera crept up to the open doorway and peered around the corner in time to meet the eye of someone coming the other way.

"Hey! They're here already!" The woman was younger than Venera and had prominent cheekbones and long stringy hair. She was dressed in the dark leathers of the city. Venera leaped into her path and leveled the pistol an inch from her face.

"Don't move."

"Shills!" somebody else yelled.

Venera didn't know what a shill was, but yelled "No!" anyway. "I'm the new owner of this house."

The stringy-haired woman was staring cross-eyed at the gun barrel. Venera spared a glance past her into a long low chamber that looked like it had originally been a wine cellar. Lanterns burned at strategic points, lighting up what was obviously somebody's hideout: there were cots, stacks of crates, even a couple of tables with maps unrolled on them. Half a dozen people were rushing about grabbing up stuff and making for an exit in the opposite wall. Several more were training guns on Venera.

"Ah." She looked around the other side of the stringy-haired head. The men with the guns were glancing inquiringly at one of their number. Though of similar age, with his flashing eyes and ironic half-smile he stood out from the rest of these youths as a professor might stand out from his students. "Hello," Venera said to him. She withdrew her pistol and holstered it, registering the surprise on his face with some satisfaction.

"You'd better hurry with your packing," she said before anyone could move. "They'll be here any minute."

The guns were still trained on her, but the confident-looking youth stepped forward, squinting at her over his own weapon. He had a neatly trimmed moustache and what looked like a dueling scar on his cheek. "Who are you?" he demanded in an amused upper-class drawl.

She bowed. "Amandera Thrace-Guiles, at your service. Or perhaps, it's the other way around."

He sneered. "We're no one's servants. And unfortunate for you that you've seen us. Now we'll have to—"

"Stow it," she snapped. "I'm not playing your game, either for your side or for Spyre's. I have my own agenda, and it might benefit your own goals to consider me a possible ally."

Again the sense of amused surprise. Venera could hear voices outside in the hall now. "Be very quiet," she said, "and snuff those lights." Then she stepped back, grabbed the edges of the doors, and shut them.

Lanterns bobbed down the corridor. "Lady Thrace-Guiles?" It was Aday.

"Here. My lantern went out. In any case there seems to be nothing of interest this way. Shall we investigate the upper floors?"

"Perhaps." Aday peered about himself in distaste. "This appears to be a commoner's area. Yes, let's retrace our steps."

They walked in silence, and Venera strained to hear any betraying noise from the chamber behind them. There was none; finally, Aday said, "To what do we owe the honor of your visit? Is Buridan rejoining the great nations? Are you going to restart the trade in horses?"

Venera snorted. "You know perfectly well there was no room to keep such animals in the tower. We had barely enough to eat from the rooftop gardens and nets we strung under the world. No, there are no horses anymore. And I am the last of my line."

"Ah." They began to climb the long-disused steps to the upper chambers. "As to your being the last of the line . . . lines can be rejuvenated," said Aday delicately. "And as to the horses . . . I am happy to say that you are in error in that case."

She cast a sidelong glance at him. "What do you mean? Don't toy with me."

Aday smiled, appearing confident for the first time. "There *are* horses, my lady. Raised and bred at government expense in paddocks on Greater Spyre. They have always been here, all these years. They have been awaiting your return."

9

VENERA WAS NINE-TENTHS asleep and imagining that the pillow she clutched was Chaison's back. Such feelings of safety and belonging were so rare for her that by contrast the rest of her life seemed a wasteland. It was as though everything she had ever done, every school lesson and contest with her sisters, every panicky interview with her father, all the manipulations and lies, had been erased by this: the quiet, his breathing, his scent, and his neck against her chin.

"Rise and shine, my lady!"

Garth Diamandis threw back the room's curtains, revealing a brick wall. He glowered at it as scraps of velvet tore away in his fingers. Dust pillared around him in the lantern light.

Venera sat up and a knife blade of pain shot up her jaw. "Get out!" She thrashed about for a second, looking for a weapon. "Get out!" Her hands fell on the lantern and—not without thinking, but rather with malicious pleasure—she threw it at him as hard as she could.

Garth ducked and the lantern broke against the wall. The candle flame touched the curtains and they caught fire instantly.

"Oh! Not a good idea!" He tore down the curtains and, fetching a poker from the fireplace, began beating the flames.

"Did you not *hear* me?" She cast the musty covers aside and ran at him. Grabbing up a broken splinter of a chair leg, she brandished it like a sword. "Get *out!*"

He parried easily and with a flick of the wrist sent her makeshift sword flying. Then he jabbed her in the stomach with the poker.

"Ooff!" She sat down. Garth continued beating out the flames. Smoke was filling the ancient bedchamber of the Buridan clan.

When Venera had her breath back she stood up and walked to a side table. Returning with a jug of water, she upended it over the smouldering cloth. Then she dropped the jug indifferently—it shattered—and glared at Garth.

"I was asleep," she said.

He turned to her, a muscle jumping in his own jaw. She saw for the first time that his eyes were red. Had he slept?

"What's the matter?" she asked.

With a heavy sigh he turned and walked away. Venera made to follow, realized she was naked, and turned to don her clothing. When she found him again he was sitting in the antechamber, fiddling with his bootstraps.

"It's her, isn't it?" she asked. "You've been looking for her?"

Startled, he looked up at her. "How did you—"

"I'm a student of human nature, Garth." She turned around. "Lace me up, please."

"You could have burned the whole place down," he grumbled as he tugged—a little too hard—on her corset strings.

"My self-control isn't good when I'm surprised," she said with a shrug. "Now you know."

"Aye." He grabbed her hips and turned her around to face him. "You usually hide your pain as well as someone twice your age."

"I choose to take that as a compliment." Conscious of his hands on her, she stepped back. "But you're evading the question—did you find her? Your expression suggests bad news."

He stood up. "It doesn't concern you." He began to walk away.

Venera gnawed her lip, thinking about apologizing for attacking him. It got no further than thinking. "Well," she said after following him for a while, "for what reason did you rouse me at such an ungodly . . . ." She looked around. "What time is it?"

"It's midmorning." He glanced around as well; the chambers of the estate were cast in gloom save where the occasional lantern burned. "The house is entombed, remember?"

"Oh! The appointment!"

"Yes. The horse masters are waiting in the front hall. They're mighty nervous, since neither in their lifetimes nor those of their line stretching back centuries has anyone ever audited their work."

"I'm not auditing, Garth. I just want to meet some horses."

"And you may—but we have a bigger problem."

"What's that?" She paused to look at herself in a faded mirror. Somewhere downstairs she heard things being moved; they had hired a work gang to clean the building, just before fatigue had caught up with her and forced her to take refuge in that mildewed bedchamber.

"There's a second delegation waiting for you," Diamandis explained. "A pack of majordomos from the great families."

She stopped walking. "Ah. A challenge?"

"In a manner of speaking. You've been invited to attend a confirmation ceremony. To formally establish your identity and tites."

"Of course, of course . . ." She started walking again. "Damn, they're a step ahead of us. We'll have to turn that around." Venera pondered this as they trotted down the sweeping front steps. "Garth, do I smell like smoke?"

"Alas, my lady, you have about you the piquant aroma of a flaming curtain."

"Well, there's nothing to be done about it, I suppose. Are those the challengers?" She pointed to a group of ornately dressed men who stood in the middle of the archway. Behind them, a motley group of men in work clothes milled uncertainly. "Those would be the horsemen, then."

"Gentlemen," she said to the horsemen with a smile as she walked past the officials. "I'm so sorry to have kept you waiting."

"Ahem," said an authoritative voice behind her. Venera made herself finish shaking hands before she turned. "Yes?" she said with a sweet smile. "What can I do for you?"

The graying man with the lined face and dueling scars said, "You are summoned to appear—"

"I'm sorry, did you make an appointment?"

"—to appear before the—what?"

"An appointment." She leaned closer. "Did you make one?"

Unable to ignore protocol, he said "No" with sarcastic reluctance.

Venera waved a hand to dismiss him. "Then take it up with my manservant. These people have priority at the moment. They made an appointment."

An amused glint came into his eye. Venera realized, reluctantly, that this wasn't some flunky she was addressing, but a seasoned veteran of one of the great nations. And since she had just tried to set fire to her new mansion and kill her one and only friend in this godforsaken place, it could be that her judgement wasn't quite what it should be today.

She glanced at Diamandis, who was visibly holding his tongue. With a deep sigh she bowed to the delegation. "I'm sorry. Where are my manners. If we conduct our business briefly, I can make my other appointment without ruffling feathers on that end as well. Who do I have the honor of addressing?"

Very slightly mollified, he said, "I am Jacoby Sarto of the nation of Sacrus. Your . . . return from the dead . . . has caused quite a stir amongst the great nations, lady. There are claims of proof that you must provide before you are accepted for who you are."

"I know," she said simply.

"Thursday next," he said, "at four o'clock in the council offices. Bring your proofs." He turned to go.

"Oh. Oh dear." He turned back, a dangerous look in his eye. Venera looked abjectly apologetic. "It's a very small problem—more of an opportunity, really. I happen to have become entangled in . . . a number of obligations that day. My former debtors and creditors . . . but I'm not trying to dodge your request! Far from it. Why don't we say eight o'clock P.M. in the main salon of my home? Such a date would allow me to fulfil my obligations and—"

"Whatever." He turned to confer with the others. The conference was brief. "So be it." He stepped close to her and looked down at her, the way her father used to do when she was young. Despite herself, Venera quailed inside—but she didn't blink, just as she had never reacted to her father's threats. "No games," he said very quietly. "Your life is at stake here." Then he gestured sharply to the others and they followed him away.

Garth leaned in and muttered, "What obligations? You have nothing planned that day."

"We do now," she said as she watched Sarto and his companions walk away. She told Garth what she had in mind, and his eyes widened in shock.

"In a week? The place is a shambles!"

"Then you know what you're going to be doing the rest of the day," she said tartly. "Hire as many people as you need—cash in a few of my gems. And Garth," she said as he turned to go. "I apologize for earlier."

He snorted. "I've had worse reactions first thing in the morning. But I expected better from you."

For some reason those parting words stung far more than any of the things she'd imagined he might say.

"YOU HAVEN'T TALKED about the horses," he said late that evening. Garth was pushing the far end of a hugely heavy wine rack while Venera hauled on the near side. Slowly, the wooden behemoth grated another few inches across the cellar floor. "How— oof!—what did you think of them?"

"I'm still sorting it out in my own mind," she said, pausing to set her feet better against the riveted iron decking that underlay her estate. "They were beautiful, and grotesque. Dali horses, the handlers called them. Apparently, a Dali is any four-legged beast raised under lower gravity than it was evolved to like."

Garth nodded and they pushed and pulled for a while. The rack was approaching the wall where the little cell of rebels had made their entrance—a hole pounded in the brickwork that led to an abandoned air shaft. Garth had explored a few yards of the tunnel beyond; Venera was afraid the rebels might have left traps behind.

"It was the smell I noticed first," she said as they took another break. "Not like any fish or bird I'd ever encountered. Foul but you could get used to it, I suppose. They had the horses in a place called a paddock—a kind of slave pen for animals. But the beasts . . . they were huge!"

Voices and loud thuds filtered in from the estate's central hall-way. Two of the work gangs Garth had hired that day were arguing over who should start work in the kitchens first.

Shadows flickered past the cellar door. The estate was crawling with people now. Lanterns were lit everywhere and shouted conversations echoed down, along with hammering, sawing, and the rumble of rolling carts. Venera hoped the racket would keep the neighbors up. She had a week to make this place fit for guests and that meant working kitchens, a ballroom with no crumbling plasterwork and free of the smell of decay—and, of course, a fully stocked wine cellar. The rebel gang had removed all evidence of themselves when they retreated but had left behind the hole by which they'd gained entrance. Because the mansion had only one entrance—the back doors had not yet been uncovered—Venera had decided it prudent to keep this bolt-hole. But if she was going to have a secret exit, it had to be secret; hence the wine rack.

"Okay," she said when they had it about three feet from the wall. "I'm going to grease the floor under the hole, so we can slide the rack to one side if we need to get out in a hurry." She plonked down the can she'd taken from one of the workmen and rolled up her sleeves.

"We'll have to survey for traps sometime," he said reasonably.

Venera squinted up at him. "Maybe, but not tonight. You look like you're about to collapse, Garth. Is it the gravity?"

He nodded, wincing. "That, and simple age. This is more activity than I've had in a long while, when you factor in the new weight. I thought I was in good shape, but . . ."

"Well, I hereby order you to take two days off. I'll manage the workmen. Take one day to rest up, and maybe on the second you tend to the . . . uh, that matter that you won't talk to me about."

"What matter?" he said innocently.

"It's all right." She smiled. "I understand. You've been in exile for a long time. Plenty of time to think about the men who put you there. Given that much time, I'd bet you've worked out your revenge in exquisite detail."

Garth looked shocked. "Revenge? No, that's not—oh, I suppose in the first few months I thought about it a lot. But you get over anger, you know. After a few years, perspective sets in."

"Yes, and that's the danger, isn't it? In my family, we were taught to nurture our grudges lest we forget."

"But why?" He looked genuinely distressed for some reason.

"Because once you forgive," she said, as if explaining something to a small child, "you set yourself up for another betrayal."

"That's what you were taught?"

"Never let an insult pass," she said, half-conscious that she was reciting lines her father and sisters had spoken to her many times. She ticked the points off on her fingers. "Never let a slight pass, never forget, build realistic plans for your revenges. You're either up or down from other people and you want always to be up. If they hurt you, you *must* knock them down."

Now he looked sad. "Is that why you're doing all this?" He gestured at the walls. "To get back at someone?"

"To *get back,* at all," she said earnestly, "I must have my revenge. Else I am brought low forever and can never go home. For otherwise—" Her voice caught.

For otherwise, I have no reason to return.

His expression of compassion on anyone else would have maddened her. "You were telling me about the horses," he said quietly.

"Ah. Yes." Grateful of the distraction, she said, "Well, they have these huge barrel-shaped bodies and elegant long necks. Long heads like on my ring." She held it up, splaying her fingers. "But their legs! Garth, their legs are twice the length of their bodies—like spider's legs, impossibly long and thin. They stalked around the paddock like . . . well, like spiders! I don't know how else to describe it. They were like a dream that's just tipping over to become a nightmare. I'm not sure I want to see them again."

He nodded. "There are cattle loose between some of the estates. I've seen them; they look similar. You have to understand, there's no room on the city wheels to raise livestock."

Venera pried open the lid of the grease can and picked up a brush. "But now that the nation of Buridan has returned, the horses are our responsibility. There are costs . . . it seems a dozen or more great nations have acted as caretakers for one or another part of the Buridan estate. Some are tenants of ours who haven't paid rent in centuries. Others are like Guinevera, who've been tending the horses. There's an immense web of relationships and dependencies here, and we have a little under a week to figure it all out."

Garth thought about it for a while. "First of all," he said eventually, "you need to bring a foal or two up here and raise it in the estate." He grimaced at her expression. "I know what I just said, but it's an important symbol. Besides, these rooms will just fill up with people if you give them a chance. Why not set some aside for the horses now?"

"I'll think about that."

They cleared out the space behind the rack and slid it against the wall. It fit comfortably over the exit hole. As they stood back to admire their work, Garth said, "It's a funny thing about time, you know. It sweeps away anger and hate. But it leaves love untouched."

She threaded her hand through his arm. "Ah, Garth, you're so sentimental. Did it ever occur to you that's why you ended up scrabbling about on Greater Spyre for the past twenty years?"

He looked her in the eye. "Truthfully, no. That had never occurred to me. If anything, I'd say I ended up there because I didn't love well enough, not because I ever loved too well."

She sighed. "You're hopeless. It's a good thing I'm here to take care of you."

"And here I thought it was I taking care of you."

They left the cellar and reentered the bedlam of construction that had taken over the manor.

THE HEADACHE BEGAN that night.

Venera knew exactly what it was; she'd suffered these before. All day her jaw had been bothering her; it was like an iron hand was inside her throat, reaching up to clench her skull. Around dinner a strange pulsating squiggly spot appeared in her vision and slowly expanded until she could see nothing around it. She retired to her room and waited.

How long was this one going to last? They could go on for days, and she didn't have days. Venera paced up and down, stumbling, wondering whether she could just sleep it off. But no, she had mounds of paperwork to go through and no time.

She called Garth. He exclaimed when he saw her and ran to her side. "You're white as a new wall!"

"Never mind," she said, detaching herself from him and climbing into bed. "Bring in the accounts books. It's just a headache. I get them. I'm sick but we need to go through these papers."

He started to read the details of Buridan's various contracts. Each word was like a little explosion in her head. Venera tried to concentrate, but after ten minutes she suddenly leaned over the edge of the bed and retched.

"You need to sleep!" Garth's hands were on her shoulders. He eased her back on the bed.

"Don't be ridiculous," she mumbled. "If we don't get this stuff straight, we won't convince the council and they'll cart us both away in chains." A blossom of agony had unfurled behind her left eye. Despite her brave words Venera knew she was down for however long the migraine decided to hold her.

Garth darkened the lamps and tiptoed around while she lay sprawled like a discarded doll. Distant hammering sounded like it was coming from inside her own head, but she couldn't hold up the renovations.

Sleep eventually came, but she awoke to pain that was abstract only until she moved her head and opened one eye. *This is how it's going to be.* These headaches were the bullet's fault; when it smashed her jaw it had tripped some switch inside her head and now agony ambushed her at the worst times. Always before, she'd had the safe haven of her bedroom at home to retreat to—her time on the Rook had been mercifully free of such episodes. She used such times to indulge in her worst behavior: whining, accusing, insulting anyone who came near her, and demanding that her every whim be catered to. She wallowed in self-pity, letting everyone know that she was the sad victim of fate and that no one, ever, had felt the agonies she was enduring so bravely.

But she really was going to die if she let the thing rule her this time. It wasn't that there was nobody around to indulge her; but in a moment of clarity she realized that all the sympathy in the world wasn't going to save her life if she didn't follow through on the deception she and Garth had planned. So, halfway through morning, Venera resolutely climbed out of bed. She tied a silk sash over her eyes, jammed candle wax in her ears, and picked up an empty chamber pot. Carrying this, she tottered out of the room. "Bring me a dressing gown," she said in reply to a half-heard question from a maid. "And fetch Master Flance."

Blindfolded, half-deaf, she nonetheless managed to make her rounds of the work crews, while Garth followed her and read from the books. She told him what points to underline for her to look at later; inquired of the work and made suggestions; and, every now and then, she turned aside to daintily vomit into the chamber pot. Her world narrowed down to the feel of carpet or stone under her feet, the murmur of words in her ear, and the cataclysmic pounding that reverberated inside her skull. She kept going by imagining herself whipping, shooting, stomping on, and setting fire to Jacoby Sarto and the rest of this self-important council who had the temerity to oppose her will. This interior savagery was invisible from without, as she mumbled and queried politely, and let herself be led about.

All of this busywork seemed to be getting her somewhere, but that evening when she collapsed onto her bed, Venera realized that she had no memory of anything she had said or done that day. It was all obscured by the angry red haze of pain that had followed her everywhere.

She was doomed. She'd never be ready in time for the interrogation the council had planned. Venera rolled over, cried into her pillow, and finally just lay there, accepting her fate. The bullet had defeated her.

With that understanding came a kind of peace, but she was in too much pain to analyze it. She just lay there, dry-eyed, frowning, until sleep overcame her.

10

"WHAT IS *THIS?*" Jacoby Sarto glared at the rickshaws cluster-
ing in the courtyard below the Buridan estate's newly rebuilt entrance. It was seven P.M. and Candesce was extinguishing itself, its
amber glories drenching the building tops. Down in the purpled
courtyard the upstart princess's new footmen were lighting lanterns to guide in dozens of carts and palanquins from the crowded
alley.

Someone of a minor noble nation had heard him and turned,
smirking. "You didn't receive an invitation?" asked the impertinent youth. "It's a gala reception!"

"Bah!" Sarto turned to his companion, the duke of Ennersin.
"What is she up to? This is a feeding frenzy. I'll wager half these
people have come to gawk at the legendary Buridans, and the
other half to watch us drag her out of the place in chains. What
does she gain out of such a spectacle?"

"I'm afraid we'll find out shortly," said the duke. He was as
stocky as Sarto, with similarly graying temples and the sort of
paternal scowl that could freeze the blood of anyone under forty.
Together the two men radiated gravitas to such an extent that the
crowds automatically parted for them. True, most of those assembling here knew them, by sight and reputation at least. The nations of Sacrus and Ennersin were feared and respected by all.
—All, it seemed, save for newly reborn Buridan. These two were
here tonight to make sure that this new situation didn't last.

"In any case, such entertainments as this are rare, Jacoby. It's
sure to attract the curious and the morbid, yes. But it's the third

audience that worries me," Duke Ennersin commented as they strode up the steps to the entrance.

Sarto glared at a footman who had the temerity to approach them at the entrance. "What third audience?"

"Do you see the Guineveras there? They've been keeping Buridan's horses for generations. Make no mistake, they'd be happy to be free of the burden—or to own the beasts outright."

"Which they will after tonight."

"I wouldn't be too sure of that," said Ennersin. "Proof that this Amandera Thrace-Guiles is an imposter is not proof that the real heirs aren't out there."

"What are you saying, man? She's been in the tower! Clearly it's empty after all. There are no heirs to be had."

"Not there, no . . . But don't forget there are sixteen nations that claim to be related by blood to the Thrace-Guileses. The moment this Amandera's declared a fake the other pretenders will pounce on the property rights. It'll be a legal free-for-all—maybe even a civil war. Many of these people are here to warn their nations the instant it becomes a possibility."

"Ridiculous!" Sarto forgot what he was going to say next, as they entered the lofting front hall of the Buridan estate.

It smelled of fresh paint and drying plaster. Lanterns and braziers burned along the pillared staircases, lighting a frescoed ceiling crawling with allegorical figures. The painted blues, yellows, and reds were freshly cleaned and vibrant to the point of being nauseating, as were the heroic poses of the men and half-clad women variously hanging off, riding, or being devoured by hundreds of ridiculously posed horses. Sarto gaped at this vision for a while, then shuddered. "The past is sometimes best left buried," he said.

Ennersin chuckled. "Or at least strategically unlit."

Sarto had been expecting chaos inside the estate; after all, nobody had set foot in here in centuries, so Thrace-Guiles's new servants would be unfamiliar with the layout of their own home.

They would be a motley collection of rejects and near-criminals hired from the dregs of Lesser Spyre, after all, and he fully expected to see waiters spilling drinks down the decolletage of the ladies when they weren't banging into one another in their haste to please.

There was none of that. Instead, a string quartet played a soothing pavane in the corner, while men and women in black tails and white gloves glided to and fro, gracefully presenting silver platters and unobtrusively refilling casually tilted glasses. The waitstaff were, in fact, almost mesmerizing in their movements; they were better than Sarto's own servants.

"Where did she get this chattel?" he muttered as a man with a stentorian voice announced their arrival. Lady Pamela Anseratte, who had known Sarto for decades and was quite unafraid of him, laughed and trotted over in a swirl of skirts. "Oh, she's a clever one, this Thrace-Guiles," she said, laying her lace-covered hand on Sarto's arm. "She's hired the acrobats of the Spyre Circus to serve drinks! I hear they rehearsed blindfolded."

Indeed, Sarto glanced around and realized there was a young lady with the compact muscled body of a dancer standing at his elbow. She held out a glass. "Champagne?" Automatically, he took it, and she vanished into the crowd without a sound.

"Well, we'll credit the woman with being a genius in domestic matters," he growled. "But surely you haven't been taken in by her act, Pamela? She's an imposter!"

"That's as may be," said the lady with a flick of her fan. "But your imposter has just forgiven Virilio's debt to Buridan. It seems that with interest it would now be worth enough to outfit a small fleet of merchant ships! And she's just erased it! Here, look! There's August Virilio himself, drinking himself into happy idiocy under that stallion statue."

Sarto stared. The limestone stallion appeared to be sneering over Virilio's shoulder at the small crowd of hangers-on he was holding forth to. He was conspicuously unmasked, like most of the other council representatives. The place was crowded with masked faces, though—some immediately identifiable, others unfamiliar even to his experienced eye. "Who are all these people?" he wondered aloud.

"Debtors, apparently," said Lady Pamela with some relish. "And creditors . . . everyone who's taken care of Buridan's affairs or profited by their absence over the past two hundred years. They all look . . . happy, don't you think, Jacoby?"

Ennersin cleared his throat and leaned in to say, "Thrace-Guiles has clearly been doing her homework."

Despite himself, Sarto was impressed. This woman was continuing to confound his expectations. Was it possible that she might go on doing so? The thought was unexpected—and nothing unexpected had happened in Jacoby Sarto's life in a very long time.

He resisted where this line of thought led; after all, he had his instructions. Sarto dashed his champagne glass on the floor. Heads turned. "Let her enjoy her little party," he said in his darkest voice. "Amandera Thrace-Guiles, or whatever her real name is, has about one hour of freedom left.

"And no more than a day to live."

VENERA STRODE THROUGH the crowd, nodding and smiling. She felt unsteady and vulnerable, and though her headache had finally faded she had to rein in an automatic cringe-reaction to bright lights and loud sounds. She felt hideously unready for the evening and had overdressed to compensate. Most of the people in Spyre wore dark colors, so she had chosen to dress in red—her corset was a glossy crimson inset with designs sewn in scarlet thread, with a wide-shouldered, open jacket atop that. She wore a necklace from the Anetene hoard. Her skin was recovering from the burns she'd suffered near Candesce, but the contrasts were still effective. To hide the scar on her chin she'd adopted one of the strange local skullcaps, this one of black feathers. It swept up behind her ears and down to a point in the middle of her forehead, where a single red Anetene gem glowed above her heavily drawn eyebrows—but it also thrust two small wings along her jawline. They tickled her chin annoyingly, but that was a small distraction compared with the sensations that the ankle-length skirt gave her. Dresses and skirts were considered obscene in most of Virga, where one might become weightless at any time. Back home, the prostitutes wore them. Venera wore a pair of breeches under the thing, which made her feel a bit better, but the long heavy drape still moved and turned like it had a mind of its own.

The one spot of white in her apparel was the fan she held before her like a shield. Nobody but Garth would know that its near side was covered with names and family trees, drawn in tiny spiked letters. She hadn't had time to read the complicated genealogies and financial records of Buridan and its dependents; this fan was her lifeline.

As she recovered from her migraine in the last day or so, the reconstruction work had caught up and the servants learned where everything was. To her relief Garth had orchestrated the ball without supervision, making sometimes brilliant decisions. Twenty years of pent-up social appetite, she supposed. The estate's pantries had been cleared of rats and spiders and restocked; the ancient plumbing system had been largely replaced (not without messy accidents) and the gas lines to the stoves reconnected.

In a way, she was grateful for having been distracted these past few days. This afternoon she'd had a brief moment with nothing to do, and into her mind had drifted memories of Chaison. Standing in her chambers, her hand half-lifted to her hair, she was suddenly miserable. Pain and anxiety had masked her grief until now.

She had to battle through it all—play her part. So now she marched up to a tight knot of masked nobles from the mysterious nation of Faddeste and bowed. "Welcome to my house. Speaking as someone who has seen few human beings in her life, outside her immediate family, I know how much it must cost you to attend a crowded event such as this."

"We find it . . . hard." The speaker could be a man or a woman, it was impossible to tell. Its accent was so thick she had to puzzle out the words. Tall and thickly robed, this ambassador from a ten-acre nation flicked a finger at the sweeping dancers now beginning to fill up the center of the hall. "Such frivolity should be banned. How are you so calm? Not raised to this, crowd should frighten."

Venera bowed. "I lived in my imagination as a girl." That much was true. "Lacking real people to talk to, I invented a whole court—a whole nation!—who followed me everywhere. I was never alone. So perhaps this isn't so strange for me."

"Doubtful. We don't believe you are of Buridan."

"Hmm. I could say the same—how do I know you're really from Faddeste?"

"Sacrilege!" But the robed figure didn't turn away.

"Whether either of us is who we say we are," said Venera with a smug smile, "it remains a fact that Buridan owes Faddeste twenty thousand Spyre sovereigns. Imposter or not, I am willing to repay that debt."

Now she stepped in close, raising one black eyebrow and glancing around at the crowd. "Do you trust the pretenders in the crowd to do the same, if they acquire the title to Buridan? Think hard on that."

The ambassador reared back as though afraid Venera would touch it. "You have money?"

"Go see Master Flance." She pointed at Garth who, despite being masked, had characteristically surrounded himself with women young and old. All were laughing at some story he was telling. Seeing this, for a moment Venera forgot her worries and felt a pulse of warmth for the aging dandy. She turned back to the Faddestes, but they were already maneuvering across the dance floor like a frightened but determined flock of crows.

She blew out a held breath. Seven or eight more minor nations to bribe, and no time to do it. All the members of the Spyre council were here now, some clustered in little groups talking and pointing at her. It would all be decided soon, one way or another.

Before she could reach her next target, a majordomo in the livery of the Spyre Council approached and bowed. "They are ready for you upstairs, madam," he said coolly.

She kept her gaze fixed on the top of his head as she bowed in return. All eyes were on her, she was certain. This was the moment when all would be decided.

As she clattered up the marble steps she tried to remember the lines and gambits she had crammed into her head over the past day or so. It hadn't been enough time, and the hangover of her migraine had interfered. She was not ready; she just had herself, the passing lanterns, the looming shadows above, and the single rectangle of light from a pair of doors in the upstairs hall. She told herself to slow down, control her breathing, count to ten—but finally just cursed and strode down the newly laid crimson carpet to pivot on one heel and step into the room.

Jacoby Sarto's leonine features crinkled into something like a smirk as he saw her. He was placing the final chair behind the long conference table in the high-ceilinged minor reception hall. Damn him, he'd moved everything! Where Venera had contrived a single long table with chairs along two sides, with her at the end, Sarto had turned the table sideways, crammed all the seats on one side of it (behind it, now), and left one solitary chair in the center of the carpet. What had been a conference room was now a court, with her as the defendant.

The rest of the council were standing around behind Sarto as the servants finished the new placement.

She had an overwhelming urge to pick a seat behind the table and put her feet up, then point to the solitary position and ask, "Who sits there?" Only memory of how badly her recent outbursts had gone stopped her.

Well, he had won this round, but she wasn't going to let him revel in it. Venera stopped one of the servants and said, "Bring me a side table, and a bottle of wine and a glass. Some cheese might be good too." She sat graciously in the exposed chair and draped her skirts as she'd seen the other ladies do. Then she locked eyes with Sarto and smiled.

The others began to take their places. There were twelve of them. Jacoby Sarto of Sacrus, who was rumored to be merely an errand boy to the true heads of the family, sat on the far left. The arch-conservative duke Ennersin, who had conspicuously arrived with Sarto, sat next to him, frowning in disapproval at Venera. She could count on those two to oppose her confirmation. Of the others . . .

Pamela Anseratte was smiling at something, but wouldn't meet Venera's eye. Principe Guinevera *was* trying to meet her eye and apparently attempting to wink; he took up two spaces at the table and his fleshy hands were planted on the tabletop as if he were, at any second, about to leap to his feet and proclaim something. Next to him sat August Virilio, who looked contented, half-asleep even—and probably was, after the heroic drinking he'd gotten up to after she forgave his nation's debt. These three were on her side—or so she hoped.

The other great families were represented by minor members and, in three cases, by ambassadors. Two of the ambassadors were cloaked and masked; the families in question, Garrat and Oxorn, were mysterious, isolate, and paranoid as only the ancients of Greater Spyre could be. Nobody knew what their nations produced—only that it went for fabulous prices and threat of death on exposure in the outside world.

Three out of twelve for sure. Maybe three others if her reckless divestment of Buridan's wealth had done what she hoped. But it was a big if. She was going to need every ounce of cunning and every resource to get through the evening free and intact.

The council all sat and waited while Venera's new servants placed decanters of wine and tall glasses on the table. Then Pamela Anseratte stood and smiled around the table. "Welcome, everyone. I trust the nations are well and that the hospitality of our host has been sampled and appreciated by all? Yes? Then let's begin. We're gathered here tonight to decide whether to reinstate Buridan as an active nation, in the person of the woman who here claims to be Amandera Thrace-Guiles, heir of said nation. I—"

"Why are you alone?" Duke Ennersin was speaking directly to Venera. "Why are we to take this one person's word for who she is? Where is the rest of her nation? Why has she appeared here, now, after an absence of centuries?"

"Yes, yes, we're going to get to those questions," soothed Lady Anseratte. "First, however, we have some formalities to clear away. Amandera Thrace-Guiles's claim is pointless and instantly void if she cannot produce documents indicating her paternity and ancestry, as well as the notarized deeds and titles of her nation, plus the key." She beamed at Venera. "You have all those things?"

Silently, Venera rose and walked to the table. She placed the thick sheaf of papers she'd brought in front of Anseratte. Then she unscrewed the heavy signet ring from her finger and placed it atop the stack.

This was her opening move, but she couldn't count on its effect.

"I see," said Lady Anseratte. "May I examine the ring?" Venera nodded, returning to her seat. Lady Anseratte took a flat box with some lights on it and hovered it over the ring. The box glowed and made a musical bonging sound.

"Duly authenticated," said the lady. She carefully placed the ring to one side and opened the sheaf. Many of its contents were genuine. Venera had found the deeds and titles in the tower. It had been the work of several careful days to extend the family tree by several centuries and insert herself at its end. She had intended to use her own not-inconsiderable talents at forgery but had been indisposed, and Garth had come through, displaying surprising skills. He was not just a gigolo in his previous life, evidently. As the papers were passed up and down the table Venera kept a bland expression on her face. She tried the wine and adjusted the fall of her skirt again.

"Convincing," said Jacoby Sarto after flipping through the

papers. "But just because something is convincing that doesn't mean it's true. It's merely convincing. What can you do to establish the truth of your claim?"

Venera tilted her head to one side. "It would be impossible to do so to everyone's satisfaction, sir, just as it would be impossible for you to prove that you are, without doubt, Jacoby Sarto of Nation Sacrus. I rather think the onus is on this council to disprove my claim, if they can."

August Virilio opened one eye slightly. "Why don't we start with your story? I always like a good story after supper."

"Excellent idea," said Pamela Anseratte. "Duke Ennersin asked why it is that you are here before us now, of all times. Can you explain why your nation has hidden away so thoroughly for so long?"

Venera actually knew the answer to that one—it had been written in the contorted bodies of the soldiers inside the tower, and in the scrawled final confessions of the dead woman in the bedchamber.

Steepling her hands, Venera smiled directly at Jacoby Sarto and said, "The answer is simple. We knew that if we left Buridan Tower, we would be killed."

This was gambit number two.

The council members expressed various shades of surprise, shock, and satisfaction at her revelation. Jacoby Sarto crossed his arms and sat back. "Who would do this?" asked Anseratte. She was still standing and now leaned forward over the table.

"The isolation of Buridan Tower wasn't an accident," said Venera. "Or, at least, not entirely. It was the result of an attack—and the attackers were two of the great nations present at this table tonight."

August Virilio smiled sleepily, but Principe Guinevera leapt to his feet, knocking his chair over. "*Who?*" he raged. "Name them, fair lady, and we will see justice done!"

"I did not come here to open old wounds," said Venera. "Although I recognize that my position here is perilous, I had no choice but to leave the tower. Everyone else there is dead—save myself and my manservant. Some bird-borne illness took the last five of our people a month ago. I consigned their bodies to the winds of Virga, as we have been doing for centuries now. Before that we were dwindling, despite careful and sometimes repugnant breeding restrictions and constant austerity. . . . We lived on birds and airfish we caught with nets, and supplemented our diets with vegetables we grew in the abandoned bedrooms of our ancestors. Had I died in that place, then our enemies would truly have won. I chose a last throw of the die and came here."

"But the war of which you speak . . . it was centuries ago," said Lady Anseratte. "Why did you suppose that you would still be targeted after so long?"

Venera shrugged. "We had telescopes. We could see that our enemies' nations were thriving. And we could also clearly see that sentries armed with machine guns ringed the tower. I was raised to believe that if we entered the elevator and tried to reach Lesser Spyre, those machine gunners would destroy us before we rose more than a hundred meters."

"Oh, no!" Guinevera looked acutely distressed. "The sentries were there for your protection, madam! They were to keep interlopers out, not to box you in!"

"Well." Venera looked down. "Father thought so, but he also said that we were so reduced that we could not risk a single soul to find out. And isolation . . . becomes a habit." She looked pointedly at the ambassadors of Oxorn and Garrat.

Sarto guffawed loudly. "Oh, come on! What about the dozens of attempts that have been made to contact the tower? Semaphore, loudspeakers, smoke signals, for God's sake. They've all been tried and nobody ever responded."

"I am not aware that anyone has tried to contact us during my lifetime," said Venera. This was true, as she'd learned in the past days. Sarto would have to concede the point. "And I can't speak to my ancestors' motives for staying silent."

"That's as may be," Sarto continued. "Look, I'll play it straight. Sacrus was involved in the original atrocity." He held up a hand when Guinevera protested loudly. "But gentlemen and ladies, that was centuries ago. We are prepared to admit our crime and make reparations to the council when this woman is exposed for the fraud that she is."

"And if she's not?" asked Guinevera angrily.

"Then to the nation of Buridan directly," said Sarto. "I just wanted to clear the air. We can't name our coconspirators because, after all this time, the records have been lost. But having admitted our part in the affair, and having proposed that we pay reparations, I can now continue to oppose this woman's claim without any appearance of conflict."

Venera frowned. Her second gambit had failed.

If Sacrus had wanted to keep their involvement a secret, she might have had leverage over Sarto. Maybe even enough to swing his vote. As it was he'd adroitly sidestepped the trap.

Lady Anseratte looked up and down the table. "Is the other conspirator's nation similarly honorable? Will they admit their part?" There was a long and uncomfortable silence.

"Well, then," said Pamela Anseratte. "Let us examine the details of your inheritances."

From here the interview deteriorated into minutiae as the council members pulled out individual documents and points of law and debated them endlessly. Venera was tired, and every time she blinked to clear her vision, she worried that a new migraine might be reaching to crush her. Pamela Anseratte conducted the meeting as if she had boundless energy, but Venera—and everyone else—wilted under the onslaught of detail.

Sarto used sarcasm, wit, guile, and bureaucracy to try to torpedo her claim, but after several hours it became clear that he wasn't making headway. Venera perked up a bit. *I could win this*, she realized—simultaneously realizing just how certain she'd been that she wouldn't.

Finally Lady Anseratte said, "Any further points?" and nobody answered. "Well," she said brightly, "we might as well proceed to a vote."

"Hang on," said Sarto. He stood heavily. "I've got something to say." Everyone waited.

"This woman is a fraud. We all know it. It's inconceivable that this family could have sustained themselves and their retainers for centuries within a single tower, cut off from the outside world—"

"Not inconceivable," said the ambassador of Oxorn from behind her griffin mask. "Quite possible."

Sarto glared at her. "What did they do for clothes? For even the tiniest item of utility, such as forks or pens? Do you really believe they have an entire industrial base squirreled away in that tower?" He shook his head.

"It's equally inconceivable that someone raised in such total isolation should, upon being dropped into society and all its machinations, conduct herself like a veteran! Did she rehearse social banter with her *dolls*? Did she learn to dance with her rocking horse? It's preposterous on the face of it.

"And we all know why her claim has any chance of success. It's because she's bought off everyone who might oppose it. Buridan has tremendous assets—estates, ships, buildings, and industries here and on Greater Spyre that have been administered by other nations in absentia, for generations. She's promised to give those nations the assets they've tended! For the rest, she's proposing to beggar Buridan by paying all its debts here and now. When she's done Buridan will have nothing to its name but a herd of gangly equines."

"And this house," said Venera primly. "I don't propose to give that up." There was some stifled laughter around the table.

"It's a transparent fraud!" Sarto turned to glare at the other council members. "Forget about the formal details of her claim—in fact, let it be read that there's nothing to criticize about it. That doesn't matter. We all know the truth. She is insulting the name of a great nation of Spyre! Do you actually propose to let her get away with it?"

He was winning them over. Venera had one last hand to play, and it was her weakest. She stood up.

"Then who am I?" She strode up to the table and leaned across it to look Sarto in the eye. "If I'm a fraud I must have come from somewhere. Was I manufactured by one of the other nations, then? If so, which one? Spyre is secretive, but not so much so that we don't all keep tabs on one another's genealogies. Nobody's missing from the rosters, are they?

"And yet!" She turned to address the rest of the council. "Gaze upon me and tell me to my face that you don't believe I am noble born." She sneered at Sarto. "It's evident in my every gesture, in how I speak, how I address the servants. Jacoby Sarto says that he knows I am a fraud. Yet you know I am a peer!

"So then where did I come from?" She turned to Sarto again. "If Jacoby Sarto believes I did not come from Buridan Tower, then he must have some idea of where I did. What do you know, Sir Sarto, that you're not telling the rest of us? Do you have some proof that you're not sharing? A name, perhaps?"

He opened his mouth—and hesitated.

They locked eyes and she saw him realize what she was willing to do. The key to Candesce was almost visible in the air between them; it was the real subject of tonight's deliberations.

"Sacrus has many secrets, as we've seen tonight," she said quietly. "Is there some further secret you have, Sir Sarto, that you wish to share with the council? A name, perhaps? One that might be recognized by the others present? A name that could be tied to recent events, to rumors and legends that have percolated through the principalities in recent weeks?" She saw puzzled frowns on several faces—and Sarto's eyes widened as he heard her tread the edge of the one revelation Sacrus did not want made public.

He looked down. "Perhaps I went too far in my accusations," he said almost inaudibly. "I retract my statements."

Duke Ennersin leaned back in his chair, open-mouthed. And Jacoby Sarto meekly sat down.

Venera returned to her seat. *If I lose, everyone learns that you have the key,* she thought as she settled herself on the velvet cushion. She took a sip of wine and kept her expression neutral as Pamela Anseratte stood again.

"Well," said the lady in a cautious tone, "if there are no more outbursts . . . let us put it to a vote."

Venera couldn't help but lean forward a bit.

"All those who favor this young lady's claim, and who wish to recognize the return of Buridan to Spyre and to this council, raise your right hand."

Guinevera's hand shot up. Beside him, August Virilio languidly pushed his into the air. Pamela Anseratte raised her own hand.

Oxorn's hand went up. Then, Garrat's ambassador raised his.

That made five. Venera let out the breath she'd been keeping. It was over. She had failed—

Jacoby Sarto raised his hand.

His expression was exquisite—a mixture of distaste and resignation that you might see in a man who's just volunteered to dig up a grave. Duke Ennersin was staring at him in total disbelief and slowly turning purple.

Lady Anseratte's only show of surprise was a minute frown. "All those opposed?" she said.

Ennersin threw his hand in the air. Five others went up.

"And no abstentions," said Anseratte. "We appear to have a tie."

Jacoby Sarto slumped back in his chair. "Well, then," he said quietly. "I move we take the matter to the council investigative team. Let them visit the tower and conduct a thorough—"

"*Don't I get a vote?*"

They all turned to stare at Venera. She sat up straighter, clearing her throat. "Well, it seems to me . . ." She shrugged. "It's just that this meeting was called to confirm my identity and claim to being head of Buridan. Confirmation implies a presumption that I am who I say I am. I *am* Buridan unless proven otherwise. And Buridan is a member of the council. So I should have a vote."

"This is outrageous!" Duke Ennersin had had enough. He threw back his chair and stalked around the table. "You have the temerity to suggest that you—"

"She's right."

The voice was quiet and languid, almost indifferent—but it stopped Ennersin in his tracks. His head ratcheted around slowly, as if pulled by unwilling forces to look at the man who had spoken.

August Virilio was lounging back in his chair, his hands steepled in front of him. "Article five, section twelve, paragraph two of the charter," he said in a reasonable tone. "Identity is presumptive if there is no other proven heir. And Buridan is a member of the council. Its title was never suspended."

"A mere formality! A courtesy!" But Ennersin's voice had lost its certainty. He appealed to Pamela Anseratte, but she simply spread her hands and smiled.

Then, looking around him at Venera, she said, "It appears you are right, dear. You do get a vote. Would you care to . . . ?"

Venera smiled and raised her right hand. "I vote in favor," she said.

SHE WAS SURE you could hear Ennersin outside and down the street. Venera smiled as she shepherded her guests to the door. She was delirious with relief and was sure it showed in her ridiculous grin. Her soiree was winding down, though naturally the doors and lounges would be open all night for any stragglers. But the council members were tired; no one would criticize them for leaving early.

Ennersin was yelling at Jacoby Sarto. It was music to Venera's ears.

She looked for Garth but couldn't see him at first. Then—there he was, sidling in the entrance. He'd changed to inconspicuous street clothes. Had he been preparing to sneak away? Venera pictured him leaving through the wine cellar exit to avoid the council's troops. Then he could have circled around to stand with the street rabble who were waiting to hear the results of the vote. She smiled; it was what she might have done.

There went Ennersin, sweeping by Garth without noticing him. Diamandis watched him go in distaste, then turned and saw Venera watching him. He spread his hands and shrugged. She made a dismissive gesture and smiled back.

Time to mingle; the party wasn't over yet and her head felt fine. It felt good to reinforce her win with a gracious turn about the room. For a while everything was a blur of smiling faces and congratulations. Then she found herself shaking someone's hand (the hundredth, it must have been) and looked up to find it was Jacoby Sarto's.

"Well played, Ms. Fanning," he said. There was no irony in his voice.

She glanced around. They were miraculously alone for the moment. Probably a single glance from under Sarto's wiry brows had been enough to clear a circle.

All she could think of to say was, "Thank you." It struck her as hopelessly inadequate for the situation, but all her strategies had been played out. To her surprise, Sarto smiled.

"I've lost Ennersin's confidence," he said. "It's going to take me years to regain some allies I abandoned today."

"Oh?" The mystery of his reversal during the vote deepened. Not one to prevaricate, Venera said, "Why?"

He appeared puzzled. "Why did I vote for you?"

"No—I know why." The key was again unspoken-of between them. "I mean," she said, "why did you come out so publicly against me in the first place, if you knew I had that to hang over you?"

"Ah." It was his turn to look around them. Satisfied that no one was within earshot, he said, "I was entrusted with the safety of Sacrus's assets. You're considered one of them. If I could acquire you, I was to do that. If not, and you threatened to reveal . . . certain details . . . well, I was to contrive a murderous rage." He opened his jacket slightly and she saw the large pistol he had holstered there. "You would not have had a chance to say what you know," he said with a slight smile.

"So why didn't you . . ."

"It is useful to have an acknowledged heir of Buridan controlling that estate. This way we avoid a nasty succession conflict, which Sacrus would view as an unnecessary . . . distraction, right now. Besides." Sarto shrugged. "There are few moments in a man's life when he has the opportunity to make a choice on his own. I simply did not want to shoot you."

"And why tell me this now?"

His mouth didn't change from its accustomed frown, but the lines around Sarto's eyes might have crinkled a little bit—an almost-smile.

"It will be easy for me to tell my masters that the pistol was taken from me at your door," he said. "Without an opportunity to acquire or silence you, letting you win was the expedient option. My masters know that." He turned away, then looked back with a scowl. "I hope you won't give me reason to regret my decision."

"Surely not. And my apologies for inconveniencing you."

He laughed at the edge in her voice.

"You may think you're free," he said as the crowd parted to let him through, "but Sacrus still owns you. Never forget that."

Venera kept her smile bright, but his parting words worried at her for the rest of the evening.

11

MUSCLES ACHING, VENERA swung down from the saddle of her horse. It was two weeks since the confirmation and she had lost no time in establishing her rule over Buridan—which, she had decided, had to include becoming a master rider.

She'd knocked down two walls and sealed up the ends of one of the high-ceilinged cellar corridors, forming one long narrow room where her steed could trot. There were stalls at one end of this, and two workmen were industriously scattering straw and sand over the flagstones. "Deeper," Venera told them. "We need several inches of it everywhere."

"Yes, ma'am." The men seemed unusually enthusiastic and focused on their task. Maybe they had heard that the new foals were to arrive later today. Probably it was just being in proximity with the one horse now residing here. Venera hadn't yet met anyone who didn't share that strange, apparently ancient love for horses that seemed inbuilt in humans.

Venera herself wasn't immune to it. She patted Domenico and walked down the length of the long room, trailing one hand along the low fence that bisected it lengthwise. Her horsemaster stood at the far end, a clipboard clutched in his hand; he was arguing quietly with someone. "Is everything all right, gentlemen?" Venera asked.

The other man turned, lamplight slanting across his gnomish features, and Venera said "Oh!" before she could stop herself.

Samson Odess screwed his fishlike face up into a smile and practically lunged over to shake her hand.

"I'm honored to meet you, Lady Amandera Thrace-Guiles!" His eyes betrayed no recognition, and Venera realized that she was standing in heavy shadow. "Liris is honored to offer you some land to stable your horses. You see, we're diversifying and—"

She grinned weakly. It was too soon for this! She had hoped that the men and women of Liris would be consumed by their own internal matters, at least long enough for her new identity to become fixed. If Odess recognized her the news would be bound to percolate through the Fair. She didn't believe in its vaunted secrecy any more than she believed that good always triumphed.

She let go of Odess's hand before he could get entirely into his sales pitch, and turned away. "Charmed I'm sure. Flance! Can you deal with this?"

"Oh, but Master Flance was unable to resolve one little matter," said the horsemaster, stepping around Odess.

"Deal with it!" she snarled. She glimpsed a startled look in Odess's eye before she swept by the two men and into the outer hallway.

Well, that had been an unexpected surge of adrenaline! She laughed at herself as she strode quickly through the vaulted, white-washed spaces. In the half-minute it took her to slow down to a stroll, Venera took several turns and ended up in an area of the cellars she didn't know.

Someone cleared their throat. Venera turned to find a man in servant's livery approaching. He looked only vaguely familiar but that was hardly surprising, considering the number of people she'd hired recently.

"Ma'am, this area hasn't been cleaned up yet. Are you looking for something in particular?"

"No. I'm lost. Where did you just come from?"

"This way." The man walked back the way they had both come. He was right about the state of the cellars; this passage hadn't been reconstructed and was only minimally cleaned. Black portraits still hung on the walls, here and there an eye glaring out from behind centuries of dust and soot. The lanterns were widely spaced and a few men visible down a side way were reduced to silhouettes, their backdrop some bright distant doors.

"Down this way." Her guide indicated a black stairwell Venera hadn't seen before. Narrow and unlit, it plummeted steeply down.

Venera stopped. "What the—" Then she saw the pistol in his hand.

"Move," grated the man. "Now."

She almost called his bluff. One of those quick sidesteps Chaison had taught her, then a foot sweep . . . he would be on the floor before he knew it. But she hesitated just long enough for him to step out of reach. Caught unprepared for once, Venera stumbled into the blackness with him behind her.

"YOU'RE IN A lot of trouble," she said.

"We're not afraid of the authorities." said her kidnapper contemptuously.

"I'm not talking about the authorities. I'm talking about me." The stairs had ended on a narrow shelf above an indistinct, dark body of water. It was dank and cold down here; looking left and right she saw that she was standing on the edge of a large tank—a cistern, no doubt.

"We've been watching you," said the shadowy figure behind her. "I assure you we know what you're capable of." The pistol was in her back again and he was pushing her hard enough that she had trouble keeping her feet. Angrily she hurried ahead and emerged onto the flagstones next to the water. "I didn't know I had this," she commented as she turned right, toward the source of the light.

"It's not yours. This is part of the municipal water supply," said a half-familiar voice up ahead.

She eyed the black depths. Jump in? There might be a culvert she could swim through, the way heroes did in romance novels. Those heroes never drowned in the dark, though, and besides, even if she made it out of here her appearance, soaking wet, in the streets of the city was bound to cause a scandal. She did not need that right now.

There was an open area at the far end of the tank. The same tables and crates she'd seen in the wine cellar were set up here, and the same young revolutionaries were sitting on them. Standing next to a lantern-lit desk was the youth with straight black hair and oval eyes. He was dressed in the long coat and tails she'd seen fashionable men wearing on the streets of the wheel; with his arms crossed the coat belled out enough for her to see the two pistols holstered at his waist. She was suddenly reminded of Garth's apparel, which was like a down-at-heel version of the same costume.

"What's the meaning of this?" she snapped, even as she counted people and exits (there was one of the latter, a closed iron door). "You're not being very neighborly," she added more softly.

"Sit her down and tie her up," said the black-haired youth. He had a high tenor voice, not unmanly but refined, his words very precise. His eyes were gray and cold.

"Yes, Bryce." The man who'd led her here sat her down on a stout wooden chair next to the table and, pulling her arms back, proceeded to tie a clumsy knot around her wrists.

Venera craned her neck to look back. "You obviously don't do this much," she said. Then, spearing this Bryce fellow with a sharp eye, she added, "Kidnapping is precision work. You people don't strike me as being organized enough to pull it off."

Bryce's eyebrows shot up, that same look of surprise he'd shown in the cellar. "If you'd been following our escapades you'd know what we're capable of."

"Bombing innocent crowds, yes," she said acidly. "Hero's work, that."

He shrugged, but looked uncomfortable. "That one was meant for the committee members," he admitted. "It fell back and killed the man who threw it. That *was* a soldier's death."

She nodded. "Like most soldiers' deaths, painfully unnecessary. What do you want?"

Bryce spun another chair around and sat down in it, folding his arms over its back. "We intend to bring down the great nations," he said simply.

Venera considered how to reply. After a moment she said, "How can kidnapping me get you any closer to doing that? I'm an outsider; I'm sure nobody cares much whether I live or die. And nobody will ransom me."

"True," he agreed with a shrug. "But if you go missing, you'll soon be declared a fraud and the title to Buridan will go up for grabs. It'll be a free-for-all, and we intend to make sure that it starts a civil war."

As plans went, it struck Venera as eminently practical—but this was not a good time to be smiling and nodding.

She thought for a while. All she could hear was the slow drip, drip of water from rusted ceiling pipes; doubtless no one would hear any cries for help. "I suppose you've been following my story," she said eventually. "Do you believe that I'm Amandera Thrace-Guiles, heir of Buridan?"

He waved a hand negligently. "Couldn't care less. Actually, I think you are an imposter, but why does it matter? You'll soon be out of the picture."

"But what if I *am* an imposter?" She watched his face closely as she spoke. "Where do you suppose I came from?"

Now he looked puzzled. "Here . . . but your accent is foreign. Are you from outside Spyre?"

She nodded. "Outside Spyre, and consequently I have no loyalty for any of the factions here. But I do have one thing—I've come into a great deal of money and influence, using my own wits."

He leaned back, laughing. "So what are you saying?" he asked. "That you're a sympathizer? More like an opportunist; so why should I have anything but contempt for that?"

"Because this power . . . is only a means to an end," she said. "I'm not interested in who governs or even who ends up with the money I've gained. I have my own agenda."

He snorted. "How vague and intriguing. Well, I'm sure I can't help you with this ill-defined 'agenda.' We're only interested in people who *believe*. People who know that there's another way to govern than the tyrannies we have here. I'm talking about emergent government, which you as a barbarian have probably never even heard of."

"Emergent?" Now it was Venera's turn to be startled. "That's just a myth. Government emerging spontaneously as a property of people's interactions . . . it doesn't work."

"Oh, but it does." He fished inside his jacket and came out with a small, heavily worn black book. "This is the proof. And the key to bringing it back." He held the book up for her to see; with her limited mobility, Venera could just make out the title: *Rights Currencies, 29th Edition.*

"It's the manual," he said. "The original manual, taken from the secret libraries of one of the great nations. This book explains how currency-based emergent government works and provides an example." He opened the book and withdrew several tightly folded bills. These he unfolded on the table where she could see them. "People have always had codes of conduct," said Bryce as he stared lovingly at the money, "but they were originally put together hit-or-miss, with anecdotal evidence to back them up, and using armies and policemen to enforce them. This is a system based on the human habit of buying and selling—only you can't use this money to buy *things*. Each bill stands for a particular *right*."

She leaned over to see. One pink rectangle had the word JUDGE-MENT printed on it above two columns of tiny words. "The text shows which other bills you can trade this one for," said Bryce helpfully. "On the flip side is a description of what you can do if you've got it. This one lets you try court cases if you've also got some other types of bill, but you have to trade this one to judge a trial. The idea is you can only sell it to someone who doesn't have the correct combination to judge and hopefully whoever they sell it to sells it back to you. So the system's not static; it has to be sustained through continual transactions."

She looked at another bill. It said GET OUT OF JAIL FREE. The book

Bryce was holding, if it was genuine, was priceless. People had been looking for these lost principles for longer than they'd been trying to find the last key to Candesce. Venera had never believed they really existed.

Pointedly, she shrugged. "So?"

The young revolutionary snatched up the bills. "Currencies like this can't just be *made*," he proclaimed, exhibiting a certain youthful zeal that she would have found endearing in other circumstances. "The rights, the classifications, number of denominations, who you can trade to—all of those details have to be calculated with the use of massive simulations of whole human societies. Simulate the society in a computing machine, and test different interactions . . . then compile a list of ratios and relations between the bills. Put them in circulation, and an ordered society emerges from the transactions—without institutions getting in the way. Simple."

"Right," said Venera. "And I'm betting that this book wasn't designed for a world like Virga, was it? Isn't this a set of rules for people who live on a flat world—a 'planet'? The legend says that's why the emergent systems were lost, because their rules didn't apply here."

"Not the old ratios, it's true," he admitted. "But the core bills . . . they're sound. You can at least use them to minimize your institutions even if you can't eliminate them completely. We intend to prove it, starting here."

"Well, that's very ambitious." Venera suddenly noticed the way he was looking at her. She was tied with her arms back and her breasts thrust at this young man and he was obviously enjoying her predicament. For the first time since being brought down here, she found herself genuinely off-balance.

She struggled to regain her line of thought. "Anyway, this is all beside the point. Which is, that I am in a greater position to help you as a free woman than as a social pariah—or dead. After all, this civil war of yours probably won't happen. As you say, the great nations have too big a stake in stability. And if it doesn't happen, then what? It's back to the drawing board, minus one hideout for you. Back to bombing and other ineffectual terrorist tactics."

Bryce closed the book and restored it to his jacket. "What of it? We've already lost this place. If the war doesn't happen there's no downside."

"But consider what you could do if you had an ally—a patroness—with wealth and resources, and more experience than you in covert activities." She looked him straight in the eye. "I've killed a number of men in my time. I've built and run my own spy organization. —No, I'm not Amandera Thrace-Guiles. I'm someone infinitely more capable than a mere heir to a backward nation on this backward little wheel. And with power, and wealth, and influence . . . I can help you."

"No deal." He stood up and gestured to the others to follow him as he walked to the metal door.

"A printing press!" she called after him. He looked back, puzzled. "In order for that money to work," she continued, "don't you need to mint thousands of copies of the bills and put them into circulation? It has to be used by everybody to work, right? So where's your printing press?"

He glanced at his people. "It'll happen."

"Oh? What if I offered you your own mint—delivery of the presses in a month—as well as a solid budget to print your money?"

Bryce appeared to think about it, then reached for the door handle.

"And what if you had an impregnable place to house the press?" she called, frantically reaching for the only other thing she could think to offer. *"What if Buridan Tower was yours?"*

One of his lieutenants put a hand on Bryce's arm. He glared at the man, then made a sour face and turned. "Why on Spyre would we trust you to keep your end of the bargain?"

"The tower contains proof that I'm an imposter," she said quickly. "The council is going to want to visit it, I'm sure of it— but how can I clean it up and make it presentable? None of my new servants could be trusted with the secret. But you could—and you could take photographs, do what you need to do to assemble proof that I'm not the heir. So you'll have that to hold over me. You'll have the tower, you'll have money, and as much influence as I can spare for you."

He was thinking about it, she could tell—and the others were impressed as well. "Best of all," she added before he could change his mind, "if my deception is ultimately revealed, you may get your civil war anyway. What could be better?"

Bryce walked slowly back to her. "Again I say, why should we trust you? If there's proof as you say in Buridan Tower . . . if you'd even let us get there before the police descended on us . . . Too many ifs, Ms. Thrace-Guiles."

"I'll draft you a note right now," she said. "Made out to the night watch at the elevators, to let your people ride the elevator down to Buridan Tower. You can do it right now and release me after you're sure I'm right."

"And be trapped there when your charade is exposed?"

That was just too much for Venera. "Then forget it, you bastard!" she yelled at him. "Go on, get out! I'm sure you're far too busy playing the romantic revolutionary leader. Go and sacrifice the lives of a few more of your friends to convince the rest of them that you're actually doing something. Oh, and blow up a few women and babies for good measure. I'm sure that'll make you feel better—or start your damned war and kill ten thousand innocents, I don't care! Just get out of my sight!"

Bryce's face darkened with anger, but he didn't move. Finally he stalked over and scowled at her. Venera glared back.

"Bring this woman some paper," he said. "You'll write that note," he said in a low voice, "and we'll see what we can find in Buridan Tower."

THE STREETS HAD not changed since his childhood. Garth Diamandis strode familiar ways, but after such a long absence it was as if he saw them with new eyes. His town-wheel, officially known as Wheel 3, had been called Hammerlong for centuries. Its riveted iron diameter spanned nearly a mile, and the inside surface on which the buildings were set was nearly half that wide. It had spun for five hundred years. In that time, the layout of Hammerlong's gargoyled buildings had been rearranged—or not where they accommodated stubborn holdouts—dozens of times. New edifices had hiked their buttresses over the shoulders of older ones as the population grew, then shrank, then grew again. The wheel had been fixed, reinforced, rejigged, and thrown out of whack by weight imbalances so often that its constant creaking and groaning was like background music to the citizens who lived there. The smell of rust permeated everything.

With finite space, the citizens of the wheel had jammed new buildings in between existing ones; corkscrewed them inward and outward from the rim; overgrown what was original with the new. Streamlined towers hung like knife blades below the rim, their bottom-most floors straining under nearly two gravities while the stacked apartments overhead converged to shadow the streets and a second layer of avenues, then a third, were built up where weight diminished. Ying-yang stairs, elevator cables, ancient rust-dribbling spokes, and leaking pipes all knotted together at the smoke-wreathed axis. Ships and shuttles clustered there like grazing flies.

Hammerlong seemed designed for skulking and the population did just that. Most were citizens of nations based on Greater Spyre, after all, so they brought the paranoia of that realm with them to the city. Those born and raised in Hammerlong and the other wheels were more open, but they formed a separate class and had fewer rights in their own towns. Left to their own devices, they cultivated a second economy and culture in the alleys, air shafts, and crawlspaces of the layered city.

Garth was on a third-level street when the full force of nostalgia hit him. He had to stop, his imagination filling in gaps in the crowds that scurried to and fro like so many black-clad ants. He saw the young dandies of his youth, swaggering and hipshot to display their pistols; the young ingenues leaning on their balconies high above, their attention apparently elsewhere. He had walked or run or fled down these ways dozens of times.

Some of his old compatriots were dead, he knew, some had moved on to build prosperous families and deny their youths. Others . . . the prisons were still full, one of Venera Fanning's new carpenters had told him this morning. And, if one knew where to look, and how to read . . . there, yes, he saw a thin scrawl of graffiti on a wall ten feet beyond the parapet. Made with chalk, it was barely visible unless you knew to look for it. REPEAL EDICT 1, said the spiky letters.

Garth smiled. Ah, the naivete of youth! Edict 1 had been passed so long ago that most citizens of Spyre didn't even know it existed, nor would they have understood its significance if it were described to them. The hotheaded youth of Spyre were still political, it seemed, and still as incompetent at promoting their politics as in his day. Witness that appalling bomb attack the other day.

The memory chased all sentimentality out of Garth's mind. His mouth set in a stoic frown, he continued on down the street, digging his hands deep into his coat pockets and avoiding the glances of the few women who frequented the walkway. His aching feet carried him to stairs and more stairs, and his knees and hips began to protest at the labor. The last time he'd gone this way he'd been able to run all the way up.

Hundreds of feet above the official street level of Hammerlong, a bridge had been thrown between two buildings back in the carefree Reconstructionist period. Culture and art had flourished here before the time of the preservationists, even before the insular paranoia that had swallowed all the great nations.

The bridge was two stories tall and faced with leaded glass windows that caught the light of Candesce. It wasn't used by occupants of either tower; the forges of one had little use for the papermaking enterprise in the other. For decades, the lofting, sunlit spaces of the bridge had been used by bohemian artists—and the agitators and revolutionaries who loved them.

Garth's heart was pounding as he took the last few steps up a wrought-iron fire escape at the center of the span. He paused to catch his breath next to the wrought-iron curlicues of the door, and listened to the scratchy gramophone music that emanated from it. Then he rapped on the door.

The gramophone stopped. He heard scrambling noises, muffled voices. Then the door cracked open an inch. "Yes?" a man said belligerently.

"Sorry to disturb you," Garth said with a broad smile. "I'm looking for someone."

"Well, they're not here." The door started to close.

Garth laughed richly. "I'm not with the secret police, young pup. I used to live here."

The door hesitated. "I painted this iron about . . . oh, twenty years ago," Garth said, tracing his finger along the curves of metal. "It was rusting out, just like the one in the back bathroom. Do the pipes still knock when you run the water?"

"What do you want?" The voice held a little less harshness.

Garth withdrew his hand from the remembered metal. With difficulty he brought his attention back to the present. "I know she doesn't live here now," he said. "Too much time has passed. But I had to start somewhere and this was the last place we were together. I don't suppose you know . . . any of the former occupants of the place?"

"Just a minute." The door closed, then opened again, widely this time. "Come in." Garth stepped into the sunlit space and was overwhelmed by memory.

The factory planks paving the floor had proven perfect for dancing. He remembered stepping into and out of that parallelogram of sunlight—though there had been a table next to it and he'd banged his hip—while she sang along with the gramophone. That same gramophone sat on a windowsill now, guarded by twin potted orange trees. A mobile of candles and wire turned slowly in the dusty sunlight, entangling his view of the loft behind it. Where he'd slept, and made love, and played his dulcimer for years . . .

"Who are you after?" A young woman with cropped black hair stood before him. She wore a man's clothing and held a tattoo needle loosely in one hand. Another woman sat at the table behind her, shoulder bared and bleeding.

Garth took a deep breath and committed the name to speech for the first time in twenty years. "Her name is Selene. Selene Diamandis . . ."

12

SPYRE WAS AWE inspiring even at a distance of ten miles. Venera held onto netting in a rear-facing doorway of the passenger liner *Glorious Dawn* and watched the vast blued circle recede in the distance. First one cloud shot by to obscure a quadrant of her view, then another, then a small team of them that whirled slowly in the ship's wake. They chopped Spyre up into fragmented images: a curve of green trees here, a glint of window in some tower (Liris?). Then, instead of clouds, it was blockhouses and barbed wire flicking by. They were passing the perimeter. She was free.

She turned, facing into the interior of the ship. The velvet-walled galleries were crowded with passengers, mostly visiting delegations returning from the Fair. But a few of the men and women were dressed in the iron and leather of a major nation: Buridan. Her retainers, maids, the Buridan trade delegation . . . she wasn't free yet, not until she had found a way to evade all of them.

Now that she was undisputed head of the nation of Buridan, Venera had new rights. The right to travel freely, for example; it had taken only a simple request and a travel visa had been delivered to her the next day. Of course she couldn't simply wave good-bye and leave. Nobody was fully convinced that she was who she said she was. So, it had been necessary for her to invent a pointless trade tour of the principalities to justify this trip. And that in turn meant that she could not be traveling alone.

Still, after weeks of running, of being captured by Liris and made chattel; after run-ins with bombers and bombs, hostile nobility, and mad botanists—after all of that, she had simply boarded a ship and left. Life was never like you imagined it would be.

And she could just keep going, she knew—all the way back to her home in Rush. The idea was tempting, but it wasn't why she had undertaken this expedition. It was too soon to return home. She didn't yet have enough power to undertake the revenge she planned against the Pilot of Slipstream. If she left now it would be as a thief, with only what she could carry to see her home. No, when she finally did leave Spyre, it must be with power at her back.

The only way to get that power was to increase her holdings here, as well as the faith of the people in her. So, like Liris and all the other nations of Spyre, Buridan would visit the outer world to find *customers*.

Her smile faltered as the last of the barbed wire and mines swept by to vanish among the clouds. True, if she just kept going she wouldn't miss anything of Spyre, she mused. Yet even as she thought this Venera experienced a little flash of memory: of Garth Diamandis laughing in sunlight, then of Eilen leaning on a wall after drinking too much at the party.

Last night Venera too had drunk too much wine, with Garth Diamandis. Sitting in a lounge that smelled of fresh paint and plaster, they had listened to the night noises of the house and talked.

"You're not kidding either of us," he'd said. "You're leaving for good. I know that. So let me tell you now, while I can, that you've stripped many years off my shoulders, Lady Venera Fanning. I hope you find your home intact and waiting for you." He toasted her then.

"I'll prove you wrong about me yet," she'd said. "But what about you? When all of this really is finished with, what are you going to do? Fade into the alleys of the town-wheels? Return to your life as a gigolo?"

He shook his head with a smile. "The past is the past. I'm interested in the future. Venera . . . I found her."

Venera had smiled, genuinely happy for him. "Ah. Your mysterious woman. Your prime mover. Well, I'm glad."

He'd nodded vigorously. "She's sent me a letter, telling where and when we can meet. In the morning, you'll head for the docks and your destiny, and I'll be off to the city and mine. So you see, we've both won."

They toasted one another, and Spyre and eventually the whole world before the night became a happy blur.

She kicked off from the ship's netting, almost colliding with one of the crew, and began hauling her way up the corridor to the bow of the ship. One of her new maids fell into formation next to her.

"Is there something wrong, lady?" The maid, Brydda, wrung her hands. Her normally sour face looked even more prudish as she frowned. "Is it leaving Spyre that's upset you so?"

Venera barked a laugh. "It couldn't happen soon enough. No." She kept hand-walking up the rope that led to the bow.

"Can I do anything for you?"

She shot Brydda an appraising look. "You've traveled before, haven't you? You were put onto my staff by the council, I'll bet. To watch me."

"Madam!"

"Oh, don't deny it. Just come with. I need a . . . distraction. You can point out the sights as we go."

"Yes, madam."

They arrived at a forward observation lounge in time for the ship to exit the cloud banks. The *Glorious Dawn* was a typical passenger vessel: a spindle-shaped wooden shell one hundred fifty feet long and forty wide, its surface punctuated with rows of windows and open wickerwork galleries. Big jet nacelles were mounted on short arms at the stern, their whine subdued right now as the ship made a scant fifteen miles per hour through the thinning clouds. The ship's interior was subdivided into staterooms and common areas and contained two big exercise centrifuges. With the engine sound a constant undertone, Venera could easily hear the clink of glassware in the kitchens, muted conversations, and somewhere, a string quartet tuning up. The lounge smelled of coffee and fresh air.

Such a contrast to the *Rook*, the last ship she had flown on. When she'd left it the Slipstream cruiser had stank of unwashed men, stale air, and rocket exhaust. Its hull had been peppered with bullet holes and scorched by explosions. The engines' roar would pierce your dreams as you slept and the only voices were those of arguing, cursing airmen.

The *Glorious Dawn* was just like every vessel she had ever traveled on prior to the *Rook*. Its luxuries and details were appropriate to one of Venera's station in life; she should be able to put the ship on like a favorite glove. In the normal course of affairs she would never have set foot on a ship like the *Rook*, much less would she have seen it through battle and boarding, pursuit and silent running.

Yet the quiet comforts of the *Glorious Dawn* annoyed her. Venera went right up to the main window of the lounge and peered out. "Tell me where we are," she commanded the maid.

Candesce lay ahead, its brilliance too intense to be looked at directly. Venera well knew that light; it had burned her as she'd fled from its embrace. She shielded her eyes with her hand and looked past it.

She saw the principalities of Candesce. Although she had spent a week in a charcoal-harvester's cabin perched on a burnt arm of the sargasso of Leaf's Choir, that place had been too close to Candesce; the white air cradling the Sun of Suns washed out any details that lay past it. Here, for the first time, she had a clear view of the nations that surrounded that biggest of Virga's artificial lights. And the sight was breathtaking.

Candesce lay at the center of the world, a beacon and a heart to Virga. Anything within a hundred miles of the Sun of Suns simply vanished in flame, a fact that the principalities exploited to dispose of trash, industrial wastes, and the bodies of their dead. This forbidden zone was completely empty, so Venera could see the whole inner surface of the two-hundred-mile-diameter bubble formed by it. On the far side of Candesce that surface was just a smooth speckled gray-green; in the middle distances Venera could make out dots and glitter, and individual beads of leaf color. As she turned to follow the curve of the material toward her the dots became buildings and the glints became the mirrored surfaces of house-sized spheres of water. The beads of green grew filigreed detail and became forests—dozens or hundreds of trees at a time with their roots intertwined around some buried ball of dirt and rocks.

Candesce presided at the center of a cloud of city whose inner extent was two hundred miles in diameter—and whose outer reaches could only be guessed at. The fog of habitations and farms receded into blue dimness, behind lattices of white cloud. Back in the darkening airs a hundred or two hundred miles away, smaller suns glowed.

"These are the principalities," said Brydda, sweeping her arm to take in the sight. "Sixty-four nations, countless millions of people moving at the mercy of Candesce's heat."

Venera glanced at her. "What do you mean by that? 'At the mercy of'?"

The maid looked chagrined. "Well, they can't keep station where they please, the way Spyre does. Spyre is fixed in the air, madam, always has been. But these—" she dismissed the principalities with a wave—"they go where the breezes send them. All that keeps them together as nations is the stability of the circulation patterns."

Venera nodded. The cluster of nations she'd grown up in, Meridian, worked the same way. Candesce's prodigious heat had to go somewhere, and beyond the exclusion zone it must form the air into Hadley cells: semistable up- and downdrafts. You could enter such a cell at the bottom, near Candesce, and be lofted a hundred miles up, then swept horizontally for another hundred miles, then down again until you reached your starting point. The Meridian Hadley cell was huge—a thousand miles across and twice that in depth—and nearly permanent. Down here in the principalities the heat would make the cells less stable, but quicker and stronger.

"So there's one nation per Hadley cell?" she asked. "That seems altogether too well-organized."

The maid laughed. "It's not that simple. The cells break up and merge, but it takes time. Every time Candesce goes into its night-cycle the heat stops going out and the cells falter. Candesce always comes back on in time to start them up again but not without consequence."

Venera understood what she meant by *consequence*. Without predictable airflow, whole countries could break apart, their provinces drifting away from one another, mixing with neighbors and enemies. It had happened often enough in Meridian, where the population was light and obstacles few. Down here, such an event would be catastrophic.

Brydda continued her monologue, pointing out border beacons and other sights of interest. Venera half-listened, musing at something she'd known intellectually but not grasped until this moment. She had been inside—had for one night been in control of—the most powerful device in the word. Whole cities rose and fell in a slow majestic dance driven by Candesce—as did forests, mists of green food crops and isolated buildings, clouds and ships and factories, supply nets a mile across, whale and bird paddocks. Ships and dolphins and ropeways and flapping, foot-finned humans threaded through it all.

She'd had ultimate power in her hands and had let it go without a thought. Strange.

Venera turned her attention back to Brydda. As the *Glorious Dawn* turned, however, she saw that Spyre lay in a kind of dimple in the surface of the bubble. The giant cylinder disrupted the smooth winds of the cells that surrounded it. Wrapped in its own weather,

Spyre was an irritant, a mote in the gargantuan orb of the principalities.

"How they must hate you," she murmured.

SLIPSTREAM HAD AN ambassador at the Fitzmann States, an old and respected principality near Spyre. So it was that Buridan's trade delegation made its first stop there.

For two days Venera feted the local wealthy and talked horses—horses as luxury items, horses as tourist draws, as symbols of state power and a connection to the lost origins of Virga. She convinced no one, but since she was hosting the parties, her guests went away entertained and slightly tipsy. The arrangement suited everyone.

There was nothing scheduled for the third morning, and Venera awoke early with a very strange notion in her head.

Leave now.

She could do it. Oh, it would be so simple. She imagined her marriage bed in her chambers in Rush, and a wave of sorrow came over her. She was up and dressed before her thinking caught up to her actions. She hesitated, while Candesce and the rest of the capital town of Fitzmann still slept. She paced in front of her rented apartment's big windows, shaking her head and muttering. Every now and then she would glance out the window at the dark silhouette of the Slipstream ambassador's residence. She need only make it there and claim asylum and Spyre and all its machinations would lie behind her.

Slowly, as if her mind were on something else, she slipped a pistol into her bag and reached for a set of wings inside the closet. At that moment there came a knock on her door.

Venera came to herself, shocked to see what she had been doing. She leaned against the wall for a moment, debating whether to step into the closet and shut herself in it. Then she cursed and walked to the door of the suite. "Who's there?" she asked testily.

"It's Brydda, ma'am. I've a letter for you."

"A letter?" She threw open the door and glared at the maid, who was dressed in a nightgown and clutching a white envelope in one hand. She saw Brydda's eyes widen as she took in Venera's fully dressed state. Venera snatched the letter from her and said, "Lucky thing that I couldn't sleep. But how dare you come to disturb me in the middle of the night over this!"

"I'm sorry!" Brydda curtsied miserably. "The man who delivered it was very insistent that you read it now. He says he needs a signed receipt from you saying you've read it—and he's waiting in the foyer . . ."

Venera flipped the envelope over. The words *Amandera Thrace-Guiles* were written on it. There was no other seal or indication of its origin. Uneasy, Venera retreated into the room. "Wait there a moment." She went over to the writing desk; not seeing a letter opener anywhere handy, she slit the envelope open using the knife she'd been keeping in her vest. Then she unfolded the single sheet under the green desk lamp.

TO: *Venera Fanning*
FROM: —
SUBJECT: *Master Flance, otherwise known as Garth Diamandis*

We have arrested your accomplice (above-named). As an exiled criminal he has no rights in Greater or Lesser Spyre. If you want him to continue living, you will return immediately to Spyre and await our instructions.

She swore and knocked over the writing desk. The lamp broke and went out. "My lady!" shouted Brydda from the doorway.

"Shut up! Get out! Don't disturb me again!" She slammed the door in the maid's face and began pacing, the letter mangled in her fist.

How dare they! This was obviously Sacrus asserting their hold over her—but in the most clumsy and insulting manner possible. There was a message in their bluntness and it was simple: they had neither the need nor the patience to treat her carefully. She would do as they asked, or they would kill Garth.

Like Garth, they must have thought she was going to run. So why not let her do it? They didn't appear to be concerned that she might alert Slipstream to the theft of the key to Candesce because they had let her get this far. That was odd—or not so odd, when you considered that the leaders of Sacrus must be as insular and decadent as any of the other pocket nations on the wheel. But why not just let her go?

They must have decided that they needed Buridan's stability. She probably shouldn't read too much into the decision. They could just as easily change their minds and have her killed at any moment.

Anyway, the reasons didn't matter. They had Garth—she had no reason to doubt that—and if she didn't return to Spyre immediately, his death would be her fault.

As her initial anger wore off, Venera sat down on a divan and, reaching into her jacket, brought out the bullet that nestled there. She turned it over in her hands for half an hour and then as Candesce began to ignite in the distant sky, she made her decision.

She slid the dagger back into her vest.

She took the wings from inside the closet and stepped into the hallway. Brydda was asleep in a wing chair under a tall leaded-glass window. Venera walked past her to the servant's stairs and headed for the roof.

Gold-touched by the awakening Sun of Suns, she took flight in the high winds and lower gravity of the rooftop.

Venera rose on the air, losing weight rapidly as the wind disengaged her from the spin of the town-wheel. High above the buildings, among turning cables and hovering birds, she turned her back on the apartment and on the trade delegation of Buridan. She turned her back on Garth Diamandis, and flew toward the residence of the ambassador of Slipstream.

VARIOUS SCENARIOS HAD played themselves out in her mind as she flew. The first was that she could pretend to be the estranged wife of one of the sailors on the Rook. Wringing her hands, she could look pathetic and demand news of the expedition.

Venera wasn't good at looking pathetic. Besides, they could legitimately ask what she was doing here, thousands of miles away from Slipstream.

She could claim to be a traveling merchant. Then why ask after the expedition? Perhaps she should say she was from Hale, not Slipstream, a distant relative of Venera Fanning needing news of her.

These and other options ran through her mind as Venera waited next to the tall scrolled doors of the ambassador's office. The moment the door lock clicked she pushed her way inside and said to the surprised secretary, "My name is Venera Fanning. I need to talk to the ambassador."

The man turned white as a sheet. He practically ran for the inner office and there was a hurried, loud conversation there. Then he stuck his head out the door and said, "You can't be seen here."

"Too late for that, if anyone's watching." She closed the outer door and walked to the inner. The secretary threw it open and stepped aside.

The ambassador of Slipstream was a middle-aged woman with iron-gray hair and the kind of stern features usually reserved for suspicious aunts, school principals, and morals crusaders. She glared at Venera and gestured for her to sit in one of the red leather wing chairs that faced her dark teak desk. "So you're alive," she said as she lowered herself heavily on her side.

"Why shouldn't I be?" Venera was suddenly anxious to the point of panic. "What happened to the others?"

The ambassador sent her a measuring look. "You were separated from your husband's expedition?"

"Yes! I've had no news. Just . . . rumors."

"The expeditionary force was destroyed," said the ambassador.

She grimaced apologetically. "Your husband's flagship apparently rammed a Falcon dreadnought, causing a massive explosion that tore both vessels apart. All hands are presumed lost."

"I see . . ." She felt sick, as though this were the first time she'd heard this news.

"I don't think you do see," said the ambassador. She snapped her fingers and her secretary left, returning with a silver tray and two glasses of wine.

"You've shown up at an awkward time," continued the ambassador. "One of your husband's ships did make it back to Rush. The *Severance* limped back into port a couple of weeks ago, and its hull was full of holes. Naturally the people assumed she was the vanguard of a return from the battle with Mavery. But no—the airmen disembarked and they were laughing, crying, claiming a great victory and waving away all talk of Mavery. 'No,' they say, 'we've beaten *Falcon*! By the genius of the Pilot and Admiral Fanning, we've forestalled an invasion and saved Slipstream!'

"Can the Pilot deny it? If Fanning himself had returned, with the other ships . . . maybe not. If the airmen of the *Severance* hadn't started throwing around impossible amounts of money, displaying rich jewels and gold chains and talking wildly about a pirate's hoard . . . Well, you see the problem. Falcon is supposed to be an *ally*. And the Pilot's been caught with his pants below his knees, completely unaware of a threat to his nation until after his most popular admiral has extinguished that threat.

"He ordered the crew rounded up on charges of treason. The official story is that Fanning took some ships on a raid into Falcon and busted open one of their treasuries. He's being court-martialed in absentia as a traitor and pirate."

"Therefore," said Venera, "if I were to return now . . ."

"You'd be tried as an accessory, at the very least." The ambassador steepled her hands and leaned forward minutely in her chair. "Legally, I'm bound to turn you over for extradition. Except that should I do so, you'd likely become a lightning rod for dissent. After the riots—"

"What riots?"

"Well." She looked uncomfortable. "The Pilot was a bit . . . slow to act. He didn't round up all of the *Severance*'s airmen quickly enough. And he didn't stem the tide until a good deal of money had flowed into the streets. Apparently these were no mere trinkets the men were showing off—and they're not treasury items either; they're *plunder*, pure and simple, and ancient to boot. And the people, the people believe the *Severance*, not the Pilot.

"Our last dispatch—that was two days ago—says that the bulk of the crew and officers made it back to the *Severance* and bottled themselves up in it. It's out there now, floating a hundred yards off the admiralty. The Pilot ordered it blown up, and that's when rioting started in the city."

"If you returned now," said the secretary, "there'd be even more bloodshed."

"—And likely your blood would be spilled as an example to others." The ambassador shook her head. "It gets worse too. The navy's refused the Pilot's command. They won't blow up the *Severance*. They want to know what happened. They're trying to talk the crew out and there's a three-way standoff now between the Pilot's soldiers, the navy, and the *Severance* herself. It's a real mess."

Venera's pulse was pounding. She wanted to be there, in the admiralty. She knew Chaison's peers, she could rally those men to fight back. They all hated the Pilot, after all.

She slumped back in her chair. "Thank you for telling me this." She thought for a minute, then glanced up at the ambassador. "Are you going to have me arrested?"

The older woman shook her head, half-smiling. "Not if you make a discreet enough exit from my office. I suggest the back stairs. I can't see how sending you home in chains would do anything but fan the flames at this point."

"Thank you." She stood and looked toward the door the ambassador had pointed at. "I won't forget this."

"Just so long as you never tell anyone that you saw me," said the ambassador with an ironic smile. "So what will you do?"

"I don't know."

"If you stay here in the capital, we might be able to help you—set you up with a job and a place to stay," said the ambassador sympathetically. "It would be below your station, I'm afraid, at least to start . . ."

"Thanks, I'll consider it. —And don't worry, if I see you again, I won't be Venera Fanning anymore." Dazed, she pushed through the door into a utilitarian hallway that led to gray tradesman's stairs. She barely heard the words "Good luck" before the door closed behind her.

Venera went down one flight then sat on a step and put her chin in her hands. She was trembling but dry-eyed.

Now what? The news about the *Severance* had been electrifying. She should board the next ship she could find that was headed for the Meridian countries and . . . but it might take weeks to get there. She would arrive after the crisis was resolved, if it hadn't been already.

There was one man who could have helped her. Hayden Griffin was flying a fast racing bike, a simple jet engine with a saddle. She'd last seen him at Candesce as the Sun of Suns blossomed into incandescent life. He was opening the throttle—racing for home—and surely by now he was back in Slipstream. If she'd gone with him when he offered her his hand, none of her present troubles would have happened.

Yet she couldn't do it. Venera had killed Hayden's lover not ten minutes before and simply could not believe that he wouldn't murder her in return if he got the chance.

She hadn't wanted to kill Aubri Mahallan. The woman had lied about her intentions; she had joined the Fanning expedition with the intention of crippling Candesce's defenses. She worked for the outsiders, the alien Artificial Nature that lurked somewhere beyond the skin of Virga. Had Venera not prevented it, Mahallan would have let those incomprehensible forces into Virga and nothing would now be as it was.

Once again Venera took out the bullet and turned it over in her fingers. She had killed the captain of the Rook and his bridge crew—shot them with a pistol—in order to save the lives of everyone aboard. Captain Sembry had been about to fire the Rook's scuttling charges during their battle with the pirates. She had shot several other people in battle and killed Mahallan to save the world itself. Just like she'd shot the man who had been about to kill Chaison, on the day they'd met. . . .

She had killed those people either because of a higher purpose or from naked self-interest. She could admit to being ruthless and callous, even heartless, but Venera did not see herself as fundamentally selfish. She had been bred and raised to be selfish, but she didn't want to be like her sisters or her father. That was the whole reason why she'd escaped life in Hale at her first opportunity.

Venera cursed. If she flew away from Garth Diamandis and the key to Candesce now, she would be admitting that she had killed Aubri Mahallan not to save the world but out of pure spite. She'd be admitting that she'd shot Sembry in the forehead solely to preserve her own life. Could she even claim to have been trying to save Chaison too?

All her stratagems collapsed. Venera returned the bullet to her pocket, stood, and continued down the steps.

When she reached the street she looked around until she spotted the apartment where at this moment Brydda and the rest of the Buridan trade delegation must be frantically searching for her. Leaden with defeat and anger, she let her feet carry her in that direction.

13

THERE WERE PLENTY of people waiting for Venera at the docks, but Garth was not among them. —Oh, she had accountants aplenty, maids and masters of protocol, porters and reporters and doctors, couriers and dignitaries from the nations of Spyre that had decided to conspicuously ally with Buridan. There was lots to do. But as she signed documents and ordered people about, Venera felt the old familiar pain radiating up from her jaw. Today's headache would be a killer.

She had to provide some explanation for why she'd returned early from the expedition, if only for the council representatives with their clipboards and frowns. "We were successful beyond expectations," she said, pinioning Brydda with a warning glare. "A customer has come forward who will satisfy all of our needs for quite some time. There was simply no need to continue with an expensive journey when we'd already achieved our goal."

This was far more information than most nations ever released about their customers, so the council would have to be content with it.

The return of the ruler of Buridan was a hectic affair, and it took until near dinnertime before Venera was able to escape to her apartment to contemplate her next move. There had been no messages from Sacrus, neither demands nor threats. They thought they had her in their pocket now, she supposed, so they could turn their attention to more important matters for a while. But those more important matters were her concern too.

She had a meal sent up and summoned the chief butler. "I do not wish to be disturbed for any reason," she told him. "I will be working here until very late." He bowed impassively and she closed and locked the door.

In the course of renovations some workmen had knocked a hole in one of her bedroom walls. She had chastised them roundly for it, then discovered that there was an airspace behind it—an old chimney, long disused. "Work in some other room," she told the men. "I'll hire more reliable men to fix this." But she hadn't fixed it.

Ten minutes after locking the door, she was easing down a rope ladder that hung in the chimney. The huge portrait of Giles Thrace-Guiles that normally covered the hole had been set aside. At the bottom of the shaft she pried back a pewter fireplace grate decorated with dolphins and naked women and dusted herself off in a former servant's bedroom that she'd recast as a storage closet.

It was easy to nip across the hall and into the wine cellar and slide aside the rack on its oiled track. Then she was in the rebels' bolt-hole and momentarily free of Buridan, Sacrus, and everything else—except, perhaps, the nagging of her new and still unfamiliar conscience.

THE INSANE ORGAN music from Buridan Tower's broken pipeworks had ceased. Not that it was silent as Venera stepped out of the filigreed elevator; the whole place still hummed to the rush and flap of wind. But at least you could ignore it now.

"Iron lady's here!" shouted one of the men waiting in the chamber. Venera frowned as she heard the term being relayed down the halls. There were three guards in the elevator chamber and doubtless more lurking outside. She clasped her hands behind her back and strode for the archway, daring them to stop her. They did not.

The elevator room opened off the highest gallery of the tower's vast atrium. It was also the smallest, as the space widened as it fell. The effect from here was dizzying: she seemed suspended

high above a cavern walled by railings. Venera stood there looking down while Bryce's followers silently surrounded her. Echoes
of hammering and sawing drifted up from below.

After a while there was a chattering of feet on the steps and
then Bryce himself appeared. He was covered in plaster dust and
his hair was disarrayed. "What?" he said. "Are they coming?"

"No," said Venera with a half-smile. "At least not yet. Which is
not to say that I won't need to give a tour at some point. But you're
safe for now."

He crossed his arms, frowning. "Then why are you here?"

"Because this tower is mine," she said simply. "I wanted to
remind you of the fact."

Waving away the makeshift honor guard, he strode over to
lean on the railing beside her. "You've got a nerve," he said. "I
seem to remember the last time we spoke, you were tied to a
chair."

"Maybe next time it'll be your turn."

"You think you have us bottled up in here?"

"What would be the use in that?"

"Revenge. Besides, you're a dust-blood—a noble. You can't
possibly be on our side."

She examined her nails. "I haven't got a side."

"That is the dust-blood side," said Bryce with a sneer. "There's
those that care for the people; that's one side. The other side is
anybody else."

"I care for my people," she said with a shrug, then, to needle
him, "I care for my horses too."

He turned away, balling his hands into fists. "Where's our printing press?" he asked after a moment.

"On its way. But I have something more important to talk to
you about. Only to you. A . . . job I need done."

He glanced back at her; behind the disdain, she could see he
was intrigued. "Let's go somewhere better suited to talking," he
said.

"More chairs, less rope?"

He winced. "Something like that."

"YOU CAN SEE Sacrus from here," she said. "It's a big sprawl-ing estate, miles of it. If anybody is your enemy, I'd think it was them."

"Among others." The venue was the tower's library, a high space full of gothic arches and decaying draperies that hung like the forelocks of defeated men from the dust-rimed window case-ments. Venera had prowled through it when she and Garth were alone here and who knew?—some of those dusty spines settling into the shelves might be priceless. She hadn't had time to find out; but Bryce's people had tidied up and there were even a few tomes open on the side tables next to several cracked leather arm-chairs.

Evening light shone hazily through the diamond-shaped win-dowpanes. She was reminded of another room, hundreds of miles away in the nation of Gehellen, and a gun battle. She had shot a woman there before Chaison's favorite staffer shattered the win-dows and they all jumped out.

Bryce settled himself into an ancient half-collapsed armchair that had long ago adhered to the floor like a barnacle. "Our goals are simple," he said. "We want to return to the old ways of gov-ernment, from the days before Virga turned its back on advanced technologies."

"There was a reason why we did that," she said. "The out-siders—"

He waved a hand dismissively. "I know the stories, about this 'Artificial Nature' from beyond the skin of the world that threat-ens us. They're just a fairy tale to keep the people down."

Venera shook her head. "I knew an agent from outside. She worked for me, betrayed me. I killed her."

"Had her killed?"

"Killed her. With my sword." She allowed her mask to slip for a second, aiming an expression of pure fury at Bryce. "Just who do you think you're talking to?" she said in a low voice.

Bryce nodded his head. "Take it as read that I know you're not an ordinary courtier," he said. "I'm not going to believe any stories you tell without some proof, though. What I was trying to say was that our goal is to reintroduce computation machines into Virga and spread the doctrine of emergent democracy everywhere, so that people can overthrow all their institution-based governments, and emergent utopias can flourish again. We're prepared to kill anybody who gets in our way."

"I'm quite happy to help you with that," she said, "because I know you'll never be able to do it. If I thought you could do what you say . . ." She smiled. "But you might accomplish much, and on the way you can be of assistance to me."

"And what do you want?" he asked. "More power?"

"That would help. But let's get back to Sacrus. They—"

"They're your enemies," he said. "I'm not interested in helping you settle a vendetta."

"They're your enemies too, and I have no vendetta to settle," she said. "In any case I'm not interested in making a frontal assault on them. I just want to visit for an evening."

Bryce stared at her for a second, then burst into laughter. "What are you proposing? That we hit Sacrus?"

"Yes."

He stopped laughing. He shook his head. "Might as well just march everybody straight into prison," he said. "Or a vivisectionist's operating room. Sacrus is the last place in Spyre any sane person would go."

Venera just looked at him for a while. Finally she said, "Either you or one of your lieutenants works for them."

Bryce looked startled, then he scowled at her. "You've said ridiculous things before, but that one takes the prize. Why could you possibly—"

"Jacoby Sarto said something that got me thinking," she interrupted. "Sacrus's product is control, right? They sell it, like fine wine. They practice it as well; did you know that many, maybe most of the minor nations of Spyre are under their thumb? They make a hobby of pulling the strings of people, institutions—whole countries. I'm not so big a fool as to believe that a band of agitators like yours has escaped their attention. One of you works for them—for all I know, your whole organization is a project of theirs."

"What proof do you have?"

"My . . . lieutenant, Flance, whom you have yet to meet, has spent many nights walking the fields and plazas of Greater Spyre. He knows every passage, hedgerow, and hiding place on that decrepit wheel. But he's not the only one. There's others who creep about at night, and he's followed them on occasion. Many times, such parties either started or ended up at Sacrus."

Bryce scoffed. "I've seen a nation that was controlled by them," Venera continued. "I know how they operate. Look, they have to train their people somehow. To them, Greater Spyre is a . . . a paddock, like the one where I keep my horses. It's their school. They send their people out to take over neighbors, foment unrest, create scandals, and conduct intrigues. I'd be very surprised if they didn't do that up in the city as well. So, tell me I'm wrong. Tell me you're not working for them. And if not, look me in the eye and tell me that you're impervious to infiltration and manipulation."

He shrugged but she could tell he was angry. "I'm not a fool," he said after a while. "Anything's possible. But you're still speculating."

"Well I *was* speculating . . . but then I decided to do some research." She held up a sheaf of news clippings. "The news broadsheets of Lesser Spyre are highly partisan, but they don't disagree on facts. On the run-up to my party I spent a couple of afternoons reading news from the past couple of years. This gave me a chance to check on the places and properties that your group has targeted since you first appeared. Quite an impressive list, by the way. But every single one of these incidents has hurt a rival of Sacrus. Not one has touched them."

Bryce looked genuinely rattled for the first time in their brief acquaintance. Venera savored the moment. "I haven't been deliberately neglecting them," he said. "This must be a coincidence."

"Or manipulation. Are you so sure that you're the real leader of this rabble?"

Bryce began to look slightly green. "You don't think it's me."

Venera shook her head. "I'm not *totally* sure that you aren't the one working for them. But you're not"—she almost said *competent*, but turned it into—"ruthless enough. You don't have their style. But you don't make decisions without consulting your lieutenants, do you? And I don't know them. Chances are, you don't really know them either."

"You think I'm a puppet." He looked stricken. "That all along . . . So what—"

"I propose that we flush out their agent, if he exists."

He leaned forward and now there was no hesitation in his eyes. "How?"

She smiled. "Here, Bryce, is where your interests and mine begin to converge."

"I'LL SPEAK ONLY to Moss," said the silhouetted figure. It had appeared without warning on the edge of the rooftop of Liris, startling the night guard nearly out of his wits. As he fumbled for his long-neglected rifle, the shape moved toward him with a lithe, half-remembered step. "This is urgent, man!"

"Citizen Fanning! I—uh, yes, let me make the call." He ran over to the speaking tube and hauled on the bell cord next to it. "She's back—wants to talk to the botanist," he said. Then he turned back to Venera. "How did you get up here?"

"Grappling hook, rope . . ." She shrugged. "Not hard. You should bear that in mind. Sacrus may still hold a grudge."

Shouts and footsteps echoed up through the open shaft of the central courtyard. "Tell them to be quiet!" she hissed. "They'll wake the whole building."

The watchman nodded and spoke into the tube again. Venera walked over to look down at the tree-choked courtyard far below. She could see lanterns hurrying to and fro down there. Finally the iron-bound rooftop door creaked open and figures gestured to her to follow.

Moss was waiting for her in a gallery on the third floor. He was wrapped in a vast purple nightgown and his hair disheveled. His desperate, unfocused eyes glinted in the lantern light. "W-what is the m-meaning of this?"

"I'm sorry for rousting you out of bed so late at night," she said, eyeing the absurd gown. *We must look quite the couple*, she mused, considering her own efficient black and the sword and pistols at her belt. "I have something urgent to discuss with you."

He narrowed his eyes, then glanced at the watchman and soldiers who had escorted her down here. "L-l-leave us. I, I'll be all right." With a slight bow he turned and led her to his chamber.

"You could have taken over Margit's apartments, you know," said Venera as she glanced around the untidy, tiny chamber with its single bed, writing desk, and wardrobe. "It's your right. You *are* the botanist, after all."

Moss indicated for her to take the single wooden chair; he managed one of his mangled smiles as he plunked himself down on the bed. "Wh-who says I w-w-won't?" he said. "H-have to get the sm-smell out first."

Venera laughed, then winced at the shards of pain that shot through her jaw and skull. "Good for you," she said past gritted teeth. "I trust you've been well since I left?" He shrugged. "And Liris? Made any new sales?"

"W-what do you want?"

Tired and in pain as she was, Venera would have been more than happy to come to the point. But, "First of all, I have to ask you something," she said. "Do you know who I am?"

"Of c-course. You are V-Venera F-Fanning, from—"

"Oh, but I'm not. —At least, not anymore." She grimaced at his annoyed expression. "I have a new name, Moss. Have you heard of Amandera Thrace-Guiles?"

His reaction was comically perfect. He stared, his eyes wide and his mouth open, for a good five seconds. Then he brayed his difficult laugh. "Odess was r-right! And h-here I thought he was m-mistaking every new face for s-somebody he knew." He laughed again.

Venera examined her nails coolly. "I'm glad I amuse you," she said. "But my own adventures hardly seem unique these days."

The grin left his face. "Wh-what do you mean?"

"Not that you have any obligation to tell me anything," she said, "but . . . surely you've seen that there are odd things afoot in Greater Spyre. Gangs of soldiers wandering in the dark . . . backroom alliances being made and broken. Something's afoot, don't you agree?"

He sat up straight. "Th-the Fair is full of rumors. Some of the l-lesser nations have been losing people."

"Losing them? What do you mean?"

"When the f-first of our people v-vanished, we assumed M-Margit's supporters were leaving. I th-thought it was o-only us. But others have also lost people."

"How many of yours have left?" she asked seriously.

He held up one hand, fingers splayed. Five, then. For a miniature nation like Liris, that was too many.

Moss stood up, walked to the door, and listened at it for a moment. Then he turned and leaned on it. "Sacrus," he said flatly.

"It can't be a coincidence," she said. "I came here to talk to you about them. They . . . they have one of my people. Moss, you know what they're capable of. I have to get him back."

Her words had a powerful effect on Moss. He drew himself up to his full height and for a moment his face lost its devastated expression; in that moment she glimpsed the determined, intelligent man who hid deep inside his ravaged psyche. Then his features collapsed back to their normal, woebegone state. He raised shaking hands and pressed his palms against his ears.

He said something, almost unintelligibly; after a moment Venera realized he'd said, "Are they toying with th-these recruits?"

"No," she countered hastily. "My man is a prisoner. The recruits or whatever they are . . . Moss, Sacrus has a reason to want an army of their own, possibly for the first time. They've finally discovered an ambition worth leaving their own doorstep." She said this with contempt, but in her imagination she saw the vast glowing bubble of nations that made up the principalities of Candesce. "They don't have the population to support what I think they're planning. But it wouldn't surprise me if they've been recruiting from the more secretive nations. Maybe they've always done it but never needed them all before. Now they're activating them."

Puzzlement spread slowly across Moss's face. "An a-army? What for?"

Venera took a deep breath, then said, "They believe they have the means to conquer the principalities of Candesce."

He stared at her. "A-and do they?"

"Yes," she admitted, looking at her hands. "I brought it to them."

He said nothing; Venera's mind was already racing ahead. "Their force must be small by my standards," she said. "Maybe two thousand people. They'd be overwhelmed in any fair fight but they don't intend to fight fair. If we could warn the principalities, they could blockade Spyre. But we'd need to get a ship out."

"Uh-unlikely," said Moss with a sour expression. "One thing I d-do know about Sacrus is that they have been buying ships."

"What else can we do?" she asked tiredly. "Attack them ourselves?"

"Y-you didn't come to ask me to h-help you do that?"

She laughed humorlessly. "Buridan and Liris against Sacrus? That would be suicidal."

He nodded, but suddenly had a faraway look in his eye. "No," Venera continued. "I came to ask you to help me break into Sacrus's prison and extract my man. I have a plan that I think will work. Margit told me where they keep their 'acquisitions.' I believe they view people as objects too, so he's likely to be in that place."

"Th-they guard their lands on the ground and a-above it," said Moss skeptically.

"I don't intend to come in by either route," she said. "But I need a squad of soldiers, at least a score of them. I have some of the forces I need, or I will." She half-smiled. "But I need others I can trust. Will your people do it?"

Now it was his turn to smile. "S-strike a blow against Sacrus? Of c-course! But once the other nations who've l-lost people find out it was S-Sacrus that stole them, y-you'll have more allies. A d-dozen at least."

Venera hadn't considered such a possibility. *Allies?* "I suppose we could count on one or two of the countries whose debts we forgave," she said slowly. "A couple of others might join us just out of devilment." She was thinking of Pamela Anseratte as she said this. Then she shook her head. "No—it's still not enough."

Moss gave his damaged laugh. "Y-you've f-forgotten the most important faction, Venera," he said. "And they have no l-love for Sacrus."

Venera rubbed her eyes. She was too tired and her head hurt too much to guess his meaning. "Who?" she asked irritably.

Moss opened the door and bowed slightly as he held it for her. "You c-came in s-secret. You should return before Candesce l-lights. We will assemble a force f-for you.

"And I will t-talk . . . to the preservationists."

14

"THIS IS THE window she was signaling from," said Bryce. He had his arms folded tightly to his chest and a muscle jumped in his jaw. Long tonguelike curls of wallpaper trembled over his shoulder in the constantly moving air. "I watched her send the whole message, clicking the little door of her lantern like she'd been doing light codes her whole life. She didn't even bother to encrypt it."

Venera had gotten the story out of him in fits and starts, as memory and anger distracted him in turn. Cassia had been one of Bryce's first recruits. They had argued with their foreheads together in the dark bars that peppered Lesser Spyre's red-light district, and defaced buildings and thrown rocks at council parades. It was her urging that had led him down the path to terrorism, he admitted. "And all along, I was a project of hers—some kind of entrance exam to the academy of traitors in Sacrus!" He slammed his fist against the wall.

"Well." Venera shaded her eyes with her hand and peered through the freshly installed glass. "In the end, you were the one who fooled her. And she's the one pent up in a locker downstairs."

He didn't look mollified. The false attack plan had been Venera's idea, after all; all Bryce had done was bring his lieutenants together to reveal the target of their next bombing, a Sacrus warehouse in Lesser Spyre. All three of the lieutenants had expressed enthusiasm, Cassia perhaps most of all. But as soon as the planning meeting broke up she had come down to this disused pantry midway up the side of Buridan Tower—and had started signaling.

Venera could see why she would have favored this room for

more than its writhing, peeled wallpaper. From here you had a clear line of sight to the walls of Sacrus, which ran in uneven mazelike lines just past a hedge of trees and a preservationist siding. From the center of the vast estate, a single monolithic building rose hundreds of feet into the afternoon air. Venera imagined a tiny flicker of light appearing somewhere on the side of that edifice—the rapid blink-blink of a message or instruction for Cassia. Bryce was having the place watched round the clock, but so far Sacrus had not responded to Cassia's warning.

"'Target is Coaver Street warehouse in two days,' she told them." Bryce shook his head in disgust. "'Urge evac of assets unless I can change target.'"

"You've done well," said Venera. She turned and sat on the window casement. "Listen, I know you're upset—you feel unmanned. Fair enough, it's a humiliation. No more so than this, though." She held out a sheet of paper—a letter that had arrived for her this morning. She watched Bryce unfold it sullenly.

"'Vote for Proposition forty-four at council tomorrow,'" he read. "What's that mean?"

She grimaced. "Proposition forty-four gives Sacrus control of the docks at Upper Spyre. Supposedly it's a demotion, since the docks aren't used much. Sacrus has modestly agreed to take that job and give up a plumb post in the exchequer that they've held for decades. Nobody's likely to object."

Bryce managed a grim smile. "So they're ordering you around like a lackey now?"

"At least they respected you enough to manipulate you instead," she said. "And don't forget, Bryce: your people follow you. Cassia recognized the leader in you, otherwise she wouldn't have singled you out for her attention. She may have been manipulating you all this time—but she was also training you."

He grumbled, but she could see her words had pleased him. At that moment, though, they heard rapid footsteps in the hall outside. Gray-haired Pasternak, one of Bryce's remaining two lieutenants, stuck his head in the doorway and said, "They're here."

Venera spared a last glance out the window. From up here the airfall was an insubstantial mesh of fabric where ground should be. Rushing clouds spun by beneath that faint skein, which she knew was really a gridwork of I-beams and stout cable—the tough inner skeleton of Spyre, visible now that the skin was stripped away. A small jumble of gantries and cranes perched timidly at the edge of the ruined land. The official story was that Amandera Thrace-Guiles was trying to build a bridge across the airfall to rejoin Buridan Tower to the rest of Spyre.

She followed Bryce out of the room. The truth was that the bridge site was a ruse, a distraction to cover up the real link between Buridan and the rest of the world. In the few days that had passed since Venera's conversation with Moss, a great deal of activity had taken place in the pipeworks that Venera and Garth had used to reach Buridan Tower the first time. A camouflaged entrance had been built near the railway siding a few hundred yards back from the airfall's edge. A man, or even a large group of men, could jump off a slow-moving train and after a sprint under some trees be in a hidden tunnel that led all the way to the tower. True, there were still long sections where men had to walk separated by thirty feet or more lest the pipe give way . . . but that would be fixed.

As she and Bryce strode down the long ramp that coiled from the tower's top to its bottom, they passed numerous work sites, each comprising half a dozen or more men and women. It was much like the controlled chaos of her estate's renovation, except that these people weren't fixing the plaster. They were assembling weapons, inventorying armor and supplies, and fencing in the ballrooms. Bryce's entire organization was here, as well as gray-eyed soldiers from Liris and exotics from allies of that country. They had started arriving last night, after Bryce gave the all-clear that he'd found his traitor.

Bryce's people were still in shock. They watched the newcomers with mixed loathing and suspicion; but the shock of Cassia's betrayal had been effective, and their loyalty to him still held.

Venera knew they would need something to do—and soon—or their natural hatred of the status quo would assert itself. They were born agitators, cutthroats, and bomb builders, but that was why they would be useful.

A new group was just tromping up from the stairs to the pipeworks as Venera and Bryce reached the main hall. They wore oilstained leathers and outlandish fur hats. Venera had seen these uniforms at a distance, usually wreathed in steam from some engine they were working on. These burly men were from the Preservation Society of Spyre, and they were sworn enemies of Sacrus.

For the moment they were acting more like overawed boys, though, staring around at the inside of Buridan Tower like they'd been transported into a storybook. In a sense, they had; the preservationists were indoctrinated in the history of the airfall, which remained the greatest threat to Spyre's structural integrity and which all now knew had been caused partly by Sacrus. Buridan Tower had probably been a symbol to them for centuries of defiance against decay and treachery. To stand inside it now was clearly a shock.

Good. She could use that fact.

"Gentlemen." She curtsied to the group. "I am Amandera Thrace-Guiles. If you'll follow me, I'll show you where you can freshen up, and then we can get started."

They murmured amongst themselves as they walked behind her. Venera exchanged a glance with Bryce, who seemed amused at her formality.

The preservationists headed off to the washrooms and Venera and Bryce turned the other way, entering the tower's now-familiar library. Venera had ordered some of the emptied armor of the tower's long-ago attackers mounted here. The holed and burned crests of Sacrus and its allies were quite visible on breastplate and shoulder. As a pointed message, Venera'd had the suits posed like sentries around the long map table in the middle of the room. One even held a lantern.

Bryce's lieutenants were already at the table, pointing to

things and talking in low tones with the commander of the Liris detachment. As the preservationists trooped back in, the other generals and colonels entered from a door opposite. Moss had exceeded Venera's wildest expectations: at the head of this group were generals from Carasthant and Scoman, old allies of Liris in its war with Vatoris—and they had brought friends of their own. Most prominent was the towering, frizzy-haired Corinne, princess of Fin. Normally Venera didn't like women who were social equals—in Hale they always represented a threat—but she'd taken an instant liking to Corinne.

Venera nodded around at them all. "Welcome," she said. "This is an extraordinary meeting. Circumstances are dire. I'm sure you all know by now that Sacrus has recruited an army, plundering its neighbors of manpower in the process. So far the council at Lesser Spyre is acting like it never happened. I think they're in a tailspin. Does anyone here believe that the council should be the ones to deal with the situation?"

There were grins round the table. One of the preservationists held up a hand. He would have been handsome were it not for the beard—Venera hated beards—that obscured the lower half of his face. "You're on the council," he said. "Can't you bring a motion for them to act?"

"I can, but the next morning I'll receive the head of my man Flance in the mail," she said. "Sacrus has him. So I'm highly motivated, though not in the ways that Sacrus probably expects. Still . . . I won't act through the council."

"Sacrus blocked one of our main lines," said the preservationist. "All of Spyre is in danger unless we can get a counterbalance running through their land. Beyond that, we don't give a damn who they conquer."

It was Venera's turn to nod. The preservationists were dedicated to keeping the giant wheel together. Most of their decisions were therefore pragmatic and dealt with engineering issues. They wouldn't care if they were ruled by the council or Sacrus itself, as long as the engineering was sound.

"Are you saying they could buy your loyalty by just giving you a siding?" she asked.

"They could," said the bearded man. There were protests up and down the table, but Venera smiled.

"I applaud your honesty," she said. "Your problem is that you'd need to give them a reason before they did that. They've never had any use for you and you've never been a threat to them. So you've come here to buy that leverage?"

He shrugged. "Or see them destroyed. It's all the same to us."

Bryce leaned out to look at the man. "And the fact that they used poison gas to kill twenty-five of your workers a generation ago . . . ?"

". . . Gives us a certain bias in the *destroy* direction. Who are you?" added the bearded man, who had been briefed on the identities of the other players.

With obvious distaste, Bryce said what they'd decided he would say: "Bryce. Chief of intelligence for Buridan." He nodded at Venera.

"You've a *spy network?*" The preservationist grinned at her ironically.

"I do, Mister . . . ?"

"Thinblood." It could have been a name or a title.

"I do, Mr. Thinblood—and *you've* got a secret warehouse full of artillery at junction sixteen," she said with a return smile. Thinblood turned red; out of the corner of her eye Venera saw Princess Corinne stifle a laugh.

"We are all to be taken seriously," Venera went on. "As is Sacrus. Let's return to discussing them."

"Hang on," said Thinblood. "What are we discussing? War?"

She shook her head. "Not yet. But clearly, Sacrus needs its wings clipped."

The lean, cadaverous general from Carasthant made a violent shushing gesture that made everyone turn to stare at him. "What can little guppies like us do?" he said in a buzzing voice that seemed to emanate from his bobbing Adam's appple. "Begging your pardon, Madam Buridan, Mr. Preservationist sir. Do you propose we take down a shark by worrying at its gills?"

His compatriot from Scoman waggled his head in agreement. The one tiny clock built into his armor clicked ahead a second. "Sacrus is bounded by high walls and barbed wire," he said over the quiet snicking of his clothing, "and they have sniper towers and machine-gun positions. Even if we fought our way in, what would we do? Piss on their lawn?"

That was an expression Venera had never heard before.

Venera had thought long and hard about what to say when this question came up. These men and women were gathered here because their homes had all been injured or insulted by Sacrus—but were they here merely to vent their indignation? Would they back down in the face of actual action?

She didn't want to tell them that she knew what Sacrus was up to. The key to Candesce was a prize worth betraying old friends for. If they knew Sacrus had it, half these people would defect to Sacrus's side immediately, and the other half would proceed to plan how to get it themselves. It might turn into a night of long knives inside Buridan Tower.

"Sacrus's primary assets lie inside the Grey Infirmary," she said. "Whatever it is that they manufacture and sell, that is its origin. At the very least, we need to know what we're up against, what they're planning to do. I propose that we invade the Grey Infirmary."

There was a momentary, stunned silence from the new arrivals. Princess Corinne's broad sunburnt face was squinched up in a failed attempt to hide a smile. Then Thinblood, the Carasthant general, and two of the minor house representatives all started talking at once.

"Impossible!" she heard, and "Suicide!" through the general babble. Venera let it run on for a minute or so, then held up her hand.

"Consider the benefits if it could be done," she said. "We could rescue my man Flance, assuming he's there. We could find out what Sacrus trades in—though I think we all know—but in any case find out what its tools and devices are. We might be able to seize their records. Certainly we can find out what it is they're doing.

"If we want, we can blow up the tower.

"And it *can* be done," she said. "I admit I was pretty hopeless myself until last night. We'd talked through all sorts of plans, from sneaking over the walls to shimmying down ropes from Lesser Spyre. All our scenarios ended up with us being machine-gunned, either on the way in or on the way out. Then I had a long talk with Princess Corinne, here."

Corinne nodded violently; her hair followed her head's motion a fraction of a second late. "We can get into the Grey Infirmary," she brayed. "And out again safely."

There was another chorus of protests and again Venera held up her hand. "I could tell you," she said, "but it might be more convincing to *show* you. Come." And she headed for the doors.

THE ROAR FROM the airfall was more visceral than audible here in the lowest of Buridan's pipes. Bryce's people had lowered ladders down here when they came to cut away the maddening random organ that had been created accidentally in Buridan's destruction. The corroded metal surface gleamed wetly, and as Venera stepped off the ladder she slipped and almost fell. She stared up at the ring of faces twenty feet above her.

"Well, come on," she said. "If I'm brave enough to come down here, you can be too."

Thinblood ignored the ladder and vaulted down, landing beside her with a smug thump. Instantly the surface under their feet began swaying and little flakes of rust showered down. "The ladder's here to save the pipe, not your feet," Venera said loudly. Thinblood looked abashed; the others clambered down the ladder meekly.

The ladder descended the vertical part of the pipe and they now stood where it bent into a horizontal direction. This tunnel was ten feet wide and who knew what it might originally have carried—horse manure, Venera suspected. Whatever the case, it now ended twenty feet away. Late afternoon sunlight hurried shadows across the jagged circle of torn metal. It was from there that the roar originated.

"Come." Without hesitation Venera walked to within five feet of the opening, then went down on one knee. She pointed. "There! Sacrus!"

They could barely have heard her over the roar of the thin air; it didn't matter. It was clear what she was pointing at.

The pipe they stood in thrust forty or fifty feet into the airstream below the curve of Spyre's hull. Luckily this opening faced away from the headwind, though suction pulled at Venera relentlessly and the air was so thin she was starting to pant already. The pipe hung low enough to provide a vantage point from which a long stretch of Spyre's hull was visible—miles of it, in fact. Way out there, near the little world's upside-down horizon, a cluster of pipes much like this one—but intact—jutted into the airflow. Nestled among them was a glassed-in machine-gun blister, similar to the one Venera had first visited underneath Garth Diamandis's hovel.

"That's the underside of the Grey Infirmary," she yelled at the motley collection of generals and revolutionaries crowding at her shoulder. Someone cupped hand to ear and looked quizzical. "Infirmary! In! Firm!" She jabbed her finger at the distant pipes. The quizzical person smiled and nodded.

Venera backed up cautiously and the others scuttled ahead of her. At the pipe's bend where breathing was a bit easier and the noise and vibration not so mind-numbing, she braced her rump against the wall and her feet in the mulch of rust lining the bottom of the pipe. "We brought down telescopes and checked out that machine-gun post. It's abandoned, like most of the hull positions. The entrance is probably bricked up, most likely forgotten.

It's been hundreds of years since anybody tried to assault Spyre from the outside."

She could barely make out the buzzing words of Carasthant's general. "You propose to get in through that? How? By jumping off the world and grabbing the pipes as they pass?"

Venera nodded. When they all stared back uncomprehending, she sighed and turned to Princess Corinne. "Show them," she said.

Corinne was carrying a bulky backpack. She wrestled this off and plunked it down in the rust. "This," she said with a dramatic flourish, "is how we will get to Sacrus.

"It is called a *parachute*."

SHE HAD TO focus on her jaw. Venera's face was buried in the voluminous shoulder of her leather coat; her hands clutched the rope that twisted and shuddered in her grip. In the chattering roar of a four-hundred-mile-per-hour wind there was no room for distractions, or even thought.

Her teeth were clenched around a mouthpiece of Fin design. A rubber hose led from this to a metal bottle that, Corinne had explained, held a large quantity of squashed air. It was that ingredient of the air the *Rook's* engineers had called *oxygen*; Venera's first breath of it had made her giddy.

Every now and then the wind flipped her over or dragged her head to the side and Venera saw where she was: wrapped in leathers, goggled and masked, and hanging from a thin rope inches below the underside of Spyre.

All she had to do was keep her body arrow-straight and keep that mouthpiece in. Venera was tied to the line, which was being let out quite rapidly from the edge of the airfall. Ten soldiers had already gone this way before her so it must be possible.

It was night, but distant cities and even more distant suns cast enough light to silver the misty clouds that approached Spyre like curious fish. She saw how the clouds would nuzzle Spyre cautiously only to be rebuffed by its whirling rotation. They recoiled, formed cautious spirals, and danced around the great cylinder as if trying to find a way in. Dark speckles—flocks of piranhawks and sharks—browsed among them, and there in great black formations were the barbed wire and blockhouses of the sentries.

To be among the clouds with nothing above or below seemed perfectly normal to Venera. If she fell she only had to open her parachute and she'd come to a stop long before hitting the barbed wire. It wasn't the prospect of falling that made her heart pound—it was the savage headwind that was trying to snatch her breath away.

The rope shuddered and she grabbed it spasmodically. Then she felt a hand grab her ankle.

The soldiers hauled her through a curtain of speed ivy and into a narrow gun emplacement. This one was dry and empty, its tidiness somehow in keeping with Sacrus's fastidious attention to detail. Bryce was already here and he unceremoniously yanked the air line from Venera's mouth. —Or tried; she bit down on it tenaciously for a second, glaring at him, before relenting and opening her mouth. He shot her a look of annoyance and tied it and her unopened parachute to the line. This he let out through the speed ivy, to be reeled back to Buridan for its next user.

Princess Corinne's idea had sounded insane, but she merely shrugged, saying, "We do this sort of thing all the time." Of course, she was from Fin, which explained much. That pocket nation inhabited one of Spyre's gigantic ailerons, a wing hundreds of feet in length that jutted straight down into the airstream. Originally colonized by escaped criminals, Fin had grown over the centuries from a cold and dark subbasement complex into a bright and independent—if strange—realm. The Fins didn't really consider themselves citizens of Spyre at all. They were creatures of the air.

Over the years they had installed hundreds of windows in the giant metal vane as well as hatches and winches. They were suspected of being smugglers, and Corinne had proudly confirmed that. "We alone are able to slip in and out of Spyre at will," she'd told Venera. And, as their population expanded, they had colonized five of the other twelve fins by the same means they were using to break into Sacrus.

To reach Sacrus, one of Corinne's men had donned a parachute and taken hold of a rope that had a big three-barbed hook on its end. He had unceremoniously stepped into the howling airfall and was snatched down and away like a fleck of dust.

Venera had been watching from the tower and saw his parachute balloon open a second later. Instantly, he stopped falling away from Spyre and began curving back toward the hull. Down only operated as long as you were part of the spinning structure, after all; freed of the high speed imparted by Spyre's rotation, he'd come to a stop in the air. He could have hovered there, scant feet from the hull, for hours. The only problem was the rope he held, which was still connected to Buridan.

The big wooden spool that was unreeling it was starting to smoke. Any second now it would reach its end and the snap would probably take his hands off. Yet he calmly stood there on the dark air, waiting for Sacrus to shoot past.

As the pipes and machine-gun nest leaped toward him he lifted the hook and, with anticlimactic ease, tossed it ahead of the rushing metal. The hook caught, the rope whipped up and into the envelope of speeding air surrounding the hull, and Corinne's man saluted before disappearing over Spyre's horizon. They'd recovered him when he came around again.

Now, brilliant light etched the cramped gun emplacement with the caustic sharpness of a black-and-white photograph. One of the men was employing a welding torch on the hatch at the top of the steps. "Sealed ages ago, like we thought," shouted Bryce, jabbing a thumb at the ceiling. "Judging from the pipes, we're under the sewage stacks. There's probably toilets above us."

"Perfect." They needed a staging ground from which to assault the tower. "Do you think they'll hear us?"

Bryce grimaced. "Well, there could be fifty guys sitting around up there taking bets on how long it'll take us to burn the hatch open. We'll find out soon enough."

Suddenly the ceiling blew out around the welder. He retreated in a shower of sparks, cursing, and a new wind filled the little space. Before anybody else could move Thinblood leaped over to the hole and jammed some sort of contraption up it. He folded, pulled—and the wind stopped. The hole the welder had made was now blocked by something.

"Patch hatch," said Thinblood, wiping dust off his face. "We'd better go up. They might have heard the pop or felt the pressure drop."

Without waiting he pressed against his temporary hatch, which gave way with a rubbery slapping sound. Thinblood pushed his way up and out of sight. Bryce was right behind him.

Both were standing with their guns drawn when Venera fought her way past the suction to sprawl on a filthy floor. She stood up, brushing herself off, and looked around. "It is indeed a men's room."

Or was it? In the weak light of Thinblood's lantern she could see that the chamber was lined in tiles that had once been white but which had long since taken on the color of rust and dirt. Long streaks ran down the wall to dark pools on the floor. Venera expected to see the usual washroom fixtures along the walls, but other than a metal sink there was nothing. She had an uneasy feeling that she knew what sort of room this was, but it didn't come to her until Thinblood said, "Operating theater. Disused."

Bryce was prying at a metal chute mounted in one wall. It creaked open and he stared down into darkness for a second. "A convenient method of disposal for body parts or even whole people," he said. "I'm thinking more like an autopsy room."

"Vivisectionist's lounge?" Thinblood was getting into the game.

"Shut up," said Venera. She'd gone over to the room's one door and was listening at it. "It seems quiet."

"Well, it is the middle of the night," the preservationist commented. More members of their team were meanwhile popping up out of the floor like Jacks-in-the-box. *Minus the windup music,* Venera mused.

Soon there were twenty of them crowded together in the ominous little room. Venera cracked the door and peered out into a larger, dark space full of pipes, boilers, and metal tanks. This was the maintenance level for the tower, it seemed. That was logical.

"Is everyone clear on what we're doing?" she asked.

Thinblood shook his head. "Not even remotely."

"We are after my man Flance," she said, "as well as information about what Sacrus is up to. If we have to fight, we cause enough mayhem to make Sacrus rethink its strategy. Hence the charges." She nodded at the heavy canvas bag one of the Liris soldiers was toting. "Our first order of business is to secure this level, then set some of those charges. Let's do it."

She led the soldiers of half a dozen nations as they stepped out of their bridgehead and into the dark of enemy territory.

15

EVERYTHING IN THE Grey Infirmary seemed designed to promote a feeling of paranoia. The corridors were hung with huge black felt drapes that swayed and twitched slightly in the moving air, giving the constant impression that there was someone hiding behind them. The halls were lit by lanterns fixed on metal posts; you could swivel the post and aim the light here and there, but there was no way to illuminate your entire surroundings at any point. The floors were muffled under deep crimson carpeting. You could sneak up on anybody here. There were no signs, doors were hidden behind the drapery, and all the corridors looked alike.

It reminded Venera unpleasantly of the palace at Hale. Her father's own madness had been deepening in the days before she succeeded in escaping to a life with Chaison. The Pilot had all the paintings in the palace covered, the mirrors likewise. He took to walking the hallways at night, a sword in his hand, convinced as he was that conspirators waited around every corner. These nocturnal strolls were great for the actual conspirators, who knew exactly where he was and so could avoid him easily. Those conspirators— almost entirely comprising members of his own family—would bring him down one day soon. Venera had not received any letters bragging of his downfall while she lived in Rush; but there could well be one waiting when or if she ever returned to Slipstream.

That was the madness of one man. Sacrus, though, had done more than generalize such paranoia: it had institutionalized it. The Grey Infirmary was a monument to suspicion and a testament to the idea that distrust was to be encouraged. "Don't pull on the curtains to look for doors," Venera cautioned the men as they rounded a corner and lost sight of the stairs to the basement. "They may be rigged to an alarm."

Thinblood scoffed. "Why do something like that?"

"So only the people who know where the doors are can find them," she said. "People trying to escape—or interlopers like us—set off the bells. Luckily there's another way to find them." She pointed at the carpet. "Look for worn patches. They signify higher traffic."

The corridor they were in seemed to circle some large inner area. Opposite the basement stairs they found the broad steps of an exit, and next to it stairs going up. It wasn't until they had nearly circled back to the basement stairs that they found a door letting into the interior. Next to a patch of slightly worn carpet, Venera eased the curtains to the side and laid her hand on a cold iron door with a simple latch. She eased the door open a crack—it made no sound—and peered in.

The room was as big as an auditorium, but there was no stage. Instead, dozens of long glass tanks stood on tables under small electric lights. The lights flickered slightly, their power no doubt influenced by the jamming signal that emanated from Candesce.

Each tank was filled with water, and lying prone in them were men—handcuffed, blindfolded, and with their noses and mouths just poking out of the water. Next to each tank was a stool and perched on several of these were women who appeared to be reading books.

"What is it?" Thinblood was asking. Venera waved at him impatiently and tried to get a better sense of what was going on here. After a moment she realized that the women's lips were moving. They were reading to the men in the tanks.

". . . I am the angel that fills your sky. Can you see me? I come to you naked, my breasts are full and straining for your touch."

Bryce put a hand on her shoulder and his head above hers. "What are they doing?"

"They seem to be reading pornography," she whispered, shaking her head.

". . . Touch me, oh touch me, exalted one. I need you. You are my only hope.

"Yet who am I, this trembling bird in your hand. I am more than one woman, I am a multitude, all dependent on you. . . . I am Falcon Formation, and I need you in all ways that a man can be needed . . ."

Venera fell back, landing on her elbows on the deep carpet. "Shut it!" Bryce raised an eyebrow at her reaction but eased the door closed. He twitched the curtain back into place.

"What was that all about?" asked Thinblood.

Venera got to her feet. "I just found out who one of Sacrus's clients is," she said. She felt nauseated.

"Can we seal off this door?" she asked. "Prevent anyone getting out and coming at us from behind?"

Bryce frowned. "That presents its own dangers. We could as easily trap ourselves."

She shrugged. "But we have *grenades*, and we're not afraid to use them." She squinted at him. "Are we?"

Thinblood laughed. "Would a welding torch applied to the hinges do the trick? We'll have to leave a tiny team behind to do that."

"Two men, then."

They went back to the upward-leading stairs. The second level presented a corridor identical to the one below. The same muffled silence hung over everything here. "Ah," said Venera, "such delicate decorative instincts they have."

Thinblood was pacing along bent over, hands behind his back. He stared at the floor mumbling "hmmm, hmmm." After a few seconds he pointed. "Door here."

Venera twitched back the curtain to reveal an ironbound door with a barred window. She had to stand on her tiptoes to see through it to the long corridor full of similar doors beyond. "This looks like a cell block." She rattled the door handle. "Locked."

"*Hello?*" The voice had come from the other side of the door. Venera motioned for the others to get out of sight, then summoned a laconic, sugary voice and said, "Is this where I can find my little captain?" She giggled.

"Wha—?" Two eyes appeared at the door, blinking in surprise at her. Just in time, Venera had yanked off her black jacket and shirt, revealing the strategic strappery that maximized her figure. "Who the hell are you?" said the man on the other side of the door.

"I'm your present," whispered Venera. "That is, if you're Captain Sendriks. . . . I'd like it if you were," she added petulantly. "I'm tired of tromping around these stupid corridors in nothing but my assets. I could catch a cold."

A moment later the latch clicked and seconds after that Venera was inside with a pistol under the chin of the surprised guard. Her men flowed around her like water filling a pipe; as she gestured for her new prisoner to kneel Thinblood said, "It's clear on this end, but there's another man around the corner yonder."

"Level a pistol at him and he'll fall into line." She watched one of the soldiers from Liris tying up her man, then said, "It is cold in here. Bryce, where's my jacket?"

"Haven't seen it," he said innocently. Venera glared at him, then went to collect it herself.

The corridor held a faint undertone of coughing and quizzical voices, which came from behind the other doors. This was indeed a cell block. Venera raced from door to door. "Up! Yes, you! Who are you? How long have you been here?"

There were men and women here. There were children as well. They wore a wide mix of clothing, some familiar from her days in Spyre, some foreign, perhaps of the principalities. Their accents, when they answered her hesitantly, were similarly diverse. All seemed well fed but they were haggard with fear and lack of sleep.

Garth Diamandis was not among them.

Venera didn't hide her disappointment. "Tell me where the rest of the prisoners are or I'll blow your head off," she told the guard. She had him on his knees with his face pressed against the wall, her pistol against the back of his head. "Bear in mind," she added, "that we'll find them ourselves if we have to, it'll just take longer. What do you say?"

He proceeded to give a detailed account of the layout of the tower, including where the night watch were stationed and when their rounds were. So far Venera hadn't seen any sign of watchmen; for a nation gearing up for war, Sacrus seemed extremely lax. She said so and her prisoner laughed, a tad hysterically.

"Nobody's ever gotten in or out of here," he mumbled against the plaster. "Who would break in? And from where?" He tried unsuccessfully to shake his head. "You people are insane."

"A common enough trait in Spyre," she sniffed. "Your mistake, then."

"You don't understand," he croaked. "But you will."

She had already noted that he wore armor that was light and utilitarian, and his holstered weapons had been similarly simple. This functionalism, which contrasted dramatically with the outlandish costumes of most of her people, made her more uneasy about Sacrus's abilities than anything he'd said.

They spent some time trying to get more out of him and his companion. Neither they nor the prisoners they spoke to knew what Sacrus's plan was—only that a general mobilization was underway. The prisoners themselves were from all over the principalities; some had recently gone missing within Spyre itself.

"They're enough evidence to haul Sacrus before the high court on crimes against the polity," crowed Bryce. "If we can just get some of these people out of here."

Venera shook her head. "They may be enough to get the rest of Spyre up in arms. But until we can come up with a decent plan for getting them out alive, they're safer where they are. Let them loose now and they'll give us away, and probably try to run the gauntlet of machine guns and barbed wire on their way to the outer walls. At least let's find them some weapons and a direction to run in."

Bryce and Thinblood exchanged glances. Then Bryce quirked his irritating smile. "I have an idea," he said. "Let's strike a compromise . . ."

THERE WERE PLENTY of cells in the block, but Garth was in none of them. While Venera searched for him, Thinblood took the bulk of the team to look for the night watch. Nearly fifteen minutes had passed before he reappeared.

Thinblood was jubilant. "Both floors are secure," he said. "We left the watchmen in a closet we found. And my welder has sealed off the main doors and a side entrance. He's a model of efficiency, that one."

Bryce put a hand on Venera's arm. "Your man doesn't seem to be here. We have to look to our other objectives."

She shrugged him off, gritting her teeth so as not to snap some withering retort. "All right, then," she said. "There's more to this tower upstairs. Let's find out what Sacrus is up to."

The next floor was different. Here the velvet-covered walls and darkness gave way to marble and bright, annoyingly uneven electric light. Venera heard the sound of voices and chatter of a mechanical typewriter coming from an open door about thirty feet to the left. Crouching under the lee of the steps with the others, she scowled and said, "The time for subtlety may be past."

"Wait." Thinblood pointed the other way. Venera craned her neck and saw the heavy vault-style door even as Thinblood said, "Sacrus is reputed to keep their most secret weapons in this place. Do you think . . . ?"

"I think I saw some of those weapons being made downstairs," she said, thinking of the fish-tank room. "But you're right. It's just too tempting." The door was surrounded by big signs saying VALID PERSONNEL ONLY, and two men with rifles slouched in front of it. "How do we get past them?"

One of Corinne's men cleared his throat quietly. He drew something from his backpack and after a moment his companions did likewise. They strung the small compound bows with quick economical movements. Seeing this, Venera and the other leaders climbed back down and out of the way.

"Count of three," said the man at the top. "You take the one on the right, we'll do the one on the left. One, two—"

All four of Corinne's soldiers jumped out of the stairwell and rolled into crouches. Their shoulder muscles creased in unison as they drew back and Venera heard an intake of breath and "What the—" from off to the right and then they let loose.

There was a grunt, a thud, then another. The archers whirled around, looking for another target.

The sound of typing continued.

"Take out that office," Venera instructed the archers as she stepped into the hallway. "We'll go for the vault."

The heavy door had a thick glass window in it. Venera shaded her eyes with her hands and stared through for a few seconds. She whistled. "I think we've found the mother lode."

The chamber beyond was large—it took up most of this level. There were no windows and its distant walls were draped in black like the corridors downstairs. Its brick floor was crisscrossed by red carpets; in the squares they defined, pedestals large and small stood under cones of light. Each pedestal supported some device—brass canisters here, a fluted riflelike weapon there. Large jars full of thick brown fluid gleamed near things like bushes made of knives. There was nothing in there that looked innocuous, nothing Venera would have willingly wanted to touch. But all were on display as if they were treasures.

She supposed they were that; this might be the vault that held Sacrus's dearest assets.

The view was obscured suddenly. Venera found herself staring into the cold gray eyes of a soldier, who mouthed something she couldn't hear through the glass.

Deception wasn't going to work this time. "We've been seen," she said even as a loud alarm bell suddenly filled the corridor with jangling echoes.

"Can we blow this?" Thinblood was asking one of his men. The soldier shook his head.

"Not without taking time to figure out the vulnerable points . . . maybe doing some drilling . . ."

Thinblood looked at Venera, who shrugged. "It's going to be a firefight from now on," she said. "Better get downstairs and free those prisoners. Then we can—" Something bright and sudden flashed in her peripheral vision and there was a loud *clang!*

She stared in dumb surprise at the metal bars that now blocked the way to the stairwell. "Blow them!" she shouted, pulling out her preservationist-built machine pistol. "This is no time for subtlety!"

At that moment there was an eruption of noise from the far end of the corridor. Venera dove to the floor as impacting bullets sprayed marble dust and plaster at her. The others either flattened as well or staggered back against the wall. Blood spattered over the threaded stonework.

Now a smoke grenade was tumbling toward her, each end-over-end bounce sending a gout of black into the air. It stopped just outside the bars then disappeared in a growing pyramid of darkness. Past that Venera heard shouted orders, gunshots.

"You will lie facedown on the floor and put your hands behind your necks! Anyone we do not find in that position will be shot! You have five seconds and then we will shoot everything that sticks up more than a foot off the floor."

All she could hear after that was machine gun fire.

THE COMMANDANT HELD the mimeographed picture of Venera next to her head and compared the two. "You look older in real life," he said in apparent disappointment. She glared at him but said nothing.

"Really," he continued in apparent amazement, "what did you think you were going to achieve? Invading *Sacrus*? We've forgotten more tricks of incursion and sabotage than you people ever knew."

Twelve of Venera's people knelt around her on the floor of a storage room that opened off the third-floor corridor. Mops and brooms loomed over her; a single flickering bulb illuminated the three men with machine guns who were standing over the prisoners. Two more soldiers had been tying their hands behind their backs but the process had stalled out briefly as they ran out of rope. The commandant, who had at first seemed flustered and shocked, had soon recovered his poise and now appeared to be genuinely enjoying himself.

"You did a good job of sealing off the front doors, but my superiors were able to slip this through the crack." He waggled the mimeograph at Venera. He was a beefy man with an oddly asymmetrical face; one of his eyes was markedly higher than the other, and his upper lip lifted on the left, giving him a permanent look of incredulity. "They also slipped in some instructions on how we're to proceed while they cut through your welding job. It seems we had a—" He flipped the sheet over to read the back. "—A certain Garth Diamandis in our custody, as guarantor of your good behavior. Our arrangement was very clear. Should you fail to obey our orders, we were to kill this Diamandis. I'd say that your little incursion tonight constitutes disobedience, wouldn't you?"

Venera drew back her lips in a snarl. "Someday they're going to name a disease after you."

The commandant sighed. "I just wanted you to know that I've issued the order. He's being terminated, oh, even as we speak. And—" he laughed heartily "—I had an inspiration! The manner of his passing is quite hideous. You'll be impressed when you see—"

A soldier clattered to a stop at the door to the office. "The lower floors are secure, sir," he said. "They had tied up the night watch and the guards in the prison. In addition, we found ten of these in the basement." He handed the commandant one of the charges Venera's people had set.

Venera exchanged a glance with Bryce, whose hands were still untied.

"Well, look at this." The commandant knelt in front of Venera.

"A little clockwork bomb. Why, it's so intricately made, I can only think of one place it might have come from." He arched an eyebrow at the knot of prisoners. "Are any of you from Scoman, by any chance?" He didn't wait for an answer, but turned the mechanism over under Venera's nose. "How does it work? Is it a timer?"

She said nothing; he shrugged and said, "I think I can figure it out. You turn this dial to give yourself . . . what? Ten minutes? If you don't reset it before it winds down to zero it explodes."

A muffled report sounded from somewhere in the building. A gunshot? The commandant glanced at his men; one turned and left the room. "I suppose one or two of your compatriots might still be loose," he admitted. "But we'll round them up soon enough."

He was just opening his mouth to add something else when the lights went out. The building rocked to a distant blast.

Instant pandemonium—somebody stepped on Venera and crumpled her to the floor while some sort of struggle erupted just to her right; one of the machine guns went off, apparently into the ceiling, lighting the space with a momentary red flicker. All she saw was people rearing up, falling down, tumbling like scattered chessmen. She strained but couldn't get free of the ropes that bound her hands behind her.

Another explosion, then another. How many of those bombs had they said they'd found? She was sure they'd planted at least twelve.

Now somebody fell on her in a horrifyingly limp tangle and she screamed but nobody could hear her over the shouts, cries, and shots.

More machine gun fire, terrifyingly close but apparently directed out the door. Venera wormed out from under the wet body and found a corner to huddle in, hands jammed into the spot where walls and floor met. She cursed the dark and chaos and expected to receive a bullet in the head any second.

Silence and heavy breathing. Distant shouts. Somebody lit a match.

Bryce and Thinblood stood back to back. Each held a machine

gun. Another gun lay under the body of the commandant, whose lopsided face was frozen in an expression of genuine surprise. The room was awash with men who were holding one another by the throat, or feet, or wrists, all atop the tiled bodies of the soldiers who were still tied up. Dark blood was spattered up the wall and over everybody. Venera looked down at herself and saw that her own clothes were glistening with the stuff.

"Get them untied!" Somebody flipped a knife into his hand and began bending and slashing at the ropes. When he reached Venera she saw that it was one of the archers. Venera leaned forward, knocking her forehead against the floor as he roughly grabbed her arms and cut.

"The prisoners are loose!" Bryce hauled her to her feet just as the match went out. "Somebody find a bloody lantern! We've got to get out of here!" They burst into the corridor just as the lights resumed a dim glow. There were bodies all over the place and bullet holes in the walls, and she heard shots and shouts coming from the stairwell.

"Good idea to leave those men in the cells," she said to Bryce. "A command decision."

He grinned. They had given two men some spare weapons and grenades and, out of sight of the tied-up guards, put them in a cell with a broken lock. They were to free the prisoners and arm them if the rest of the team didn't return in good time.

The soldiers recovered their guns and armor from a pile outside the storage room and one by one loped toward the T-intersection next to the stairwell. A firefight had broken out down there. Venera had her pistol in her hand but ended up in the rear, down on all fours as bullets sprayed overhead.

For a few minutes there was shouting and shooting. When it became clear that the men in the stairwell were of Sacrus, somebody threw a grenade at them, but more shots were coming from the side—the top right arm of the T from Venera's perspective. That was the direction the commandant's men had originally come from. The stairwell was at the very top of the T, the storage room behind her.

Now it was chaos and shooting again. Venera crawled to the left, to the spot where the metal cage had descended earlier. It was gone. She raised her head slightly and saw, through smoke and dim light, that the great metal door to the treasure room was open.

Bryce and the others had made it into the now-cleared stairwell but Venera had been too slow. Soldiers of Sacrus emerged from clouds of gunsmoke, faceless in the faint light. Venera scrambled to her feet, slipped on blood, and half-fell through the doorway into the treasure room. Her feet found purchase on the carpet and she pressed her whole body against the cold door. It slowly creaked shut, ringing from bullet impacts at the last instant.

She spun the wheel in the center of the portal and turned around to lean on it. A sound hangover echoed through her head for a few seconds; or was she still hearing the battle, but muffled by iron and stone?

Stepping forward she lifted her arms, saw blood all over them. Something caught her foot and she stumbled. Looking down she saw that it was another body—a soldier of Sacrus, maybe the very one with whom she'd locked eyes through the little glass window in the door. He lay on his back, arms flung about and blood pooling behind his head.

His abdomen had been cut wide open and his entrails trailed along the floor.

A new wash of fear came over Venera. She backed against the door and brought up her pistol to check it. Wouldn't do to have a misfire due to blood in the barrel. For a few moments she stood perfectly still, listening and, finally, looking about at the place she had come to.

The huge square room was lit better than the hallway had been, by small electric spotlights that hung over dozens of pedestals. She had glimpsed those earlier, the canisters and boxes atop them now glowing in surreal majesty. There was nobody else in sight, but she thought she could see another door opposite the one through which she'd entered.

A woman chuckled somewhere; the chuckle turned into a laugh of childish delight.

Venera made her way around the room's perimeter in quick sprints, ducking from pedestal to pedestal. It was hard to tell where the laughter was coming from because sounds echoed off the high ceiling. Faintly, through the floor, she could still hear the noise of battle.

The laugh came again—this time from only a few yards away. Venera rounded a broad pedestal surmounted by some kind of cannon and stopped dead, pistol forgotten in her hand.

A big clockwork mechanism had been shoved off the next pedestal and now lay shattered on the floor. Little wisps of smoke rose from it. The pedestal itself was covered with the remains of a man.

Somebody was kneeling in the gore and viscera that dripped over the edges of the pedestal. It was a woman, completely nude, and she was bathing—no, wallowing—in the blood and slippery things she was hauling out of the man's torso. She stroked her skin with something, squeezing it as if it were a wet sponge, and gave a little mewl of delight.

Venera raised the pistol and aimed carefully. "Margit! What have you done?"

The former botanist of Liris cocked her head at Venera. She grinned, holding up two crimson hands.

"Don't you get it?" she said. "It's cherries! Red, red cherries, full and ripe."

"Wh-who—" Venera had suddenly remembered the commandant's boast. He had found a hideous death for Garth, he'd said. She stepped forward, staring past a haze of nausea at the few scraps of clothing she could recognize. Those boots—they were Sacrus army issue.

"They trusted me," said Margit as she lowered herself into the sticky mass she was massaging. "These two knew me—so they let me in. When the bombs went off, the wall and door parted a bit—the hinges sprung! I just pushed it open and ran right out of my little room! Nobody there to stop me. So I came here and brought him with me."

"Brought who?"

Margit raised a hand to point at something lying in the shadows of another pedestal. "The one they'd just given to me. My present."

"Garth!" Venera ran over to him. He was on his side, unconscious but breathing. His hands were tied behind his back. Venera knelt to undo the knots, putting her pistol down when she decided Margit was too far into her own delusions to notice.

Far gone she might be, but she'd killed at least two men in this room. "You must have ambushed them," said Venera, making it into a question.

"Oh yes. I was dressed oh-so respectably and had my prisoner with me. They were staring out the window, you people were shooting and thrashing about somewhere out of sight, and I just popped up there in front of them. 'Let me in!' Oh, I looked so scared. As soon as their backs were to me I mowed them down."

"There were only two?"

Margit clucked reproachfully. "How many people do you put inside a locked vault? Two was overkill, but you see the doors don't open from the outside. That's a *precaution*." She enunciated the word cheerfully.

Venera slapped Garth lightly; he groaned and mumbled something, batting feebly at her hand.

She looked up at Margit again. "Why come here?"

Margit stood up, dripping. "You know why," she said, suddenly serious. "For *that*." She pointed, straight-armed, at something on the floor.

It was crimson now, but there was no mistaking the cylindrical shape of the key to Candesce. When Venera saw it she gasped and raised the pistol again, cocking it as she tried to haul Garth to his feet with her other hand.

Margit frowned. "Don't deny me my destiny, Venera. Behold!" She struck one of her poses, throwing her arms out in the spotlight. "You gaze upon the queen of Candesce!"

"V-Venera?" Garth blinked at her, then focused past her at Margit. "What the—"

"Quickly now, Garth." She half-carried him over to the blood-smeared stones where the key lay. She let go of him and reached to scoop it up, still keeping a bead on Margit.

The botanist simply stood there, awash in light and gore, and watched as Venera and Garth backed away.

She was still watching when they made it to the chamber's other door and spun the wheel to open it.

16

VENERA'S PARACHUTE YANKED at her shoulders viciously. All the breath drove out of her, the world spun, and then a sublime calm seemed to ease into the world: the savage wind diminished, became gentle, and the roar of gunfire faded. Weight, too, slackened and in moments she found she had come to a stop in dawn-lit air that was crisp but hinted at a warm day to come.

All around her other parachutes had bloomed like night flowers. There were shouts, screaming—but also laughter. Corinne's people were taking charge; the air below Spyre was their territory. "Catch this rope!" one of them commanded, tossing a length at Venera. She grabbed it and he began to draw her in.

The knot of people waited a hundred feet from the madly spinning hull of Spyre. Twenty had arrived here in the early morning hours, but more than seventy were leaving. There hadn't been enough parachutes, but Sacrus had helpfully decorated its corridors with heavy black drapes. Many of these were now held by former prisoners. Having belled with air to brake them, the black squares were now twisting like smoke and were starting to get in the way as people tried to grab one another by wrist, fingertip, or foot.

She pulled herself up Garth's leg, hooked a hand in his belt, and met him at eye level. "Are you okay?" He still seemed disoriented and for a moment he just stared back at her.

"Did you come for me?" His voice was hoarse and she didn't like to think why. There were burn marks on his cheeks and hands and he looked thinner and older than ever.

Venera smoothed the backs of her fingers down the side of his face. "I came for you," she said, and was surprised to see tears start in his eyes.

Of course, she'd also gone in to find the key to Candesce—but now wasn't the politic time to say that.

"Listen up!" It was the leader of Corinne's troupe. "We've just passed Fin and I let out the signal flare. In a couple of minutes it's going to come by again and they'll have lowered a net! We're going to land in that net, all of us. Then we'll be drawn up into Fin. We need to stick together or people will get left behind."

"Isn't Sacrus going to pass us first?" somebody asked.

"Yes. So everybody with a gun get to the top. And unravel those drapes, we can use them to hide behind."

As Spyre rotated, first Buridan, then Sacrus would go by before Fin came around again. The soldiers of Sacrus had been right on their heels as Venera's group crowded into the basement. Doubtless they would be bringing heavy machine guns down, or grenades or—it didn't bear thinking about because there was nothing to be done. For a few seconds at least, Venera and her people were going to be helpless targets pinioned in air.

"Ouch!" said a woman near Venera's feet. "I—*ouch!* Hey, ohmigod—" She screamed suddenly, a frantic yelp that grew into a wail.

Venera spun around to look. Dark shapes flickered around the woman's silhouette, half-seen but growing in number. "Piranhawks!" someone shouted.

A second later there were thousands of them, a swirling cloud that completely enveloped the screaming woman. Her cries turned to horrible retching sounds and then stopped. Buzzing wings were everywhere, caressing Venera's throat and tossing her hair, but so far nothing had bitten her.

Nobody spoke. Nobody moved, and after a minute the cloud of piranhawks began to smear away into the air. They left behind a coiling cloud of black feathers and atomized red, at its heart a horrible thing bereft of blood and flesh.

"Brace yourselves! Here comes the airfall!" Venera looked up in time to see the latticework of girders that supported Buridan Tower flash past. In the next instant a fist of wind hit her.

Garth was nearly torn from her grasp by the pounding air. Two people who had refused to untie themselves from the black drapes were simply blown away, disappearing in moments into a distance blurred with barbed wire and mines. Others simply let go of their neighbors for a second and found themselves being drawn slowly, leisurely away as the airfall passed by and calmer air returned.

"Catch the rope! Catch it!" She watched the lines being tossed and frantic lunges to catch them; then one of the men who'd drifted a few yards away shuddered and spun. Dark lines stood in the air behind him for an instant before snapping and becoming thousands of red droplets. She heard machine gun fire.

"Sacrus! Return fire!" Everybody opened up on the small knot of pipes and the machine gun nest as it swept down and at them. Tracer rounds framed and dissected a vision of mauve cloud and amber sunlight. Venera blinked and couldn't see, waved her pistol hesitantly. Then Sacrus lofted up and away and the firing ceased.

"Get ready!"

Ready? Ready for what—the net caught her limp and unresisting and that probably saved Venera from a broken neck. As thin cords dug into her face and hands she was hauled into speeding air again, faster and faster until all breath was sucked out of her and spots danced in her eyes. Just as the howl and tearing fingers of the hurricane became intolerable it ceased so abruptly that she just lay for a while, staring at nothing. Gradually she made out voices, sounds of something heavy being shut as the wind sound cut out. Lantern light glowed below a metal ceiling where shadows of people hove to and fro. She rolled over.

Garth Diamandis was sitting up next to her. He probed at the back of his head carefully, then darted his eyes back and forth at the people who surrounded them. "Where are we?"

"Among friends," she said. "Safe. At least for now."

BLOOD SLID DOWN the drain, miniature rivers in the greater flow of water. After all that had happened, Venera was surprised to find that none of it was hers. By rights she should have been riddled with holes last night.

The facilities of Fin were primitive but the water was wonderfully hot. She dallied in the rusted metal cabinet that stood in for a shower, letting the stuff run over and off her in sheets, holding her face under it. Not thinking, though her hands still shook.

A loud banging startled her and she almost slipped. Venera flung open the sheet-metal door. "What?"

Bryce stood there. His glower turned to distraction as he took in her naked form. In a moment of reflected vision, she saw his gaze lower, pause, drop, pause again. Then he caught himself and met her eyes. "You're going to use up all the hot water," he said in a reasonable tone.

She slammed the door but it was too late; she could practically feel the line drawn down her body by his eyes. "So what if I use it all?" she said gamely. "You're a man—take yours cold."

"Not if I don't have to." She heard rattling around the side of the enclosure. "There's a master valve here, but I'm not sure whether it's for the cold or the hot. I'll give it a few turns . . ."

She threw the door open again and stalked past him to grab the rag they'd told her was her towel. Wrapping it around herself as best she could, she did a double take as she saw him watching her again. "Well?" she said. "What are you waiting for?"

"Huh?"

"Get in there." She crossed her arms and waited. Bryce turned his back to her as he undressed, but she didn't give him any relief. It was her turn to admire. With a sour glance that held more than a little humor, he stepped into the stall.

Venera leaned over to look at the side of the enclosure; there was the valve he'd mentioned. It was momentarily tempting to give a few turns—she could imagine his shouts quite vividly—but no. She was an adult, after all.

She left the enclosure and stepped gingerly over the grillwork floor to the little closet Fin had prepared for her. Despite the stares of those billeted in the hallway, she made her way to where Garth Diamandis lay. He was awake but listless. Still, he half-smiled as he saw her.

"Ah, that you should dress so for me," he murmured.

Venera smoothed the hair back from his brow. "What's wrong?"

He looked away, lips twisting. Then: "It was her. She betrayed me to them."

"Your woman? —Wife? Mistress?"

A heavy sigh escaped him. "My daughter."

Venera stepped back, shocked. For a moment she had no idea what to say, because her whole understanding of this man had been changed in one stroke. "Oh, Garth," she said stupidly. "I'm so sorry." *We daughters will do that,* she thought; but she didn't say it.

She held his hand for a minute until he gently disengaged it and turned on his side. "You must be cold," he said. "Go get some rest." So, reluctantly, she left him on his cot in the hallway.

She mused about this surprising new Garth as she threaded her way back to her sleeping station. It was hard navigating the place; the nation of Fin was less than thirty feet wide at its broadest point. Since it was literally a fin, an aileron for controlling Spyre's spin and direction, the place was streamlined and reinforced inside by crisscrossing girders. The citizens of the pocket nation had built floors and chambers all through the vertical wing and grudgingly added several ladder wells. Where Garth lay was not a corridor as such, however—just a more or less labyrinthine route between the rooms that were strung the length of the level. Privacy was to be had only within the sleeping chambers, where the ever-present roar of air just behind the walls drowned all other sounds.

Fin didn't have the capacity for an extra seventy or so people. Venera had been informed by an impatient Corinne that they must all leave by nightfall. That suited her fine—she had a meeting with the council later today in any case. But she needed to sleep first. So she was grateful for the little bed they'd prepared behind a set of metal cabinets. You had to squeeze around the last cabinet to get in here and there were no windows; still, it had an air of privacy. She rolled out of the towel and under the blanket.

Venera willed herself to sleep, but she was still a mass of nerves from the events of the night. And, she had to admit, there was something else keeping her awake . . .

A blundering noise jolted her into sitting up. She groped for a nonexistent weapon. Somebody was blocking the light that leaked around the cabinets. "Who—"

"Oh, no! You!" Bryce stood there, his nakedness punctuated by the towel at his waist. His hands were on his hips.

Venera snatched up the blanket. "Don't tell me they put you in with me."

"Said there wasn't any room. Last good place was here." He crossed his arms. "Well?"

"Well what?"

"You've had at least fifteen minutes to sleep. My turn."

"Your—?" She reached for one of her boots and threw it at him. "Get out! This is my room!" Bryce ducked adroitly and stepped up, grabbing at her wrist. She rabbit-punched him in the stomach; the only effect was that his towel fell off.

He took advantage of her surprise to make a play for the bed. She managed to keep him from taking it but he did grab the blanket. She pulled it back; she kicked him and he toppled onto the mattress. He sprawled, laying claim to as much of it as he could, and pushed her to the edge.

"No you don't! My bed!" She tried to climb over him, aiming to reconquer the corner, but his hand was on her wrist then her shoulder and her breast and his other gripped the inside of her thigh. Bryce picked her up that way and would have thrown her off the bed if she hadn't squirmed her way loose. She landed straddling him and grabbed for the sheets on either side of his shoulders so when he pushed at her she had a good grip.

He was getting hard against her pubic bone and his hands were on her breasts again. Venera mashed her palm against his face and reared back but now his hands were on her hips and he was pulling her hard against him. They rocked together and she clawed at his chest.

Grabbing him around the shoulders she kissed him, feeling her nipples tease the hairs on his chest. All their movement was making him slide against her wetness and suddenly he was inside her. Venera gasped and reared up, pushing down on him with all her weight.

She leaned forward until they were nose to nose. "My bed," she hissed, grinning.

They were locked together now and each motion by one made the other respond. She had a hand behind his neck and his were behind her spreading her as they kissed and the bed shook and threatened to collapse. She bucked and rode him like the Buridan must have ridden their horses, all pounding muscle under her until wave after wave of pleasure mounted up her core and she came with a loud cry. Moments later he did the same, bouncing her up and nearly off of him. She held on and rode it out, then collapsed on the bellows of his chest.

"See?" he said. "You *can* share."

Well.

Venera wasn't about to dignify his statement with a response; but this was certainly going to change things. Now sleep really was coming over her, though, and she had no ability to think more about it. She nuzzled his shoulder.

Damn it.

THE SPYRE COUNCIL building was satisfyingly grandiose. It sprawled like a well-fed spider over an acre of town-wheel, with outbuildings and annexes like black-roofed legs half-encircling the nearby streets, plazas, and offices of the bureaucracy. The back of the spider was an ornate glass and wrought-iron dome surmounted by an absurdly dramatic black statue of a woman thrusting a sword into the air. The statue must have been thirty feet tall. Venera admired it as she strolled up the broad ramp that led to the council chamber.

She was aware of many eyes watching her. Word had gotten around quickly of the events last night, and Lesser Spyre was quietly but visibly tense. Shops had closed early; people hurried through the streets. The architecture of the spider did not permit large assemblies—Spyre was not the sort of place to encourage mass demonstrations—but the people were a presence here nonetheless, standing in groups of two to ten to twenty on street corners and under the shadowy canopies of bridges. It was their presence, and not memory or reason, that convinced Venera that she had today done something highly significant.

Her own appearance must confirm that. She wore a high-collared black leather coat over a scarlet blouse, with her bleached shock of hair standing straight up and silver trefoil-shaped bangles the size of her hand hanging from her ears. Her makeup was dark—she'd redrawn her brows as two obsessively black lines. Trailing behind her in a V-formation like a flock of grim birds were two dozen people, all similarly startling to look upon. Some appeared pale and unsteady, their faces and exposed hands bearing bruises and burn marks. Others attended these souls, and marching behind like giant tin toys were soldiers of Liris and various preservationist factions. Venera knew that Bryce's people peppered the crowds, there to listen and give an alert if necessary.

"Do you think Jacoby Sarto brings his gun to council meetings?" she asked offhandedly. Corinne, who was walking beside her, guffawed.

"Here," she said, handing Venera a large black pistol, "try to take this in and see what happens. No, seriously. If they don't stop you, then he's probably got one too. You may need to get the drop on him."

"I can do that." She took the pistol and slipped it into her jacket, which promptly dragged down her right collar. She transferred it to the back of her belt.

"Not *too* obvious," said Corinne doubtfully.

A preservationist runner puffed to a stop next to her and saluted. "They're on the move, ma'am. Five groups of a hundred or more each were just seen exiting the grounds of Sacrus. They're in no-man's-land now but they have nowhere to go except through their neighbors. Of course, they own most of those estates . . ."

"What have they got?" she asked. "Artillery?"

He nodded. "We're moving to secure the elevator cables, but they're doing the same thing," he continued. "There's been no shots fired yet . . ."

"All right." She dismissed the details with a wave of her hand. "Let me see what we can do in council. We'll talk after that." He nodded and backed off.

The big front doors of the building were for council members only. The ceremonial guards there, with their plumed helmets and giant muskets, raised their palms solemnly to exclude the people following Venera. She turned and gestured with her chin for them to go around the side; she'd been told there was a second, more-traveled entrance there for diplomats, attachés, and other functionaries. She strode alone into the frescoed portico that half-circled the chamber itself.

The bronze council chamber doors were open and a small crowd was milling there. She recognized the other members; they were just filing in.

Jacoby Sarto was talking to Pamela Anseratte. He looked relaxed. She looked tense. He spotted Venera and, surprisingly, smiled.

"Ah, there you are," he said, strolling over to her. Venera glanced around to see what other people—or pillars or statues to hide behind—were nearby, and started to reach for the pistol. But Sarto simply took her arm and led her a bit to the side of the group.

"The preservationists and lesser countries are following you right now," he said. "But I can't see that continuing, can you? The only leverage you've got is the name of Buridan."

She extricated her arm and smiled back at him. "Well, that depends on the outcome of this meeting, I should think," she said. He nodded affably.

"I'm here to engineer a crisis," he said. "How about you?"

"I should have thought we were already in a crisis," she said cautiously. "Your troops are on the move."

"And we've seized the docks," he said. "But that may not be enough to serve either of our interests." She tried to read his expression, but Sarto was a master politician. He gave no sign that Spyre was balanced on the edge of its greatest crisis in centuries.

"Our interests aren't the same," he continued, "but they're surprisingly . . . compatible. You're after power, but not so much power as you'd have to have if you used the key again. It's difficult—you possess the ultimate weapon but no way to use it to get what you want. But the blunt fact is that as long as we hold the docks, the little trinket you stole from us last night is even worse than useless to you," he said. "It's an active liability."

She stared at him.

Apparently oblivious to her expression, Sarto continued as though he were discussing the budget for municipal plumbing contracts. "On the other hand, the polarization of allegiance you're generating is useful to us. I've been impressed, Ms. Fanning, by your abilities—last night's raid came as a complete surprise, advantageous as it's turned out to be. You got what you wanted, we get what we want, which is to flush out our enemies. The only matter of dispute between us, privately, is that ivory wand you took."

"You want it back?"

He nodded.

"Go fuck yourself!" She started to stalk toward the giant doorway but couldn't resist turning and saying, "You tortured my man Garth! You think this is a game?"

"The only way to win," he said so quietly that the others couldn't hear, "is to treat it as one." Now his expression was serious, his gray eyes cold as a statue's.

It was suddenly clear to Venera that Sacrus already knew what she had been planning to say and do here today—and they approved. She made an excellent enemy for them to rally their own forces around. If they had needed an excuse to extend martial law over their neighbors, she had provided it. If civil war came, they would have their justification for marshaling the ancient Spyre fleet. The civil war would provide a nice smokescreen behind which they could seize Candesce. It wouldn't matter then whether they won or lost back home.

She had given them the enemy they needed. Sarto's candid admission of the fact was a clear overture from him.

Venera hesitated. Then, deliberately clamping down on her anger, she walked back to him. They were now the only council members remaining in the hall. The others had taken their seats, and she saw one or two craning their necks to watch their confrontation.

"What do I get if I return the key?" she asked.

He smiled again. "What you want. Power. For the rest, take your satisfaction by attacking us. We know you'll be sincere. We're counting on it. Only return the key, and at the end of the war you'll get everything you want. You know we can deliver." He held out his hand, palm up.

She laughed lightly, though she felt sick. "I don't have it with me," she said. "And besides, I have no reason to trust you. None at all."

Now Sarto looked annoyed. "We thought you'd say that. You need a guarantee, a token of our sincerity. My masters have . . . instructed me . . . to provide you with one."

She laughed bitterly. "What could you possibly give me that would convince me you were sincere?"

His expression darkened even further; for the first time he looked genuinely angry. Sarto spoke a single word. Venera gaped at him in undisguised astonishment, then laughed again. It was the bray of disdain she reserved for putting people down, and she was sure Sarto knew it.

However, he merely bowed slightly and turned to indicate that she should precede him into the chamber. The doors were wide, and so they entered side by side. As they did so Venera caught sight of Sarto's expression and was amazed. In a few seconds he had undergone a gruesome transformation from the merely dark expression he'd displayed outside to a mask of twisted fury. By the time they split up halfway across the polished marble floor he looked like he was ready to murder someone. Venera kept her own expression neutral, her eyes straight ahead of her as she climbed the red-carpeted steps to the long disused seat of Buridan.

The council members had been chatting, but one by one they fell silent and stared. Several of those were gazes of surprise; although they were masked, the ministers from Oxorn and Garrat were leaning forward in their seats as if unsure whether to run or dive under their chairs. August Virilio's usual expression of polite disdain was gone, in its place a brooding anger that seemed transplanted from an entirely different man.

Pamela Anseratte stood as soon as they were seated, and banged her gavel on a little table. "We were supposed to be gathering today to discuss the change of stewardship of the Spyre docks," she began. "But obviously—"

"*She has started a war!*"

Jacoby Sarto was on his feet before the echoes of his voice died out—and so were the rest of the ministers. For a long moment everyone was talking at once while Anseratte pounded her gavel ineffectually. Then Sarto held up one hand in a magisterial gesture. He gravely hoisted a stack of papers over his head. "I hold the signed declarations in my hand," he rumbled. "This is nothing less than the start of that civil conflict we have all been dreading—an unprovoked, vicious attack in the heartland of Sacrus itself—"

"To rescue those people you kidnapped," Venera said. She remained obstinately in her seat. "Citizens of sovereign states, abducted from their homes by agents of Sacrus."

"Impudence!" roared Sarto. Half the members were still on their feet; in the pillared gallery that opened up behind the council pew, the coteries of ministers, secretaries, courtiers, and generals that each council member held in reserve were glaring at one another and at her. Several clenched the pommels of half-drawn swords.

"I have a partial list of names," continued Venera, "of those we rescued from Sacrus's dungeon last night. They include," she shouted to drown out hecklers from the gallery, "citizens of every nation represented on this council, including Buridan. The council will not deny that I had every right to seek the repatriation of my own kinsman?" She looked around, locking eyes with the unmasked members.

Principe Guinevera's jowls quivered as he thunked solidly into his seat. "You're not going to claim that Sacrus stole one of my citizens? Surely—" He stopped as he saw her scan the list and then hold up her hand.

"Her name is Melissa Ferania," said Venera.

"Ferania, Ferania . . . I know that name . . ." Guinevera's brows knit. "It was a suicide. They never found a body."

Venera smiled. "Well, you'll find her right now if you turn your head." She gestured to the gallery.

The whole council craned their necks to look. People had been filing into the Buridan section of the gallery for several minutes; in the ruckus nobody on the council had noticed.

On cue, Melissa Ferania stood up and bowed to Guinevera.

"Oh my dear, my dear child," he said, tears starting at the corners of his eyes.

"I have more names," said Venera, eyeing Jacoby Sarto. Everyone else was staring into the gallery and he took the opportunity to meet her eye and nod slightly.

Venera felt a sinking sensation in the pit of her stomach.

She had stage-managed this confrontation for maximum effect, calling for volunteers from the recently rescued to attend the scheduled council meeting with her. Garth alone had refused to come; pale and still refusing to talk about his experience in the tower, he had remained outside in the street. But there were prisoners from Liris here as well as half a dozen other minor nations. As her trump card, she had brought people taken from the great nations of the council itself.

Sarto seemed more than unfazed at this tactic. He seemed *satisfied*.

She realized that a black silence had descended on the chamber. Everyone was looking at her. Clearing her throat, she said—her own words sounding distant to herself—"I move for immediate censure of Sacrus and the suspension of its rights on the council of Spyre. Pending, uh . . . pending a thorough investigation of their recent activities."

For once, Pamela Anseratte looked out of her depth. "Ah . . . what?" She pulled her gaze back from the gallery.

August Virilio laughed. "She wants us to expel Sacrus. A marvelous idea if I do say so myself—however impractical it may be."

Venera rallied herself. She shrugged. "Gain a seat, lose a seat . . . besides," she said more loudly, "it's a matter of justice."

Virilio toyed with a pen. "Maybe. Maybe—but Buridan forgot its own declaration of war before it invaded Sacrus. That nullifies your moral high ground, my dear."

"It doesn't nullify *them*." She swept her arm to indicate the people behind her.

"Yes, marvelous grandstanding," said Virilio drily. "No doubt the majority of our council members are properly shocked at your revelation. Yet we must deal with practicalities. Sacrus is too important to Spyre to be turfed off the council for these misdemeanors, however serious they may seem. In fact, Jacoby Sarto was just now leveling some serious charges against *you*."

There was more shouting and hand waving—and yet, for a few moments, it seemed to Venera as though she were alone in the room with Jacoby Sarto. She looked to him, and he met her gaze. All expression had drained from his face.

When he opened his mouth again it would be to reveal her true identity to these people: he would name her as Venera Fanning and the sound of her name would act like a vast hand, toppling the whole edifice she had built. Though most of her allies knew or suspected she was an imposter, it had been neither polite nor expedient for them to admit it. If forced to admit what they already knew, however, they would find her the perfect person to blame for the impending war. All her allies would desert her, or if they didn't at least they would cease listening to her. Sarto had the power to cast her out, have her imprisoned . . . if she didn't counter with her own bombshell.

This was the great gamble she had known she would have to take if she came here today. She had rehearsed it in her mind over and over: Sarto would reveal that she was the notorious Venera Fanning, who was implicated in dastardly scandals in the principalities. Opinion would turn against her and so, in turn, she would have to tell the people of Spyre another great secret. She would reveal the existence of the key to Candesce and declare that it was the cause of the coming war—a war engineered by Sacrus for its own convenience.

And now the moment had come. Sarto blinked slowly, looked away from her, and said, "I have here my own list. It is a list of innocent civilians killed last night by Amandera Thrace-Guiles and her men."

Braced as she was for one outcome, it took Venera some seconds to understand what Sarto had said. He had called her *Amandera Thrace-Guiles*. He was not going to reveal her secret.

And in return, he expected her not to reveal his.

The council members were shouting; Guinevera was embracing his long-lost countrywoman and weeping openly; August Virilio had his arms crossed as he stared around in obvious disgust. Swords had been drawn in the gallery and the ceremonial guards were rushing to do their job for the first time in their lives. Abject, shoulders slumped, Pamela Anseratte stood with gesturing people and words swirling around her, her hand holding a slip of paper that might have been her original agenda for the meeting.

It all felt distant and half-real to Venera. She had to make a decision, right now.

Jacoby Sarto's eyes were drilling into her.

She cleared her throat, hesitated one last second, and reached behind her.

17

TREBLE WAS A musician by day and a member of Bryce's underground by night. He'd always known that he might be called upon to abandon his façade of serene artistry and fight in the cause—though like some of the others in the secret organization, he was uneasy with the direction things had taken lately. Bryce was becoming altogether too cozy with the imposing Amandera Thrace-Guiles.

Not that it mattered anymore, as of this minute. Clinging to a knuckle of masonry high on the side of the Lesser Spyre Ministry of Justice, Treble was in an ideal position to watch the city descend into anarchy.

Treble had gained access to the building disguised as a petitioner seeking information about an imprisoned relative. His assignment was to plant some false records in a Ministry file cabinet on the twelfth floor. He evaded the guards adroitly, made his way up the creaking stairs with no difficulty, and had just ensconced himself in the records office when two things happened simultaneously: the staccato sound of gunfire echoed in through the half-open window; and three minor bureaucrats approached the office, talking and laughing loudly.

This was why Treble found himself clutching a rounded chunk of masonry that might once have been a gargoyle, and why he was staring in fascination at the streets that lay below and wrapped up and around the ring of the town-wheel. He hardly knew where to look. Little puffs of smoke were appearing around the Spyre docks directly overhead. The buildings there hovered in midair like child's toys floating in a bathtub and seldom moved; now several were gliding slowly—and ominously—on collision courses. Several ships had cast off. Meanwhile, halfway up the curve of the wheel, some other commotion had sprung up around the Buridan estate. Barnacled as it was by other buildings, he could never have identified the place had he not been familiar with the layout but it was clearly the source of that tall pillar of smoke that stood up two hundred feet before bending over and wrapping itself in a fading spiral around and around the inner space of the wheel.

People were running in the avenue below. Ever the conscientious spy, Treble shifted his position so that he straddled the masonry. He checked his watch, then pulled out a frayed notebook and a stub pencil. He dabbed the pencil on the tip of his tongue then squinted around.

Item one: at four-fourteen o'clock, the preservationists broke our agreement by attempting to prevent Sacrus from occupying the docks. At least, that was what Treble assumed was happening. The hastily scrawled note from Bryce that had mobilized the resistance told of arguments during the Sacrus raid last night, hasty plans made and discarded in the heat of the moment. Thrace-Guiles wanted to rally the nations of Greater Spyre that had lost people to Sacrus. The preservationists had their own agenda, which involved cowing Sacrus into letting them run a railway line through the middle of the great nation's lands. Sacrus itself was moving and activating its allies. So much was clear; but in the background of this fairly clear political situation, a greater upheaval was taking place.

Bryce had said on more than one occasion that Spyre was like the mainspring of a watch wound too tight. A single tap in the right place might cause a vicious uncoiling—a *snap*. Many in Spyre had read about the Pantry War with envy; over centuries a thousand resentments and grudges had built up between the pocket nations and it was glorious to watch someone else finally try to settle a score. Everyone kept ledgers accounting who had slighted whom and when. Nothing was forgotten and behind their ivy-and-moss-softened walls, the monarchs and presidents of nations little bigger than swimming pools spent their lives plotting their revenges.

The well-planned atrocities of the resistance were little trip-hammer blows on the watch's case, each one an attempt to break the mechanism. Tap the watch, shake it, and listen. Tap it again. That had been Bryce's strategy.

Sacrus and Buridan had hit the sweet spot. Shopfronts were slamming all over the place, like air-clams caught in a beam of sunlight, while gangs of men carrying truncheons and knives seemed to materialize like smoke out of the alleys. It was time for a settling of scores.

Item two: chaos in the streets. Maybe time to distribute currency?

Treble peered at the line of smoke coiling inside the wheel. *Item three: Sacrus seems to have had more agents in place in the city than we thought. They appear to be moving against Buridan without council approval. So . . . Item four: council no longer effective?*

He underlined the last sentence, then thought better and crossed it out. Obviously the council was no longer in control.

He leaned over and examined the flagstoned street a hundred feet below. Some of those running figures were recognizable. In fact . . .

Was that Amandera Thrace-Guiles? He shaded his eyes against Candesce's fire and looked again. Yes, he recognized the shock of bleached hair that surmounted her head. She was hurrying along the avenue with one arm raised to shoulder height. Apparently she was aiming a pistol at the man walking ahead of her. Oh that was definitely her then.

Around her a mob swirled. Treble recognized some of his compatriots; there were others, assorted preservationists, soldiers of minor nations, even one or two council guards. Were they escorting Thrace-Guiles or protecting someone else Treble hadn't spotted?

Item five: council meeting ended around four o'clock.

He sighted in the direction Thrace-Guiles's party was taking. They were headed for the Buridan estate. From ground level they probably couldn't tell that place was besieged. At this rate they might walk right into a crowd of Sacrus soldiers.

Treble could still hear voices in the room behind him. He tapped the file folder in his coat pocket and frowned. Then with a shrug he swung off his masonry perch and through the opened window.

The three bureaucrats stared at him in shock. Treble felt the way he did when he dropped a note in performance; he grinned apologetically, said, "Here, file this," and tossed his now-redundant folder to one of the men. Then he ran out the door and made for the stairs.

GARTH DIAMANDIS STAGGERED and reached out to steady himself against the wall of a building. He had to keep up; Venera Fanning was striding in great steps along the avenue, her pistol held unwaveringly to Jacoby Sarto's head. But Garth was confused; people were running and shouting while overhead even lines of smoke divided the sky. This was Lesser Spyre, he was sure of that. The granite voice of his interrogator still echoed in Garth's mind, though, and his arms and legs bellowed pain from the many burns and cuts that ribbed them.

He had insisted on coming today and now he regretted it. Once upon a time he'd been a young man and able to bounce back from anything. Not so anymore. The gravity here weighed heavily on him and for the first time he wished he was back on Greater Spyre where he could still climb trees like a boy. Alone all those years, he had reached an accommodation with himself and his past; there'd been days when he enjoyed himself as if he really were a youth again. And then the woman who now stalked down the center of the avenue ahead of him had appeared, like a burning cross in the sky, and proceeded to turn his solitary life upside down.

He'd thought about abandoning Venera dozens of times. She was self-reliance personified, after all. She wouldn't miss him. Once or twice he had gotten as far as stepping out the door of the

Buridan estate. Looking down those half-familiar, secretive streets, he had realized that he had nowhere to go—nowhere, that is, unless he could find Selene, the daughter of the woman whose love had caused Garth's exile.

Logic told him that now was the time. Venera was bound to lose this foolish war she'd started with Sacrus. The prudent course for Garth would be to run and hide, lick his wounds in secret and then . . .

Ah. It was this *and then* that was the problem. He had found Selene, and she had turned him over to Sacrus. She was theirs—a recruit, like the ones Moss claimed had left many of Spyre's sovereign lands. Sacrus had promised Selene something, had lied to her; they must have. But Garth was too old to fight them and too old to think of all the clever and true words that might win his daughter's heart.

Selene, his kin, had betrayed him. And Venera Fanning, who owed him nothing, had risked her life to save his.

He pushed himself off from the wall and struggled to catch up to her.

A man ran down the broad steps of the Justice ministry. He waved his arms over his head. "Don't go that way! Not safe!"

Venera paused and glanced at him. "You're one of Bryce's."

"That I am, Miss Thrace-Guiles." Garth half-smiled at the man's bravado; these democrats refused to address people by their titles. Venera didn't seem to notice, and they had a hurried conversation that Garth couldn't hear.

"There you are." He turned to find the preservationist, Thinblood, sauntering up behind him. He grinned at Garth. "You ran off like a startled hare when she came out of the council chamber."

Garth grunted. Thinblood seemed to have decided he was an old man who needed coddling. It was annoying. He had to admit to himself that it was a relief to have him here, though. The rest of this motley party consisted mostly of Venera's other freed prisoners and they made for bad company, for much the same reasons as Garth supposed he did. They all looked apprehensive and tired. It didn't help that their presence at council didn't seem to have made a dent in Sacrus's support.

Garth and Thinblood had been talking under an awning across the street when Venera Fanning appeared at the official's entrance to the council chamber. She backed out slowly, her posture strange. As she emerged further it became clear that she was holding a gun and aiming it at someone. That someone had turned out to be Jacoby Sarto.

Before he knew it Garth was by her side. "What are you doing?" he heard himself shouting. She'd merely grimaced and kept backing up.

"Things didn't go our way," she'd said. Past Sarto, the council guards were lining up with their rifles aimed at her. At the same time, the commoner's doors around the long curve of the building were thrown open. A hoard of people spilled out, some of them fighting openly. Venera's supporters ran to her side as Bryce's agents appeared from nowhere to act as crowd control. And then a gasp went up from the watching crowd as Principe Guinevera and Pamela Anseratte pushed the council guards aside and came to stand at Venera's side.

"The lines have been drawn," Anseratte said to the council guards. "Sacrus is not on the council's side. Stand down."

Reluctantly, the guards lowered their rifles.

Garth leaned close to Venera. "Did he tell them your . . . secret?" But she shook her head.

Maybe it was having Thinblood's reassuring hand on his shoulder, but as Venera argued now with Bryce's spy, the fog of fatigue and pain lifted enough for Garth to begin to wonder about that. Jacoby Sarto had not told the council who Venera really was? That made no sense. Right now Amandera Thrace-Guiles was the darling of the old countries. She was the resurrected victim of Sacrus's historical arrogance; she was a champion. If Sarto wanted to deflate Sacrus's opposition all he had to do was reveal that she was a fake.

"Why did she do it?" he wondered aloud. Thinblood laughed.

"You're trying to second-guess our Amandera?" He shook his head. "She's got too much fire in her blood, that's clear enough. Obviously she saw a chance to take Sarto and she went with it."

Garth shook his head. "The woman I know wouldn't see Sarto as a prize to be taken. She'd think him a burden and be happy to be rid of him. And if he's a prisoner why doesn't he seem more concerned?" Sarto was standing with his arms crossed, waiting patiently for Venera to finish her conversation. He seemed more to be with her than taken by her. Garth seemed to be the only who had noticed this.

"Attention!" Venera raised her pistol and for a moment he thought she was about to fire off a round. She already had the attention of everyone in sight, though, and seemed to realize it. "Buridan is under siege!" she cried. "Our ancient house is surrounded by Sacrus's people. We can't go back there."

Garth hurried over. "What are we going to do? They've moved faster than we anticipated."

She nodded grimly. "Apparently their ground forces are moving to surround the elevator cables. —The ones they can get to, that is."

"Most of our allies are on Greater Spyre," he said. If Sacrus isolated them up here in the city, they would have to rely on the preservationists, and a few clear-headed leaders such as Moss, to organize the forces down there.

For a moment that thought filled Garth with hope. If Venera was sidelined at this stage, she might be able to avoid being drawn into the heart of the coming conflagration. A checkmated Buridan might survive with honor, no matter who won.

Clearly Venera had no intention of going down that road. "We need to get down there," she was saying. "Sacrus doesn't control all the elevators. Pamela, your country's line, where is it?"

Anseratte shook her head. "It's two wheels away from here. We might make it, but if Sacrus already has men in the streets they've probably taken the axis cable cars as well."

Guinevera shook his head too. "Our line comes down about a mile from Carrangate. They're an old ally of Sacrus. They could use us for target practice on our way down."

"What about Liris?" It was one of Moss's men, standing alertly with a proud look in his eye. "Lady, we are the only nation in Spyre that has recently fought a war. There may not be many of us, but . . ."

She turned a dazzling smile on the man. "Thank you. Yes—but your elevator is above the Fair, isn't it?"

"And the Fair, m'lady, is six blocks up the wheel, that way." He pointed off to the left.

"This way!" Venera gestured for Sarto to precede her, then stalked toward the distant pile of buttresses and roofs that was the Fair.

Garth followed, but as the fog of exhaustion and pain slowly lifted from him he found himself considering their chances. It was folly for Venera to involve herself in this war. Sidelined, she might be safe.

Sacrus had known what to reveal about her to draw her fangs, but they had chosen not to reveal it. The only person on this side of the conflict who knew was Garth himself. If word got out, Venera would naturally assume that it was Sacrus's doing. It would be so simple . . .

Troubled but determined to follow this thought to its conclusion, Garth put an extra effort into his footsteps and kept up with Venera as she made for the Fair.

LIRIS PERCHED ON the very lip of the abyss. At sunoff the building's roof was soaked with light, all gold and purple and rose. The sky that opened beyond the battlement was open to all sides; Venera could almost imagine that she was back in the provinces of Meridian, where the town-wheels were small and manageable and you could fly through the free air whenever you chose. She leaned out, the better to lose herself in the radiance.

Tents had been set up on the rooftop behind her, and Moss was holding court to a wild variety of Spyre dignitaries. They came in all shapes and sizes, masked and unmasked, lords and ladies and diplomats and generalissimos. United by their fear of Sacrus and its allies, they were hastily assembling a battle plan while their tiny armies traveled here from across Greater Spyre. Venera had looked for those armies earlier—but who could spot a dozen men here or there making their way between the mazelike walls of the estates?

It would be an eerie journey, she knew. Garth had shown her the overgrown gates to estates whose windows were slathered with black paint, whose occupants had not been seen in generations. Smoke drifted from their chimneys; someone was home. The soldiers of her alliance might stop at one or two of those gateways and shout and rattle the iron, hoping to find allies within. But there would be no answer, unless it be a rifle shot from behind a wall.

For the first time in days, Venera found herself idle. She was too tired to look for something to do, and so as she gazed out at the endless skies that familiar deep melancholy stole over her. This time, she let it happen.

She wanted Chaison back. It was time to admit it. There were many moments every day when Venera longed to turn to him and grin, and say, "Look what I did!" or "Have you ever seen anything like it?" She'd had such a moment only an hour ago, as the first of the Dali horses were led into their new paddock in the far corner of Liris's lot. The spindly steeds had been trained to be ridden and she had mounted up herself and trotted one in a circle. Oh, she'd wanted to catch someone's eye at that moment! But she was Amandera Thrace-Guiles now. There was no one to appeal to, not even Garth, who had been making himself scarce since their arrival.

She heard a footstep behind her. Bryce leaned on the stones and casually reached out to take her hand. She almost snatched it back, but his touch awoke something in her. This was not the man she wanted; but there was some value in him wanting her. She smiled at him.

"All the pawns and knights are in play," he said. His thumb rubbed the back of her hand. "It's our opponent's move. What would you like to do while we wait?"

Venera's pulse quickened. His strong fingers were kneading her hand now, almost painfully.

"Uh . . . ," she said, then before she could talk herself out of it, "they've given me an actual room this time."

"Well." He smiled ironically. "That's an honor. Let's go try it out."

He walked toward the stairs. Venera hesitated, turning to look out at the dimming sky. No: the pang was still there, and no amount of time with Bryce was going to make it go away. But what was she to do?

Venera followed him down the stairs, her excitement mounting. Several people hailed her but she simply waved and hurried past. "This way," she said, grabbing Bryce's arm as he made to descend the main stairs. She dragged him through a doorway hidden behind a faded tapestry. This led to a narrow and dusty little corridor with several doors leading off of it. Hers was at the end.

She barely had time to open the door before his arms were around her waist. He kissed her with passionate force and together they staggered back to the bed under its little pebbled-glass window.

"Shut the door!" she gasped, and as he went to comply she undid her blouse. As he knelt on the bed she guided his hand under the silk. They kept their mouths locked together as they undressed one another, then she took his cock in her hands and didn't let go as they sank back onto the cushions.

Later as they sprawled across the demolished bed, he turned to her and said, "Are we partners?"

Venera blinked at him for a moment. Her mind had been entirely elsewhere—or, more exact, nowhere. "What?"

He shrugged onto his side and his hand casually fell on her hip. "Am I your employee? Or are we pursuing parallel interests?"

"Oh. Well, that's your decision, isn't it?"

"Hmm." He smiled, but she could tell he wasn't satisfied with that reply. "My people have been acting as your spies for the past few days. They're not happy about it. Truth to tell, Amandera, I'm not happy about it."

"Aaahhh . . ." She stretched and leaned back. "So the past hour was your way of softening me up for this conversation?"

"Well, no, but if there's going to be a good strategic moment to raise the issue, this has got to be it." She laughed at his audacity. He was no longer smiling, though.

"You'd be mistaken if you thought I was picking sides in this war," he said. "I don't give a damn whether it's Sacrus or your faction that wins. It's still titled nobles and it'll make no difference to the common people."

Now she sat up. "You want your printing press."

"I have my printing press. I forged your signature on some orders and it was delivered yesterday. Those of my people who aren't in the field right now are running it. Turning out bills by the thousands."

She examined his face in the candlelight. "So . . . how many of your people really are in the field?"

"A half-dozen."

"You told me they were all out!" She glared at him as a spasm of pain shot up her jaw. "A half-dozen? Is this why we had no warning that the estate was being attacked? Because you were keeping a handful of people where they'd be visible to me? —So I'd think they were all out?"

"That's about the size of it, yes."

She punched him in the chest. "You lost me my estate! My house! What else have you given to Sacrus?"

"Sacrus is not my affair," he said. Bryce was deadly earnest now. Clearly she had misjudged him. "Restoring emergent democracy in Virga is my only interest," he said. "But I don't want you to die in this war, and I'm sorry about your house if it's any consolation. But what choice did I have? If everything descends into chaos, when am I going to get my ink? My paper? When were you going to do what I needed you to do? Look me in the eye and tell me it was a priority for you."

Venera groaned. "Oh, Bryce. This is the worst possible time . . ."

"—The only time I have!"

"All right, all right, I see your point." She glowered at the plaster ceiling. "What if . . . what if I send some of my people in to run the press? We don't need trained insurgents to do that. All I want is to get your people out in the field! I'll give you as much ink and paper as you want."

He flopped onto his back. "I'll think about that."

There was a brief silence.

"You could have asked," she said.

"I did!"

Venera was trying to think of some way to reply to that when there was a loud bang and she found herself inside a storm of glass, shouting in surprise and trying to jump out of the way, banging her chin while shards like claws scrawled up her ribs and along her thigh.

Scratched and stunned, she sat up to find herself on the floor. Bryce was kneeling next to her. The candle had gone out and she sensed rather than saw the carpet of broken glass between her and her boots. The little window gaped, the leading bent and twisted to let in a puff of cold night air. "What was . . ." Now she heard gunfire.

"Oh shit." Bryce stood up and reached down to draw her to her feet. "We've got to get out there.

"Sacrus has arrived."

18

THERE WAS STILL a splinter in the ball of her foot but Venera had no time to find it and dig it out. She and Bryce raced up the stairs to the roof as shouts and thundering feet began to sound on the steps below.

They reached the roof and Bryce immediately ran off somewhere to the right. "I need to get to the semaphore!" he shouted before disappearing into the gloom. All the lanterns had been put out, Venera realized; she could just see the silhouettes of the tents where her people had been meeting. The black cutout shapes of men roved to and fro and she made out the gleam of a rifle barrel here and there. It was strangely quiet, though.

She found the flap to the main tent, more by instinct than anything else, and stepped in. Lanterns were still lit here, and Thinblood, Pamela Anseratte, Principe Guinevera, Moss, and the other leaders were all standing around a map table. They all looked over as she entered.

"Ah, there you are," said Guinevera in a strangely jovial tone. "We think we know what they're up to."

She moved over to the table to look at the map. Little counters representing Sacrus's forces were scattered around the unrolled rectangle of Greater Spyre. A big handful of tokens was clustered at the very edge of the sheet, where Liris had its land.

"It's an insane amount of men," said Thinblood. He appeared nervous. "We think over a thousand. Never seen anything like it in Spyre."

Guinevera snorted. "Obviously they hope to capture our entire command all at once and end the war before it begins. And it looks like they stand a good chance of succeeding. What do you think, Venera?"

"Well, I—" She froze.

They were all staring at her. All silent.

Guinevera reached into his brocaded coat and drew out a sheet of paper. With shocking violence he slammed it down on the table in front of her. Venera found herself looking at a poor likeness of herself—with her former hairstyle—on a poster that said, WANTED FOR EXTRADITION TO GEHELLEN, VENERA FANNING.

"So it's true," said Guinevera. His voice was husky with anger, and his hand, still flattening the poster, was shaking.

She chewed her lip and tried to stare him down. "This is hardly the time—"

"This *is* the time!" he bellowed. "You have *started a war!*"

"Sacrus started it," she said. "They started it when they—"

But he struck her full across the face and she spun to the floor.

She tasted blood in her mouth. Where was Bryce? Why wasn't Moss rushing to her defense?

Why wasn't Chaison here?

Guinevera reared over her, his dense mass making her flinch back. "Don't try to blame others for what you've done! You brought this catastrophe on us, imposter! I say we hang her over the battlement and let Sacrus use her for target practice." He reached down to take her arm as Venera scrambled to get her feet under her.

Light knifed through the tent's entrance flap and then miraculously the whole tent lifted up as though tugged off the roof by a giant. The giant's cough was still echoing in Venera's ears as the tent sailed into the permanent maelstrom at the edge of the world and was snatched away like a torn kerchief.

Another bright explosion, and everyone ducked. Then they were all running and shouting at once and soldiers were popping up to fire their blunderbusses then squatting to refill them as trails of smoke and fire corkscrewed overhead. Venera's ears were still ringing, everything strangely aloof as she stood up and watched

the big map on the table lift in the sudden breeze and slide horizontally into the night.

Who had it been? she wondered dimly. Had Moss turned on
her? Or had Odess said something injudicious? Probably some
soldier or servant of Liris had spoken out of turn . . . But then,
maybe Jacoby Sarto had become bored of his confinement and
decided to liven things up a bit.

Venera was half-aware that the squat cube of Liris was surrounded on three sides by an arcing constellation of torches. The
red light served to illuminate the grim faces of the soldiers rushing past her. She raised her hand to stop one of them, then thought
better of it. What if Guinevera had remembered to order her
arrest? —Or death? As she thought about her new situation, Venera began to be afraid.

Maybe she should go inside. Liris had stout walls, and she
still had friends there—she was almost sure of that. She could,
what—go chat with Jacoby Sarto in his cell?

And where was Bryce? Semaphore, that was it; he'd gone to
send a semaphore. She forced herself to think: the semaphore station was over there . . . where a big gap now yawned in the side
of the battlement. Some soldiers were laying planks across it.

"Oh no." No no no.

Deep inside Venera a quiet snide voice that had always been
there was saying, "Of course, of course. They all abandon you in
the end." She shouldn't be surprised at this turn of events; she had
even planned for it, in the days following her confirmation. It
shouldn't come as a shock to her. So it seemed strange to watch
herself, as if from outside, as she hunkered down next to the elevator mechanism at the center of the roof, and wrapped her arms
around herself and cried.

I don't do this. She wiped at her face. I don't.

Maybe she did, though; she couldn't clearly remember those
minutes in Candesce after she had killed Aubri Mahallan and she
had been alone. Hayden Griffin had pulled Mahallan's body out of
sight, leaving a few bright drops of blood to twirl in the weightless

air. Griffin was her only way out of Candesce, and Venera had just killed his lover. It hardly mattered that she'd done it to save the world from Mahallan and her allies. No one would ever know, and she was certain she would die there; she had only to wait for Candesce to open its fusion eyes and bring morning to the world.

Griffin had asked her to come with him. He had said he wouldn't kill her; Venera hadn't believed him. It was too big a risk. In the end she had snuck after him and ridden out of Candesce on the cargo net he was towing. Now the thought of running to the stairs and throwing herself on the mercy of her former compatriots filled her with a similar dread. Better to make herself very small here and risk being found by Guinevera or his men than to find out that even Liris now rejected her.

"There they are!" Someone pointed excitedly. Staccato runs of gunfire sounded in the distance—they were oddly distant, in fact. If Venera had cared about anything at that moment she might have stood up to look.

"We're gonna outflank them!"

Something blew up on the outskirts of Liris's territory. The orange mushroom lit the whole world for a moment, a flicker of estates and ornamental ponds overhead. Her ground forces must have made it here just after Sacrus's.

Well. Not my forces, she thought bitterly. *Not anymore.*

"There she is!" Venera jerked and tried to back up but she was already pressed against the elevator platform. A squat silhouette reared up in front of her and something whipped toward her. She cringed. Nothing happened; after a moment she looked up.

An open hand hovered a few inches above her. A distant flicker of red lit the extended hand and behind it, the toadish features of Samson Odess. His broad face wore an expression of concern. "Venera, are you hurt?"

"N-no . . ." Suspiciously, she reached to take his hand. He drew her to her feet and draped an arm across her shoulder.

"Quickly now," he said as he drew her toward the stairs. "While everyone's busy."

"What—" She was having trouble finding words. "What are you doing?"

He stopped, reared back, and stared at her. "I'm taking you home."

"Home? Whose home?"

"Yours, you silly woman. Liris."

"But why are you helping me?"

Now he looked annoyed. "You never ceased to be a citizen of Liris, Venera. And technically, I never stopped being your boss. You're still my responsibility, you know. Come on."

She paused at the top of the steps and looked around. The soldiers who had crowded the roof all seemed to be leaping off one side, in momentary silhouetted flashes showing an arm brandishing a blunderbuss, another waving a sword. There was fighting down in the bramble-choked lot that surrounded Liris. Farther out, she glimpsed squads of men running back and forth, some piling up debris to form barricades, others raising archaic weapons.

"Venera! Get off the roof!" She blinked and turned to follow Odess.

They descended several levels and Venera found herself entering, of all places, the apartments of the former botanist. The furniture and art that had borne the stamp of Margit of Sacrus was gone, and there were still burn marks on the walls and ceiling. Someone had moved in new couches and chairs, and one particularly charred wall was covered with a crepuscular tapestry depicting cherry trees shooting beams of light all over an idealized tableau of dryads and fairies.

Venera sat down under a dryad and looked around. Eilen was there with the rest of the diplomatic corps. "Bring a blanket," said Odess, "and a stiff drink. She's in shock." Eilen ran to fetch a comforter and somebody else shoved a tumbler of amber liquid into Venera's hand. She stared at it for a moment, then drank.

For a few minutes she listened without comprehension to their conversation; then as if a switch had been thrown somewhere inside her, she realized where she must be and she understood something. She looked at Odess. "This is your new office," she said.

They all stopped talking. Odess came to sit next to her. "That's right," he said. "The diplomatic corps has been exalted since you left."

Eilen laughed. "We're the new stars of Liris! Not that the cherry trees are any less important, but—"

"Moss understands that we need to open up to the outside world," interrupted Odess. "It could never have happened under Margit."

Venera half-smiled. "I suppose I can take some credit for making that possible."

"My dear lady!" Odess patted her hand. "The credit is all yours! Liris has come alive again because of you. You don't think we would abandon you in your hour of need, do you?"

"You will always have a place here," said Eilen.

Venera started to cry.

"WE WOULD NEVER have told," Odess said a few minutes later. "None of us."

Venera grimaced. She stood at a mirror where she was dabbing at her eyes, trying to erase the evidence of tears. She didn't know what had come over her. A momentary madness; at least it was only the Lirisians who had witnessed her little breakdown. "I suppose it was Sarto," she said. "It hardly matters now. I can't show my face up there without Guinevera putting a bullet in me."

Odess hmmphed, wrapping his arms around his barrel chest and pacing. "Guinevera has impressed no one since he arrived. Why should any of your other allies listen to him?"

She turned, raising an eyebrow. "Because he's the ruler of a council nation?"

Odess made a flicking motion. "Aside from that."

With a shake of her head Venera returned to the divan. She

could hear gunfire and shouting through the opened window, but it was filtered through the roar of the world-edge winds that tumbled above the courtyard shaft. You could almost ignore it.

In similar fashion, Venera could almost ignore the emotions overflowing her. She'd always survived through keeping a cool head and this was no time to have that desert her. It was inconvenient that she felt so abandoned and lost. Inconvenient to feel so grateful for the simple company of her former coworkers. She needed to recover her poise, then act in her own interests as she always had before.

There was a commotion in the corridor, then someone burst through the doors. He was covered in soot and dust, his hair a shock, the left arm of his jacket in tatters.

Venera leaped to her feet. "Garth!"

"There you are!" He rushed over and hugged her fiercely. "You're alive!"

"I'm—oof! Fine. But what happened to you?"

He stepped back, keeping his hands on her arms. Garth had a crazed look in his eye she'd never seen before. He wouldn't meet her gaze. "I was looking for you," he said. "Outside. The rest of them, they're all out there, fighting around the foot of the building. Sacrus has ringed us, they want something here very badly, and our relief force is trying to break through from the outside. So Anseratte and Thinblood are leading the Liris squads in an attempt to break out—make a corridor . . ."

Venera nodded. The irony was that this fight was almost certainly about her, but Anseratte and the others wouldn't know it. Sacrus wanted the key and they knew Venera was here. Naturally they would throw whatever they had at Liris to get it.

If Guinevera had thrown her over the walls half an hour ago, the battle would already be over.

Garth toyed with the ripped fringe of his coat for a moment, then burst out with, "Venera, I am so, so sorry!"

"What?" She shook her head, uncomprehending. "Things aren't

so bad. Or do you mean . . . ?" She thought of Bryce, who might be lying twisted and broken at the foot of the wall. "Oh," she said, a twisting feeling running through her.

He had just opened his mouth—doubtless to tell her that Bryce was dead—when the noises outside changed. The gunfire, which had been muffled with distance and indirection, suddenly sounded loud and close. Shouts and screams rang through the open windows.

Venera ran over, and with Odess and Eilen craned her neck to look up the shaft of the courtyard. There were people on the roof.

She and Odess exchanged a look. "Are those our . . . ?" she started to say, but the answer was clear.

"Sacrus is inside the walls!" The cry was taken up by the others and everyone ran for the doors, streaming past Garth Diamandis, who was speaking but inaudible through the jumble of shouts.

Venera paused long enough to shrug at him, then grabbed his arm and hauled him after her into the corridor.

The whole population of Liris was running up the stairs. They carried pikes, kitchen knives, makeshift shields, and clubs. None had on more than the clothing they normally wore, but that meant they were formidably armored. There were one or two soldiers in the mix—probably the men who had been guarding Jacoby Sarto. They were frantically trying to keep order in the pushing mass of people.

Garth stared at the crowd and shook his head. "We'll never get through that."

Venera eyed the window. "I have an idea."

As she slung her leg over the lintel Garth poked his head out next to her and looked up. "It's risky," he said. "Somebody could just kick us off before we can get to our feet."

"In this gravity, you're looking at a sprained ankle. Come on." She climbed rapidly, emerging from the stairs into the light of flares and the sound of gunfire. Half the country was struggling with something at the far end of the roof. Venera blinked and squinted, and realized what it was: they were trying to dislodge a stout ladder that had been swung against the battlements. Even as that came clear to her, she saw the gray cross-hatch of another emerge from the darkness to thud against the stonework.

Withering fire from below prevented the Lirisians from getting near the things. They were forced to crouch a few feet back and poke at them with their pikes.

A third ladder appeared and now men were swarming onto the roof. The Lirisians stood up. Venera saw Eilen raise a rusted old sword as a figure in red-painted iron armor reared above her.

Venera raised her pistol and fired. She walked toward Eilen, firing steadily until the man who'd threatened her friend fell. He wasn't dead—his armor was so thick that the bullets probably hadn't penetrated—but she'd rattled his skull for sure.

She was five feet away when her pistol clicked empty. This was the gun Corinne had given her; she had no idea whether it took the same caliber of bullets as anything the Lirisians used. Examining it quickly, she decided she didn't even know how to breech it to check. At that moment two men like metal beetles surmounted the battlement, firelight glistening off their carapaces.

She tripped Eilen and when the woman had fallen behind her Venera stepped between her and the two men. She drop-kicked the leader and he windmilled his arms for a moment before falling back. The force of her kick had propelled Venera back ten feet. She landed badly, located Eilen, and shouted, "Come on!"

Moss straight-armed a pike into the helmet of the other man. Beside him Odess shoved a lighted torch at a third who was stepping off the ladder. Gunfire sounded and somebody fell but she couldn't see who through the press of bodies.

She grabbed Eilen's arm. "We need guns! Are there more in the lockers?"

Eilen shook her head. "We barely had enough for the soldiers. There's that." She pointed.

Around the corner of the courtyard shaft, the ancient, filigreed morning gun still sat on a tripod under its little canopy. Venera started to laugh but the sound died in her throat. "Come on!"

The two women wrestled the weapon off its stand. It was a massive thing and though it weighed little in this gravity it was difficult to maneuver. "Do we have shells?" Venera asked.

"Bullets, no shells," said Eilen. "There's black powder in that bin."

Venera opened the gun's breech. It was of a pointlessly primitive design. You poured black powder into it and then inserted the bullet and closed the breech. It had a spark wheel instead of a percussion trigger. "Well, then, come on."

Eilen grabbed up the box of bullets and a sack of powder and they ran along the inner edge of the roof. In the darkness and confusion Eilen stumbled, and Venera watched as the bullets spilled out into the air over the courtyard. Eilen screamed in frustration.

One bullet spun on the flagstones at Venera's feet. Cradling the gun, she bent to pick up the metal slug. A wave of cold prickles swept over her shoulders and up her neck.

This bullet was identical to the one that nestled inside her jacket—identical save for the fact that it had never been fired.

The bullet she carried—that had sailed a thousand miles through the airs and clouds of Virga, avoiding cities and farms, adeptly swerving to avoid fish and rocks and oceanic balls of water—this bullet that had lined up on Slipstream and the city of Rush and the window in the admiralty where Venera stood so innocently; had smashed the glass in a split-second and buried itself in her jaw, spinning her around and nailing a sense of injured outrage to Venera forever—it had come from here. It had not been fired in combat. Not in spite. Not for any murderous purpose, but for tradition, and to celebrate the calmness of a morning like any other.

Venera had fantasized about this moment many times. She had rehearsed what she would say to the owner of the gun when she finally found him. It was a high, grand, and glorious speech that, in her imagination, always ended with her putting a bullet in the villain. Cradling this picture of revenge to herself had gotten her through many nights, many cocktail parties where out of the corner of her eye she could see the ladies of the admiralty pointing to her scar and murmuring to one another behind their fans.

"Huh," she said.

"Venera? Are you all right?"

Venera shook her head violently. "Powder. Quick!" She held out the gun and Eilen filled it. Then she jammed the clean new bullet into the breech and closed it. She lofted the gun and spun the wheel.

"Everybody down!" Nobody heard her but luckily a gap opened in the line at the last second. The gun made a huge noise and nearly blew Venera off the roof. When the vast plume of smoke cleared she saw nearly everybody in sight recovering from having ducked.

It might not be powerful or accurate, but the thing was loud. That fact might just save them.

She ran toward the Lirisians. "The cannons! Start shouting stuff about cannons!" She breeched the smoking weapon and handed it to Eilen. "Reload."

"But we lost the rest of the bullets."

"We've got one." She reached into her jacket pocket. There it was, its contours familiar from years of touching. She brought out her bullet. Her fingers trembled now as she held it up to the red flare-light.

"Damn you anyway," she whispered to it.

Eilen glanced up, said, "Oh," and held up the gun. There was no time for ceremony; Venera slid the hated slug into the breech and it fit perfectly. She clicked it shut.

"Out of my way!" She crossed the roof in great bounding steps, dodging between fighting men to reach the battlement where the ladders jutted up. The gunfire from below had stopped; the snipers didn't want to hit their own men as they topped the wall.

Venera hopped up onto a crenelation and sighted nearly straight down. She saw the startled eyes of a Sacrus soldier between her feet, and half a dozen heads below his. She spun the spark wheel.

The explosion lifted her off her feet. Everything disappeared behind a ball of smoke. When she staggered upright some yards away Venera found herself surrounded by cheering people. Several of Sacrus's soldiers were being thrown off the roof and for the moment no more were appearing. As the smoke cleared she saw that the top of the ladder she'd fired down was missing.

"Keep filling it," she said, thrusting the gun at Eilen. "Bullets don't matter—as long as it's bright and loud."

Moss's grinning face emerged from the gloom. "They're hesitating!"

She nodded. Sacrus didn't have so many people that they could afford to sacrifice them in wave attacks. The darkness and confusion would help; and though they had probably heard it every day of their lives, the thunderous sound of the morning gun at this close range would give pause to the men holding the ladders.

"It's not going to keep them at bay for long, though," she said. "Where are the rest of our people?"

Now Moss frowned. "T-trapped, I fear. Guinevera l-led them into an ambush. Now they have their backs to the open air." He pointed toward the edge of the world and the night skies beyond.

Venera hopped up on the edge of the elevator platform and took a quick look around. Sacrus's people were spread in a thin line around two of the approaches to Liris. On their third side ragged girders and scoured metal jutted off the end of the world. And on the fourth—behind her—a jumble of brambles, thornbushes, and broken masonry formed a natural barrier that Sacrus wasn't bothering to police.

In the darkness beyond, hundreds of torches lit the contours of an army small by Venera's standards but huge for Spyre. There might be no more than a thousand men there, but that was all the forces that opposed Sacrus on this world.

Spreading away behind that army was the maze of estates

that made up Greater Spyre. Somewhere out there was the long low building where the hollowed bomb hung, with its promise of escape.

She turned to Moss. "You need to break through Sacrus's lines. Otherwise, they'll overwhelm us and then they can turn and face our army with a secure fortress behind them."

He nodded. "But all our leaders are t-trapped."

"Well, not all." She strode across the roof to the battlements that overlooked the bramble-choked acres. He came to stand at her side. Together they gazed out at the army that lay tantalizingly out of reach.

"If the semaphore were working—" She stopped, remembering Bryce. Moss shook his head anyway.

"S-Sacrus has encircled the t-tower. They would read every letter."

"But we need to coordinate an attack—from outside and inside at the same time. To break through . . ."

He shrugged. "Simple matter. If we c-can get one p-person through the lines."

She speculated. If she showed up there among the brambles, would the generals of that army have her arrested? How far had news of her deceptions spread?

"Get them ready," she said. "Everyone into armor, everyone armed. I'll be back in two minutes." She headed for the stairs.

"Where are you g-going?"

She shot him a grim smile. "To check in on our bargaining chip."

VENERA RAN THROUGH empty halls to the old prison on the main floor.

As she'd suspected, the guards had deserted their posts when the roof was attacked. The main door was ajar; Venera slowed when she saw this. Warily, she toed it open and aimed her pistol through. There was nobody in the antechamber. She sidled in.

"Hello?" That was Jacoby Sarto's voice. Venera had never heard him sound worried, but he was clearly rattled by what was happening. *He's never been in a battle before*, she realized—nor had any of these people. It was shocking to think that she was the veteran here.

Venera went on her tiptoes to look through the door's little window into the green-walled reception room. Sarto was the sole occupant of a bench designed to seat thirty; he sat in the very center of a room that could have held a hundred. He squinted at the door, then said, "Fanning?"

She threw open the door and stepped in. "Did you tell them?"

He appeared puzzled. "Tell who what?"

She showed him her pistol; he wouldn't know it was empty. "Don't play games, Sarto. Someone told Guinevera who I really am. Was it you?"

He smiled with a trace of his usual arrogance. He stood up and adjusted the sleeves of the formal shirt he still wore. "Things not going your way out there?"

"Two points," said Venera, holding up two fingers. "First: I'm holding a gun on you. Second: you're rapidly becoming expendable."

"All right, all right," he said irritably. "Don't be so prickly. After all, I came here of my own free will."

"And that's supposed to impress me?" She leaned on the doorjamb and crossed her arms.

"Think about it," he said. "What do I have to gain from revealing who you are?"

"I don't know. Suppose you tell me?"

Now he scowled at her, as if she were some common servant girl who'd had the temerity to interrupt him while he was talking. "I have spent thirty-two years learning the ins and outs of council politics. All that time, becoming an expert—maybe *the* expert—on Spyre, learning who is beholden to who, who's ambitious, and who just wants to keep their heads down. I have been the public face of Sacrus for much of that time, their most important operative, because for all those years, Spyre's politics were all that mattered. But look at what's happening." He waved a hand to indicate the siege and battle going on beyond Liris's thick walls. "Everything that made me valuable is being swept away."

This was not what Venera had been expecting to hear from him. She came into the room and sat down on a bench facing Sarto. He looked at her levelly and said, "Change is inconceivable to most people in Spyre; to them a catastrophe is a tree falling across their fence. A vast political upheaval would be somebody snubbing somebody else at a party. That's the system I was bred and trained to work in. But my masters have always known that there's much bigger game out there. They've been biding their time, lo these many centuries. Now they finally have in their grasp a tool with which to conquer the world—the *real* world, not just this squalid imitation we're standing in. On the scale of Sacrus's new ambitions, all of my accomplishments count for nothing."

Venera nodded slowly. "Spyre is having all its borders redrawn around you. Even if they never get the key from me, Sacrus will be facing a new Spyre once the fighting stops. I'll bet they've been grooming someone young and malleable to take your place in that new world."

He grimaced. "No one likes to be discarded. I could see it coming, though. It was inevitable, really, unless . . ."

"Unless you could prove your continuing usefulness to your masters," she said. "Say, by personally bringing them the key?"

He shrugged. "Yesterday's council meeting would otherwise have been my last public performance. At least here, as your, uh, guest, I might have the opportunity to act as Sacrus's negotiator. Think about it—you're surrounded, outgunned; you're approaching the point where you have to admit you're going to lose. But I can tell you the semaphore codes to signal our commanders that we've reached an accommodation. As long as you had power here, you could have functioned as the perfect traitor. A few bad orders, your forces ordered into a trap, then it's over the wall for you and me, the key safely into my master's hands, you on your way home to wherever it is you came from."

Venera tamped down on her anger. Sarto was used to dealing in cold political equations; so was she, for that matter. What he was proposing shouldn't shock her. "But if I'm disgraced, I can't betray my people."

"Your usefulness plummets," he said with a nod. "So, no, I didn't tattle on you. You're hardly of any value now, are you? All you've got is the key. If your own side's turned against you, your only remaining option is to throw yourself on the mercy of Sacrus. Which might win me some points if I'm the one who brings you in, but not as much, and—"

"—And I have no reason to expect good treatment from them," she finished. "So why should I do it?"

He stood up—slowly, mindful of her gun—and walked a little distance away. He gazed up at the room's little windows. "What other option do you have?" he asked.

She thought at first that he'd said this rhetorically, but something about his tone . . . It had sounded like a genuine question.

Venera sat there for a while, thinking. She went over the incident with the council members on the roof; who could have outed her? Everything depended on that—and on when it had happened. Sarto said nothing, merely waited patiently with his arms crossed, staring idly up at the little window.

Finally she nodded and stood up. "All right," she said. "Jacoby, I think we can still come to an . . . accommodation. Here's what I'm thinking . . ."

19

AS SOMETIMES HAPPENED at the worst of moments, Venera lost her sense of gravity just before she hit the ground. The upthrusting spears of brush and stunted trees flipped around and became abstract decorations on a vast wall she was approaching. Her feet dangled over sideways buildings and the pikes of soldiers. Then the wall hit her and she bounced and tumbled like a rag doll. Strangely, it didn't hurt at all—perhaps not so strangely, granted that she was swaddled in armor.

She unscrewed her helmet and looked up into a couple dozen gun barrels. They were all different, like a museum display taken down and offered to her; in her dazed state she almost reached to grab one. But there were hands holding them tightly and grim men behind the hands.

When she and Sarto had reached the rooftop of Liris they found a theatrical jumble of bodies, torn tenting, and brazier fires surrounded by huddling men in outlandish armor. At the center of it all, the thick metal cable rose up and out of sight into the turbulent mists; that cable glowed gold now as distant Candesce awoke.

She had spotted Moss and headed over, keeping her head down in case there were snipers. He looked up, lines of exhaustion apparent around his eyes; glancing past her, he spotted Sarto. "What's this?"

"We need to break this siege. I'm going over the wall, and Sarto is coming with me."

Moss blinked, but his permanently shocked expression revealed none of his thoughts. "What for?"

"I don't know whether the commanders of our encircling force have been told that I'm an imposter and a traitor. I need to bring Jacoby Sarto in case I need a . . . ticket, I suppose you could call it . . . into their good graces."

He nodded reluctantly. "And how do you p-propose to reach our force? S-Sacrus is between us and them."

Now she grinned. "Well, you couldn't do this with all of us, but I propose that we jump."

Of course they'd had help from an ancient catapult that Liris had once used to fire mail and parcels over an enemy nation to an ally some three miles away. Venera had seen it on her second day here; with a little effort, it had been refitted to seat two people. But nobody, least of all her, knew whether it would still work. Her only consolation had been the low gravity in Spyre.

Now Venera had two possible scripts she could follow, one if these were soldiers of the council alliance, one if they owed their allegiance to Sacrus. But which were they? The fall had been so disorienting that she couldn't tell where they'd ended up. So she merely put up her hands and smiled, and said, "Hello."

Beside her Jacoby Sarto groaned and rolled over. Instantly another dozen guns aimed at him. "I think we're not that much of a threat," Venera said mildly. She received a kick in the back (which she barely felt through the metal) for her humor.

A throb of pain shot through her jaw—and an odd thing happened. Such spasms of pain had plagued her for years, ever since the day she woke up in Rush's military infirmary, her head bandaged like a delicate vase about to be shipped via the postal system. Each stab of pain had come with its own little thought, whose content varied somewhat but always translated roughly to either *I'm all alone* or *I'm going to kill them*. Fear and fury, they stabbed her repeatedly throughout each day. The fierce headaches that often built over the hours just added to her meanness.

But she'd taken the bullet that struck her jaw and blown it back out the very same gun that had shot her. So, when her jaw cramped this time, instead of her usual misery Venera had a flash of memory: the morning gun going off with a tremendous explosion in her hands, bucking and kicking and sending her flying backward into the Lirisians. She had no idea what the feeling accompanying that had been, but she liked it.

So she grinned crookedly and stood up. Dusting herself off, she said with dignity, "I am Amandera Thrace-Guiles, and this is Jacoby Sarto of the Spyre Council. We need to talk to your commanders."

"YOU HAVE A reputation for being foolhardy," said the army commander, his gray moustaches waggling. "But that was ridiculous."

It turned out that they'd nearly overshot both Sacrus and Council Alliance positions. Luckily several hundred pairs of eyes had tracked their progress across the rolled-up sky of Spyre and it was her army that had gotten to Venera and Jacoby first. Sarto didn't seem too upset about the outcome, which was telling. What was even more significant was that everyone was calling her "Lady Thrace-Guiles," which meant that word of her deceptions hadn't made it out of Liris. Here, Venera was still a respected leader.

She preened at the commander's back-handed compliment. He stood with his back to a brick wall, a swaying lamp nodding shadows across the buttons of his jacket. Aides and colonels bustled about, some shoving little counters across the map board, others reading or writing dispatches.

Venera smelled engine oil and wet cement. The alliance army had set up its headquarters in a preservationist roundhouse about a mile from Liris; these walls were thick enough to stop anything Sacrus had so far fired. For the first time in days, Venera felt a little safe.

"I wouldn't have had to be foolhardy if the situation weren't so dire," she said. It was tempting to upbraid this man for hesitating to send his forces to relieve Liris; but Venera found herself uninterested anymore in taking such familiar pleasures. She merely said, "Tell me what's been happening out here."

The commander leaned over the board and began pointing at the little wooden counters. "There've been engagements all across Greater Spyre," he said. "Sacrus has won most of them."

"So what are they doing? Conquering countries?"

"In one or two cases, yes. Mostly they've been cutting the preservationist's railway lines. And they've taken or severed all the elevator cables."

"Severed?" Even to an outsider like her this was a startling development.

One of the aides shrugged. "Easy enough to do. They just use them for target practice. Except for the ones at the edge of the world, like Liris. The winds around those lines deflect the bullets."

She raised her eyebrows. "Why don't they just use more high-powered guns on them?"

The aide shook his head. "Ancient treaty. Places limits on muzzle velocities. It's to prevent accidental punctures of the world's skin."

"—Not significant, anyway," said the commander with an impatient gesture. "The war will be decided here on Greater Spyre. The city will just have to wait it out."

"No, it can't wait," she said. "That's what this is all about. Not the city, but the docks."

"The docks?" The commander stared at her. "That's the last thing we're going to worry about."

"I know, and Sacrus is counting on that." She glared at him. "Everything that's happening down here is a diversion from their real target. Everything except . . ." She nodded at Liris.

Now they were looking at each other with faintly embarrassed unease. "Lady Thrace-Guiles," said the commander, "war is a very particular art. Perhaps you should leave such details to those who've made it their careers."

Venera opened her mouth to yell at him, thought better, and

took a deep breath instead. "Can we at least be agreed that we need to break Sacrus's hold on Liris?"

"Yes," he said with a vigorous nod. "We need to ensure the safety of our leadership. For that purpose," he pointed at the table, "I am advocating a direct assault along the innermost wall."

A moment of great temptation made Venera hesitate. The commander was proposing to go straight for the walls and leave the group trapped at the world's edge to its fate. He didn't know that his objective was actually there. They'd made themselves her enemies and Venera could just . . . forget to tell him. Leave Guinevera and the others to Sacrus's mercy now that she had the army.

She couldn't claim not to have known, though, unless the Lirisians went along with it. And she was tired of deceptions. She sighed and said, "Liris is a critical objective, yes, but the rest of our leadership is actually trapped with the Lirisian army at the edge of the world." There were startled looks up and down the table. "Yes—Master Thinblood, Principe Guinevera, and Pamela Anseratte, among others, are among those pinned down in the hurricane zone. I'm sure you were concerned for the safety of that group, but they're even more important than you probably knew."

The commander frowned down at the map. On it, Liris was a square encircled by red wooden tokens representing Sacrus's army. This circle squashed a knot of blue tokens against the bottom edge of the map: the Lirisian army, trapped at the edge of the world. Left of the encirclement was a no-man's-land of tough brush that had so far resisted burning. Left of that, the preservationist siding and army encampment where they now stood.

"This is a problem," said the commander. He thought for a moment, then said, "There are certain snakes that coil around their victims and choke them to death." She raised an eyebrow, but he continued, "One of their characteristics, so I've been told, is that if you try to remove them they tighten their grip. Right now Sacrus has both Liris and our leaders in its coils, and if we try to break through to one they will simply strangle the other."

To relieve the Lirisian army, they would have to force a wedge under Liris, with the edge of the world at their right side. To do this they would trade off their ability to threaten Sacrus along the inner sides of Liris—freeing those troops up to assault the walls of Liris. Conversely, the best way to relieve Liris would be to come at it from the inner side, which meant swinging the army away from the world's edge—thus giving Sacrus a free hand against the trapped force.

Venera examined the map; it didn't tell her anything she didn't already know. "We have to fool them into making the wrong choice," she said.

"Yes, but how are we going to do that?" He shook his head. "Even if we did, they can maneuver just as fast as we can. They have less ground to cover than we do to redeploy their forces."

"As to how we'll fool the snake into uncoiling," she said, "it helps to have your own snake to consult with." She turned and waved to some figures standing a few yards away. Jacoby Sarto emerged from the shadows; he was a silhouette against klieg lights that pinioned a pair of hulking locomotives in the center of the roundhouse. He was accompanied by two armed soldiers and a member of Bryce's underground.

The commander bowed to Sarto but then said, "I'm afraid we cannot trust this man. He is of the enemy."

"Lord Sarto has seen the light," said Venera. "He has agreed to help us."

"Pah!" The commander sneered. "Sacrus are masters of deception. How can we trust him?"

"The politics are complex," she said. "But we have very good reasons to trust him. I do. That is why I brought him."

There were more glances thrown between the colonels and the aides. The commander twitched a frown for just a moment, then said, "No. I understand the dilemma we're in, but my sovereign and commanding officer is Principe Guinevera, and he's in danger. Politically, saving our leadership has to be the priority. I'll not countenance any plan that weakens our chance of doing that."

Jacoby Sarto laughed. It was an ugly, contemptuous sound,

delivered by a man who had spent decades using his voice to whither other men's courage. The commander glared at him. "I fail to see the humor in any of this, Lord Sarto."

"Forgivable," said Sarto drily, "as you're not aware of Sacrus's objectives. They want Liris, not your management. They haven't crushed the soldiers pinned down at the world's edge because they're dangling them as bait."

"What could they possibly want with Liris?"

"Me," said Venera, "because they surely think I'm still there. —And the elevator cable. They need to cut it. All they have to do is capture me or make it impossible for me to leave Greater Spyre. Then they've won. It will just be a matter of time."

Now it was the commander's turn to laugh. "I think you vastly overrate your own value and underrate the potential of this army," he said, sweeping his arm to indicate the paltry hundreds gathered in the cavernous shed. "You alone can't hold this alliance together, Lady Thrace-Guiles. And I said it before, the elevator cables are of little strategic interest."

Venera was furious. She wanted to tell him that she'd seen more men gathered at circuses in Rush than he had in his vaunted army. But, remembering how she had thrown a lighted lamp at Garth in anger and his gentle chiding after, she bit back on what she wanted to say and instead said, "You'll change your mind once you know the true strategic situation. Sacrus wants—" She stopped as Sarto touched her arm.

He was shaking his head. "This is not the right audience," he said quietly.

"Um." In an instant her understanding of the situation flipped around. When she had walked in here she had seen this knot of officers in one corner of the roundhouse and assumed that they were debating their plan of attack. But that wasn't what they were doing at all. They had been huddling here, as far as possible from the men they must command. They weren't planning; they were hesitating.

"Hmmm . . ." She quirked a transparently false smile at the

commander. "If you men will excuse me for a few minutes?" He looked puzzled, then annoyed, then amused. Venera took Sarto's arm and led him away from the table.

"What are you going to do?" he asked.

She stopped in an area of blank floor stained over the decades by engine oil and grease. At first Venera didn't meet Sarto's eyes. She was looking around at the towering wrought-iron pillars, the tessellated windows in the ceiling, the smoky beams of light that intersected on the black backs of the locomotives. A deep knot of some kind, loosened when she cried in Eilen's arms, was unraveling.

"They talk about places as being our homes," she mused. "It's not the place, really, but the people."

"I'm sure I don't know what you mean," he said. His dry irony had no effect on Venera. She merely shrugged.

"You were right," she said. He cocked his head to one side, crossing his arms, and waited. "After the confirmation, when you said I was still Sacrus's," she went on. "And in the council chamber, even when we talked in your cell earlier tonight. Even now. As long as I wanted to leave Spyre, I was theirs. As long as they've known what to dangle in front of me, there was nothing I could do but what they wanted me to do."

"Haven't I said that repeatedly?" He sounded annoyed.

"All along, there's been a way to break their hold on me," she said. "I just haven't had the courage to do it."

He grumbled, "I'd like to think I made the right choice by throwing in with you. Takes you long enough to come to a decision, though."

Venera laughed. "All right. Let's do this." She started to walk toward the locomotives.

"*There you are!*" Venera stumbled, cursed, and then flung out her arms.

"Bryce!" He hugged her, but hesitantly—and she knew not to display too much enthusiasm herself. No one knew they were lovers; that knowledge would be one more piece of leverage against them. So she disengaged from him quickly and stepped back. "What happened? I saw the semaphore station blown up. We all assumed you were . . ."

He shook his head. In the secondhand light he did look a bit disheveled and soot-stained. "A bunch of us got knocked off the roof, but none of us were hurt." He laughed. "We landed in the brambles and then had to claw our way through with Sacrus's boys firing at our arses all the way. Damn near got shot by our own side as well, before we convinced them who we were."

Now she did hug him and damn the consequences. "Have you been able to contact any of our—your people?"

He nodded. "There's a semaphore station on the roof. The whole Buridan network's in contact. Do you have orders?"

As Venera realized what was possible, she grinned. "Yes!" She took Bryce by one arm and Sarto by the other and dragged them across the floor. "I think I know a way to break the siege and save the other commanders. You need to get up there and get Buridan to send us something. Jacoby, you get up there too. You need to convince Sacrus that I'm ready to double-cross my people." She pushed them both away.

"And what are you going to do?" asked Bryce.

She smiled past the throbbing in her jaw. "What I do best," she said. "I'll set the ball rolling."

Venera stalked over to the black, bedewed snout of a locomotive and pulled herself up to stand in front of its headlamp. She was drenched in light from it and the overhead spots, aware that her pale face and hands must be as bright as lantern flames against the dark metal surrounding her. She raised her arms.

"It is tiiiiiime!"

She screamed it with all her might, squeezed all the anger and the pain from her twisted family and poisonous intrigues of her youth, the indifferent bullet and her loss of her husband Chaison, the blood on her hands after she stabbed Aubri Mahallan, the smoke from her pistols as she shot men and women alike, all of it into that one word. As the echoes subsided everyone in the roundhouse came to their feet. All eyes were on her and that was exactly right, exactly how it should be.

"Today the old debts will be settled! Two hundred years and more the truth has waited in Buridan Tower—the truth of what Sacrus is and what they have done! Nearly too late, but not too late, because you, here today, will be the ones to settle those debts and at the same time prevent Sacrus from ever committing such atrocities again!

"Let me describe my home. Let me describe Buridan Tower!" Out of the corner of her eye she saw the army commanders running from their map table, but they had to shoulder their way through hundreds of soldiers to reach her, and the soldiers were raptly attentive to her alone. "Like a vast musical instrument, a flute thrust into the sky and played on by the ceaseless hurricane winds of the airfall. Cold, its corridors decorated with grit and wavering, torn ribbons that once were tapestries. Wet, with nothing to burn except the feathers of birds. Never silent, never still as the beams it stands on sway under the onslaught of air. A roaring tomb, that is Buridan Tower! That is what Sacrus made. It is what they promise to make of your homes as well, make no mistake.

"That's right," she nodded. "You're fighting for far more than you may know. This isn't just a matter of historical grudges, nor is it a skirmish over Sacrus's kidnapping and torture of your women and children. This is about your future. Do you want all of Spyre to become like Buridan, an empty tomb, a capricious playground for the winds? Because that is what Sacrus has planned for Spyre."

The officers had stopped at the head of the crowd. She could see that the commander was about to order her to be taken off her perch, so Venera hurried on to her main point. "You have not been told the truth about this war! Before we leave this place you need to know why Sacrus has moved against us all. It is because they believe they have outgrown Spyre the way a wasp outgrows its cocoon. Centuries ago they attacked and destroyed Buridan to gain a treasure from us. They failed to capture it but never gave up their ambition. Ever since Buridan's fall they have bided their time, awaiting the chance to get their hands on something Buridan has guarded for the sake of Spyre since the very beginning of time." She was really winding herself up now and for the moment the officers had stopped, curious no doubt about what she was about to say.

"Since the creation of Spyre my family has guarded one of the most powerful relics in the world! It was for the sake of this trust that we kept to Buridan Tower for generations, not venturing out because we feared Sacrus would learn that the tower is not the empty shell they believed—afraid they would learn that it can be entered. The thing we guarded is so dangerous that my brothers and sisters, my parents, grandparents, and their grandparents, all sacrificed their lives to prevent even a hint of its existence from escaping our walls.

"Time came when we could no longer sustain ourselves," she said more softly, "and I had to venture forth." Dimly, Venera wondered at this grand fib she was making up on the spot; it was a rousing story, and if it proved rousing enough then nobody would believe Guinevera if he survived to accuse her of being an imposter.

"As soon as I came forth," she said, "Sacrus knew that Buridan had survived, and they knew why we had stayed hidden. They knew that I carried with me the last key to Candesce!"

She stopped, letting the echoes reverberate. Crossing her arms, she gazed out at the army, waiting. Two seconds, five, ten, and then they were muttering, talking, turning to one another with frowns and nods. Some who prided themselves on knowing old legends told the men standing next to them about the keys; word began to spread through the ranks. In the front row, the officers were looking at one another in consternation.

Venera raised a hand for silence. "That is what this war is about," she said. "Sacrus has known of the existence of this key for centuries. They tried to take it once, and Buridan and its allies resisted. Now they are after it again. If they get it, they will no longer need Spyre. To them it is like the hated chrysalis that has confined them for generations. They will shed it, and they don't care if it unravels in pieces as they fly toward the light. At best, Spyre will prove a good capital for the world-spanning empire they plan—once they've scoured it clean of all the old estates, that is. Yes, this cylinder will make a fine park for the palace of Virga's new rulers. They'll need room for the governors of their new provinces, for prisoners, slaves, treasure houses, and barracks. They might not knock down all the buildings. But you and yours . . . well, I hope you have relatives in one of the principalities, because rabble like us won't be allowed to live here anymore."

The soldiers were starting to argue and shout. Belatedly the officers had realized that they weren't in control anymore; several darted at the locomotive but Venera crouched and glared at them, as if she was ready to pounce on them. They backed away.

She stood up, onto her tiptoes as she flung one fist high over her head. "We have to stop them! The key must be protected, for without it Spyre itself is doomed. You fight for more than your lives—more than your homes. You are all that stands between Sacrus and the slow strangulation of the very world!

"Will you stop them?" They shouted yes. "Will you?" They screamed it.

Venera had never seen anyone give a speech like this, but she'd heard Chaison work a crowd and had read about such moments in books. It all took her back to those romantic stories she'd devoured as a little girl in her pink bedroom. Outrageous theatricality, but none of these men had ever seen its like either; few had probably ever been in a theater. For most this roundhouse was the furthest they had ever been from home, and the looming locomotive was something they had only ever glimpsed in the far distance. They stood among peers who before today had been dots seen through telescopes and they were learning that however strange and foreign they were, all were united in their loyalty to Spyre itself. Of course the moment made them mad.

Fist still raised, Venera smiled down at the commander who shook his head in defeat.

Bryce and Jacoby Sarto clambered along the side of the loco-motive to join her. "What's the news?" she asked over the roar of the army at her feet.

Bryce blinked at the scene. "Uh . . . they're on their way."

Sarto nodded. "I semaphored the Sacrus army commander. Told him you realize your situation is hopeless, that you're going to lead your army into a trap."

She grinned. "Good." She turned back to the crowd and raised her fist again.

"It! Is! Tiiiiiiiiiime!"

20

THE SOUND OF bullets hitting Liris's walls reminded Garth Diamandis of those occasional big drops that fall from trees after a rain. Silence, then a *pat* followed in this case by the distant sound of a shot. From the gunslit where he was watching he could see the army of the Council Alliance assembling next to the rust-streaked roundhouse. In the early morning light it seemed like a dark carpet moving, in ominous silence, in the direction of Liris. Little puffs of smoke arose from the Sacrus line but the firing was undisciplined.

"Come away from there," said Venera's friend Eilen. They stood in a musty closet crammed with door lintels, broken drawers, cracked table legs: useless junk, but impossible for a tiny nation like Liris to throw away. Lantern light from the corridor shone through Eilen's hair. She could have been attractive, a habitual part of his mind noted. At one time, he could have helped her with that.

"I have a good view of the Sacrus camp," he said. "And it's too dangerous to be on the roof right now."

"You'll get a bullet in the eye," she said. He grunted and turned back to the view, and after a moment he heard her leave.

He couldn't tell her that he had recognized one of the uniformed figures moving down there. Maybe two of them, he couldn't be sure. Garth was sure that Eilen would tell him he was suffering an old man's delusions if he said he'd recognized his daughter among the hundreds of crimson uniforms.

He could be imagining it. He'd had scant moments to absorb the sight of her before she'd signaled her superiors and Sacrus's thugs had moved in on him. Yet Garth had an eye for women, was able to recall the smallest detail about how this or that one moved or held herself. He could deduce much about character and vulnerability by a woman's stance and habitual gestures; and he damned well knew how to recognize one at a distance. That was Selene standing hipshot by that tent, he was sure of it.

Garth cursed under his breath. He'd never been one to probe at sore spots, but ever since they'd thrown him into that stinking cell in the Grey Infirmary, his thoughts had pivoted around the moment of Selene's betrayal.

He had told her that he was her father, just before she betrayed him. In the seconds between, he'd seen the doubt in her eye— and then the mad-eyed woman with the pink hair had come to stand next to Selene.

"He said he's my father," Selene murmured as the soldiers cuffed Garth. The pink-haired woman laughed.

"And who knows?" Selene had said. "He might well be." She had laughed again, and Garth had glimpsed a terrible light in his daughter's eye just before he was hauled out of her sight.

There it was again, that mop of blossom-colored hair poking out from under a gray army cap. She was an officer. The last time Garth had seen her had been in a bizarre fever dream where Venera was whispering his name urgently. This woman had been there, among glass cases, but she was naked and laved with crimson from head to toe. Venera had spoken her name then, but Garth didn't remember it.

The sound of firing suddenly intensified. Garth craned his neck to look in the direction of the roundhouse. Sacrus's forces were moving out to engage the council troops on the inside of Liris. Behind him, though, he could see an equally large contingent of Sacrus's soldiers circling back around the building. Headed toward the edge of the world.

Garth had some inkling of what the council army was doing. They were pressing up against the no-man's-land of thorn and tumbled masonry, a scant hundred yards from the walls of Liris.

From there they could turn left or right—inward or toward the world's edge—at a moment's notice. Sacrus would have to split their forces into two to guard against both possibilities.

It was an intelligent plan and for a moment Garth's spirits lifted. Then he saw more of Sacrus's men abandon their positions below him. They were leaving a noisy and smoke-wreathed band of some two hundred men to defend the inward side while the rest of their forces marched behind Liris and out of sight from the roundhouse. They clearly expected the council army to split right and try to relieve Guinevera and Anseratte at the hurricane-wracked world's edge. But how did they know what the council was planning?

He cursed and jumped down off the ancient credenza he'd been perched upon. The corridors were stuffed with armed people, old men and women mostly (strange how he thought of other people his age as old, but not himself). He elbowed his way through them carelessly. "Where the hell is Moss?"

Someone pointed down a narrow, packed hallway. Liris's new botanist was deep in discussion with the only one of Bryce's men left inside the walls. "I need semaphore flags," Garth shouted over two shoulders. "We have to warn the troops what Sacrus is doing!"

To his credit, Moss didn't even blink. He raised a hand, pointed to one man, then held up two fingers. "Forward stores," he said. He pointed to another man and then at Garth. "Go with."

It took precious minutes for Garth and his new helper to locate the flags. Then they had to fight their way to the stairs. They emerged outside to the mind-numbing roar of the winds and an almost continual sound of gunfire. Ducking low, they ran for the edge of the roof.

"THEY EXPECT YOU to act as if you don't know about the key," Venera was explaining for the tenth time. She was surrounded by nervous officers and staffers; the gray-mustachioed army commander stood with his arms crossed, glowering as she drew on the ground with a stick. "If you don't know about it, then the obvious strategic goal is to relieve Guinevera's force. Jacoby Sarto has told them that we are going to do that. This frees Sacrus to take Liris, their real objective."

The commander nodded reluctantly. A bullet whined past somewhere too near for comfort. They stood behind a screen of brush on the edge of no-man's-land. An arc of soldiers surrounded them, far too few for Venera's taste. This force would hardly qualify as a company in Chaison's army. Yet Sacrus didn't have much more.

"So," she continued. "We feint right then strike left. I humbly suggest that we start with sustained fire into Sacrus's position on the edge-side of no-man's-land."

There was some talk among the officers—far too much of it to suit her—then the commander said, "It's too risky. And I remain skeptical about your story."

He didn't believe the key was real. Venera was tempted to take it out and show it to him, but that might backfire. Who could believe a whole war would be fought over an ivory wand?

While she and the commander were scowling at one another Bryce ran up, puffing. "They're here!" Venera turned to look where he pointed.

She turned back, grinning broadly. "Commander, would you be more amenable to my plan if you had a secret weapon to help with it?"

The commander and all the officers fell silent as they saw what was approaching. Slowly, the commander began to smile.

"DAMN IT, THEY'RE ignoring us!" Garth ducked as another volley of fire from below raked the edge of the roof. His assistant slumped onto the flagstones next to him, shaking his head.

"Maybe they don't see us," he said.

"Oh, they see us all right. They just don't believe us." Garth risked a glance over the stones. The council army was pressing hard against the barricades hastily thrown up by Sacrus on the inward side of Liris. The bulk of their army was hovering on the far side of the building, ready to speed toward the edge as soon as they were given the word.

Another ladder thunked against the wall. That made four in as many seconds. Garth pushed his companion. "Back to the stairs!" Sacrus were moving to take Liris. There was nothing anyone could do to stop them.

Garth stood up to run and hesitated for just a second. He couldn't stop himself from looking down through the gunfire and smoke to find his daughter. The ground around Liris was boiling with men; he couldn't see her.

Something hit him hard and he spun around, toppling to the flagstones. A bullet—was he dead? Garth clawed at his shoulder, saw a bright scar on the metal of his armor but no hole.

"Sir!" Damn him, his helper was running back to save him. "No, get to the stairs, damnit!" Garth yelled, but it was too late. A dozen bullets hit the man and some of those went right through his armor. He fell and slid forward, and died at Garth's feet.

Garth had never even learned his name.

Up they came now, soldier after soldier hopping onto Liris's roof. One loped forward, ignoring rifle fire from the stairs, and pitched a firebomb into the central courtyard. The cherry trees were protected under a siege roof, but a few more of those and they would burn.

Swearing, he tried to stand. Something hit him again and he fell back. This time when he looked up, it was to see the black globe of a Sacrus helmet hovering above him, and a rifle barrel inches from his face.

Garth fell back, groaning, and closed his eyes.

"WE'VE LOST OUR momentum," said Bryce. He and Venera were crouched behind an upthrust block of brickwork from some ancient, abandoned building. A hundred feet ahead of them, men were dying in a futile attack on the Sacrus barricade.

She nodded, but the council officers were already ordering a retreat. For a few seconds she watched the soldiers scampering back under relentless fire. Then she cocked an eyebrow at Bryce and grinned.

"*We've* lost our momentum? When did you decide this was your fight?"

"People are dying," he said angrily. "Anyway, if what you say is true, there's far more at stake than any of us knew." She shrugged and glanced again at the retreat, but then noticed he was staring at her.

"What?"

"Who are you, really? Surely not Amandera Thrace-Guiles?"

Venera laughed. He hadn't been there for her moment of humiliation at the feet of Guinevera—had, in fact, been flying through the air over brambles and scrub just about then.

She stuck out her hand for him to shake. "Venera Fanning. Pleased to meet you."

He shook it, a puzzled expression on his face, but then a new commotion distracted him. "Look! Your friends . . ."

Through the drifting smoke she could see a dozen spindly ladders wobbling against the building's walls. Men were swarming up them and there was fighting on the roof. In seconds she could lose the people who had become most precious to her. "Come on!"

They braved rifle fire and ran back. The army commander was crouched over a map. He looked up grimly as Venera approached. "Can you feel it?" When she frowned, he pointed down at the ground. Now she realized that for some time now, she had been feeling a slow, almost subliminal sensation of rising and falling. It was the kind of faint instability of weight that you sometimes felt when a town's engines were working to spin it back up to speed.

"I think Sacrus cut one too many cables."

"Let the preservationists deal with it when we're finished," she said. "Right now we need to cut down those ladders."

He shook his head. "Don't you understand? This is more than just a piece or two falling off the world. Something's happened. It—we . . ." She realized that he was very, very frightened. So were the officers kneeling with him.

Venera felt it again, that long slow waver, unsettling to the inner ear. Way out past the smoke, it seemed like the curving landscape of Spyre was crawling, somehow, like the itchy skin of a giant beast twitching in slow motion.

"We can't do anything about that," she said. "We have to focus on saving lives here and now! Look, I don't think there's more than three dozen men on those barricades. The rest of their men are waiting on the far side for us to try to relieve Guinevera."

With an effort he pulled himself together. "Your plan . . . Can you do it?"

"They'll start to pull back as soon as they realize we're concentrating here," she said. "When they do, we'll have them."

"All right. We have to . . . do something." He got to his feet and began issuing orders. The frightened officers sprinted off in all directions. Venera and Bryce ran back in the direction of the roundhouse and as they passed the fringe of the no-man's-land she saw scores of men standing up from concealment in the bushes. Suddenly they were all bellowing and as more popped up from unexpected places Venera found herself being swept back by a vast mob of howling armored men. She and Bryce fought their way forward as hundreds of bodies plunged past them. She had no time to look back but could imagine the Sacrus barricades being overwhelmed in seconds; the ladders would tremble and fall, and when they rose again it would be council soldiers climbing them.

A small copse of trees stood at the end of no-man's-land; bedraggled and half-burnt, they still made a good screen for what hid behind them. Venera smelled the things before she saw them, and her spirits soared as she heard their nervous snorting and stamping.

With murmurs and an outstretched hand, she approached the

Dali horse. A dozen others stood huddled together, flanks twitching, their heads a dozen feet off the earth. All were saddled and some of the horsemen were already mounted.

Bryce stopped short, a wondering expression on his face. Venera put her hand on the rope ladder that led up to her beast's saddle, then looked back at him. "See to your people," she said. "Run your presses. If I live, I'll see you after."

He smiled and for a moment looked boyishly mischievous. "The presses have been running for days, and I've sent my messages. But just in case . . . here." He dug inside his jacket and handed her a cloth-wrapped square. Venera unwrapped it, puzzled, then laughed out loud. It was a brand-new copy of the book *Rights Currencies*. She raised it to her nose and smelled the fresh ink, then stuffed it in her own jacket.

She laughed again as Bryce stepped back and the rest of her force mounted up behind her. Venera turned and waved to them, and as Bryce ran back toward the roundhouse and safety, she yelled, "Come on! They're not going to be expecting this!"

GARTH COULD SEE it all. They'd tied his hands behind him and stood him near the body of the man who'd come with him to the roof. From behind him came the sounds of Sacrus's forces mopping up on the lower floors of Liris. Prisoners were being led onto the roof under the direction of Margit, who had climbed up the ladder with ferocious energy a few minutes before.

Garth had turned away when his daughter stepped onto the roof behind her.

Turning, he saw what was developing under the shadow of the building, and despite all the tragedy it made him smile.

A dozen horses, each one at least ten feet tall at the shoulder, were stepping daintily but rapidly through no-man's-land. The closely packed thornbushes and tumbled masonry were no barrier to them at all. Each mount held two riders except the one in the lead. Venera Fanning rode that one, a rifle held high over her head. Garth could see that her mouth was wide open—mother of Virga, was she howling some outlandish battle cry? Garth had to laugh.

"What's so funny, you?" A soldier cuffed him on the side of his head. Garth looked him in the eye and nodded in Venera's direction.

"That," he said.

After he finished swearing, the man ran toward Margit, shouting, "Sir! Sir!" Garth turned back to the view.

Sacrus had taken Liris with a comparatively small force and were now depleted on the Spyre side of the building. The bulk of the council army was wheeling in that direction, pushing back the few defenders on the barricades. They'd take the siege ladders on that side in no time. It shouldn't have been a problem for Sacrus; they now held the roof and could lower ladders, ropes, and platforms to relieve their own forces from the other side of the building. Now that they knew where the council army was going, their ground forces had started running back in that direction from the world's edge. This seemed safe because they had a large force below no-man's-land to block any access from the direction of the roundhouse.

But Venera's cavalry had just crossed over no-man's-land and were now stepping into the strip of cleared land next to the building. Without hesitation they turned right and galloped at the rear of the Sacrus line. Simultaneously those council troops fronting the roundhouse assaulted them head-on.

A hysterical laugh pierced the air. Garth turned to see Margit perched atop the wall. She was staring down at the horses with a wild look in her eye. "I'm seeing things in broad daylight now," she said, and laughed again. "This is a strange dream, this one. Things with four legs . . . taller than a man . . ."

Selene reached up to take Margit's arm but the former botanist batted her hand aside. Stepping back, her face full of doubt, Selene looked around—and her eyes met Garth's. He frowned and shook his head slowly.

Angrily, she turned away.

The twelve horses stepped over a barricade while their riders shot the men behind it. The horses were armored, Garth saw, although he was sure it wouldn't prove too effective under direct fire. Sacrus's men weren't firing, though. They were too amazed at what they were seeing. The beasts towered over them, huge masses of muscle on impossibly long legs, festooned with sheet metal barding that half-hid their giant eyes and broad teeth. The monsters were overtop and past and wheeling before the defenders could organize. And by then bullets and flicking hooves were finding them, and they all fell.

Margit stood there and watched while the commanders on the ground shouted and waved. The other men on the rooftop stared at the fiasco unfolding below them, then looked to Margit. The seconds dragged.

In that time the horses reached a point midway between the bottled-up council leadership and the Sacrus force below no-man's-land. Now they split into two squads of six. Venera led hers in a thunderous charge directly at the men who had pinned down Guinevera and the Liris army.

Selene jumped onto the wall beside Margit. She stared for a second, then cursed, and whirling, shouted, "Shoot! Shoot, you idiots! They're going to—"

Margit seemed to wake out of her trance. She stepped grandly down from the wall and frowned at the line of prisoners that had been led onto the roof. She strolled over, loosening a pistol at her belt.

"Where is Venera Fanning?" she shouted.

A sick feeling came over Garth. He watched Margit walk up and down the line, saw her pause before Moss, sneer at Samson Odess, and finally stop in front of Eilen.

"You were her friend," she said. "You'll know where she is." She raised the pistol and aimed it between Eilen's eyes.

Garth tried to run over to her but a soldier kicked his legs out from under him and only the light gravity saved him from breaking his nose as he fell. "She's right there!" Garth hollered at Margit. "Riding a horse! You were just looking at her."

Margit glanced back. Her eyes found Garth lying prone on the flagstones.

"Don't be ridiculous," she said with a smile. "Those things weren't *real*."

She shot Eilen in the head.

Venera's friend flopped to the rooftop in a tumble of limbs. The other captives screamed and quailed. "Where is she?" shrieked Margit, waving the pistol. Now, too late, Selene was running to her side. The younger woman put her hand on Margit's arm, spoke in her ear, tugged her away from the prisoners.

As she led Margit away Selene glanced over at Garth. It was his turn to look away.

There was a lot of running and shouting then, though little shooting because, he supposed, the men on the roof were afraid of hitting their own men. Garth didn't care. He lay on his stomach, with his cheek pressed against the cold stone, and cried.

Someone hauled him to his feet. Dimly he realized that a great roaring sound was coming from beyond the roof's edge. Now the men on the roof did start firing—and cursing, and looking at one another helplessly.

Garth knew exactly what had happened. Venera had broken the line around Guinevera's men. They were pouring out of their defensive position and attacking Sacrus's force beneath no-man's-land. That group was now itself isolated and surrounded.

He wouldn't be surprised if Venera herself had moved on, perhaps circling the building to connect up with the main bulk of the council army. If she did that, then none of the ladders and elevator platforms to this roof would be safe for Sacrus.

"Come on." Garth was hauled to his feet and pushed to the middle of the roof. He coughed and realized that black smoke was pouring up from the courtyard. The prisoners were wailing and screaming.

Margit's soldiers had set the cherry trees alight.

"Get on the platform or I'll shoot you." Garth blinked, and saw that he was standing next to the elevator that climbed Liris's cable. Margit and Selene were already on the platform, with a crowd of soldiers and several Liris prisoners, including Moss and Odess.

He climbed aboard.

Margit smiled with supreme confidence. "This," she said as if to no one in particular, "is where we'll defeat her."

VENERA LOOKED DOWN from her saddle at Guinevera, who stared at her with his bloody sword half-raised. "You spoke out of turn, Principe," she called down. "Even if I wasn't Buridan before, I am now."

He ducked his head slightly, conceding the point. "We're grateful, Fanning," he said.

Venera finally let herself feel her triumph and relief, and slumped a bit in her saddle. Fragmentary memories of the past minutes came and went; who would have thought that the skin of Spyre would *bounce* under the gallop of a horse?

Scattered gunfire echoed around the corner of the building, but Sacrus's army was in full retreat. Their force below no-man's-land had surrendered. No one had any stomach for fighting anyway; Sacrus and council soldiers stood side by side, exchanging uneasy glances as another long slow undulation moved through the ground. Council troops were swarming up the sides of Liris, but there was no sound from up there and an ominous flag of black smoke was fluttering from the roofline.

Seeing that, Venera's anxiety about her friends returned. Garth, Eilen, and Moss—what had become of them during Sacrus's brief occupation? Her eyes were drawn to the cable that stretched from Liris up to Lesser Spyre. It seemed oddly slack, and somehow that tiny detail filled her with more fear than anything else she'd seen today.

Closer at hand, she spotted Jacoby Sarto walking, unescorted, past ranks of huddling Sacrus prisoners. He looked up at her, his face eloquently expressing the unease she too felt.

Another undulation, stronger this time. She saw trees sway, and a sharp *crack!* echoed from Liris's masonry wall. Some of the soldiers cried out.

Guinevera looked around. Ever the dramatist, his florid lips quivered as he said, "This should have been our moment of triumph. But what have we won? What have we done to Spyre?"

Venera did her best to look unimpressed, though she was worried too. "Look, there's no way to know," she said. That was a lie: she could feel it, they all could. Something was wrong.

A captain ran up. He saluted them both but it was almost an afterthought. "Ma'am," he said to Venera. "It's . . . they're waiting for you. On the roof."

A cold feeling came over her. For just a second she remembered lying on the marble floor of the Rush admiralty, bleeding from the mouth and sure she would die there alone. And then, curled around herself inside Candesce, feeling the Sun of Suns come to life, minutes to go before she was burnt alive. She'd almost lost it all. She could lose it all now.

She flipped down the little ladder attached to her saddle and climbed down. Her thighs and lower back spasmed with pain, but there was no echo from her jaw. She wouldn't have cared if there had been. As a tremor ran through the earth Jacoby Sarto reached to steady her. She looked him in the eye.

"If you come with me," she said, "whose side will you be on?"

He shrugged and staggered as the ground lurched again. "I don't think sides matter anymore," he said.

"Then come." They ran for the ladders.

21

ALL ACROSS SPYRE, metal that had been without voice for
a thousand years was groaning. The distant moan seemed half-
real to Venera, here at the world's edge where the roar of the
wind was perpetual; but it was there. Spyre was waking, trembling, and dying. Everybody knew it.

She put one hand over the other and tried to focus on the rungs
above her. She could see the peaked helmets of some of Guinevera's men up there and was pathetically glad that she wouldn't have
to face this alone.

Sarto was climbing a ladder next to hers. Even a month ago,
the very idea of trusting him would have seemed insane to her.
And anyway, if she were some romantic heroine and this were
the sort of story that would turn out well, it would be her lover
Bryce offering to go into danger at her side—not a man who until recently she would have been perfectly happy to see skewered
on a pike.

"Pfah," she said, and climbed out onto the roof.

Thick smoke crawled out of the broad square opening in the
center of the roof. Black and ominous, it billowed up twenty feet
and then was torn to ribbons by the world's-edge hurricanes. The
smoke made an undulating black tapestry behind Margit, her soldiers, and their hostages.

The elevator platform had been raised six feet. It was closely
ringed by council troops whose weapons were aimed at Margit and
her people. Venera recognized Garth Diamandis, Moss, and little
Samson Odess among the captives. All had gun muzzles pressed
against their cheeks.

A young woman in a uniform stood next to Margit. With Garth's face hovering just behind her own Venera could be in no doubt as to who she was; she had the same high cheekbones and gray eyes as her father.

Her gaze was fixed on Margit, her face expressionless.

"Come closer, Venera," called Margit. She held a pistol and had propped her elbow on her hip, aiming it casually upward. "Don't be shy."

Venera cursed under her breath. Margit had managed to corral all of her friends—no, not all. Where was Eilen? She glanced around the roof, not seeing her among the other newly freed Lirisians. Maybe she was downstairs fighting the fires; that was probably it. . . .

Her eye was drawn despite herself to a huddled figure lying on the roof. Freed of life, Eilen was difficult to recognize; her clothes were no longer clothes but some odd drapes of cloth covering a shape whose limbs weren't bent in any human pose. She stared straight up, her face a blank under the burnt wound in her forehead.

"Oh no . . ." Venera ran to her and knelt. She reached out, hesitated, then looked up at Margit.

Black smoke roiled behind the former botanist of Liris. She smiled triumphantly. "Always wanted an excuse to do that," she said. "And I'd love an excuse to do the same to these." Her pistol waved at the prisoners behind her. "But that's not going to happen, is it? Because you're going to . . ." She seemed to lose the thread of what she was saying, staring off into the distance for a few seconds. Then, starting, she looked at Venera again and said, "Going to give me the key to Candesce."

Venera glanced behind her. None of the army staff who knew about the key were here. Neither was Guinevera nor Pamela Anseratte. There was no one to prevent her from making such a deal.

Margit barked a surprised laugh. "Is this your solution? You thought to do a trade, did you?" Jacoby Sarto had stepped into view, paces behind Venera. Margit was sneering at him with undisguised contempt.

"That man-shaped thing might have been valuable once, but not anymore. It's not worth the least of these fools." She flipped up the pistol and fired; instantly hundreds of weapons rose across the roof, hammers cocking, men straining. Venera's heart was thudding painfully in her chest; she raised a hand, lowered it slowly. Gratefully, she saw the council soldiers obey her gesture and relax slightly.

She ventured a look behind her. Jacoby Sarto was staring down at a hole in the rooftop, right between his feet. His face was dark with anger, but his shoulders were slumped in defeat. He had nothing now, and he knew it.

"Your choice is clear, oh would-be queen of Candesce," shouted Margit over the shuddering of the wind. "You can keep your trophy, and maybe even use it again if you can evade us. Maybe these soldiers will follow you all the way to Candesce, though I doubt it. But go ahead: all you have to do is give the order and they'll fire. I'll be dead—and so will your friends. But you can walk away with your trinket.

"Or," she said with relish, "you can hand it to me now. Then I'll let your friends go—well, all save one, maybe. I need some guarantee that you won't have us shot on our way up to the docks. But I promise I'll let the last one go when we get there. Sacrus keeps its promises."

Venera played for time. "And who's going to use the key when you get to Candesce? Not you."

Margit shrugged. "They are wise, those that made me and healed me after you . . ." Her brows knit as though she were trying to remember something. "You . . . Those that made me—yes, those ones, not this one and his former cronies." She nodded to Sarto. "No, Sacrus underwent a . . . change of government . . . some weeks ago. People with a far better understanding of what the key represents, and who we might bargain with using it, are in charge now. Their glory shall extend beyond merely cowing the principalities with some show of force from the Sun of Suns. The bargain they've struck . . . the forces they've struck it with . . . well, suffice it to say, Virga itself will be our toy when they're done."

An ugly suspicion was forming in Venera's mind. "Do these forces have a name? Maybe—Artificial Nature?"

Margit shrugged again, looking pleased. "A lady doesn't tell." Then her expression hardened. She extended her hand. "Hand it over. Now. We have a lot to do, and you're wasting my time."

The rooftop trembled under Venera's feet. Past the pall of smoke, Spyre itself shimmered like a dissolving dream.

She'd almost had the power she needed; power to take revenge against the Pilot of Slipstream for the death of her husband. Enough wealth to set herself up somewhere in independence. Maybe she was even growing past the need for vengeance. It was possible she could have stayed here with her newfound friends, maybe in the mansion of Buridan in Lesser Spyre. Such possibilities had trembled just out of reach ever since her arrival among these baroque, ancient, and inward-turned people. It had all been within her grasp.

And Margit was right: she could still turn away. The key was hers and with it untold power and riches if she chose to exercise it. True, she would have to move immediately to secure her own safety, else the council would try to take it from her. But she was sure she could do that, with Sarto's help and Bryce's. Maybe Spyre would survive, if they spun its rotation down in time and repaired it under lesser gravity. She could still have Buridan, her place on the council, and power. All she had to do was sacrifice the prisoners who stood watching her now.

The Venera Fanning who had woken in Garth Diamandis's bed those scant weeks ago could have done that.

She reached slowly into her jacket and brought out the slim white wand that had caused so much grief—and doubtless would be the cause of much more. Step by step she closed the distance between herself and Margit's outstretched hand. Venera raised her hand and Margit leaned forward, but Venera would not look her in the eye.

Selene Diamandis put her foot in Margit's lower back and pushed.

As the former botanist sprawled onto Venera, bringing them both down, Selene pulled her own pistol and aimed it at the face of the man whose gun was touching Garth's ear. "Father, jump!" she cried.

Margit snarled and punched Venera in the chin. The explosion of pain was nothing compared to the spasms she usually got there so Venera didn't even blink. She grabbed Margit's wrist and the two rolled over and away from the platform.

"Lower your guns," Selene was shouting. Venera caught a confused glimpse of men and women stepping out of the way as she and Margit tumbled to the edge of the roof by the courtyard. Nobody moved to help her—if anyone laid a hand on either her or Margit, everyone would start shooting.

Margit elbowed Venera in the face and her head snapped back. She had an upside-down view of the courtyard below; it was an inferno.

"That red looks good on the trees, don't you think?" Margit muttered. She struck Venera again. Dazed, Venera couldn't recover fast enough and suddenly found Margit standing over her, pistol aimed at her.

"The key," she said, "or you die."

A shadow flickered from overhead. Margit glanced up, said, "What—," and then Moss collided with her and the two of them sailed off the roof. In the blink of an eye they were gone, disappearing silently into the smoke.

No one spoke. On her knees, gazing into the fire, Venera realized that she was waiting like everyone else for the end: a scream, a crash, or some other evidence that Margit and Moss had landed. It didn't come. There was only the dry crackle of the flames. Someone coughed and the spell was broken. Venera took a proffered arm and stood up.

It was Samson Odess who had helped her to her feet. A short distance away Garth Diamandis was hugging his daughter fiercely as the remaining Sacrus troops climbed down from the platform. The building was swaying, its stones cracking and grinding now. The whole landscape of Spyre was transforming as trees fell and buildings quivered on the verge of collapse. Soldiers and officers of both sides looked at one another in wonder and terror. Their alliances suddenly didn't matter.

Odess pointed to the grandly spinning town-wheels miles overhead. "Come on," he said. "Lesser Spyre will survive when the world comes apart. It'll all fall away from the town-wheels."

Venera followed his gaze, then looked around. The little elevator platform might hold twelve or fifteen people; she could save her friends. Then what? Repeat the standoff she'd just undergone, this time at the docks? Sacrus's leaders were there. They probably held the entire city by now.

"Who are you going to save, Samson?" she asked him. "These are your people now. You're the senior official in Liris—you're the new botanist now, do you understand? These people are your responsibility."

She saw the realization hit him, but the result wasn't what she might have expected. Samson seemed to stand a little taller. His eyes, which had always darted around nervously, were now steady. He walked over to where Eilen lay crumpled. Kneeling, he arranged her limbs and closed her eyes so that it looked like she was sleeping with her cheek and the palm of one hand pressed against the stones of Liris. Then he looked up at Venera. "We have to save them all," he said.

It seemed hopeless, if the very fabric of Spyre was about to come apart around them. Even burying the dead in the thin earth of their ancestral home seemed pointless. In hours or minutes they would be emptied into the airs of Virga. The alternative for the living was to rise to the city, to probably become prisoners in Lesser Spyre.

The air . . .

"I know what to do," Venera said. "Gather all your people. We might just make it if we go now."

"Where?" he asked. "If the whole world's coming apart—"

"Fin," she shouted as she ran to the edge of the roof. "We have to get to Fin!"

SHE MOUNTED HER horse and led them at a walk. At first only a trickle of people followed, just those who had been on the rooftop, but soon soldiers of Liris and Sacrus threw down their weapons and joined the crowd. Their officers trailed them. Guinevera and Anseratte appeared, but they were silent when anyone asked them what to do.

As they passed the roundhouse Bryce emerged with some of his own followers. They fell into step next to Venera's horse but, while their eyes met, they exchanged no words. Both knew that their time together had ended, as certainly as Spyre's.

In the clear daylight, Venera was able to behold the intricacies of Greater Spyre's estates for the first and last time. Always before she had skulked past them at night or raced along the few awning-covered roads that were tolerated by this paranoid civilization. Now, atop a ten-foot-tall beast striding the narrow strip of no-man's-land between the walls, she could see it all. She was glad she had never known before what lay here.

The work of untold ages, of countless lives, had gone into the making of Spyre. There was not a square inch of it that was untouched by some lifetime of contemplation and planning. Any garden corner or low stone wall could tell a thousand tales of lovers who'd met there, children who built forts or cried alone, of petty disputes with neighbors settled there with blood or marriage. Time had never stopped in Spyre, but it had slowed like the sluggish blood of some fantastically old beast, and now for generations the people had lived nearly identical lives. Their hopes and dreams were channeled by the walls under which they walked—influenced by the same storybooks, paintings, and music as their ancestors—until they had become gray copies of their parents or grandparents. Each had added perhaps one small item to Spyre's vast stockpile of bric-a-brac, unknowingly placing one more barrier before any thoughts of flight their own children might nurture. Strange languages never spoken by more than a dozen people thrived. Venera had been told how the lightless inner rooms of some estates had become bizarre shrines as beloved patriarchs died and because of tradition or fear no one could touch the body. More than one nation had died too as its own mausoleum ate it from the inside, its last inhabitants living out their lives in an ivy-strangled gatehouse without once stepping beyond the walls.

Now the staggered rows of hedge and wall were toppling. From half-hidden buildings came the sound of glass shattering as pillars shifted. Doors unopened for centuries suddenly gaped revealing blackness or sights that seared themselves into memory but not the understanding—glimpses, as they were, of cultures and rituals gone so insular and self-referential as to be forever opaque to outsiders.

And now the people were visible, running outside as the ground quaked and the metal skin of Spyre groaned beneath them. They were like grubs ejected from a wasp's nest split by some indifferent boy; many lay thrashing on the ground, unable to cope with the strangeness of the greater world they had been thrown into. Others ran screaming, or tore at themselves or one another, or stood mutely or laughed.

As a many-veranda'd manor collapsed in on itself Venera caught a glimpse of the people still inside: the very old, parchment hands crossed over their laps as they sat unmoved beneath their collapsing ceilings; and the panicked who stood staring wide-eyed at open fields where walls had been. The building's floors came down one atop the other, pancaking in a wallop of dust, and they were all gone.

"Liris's cable has snapped," someone said. Venera didn't look around. She felt strangely calm; after all, what lay ahead of them all but a return to the skies of Virga? She knew those skies, had flown in them many times. There, of course, lay the irony: for those who fell into the air with the cascading pieces of the great wheel, this would not be the end, but a beginning. Few, if any, could comprehend that. So she said nothing.

And for her? She had saved herself from her scheming sisters and her father's homicidal court by marrying a dashing commodore. In the end he had lived up to her expectations, but he had also died. Venera had been taught exactly one way to deal with such crises, which was through vengeance. Now she patted the front of her jacket, where the key to Candesce nestled once again in its inner pocket. It was a useless trinket, she realized; nothing worthwhile had come of using it and nothing would.

For her, what was ending here was the luxury of being able to hide within herself. If she was to survive, she would have to begin to take other people's emotions seriously. Lacking power, she must accommodate.

Glancing affectionately at Garth, who was talking intensely with his red-uniformed daughter, Venera had to admit that the prospect wasn't so frightening as it used to be.

It became harder to walk as gravity began to vary between nearly nothing and something crushingly more than one g. Her horse balked and Venera had to dismount; and when he ran off, she shrugged and fell into step next to Bryce and Sarto, who were arguing politics to distract themselves. They paused to smile at her, then continued. Slowly, with many pauses and some panicked milling about as gaps appeared in the land ahead, they made their way to Fin.

They were nearly there when Buridan finally consigned itself to the air. The shouting and pointing made Venera lift her eyes from the splitting soil, and she was in time to see the black tower fold its spiderweb of girders around itself like a man spinning a robe over his shoulders. Then it lowered itself in stately majesty through the gaping rent in the land until only blue sky remained.

She looked at Bryce. He shrugged. "They knew it might happen.

I told them to scatter all the copies of the book and currency to the winds if they fell. They're to seed the skies of Virga with democracy. I hope that's a good enough task to keep them sane for the next few minutes; and then, maybe, they'll be able to see to their own safety."

The tower would quickly disintegrate as it arrowed through the skies. Its pieces would become missiles that might do vast harm to the houses and farms of the neighboring principalities; much more so would be the larger shreds of Spyre itself when it all finally went. That was tragic; but the new citizens of Buridan, and the men and women of Bryce's organization, would soon find themselves gliding through a warm blue sky. They might kick their way from stone to tumbling stone and so make their way out of the wreckage. And then they would be like everyone else in the world: sunlit and free in an endless sky.

Venera smiled. Ahead she saw the doors of the low bunker that led to Fin, and broke into a run. "We're there!"

Her logic had been simple. Fin was a wing, aerodynamic like nothing else in Spyre. Of all the parts that might come loose and fall in the next little while, it was bound to travel fastest and farthest. So, it would almost certainly outrun the rest of the wreckage. And Venera had a hunch that Fin's inhabitants had given thought, over the centuries, about what they would do when Spyre died.

She was right. Although the guards at the door were initially reluctant to let in the mob, Corinne appeared and ordered them to stand down. As the motley collection of soldiers and citizens streamed down the steps she turned to Venera and grinned, just a little hysterically. "We have parachutes," she said. "And the fin can be detached and let drop. It was always our plan of last resort if we ever got invaded. Now . . ." She shrugged.

"But do you have boats? Bikes? Any means of traveling once we're in the air?" Corinne grinned and nodded, and Venera let out a sigh of relief. She had led her people to the right place.

Spyre's final death agony began as the last were stumbling inside. Venera stood with Corinne, Bryce, and Sarto at the top of the stairs and watched a bright line start at the rim of the world, high up past the sedately spinning wheels of Lesser Spyre. The line became a visible split, its edges pulling in trees and buildings; and Spyre peeled apart from that point. Its ancient fusion engines had proven incapable of slowing it safely—it might have been the stress they generated as much as centripetal force that finally did in the titanium structure. The details didn't matter; all that Venera saw was a thousand ancient cultures ending in one stroke of burgeoning sunlight.

A trembling shockwave raced around the curve of the world. It was beautiful in the blued distance but Venera knew it was headed straight for her. She should go inside before it arrived. She didn't move.

Other splits appeared in the peeling halves of the world and now the land simply shredded like paper. A roar like the howl of a furious god was approaching and a tremble went through the ground as gravity failed for good.

Just before Bryce grabbed her wrist and hauled her inside, Venera saw a herd of Dali horses gallop with grace and courage off the rim of the world.

They would survive, she was sure. Kicking and neighing, they would sail through the skies of Virga until they landed in the lap of someone unsuspecting. Gravity would be found for them, somewhere; they were too mythic and beautiful to be left to die.

Then Corinne's men threw the levers that detached Fin from the rest of Spyre. Suddenly weightless, Venera hovered in the open doorway and watched a wall of speed ivy recede very quickly and disappear behind the clouds.

Nobody spoke as she drifted inside. Hollow-eyed men and women glanced at one another, all crowded together in the thin antechamber of the tiny nation. They were all refugees now; it was clear from their faces that they expected some terrible fate to befall them, perhaps within the next few minutes. None could imagine what that might be, of course, and seeing that confusion, Venera didn't know whether to laugh or cry for them.

"Relax," she said to a weeping woman. "This is a time to hope, not to despair. You'll like where we're going."

Silence. Then somebody said, "And where is that?"

Somebody else said, "Home."

Venera looked over, puzzled. The voice hadn't been familiar, but the accent . . .

A man was looking back at her steadily. He held one of Fin's metal stanchions with one hand but otherwise looked quite comfortable in freefall. She did recognize the rags he was wearing, though—they marked him as one of the prisoners she had liberated from the Grey Infirmary.

"You're not from here," she said.

He grinned. "And you're not Amandera Thrace-Guiles," he said. "You're the admiral's wife."

A shock went through her. "What?"

"I only saw you from a distance when they rescued us," said the man. "And then lost sight of you when we got here to Fin. Everyone was talking about the mysterious lady of Buridan. But now I see you up close, I know you."

"Your accent," she said. "It's *Slipstream*."

He nodded. "I was part of the expedition, ma'am—aboard the *Arrest*. I was there for the big battle, when we defeated Falcon Formation. When your husband defeated them. I saw him plunge the *Rook* into the enemy's dreadnought like a knife into another man's heart. Had time to watch the bastard blow up, before they netted me out of the air and threw me into prison." He grimaced in anger.

Venera's heart was in her throat. "You saw . . . Chaison die?"

"Die?" The ex-airman looked at her incredulously. "*Die?* He's not dead. I spent two weeks in the same cell with him before Falcon traded me to Sacrus like a sack of grain."

Venera's vision grayed and she would have fallen over had she been under gravity. Oblivious, the other continued: "I might'a wished he were dead a couple times over those weeks. It's hard sharing your space with another man, particularly one you've respected. You come to see all his faults."

Venera recovered enough to croak, "Yes, I know how he can be." Then she turned away to hide her tears.

The giant metal wing shuddered as it knifed through the air. Past the opened doorway, where Bryce and Sarto were silhouetted, the sky seemed to be boiling. Cloud and air were being torn by the shattering of a world. The sound of it finally caught up with Fin, a cacophony like a belfry being blown up that went on and on. It was a knell that should warn the principalities in time for them to mount some sort of emergency response. Nothing could be done, though, if square miles of metal skin were to plow into a town-wheel somewhere.

To Venera, the churning air and the noise of it all seemed to originate in her own heart. He was alive! Absurdly, the image came to her of how she would tell him this story—tell him about Garth rescuing her, about her first impressions of Spyre as seen from a roofless crumbling cube of stone; about Lesser Spyre and Sacrus and Buridan Tower. Moments ago they had been mere facts, memories of a confused and drifting time. With the possibility that she could tell him about them, they suddenly became episodes of a great drama, a rousing tale she would laugh and cry to tell.

She turned to Garth, grinning wildly. "Did you hear that? He's alive!"

Garth smiled weakly.

Venera shook him by the shoulders. "Don't you understand? There is a place for you, for all of you, if you've the courage to get there. Come with me. Come to Slipstream, and on to Falcon, where he's imprisoned. We'll free him and then you'll have a home again. I swear it."

He didn't move, just kept his grip on his daughter while the wind whistled through Fin and the rest of the refugees looked from him to Venera and back again.

"Well, what are you scared of?" she demanded. "Are you afraid I can't do what I say?"

Now Garth smiled ruefully and shook his head. "No, Venera," he said. "I'm afraid that you can."

She laughed and went to the door. Bracing her hands and feet on the cold metal, she looked out. The gray turbulence of Spyre's destruction was fading with the distance. In its place was endless blue.

"You'll see," she said into the rushing air. "It'll all work out. I'll make sure of it."